Three Strangers

A Trilogy in Black and White

This character-driven novel is set in central Florida in 1957 near the end of the Jim Crow era. An eleven-year-old white girl, a nineteen-year-old black man, and a forty-two year old white woman are all going through personal struggles. In the midst of these, they have brief, yet meaningful, encounters that begin to shift some of their thinking.

Publisher's notes:
This is a work of fiction and should be considered as such. For events based on fact, most names have been changed to protect the innocent, and the guilty.

Comments about Jackie Robinson, Nat King Cole, Harry Moore, and Willie Edwards are based on actual incidents. The story in "James" about Junior Jackson and the taxi driver at the bus station in Lakeland actually happened to Mr. Willie Horton of the Detroit Tigers. Arriving in Lakeland for Spring Training in 1961, Mr. Horton was not allowed to take a taxi to the stadium, nor room with the white players. He lived with local African-American families, including the family of Beverly Brooks Boatwright, my advisor on African-American dialect mentioned in the acknowledgments.

Three Strangers

A Trilogy in Black and White

A novel by
Evelyn Parrish Gifun

Pine Top Publishing

Gifun, Evelyn Parrish
    Three Strangers: A Trilogy in Black and White

Pine Top Publishing
www.PineTopPublishing.com

ISBN 978-1-4675-5177-9

Quote from *The Gabriel Horn* by Felix Holt (1951),
courtesy of E. P. Dutton & Co.

This book was printed in the United States of America.

Acknowledgments

Dialect:

The regional dialects, both white and African American, are an important aspect of the novel for capturing the flavor of the period. Both dialects are meant to represent only the time and place in which the novel is set, not Southern speech in general. The white dialect is based on my own experiences growing up in central Florida, which, in the 1950s, was still the Deep South.

For the African-American dialect, I'm indebted to Lakeland native Beverly Brooks Boatwright, introduced to me by her former co-worker, my nephew Erv Fallin. Beverly gave generously of her time, providing priceless help with the dialect and expressions from the period and the region. I thank her for sharing memories, and adding some humor and vibrancy to "James." She seemed like an old friend when we finally met after months of emails, and I look forward to a long friendship.

I also drew from dialect used by fellow Floridian and renowned author the late Zora Neale Hurston in the novel, *Their Eyes Were Watching God.*

I owe a huge debt of gratitude to my husband, Frederick Gifun. Not only did he cook many delicious dinners while I worked on the book, he also faithfully read, reread, and improved the manuscript. And he offered encouragement and support when I needed it.

Special thanks to Pamela Hill Costa, Charles Costa, and my daughter Donna Gifun for early feedback, careful editing, and encouragement. Thanks also to Claire T. Carney, Linda Richter, Betty Jeanne Nooth, Joyce Miller, and my daughter Gina Gifun for their reviews and insights.

Thanks to the following for sharing memories:

Classmates and friends: Kay Hinson Besecker, G. Randall Cravey, Thomas (Tommy) M. Fortner, F. G. (Jerry) Miller, Ernestine Barley Rancourt, Patricia Harrelson Shannon, Paul J. Sheffield, Sharon Godwin Starling, and my former neighbor Louise Prine Albritton.

My late parents, Flem and Evie Hatchett Parrish, for their stories, my cousin Carol Selph Mears, my sister-in-law the late Freida Crane Parrish, and my late brother Paul E. Parrish. I'll always treasure my wonderful telephone conversations with Paul, whose memory of the time was detailed and colorful.

Mr. Glover Johnson who worked during the summer at the Kittansett Club in Marion, Massachusetts where an elderly woman I worked for was a member. Mr. Johnson, an African American who grew up on a farm in North Florida, sat for an interview with me. I was amazed to learn that his mother didn't work in the fields, because my mother did, as does the mother of my eleven-year-old character, Lora Lee.

Lakeland history:
Thanks to Kevin Logan, Lakeland Public Library; Sharon McCawley, City of Lakeland; and Barbara Harrison, retired, Lakeland General Hospital (Morrell).

Inspiration:
Two brief encounters with African-American strangers inspired me to tell the stories in this novel.
The first was with a man who gave me a gift when I was a little girl. Although a small gift, it was significant for me because I didn't know any African-Americans, and it planted seeds of doubts about the culture's racial stereotypes.
Decades later, the second was with a young man who handed me a rose at Lake Mirror one New Year's Eve. His gesture reminded me of the first time an African-American man in Lakeland gave me a gift, and renewed my resolve to write this novel.

Design:
Mere thanks are not sufficient to express my gratitude to artist and educator, Debra Smook, who has worked diligently in formatting the text, art work in the three sections, and the cover. Her amazing patience and pleasant demeanor gave me the leeway to make numerous revisions—tweaking and polishing. In working with her, I have improved the novel and gained a friend. I am truly grateful.

To my husband, Fred,
and the anonymous, compassionate, African-American man
who gave a little white girl a small gift with a large impact.

"Sometimes I feel discriminated against, but it does not make
me angry. It merely astonishes me. How *can* any deny
themselves the pleasure of my company? It's beyond me."

Zora Neale Hurston

Book I

Lora Lee
A Heart with Wonder

◊

Will you be a diamond, little girl,
hidden under feedsack and freckles?

Cast of Characters

Lora Lee Baker, 11 (6th grade)

Family:
Ruth (Hall), mother, 52
Caleb, father, 55
Billy, 18, brother; fiancée Patty; friends: Joe, Pete, Scooter,
Wayne Ben, 22, brother; wife Hannah, 18 (live in Mulberry)
Linda, 25, sister; husband Tim, 26; daughter Hope, 13 months
    (live in Lakeland)
Rose Dobbins, 35, aunt (Ruth's youngest sister); husband Roger, 37;
    son P. J., 9; daughter Lucy, 4 (live in Lakeland)
Clara Hall, 75, Grandmother (Ruth's mother, lives in Georgia)
Bessie, 84, great aunt (Clara's sister, lives in Lakeland)

School:
Rita, bus driver
Leroy, 11 (5th grade), neighbor, rides bus
Station wagon (bus) kids: Herman, 15 (8th grade), Levi, 10 (4th),
    Julie, 9 (3rd)
Deborah, 14 (8th grade)
Bruce, 14 (8th grade)
Stone, 13 (5th grade)
Classmates: Arnold, Cynthia, David, Ella, Emily, Grace, Jimmy,
    Lawrence, Lola, Mary Sue, Perry
Teachers: Mrs. Hoffman, 6th grade
    Mr. Docker, 8th grade (principal)
    Mrs. Carter, 7th grade (6th grade arithmetic)

Church:
Missy, 12
Howlie May, 13
Arnold, 11 (also at school)
Grace, 12 (also at school)
Reverend Booker

Dime Store:
Anna Love, clerk, and former neighbor

Sunday

"All right, Lora Lee, you hafta git up now," Ruth called from the kitchen in a tone that told Lora Lee that was her last warning.

Lora Lee rubbed her eyes, yawned, and gradually became aware of the intermingled smells of bacon and coffee. She sat up, pushed her tangled brown hair out of her eyes, and studied the light and shadows on the old wood floor.

A few times she'd tried to convince her mother to let her stay home, and Ruth had lost patience with her. When she'd asked the night before, Ruth said, "Lora Lee Baker, you need to go to church. That's where you learn about the *Bible* an' livin' right, an' the trials an' tribulations that other people have faced, so maybe you can avoid 'em."

Lora Lee wanted to say, "Yeah, I shore don't wanna git throwed into a lion's den or a fiery furnace," but she knew that would get her in big trouble. So she simply mumbled, "Yes, ma'am."

Ruth added, "An', Lora Lee, I don't want to hear about this no more."

"Yes, ma'am," Lora Lee answered, resigned to her fate.

She wondered what she'd wear to church, and she looked at the corner of the room where her clothes hung from an old blue broomstick, which served as a clothes rod. Because it was in the corner, there wasn't much room to hang things, but that wasn't a problem because she didn't have many clothes to hang. She thought a man must've had the bedroom before because the broomstick was so high she had to stand on her tiptoes to reach it. "I wish I had some more clothes," she thought, looking away.

Her parents normally did all right on the farm, but all farmers had bad years, and they had two mortgages to pay, since in addition to the 120-acre farm, they'd recently purchased an eighty-acre farm, and they sometimes had repairs to their tractor and pick-up truck. Mostly though, they just didn't think about Lora Lee's wardrobe. Occasionally, during the hot summers when there was no work for Ruth in the fields, she'd make her a dress out of feedsacks from cow feed. Fortunately, there were some pretty prints, but it still looked like feedsack cloth. She always got to buy an Easter dress to wear to church, but she didn't get many store-bought dresses.

Lora Lee swung her thin legs over the edge of the bed and felt the cool floor under her bare feet. Sighing, she moved her eleven-year-old body past her dresser, down the hallway, and into the bathroom. As she washed her hands, she smelled the soap and was glad that they had some store-bought soap; before, they'd used the lye soap her mother had made out of hog fat and lye, and Lora Lee didn't like the smell.

She splashed water on her face to wash the sleep out of her hazel eyes, wiped with a towel, and studied herself in the mirror. She saw her thin arms and shrugged her shoulders. She figured there was nothing she could do about being skinny; she ate plenty. The previous summer, Ruth had given her a spoonful of Hadacol daily trying to improve her appetite. Lora Lee didn't think there was anything wrong with her appetite, but she thought there was plenty wrong with Hadacol; she hated the taste and shuddered every time she took it. She wanted to whine each time, but she knew better. Touching her straight hair, which was just down to her shoulders, she thought, "I wish I had long hair. An' curls."

Disgusted by the freckles on her face, she turned away from the mirror. She went back to her bedroom, put on her white sweater, the only one she had, and slid her cold feet into her old shoes. Then she went across the hallway to the kitchen to see what her mother had fixed for breakfast to go with the bacon she smelled.

About seven feet wide, the hallway ran the length of the house and allowed some airflow. Of course, it had screen doors on each end to keep out flies and mosquitoes, but some always got in. The kitchen and living room were on one side of the hallway, and two bedrooms and a bathroom were on the other side. The bathroom, which the family had added, was between Lora Lee's and her parents' bedrooms. Her brother Billy's bedroom was on the side of the front porch, and opened only onto the porch.

The kitchen was directly across the hall from Lora Lee's bedroom, and was spacious enough to accommodate a large oak table, which had belonged to her grandmother Baker, and was needed when all the kids and their spouses were there. The window behind the table had tan curtains with little white rosebuds. A small, bare window over the sink looked out on orange trees and a clothesline. A brown and white linoleum covered the floor, and the wooden walls—like those in the rest of the house—had been painted white sometime in the distant past. The newer plywood cabinets had never been painted.

"Oh goodie! Cream of Wheat," Lora Lee said, in spite of her desire to remain a little moody—she was well aware of the fine line between pouting and the little bit of moodiness she could get away with. Often, her mother made oatmeal on Sunday morning, and Lora Lee didn't like it unless she put enough sugar in it to make it like dessert, and Ruth scolded her when she saw her do it. She loved Cream of Wheat and figured her mother had made it because she knew Lora Lee didn't want to go to church that day.

On the table was a *Life* magazine from March 4, 1957, with a picture of Queen Elizabeth and Prince Philip on the cover. As Lora Lee picked it up, she realized it was over two months old. "This magazine's got a purty picture of Queen Elizabeth, Mama. Did Aunt Rose give it to ya, an' can I have it? I like Queen Elizabeth."

Her mother was standing at the sink in an everyday dress with an apron tied around her waist. "Yes, she did, and you can have it after I git around to readin' it. I'm int'rested in that article about tradin' stamps. The cover says half the families in this country save 'em." She finished her coffee and put her cup in the sink.

Ruth's hair was almost all gray and she'd put on some extra pounds when she entered her fifties, but her hazel eyes were bright, and she still worked like a man on the farm. Her shoulder-length hair was loose around her face, but Lora Lee knew she would put it up before church with one of those hair rats that fit around her head in a semi-circle.

"What are tradin' stamps?" Lora Lee asked. She heard a chicken cackling out back to announce the arrival of her egg.

"That's what S&H green stamps are, an' we've got a couple of books. You know, when we buy groceries an' they give us green stamps, an' we paste 'em in a book an' redeem 'em for somethin' in the S&H store."

"Oh yeah. Can we git toys with 'em?" Lora Lee asked hopefully.

"I don't know. I have to look at the catalog to see what they have, but I'm hopin' I can git a step stool for this kitchen, for one thing."

"Oh shoot," Lora Lee thought. "I won't be gittin' no toys."

"Why don't you wear your new dress today?" her mother suggested, "that nice dress you got for Easter. But you'll have to wear your sweater. It's a bit cool this mornin'. It shore don't feel like May in Florida."

"Yes, ma'am, I will."

Lora Lee saw the empty milk bucket on the counter, with the cloth that Ruth used to strain the milk stretched over it to dry. She knew her mother had already milked, and rinsed the cloth. Either Billy or Ruth milked every morning and evening until the cow bred again and her milk dried up. They liked having fresh butter and fresh milk, which they called "sweet milk" to distinguish it from other types of milk, like buttermilk.

Lora Lee thought for a moment, and since her mother had asked her to wear her Easter dress, she decided to ask her for something. "Mama, can Missy come home wi' me today?"

"No, she cain't," Ruth answered impatiently. "You know I don't like you hangin' around with her. I hear tell her mama let her go to Lakeland with that Stewart Andrews. That boy's eighteen years old an' ever'body knows he's up to no good. I wish that woman would just hightail it on outta this county an' back to where she came from."

Lora Lee didn't say anything. Missy didn't tell her about Stewart Andrews, and she wondered if that was true.

"An' don't keep askin' me," Ruth said as she left the kitchen.

Ruth didn't like her hanging around with Missy for the same reason Lora Lee liked to. Missy was two years older, and she knew a lot more about a lot of things than Lora Lee did. She told Lora Lee about the birds and the bees, and Ruth was still angry about that. Lora Lee overheard her talking to Caleb and she called her "that Little Missy Know-It-All."

"When I ask Mama questions," she thought, "she always says the same thing, 'I'll tell you when you're older.' I wuz already nine years ole when Missy tol' me. I don't reckon Mama woulda ever tol' me. 'Where do babies come from?' 'The stork brings 'em.' 'How come I have a belly button?' 'I'll tell you when you're older.' Well, now she don't hafta tell me."

Missy and her mother, Maxine, had moved to Bradley Junction two years earlier from Tampa, and Ruth was suspicious of anyone from a big city. And Maxine was divorced. Ruth didn't trust divorced women at all. Lora Lee had heard her and her aunt Rose talking about Maxine and calling her "that grass widow." Lora Lee didn't know exactly what that meant, but she could tell by the way they said it that it was not good.

She stirred a chunk of butter into her Cream of Wheat. As she slowly savored it, she tried to think of something interesting she could do that afternoon. She didn't think either her sister or brother would visit. "I really wish Missy could come home wi' me," she thought. There was no other girl in the small church that Lora Lee considered a good friend.

The girl who'd been her best friend had moved away just a few months before Missy moved there. They'd taken turns going home with each other, spending the afternoon together, and returning to church that night. That made Sundays a lot more fun. Lora Lee had actually looked forward to church when her friend was there.

She didn't really mind church—most of the time she liked it—but she needed something else to do on Sunday besides that, and she wanted an occasional break. Sunday school was at 9:45; the church service was at 11:00 and it went until 12:00 or later. Then her parents stood around in front of the church and talked to people.

When they got home, Ruth had to cook. By the time they finished eating, it was usually around 2:00, and Lora Lee often had to wash the dishes. That left her about three free hours before she had to get ready to go back to church, and if a friend was with her, those hours flew by. When they were younger, they'd play games, but now they usually just talked or looked at magazines Lora Lee's aunt Rose had given her with pictures of Elvis Presley, Tommy Sands, and Ricky Nelson. Lora Lee loved Elvis, but her heart beat faster when she looked at Tommy Sands.

On Sunday evening, the Baptist Training Union classes met at 6:15; the church service was at 7:30 and lasted an hour. It was almost time for bed when they finished eating, usually leftovers from the afternoon meal.

The family attended the Bradley Baptist Church, which was ten miles away in Bradley Junction, a community of only a few hundred people. Most of the men worked for local phosphate companies, and most of the women were housewives. The "downtown" area had a train station, a post office, a garage, a drug store, a small gas station, and a small grocery store, where Lora Lee's family did most of their grocery shopping. Highway 37 and the railroad ran through the town. The north-south railroad tracks were the basic separation of the white and Negro sections.

Lora Lee was thinking about what she'd do that afternoon when her father passed by and tousled her tangled brown hair. As he got a glass of water, she noticed that he was dressed for church. He had on blue slacks, a long-sleeved white shirt, and a red and blue striped tie; and she knew he'd be putting on his blue suit jacket when they got to church. She wondered how he could stand those clothes. He almost always wore a suit on Sunday morning no matter how hot it was, and when they went to a funeral, he always wore a suit and tie, but he sometimes wore a short-sleeved shirt.

"I like that tie, Daddy," she said, smiling. She knew her sister, Linda, had given it to him for Christmas.

"Well, thank you, Double L," he said. Lora Lee felt warm inside. She liked being called "Double L" by him.

She thought he was a good-looking man. His brown hair was graying and he had light blue—almost gray—eyes that she loved when they twinkled, and feared when he was angry, which was too often. When she was little, she'd climb up on his lap in the morning and he'd give her coffee from a spoon. He put plenty of milk and sugar in his coffee, so Lora Lee liked it. And she loved her daddy.

"You better hurry," he said as he winked at her.

Lora Lee smiled and moaned, "Oh, Daddy!" From the time she was little, both eyes always closed when she tried to wink. As she got older, she was embarrassed by her failure and stopped trying, except occasionally when she was alone. Caleb never mentioned it, but when no one else was around, he'd tease her by winking.

"Billy still on day shift?" she asked about her eighteen-year-old brother.

"Yep. Today an' tomorrah. Then he's off Tuesday an' Wednesday, an' starts the midnight shift on Thursday."

Billy worked for the American Cyanamid Phosphate Company in Brewster. To reach the phosphate, huge draglines were used for strip-mining, and the process created deep craters. Central Florida had several phosphate companies, and the small town of Mulberry, eighteen miles from the farm, was called the "Phosphate Capital of the World." The emblem on Billy's class ring from Mulberry High School contained a mulberry tree and a dragline. Central Florida showed the results of the strip-mining with phosphate pits full of water scattered over the landscape. Often stocked with fish, the unnamed pits were identified by numbers.

Lora Lee shoveled her last bite into her mouth, put her dish in the sink, and went to get dressed. Caleb's twinkling eyes watched her leave the kitchen, and he realized that his little girl, at eleven, was getting taller. He ran his fingers through his short, straight hair and worried for a moment about what the future held. He did not look forward to boys hanging around another daughter—this one his baby—but he realized that he had some years left before he'd have to face that.

In her room, Lora Lee took down her Easter dress, and her heart skipped a beat when she saw the big spider on the wall behind her clothes. She shuddered. "Durn it, Spider! Why don't you go somewhere else?" Since big spiders ate roaches and mosquitoes, her father wouldn't kill them, but she was afraid of them, and that one was often on the wall or ceiling.

By the time she finished dressing, Caleb was in their '56 Dodge impatiently blowing the horn. She loved that car. It had a push-button transmission, which was on the dash on the driver's left. Caleb had sat close to her once and let her drive the car in the open space in front of the house, although she could barely see over the steering wheel. She went forward a little ways, stopped, backed up a little, stopped, and went forward a little. "Anybody could drive this car," she said. "Ya don't even hafta shift any gears; jus' mash the buttons."

She heard the horn blow again as she hurriedly buckled her sandals and ran out the door to the porch right ahead of her mother. "Have you got your Sunday school book?" Ruth asked. "And I told you to wear your sweater. It's cool this mornin'."

Lora Lee ran back to her room and grabbed the book and her sweater. She glanced at the spider to make sure it was still in the same place.

She ran outside and as soon as she hopped down from the steps, her father's white bird dog, King, jumped up on her. "King!" she yelled, pushing him off. Lora Lee felt sorry for him because he didn't get much attention, but she didn't like him jumping on her. Caleb used him for hunting quail during bird season, but Ruth fed him. Lora Lee and Billy would sometimes pet him, but she didn't think Caleb ever did, and King was his dog. He had two bird dogs before Queen, King's mother, died. She wished they didn't have King, and that she could have a little dog of her own, but she knew her father would always have a bird dog for hunting quail. She quickly brushed off her dress before she got in the car.

♥   ♥   ♥

In the back seat, Lora Lee was reading the day's lesson. She often read it on the way to church, and today was no exception. Neither was Ruth's reaction.

"I don't know why you don't study your lesson ahead of time, Lora Lee," she scolded. "I know good an' well you have plenty of time."

Lora Lee sat in the back seat behind her mother who couldn't see her unless she turned around. She noticed that Ruth had fixed her hair with her hair rat, which Lora Lee called a sausage because it looked like one. Ruth collected some of her hair and sewed it into a piece of nylon stocking. She used bobby pins to pin the ends of the rat in the front of her hair, pushed her hair up over it, and tucked the hair in, making a nice roll around her head.

Lora Lee sat quietly, waiting to see if she'd have to respond. When Ruth didn't say anything else, Lora Lee breathed a quiet sigh of relief.

As they passed their pasture, she saw the cows near the barbed wire fence, standing and lying in the shade of the trees along the fencerow. Their Brahma bull stood among them like the big chief. Denny Boy was cream colored with smudges of gray, and all gray around his hump and head. She thought about the young bull he had been.

When Caleb first bought the calf, he'd kept him in the orange grove close to the house because Brahmas had a wild streak and could be vicious, so Caleb wanted him to be around the family and get used to them. Lora Lee had treated him like a pet. Sometimes she'd sit near him when he was lying down, and he'd rest his head in her lap while she petted him. After Denny Boy got older and was put in the pasture, Caleb would walk out to him with a bucket of grain, but he always kept an eye on him, and Lora Lee could only pet him through the barbed wire fence. She missed their closeness, but he was a big bull now.

Lora Lee had just started reading again when they got to the large oaks near the curve in the road, and Caleb said, "Look, there's two fox squirrels." She looked. That was the only place she ever saw fox squirrels They were larger than the other squirrels, and brown was mixed in with their gray coloring. She thought they were much prettier than the others.

"They're so purty," Ruth said.

Lora Lee returned to her lesson, which was on the *Bible* story of Jonah and the whale. She read for a little while, and then she started thinking. "Even if there was a fish big enough ta swallow a man whole, he couldn' live in a fish's belly. It wouldn' be like a little room—there ain't no extry space in nothin's belly. An' there wouldn' be no air ta breathe, either." She'd seen hogs' insides when they butchered them.

"Good golly!" she said, still deep in thought.

"Lora Lee," her father said sharply. "Don't ya know that's just another way of usin' God's name in vain? Don't you say that ag'in!"

"Well, what can I say?" she asked innocently, looking at him. "I cain't say 'gosh' or 'golly.' They don't mean 'God' ta me, Daddy."

Caleb was staring at the road. "They're jus' substitutes for 'God.'"

His tone told her she would be wise not to say it anymore. But she knew she would be better off saying, "Good golly" than sharing her thoughts on Jonah and the whale. "Yes, sir." she said, looking at her lesson.

"You can say 'Good night!'" Ruth said.

"Good night!" Lora Lee muttered looking up, and although she could only see the side of her father's face, she saw his cheek move and could tell he was smiling. And she smiled as she returned to her lesson.

When they passed the Number 4 phosphate pit, Caleb said, "Look at that. People out there fishin' on a Sunday."

"I guess they don't know no better," Ruth said. "It's a shame."

Lora Lee glanced at a boat with a couple and two children in it, all of them holding fishing poles.

By the time they got to the church, she'd finished reading her lesson. Caleb parked in their usual spot under the big oak at the side of the building, so the car would be in the shade. The car windows were left open, and the keys were left in the ignition, as they always were.

In her Sunday school class, Lora Lee sat quietly while Mrs. Jones taught the lesson. Toward the end of the class, she asked, "Miz Jones, how could a whale swallow a whole man?"

"Well, the Bible don't say it wuz a whale," Mrs. Jones replied. "The Bible says God made a big fish to swallow Jonah. An' if God made it for that purpose, then it would work out jus' the way He planned. That wuz a good question, Lora Lee. Does anybody else have any questions?"

Lora Lee accepted defeat. She knew she couldn't argue with that, so she decided to let Jonah and the big fish rest in peace.

When the class ended, she went straight outside to the water fountain by the side of the church. She was enjoying the cool water and wondering if Missy would come, when suddenly a hand shoved her face into the water.

"Tryin' ta wash yore freckles off?" Howlie May asked, and laughed.

"You better quit it, Howlie May!" she said, wishing she were a little bigger. She wiped her wet face with the back of her hand. "Why don't ya quit pesterin' me, an' pick on somebody yore own size!"

"Look at you gittin' all riled up." Howlie May snickered. "Too bad, so sad. The water didn' wash any a 'em off. You still ugly. You look like ya got the measles all the time."

"Nuh-uh," Lora Lee said, trying to think of something smart enough to shut her up. "Somebody oughta bless her out," she thought. "I wish I could do it. That crazy girl's meaner 'an a snake."

Howlie May was fourteen and a lot bigger than her. Lora Lee thought Howlie May hated her, and she knew she hated Howlie May. She hated her for making fun of the freckles that covered her nose and much of her face, mostly because she hated the freckles herself.

When Missy was around, Howlie May never made fun of her. Missy was smaller and a year younger than Howlie May, but her sharp eyes and squared shoulders showed a strong will and determination, and Howlie May was afraid to upset her.

Lora Lee took another sip of water, even though she didn't want it, just to show Howlie May that she wasn't afraid. But she was mad and she felt humiliated. She knew what she'd do if she were only bigger. "One day I'll be big as her, or maybe bigger, an' I'll beat the dadgum stuffin' outta her then," she thought, even though she'd never been in a fight.

When she went into the church, she was disappointed to see that Missy wasn't there. Missy and her mother sometimes slept late and missed Sunday school, but went to the church service.

After Lora Lee turned ten, Ruth and Caleb decided she could sit with a friend on the pew behind them, provided they acted like "little ladies." Some of the girls and boys sat in the back, and she would've preferred to sit closer to the back, but she was pleased just to sit behind her parents. However, when Missy wasn't there, Lora Lee usually sat with them.

She didn't like sitting near the front, but she had no choice. Her parents sat on the third pew because Caleb was the song leader, and he needed to be close to the front.

Both she and Missy liked to sing, but during the announcements and when the preacher was preaching, they would sometimes pass notes to each other. Ruth and Caleb didn't mind, as long as they were quiet and didn't do anything distracting to others.

Before the service began, those who wanted to went to the front of the sanctuary to the choir loft behind the pulpit. Because it was a small congregation, they didn't have a regular choir. They seldom sang any special music—they just sang along with the rest of the congregation. When it was time for the sermon, they returned to their pews.

Lora Lee glanced at the Sunday bulletin to see if there was anything that might pertain to her. She noticed something on Friday, Saturday, and Sunday, but the mimeograph paper had a black smear on it and she couldn't read it. "I hope it ain't sumpin I'm gonna havta come to," she thought, assuming it wasn't. "What could be goin' on then?"

Although the mimeograph paper had a smudge, the black print was clearer than the dittos that she often got at school. That print was purple, and sometimes faint and hard to read.

Caleb stood in the front, facing the congregation. As the song leader, he chose the hymns, set the tempo, and kept time to the music. Ruth sang with the choir, so Lora Lee sat by herself until it was time for the sermon, but she had to be on her best behavior since both parents were facing her.

The first hymn Caleb chose was "Nearer My God to Thee," one of the favorite hymns. As the young pianist played the intro, Lora Lee knew it was too fast. The pianist liked fast songs, and she liked to play faster than Caleb liked to sing, and she would often start fast. When the singing began, Caleb would sing at the tempo he wanted, and the pianist would have to slow down. That's what happened, and Lora Lee looked at her to see if she was blushing. She was. "Wonder how come she don't learn that

Daddy ain't gonna sing fast 'less it's a fast song," she thought. "She mus' think you can make any song fast." Lora Lee would also have preferred faster songs, but the hymnbook they used didn't have many that were fast, and she always sang, fast or slow.

During the announcements, the Rev. Booker told them that they were going to do something unusual that week. An evangelist he knew was coming on Friday, and he'd be preaching there Friday night, Saturday night, and both services on Sunday, for a short revival. Normally, revivals ran for a week or two, but he was so fond of this preacher that he wanted to take advantage of his time in the area. "Invite yore friends an' neighbors," he said. "Brother Craig is a wonderful preacher, an' everyone who hears him will be blessed."

"So, that's what the bulletin said," she thought unhappily as she took off her sweater. "That means this week I'll be at church Wednesday night for prayer meetin', Friday an' Saturday night, plus Sunday mornin' an' night. Good golly! I mean, good night! I better not even think that or I'll say it out loud an' git myself in trouble. Shoot! Shoot! Shoot! I'll be missin' 'The Life of Riley' Friday night, an' 'The Jackie Gleason Show' Saturday night. We oughta be home in time for 'Gunsmoke.'" They'd only had a television since Christmas, and she loved her shows. "I wish I could at least bring a book ta read durin' the preachin', 'cause Missy prob'ly won't come."

Lora Lee always hoped for something entertaining to happen during the service, and occasionally, something did. She hoped the preacher would tell a joke while he was preaching and Mr. Cooper would get tickled. She looked, as she always did, for his red hair, and was relieved when she saw him on the other side of the church, just one row back. If he started laughing, she'd have a good view of him.

Mr. Cooper was around fifty, and even though his hair was still red, it was quite thin on top. That and some excess weight made him appear older. His large mid-section shook like jello when he laughed, and his infectious laugh made everybody laugh. Once he started, the whole congregation would laugh until they were all laughed out.

Lora Lee got her wish when the preacher told a joke that she didn't even think was funny. He said a lot of Christians were like a young couple he'd heard about. The boy was telling the girl how much he loved her and he said he'd do anything for her: "I'll climb the highest mountain for you an' I'll swim the widest river." And then he added, "An' I'll be over tomorrah night, if it don't rain." A few people chuckled, but Mr. Cooper apparently thought it was hilarious, and he started.

Lora Lee's happiness quotient rose immediately when she heard him. She started laughing even before she saw his shaking belly. When she looked at him, she just dissolved into the laughter. His hymn book was standing on his belly, leaning lightly against his chest, and bouncing up and down, up and down. He had thrown his head back laughing, and she figured he didn't know what was happening to the book. At first, she thought he was holding it there, but it was clearly just standing on his belly roll. As she laughed, she kept her eyes fixed on the shaking belly and the bouncing book, waiting and hoping for the book to fall. When it didn't, she found that hilarious, thinking, "That book's shakin' all over the place. How can it be stayin' on there wi' all that shakin' goin' on?"

And even in the state she was in, the words, "shakin' goin' on" reminded her of the song she'd heard on the radio just a few days earlier by Jerry Lee Lewis. "There is a whole lot of it," she thought. Remembering the song made the scene even funnier, and she knew she would remember Mr. Cooper's shaking belly and bouncing book every time she heard the song. She had an urge to surrender completely to the laughter—to just curl up on the floor so no muscles were being used for anything but laughing. But she sat on the pew watching him, laughing until her stomach ached and her face hurt and was wet with tears. The book never did fall. Fortunately, by the time everyone else was quieting down, she barely had enough energy left to laugh anymore.

Nevertheless, she had a hard time restraining herself. Her mind kept replaying the sound of his laughter, the image of his shaking belly and the bouncing book, and the phrase "a whole lotta shakin' goin' on," and she had to pinch her arm really hard to keep from laughing. "I hafta think about somethin' else," she thought, but her arm was sore before she did.

She looked around for something to distract her, and saw a fan in the hymnal rack. Her brow was covered with sweat, so she was happy to have the fan. When there was a funeral in the church, the funeral home would put out cardboard fans with wooden handles, with the name of the funeral home on one side, and a religious picture on the other. The fan she was using had Jesus praying in the Garden of Gethsemane.

Lora Lee busied herself with it and thought of Jesus being kissed and betrayed by Judas—nothing funny about that, but she couldn't think about it long. When she thought about *Little Lord Fauntleroy*, the book she was reading for her book report, she knew that would keep her occupied for a while. She was almost through reading it and she couldn't wait to get to the end to see if Little Lord Fauntleroy's mother would get to go live in the castle with him and his mean old English grandfather, the earl. After the boy's father died, the earl sent for him and his mother in the United States. The earl didn't like her because she was an American—as was Little Lord Fauntleroy, but he was his grandson—so he took the boy to live with him, and he set his mother up in a nice little cottage nearby. Little Lord Fauntleroy missed his mother, whom he called "Dearest," even though he got to visit her often.

"I hafta finish readin' it today, 'cause I belong to give my book report on Tuesday," she thought. "Oh shoot! I hafta write it with a fountain pin. I forgot about that. I better make sure we got some ink."

She spent so much time thinking about the book that the sermon was over before she knew it, and her father was announcing the invitation, the closing hymn. After each sermon, they had a hymn inviting people to go forward if they accepted Jesus as their savior, wanted to rededicate their lives, or were moving their membership from another church. If people went forward, they'd stand in the front and the congregation would sing another song while filing by to shake their hands. Lora Lee was glad no one went forward because she was ready to go home.

♥   ♥   ♥

Luckily, Sunday afternoon turned out to be more interesting than Lora Lee had expected. When they arrived home, Ruth went immediately to the kitchen, put on an apron, and told Lora Lee to change her clothes and get some water for tea. There was running water in the house from their well, but for some reason Lora Lee didn't know, it turned the tea black, and Ruth insisted on using water from the old hand pump out by the barn to make the tea a lovely red.

Lora Lee changed into her everyday clothes, and went barefoot to the pump, feeling the warm gray sand on her feet and between her toes. She heard a blue jay squawking and looked up at the mulberry tree that shaded the pump to see if it was there. She didn't see the jay, but noticed some Spanish moss hanging from the tree. "I'll hafta climb that tree an' git that moss outta there," she thought. She loved mulberries and didn't want anything to interfere with their production.

She ate them right off the tree, even though close examination showed tiny bugs (thrips) crawling around. She and her nine-year-old cousin P. J. were eating them one day, and Lora Lee mentioned the bugs to him. He looked closely at a mulberry and spat out the mouthful he had, even though he'd already eaten several handfuls. She laughed at him, but he wouldn't eat any more that day. She also loved what her father called mulberry pie. Ruth cooked the mulberries in water and sugar, and then added dumplings. Lora Lee would skim the cream off the top of the milk and put it in hers, and she thought the purple dessert was delicious.

She poured the jar of water, kept beside the pump, into the pump to prime it, and pumped enough to refill the jar. She'd pumped the bucket almost full when she heard a car a quarter of a mile away on the paved road. She stood still listening. When she heard it turn onto their dirt road, and shift into second gear, she immediately recognized the sound of the Chevrolet that belonged to her twenty-five year-old sister, Linda, and her husband, Tim.

"Goodie, goodie," she said excitedly, and pumped as fast as she could. Then she ran to the house, splashing water on the ground and on herself as she ran lopsided, with the heavy bucket weighing down her right side. A Rhode Island Red chicken that was scratching in some weeds went squawking out of her path as she rushed past. She wanted to be there when Linda got to the house with her thirteen-month old daughter, Hope.

Lora Lee wanted them to come, but they usually went to Tim's parents every other Sunday, and they had come the previous Sunday. Since the Bakers had no telephone, Ruth never knew whether or not anyone was coming, but she'd always take something from the freezer and defrost it in warm water if she didn't have a roast cooking or something else that would feed everyone. Sometimes Lora Lee's brother Ben and his wife, Hannah, would also come. Lora Lee set the bucket of water on the back porch, yelled excitedly, "Linda's here," and went running to the front yard.

In the front yard was a vine-covered, American-wire fence with a row of three Australian pines on the other side. One of them was covered with the same flame vine that covered the fence, and parts of the vine hung almost to the ground. Lora Lee and her father loved the small trumpet-shaped orange flowers that covered the vine for a couple of months in the winter, but her mother did not like it, or the Australian pines. Nor did she like the big Florida orchid tree on the left side of the yard with its purple, orchid-like flowers that Lora Lee loved. Ruth wanted all of them cut down and the fence removed, so the front area would be open, but that hadn't happened. Caleb liked the flame vine and the trees.

The fence had an unpainted, wooden-picket swinging gate, which Lora Lee flew through. As soon as the car stopped, she yanked the door open, gave Linda a quick hug, and took the baby from her lap. Little Hope was quite fond of her aunt "Lo Lee," since Lora Lee spent a lot of time taking her around showing her things, playing with her, and giving her piggy-back rides. She'd learned how to hold the baby so she was secure on her back. She'd gallop around like a horse and make whinnying sounds, and Hope would laugh and laugh. Lora Lee would bend forward and say, "Ooooh, better hold on. Yo're gonna faaalllll," and Hope would shriek with delight. Lora Lee would do almost anything to hear her laugh, and she'd gallop around until her arms were too tired to hold her anymore.

"Well, I see 'Lo Lee' already got Hope," Caleb said from the front porch. "Y'all come on in."

"Mama in the kitchen?" Linda asked, hugging her father.

"Yep," he said. "She had a feelin' y'all were comin' today, an' she's makin' a pot roast."

When Lora Lee got tired, she gave Hope to Caleb, who was sitting on the front porch with Tim, and went to get the bucket of water. She heard the conversation in the kitchen stop when she went on the porch. "Wonder what they were talkin' 'bout," she thought. "Prob'ly Linda's mean ole mother-in-law."

Several weeks earlier, she'd overheard Linda telling her mother about trouble with her mother-in-law, who, apparently, had an opinion about everything concerning the baby. Linda resented not only her interference, but Tim's failure to tell his mother to stop criticizing her parenting. Lora Lee figured that was the reason they came instead of going to see Tim's family. "That's good for me!" she thought. "Just keep it up, ole lady."

She stood on the porch trying to think of some way to keep them talking. She saw her old hard ball, picked it up, and bounced it a couple of times. It was too hard to bounce well, but it made the desired noise. Then she clomped down the steps, walked around the house, and snuck quietly up to the kitchen window. She could smell the pot roast, and her mouth started watering. She had to swallow a few times.

As she'd hoped, her mother and Linda were talking again. But they weren't talking about Tim's mother; they were talking about his brother. His brother was always going over to their house, often around mealtime; Linda didn't like that, but Tim didn't mind.

"You know, Linda," Ruth said, "your aunt Rose told me somethin' one time when she wuz havin' trouble with Roger an' his three brothers. Roger wuz always wantin' to include them in just about everything they did an' their wives were always complainin' about it." Ruth laughed. "Rose said, 'Cain't one of 'em even fart without all of 'em havin' to smell it.'"

Lora Lee had never heard her mother say "fart," and was surprised that she even knew the word. Ruth always said "passing gas" to her. Lora Lee could hear them laughing, and she needed to laugh. She clamped her mouth shut and held her nose to keep any sound of laughter from coming out as she quickly snuck back around the house. When she thought she was far enough away, she let it out. She stood by the house laughing until her sides ached.

When she went on the porch again, she didn't hear any sound coming from the kitchen, so she took the bucket of water in quietly and put it on the counter.

"I wuz jus' fixin' to call you, Lora Lee," Ruth scolded. "Where've you been?"

"I wuz just out back," she said, hoping that would satisfy her mother.

"I didn' git much of a hug earlier," Linda said, holding her arms out. "How ya been, Sis?"

"Fine," she replied, giving her sister a big hug, and feeling grateful that she'd changed the subject. "Hope's gittin' heavy."

She could hear her father and Hope on the porch. "Daddy's playing patty-cake with 'er," she thought. She heard her laughing.

"Yeah, she is. She weighs twenty-two pounds," Linda said.

"No wonder she feels heavy!" Lora Lee exclaimed. "That's more 'an four bags a sugar."

"An' that's how sweet she is, right?" Ruth asked, stirring something on the stove.

"Yep," Lora Lee replied. "She's shore sweet. An' cute as a button."

"Lora Lee, the cream's in the churn, an' it's all ready for you."

Breathing in the aroma of the pot roast, Lora Lee sat down at the table and started turning the handle of the glass churn. She wasn't crazy about churning, but it was her job, so she just accepted it as something she had to do. "I've churned three diff'runt ways," she said.

"How?" Linda asked, knowing the answer.

"This here crank churn, that ole churn grandma has with that wood thing that goes up and down in the churn, an' jus' shakin' cream in a jar."

"Yeah," Linda said. "I've done all that, too."

"What we havin' 'sides pot roast, Mama?" Lora Lee asked. She saw three other pots on the stove.

"Rice cooked in the broth from the pot roast, those little runnin' conk peas you like with salt pork, okra, corn on the cob, an' biscuits."

Lora Lee's mouth was watering. "Are we havin' any dessert?"

"No, Lora Lee," Ruth said impatiently, dropping okra pods into the pot with the peas. "When on earth did I have any time to make dessert?"

Lora Lee was a little disappointed because they seldom had dessert. However, she loved the meat and vegetables her mother cooked. She preferred fried corn bread with peas, but she knew her father preferred biscuits, and biscuits did go better with pot roast. And she sure loved hot biscuits and fresh butter.

After a while, the churn was getting hard to turn. "I'm done churnin', Mama," she said. "It's butter."

Lora Lee saw a piece of fabric on the counter with a loose piece of string on top of it. She realized that her mother had emptied a ten-pound bag of flour into her flour container. She opened a drawer, took out a ball of string the size of a big orange, and wrapped the string around it. "This ball a string's gittin' big," she said.

"No wonder," Linda replied. "We've been puttin' string on that thing forever."

"An' we've been usin' it forever, too," Ruth added, smiling. "Lora Lee, you can set the table now. Dinner's almost ready."

Lora Lee got the plates, silverware, and plain white paper napkins and took them to the table. She folded the napkins carefully.

"Linda, you could slice these tomatoes. I already washed 'em." Ruth handed her two large red tomatoes. "An' there's some cucumbers in the bottom of the icebox if you want to slice some a them."

Ruth took the churn to the sink. She took the butter out of the churn with a big spoon and put it in a bowl of water. Then she mashed the butter with the spoon a few times in the water to get any remaining milk out of it, drained the water out of the bowl, salted the butter, and put it on a dish.

After Lora Lee finished setting the table, Ruth told her to get ice for the tea, and then go tell the men to come to dinner. Lora Lee took the metal ice trays from the refrigerator freezer and filled the glasses with ice. She was glad there was enough ice in the trays and she didn't have to get the big pan of ice from the upright freezer and chip it. When there were more people, they used the extra ice.

As she neared the porch, she heard Tim ask Caleb how old the house was. They were both sitting in rocking chairs, Caleb with Hope in his arms, rocking lazily.

"Nobody seems ta know exactly," Caleb said, "but ya can tell it's been here a while. I'd really like ta know how old it is, an' how old the cabin an' the older part of this house is."

A log cabin and two houses had been built on the farm. Lora Lee found the old log cabin rather creepy because it only had one door, a Z door with slats, and two openings for windows, so it was dark in there. The openings had no windows, but they had wooden shutters that could be opened. The family used the cabin mostly to store tools, and hay for the cows. It was a little distance from the house.

The older house—the first regular wooden one—had three rooms and a porch. Everything was unfinished wood, except for the tin roof. The walls, which had exposed studs, were just one layer of plain pine boards, which served as the outside and inside walls, neither of which had ever been painted. There was no ceiling—just the tin roof. They used the older house mostly for storage; however, when they first moved there, they'd used the largest room for the kitchen because there was no plumbing or electricity, and Ruth preferred to use the old kerosene stove and ice box out there. They still had them from their house on Combee Road near Lakeland, which only had plumbing and electricity for about a year when they sold the 14-acre farm and moved to the 120-acre farm in a more remote part of Polk County, right next to the Hillsborough County line.

Rain falling on the old tin roof of the older house made so much noise that conversation was impossible. And in the summer, when the sun beat down on the roof, it was like an oven. Lora Lee was glad when they moved the kitchen to the main house, which was attached to the older one by the porch, part of which was a breezeway between the two buildings.

On hot days, they sat in the breezeway to rest or do sedentary work, like shucking corn, shelling peas, or snapping beans. And if Ruth had a repair requiring needle and thread, she'd sit out there to work. On one side of the breezeway was a wooden stand for a water bucket and pan, which was next to where the old hand pump had been—the one they'd used until they got plumbing in the house; the other side was just open. The main house did have ceilings and inside walls, all Southern pine boards about five inches wide, which had been painted white in the past, and it had unfinished wood floors, also made of pine boards. It was a plain old farmhouse, unpainted on the outside, set up on rocks a couple of feet off the ground, like most old Florida houses.

When they moved there, Lora Lee was disappointed that they didn't have a telephone, but there were no phone lines out in the country; they'd had a telephone for a while before they moved from Combee Road and she'd liked being able to call her friends. Also, she didn't like having to go to the outhouse on cold days, eating by lamplight, or having to go into that old kitchen on cold winter mornings. There was no heat in there except for the kerosene cook stove, and the walls let the cold air in.

The main house was bad enough since the only source of heat was the living room fireplace. On cold days, Caleb would build a fire while Ruth cooked breakfast. When Lora Lee got up, she'd grab her clothes and run to the living room to dress in front of the fire. When she faced the fire, her backside would be cold and her front side would get hot, and when she turned around, the opposite would happen, so she turned around a lot as she dressed. When it was really cold, Ruth would take her breakfast to the living room and let her sit in front of the fireplace to eat. Her breakfast would be on the piano bench, and Lora Lee would sit on a footstool Linda made in her home economics class when Lora Lee was little. It was made from large juice cans with stuffing around and over them, and covered with strong, red upholstery material.

They lived there for over a year before they had the house wired and got electricity, and another year before they drilled a new well, got indoor plumbing, and moved the kitchen into the main house. One Sunday before they had indoor plumbing, a girl went home with Lora Lee, and she told her she'd never heard of an outhouse. Lora Lee told Ruth that she acted like they were uncivilized.

"She asked me how come we didn' have no bathroom," Lora Lee said. "An' she's so nasty-nice. She thinks she's too good ta go to an outhouse, an' she didn' even wash her hands after she went. Anyhow, I asked her what she thought people did before they had indoor bathrooms, an' she said she never thought about it—she don't like ta think about things like that."

"Well, I declare!" Ruth said.

"I told her she didn' hafta use the outhouse, that we got plenty a palmettos she could go behine. An' I said, 'There's plenty a moss hangin' nearby, too, so ya don't even hafta use that ole toilet paper from the outhouse.'"

Ruth laughed. "What 'id she say?"

"She said she'd use the outhouse, she jus' didn' like it."

"Good thing we have toilet paper, an' don't still have to use a Sears an' Roebuck catalog." She paused. "But you know, honey. A lot of people these days haven't ever used an outhouse, even grown people. Most houses in town have had plumbin' for a long time now."

"Really? I said somethin' 'bout when we didn' have 'lectricity, an' she said, 'You didn' have no 'lectricity? How could ya live without 'lectricity? Lora Lee, yore life is crazy.' An' I said, 'Well, yore life is stupid.'"

Ruth laughed. "Obviously, she hadn' ever been anywhere where they didn' have electricity or plumbing."

"Well, she moved away, but I didn' ever ask her ta come home wi' me ag'in after that. One thing for shore! We might notta had no indoor plumbin' or 'lectricity, but we ain't stupid!"

♥   ♥   ♥

AFTER THEY FINISHED EATING, Ruth gave Hope to Lora Lee, who took her on the front porch and rocked her to sleep with Hope's head on her shoulder. She loved to rock her, and she was sorry when Linda took her and put her on a folded blanket on Ruth and Caleb's bedroom floor.

Without Hope to play with, she went to her room to read, even though she would have preferred to listen to the adults' conversation. After a few minutes, she heard her father say, "Feel like playin', Linda?"

Linda had taken piano lessons, and she played the piano for her church on Sunday morning and sometimes on Sunday evening. When she was at home, the family would usually gather around the piano and sing hymns. Caleb loved to sing. Lora Lee thought she'd skip singing and keep reading her book, but when she heard him ask, "Where's Lora Lee at?" she put her book down and headed for the living room.

"Come on in here, Lora Lee," her father said, smiling. "We need yore sweet voice."

She did enjoy singing with the family. It was better when Billy, Ben, and Hannah were there, but they always had fun no matter how many sang. Tim sang bass, Ruth sang alto, and Caleb and Lora Lee both sang the lead. Linda sang lead also, but she didn't usually sing while she was playing.

After they'd sung for about a half hour, Hope toddled into the room with her baby steps, and that finished the singing. Lora Lee watched Linda change her diaper, and then she took her again.

"Twenty-two pounds," she said. "You gonna make me strong, Hope."

"Jus' so ya know," Linda said, "we're gonna be leavin' in a little while. I hafta play the piano for church tonight." She knew that Lora Lee was always disappointed when they left, so she usually gave her a warning.

"Well, Hope can stay wi' me," Lora Lee said.

"Good gravy!" Linda laughed. "I can see you changin' her diaper."

"Mama can do that," Lora Lee responded, and she thought, "I can say 'good gravy!'" She smiled, and took Hope outside.

First, she showed her the gardenia bush with bees buzzing around the white flowers. "Bzzzzzzz, bzzzzzzz," she said, and Hope laughed. She said it again and Hope laughed a little less. When a black and yellow butterfly lit on a gardenia, Hope mumbled a sound and pointed.

"Butterfly," Lora Lee said. "Butterfly." But Hope did not attempt to say the word. She just watched it with wide eyes until it flew out of sight.

Lora Lee thought about what she could do next to entertain her, and she took her to the edge of the house to show her the doodlebug (ant lion) homes. "Look Hope, see where the doodlebugs live," she said, standing her gently on the ground.

There were several doodlebug homes in a sandy place just under the house. The bugs made little cone-shaped holes about an inch and a half wide in the sand. Lora Lee picked up a small stick about three inches long and squatted down by the house with one arm around Hope who was leaning against her. As she twirled the stick in a little sandy home, she chanted,

> Doodlebug, doodlebug,
> Fly away home.
> Yore house is on fire,
> An' yore children are gone.

Nothing happened, but Hope squealed with delight. "'G'in," she said.

Lora Lee tried another one, chanting again. This time, a little doodlebug appeared. "Look at the doodlebug!" she exclaimed, as it quickly burrowed back down, sand flying.

Hope squealed even louder, and laughter burst from her little body.

Linda called, "Lora Lee, we're fixin' ta go." And, as she expected, Lora Lee was disappointed.

"I didn' hardly git ta play wi' her at all," she whined as Linda took Hope.

And Hope wasn't happy either. "Lo Lee, Lo Lee," she called, her little hands reaching for her as she started crying.

Lora Lee had to fight back the tears. She was always upset when they left, especially now that Hope was old enough to show her love for her.

"It's just as well," Ruth said as they drove away. "I have to study my lesson for Trainin' Union, an' I bet you do, too, Lora Lee."

"Yes, ma'am," she said as she headed for her room. She quickly read her lesson. She enjoyed the BTU (Baptist Training Union) class better than she did the Sunday school class because not as many people attended in the evening, and the girls and boys were together. Also, the teacher liked to have fun, so the kids were allowed to joke around.

Lora Lee thought Arnold, who was also in her class at school, was really funny. He'd often come up with something silly that would make them laugh. One night he said, "It's a good thing my parents named me 'Arnold,' 'cause that's what ever'body calls me."

Arnold lived in the country also, but he lived across the creek on Bethlehem Road. Both Bethlehem and Albritton Roads had been part of a settlement named Chicora. When another settlement was named "New Chicora," Chicora was sometimes called "Old Chicora," often pronounced, "O-she-cora" by the kids. There'd been a school there, and Lora Lee wished the country kids still went to school out there. A post office and a few other buildings were there in the late 19th and early 20th Centuries, but the only thing left from that period was one small cemetery. The Primitive Baptist church down the road in Hillsborough County had a larger cemetery, where many of the locals were buried.

After Lora Lee read the BTU lesson, she was able to finish her book, but she decided she'd wait until Monday to start working on her book report. She knew it would be time to leave soon, so she went to the bathroom and washed her feet in the sink, putting one foot in while standing on the other foot. Then she got dressed for church, and sat on the floor, arranging her marbles on the Chinese checkerboard. She had a big steel ball that was the king and a small one that was the queen. She arranged the rest of her kingdom by the colors she liked best in descending order—the shiny clear ones first—until it was time to go.

♥   ♥   ♥

Lora Lee breathed a sigh of relief and smiled when she saw Missy in the church. Missy sometimes went to BTU, but she wasn't there that night and Lora Lee had been afraid she wouldn't be there for the service. Lora Lee noticed that her hair was in a ponytail, and she went in the row two pews behind her, leaned over, and pulled it. Missy jerked her head around, but her eyes lit up and she smiled when she saw Lora Lee. However, they didn't have much time to talk before the service, and when the preacher started preaching, they wrote notes to each other.

Under most circumstances, Lora Lee was pretty good at laughing without making any noise, but Missy was still learning that trick, so they had to be careful not to write anything funny. Missy had laughed out loud once and Lora Lee received a warning: if Missy laughed out loud again, they wouldn't be allowed to sit together anymore. Lora Lee figured she'd also probably get in trouble.

Missy wrote that she wasn't there that morning because her father had come to visit and he'd stayed all afternoon. Normally, he only visited about once a month, so she always stayed with him while he was there.

Lora Lee noticed that Missy had on a ring with a pretty green stone. She wrote that she liked her ring and asked if it was new. Missy replied that it was her birthstone, and her father had given it to her that day as a late birthday present. Lora Lee wished she had a pretty ring. She was happy for her friend, but felt a little deprived.

Just then, the preacher's voice rose as he was telling the story of Ham seeing his naked, drunken father. "An' Noah put a curse on him an' his descendants," he said. "'A servant of servants shall he be unto his brethren.' Brothers and sisters, this is where the Nigra race comes from!"

"Huh," Lora Lee thought. "An they're s'pose' ta be servants." She reflected a moment, then wrote a note to Missy about Howlie May, HM, pushing her face into the water. Missy wrote that she'd double-dog-dare HM to do that to her when she was there. She said she'd like to stick HM's face in a toilet bowl. That struck Lora Lee as funny, and it pleased her.

She was writing that she'd like to slap the fire out of HM when the preacher slammed his hand down on the pulpit to make a point. Startled by the noise, Lora Lee jumped, and Missy, who'd been watching her, spontaneously burst into laughter.

Ruth and Caleb both whirled around to look at them. The blood had already drained from Lora Lee's face and she'd put her finger to her lips to quiet Missy, who realized what she'd done and had stopped laughing. She knew Lora Lee was in trouble.

"Lora Lee, you come up here!" her father whispered sternly. Lora Lee stuck the note in her pocket, moved to their pew, and sat by her mother.

Although Missy had stopped laughing immediately, the damage was done. Knowing she was responsible for Lora Lee's predicament, she tried to think of some way she could help the situation.

Even though Lora Lee sat silently by Ruth, she didn't hear a word the preacher said. She felt embarrassed, angry at Missy for getting her in trouble—yet understanding why she'd think her jumping was funny—and worried that she might get a whipping.

Her last whipping was when she was four, and she was thinking about it when she felt a tap on her shoulder and turned her head just in time to see her mother snatch a note from Missy's hand. She looked at her mother and saw the look she gave Missy. Ruth put the note in her pocketbook.

"Oh Lord," Lora Lee prayed silently, "Please make her sit still an' be quiet." She knew that her parents wouldn't let her sit with Missy anymore and wondered if Missy was actually trying to make things worse for her. This was one time Lora Lee didn't want the church service to end.

When they sang the closing hymn, she made sure to sing loudly enough that her mother could hear her. And she stood perfectly still with her eyes closed for the closing prayer, even though the preacher called on Mr. Cooper. Normally when he prayed, Lora Lee squirmed and sighed softly before he finished his long prayer. It seemed to her that he tried to impress everyone with his prayers, but he didn't need to. People already liked him for his jovial, contagious laugh that gave them such pleasure.

He always began with several titles for God and paused after each one: "Almighty God, our Holy Father Jehovah, Lord of Hosts, Supreme Ruler of all, an' Father of our Lord an' Savior Jesus Christ." Lora Lee thought the salutation alone was long enough for a prayer, but he went on. He asked God to bless all the downtrodden and unfortunate people in the world; to cause all of the backsliders to repent and rededicate their lives; to heal all the sick, saying names and illnesses of any sick people he knew; to guide all the leaders of all the countries, "particularly the great general, President Eisenhower"; and to save all the lost souls who were headed for hell—which, fortunately, he did not name.

He also included other issues important to him, the church, and the world. Lora Lee stood still and didn't make a sound. By the time he finished, she thought her indiscretion—which was, after all, Missy's—should have been forgiven, but she knew her parents were in no mood to be impressed by her doing what they thought she should.

As soon as Mr. Cooper finished, Caleb, still standing in front of the sanctuary, motioned to Lora Lee. When she went to him, he said, "You go straight to the car, young lady!"

Lora Lee was grateful that the car was parked in a dark spot off to the side, so no one could see her. It was so dark she could barely see the colors of the car. The 1956 Dodge was a three-tone car: the top was black; the hood, trunk, and tops of the sides and fins were maroon; and the bottoms were pink. Lora Lee had been thrilled when she first saw it. She loved the maroon and pink. However, after they drove it to church, Grace, who was twelve and also in Lora Lee's class at school, was very happy to laughingly inform her the next day, that her family had called it a "nigger" car.

"How come y'all called it that?" Lora Lee asked.

"It's 'nigger' colors," Grace replied, grinning.

"Well, I like the colors," Lora Lee said half-heartedly.

"You got a 'nigger' car," Grace said, snickering as she walked away.

Lora Lee felt embarrassed. She wondered how many other people thought that. And she wondered what was wrong with her that she liked the same thing Negroes liked. She resented Grace for taking away some of her enthusiasm; she couldn't just love the car anymore without wondering if there was something wrong with her for loving it—and her parents for choosing it.

As she sat in the back seat, she watched the people standing in front of the church talking, in spite of the busy mosquitoes. Every now and then, someone would slap a bare arm or lift a foot and slap an ankle.

She saw a ten-year-old boy run up behind some teenage girls, and Lora Lee watched to see if he was going to put a rain frog down someone's back. Sometimes a boy did that, and the girl would squeal and dance around until the frog got out, or another girl got it out for her. This time, however, the girl turned around quickly, and the boy ran away.

The car windows had been left open because of the heat and soon she was busy slapping at mosquitoes. She was about to roll up the windows when she heard a soft voice call, "Lora Lee."

"What?" she responded, looking around trying to see who it was.

"It's Missy," answered the voice.

"Good gravy! Where you at, Missy?"

"Don't turn aroun'. I'm behind the car. Cain't nobody see me."

"You got me in trouble, Missy."

"I know it. Shoot! I'm really sorry. When the preacher hit the pulpit, you almost jumped off the bench. It wuz so funny, I couldn' help it."

"Yeah, he really scared me. Are you in trouble, too?"

"No. My mama don't care."

"Yo're lucky, Missy. I know my parents won't let me sit wi' ya no more."

"Well, durn it! I won't come ta church no more, then," Missy declared. "It won't be no fun, nohow, if I cain't sit wi' you."

"What wuz in that note Mama snatched from you?"

"I tol' you ta tell her it wuz all my fault—you didn' do nothin'."

Lora Lee had been watching her parents who were talking to the preacher. She imagined they were apologizing to him for their wicked, sinful daughter. She was about to suggest to Missy that she should leave, when they started for the car.

"Missy, ya gotta go!" she said urgently. "My parents are comin'."

"Okay. I jus' wonted ta tell ya I'm sorry."

Lora Lee wanted to turn around and look to see if Missy could be seen leaving, but she was afraid her parents would see her looking and they'd look. She kept her eyes glued on them. Ruth was saying something to Caleb and looking at him, but he was looking in the direction of the car. Lora Lee was afraid he saw Missy.

"It wuz bad enough she got me in trouble in the church. Now, dad-gummit, I might be in even more trouble. Daddy's prob'ly gonna beat the livin' daylights outta me. I shore don't plan on passin' no more words wi' her for a while!"

Neither Ruth nor Caleb said anything to her when they got in the car, so Lora Lee couldn't tell whether or not Caleb had seen Missy. And on the way home, the car was silent—a sure sign of trouble.

Lora Lee felt a need to explain what happened, yet knew she should be quiet. Finally, the need to explain won. "Daddy," she began.

"Lora Lee," Caleb said sternly. "You hush."

The rest of the ride was quiet, with Lora Lee filled with dread, waiting for her punishment. She didn't think about "What's My Line?" or "The $64,000 Challenge," which she got to stay up late for with her parents; the three of them always watched those shows on Sunday night. She didn't even say anything when they passed by a skunk that had been hit by a car.

"Oh my goodness! Somebody hit a pole cat," Ruth said disgustedly.

Normally, Lora Lee would hold her nose, moan, and exclaim about the awful odor, but she sat quietly just staring at the back of the seat in front of her, not holding her nose, and not caring about the smell.

And in the silence, Caleb and Ruth both felt the quiet pain emanating from the back seat.

Monday

Wᴇɴ sʜᴇ ʜᴇᴀʀᴅ ʜᴇʀ ᴍᴏᴛʜᴇʀ ᴄᴀʟʟ, "Lᴏʀᴀ Lᴇᴇ," her first thought was of Sunday night. She breathed a sigh of relief and silently thanked God that it was over. Caleb had yelled at her and told her she couldn't sit with Missy anymore, but Lora Lee already knew that, and she'd expected a whipping. She thought maybe he realized the fault was actually Missy's. Anyway, she put it all in perspective: she knew exactly what behavior was expected of her, and she knew that the same behavior was expected of her friends when they were with her, especially in church. And she was angry at Missy that she didn't seem to take that seriously enough and had gotten her in trouble.

She wanted to sleep about three more hours, but she knew she had to get up. She absolutely hated having to get up at 6:15, but the school bus came at 7:05, and she had to leave the house before 7:00 for the quarter-mile walk to the bus. "It's almost the end a May," she thought. "Jus' two more weeks a school, an' then I can sleep late. Oh, I cain't wait for school ta be out." To Lora Lee, as the end approached, time seemed to move at a snail's pace.

Normally, she laid out her clothes the night before so she wouldn't have to think about what she'd wear the first thing in the morning, but she hadn't been thinking about clothes Sunday night. Since she didn't have many clothes to choose from, she was trying to remember what she'd worn on Friday so she could wear something different, and it took her a little while. As she finally decided on the newest feedsack dress Ruth had made for her, and her sweater, she hoped she wouldn't be late for the bus.

"Mornin' Daddy," she said when she went to the kitchen.

"Mornin' Double L." Caleb was sitting in his place at the head of the table. "Come gimme some sugar."

Lora Lee smiled, hugged her father, and kissed him on the cheek. He was the only one who called her "Double L," and the only one who rubbed her tummy if she had a stomachache, or squeezed grapefruit juice for her when she was in bed with a cold. He'd squeeze a grapefruit, put a spoonful of baking soda in it, and stir it up. And he'd sit on the edge of her bed while she drank it. Lora Lee didn't know whether it helped cure her cold or not, but it made her feel special to have her father do that for her. And she did know that her stomachaches got better when he rubbed her tummy.

"I need $1.25 for lunch money for the week, Daddy."

She hurriedly ate her grits and egg, encouraged by her mother, who reminded her that Billy would be picking her up after school so they could go to the other place, which was off the Wimauma Road in Hillsborough County, about eight miles away. They called it "the other place," as though it were a name, and were often over there working when Lora Lee got home from school.

"I'll tell Rita I won't be on the bus this afternoon," Lora Lee said. "Mama, have we got any more ink?"

"There's some on my dresser, but you've got to git goin'."

"I gotta have some ink for my fountain pin to write my book report."

"Well, give me your pin an' I'll fill it for you."

While Ruth filled her pen, Lora Lee jammed her lunch money into her pocketbook and got her books. And as soon as Ruth handed her the pen, she ran out of the house with it in her hand, her pocketbook strap over her shoulder, and her three-ring notebook and schoolbooks on her chest, held securely with her arms folded over them.

Fortunately, King didn't jump on her when she went out the front door. He was usually around back if he wasn't off in the woods somewhere.

She realized, even at eleven, that she did a lot of thinking on that quarter-mile walk to and from the bus. There wasn't anything else to do; just trudge down the sandy dirt road, usually carrying her notebook and books in one hand by her side—whistling, singing, or thinking. She had quite an imagination, and she usually kept herself fairly well entertained. This morning, though, she had to run to catch the bus and she was thinking about that.

The road was straight, but when they first moved to the farm, their road—from Albritton Road to their house—had gone through an open space and then curved through woods. Lora Lee had thought the scenic winding road was pretty, but it was also spooky to an eight-year-old girl who had just moved there. Her mother walked with her to the clearing the first few mornings, but then Lora Lee had to walk alone. She often imagined something or someone would pop out from behind the palmetto patch that was on one of the curves, or behind one of the big old oak trees.

She always walked on the opposite side of the road from the palmettos even though they were only a few feet away, partly because she knew rattlesnakes might be in there. Once she got past the palmettos and the trees to the clearing, she wasn't afraid.

After they'd lived there for a few months, her father had that part of the land cleared, planted pangola grass for pasture on part of it and farmed the rest. He put a straight road along the edge of the property until it got across from the house, where it curved left and went up to the house.

Lora Lee ran as fast as she could, holding tightly to the books and notebook over her chest, but she hadn't gone far when she heard the bus. Rita, the bus driver, lived about half a mile down Albritton Road, so when Lora Lee heard the bus, she knew it would be there soon. "Golly," she thought, and corrected herself. "Dad-gummit, I'm really late, an' I'm gonna hafta run the whole way." Running that early in the morning was not easy for her, but she ran until she could see the yellow bus through the trees by the road, and then she started walking. She walked for a few seconds until she thought Rita could see her walking, and then started running again. She didn't want Rita to know how late she really was. Luckily for her, she was the first one on the bus—and the last one off—so there were no kids to pick on her for being late.

"Good gravy! I wish I didn' hafta run," she thought as she ran, gasping for breath. And she thought of what her mother would say, "If wishes were horses, all beggars would ride."

"We don't have beggars out here," she thought, "but we useta have 'em on Combee Road. I'd be scared if they came out here when I'm by myself." She remembered one time her mother had given a plate of food to a man Lora Lee thought was a tramp—she didn't know the difference between tramps and hobos; she just thought of all of them as beggars, although some of them would work for food. She'd stood in the house and stared at the man as he ate, sitting on the back porch doorsteps.

Rita turned onto their road, stopped the bus, and waited for Lora Lee. Fortunately, she liked Lora Lee a lot and seldom got impatient with her. Lora Lee didn't know it, but Rita felt sorry for her. She knew that Caleb was very strict, and she noticed right away that Lora Lee's clothes weren't as nice as the other girls'. She knew Lora Lee didn't have many clothes, and that some were made from feedsacks. Rita knew that had to be a problem for her since, as they were getting older, some of the girls paid a lot of attention to what everybody was wearing. Rita liked Lora Lee because she was well-behaved, respectful, and pleasant. So, if she didn't see her at the bus stop or on her way, she'd blow the horn and wait a few minutes to make sure she didn't leave her. Of course, she also did that for the other kids, but she didn't wait quite as long for them, and sometimes she would remind them to be on time.

"Mornin', Lora Lee," she said as Lora Lee climbed the bus steps.

"Mornin', Rita. Sorry I'm late," she said, panting.

"It's all right, honey. We got plenty a time. You doin' okay?"

"Yes, ma'am," Lora Lee replied.

Rita noticed that Lora Lee's hair looked a little straggly, as it often did. "She needs somebody to fix her hair nice," Rita thought. "I guess nobody don't ever roll her hair to put a little curl in it. Either her mama don't know how, or she don't take the time."

After Lora Lee sat down on the front seat behind her, Rita backed the big bus up and started back down Albritton Road. "Look at the red-birds," she said as they passed a pair of cardinals sitting on the barbed wire fence beside the road.

They flew right after Lora Lee saw them. "They're the purtiest birds!" she said.

Leroy, the only other school-age kid on the three-mile road, was a few months younger than Lora Lee, and lived about a mile from her. He was standing by the road waiting for the bus.

"Mornin', Leroy," Rita said.

"Mornin', Rita."

"Hey Leroy," Lora Lee said. "You got an arithmetic test today, don't ya?"

"Yeah," he said, with his head hung down. "I studied hard, by cracky, but I cain't understand the stupid stuff."

"I'll help ya," she offered.

Lora Lee was good at math, and she didn't want Leroy to have the kind of problems Arnold had. Poor Arnold just didn't understand it, and their math teacher, Mrs. Carter, would lose patience with him. One day she was helping him with a problem, and when he got the wrong answer for the third time, she started hitting him on the back with a ruler. Lora Lee saw him wince every time the ruler hit him. He didn't cry, but his eyes filled with tears and he wiped them with the back of his hand. She could tell he was embarrassed, and even though she liked Mrs. Carter, she was mad at her for a while.

"There wadn' any reason for that," Lora Lee thought, her own eyes full of tears. "He didn' do nothin' wrong. She reckon he could think better if he wuz in pain?"

Leroy was sitting on the other front seat and he moved to the seat behind Lora Lee, opened his book and handed it to her, pointing at the first problem he didn't understand. Of course, it was an "If one train's going one way at 90 miles per hour, and another train is going the other way at 70 miles per hour . . ." kind of question. Lora Lee patiently explained to him how to figure it out and was rewarded with a smile as he understood the problem. Since she was able to help him with that one, he showed her the other problems that he didn't understand. By the time they'd gone the six miles to the school in Brewster, he understood most of those, too.

"Thanks, Lora Lee," he said enthusiastically.

"Yo're welcome," she replied. "Any time."

In Brewster, everything was covered with light gray phosphate dust from the plant. The trees and cars looked gray. Lora Lee saw one car with "WASH ME" scrawled on it. "Ain't rained in a while," she thought.

After she and Leroy were dropped off, the bus picked up the high school kids in Brewster and Bradley Junction and took them to Mulberry High School, about twelve miles away. Since the bus had to be on time for them, Lora Lee and Leroy were at school an hour before starting time. And they had to wait an hour for the bus in the afternoon.

There were only about two-dozen kids from the country who went to Brewster. A different bus picked up the kids on Harper Grade and Bethlehem Road, and the school janitor used his station wagon to pick up three kids who lived further out in the country. Those three arrived soon after Lora Lee and Leroy, and they were around in the afternoon for a while after the Brewster kids went home and the bus that picked up the other country kids left.

Brewster was a phosphate town built and owned by the American Cyanamid Company, and many of their employees lived there in the company houses. Whites lived on one side of the railroad tracks, and Negroes lived on the other side. Besides the houses, Brewster had a company office building, small post office, recreation hall, basketball and tennis courts, swimming pool, barber shop, commissary, doctor's office, and drugstore. The drugstore had a soda fountain, and some booths and tables. A theater and gas station had been closed before 1957. There was no church, but the school auditorium was used on Sundays for non-denominational services.

Across the street in front of the school was a grassy park with a few trees where an occasional physical education class would play games like kick the can, or for the boys, football. But the main athletic field was on the side of the school, across another street.

While the bused kids waited for the bell to ring, they hung around the schoolyard, except when it was raining or cold. Then, they moved to the porch of the old wooden school, which extended most of the way around the inside of the L-shaped building, or went into the principal's classroom; they didn't like being in there because it was too much like regular school with him sitting at his desk. Outside, they'd swing, or just sit on the swings and talk, and play chase, hide and seek, hopscotch, Mother May I?, jacks, marbles, or some other game. And sometimes, they'd skin-the-cat on the old iron structure that had once supported seesaws, or turn somersaults over it. Lora Lee wished the seesaws were still there; that would've added one more thing they could do before and after school.

Of the three kids that the janitor picked up, Lora Lee liked the ten-year old boy, Levi, and the eight-year-old girl, Julie, but she didn't like the older boy, Herman, who was fifteen and had failed a grade. Lora Lee had seen him smoking out behind the school one morning, and she thought he was stupid; she knew he'd probably get expelled if he got caught smoking on the school grounds. And Herman would cuss right in front of girls. Even Stone, who was always picking fights, didn't cuss in front of girls. No other boys did. A little pudgy, Herman was sloppy about his appearance, and his face was covered with freckles. And he liked to spit. But none of that would have stopped her from liking him—not even the freckles or the spitting; lots of boys spit. She wouldn't have judged him for his appearance, but his personality irritated her and it seemed to fit the way he looked.

A couple of months before, Lora Lee was swinging one day after school, and Herman sat down in the other swing and started chatting. Lora Lee thought he was too lazy to swing. He never went high, and usually just sat in the swing, or twisted it up and spun around. He was telling her about something that happened at the cattle auction, something she didn't care anything about. Every now and then, when he stopped talking for a minute, he'd spit on the sand in front of him.

"I ain't gonna swing over there today," she thought, looking at the sand.

After he'd been there for a while, he stuck his hand in his pocket and said, "Bet ya cain't guess what I got in my pocket."

Without really thinking, Lora Lee asked, "Is it candy?"

Herman laughed a laugh full of ridicule.

"Is it caaaaaaandy?" he asked in a high mocking tone, and laughed more, like he'd just heard a really funny joke.

"What is it?" she asked as she stopped pumping and allowed her swing to slow down.

"Is it caaaaaaandy?" he repeated, laughing.

She had no idea what was in his pocket, and she was feeling irritated and stupid, wondering if there was some reason she should know what it was. Her brain searched for possibilities, but she couldn't think of anything. She had gradually stopped swinging, and just sat there while he repeated her question over and over, drawing out "candy" each time, and laughing like it was the funniest thing he'd ever heard. She was on the verge of tears, feeling humiliated for some reason she didn't even understand, when the station wagon horn blew, and Herman had to leave. After he left, she shed a few tears, mostly out of anger.

Her dislike for him turned to hatred, and she thought he was the most repulsive person she knew—even more than Howlie May! She thought about turning him in for smoking, but she knew nothing would be done unless he got caught in the act, and she was afraid he'd find out she told on him, and things would get even worse. "They oughta send 'im ta Chattahoochee," she thought. "That boy's crazy." The Florida State Hospital for the mentally ill is in the small city of Chattahoochee.

She wondered later why she hadn't called him "a stupid jerk" or the most awful name she could think of, but she decided that would probably have made him worse. And he was a lot bigger than her and she wasn't sure she could outrun him. She still wondered why she hadn't just got up and left. "I know most he knew I couldn' guess what wuz in his stupid pocket. He jus' wonted ta make fun a me. How come I sat there like a bump on a log when he wouldn' even tell me, an' jus' kep' on makin' fun a me?"

The whole situation made her furious, and it made her feel shame. She replayed the scenario often in her mind, each time trying to figure out what he had in his pocket. She was too embarrassed about it to even tell Missy. She thought there must be something logical that she was missing, and Missy might know and laugh at her, too.

The teasing got even worse when Herman told Bruce, who was thirteen. Whenever they saw her at school, both of them would say in unison, "Is it caaaaaaandy?" Then they'd laugh hysterically.

"I hafta forgit about that mess," Lora Lee told herself each time she started thinking about it. But she couldn't. And she started going out of her way to avoid them. Unfortunately, their classes had lunch at the same time, but she made sure she stayed as far away from them as possible in the lunch line and in the small lunchroom. Occasionally, one or both of them would walk behind her, ask, "Is it caaaaaaandy?" and laugh. Then the kids sitting near her would ask why they said that. Lora Lee would say,

"They're just actin' crazy," or "They like ta pester me," and that seemed to satisfy everybody.

She even started going to Mr. Docker's classroom in the morning and after school, until the station wagon left with Herman. At least, she took that opportunity in the afternoon to get some of her homework done while she was in there, and she didn't have to lug as many books home with her. She liked that, but wasn't feeling any gratitude toward the two boys.

When she got off the bus, she went straight to Mr. Docker's room and worked on her book report, writing slowly with her fountain pen. She got so involved in it that she was surprised when the Brewster kids started entering the room, which meant it was almost time for school to start. She hurriedly got her things together and started down the porch.

Suddenly, she heard, "Is it caaaaaandy?" When she turned, looking for the voice, she tripped on the old wooden floor, and as she fell, her books and papers flew everywhere. She looked up quickly and saw Herman standing in a doorway, laughing. Other kids were laughing, too, but she didn't look around to see who all was there.

She scrambled to her feet and started picking up her papers. "Stupid jerk!" she thought. "Now, I'm gonna be late."

♥ ♥ ♥

THE SIXTH GRADE CLASSROOM was IN A HOUSE about a block from the school building. The school, with grades one to eight, had an auditorium, a lunchroom, a library, a storage room, and only five classrooms, so some of the lower grades shared classrooms. Twenty-one kids were in the sixth grade—seven girls and fourteen boys—the largest class in the school.

Lora Lee liked being in a house and separate from the rest of the school. The only negative thing was that the class had to go to the main building for math and lunch; when it rained, she got wet because she didn't have a raincoat. The house had a classroom, a bathroom, a large kitchen, and a room with sewing machines where the sixth, seventh, and eighth grade girls had home economics. The students also used the entry room, which had some furniture, including a table and chairs.

When the school year started, the kids in her class didn't know what to call the building. One cold day, when some of the boys were on the playground, Jimmy said, "Let's go to the schoolhouse."

Arnold asked, "Which one?"

"There ain't but one," Jimmy said.

Arnold said, "Our building's a school house, too."

"Nuh-uh. It's just a house that's bein' used as a school. It ain't really no schoolhouse."

"Okay, then," Arnold decided. "Let's call it the 'house school,' an' then we'll know which place we're talkin' 'bout." And they did.

Lora Lee had to run to avoid being late. As she ran, she thought about how much better her life would be without Herman. "Of course, there's Lola an' her fan club."

Ella, Cynthia, and Mary Sue didn't instigate anything, but when Lola did, they backed her up. They'd given Lora Lee a hard time ever since she started there in the fourth grade, especially Lola. They did things that hurt Lora Lee's feelings, like looking at her while they were whispering and laughing, or looking down their noses at her like she was white trash, or making snide remarks about her freckles or her clothes. Mary Sue was rather plain, but the other three were cute. Lola had dark brown hair and blue eyes that sparkled when she laughed. Her father and Ella's and Cynthia's all worked in the company offices, or had other more respectable jobs than those who worked with the mining operation, and they lived on the "better" side of Brewster.

Lora Lee couldn't understand why Lola made fun of her, when she seemed to have everything. Lora Lee figured Lola's father made a lot more money than hers did. Lola had nice clothes and shoes, and a brand new bicycle, which she rode to school; most of the older Brewster kids rode bikes to school unless they lived within a block of the school. And all the boys seemed to like Lola. In the beginning, Lora Lee had wanted to be her friend, but after the way she treated her, Lora Lee decided that she was definitely not the kind of person she wanted for a friend. She just wished she wouldn't be mean to her, and she thought if Lola would be nice to her, the other three girls would be, too.

When Lora Lee lived on Combee Road, she had several friends at school, and all the kids were friendly. When she started at Brewster, it seemed to her that they all had their places, and she didn't fit anywhere. She hung around with Grace, the other country girl, and Emily, who also had freckles, but they were both more than a year older than her, and she sometimes felt like a fifth wheel with them.

On her way to the house school, she listened for the bell as she ran. She was glad to see Arnold and Jimmy walking up the porch steps, and she ran in right behind them, arriving just in time.

Mrs. Hoffman looked at her with surprise because Lora Lee was usually there before the bell. After all, she was at the school almost an hour early. "I marked you 'absent,' Lora Lee," she said, erasing the mark.

"Sorry, Miz Hoffman," Lora Lee said as she slid into her seat.

She really liked Mrs. Hoffman, who obviously liked the kids, and treated them really well. When they returned to the classroom after lunch, she'd often read to them. She read several of *The Bobbsey Twins* books to them, and they all loved them. But Lora Lee's favorite was the one she was reading now, *The Gabriel Horn*. It was a condensed version that left out the racy stuff, but the kids didn't know that. Although Lora Lee had trouble remembering a lot of her schoolwork, she easily remembered what Big Eli said when he was asked, once, to say the grace before a meal: "God bless our vittles, God bless our shack, God bless Aunt Soph and Uncle Zack. Amen." Aunt Soph and Uncle Zack were not impressed with his creativity, but Little Eli was. And Lora Lee was.

As Lora Lee settled in her seat, Mrs. Hoffman told them to get out a piece of paper for the spelling test. They were supposed to have the test on Friday, but they had a spelling bee Thursday afternoon, and they did poorly, so Mrs. Hoffman said they needed to study more and postponed the test until Monday. Lora Lee had done well in the spelling bee, and, as often happened, she was the last one standing. She liked spelling.

"Good gravy! I forgot we were havin' a test today," she thought. She'd gone over the words briefly on Friday, and forgot to look at them again. "I hope I 'member the stupid words." Mrs. Hoffman always gave them an extra, difficult word. If they got it right, they got five bonus points, and occasionally, Lora Lee would make 105 on a test.

Mrs. Hoffman called out all the spelling words. Then she announced, "The extra word for this week is 'theatrical.'"

Lora Lee immediately saw it in her mind. "Oh goodie, I know that," she thought. "She's givin' us that 'cause some a the words are hard."

But before she could write anything, Arnold sprang from his seat. Just the sound of the word was enough to set him off. He couldn't spell it, but he could be it. He started waving his arms around and making faces, being very theatrical. The class was in hysterics, and Arnold was in his glory.

By the time Mrs. Hoffman commanded, "Sit down, Arnold," her voice was angry. Lora Lee saw squinting eyes and a furrowed brow.

Arnold sat down, but he ignored the angry tone, and continued with his theatrics.

The class was laughing, and Mrs. Hoffman was losing patience. She yelled, "Arnold, knock it off."

There was a bottle of glue sitting on the front of his desk, and he looked at it, started giggling, and knocked it off the desk. The class roared. And Arnold was laughing so hard he slid from his chair onto the floor.

Mrs. Hoffman didn't find it funny. In fact, she was the maddest Lora Lee had ever seen her. She collected all the test papers and, slamming them down on her desk, announced that there would be no extra credit for anyone. She looked at Arnold through squinty eyes and said through gritted teeth, "Arnold, you come with me."

He'd stopped laughing, as had the rest of the class, and had slowly climbed back onto his chair. Mrs. Hoffman grabbed him by the arm and led him out the front door. The class could hear her talking in the front yard.

"Ya reckon she's gonna take 'im ta see Mr. Docker?" Jimmy asked. "It wadn' really that bad."

He went to the doorway of the classroom where he could see through the front windows. All Lora Lee had to do was turn around in her seat and she could see out. Mrs. Hoffman was facing Arnold, yelling at him, and still holding onto his arm, which she shook every now and then. Lora Lee was surprised because Mrs. Hoffman didn't usually get mad when Arnold did disruptive stuff like that. Normally, she would've laughed with the class before restoring order.

"She's yellin' at 'im," Jimmy announced, "an' jerkin' his arm. "I swear, if she keeps that up, it might jus' fall off."

Lora Lee thought Jimmy was cute. She'd had a crush on him in the fourth grade. She'd sat across the table from him, three kids on each side of the table. When someone would break wind, Jimmy would hold his nose and ask, "Who pooted?" Then he'd laugh a distinct laugh, which sounded sort of forced out like a cough. And when he laughed, all the kids at the table laughed, and they'd all try to laugh quietly to keep from getting in trouble. Jimmy would try to find the culprit, saying, "It wuz you" to somebody, or asking, "Wuz it you?" Lora Lee never admitted it, but some of the boys would laugh, nodding their heads, proudly accepting responsibility. Jimmy never did, though. He always blamed someone else.

Lora Lee realized that her knee was hurting and was surprised to see that it was skinned a little. She went to the bathroom and cleaned it with a wet paper towel. "Dadblamed Herman," she thought. It wasn't bleeding, but it smarted. Lora Lee knew her mother would probably ask her if she cleaned it, and probably put some Merthiolate on it, which Lora Lee knew would burn like crazy. She dreaded it already. Then she thought maybe she could get her to use Mercurochrome instead. They both would turn it red, but Mercurochrome wouldn't burn.

She was back in her seat when Arnold returned, and Jimmy went back to his seat. Lora Lee was watching when Mrs. Hoffman entered the house a moment later, and she saw her wipe her eyes. Lora Lee turned around quickly.

"She wuz cryin'," she thought. "Mus' be sumpin bad wrong wi' her. She wouldn' cry 'bout Arnold knockin' the glue off his desk. Pore Miz Hoffman." She decided she wouldn' tell anyone. She knew Mrs. Hoffman wouldn't want anyone to know she'd been crying, and she could count on Lora Lee to keep her secret.

Arnold sat down with a chastened demeanor, but Lora Lee saw him grin at Jimmy. She felt badly that he got in trouble for something the class all enjoyed so much, but she knew he tended to take things too far.

"Okay, class," Mrs. Hoffman said as though nothing had happened. "Please open your English books to today's lesson." Lora Lee noticed that the class was quieter than usual the rest of the day.

Physical education, the last class, was the one she disliked most, even more than geography. However, she was always happy when it came because they went outside, and the day was almost over. The sixth, seventh, and eighth grade girls were together for phys. ed. They changed into their gym clothes in the girl's bathroom and the older girls were usually dressed and out before the sixth graders got there. Lora Lee didn't like having to change in front of the others because they were all more developed than she was. She was the only one who wasn't wearing a bra, although some of them didn't seem to need one. The girls wore shorts, but Lora Lee's parents didn't approve of shorts, so she wore pedal pushers.

When she was ready to go, she saw Lola and her group near the sink looking at something on the wall, and laughing. A glance told her it was a drawing, with something written underneath. She knew it was about her and her heart sank. She wanted to take down the drawing, so she washed her hands, hoping they'd leave. She was afraid she'd cry in front of them, but when she turned around, they were gone.

She studied the paper. There was a round, hand-drawn face with dots all over it. Underneath was written, "Geuss who. Initils are LL."

"She cain't even spell!" she thought, snatching the paper off the wall. She folded it, and stuck it in her pocketbook. "I guess there's jus' too much meanness in her pretty little head to leave any room for spellin'." She slunk down onto the bench across from the lockers, swallowed hard, and fought back the tears, not wanting anyone to see evidence that she'd been crying. "How come she's doin' this? I ain't never done nothin' ta her. She ain't ever liked me since we moved here. If she did that ta Emily, she'd beat 'er up!" She felt even less like playing than usual, but she knew Mrs. Hoffman would be looking for her soon, so she got up and dragged herself outside.

They were playing volleyball, which Lora Lee wasn't fond of because she wasn't good at it, especially at returning the serves. One of the eighth graders would hit the ball so that it went real high, and Lora Lee always missed it when it went to her. She was not only afraid of missing it, but also of getting hit by it.

Of course, the first thing they did was to choose teams, something Lora Lee hated. Mrs. Hoffman chose two girls to be captains, and then the captains chose people for their teams. Lora Lee knew she'd be picked last because she always was. She was the youngest and the smallest, and, she realized, the worst player. As she expected, she was picked last. She thought it would be fairer and less embarrassing to kids like her if they chose their teams with "One potato, two potato." "That would actually be fun," she thought. "An' if that took too much time, they could jus' count off, with evens on one team, an' odds on the other."

Luckily, she ended up on the team with the girl who had the high serve, and she did all right in the game, but she could not get a serve over the net. She listened to Mrs. Hoffman tell them how to serve, but it just didn't work for her. Of course, the only time she ever had a chance to try was the three or four times it was her turn during the game. She thought if she could just practice a little, she could do it. She did manage to hit the ball over the net a few times when it went to her, and she actually had fun. And before she knew it, the school day was over.

♥ ♥ ♥

Lora Lee waited near the street for Billy, watching some girls playing hopscotch and wishing she could play, and some boys playing tag football, and looking occasionally for Billy's car. She didn't notice Herman until she heard, "Is it caaaaaaandy?" and his laughter.

She jumped and he laughed harder, and the look on his face told her that scaring her had given him a lot of pleasure. She figured he'd tell Bruce about it the next day. "I'd like ta slap the fire outta him," she thought as she looked at him with anger in her eyes, and then returned her attention to the football game.

"Is it caaaaaaandy?"

She heard a horn blow and realized she'd forgotten about Billy.

She picked up her arithmetic book, her notebook, and her sweater, and ran to the car.

"Hey gal young'un. Who's that boy?" Billy asked.

"Oh, that's that stupid Herman Kram," she said. "He's a big pest."

"Wuz he botherin' you?" Billy asked, looking at him sternly.

"He always is," Lora Lee sighed.

Billy looked to see if any cars were coming. Then he turned the corner staring at Herman. When Herman looked at the car, he saw the look Billy gave him.

And Lora Lee saw it, too—his brown eyes looked threatening. "Maybe that'll make him leave me alone," she thought. She felt warm all over with Billy's concern for her. She looked at his wavy brown hair and remembered how good-looking he was.

"Let me know if he bothers you," he said.

She thought, "I wish Billy'd beat the tar outta him," but she knew she wouldn't be telling Billy that, or about the way Herman taunted her. She figured Billy had more important things to think about than what happened to her, and she knew it was her fight, even though Herman was a big boy. Nevertheless, in that moment, she felt intense love for her brother, and she basked in that all the way home.

They stopped at the mailbox, which was on the paved road at the end of their dirt road, but there was no mail. Billy parked in the front yard, and King ran out to greet them. Lora Lee was happy that he went to Billy, jumping up on him, instead of her. She ran into the house before he could get to her.

She and Billy quickly changed their clothes. "I hafta git the eggs," she announced as they were getting some iced tea from the refrigerator.

"Don't worry. I gotta milk now. It'll be dark before we git back home." Billy yawned, stretched his arms above his head, and said, "Lord a mercy! I'd stretch a mile if I didn' hafta walk back."

Lora Lee had heard him say that many times, but she still thought it was clever. She had a love-hate relationship with Billy, and that afternoon, she loved him.

"I been working all day an' now I gotta go work some more," he said. "An' sometime this week, I gotta disk the grove, prob'ly Wednesday, and move the water pipes from the pepper rows. For cryin' out loud, you'd think I didn' even have a regular job." His agreement with Caleb was that he could live at home and work for the phosphate company, but he'd still work on the farm.

Caleb depended on him, and he didn't pay Billy. He usually had him drive the tractor to disk the grove and the field. There were two brothers around forty who sometimes worked on the farm, but one drank, and the other was slightly retarded, so Caleb didn't trust either one to drive the tractor. The grass and weeds were getting high in the grove and the two rows of heavy, sharp metal disks cut them into the soil.

Billy got a biscuit from the kitchen safe, poked a hole in it with his finger, and filled the hole with cane syrup. Then he got the milk bucket and put a little water in it to wash the cow's teats with. "Don't go off nowhere," he said.

"I won't, 'cept ta git the eggs." She got the round aluminum pan from the kitchen and went to the chicken coop behind the house. One hen was leaving the coop and cackling when Lora Lee got there. Even though the chickens roamed free, they'd usually lay their eggs in the hay-lined nests in the coop. Occasionally, Ruth would notice that she wasn't getting as many eggs as usual, and she'd complain that one of the hens was setting somewhere. Then, she and Lora Lee would look for the nest. However, when she wanted more chickens, she was glad to have them set.

Lora Lee could hear Billy calling "Guernsey, Guernsey." She knew the cow would go to him because he'd have a bucket of feed for her.

There weren't any chickens in the coop, and she was glad not to have to deal with their scolding, "Cluck, cluck, cluck," and occasional pecking, if they were about to lay an egg. She collected seven eggs, and put the pan on the kitchen counter.

She washed her hands and got herself a biscuit. She'd never eaten one like Billy's, and she didn't do it now. She knew she had time to put some cane syrup in a saucer, mix in some butter, and sop it up with the biscuit.

When Billy returned, he strained the milk through a clean cloth, put the milk in a large bowl, and put it in the refrigerator. Then they took off for the other place.

Once there, she and Billy drove slowly past the big field of watermelons with her hoping they could pick one to take home with them. She knew the price was always higher at the beginning of the season, but when they got to where her parents were working, she asked, "Daddy, can we please pick a watermelon?"

"No," Caleb said. "The price is too high now for *us* to be eatin' 'em."

Just as Lora Lee expected. And also as she expected, Ruth noticed her skinned knee and said she'd put some Merthiolate on it when they got home.

There was nothing for her to do that day, so she walked down to the narrow, shallow creek that ran through the middle of the property. She passed the open place where they could drive across the creek, and went to where the cypress trees grew. She admired the cypress knees that protruded from the water, some of nature's unique wooden sculptures.

"It's so funny how they grow," she thought. "Funny peculiar, not funny ha ha." They had a varnished cypress knee at home that had belonged to her grandmother Baker, and Lora Lee really liked it.

As she left there, she heard a hawk and looked up in time to see it circle once before it flew away. There were magnolia bay trees and some oak trees along the sides of the creek with Spanish moss dripping from them. She grabbed a piece of low-hanging moss and pulled it through her loosely closed hand a few times.

When she was back to the open place, she looked in the trees for the rat-a-tat sound she was hearing, and finally saw a redheaded woodpecker on a dead branch way up in a tree. "Hey, purty bird," she called, and it flew to another part of the creek and she could hear a faint rat-a-tat.

She slipped off her old shoes and waded in the cool, clear, shallow water. She loved feeling the sand under her feet and she wiggled her toes so that it came up between them. Near the edge, she saw some minnows about an inch long. She tried to scoop some up with her hands, but they were too fast. Stopping for a moment, she just listened to the softly trickling water.

Lora Lee liked being over there in the summer. For lunch, they'd often go to the little store in Fort Lonesome—which was almost the only thing in Fort Lonesome—and buy drinks, sardines, crackers, and sometimes, cheese. They kept a can opener, a knife, and some forks in the truck's glove compartment, and they ate the sardines right out of the cans. That was a treat for Lora Lee, something different from the kind of meals they normally had. And she got to get a Grapette to drink. She asked Caleb one day if the sardines still had the guts in them. He replied crossly, "If you want 'em, eat 'em. If you don't, don't." She took that as a "Yes," and ate them anyway.

Lora Lee drank some water from the creek a few steps upstream from where she was wading, as she had many times with her father. Caleb said it was okay to drink since it was flowing well. Then she chased some water bugs that scooted across the top of the water, but they were too fast for her. She watched a water spider run across the water, but didn't even want to catch it.

Wading in the creek reminded her of the Saturday that Jimmy had gone to her house with his father. Lora Lee had been excited to see him since she had a crush on him. Their fathers were going down to the pasture, and the two youngsters followed a ways behind them in silence until they got to the creek that was between the orange grove and the field. The creek and surrounding swamp went all the way through the property, but, as at the other place, the creek was shallow enough where it crossed the dirt road that they could drive right through it.

All the way, Lora Lee was trying hard to think of something interesting to say, but Jimmy spoke first. When he saw Caleb's fishing boat sitting in the water with oars in it, he exclaimed, "Oh boy! Le's go out in the boat."

"Good idea," Lora Lee responded as her heart skipped a beat.

The creek was only about twenty feet wide and forty feet long so they couldn't go far, but Jimmy enjoyed rowing around. Lora Lee's heart was beating fast as she sat in the boat, watching him paddle.

"Do ya use the boat much?" he asked.

"Nope. It's Daddy's fishin' boat. He jus' keeps it in the water here. We use it when we go fishin' in the pits, but we ain't gone for a long time."

"Which ones y'all go to?"

"Mostly number four. It's closest, an' Daddy almost always catches fish there."

"We go there sometimes, too," he said, and Lora Lee wished they'd be there at the same time.

When they saw their fathers coming, Jimmy paddled back to where the boat had been. They climbed out, and he secured the boat.

"That wuz fun," she said, smiling.

Jimmy looked at her, shaking his head. "Don't tell nobody we did that," he said as though they'd done something terrible.

Lora Lee felt a stab in her heart. "He don't wont the kids at school ta know," she thought. "Guess he'd be ashamed for them to know we were in a boat together." And she felt ashamed that she'd actually had a crush on him. "From now on, by cracky, I shore won't pay him no never mind."

She still thought he was cute, and she'd finally started to like him a little as a friend, but she didn't trust him, and the crush was definitely gone. "That wuz really mean a him," she thought as she finally managed to catch a water bug, which she immediately released. She was still wading in the water when she heard the truck coming with her parents and Billy in it. She looked toward the truck and saw a white sheet of rain moving toward them.

"Hurry up an' git in," her father said, "there's a white rain a comin'.'"

She grabbed her shoes and squeezed in the cab onto Billy's lap. They drove across the creek, through the surrounding woods, and through the orange grove on the other side. Caleb parked close to the old wooden farmhouse and they all rushed in just before the rain got there. A pink oleander bush was blooming in the front yard, but there was no lawn, just a continuation of the weeds and growth in the grove.

They just walked around looking at the house. It had a tin roof, with no ceiling, and when the rain hit, it was so noisy they stopped talking because they couldn't hear each other. It reminded Lora Lee of their old kitchen. When the rain slowed, Caleb said, "This place ain't in bad shape. They can move in right away."

Lora Lee started getting excited, "Who's movin' in?" she asked, wondering who'd want to live in that old house.

Caleb had met a young man at the farmers' market in Plant City who was looking for work, and Caleb had offered him a position sharecropping. He was married and had five little children under six.

"A young man an' his fam'ly," Caleb said. "Arkansas travelers."

"Have they got any furniture?" Ruth asked.

"He said they had some. I told 'im we might have some stuff they could have if they need it." He put his arm around Lora Lee. "Double L, they got a slew a little young'uns, five a 'em, an' one a 'em's a baby."

"Oh goodie," she said, and threw her arms around her father's waist.

"Well, we don't have much," Ruth said. "But we do have that bed out in the barn we used before we got your mama's bed."

"That's right," Caleb said. "I tell you, that man needs a job. They shore need some money with all a them young'uns. When they come here, they can grow plenty a vegetables ta eat. An' he seems like he'd be a good worker."

"I cain't wait ta see them little kids," Lora Lee said, "'specially the little baby."

"He showed me a picture he had in his billfold," Caleb said. "They're all little towheads, which ain't surprisin', 'cause he's got blond hair hisse'f."

"Well," Billy said as they walked out on the porch, "they'll have the best tangerines around next winter."

There was a tangerine tree right by the house. The tangerines were sweeter than their two trees at home, and they often got some to take home.

"Ya know they're dryin' up?" Caleb asked.

"Yes, sir," Billy replied. "But what juice they got is still good."

"They're good, all right," Caleb agreed.

Billy went out in the light rain and picked four wet tangerines. They stood on the porch, peeled the fruit, and tossed the peels on the ground. Then they ate the bottom part of the slices, the only part that had any juice left, and threw the rest in the grove.

When the rain stopped, Billy left in his car, and Lora Lee went in the truck with her parents. She and Billy often rode in the back of the truck, and she sometimes rode back there by herself, leaning against the cab with the wind in her face. But today the truck was wet, and even though the rain had stopped, it was still cloudy and she knew it might start raining again before they got home.

♥   ♥   ♥

On the way home, Lora Lee started thinking about the problem with Lola. After a couple of minutes, her parents' conversation ended and she started talking about it. It was the first time she'd mentioned it to her father, but her mother had witnessed her distress twice when Lora Lee had arrived home from school in tears. As she talked, she felt tightness in her throat and pinched her arm trying not to cry. But hurting herself did not work. She didn't even know why Lola didn't like her, and she felt helpless to do anything about it. Ruth put her arm around her, and Lora Lee snuggled up next to her, sobbing.

Caleb asked if she'd done something to upset the girls.

"It's mostly Lola, an' I ain't never done nothin' ta her," Lora Lee said between sobs. "She never liked me from the time we moved here. I don't know how come, but she ain't got no use for me."

Caleb waited for her to quiet down before asking, "What do they say?"

Lora Lee sat up, feeling better that her father was interested. "They use'ly jus' look at me an' whisper ta each other an' laugh. They're jus' downright mean."

"Did ya do sumpin ta any a 'em?" he asked.

"No, sir," she answered respectfully, resenting the question and wishing she'd never started talking about it. "I ain't done the first thing to 'em, an' I ain't said nothin', either. It ain't my fault they don't like me."

But she thought, "I shoulda known he'd think it wuz my fault. He always blames me when anything goes wrong—all kinds a things. Like when the strap broke on that red pocketbook I got for my ninth birthday."

Usually they didn't celebrate birthdays, so she wasn't expecting anything. She'd been thrilled when she saw it, especially since she didn't have a pocketbook, and she knew her mother had got it for her. She proudly took it to school the next day, but when she was walking home from the bus, happily swinging it by the long strap, one end of the strap came loose. When she told her parents, thinking they'd do something about it, Caleb asked her how it happened. When she told him, he said harshly, "Well, you shouldn' a been swingin' it." So added to the disappointment of the broken purse was the guilt of breaking it. And somewhere underneath were feelings of shame and humiliation.

As they rode along in the truck, Lora Lee remembered an incident with Lola. She couldn't believe how obvious the four girls had been that day. The class was in the library, and she saw them whispering and looking at her, so she decided to go near them, thinking maybe they'd stop, but they didn't. She heard Lola say, "She's ugly an' she wears ugly clothes."

Lora Lee stepped closer to them, and said, "I know y'all are talkin' 'bout me."

Cynthia, Ella, and Mary Sue looked a little uncomfortable, but Lola said, "Oh no. We're talkin' 'bout another girl who useta live here named Lora Lee."

She looked at them as if to say, "Do ya think I'm crazy?" She repeated, "I know yo're talkin' 'bout me," and just turned and walked away. "Of all the nerve!" she thought. "They mus' think I'm ugly *an' stupid.*"

She told her father about that. "I knew they were talkin' 'bout me—Lola was lookin' right at me the whole time. An' there never wuz a girl here named Lora Lee. They mus' think I'm really stupid."

"That's jus' plain mean," Ruth said. "I've seen kids bein' mean to each other, an' lots of times, it seemed like they jus' wonted somebody to pick on. The boys fight each other, an' the girls say mean things to each other. I always put a stop to that craziness. Why don't your teacher do somethin'?" Ruth had been a teacher in Georgia in a one-room schoolhouse for three years before she married Caleb and moved to Florida with him.

"My teacher don't know nothin' 'bout it. They don't do it when she's aroun'."

"Well, there mus' be sumpin you can do, Lora Lee," Caleb said. "You could give her candy or chewin' gum."

Lora Lee could not believe her ears. "Give her candy or chewin' gum!" she thought. "What a stupid thing ta say! I ain't even got none for me. Is he plannin' ta give me money ta buy some for her, an' does he reckon she'd like me if I did?" Her heart was pounding in her ears. To her, it seemed he was trying to take care of Lola, and almost like he was one of them at that moment, and like he thought there was something wrong with her. She couldn't have verbalized it, but she wanted him to be concerned about her feelings. She wished with all her might that she could have a full-blown hissy fit right there.

"She's got all the candy an' chewin' gum she wonts," she replied, "an' she's got a new bicycle, too." The bike remark was meant to remind Caleb that she didn't have one. Of course, the reason he gave for not getting her a bike was that she had no place to ride it. And that was true—she couldn't ride a bike in that Florida sand. But she wanted one and believed she'd find a place to ride it.

Lora Lee put her head down and snuggled close to her mother again. She didn't even want to look at her father after that suggestion, and she wished she could leap out of the truck. She loved her father dearly, but he'd just touched the fragment of hatred for him that resided, beneath the love, in her heart. "Give her candy!" she thought. "That's so stupid! Tellin' me ta give her candy an' chewin' gum after the way she treats me! Shoot! I wouldn' give her nothin'! An' he don't even care that I ain't got none for me! Oooooh! By cracky, he makes me so mad!"

When they turned onto the dirt road, there was a place where the sand was almost always soft. Sometimes during a dry spell, they had to shift gears to double low just to get through the sand. As they drove through hardly moving, the truck would shake and rattle like some big giant was playing with it. Lora Lee would sing, "Shift it down ta granny low, an' shake, rattle, an' roll," and they'd laugh. But she didn't sing today.

As soon as the truck stopped in the back yard, she got out and ran up on the porch before King got there. She went to her room, closed the door, and lay down on the bed with her face in her pillow. She needed to cry, but no tears came. She was so angry at her father she wanted to scream, but she couldn't do that. "Give her candy an' chewin' gum! Of all the stupid nerve!" she thought. She started beating her pillow with her fists, gritting her teeth and pounding it. She beat it until she was exhausted.

Finally, with most of the anger released, she started feeling the deep hurt. And then, the tears came.

Tuesday

A LOUD CLAP OF THUNDER AWAKENED LORA LEE, and she sat up, took a big gulp of air, and felt her heart beating furiously. "Wuz it a bomb?" she wondered. Lightning lit up her room, and she heard it popping close by, followed by more thunder that shook the house. She heard her mother walking around, probably looking to see if the lightning had struck anything she could see.

She slowly exhaled, lay back down, and started to relax a little. Thunderstorms always scared her, but she was more frightened by the thought of a bomb dropping on her. Ever since the last time her uncle Roger had visited, she'd been afraid that the Russians were going to drop a bomb nearby, or maybe even on the house. She sometimes thought about it when she went to bed at night, and lay there with her heart beating fast, imagining terrible things. Occasionally, she had bad dreams and woke up trembling with her heart pounding against her chest.

Her uncle Roger talked a lot about the Communists, and her father usually joined right in. "Ya cain't trus' them Russians one bit."

"That's right. First chance they git, they'll be bombin' us off the face a the earth."

"They won't be satisfied till the whole world's Communist."

"Bunch a Reds. We shoulda finished 'em off at the end a World War II."

Lora Lee didn't know anything about the Russians, or Communists, or the Reds, as they often called them. All she knew was that she was scared of them. She didn't like to hear the men talking about that kind of stuff, but she couldn't quite pull herself away, afraid that she might miss something important, like maybe things had gotten worse and the bombing was imminent.

Ruth opened the bedroom door. "Are you all right, Lora Lee?"

"Yes, ma'am," she answered, wishing her mother would climb in bed with her the way she had when she was younger. "That scared me, Mama. Will you sleep wi' me?"

"Yes, but I hafta tell your daddy," she said.

Lightning was a problem on the farm almost every time it rained. There were lightning rods on top of the house, fortunately, because the kitchen stove had been hit twice even with them there. Her mother was frying chicken once when the stove got hit and lightning knocked the metal fork right out of her hand. Ruth got shocked and yelled, and Lora Lee saw the fork fly through the air. The other time, her father was frying fish, the only thing he enjoyed cooking and the only thing he cooked. When the lightning struck that time, he was turning the fish and the tines of the fork, which had a wooden handle, went right through the pan. Of course, grease went on the stove and started a small fire, which Ruth quickly smothered with baking soda, and a pan lid. They liked the frying pan, so he took it to a shop and had it repaired, but it had a little piece of metal that showed where the holes had been.

As a result of those strikes and the noise they made, Lora Lee was terrified of lightning. She avoided the kitchen and bathroom as much as possible when there was lightning, and felt safest on her bed with her feet off the floor.

Ruth soon got in bed with her and she relaxed. There were still a few more loud claps of thunder, which kept her awake, and her thoughts went back to her uncle Roger. However, this time she was thinking about how he talked about Negroes. She knew her father didn't like Negroes either, but he didn't talk about them with the intensity that Roger did. It seemed to her that Roger really hated them.

Thinking about that reminded her of a conversation she'd overheard a year earlier between her brother Billy and his friend Joe. Joe was visiting one day and he and Billy walked close to where Lora Lee was playing with her doll on the opposite side of the gardenia bush in the front yard. She knew they hadn't seen her when they started talking, so she just sat down on the ground and listened quietly. They couldn't see her through the leaves of the bush.

Billy said, "An' I spent the night wi' Pete, an' we went ta Lakeland the next day, an' Scooter went with us. I wuz ten, so they woulda been twelve. We went to see Pete's aunt, who lived right by the Quarters. We were out in the back yard, an' we seen these two little colored young'uns, a boy 'bout my age, an' a girl about seven, walkin' on the railroad tracks, lookin' down at 'em. They didn't see us till they got close by, prob'ly thirty feet away. When they seen us, they turned around an' started back, an' Scooter said, 'Come on. Let's pelt 'em.' An' him an' Pete got some rocks from the railroad bed an' started hittin' the boy. He grabbed the little gal's hand, an' they took off runnin', an' we took off after 'em."

Lora Lee's heart was beating fast as she listened.

"Did y'all catch 'em?" Joe asked.

"Pete an' Scooter had ta keep stoppin' ta pick up more rocks, but we kep' up with 'em. The little gal fell down, an' while the boy wuz helpin' her up, they were really peltin' him. Fin'ly, a rock hit his head an' he grabbed his head, left the lil gal behine, an' took off for a house. An' then them sorry jerks startin' peltin' the girl. Course, she started cryin'."

Lora Lee had tears in her eyes. She never had liked Pete or Scooter. "I hope I never see them jerks ag'in," she thought. "Pore little kids. How could they throw rocks at a little girl?" She was imagining how it would feel to be hit by rocks.

"'Bout the time she got to the house," Billy continued, "two colored women come out, an' we all turned aroun' an' started walkin' away. One a 'em went out in the yard an' shook her fist an' yelled at us, 'Why don't y'all pick on somebody yo' own size? Maybe ya'd like ta try me.' She called us cowards an' brats, an' said she'd take on all three of us."

"Wow! Sounds like a mad mama hen," Joe said.

"She wuz mad, by cracky! Scared the heck outta me, an' we were a ways away from 'er by then."

"It's the first I heard about it," Joe said. "You didn' throw no rocks?"

"Nuh-uh. But that triflin', no-account Pete an' Scooter threw a slew a 'em. An' that's one time I'm glad I didn' go back on my raisin'—I feel bad jus' rememberin' the whole thing. After that boy got to the house, he looked right at me, an' I felt so ashamed, jus' bein' there. An' I had nightmares about it for a while; I wuz throwin' rocks at Nigras, or they were throwin' rocks at me."

"I'm glad I wadn' wi' y'all," Joe said.

"I guess I'm too much of a Christian ta think it's all right ta treat people like that, even colored people," Billy said. "I don't like 'em much, but I ain't gonna hurt 'em."

Lora Lee was relieved. "That's how I feel," she thought. She would have been disappointed if her brother had thrown rocks. "I don't like Nigras, either, but I wouldn' hurt 'em.' I wouldn' hurt nobody, even that stupid Lola or stupid jerk Howlie May." She thought for a minute before adding, "Well, I might hurt Herman. . . . I prob'ly would."

As Joe and Billy walked away, Lora Lee heard Joe say, "My daddy works with a Nigra man in Brewster that comes to the house ever' now an' then. Him an' Daddy sit out on the front porch an' drink ice tea an' talk. Daddy asked him ta go in the house once, but he said he's more comf'table sittin' out on the porch. I don't know why."

Lora Lee didn't know when she drifted off to sleep, but she woke up when she heard her mother in the kitchen. She lay there for a minute listening to the rooster crowing. She wanted to go back to sleep, but she thought about her book report. She still had about a page left to write; she didn't want to write it in Mr. Docker's room before school because she was afraid Mrs. Hoffman, who sometimes went to see Mr. Docker, would see her finishing it at the last minute. Mrs. Hoffman had warned them a few times about when the reports were due, so Lora Lee had no excuse for not having it done. She just always waited until the last minute.

She had intended to work on her report the day before when they got home from the other place, but she was too upset to work on it before supper, and after supper they'd watched television until Caleb turned it off at 9:30 after "I Love Lucy." She knew she should be working on the report, but she chose to watch television since she was upset. Her parents didn't know she had a report due, or anything about her homework. When she went to her room, she wrote until she got sleepy; then she turned off the light and went to bed. It was earlier than she normally went to bed, but she felt exhausted.

Actually, Lora Lee went to her bedroom at a decent time every night. Her parents, like other farmers, went to bed early and got up early, so they went right to bed when they went to their room. Consequently, they didn't know that Lora Lee often lay in bed with a library book, reading long after she should have been asleep.

When she would get up to turn off the light, she'd be very careful because the light switch made a loud click when she turned it on or off. She always tried to keep it quiet because she didn't want her mother to know that she was still awake, and she seemed to hear everything. If Ruth heard it, she'd ask the next morning what she was doing up so late. Occasionally, Lora Lee would say that she was reading, but usually, she said she forgot to do part of her homework or she was studying for a test. Actually, studying for tests would have been a good idea, and when she was taking tests, she often wished she'd done more of that, instead of reading a novel.

Sometimes Ruth would tell her to go straight to bed, and Lora Lee did, even though she wanted to read if she had a library book out. She noticed that she woke up more easily in the morning when she did go straight to bed, but that didn't change her desire to enter into the imaginary world she found in books.

When her mother called her, Lora Lee had finished the report and had everything ready to take to school. She hurriedly did her bathroom chores, dressed quickly, and went to eat. "Well, look at you," Ruth said. "I haven't seen you ready so early in a coon's age."

"I woke up early," Lora Lee said. She could have added that she didn't want to have to run for the bus again. "Is Daddy in the field?" She was relieved that he wasn't in the kitchen since she was not in the mood to have to act like nothing had happened Monday evening. She was still upset with him for telling her to give Lola candy or chewing gum.

"Yes, he is," Ruth replied, nodding her head.

Lora Lee ate her grits, fried egg, and bacon. As usual, she cut off the brown edge from her egg. Ruth fried eggs quickly and the edges browned before the yolk was done. It was the one thing Ruth cooked that Lora Lee wasn't happy with. She wished she'd cook them the way her sister Linda did. Her eggs weren't brown on the edges, and Lora Lee asked Linda why hers weren't and their mother's were.

"Mama's always in a hurry ta git things done in the mornin'," Linda said. "She's useta havin' ta git to the field as quick as she can. She's been doin' that her whole life."

"Well, when I git big, I'm gonna cook my eggs slow like you do," Lora Lee said.

She thought about that conversation as she ate her breakfast. She knew her mother worked hard. She was in the fields about as much as her father was, plus she did all the cooking and cleaning up. After a long, hard day working in the fields from early morning until dusk, Caleb would sit in his easy chair while Ruth cooked supper. After supper, Ruth cleaned up the kitchen, usually having Lora Lee do the dishes, while Caleb relaxed in front of the television. When Ruth was finally done, she only had a little while to relax before time for bed.

"I ain't gonna marry no farmer," Lora Lee thought. "I shore don't wanna hafta work like Mama does, nohow."

She finished her breakfast and got out of the house in plenty of time to walk to the bus. Strolling along, she thought about her book report, and remembered the one she did in the fifth grade on Bambi. They had to read their reports to the class, and when she was in the middle of hers, the fire alarm went off, and they had to leave the classroom for a fire drill. As they stood orderly in line waiting for permission to return to the classroom,

Arnold, who was standing behind her, asked her a question about Bambi, and said he couldn't wait to find out what happened. She figured she must have done a pretty good job if he was interested. She smiled, remembering their conversation. She hoped he and the other kids would find this report interesting, too.

♥　♥　♥

WHEN THE BUS ARRIVED, LORA LEE WAS SINGING "Long Tall Sally," happy that Rita wouldn't have to wait for her that morning. She greeted her with a big smile.

"I see yo're still in one piece after that storm last night," Rita said.

"Yeah, it woke me up," she replied. That was quite amazing in itself because Lora Lee had been known to sleep through storms like that, as well as other loud noises.

"It hit that pine tree right there by that bob wire fence on the edge a y'all's property," Rita said as they passed a tree with a split trunk.

"Lucky no cows were standin' by it," Lora Lee said as she noticed the cows eating grass in the pasture. She knew that cows could be electrocuted if they were too close to a fence or tree when lightning hit.

"Y'all got some purty calves," Rita said. "Look at them three little ones runnin' aroun'."

"I know it. An' there's more a 'em somewhere."

Rita asked Leroy about the storm also. She and Lora Lee laughed when he told them that he'd slept right through it.

"I cain't believe that," Rita said. "You missed some fireworks."

"Oh Lord!" Leroy suddenly exclaimed. Rita and Lora Lee already knew what he was going to say next. "Somebody run over a polecat!" They were all holding their noses as they passed the squished skunk lying in the middle of the road.

"Come on, buzzards," Rita said, and they all laughed.

"Somebody hit one Sunday night, too," Lora Lee said. "We smelled it comin' home from church."

"Yeah, it was still on the road yesterday mornin'," Rita said. "Still stinkin'. But there were some buzzards 'round it, an' it was gone by the afternoon."

There were ditches on both sides of the road, and Lora Lee looked out the window at the water standing in them from the night's rain, occasionally seeing long-legged white birds wading in the water and sticking their long beaks under it. On the other side of the ditches stood neat rows of longleaf pine trees about twenty feet tall, which the phosphate company had planted on company land. She liked pine trees, especially the big old trees behind their back pasture. She'd been back there with her father a couple of times when he was quail hunting. The dipping vat that they ran the cows through periodically to help keep insects off of them was in the back pasture, as were the windmill that pumped water for the cows to drink, and the salt lick that Caleb had recently built with a tin roof to protect it from the rain.

"Lookie there," Leroy exclaimed, pointing to a tall, dead tree. "There's a bald eagle."

"Shore is," Rita said.

Lora Lee saw it sitting on a limb high up in the tree. She hadn't seen many bald eagles, and she was pleased to see it.

When they arrived at the school, she decided to swing with Leroy until the station wagon appeared. As soon as she saw the car, she stopped pumping so the swing would come to a stop. However, when the car passed the swings, she didn't see Herman.

"Maybe he ain't here today," she thought, feeling happy. She smiled, gave a big push with her feet, and started her swing moving again, pumping hard to go high. "I guess he won't be botherin' me today." She didn't think Bruce would say anything to her without his buddy, Herman. "Thank heaven," she thought as the swing went higher and higher. "I wish Billy would beat 'im up—him an' Bruce." Swinging always made her feel free, like she was flying, and now she felt completely exhilarated.

Later, as she walked to the house school, she thought, "This is a lot better 'n yesterday. I didn' hafta run for the bus or for class." Then she thought about Lola's drawing in the bathroom. "I oughta draw a picture a her. See how she likes it. Lola Hornsby. I know, I could draw a head wi' horns on it an' write 'horns by.' I cain't help it if that's her name." But Lora Lee knew she wouldn't do it. She was afraid she'd get in trouble, and she didn't want to hurt Lola's feelings, even though Lola didn't seem to care about hers.

When she arrived at the house school, all the kids were standing outside. "Miz Hoffman's not here yet?" she asked Arnold, who was standing by the side of the house.

"Nope. The door's still locked," he answered. "See ya later." He looked up at the spindly oak tree right by the house, spat on the ground, and started climbing the tree.

When Mrs. Hoffman stopped her car in the driveway, she jumped out and rushed to open the door. Then she shooed everybody inside.

"She mus' notta wonted people ta know she wuz late," Lora Lee thought.

"Last one in's a rotten egg," Jimmy called.

When they were seated in the classroom, Mrs. Hoffman looked around to see if everyone was present. "Everybody's here but Arnold. Is he absent today?"

"He wuz on the bus this mornin'," Jimmy said.

"I saw 'im outside," Lora Lee said. "He wuz climbin' that tree next ta the house."

"Climbin' the tree?" Mrs. Hoffman asked, looking a little concerned. "That tree's hardly big enough to climb."

There was a noise on the roof, and everybody looked at the ceiling. Then they looked at each other.

"Oh my Lord," Mrs. Hoffman breathed. She rushed for the door and everybody followed her. They all stood in the front yard staring at Arnold, who was in the middle of the roof, straddling the peak like he was riding a horse, and grinning from ear to ear. Mrs. Hoffman didn't say a word for a minute. No one did, but there were a few nervous giggles and shaking of heads.

Finally, she spoke. "Arnold, I wont you to slowly an' carefully crawl over to the tree."

Arnold sat still for a moment. "Oh, la-de-da," he said theatrically, before hopping up. "Why would I crawl when I can jus' walk?" He stretched his arms out and walked along the peak as though on a tight rope.

Mrs. Hoffman gasped, and Lora Lee thought she held her breath until Arnold was in the tree. Then she turned to the class and very calmly said, "Y'all go on back inside now, an' try not to raise the roof while I'm gone." Then she smiled slyly and added as an afterthought, "Arnold won't be up there to hold it down anymore."

They laughed a tension-breaking laugh. Once inside, they stood by the door and windows looking out.

Mrs. Hoffman grabbed Arnold by the arm, and said angrily, "You come with me, young man. You could've killed yourself. You need to stop cuttin' up all the time, Arnold—stop clownin' around an' listen to me. What 'id I tell you just yesterday?"

The class didn't hear Arnold say anything, but Mrs. Hoffman held onto his arm and hauled him down the street, still talking. They couldn't hear what she was saying, but they could hear the tone she was using.

"By cracky, if he stopped walkin', she'd jus' drag 'im over there," Jimmy said, and they laughed.

They watched the two of them walking along. Arnold's head was down, and Mrs. Hoffman's back and shoulders were stiff. She was walking with determined steps as she gripped Arnold's arm.

"Pore Arnold," David said. "He's gone git a paddlin' from Mr. Docker."

"Does it hurt much?" Jimmy asked. "You got one last year." Everybody looked at David, wondering what Arnold was in for.

"What do ya think?" David replied. "There's a big man swingin' a paddle at yore rear end!"

Lora Lee knew what was going to happen to Arnold. She'd seen Mr. Docker paddle Stone one day after school. Mr. Docker made him bend over and grab his ankles and he used a wooden paddle that was obviously made for that purpose. He hit him ten times. Stone didn't cry, but Lora Lee knew it had to hurt.

"I guess it hurts," Jimmy said. "But I don't think that wuz bad enough for a paddlin', nohow."

"Me neither," David agreed.

"Well, did y'all see Miz Hoffman's face?" Grace asked. "She wuz really scared."

"Yeah," Lola said. "What if he fell off the roof an' broke his leg or somethin'? She'd prob'ly git in big trouble."

Lora Lee saw Lola brush a dark brown curl from her face, and noticed her ring with a shiny yellow stone. "That's so purty," she thought, feeling covetous. "I wont a ring with a stone."

"I bet she's cuttin' off the blood to his arm," Jimmy said. He went to the door, opened it, and spit into the yard.

"He's gonna git a paddlin' for shore," David said, and Lora Lee felt very sad. The way Arnold was walking with his head down made him look defeated. She wondered why he did some of the things he did, like going on the roof. He liked to show off, but he sure didn't like getting in trouble.

When they couldn't see the pair anymore, the class got quiet and they slowly went back to their seats and just sat there, each of them thinking about Arnold's fate, and feeling somewhat responsible because they enjoyed his antics. He entertained them, and now he was going to get a paddling.

"Miz Hoffman's gone an' we ain't even havin' no fun," Jimmy said. She seldom left the building while they were there, so when she did, it was usually a time of chaos.

There was a chorus of "Yeah," in response. But then the silence returned, each child lost in thought, and nobody feeling like having fun, knowing what would happen to Arnold.

Lora Lee didn't think Mrs. Hoffman should have taken Arnold to the principal, even though she'd been afraid he'd fall. Mrs. Hoffman was usually so easy going that the class was surprised by her reaction. They expected her to just scold him the way she normally did. "He wuz just havin' fun," she thought. "She knows how Arnold is. He wuz jus' bein' Arnold. It ain't fair!"

She knew Arnold tried the patience of all the teachers, and sometimes she even got aggravated at him, but he was nice and she liked him, and she felt sorry for him. As far as she knew, he was the only kid in the class whose parents were divorced. He had a stepfather, and a half sister, who was in the second grade. They'd moved to the area at the beginning of the fifth grade and Lora Lee didn't know where they were from.

She wondered if he'd get in trouble at home because of this. "Maybe his parents won't find out," she thought. She knew she'd get in big trouble at home if she got in trouble at school.

Mrs. Hoffman returned alone and she didn't say anything to the class about Arnold. She had to know how they felt when she saw the unusually quiet room and their solemn faces.

"Why don't I read to you for a while," she said, knowing how much they all loved *The Gabriel Horn*.

But as she picked up the book, Jimmy said, "No!" Then, a few more said "No!" and Jimmy said, "We don't wont ya ta read till Arnold's here. It ain't fair."

Lora Lee expected Mrs. Hoffman to correct the "ain't," but she didn't. Instead, she said, "All right then. I hope I don't need to remind you that some of you have book reports due tomorrow. An' some of you have them today. Lola, you're first."

"Oh goodie," Lora Lee thought. "I don't hafta be first. I hope Arnold comes back 'fore it's my turn. I think he'll like *Little Lord Fauntleroy*."

Three people had given their reports, each followed by a brief class discussion, before Arnold finally returned. He walked in sheepishly and took his seat. No one said anything.

Lora Lee looked closely at the side of his face to see if he'd been crying. She couldn't tell, but she hoped he hadn't.

When she read her book report, she looked at Arnold a couple of times. He was watching her and obviously paying attention. When she was done, Mrs. Hoffman said, "Good job, Lora Lee. Did you notice, class, how she told the important details of the story, but didn't go off onto little details that aren't important?"

There were a few comments, and she was happy when Arnold said, "That sounds like an int'restin' book. I'm gonna read it."

Lora Lee felt proud. "That wuz the nicest thing Miz Hoffman said 'bout anybody," she thought. "An' Arnold liked it, too."

When they were standing in the lunch line, Lora Lee remembered that Herman wasn't there that day, and she felt herself relax a little, knowing she didn't have to worry about him bothering her. She sat with Grace and Emily, both of whom ate much faster than she did, and left before she finished. They had spaghetti and green beans, and she ate most of hers, even though the beans didn't taste like her mother's.

After lunch, which was when Mrs. Hoffman usually read to the class, she didn't even mention reading. And even though Arnold was back in his seat, no one asked her to read. The room was completely quiet. After a moment, she said, "Let's all go outside an' play dodge ball."

"Does she mean she's gonna play?" Lora Lee wondered.

She did play. One of the girls had the ball first and she didn't throw hard enough to get anyone out. But Jimmy had it next and he threw the ball hard right at Mrs. Hoffman. She smiled when it hit her on the leg, and she was the first one out. The kids laughed, and a couple of boys patted Jimmy on the back. A few times, she was the first or second person out. When Arnold had the ball, everyone expected him to throw it at her, but he didn't. He had the ball three times, and he never threw it close to her. Clearly, he did not intend to hit her.

Lora Lee didn't enjoy dodge ball. She didn't like having to throw the ball because she wasn't good at hitting people, and she didn't like getting hit by the ball. It hurt and she felt like a failure—like she wasn't even good at dodging a ball. "At least, I wadn' the first one out today," she thought. But as soon as she finished the thought, the ball hit her right in her diaphragm and knocked the wind out of her. She doubled over, trying to breathe. Most of all, she didn't want to cry, but that is exactly what she did. Mrs. Hoffman ran over to her and asked if she was all right.

Lora Lee nodded her head. As soon as she could, she straightened up and stopped crying. She saw Jimmy look at her with contempt in his eyes, and Lola and Ella exchange smiles. She lowered her head, thinking, "It ain't like I wanted that ta happen. I couldn' help it." She felt disgusted with herself. "I wish I could be somebody else . . . somebody like Lola."

Mrs. Hoffman suggested that Lora Lee sit on the porch and watch, and that suited her fine. Most of the class seemed to like dodge ball, but she was happier just watching them play, especially with Mrs. Hoffman.

When they went back into the classroom, Lora Lee could tell that things had changed, and she figured dodge ball had been a great idea since nobody seemed mad anymore. They started the geography class without any complaints.

♥ ♥ ♥

AFTER SCHOOL, Lora Lee WENT TO THE NARROW ROOM between the seventh and eighth grade classrooms where the sports equipment was kept. There were containers in there for the basketballs, volleyballs, and other sports equipment. And there was a Coke machine. Lora Lee checked to see how much money she had, already knowing that she only had a nickel, but hoping she had more. She had one buffalo nickel. She looked at it and thought about how hot she was and how cool a Coke would be. "I'm buyin' me a Co-Cola," she thought as she put her nickel in the machine. Leroy was also in the room with a Coke. Without saying a word, they each held their bottles up high so they could see the bottoms. The game was to see whose bottle came from furthest away.

"Mine's from Columbus, Georgia," she said, disappointed.

"Mine's from Avon Park, Florida," he said, even more disappointed than Lora Lee.

"Well, la-de-da, I win!" she said, smiling.

When they finished their drinks, she and Leroy went to the swings. She was enjoying swinging, but when little Julie wanted to swing, she let her have her swing and went to the old seesaw bar and skinned the cat a few times. When Julie left, Lora Lee went back to swing again. Shortly thereafter, Leroy went to sit by a tree near the road to wait for the bus, and Lora Lee soon followed him.

As she walked across the schoolyard, she found a yellow pencil that had barely been used. "Oh boy!" she said, picking it up and sticking it behind her ear. Lora Lee never bought a pencil. She picked up any she saw on the ground or the floor, and unless someone saw her pick it up and said it was theirs, she kept it. She had more pencils than she needed and she found it strange that somebody could drop a pencil and not bother to pick it up. She believed her grandma's sayings, "A penny saved is a penny earned," and "Waste not, want not."

She remembered once when she'd been doing her math homework at the kitchen table with a pencil that was less than two inches long, including the eraser, which was almost gone.

Her mother noticed it and asked, "Lora Lee, don't you have another pencil?"

Lora Lee said, "Yes, ma'am. I got five more."

"Well then, why are you using that little ole thing? There's almost nothin' left to hold on to."

Lora Lee smiled and announced, proudly: "It makes me happy. I don't use it at school 'cause the kids'd make fun a me, but I like ta use it till I cain't sharpen it in the pencil sharp'ner no more. Then I use it down ta the nub, an' then I throw it away."

There were still five high school kids on the bus when it arrived at the school, and after Lora Lee and Leroy got on, the bus made a circle around the little town, and dropped them off. One of the girls liked Billy, and occasionally had asked Lora Lee about him or given her a note to give him. She didn't say anything to Lora Lee anymore though, because Billy was engaged to Patty.

When they got to Albritton Road, Lora Lee stood up and went to the back of the bus, and Leroy followed her. She picked up trash from one side of the bus and put up the windows. Leroy did the other side. Rita had asked them to do those chores, and on Friday, she gave them a quarter each. Then, when all the high school kids were off the bus, Rita would stop at the drugstore so they could buy something. She'd give them money to buy something for her, and she'd stay in her seat.

Lora Lee would usually buy a cherry Coke or a pineapple sherbet cone, and sometimes, a comic book, each of which cost a dime. She didn't tell her parents that Rita gave her money, and they never asked her where she got the money to buy comic books. Of course, some of hers came from Stone, who was twelve and in the fifth grade, but couldn't read well. He'd buy comic books, look at the pictures, and give them away, often to her. Early on, Ruth had seen her with one and asked her where she got it. "Stone gives me his funny books," she said. "He cain't even read. He jus' buys 'em, looks at 'em real fast, an' gives 'em away." Her parents probably assumed they were all from him. They didn't know about the weekly quarter or the drugstore stop, and they didn't often see her with a comic book. Also, they didn't know that Lora Lee didn't want many of Stone's because she didn't like a lot of the ones he bought. She liked the Dell comics, Disney characters, Tarzan, and westerns like Roy Rogers and Red

Ryder—she loved Little Beaver—but her favorite was the Black Phantom, a blond female heroine who wore a black mask.

When Lora Lee got off the bus, she went to the mailbox, and got the only piece of mail: a two-cent postal card from her mother's cousin in Live Oak. As she walked down the dirt road, she noticed the cows in the pasture by the road. She'd heard her father talking about moving them from the back pasture. Old Jersey was near the fence, so Lora Lee put her books down on some grass and pulled moss from an oak tree along the fencerow for her. She watched the cow as she stood there munching, until others started heading her way. She picked up her books and went on, whistling "The Happy Whistler" as she walked.

When she arrived home, no one was around, but there was a note on the kitchen table: "We're at the other place. Wash the dishes."

"Shoot," she said. "They prob'ly won't be home till after dark, an' I'll be here all by myself. I hate that!" She was afraid to be alone in the house after dark. She thought it was spooky, and she was afraid some drifter or criminal would come in.

She took a rubber band from the kitchen doorknob where they kept them, and took it to her room. She added the pencil she'd found to her five others of various sizes, put the rubber band around them, and put them in her top dresser drawer. Then she took off her shoes and changed into everyday clothes.

When she returned to the kitchen, she turned on the floor fan, and directed it at herself. She stood in front of it for a little while, feeling the wind cooling her. They'd got the fan in Lakeland the previous year. While they were in the appliance store, Lora Lee asked Caleb if they could get a radio, too, and they did. She went home happy—a fan and a radio. Of course, the fan went in her parents' bedroom at bedtime. The summer nights were so hot that Lora Lee often went to sleep with her feet up in the air, propped against the wall to keep her legs from touching the bed, and keeping them cooler. Sometime during the night, they'd slide down, but that didn't wake her.

"Well, at least I don't hafta do nothin' in the field," she thought. Sometimes she'd find a note telling her to weed something, or put out poison bait for the mole crickets on the pepper rows, or string up the pole beans. That was one job she didn't like. When they planted the pole beans, they'd put posts in the rows with a strand of wire attached at the top of the posts, and another several inches from the bottom. Then they'd run string over the top and under the bottom strands of wire, like a "V", and Lora

Lee would have to wrap the tender vines around the string, which they climbed. It wasn't such a bad job unless the vines had gotten too long and intertwined and tangled. Then separating them, without breaking them, was difficult.

Lora Lee looked around the kitchen for food. There were some leftovers in pots on the stove, and she found some conk peas—the small running conks that she loved—some creamed corn, some boiled okra, and some fried corn bread. She got a cucumber from the refrigerator, peeled and sliced some of it, and fixed a plate full of food. It was no longer warm, but she didn't care. Even though she'd eaten most of her lunch at school, she was hungry again.

She went in the living room and turned on the radio before she started eating. Because her parents seldom listened to it, the dial stayed set on a rock and roll station Lora Lee had found, and when it came on, they were playing The Platters' "The Magic Touch." Then they played Tab Hunter's "Young Love." She had a hard time eating and singing at the same time. "Good thing Mama ain't here or I couldn' sing," she thought. Ruth didn't allow singing at the table.

When she finished eating, she did the dishes after first taking several dishes out of the sink. Ruth would put everything but the pots in the sink, and Lora Lee couldn't even get to any water to wet the dishrag. She took out the glasses and a bowl, and that left her enough space. She added some washing powder and warm water to the dishes, and put some warm water in the other side of the sink to rinse them.

As she worked, she sang along with Jim Lowe's song, and she thought, "I wonder what *is* goin' on behine the green door. There's a piano playin' an' they're laughin'. Sounds like fun."

Lora Lee loved that song, but Ruth didn't like it. "That song is jus' silly," she'd say when she heard it on the radio or Lora Lee singing it. And she didn't tell Lora Lee, but she thought there was an implication that something was going on that she didn't want her eleven-year-old daughter thinking about.

When the dishes were washed, she left them draining and went outside. "King mus' be off in the woods," she thought when she didn't see him anywhere. She got Billy's old hard ball from the corner of the porch. It was a little smaller than a baseball, and she wished it wasn't quite so hard, but it was the only ball she had, so she played with it. She could tell that it had been red because there were a few red specks left on it, but it was now an ugly old black ball. Sometimes she threw it as high up as she could and caught it, and sometimes, like today, she threw it on the roof of the old kitchen, and caught it when it rolled off, over and over again. When the ball hit the tin roof, it made quite a racket, so it was better to play when no one else was home, although Ruth didn't mind if she was in the other part of the house.

After a while, she got tired of the game and decided to go get a tangerine. As she walked barefoot, she felt the warm gray sand between her toes. She smelled orange blossoms when she went near an orange tree, and stopped and pulled the limb down to savor the late blooms. There was a cluster of five small white flowers with yellow stamens. She took a few deep breaths, closed her eyes, and basked in the aroma before she continued on her way.

She loved the way the grove smelled in the spring when the trees were in bloom. Sometimes when the family was out at night, they could smell the orange blossoms as they drove past groves, and in their own grove at night, the aroma permeated the air. She didn't think even heaven could smell any better than that.

Lora Lee sought shade under the big old oak tree and stepped on a sandspur. "Ow," she muttered as she stopped and pulled it out of her foot. "I didn' even see them stupid ole sandspurs."

She'd only taken three more steps when a long black snake darted in front of her. She jumped back and her heart started pounding.

"Durn it!" she said angrily, allowing herself the privilege of saying "durn" if the situation seemed to merit it and no adults were around. She watched the snake stop near some weeds under an orange tree, and stood there for a moment looking at it.

"As long as yo're here, yo're prob'ly gonna scare me ag'in," she said. "Yo're a big snake, even longer 'an me."

She picked up a handful of sand and threw it at the snake, which whirled around facing her. She felt a little uneasy, but more determined to scare it away. She picked up a bigger handful of sand and threw it. When the snake started zooming right toward her, she took off for the house, terrified. She ran as fast as she could, never looking back until she hopped up on the porch and turned around to see where it was. She couldn't see it anywhere and didn't know if it had actually chased her, or had been satisfied to scare her away.

She fell into the rocking chair with the cowhide seat that still had short brown hairs on it, and sat for a while, breathing heavily, her heart pounding. "That snake scared the heck outta me," she thought. "I won't mess wi' no more big ole black snakes, by cracky! What would that crazy thing do if he caught me? Bite me? Wrap aroun' me like them snakes that choke ya ta death? Stupid thing really scared me! Good gravy!"

As she sat in the chair, she slowly calmed down. A couple of mourning doves lit in the yard and she watched them pecking at something in some low-growing weeds. Mourning doves sounded sad to her, so she was glad they were quiet.

A housefly lit on her arm and she hit at it and missed. She noticed there were several flies on the unscreened porch, and realized she'd discovered something to entertain her for a while. She got the fly swatter from the kitchen and started swatting. When she saw two mating, she swatted them. They were still together after she killed them, and she went and got two toothpicks and carefully separated them. She was amazed that she could see the difference between the male and female since they were so small. When she killed more flies, she examined them to see whether they were male or female. She felt quite proud of herself, realizing that she knew something most people probably didn't know, but she assumed most people didn't sit on the porch killing flies and checking them out. She figured most people had better, more interesting things to do.

Another thing she knew that she thought most people didn't know was about bananas. One day she was eating a banana, and Billy asked her for half, so she broke it in two and gave him half. She noticed that the banana did not break smoothly, one part being higher than the rest. So she carefully pulled that part and found that it was separate. Then she carefully separated the piece that was left. "Bananas are in thirds," she announced to Billy. "Look at this!"

Billy glanced at her banana. "So what?" he asked.

"Don't ya think that's sumpin? Did ya know bananas were in thirds?"

"No, an' I really don't care, nohow," he said, jumping off the porch and walking away.

"Well, I do," Lora Lee said, still feeling proud of herself, as though she'd made a significant discovery. "When I have kids, I'm gonna show 'em this. Then they'll know sumpin most people don't." She thought about showing the kids at school, but decided they wouldn't show any sign of being impressed, even if they were. "I'll show Daddy. He'll think it's int'restin'."

And he did. When she showed him, he was quite amazed. "I never knew that, Lora Lee," he said. "That's really sumpin! As many bananas as I ate, I never noticed that." She basked in her father's appreciation, and when Billy looked across the table at her, she stuck her tongue out at him.

Lora Lee still wanted a tangerine, but she was afraid to go back out there in case the snake was still around, so she got a knife and went in the grove and picked two Valencia oranges. They ripened later than some of the other oranges, so they were still nice and juicy. She didn't mind all the seeds because she loved the flavor. The other oranges had seeds, but not as many as the Valencias. She peeled one carefully, so there was plenty of the white part left on the orange, and the unbroken peel was one long piece. She held the peel by one end and swung it around, saying the ABCs as she did so. The peel broke on J. "J for Jimmy," she said. "I didn' want it to break on J. Jimmy ain't my boyfrien', an' I don't know no other J's."

She cut a round plug out of the top of the orange, put it in her mouth, chewed the juice out of it, and spit it out. She ran the knife around the inside of the orange, and sucked the juice out of it, squeezing it, as needed, to loosen the juice. When she finished, she tore it in half and ate what was left. Then she peeled the other orange, took off the white part, cut it in half, and ate it like that. She liked to eat them in different ways: sometimes she'd just eat the slices; and sometimes she'd cut pieces off the whole orange until only the juicy core was left, then chew that until the juice was gone, and spit it out.

♥ ♥ ♥

Lora Lee noticed that the afternoon was almost gone. She knew the sun would be setting before long, and she started feeling melancholy. She didn't mind being at the house alone during daylight hours, but she was scared after dark and hated being alone. She hopped off the porch and went around to the front yard. She knew the sun would be low on the horizon and she liked to watch the sunset, even though she dreaded the dark that followed it.

She went through the old wooden, swinging gate, and sat down on the sand in front of the house. She heard a mourning dove and wondered if it was one of the ones she'd seen earlier. Not long after she sat down, she felt something bite her leg, and she jumped up and brushed off a black ant. "Stupid thing," she said, noticing that she'd sat near an ant bed.

After moving over a few feet, she looked carefully at the ground, sat down, and watched the sky as the light blue turned to yellow, orange, and red. Gradually some purple appeared, and a little streak of green. She hoped her parents were seeing the sunset, but she knew there were probably trees obstructing their view.

She went back through the gate and sat down on the front porch steps thinking, "I guess Daddy ain't ever gonna hang that porch swing we brought with us from Combee Road. I want a swing. I could be swingin' right now." She sighed. "Looks like they ain't comin' home till after dark," she said out loud. "Jus' what I figgered."

She looked at the porch and thought about the three men whose bodies had lain on it in 1920, and she pictured them lying there with pennies on their eyes, and people fanning them to keep the flies off their bodies. After her family moved to the farm, they heard the story of the tragedy that happened to the three men, one of whom owned the house. The local cattlemen were used to an open range for their cattle, and when the phosphate company put up fences for the cattle they owned, they also fenced in a lot of the range the other cattle had been using, as well as their water supply. The cattlemen had cut the fence a few times, and it had been repaired. However, one night when they were cutting it, the sheriff and his deputies suddenly appeared and killed three of them. Lora Lee was fascinated that their bodies had been laid on the porch, and one day when she was playing on the porch, she lay on the floor and pretended to be dead, her arms stretched out on each side of her. She decided it wasn't much fun, so once was enough of that game.

She thought about the couple that had lived on down the dirt road in a house that nobody lived in now. The man had been planning to go with the other men to cut the fence, but his wife didn't want him to go. She asked him to get her some meat from their smokehouse before he left so she'd have some to cook for the children's breakfast the next morning before they went to school. She quietly followed him to the smokehouse, and when he went in, she closed the door and propped the post against it the way they did to keep animals out, locking him in so he couldn't go. She probably made him really mad, but she also probably saved his life. Lora Lee thought she was a smart woman.

As she watched the sunset, she saw the colors fading and darkness descending, and her melancholy intensified. She was just about to go into the house when she saw sporadic flashing of lights in the air; she wanted to see if she could catch some lightning bugs, but she was afraid to stay outside any longer.

"Now it's really dark," she thought as she entered the house, fumbling around for the light switch. After she turned on a couple of lights, she went into her room, turned on the light, closed and locked her door, closed the Venetian blinds on her windows, and curled up on her bed with her library book. If the doors to the house had had locks, she would have locked them, too. She followed that routine when she was home alone after dark. Then when she heard the truck, she'd get up and open her door and greet her parents when they entered the house—she didn't want them to know she was so afraid.

The night was quiet until the crickets, one of which sounded like it was right in her room, started their ritual. She found their sound monotonous, and with their noise, it was harder for her to hear if something else made a noise outside. And if something made a noise anywhere, Lora Lee wanted to hear it.

She was looking forward to her new library book. She'd turned in *Little Lord Fauntleroy* that afternoon when her class went to the school library, and checked out *The Call of the Wild* by Jack London. As she began reading about the big, magnificent dog, Buck, she thought about the little dog she knew for a few days.

"I wish I had a dog ta keep me comp'ny now," she said. "I wish I coulda kept that little feist."

One Saturday when Lora Lee went out in the back yard, there was a little white, shorthaired dog sitting there. She was delighted. She sat in the yard and held him and petted him until Caleb drove up on the tractor.

"Look at this cute little dog, Daddy," she said. "Can we keep him?"

Her father was not impressed. "That dog ain't nothin' but a feist," he said as though a "feist" was the worst thing a dog could be. "An' look how swelled up his stomach is. That dog's got worms. He ain't fit for nothin'."

Lora Lee felt her heart sink. "Pore little thing," she cooed, rubbing his head. It seemed to her that her father disliked him more because he was a feist than he did because he had worms.

"Let 'im alone, an' come on in the house, Lora Lee," Caleb said. "We ain't keepin' that dog."

Lora Lee went in, but she didn't eat much. And as soon as they heard the tractor leave, Ruth let her take some leftover grits and a biscuit out for the dog. He only ate a little. That afternoon, she spent a lot of time holding and petting him, and she named him "Whitey."

Sunday morning, she saw him by the side of the house when she went to the car. After church, she wanted to pet him, but she waited until her parents were taking a nap. Then, she fed him, and spent time with him. "He prob'ly is sick," she thought, "but we could give him sumpin for the worms." When she heard her parents talking, she went in the house because she didn't want her father to yell at her.

The next day, when she got home from school, the first thing she did was to look for the dog. She didn't see him at first and was afraid her father had taken him away. She called, "Whitey. Come 'ere, Whitey." And much to her delight, he sauntered over to her. She petted him, and then ran into the house to get him some food. He seemed to like cold grits and biscuits, which was about all she could find, except for one little piece of bacon. He didn't eat much, and that confirmed for her that he was sick. She stayed with him for a while, went in the house and had a snack, and then went back to be with him.

She sat on the ground and put him on her lap. She stroked him gently and talked softly to him. She told him how Lola was always saying mean things about her. The dog would wag his tail just a little every now and then, and when he did, it was a slow wag with his tail dragging on her lap. When she heard her parents' truck coming, she carefully placed him back under the house where he'd been when she called him. She thought maybe they wouldn't see him there. And she went in the house. However, being a good little dog, Whitey toddled out to greet them. When Lora Lee went on the porch, there was Whitey doing his slow wag and hoping to be petted.

Caleb just walked right past him. As he passed Lora Lee on the porch, he said, "I'm tired down."

Lora Lee knew her mother had been working all day, too, and she knew that her father would rest in his recliner while her mother cooked supper. That didn't seem fair to her, but it didn't seem to bother her mother. Of course, Lora Lee never said anything about it. She silently accepted the way things were, just as her mother did.

Ruth leaned down and patted the dog briefly as she said, "Well, bless your heart, you poor little thing."

After Caleb was in the house, Lora Lee asked, "Where do you think he came from, Mama?"

"Well, considerin' he's sick, I guess somebody got shed of 'im. He could be from anywhere 'round here. Lots of times, people will drop dogs or cats off a ways from where they live so they won't go home. Maybe somebody from Brewster dumped him out here, or it could've been somebody from way back in the country."

"It's mean ta do that," Lora Lee said.

"Yes, it is," Ruth agreed. "He looks like a nice little dog. Prob'ly made somebody a good pet."

"Well, they mus' notta loved 'im very much," Lora Lee said, with tears in her eyes.

"Maybe they didn' have much money, an' they couldn' afford to take him to the vet'inarian."

"Well, they prob'ly coulda jus' bought sumpin ta worm 'im."

"You'd think so," Ruth agreed.

The next day when Lora Lee got home from school, she called the dog, but he didn't come. She looked under the house, but he wasn't there. She sat down on the porch and cried, wondering whether her father had shot him or taken him off somewhere and dumped him out. Both possibilities made her equally unhappy, but she thought he would be better off dead. She never asked what had happened to him. And, although she thought of him occasionally, no one ever mentioned the poor little dog again.

Wednesday

LORA LEE WOKE UP ONCE DURING THE NIGHT with her heart pounding. She had the nightmare again about the Russians bombing the house, but after she realized it had just been a bad dream, she settled down and went back to sleep.

When her mother called her, she wanted to go back to sleep again. She lay there for a minute listening to the rooster crowing before she dragged herself out of bed, and went in the bathroom to pee and splash water on her face to wash the sleep out of her eyes.

She heard her father and Billy talking about mending a fence. "That top strand a bob wire's been loose for a while," Caleb said. "We gotta fix it before some a them cows git out. An', the whole thing needs ta be checked." She heard the screen door close when Billy went on the porch.

Lora Lee had chosen her dress the night before. It was her favorite store-bought dress and it was getting old. She knew it wouldn't fit her much longer because she was getting taller, so she wore it more than her other dresses.

When she went into the kitchen, Ruth said, "You're wearin' that ole dress ag'in, Lora Lee? It's lookin' a little faded."

"I don't care," she said. "I like this dress."

Caleb walked past the kitchen on his way out. "Ruth, did you tell Lora Lee I'm carryin' you to the dentist this afternoon?"

"Not yet," she answered. "I gotta go to the dentist, Lora Lee, an' we're gonna pick you up right after school. So be there by the street as soon as you git out."

Lora Lee loved going to Lakeland, but they didn't go often, because it was thirty miles away. "I wish I had some money," she thought.

As soon as she got on the bus, she told Rita that her parents were picking her up that afternoon. "We're goin' ta Lakeland. Mama has ta go to the dentist." When Leroy got on the bus, she also told him.

"Wish I wuz goin' ta Lakeland," he said.

They went around the curve in the road, and Lora Lee saw a gopher tortoise very slowly crossing the road. "Oh shoot!" she thought.

She glanced immediately at the rearview mirror and was disappointed to see Rita looking at her with twinkling eyes, and a hint of a smile. "She's gonna say somethin'," Lora Lee thought, a little embarrassed.

"Look," Leroy said, grinning, "there's a gopher."

"Wanna stop an' git 'im, Lora Lee?" Rita asked.

Lora Lee's face was flushed as she looked down. "No, thank you," she answered softly, and they all laughed.

The teasing was prompted by what had happened one afternoon a few months earlier. As the bus turned onto Albritton Road that day, Lora Lee said, "Aah! Look at that itty bitty turtle in the road."

"Ya wanna git 'im?" Rita asked, and she stopped the bus.

Lora Lee got it, and they all three said how cute it was. Leroy said he thought it was almost three inches long.

Lora Lee sat sideways on the seat with her feet in the aisle so Leroy, who sat across from her, had a good view of the turtle. She put it on her lap and it started crawling around, tentatively. After a minute, Leroy asked, "What kinda turtle do ya reckon he is?"

"I don't know," she replied. "Do you know, Rita?"

Rita said, "No, I don't know."

"He might be a snappin' turtle," Leroy said.

"What!" Lora Lee exclaimed, staring at the wild creature in her lap. "Do ya think so?" That possibility had not occurred to her. It was so small it had seemed completely harmless, but suddenly, it didn't look so cute.

"Put a pencil in front of 'im an' see if he bites it," Leroy suggested, and he leaned over and handed her a pencil.

And she did. And it did. And she shrieked, "Oh my Lord!" and simultaneously jerked her hand away from the pencil and stood up.

The turtle held on to the pencil while it fell to the floor. When it hit, it let the pencil go and pulled its little head in. In her peripheral vision, Lora Lee saw Leroy hastily put his feet up on the seat.

After the turtle bounced once, it stopped right next to Rita's seat. She quickly pulled the bus over to the side of the road, and stopped. "Okay, Lora Lee," she commanded, "git that thing outta here."

Rita had never spoken to Lora Lee like that before; however, Lora Lee remained right where she was. "Please, will you do it, Leroy?" she pleaded. She was amused when she noticed that his feet were back on the floor. She thought, "He don't want us to know he wuz scared."

Leroy shrank back in his seat. "Not me," he asserted. "I ain't touchin' that thing. That's *yore* turtle."

Lora Lee stood there watching the turtle, which was beginning to stir. "He ain't my turtle. I jus' got 'im, an' I don't even want 'im."

"You hafta git that thing outta here, Lora Lee," Rita said.

Lora Lee dreaded touching it. After seeing the way it clamped down on the pencil, she was afraid that might happen to her finger. "I'm in a fix now," she thought.

"It's li'ble ta bite me," she whined.

"Jus' pick it up the same way you did when ya got it," Rita said, and Lora Lee could tell that she was getting impatient.

Lora Lee noticed that Rita wasn't picking it up. And neither was Leroy. They were both acting like the little turtle might suddenly attack them, and that didn't inspire any confidence in her.

Finally, she decided she had to do something, so she used the bottom of her sandal to push it near the steps and turn it around so it was facing Rita. By then, it had its head pulled in. Lora Lee went down the steps, picked it up carefully, spun around, took three steps, and dropped it in the thick grass by the ditch. She watched as it scurried into the water.

After that incident, when they saw any kind of animal in the road, Lora Lee didn't say anything, but either Rita or Leroy would ask her if she wanted it. She was always a little chagrined, but she'd reply good naturedly, "No, thank you," and they'd all laugh, remembering the cute little, terrifying turtle.

When they got to where they saw the dead skunk the day before, five buzzards encircled it, and four more stood behind them waiting. "That's a mighty small animal for all a y'all ta share," Rita said. Three flew and lit in a nearby tree, but the others looked up and just took a few steps toward the side of the road. The bus swerved around them. Lora Lee turned around and looked out the back window to see if they went back to the skunk. They did.

♥   ♥   ♥

THE SCHOOL DAY WAS UNEVENTFUL UNTIL the girls' home economics class; the boys had shop during that period, and they all got together again for the math class. Some of the girls were at the sewing machines making aprons, and some were covering metal clothes hangers with embroidery thread. Lora Lee was covering a hanger. The class was almost over when Deborah, one of the seventh-grade girls, got up from a sewing machine and Lola said, "Deborah, you've got a spot on yore skirt. I think you fell off the roof."

Deborah pulled her skirt so she could see the back of it. "Oh no!" she said. "I didn' even know I started. What am I gonna do?"

Mrs. Hoffman noticed the commotion and went over to Deborah.

"Oh, Miz Hoffman," Deborah said. "I got my period an' my skirt's all messed up." She turned around so Mrs. Hoffman could see the spot.

"Well, let's see what we can do," Mrs. Hoffman said, rubbing her chin. "Can you turn your skirt around?"

"Yes, ma'am." Deborah turned it around so the spot was in the front.

"Great. Now we'll jus' git you an apron an' you can go home like that an' change your skirt. Did you ride a bike or walk?"

"I walked."

Mrs. Hoffman got the apron for Deborah and she put it on.

"There," said Mrs. Hoffman. "If anyone notices anything, it will jus' be that you're wearin' an apron."

Deborah put her hand to her face. "Oh Lord," she said, "I'll never git back in time for history class. Will someone tell Mr. Docker?"

Grace volunteered to tell him. Lora Lee had left her arithmetic book in Mr. Docker's room that morning, so she went to get her book, and was in the room when Grace told him. Mr. Docker was sitting at his desk grading papers.

Grace reported to him, "Mr. Docker, Deborah had ta go home 'cause she fell off the roof."

He jumped up out of his chair, frenzied, with his eyes open wide. "She fell off the roof?" he yelled. "Is she okay? What in God's name was she doin' on the roof?"

Lora Lee had just retrieved her book, and she watched, fascinated. "He thinks she fell off of a roof," she thought. "That's so funny. Miz Hoffman jus' brought Arnold over here yesterday for bein' on the roof. He mus' think we're outta control, an' we're all climbin' on the roof."

"No, no, no!" Grace exclaimed, waving her hands. "She's fine—she ain't hurt. She wadn' on the roof. She jus', ah, . . . she jus' got her period."

Mr. Docker stood behind his desk looking completely baffled. His mouth hung open, his eyes were glazed over, and it was obvious that his brain was working hard to put "fell off the roof," with "got her period."

Lora Lee felt the laughter building in her chest and throat.

"She got her period," Grace repeated, "an' she had ta go home. But she's comin' back an' she'll be a little late."

Mr. Docker sat down slowly, still looking confused, obviously still wondering how and where the roof fit in. He put his hands to his face and rubbed his chin.

"She's okay, Mr. Docker," Grace said as she turned to go out the door.

Lora Lee quickly went on the porch, and as soon as Grace closed the classroom door, both of them let out the laughter that was about to explode in them. They were bent over, laughing together for a couple of minutes before they went to Mrs. Carter's class.

"Did you see his face?" Grace asked, and Lora Lee nodded her head as she laughed.

Unfortunately, Mrs. Carter was getting ready to start the class, so they didn't have a chance to tell anyone what happened. But during the class, they'd look at each other occasionally, and they'd both laugh silently. Lora Lee was so glad she'd forgotten her book. She kept remembering the look on Mr. Docker's face when he thought Deborah had fallen off a roof, and the way he jumped out of his chair.

As soon as the arithmetic class was over, she told Emily. Emily had that look of disbelief on her face that she was hearing something really wonderful—something-that-would-take-her-through-the-rest-of-the-week wonderful—before she burst into laughter. Lora Lee saw Grace telling Lola and her group. She watched as they got the same look on their faces and started laughing, and she laughed with everybody. She didn't care what happened for the rest of the day—she could remember Mr. Docker and be happy.

As the class was returning to the house school, Lora Lee thought about telling Mrs. Hoffman. She knew she'd find it funny, too. So Lora Lee hurried to the house and was the first to arrive. Mrs. Hoffman was sitting at her desk, and she looked up when Lora Lee entered the room.

"Well, aren't you looking all bright-eyed an' bushy-tailed!" Mrs. Hoffman smiled, looking at Lora Lee's glowing face.

Lora Lee told her what had happened and Mrs. Hoffman roared. She was still laughing when the rest of the kids arrived. Lora Lee thought Mrs. Hoffman would also hold that picture in her mind, even though she didn't see it happen, and it would make her happy, too. She was glad she got to tell her.

Mrs. Hoffman gave the class an assignment to work on and they were working quietly, when all of a sudden, she burst out laughing. Lora Lee started laughing, and the other girls, beginning to understand why they were laughing, also began laughing. Jimmy asked, "What's so funny?" but no one replied. The boys were looking around the room and at each other trying to figure out what the girls were laughing at. Some of them were getting rather annoyed, and the girls and Mrs. Hoffman found that funny, too, so it was a while before they all settled down.

♥ ♥ ♥

AFTER SCHOOL, LORA LEE SAT LEANING AGAINST a tree near the road, waiting for her parents. Pretty soon, Leroy joined her, and they sat quietly watching some of the kids play kick ball. When little Julie kicked the ball, her shoe went flying along with the ball. Everybody laughed while Julie, who also laughed, grabbed her shoe and hobbled to first base.

"That reminds me a when I did that one time before we moved here," Lora Lee told Leroy. "My daddy wuz makin' cane syrup, an' this boy Brady from down the road wuz over. He wuz cute, an' I kinda liked 'im, so I wanted to show him my trick. I could kick off my shoe, an' it would go way up in the air an' spin aroun'. Only that time, by cracky, the stupid thing didn' go up—it went flyin' into the kettle a syrup."

"Jumpin' Jehosaphat!" Leroy laughed. "Did ya get a whippin'?"

"I thought I would, but Daddy fished it out with the bucket on the end of a pole that he used to dip the syrup out. I glanced at Brady an' he wuz jus' standin' there with big eyes looking at Daddy. I guess he figured I wuz in trouble, an' I did, too. But Daddy jus' looked at me like I wuz crazy, an' he dumped my shoe on the ground, an' said, 'You go on now.'"

"I'm surprised you didn' git a whippin'."

"Me, too. Boy, I thought he wuz gonna skin me alive. I grabbed my shoe, went an' washed it off, an' ya better b'lieve I made sure to stay outta his way for the rest a the day. He never said a word to me about it. I guess he figgered I learned my lesson, an' I did."

"What 'id you learn?"

"I learned not ta mess aroun' near Daddy's syrup kettle, an' I learned not ta show off for boys." "Course," she thought, "I might if the boy looked like Tommy Sands."

Syrup making was a yearly event when they lived on Combee Road. They grew some blue ribbon and green sugar cane on the small farm, and Caleb made syrup for the family and to sell. Lora Lee loved the whole syrup-making process, probably because she was too young to help with it. It was hard work for her sister and brothers cutting the cane stalks and stripping the leaves off without gloves. The long narrow leaves had sharp edges that sometimes cut them, and fine thorn-like fibers that got into their hands.

But for Lora Lee, it was a fun time, and she loved the murky, sweet juice—juice that some people wouldn't touch because they said it looked like dirty dishwater. Her father drove their old Chevrolet round and round the mill, pulling the pole that was connected above the device that turned the heavy metal rollers, which crushed the stalks, squeezing out the juice. Her mother fed the cane into the mill very carefully. Caleb's Uncle Jim had lost joints from two fingers in a cane mill.

After the cane was ground, the pummings—the stringy pulp that was left after the cane went through the mill—were dumped nearby, making a pile that the children played on. Lora Lee liked to turn somersaults and play on the pile, especially when cousins or friends visited.

As the cane juice came out of the mill, it went into a barrel, which was covered by a cloth to strain the juice, removing any little pieces of the pummings. When the barrel got full, buckets were used to transport the juice to the syrup kettle nearby, which was about four feet across at the top.

The syrup kettle rested on a concrete foundation, which had a space for a fire underneath, and it had a roof over it. As the cane juice simmered, whitish skimmings would rise to the top and gather along the edges of the kettle. Caleb would skim them off, or people, mostly children, would take a piece of the cane peel, run it along the edge coating it with skimmings, and eat the skimmings like candy. Lora Lee liked to do that, and sometimes she'd prepare the cane peel and get the skimmings for small children, or some who were not as familiar with the process.

People also liked to chew the cane. They used a knife to strip the peel off, and cut the stalk into small pieces. After chewing it until the juice was gone, they spit out the pulp. Lora Lee liked to chew it, but at the end when it got dry and cottony, the feel in her mouth made shivers run down her spine.

Often, neighbors and friends would go to the cane grinding and syrup cooking, and the adults would stand around talking, drinking cane juice, and watching the process while the children ate the skimmings and played. People went there from all over the area to buy the cane syrup. Lora Lee was surprised one time to see a Negro man there, buying three bottles of syrup from Caleb.

She loved the cane juice, and the atmosphere at the cane grindings. She wished they still had them and made syrup, but Caleb and the boys had been too busy just farming to put up the cane mill and kettle they had taken when they moved. They didn't even grow any cane. They used the kettle to scald hogs after they were killed so the hair could be scraped off, and Ruth had boiled Caleb's and Billy's dirty work clothes in it before she got the washing machine.

Lora Lee had just finished telling Leroy about the shoe when she saw her parents' car coming. She jumped up and walked over to the street.

"See ya later," Leroy said.

"Not if I see you first," she responded, seizing the opportunity to one-up him.

Lora Lee got in the front seat beside Ruth, who waved at Leroy, and said, "It's so hot. Let's stop an' git a Co-Cola. Anybody else wont one?"

"Does a pig like slop?!" Lora Lee replied.

"Lora Lee, I wish you'd quit sayin' that," Ruth said. "It really doesn't sound nice."

"Yes, ma'am. I hope they have Grapette, but I know most they won't."

The man behind the counter at the gas station said, "Well, lookie here. Who's this purty little girl wi' you, Mr. Baker?"

"This is my baby," Caleb said, patting her on the back as she blushed.

Lora Lee smiled. She loved for him to call her that, and she loved being the baby of the family.

The station didn't have Grapettes, so she settled for a grape Nehi. Ruth got a Hires root beer, her favorite, and Caleb got a Coca-Cola, which he drank without stopping for breath. Lora Lee figured he must have been awfully thirsty, but she couldn't imagine how he could do that, or why he'd want to. She liked to make her drink last for a long time, but Caleb usually drank his like that.

"Where's yore bottle from, Daddy?" Lora Lee asked.

Caleb held the bottle up in the air and looked at the bottom. "Columbus, Georgia," he said. "Is that far enough?"

"No, sir! One time I had one from Pinebluff, Arkansas, an' Billy had one once from Houston, Texas. An' ya know what? I just had one from Columbus, Georgia yesterday."

Caleb paid the two-cent deposit on the bottles for Ruth and Lora Lee, and they took their drinks with them. "How long ya reckon the dentist'll take?" he asked.

"I don't know," Ruth said. "That tooth's been botherin' me, an' I'm sure most he'll fill it."

When they stopped in front of the Marble Arcade Building, Caleb told them to wait for him in the park. He announced that he was going to the feed store, and to Selph's service station to get the oil changed in the car, and he probably wouldn't be back for a couple of hours. His nephew owned the station and he always took the car there for service if he could.

"I need some money, Caleb," Ruth said.

"What for?" he asked.

"I might see somethin' I need to buy."

He pulled out a five-dollar bill from his billfold and gave it to her with a look that said she needn't expect any more.

Because Lora Lee went to the same dentist as her mother, she didn't even like to be in the Marble Arcade building, but she liked that it was the tallest one in Lakeland, and it had an elevator. The ten-story building had the only elevator she'd ever been in.

Her mother pushed the button and Lora Lee looked at the dial above the elevator and saw that it was on the eighth floor. She watched as the dial went to the fourth floor and stopped. Then it stopped on the first floor.

She heard the elevator operator open the inside accordion-style metal gate, and then watched the doors open. After three people got off, the older Negro man tipped his uniform hat, and said, "Good afternoon, Ladies," as they went into the elevator. He closed the doors and the gate, and Lora Lee looked through the metal gate and counted the floors as the elevator passed them. When they reached their floor, he opened the gate and then the doors. She always thought that looked like fun, and wished she could do it. She thought she might be an elevator operator.

In the waiting room, a woman was reading a magazine, and a boy was throwing an orange up and catching it, over and over. The receptionist said, "It'll jus' be a few minutes," and Lora Lee and Ruth sat down and watched the boy.

"When I was little," Ruth said, "I used to git an orange for Christmas."

"You did?" Lora Lee questioned. "Is that all you got?"

"Some years it wuz, an' I wuz happy to git it. Oranges were somethin' special to us children—we didn' have oranges in Georgie, you know. Some years, we'd get an apple an' maybe a banana, too, but the store didn' have bananas very often."

Lora Lee just sat quietly thinking about that. "An orange for Christmas! Jus' one orange." She wasn't always happy with her Christmas present, but she thought hers had been pretty good compared to that.

The boy got called, and he and his mother went down the hall. Lora Lee noticed the magazine that his mother had put on the coffee table face down. A picture of Aunt Jemima on the back reminded her of something.

"Ya know what, Mama?" she said.

"What?"

"Our teacher wuz tellin' us about slavery today. She said they useta sell the Nigra children, an' their mamas an' daddies couldn' do nothin' about it. They'd jus' take 'em away an' sell 'em. Ain't that awful! Them little kids musta been so scared."

"I'm sure they were," Ruth said, fanning herself and Lora Lee with a folding fan she kept in her pocketbook.

"Or they'd sell the mamas an' daddies an' keep the kids. An' they didn' jus' sell one kid—they'd sell any a 'em they didn' wont. It didn' matter ta them if they sold ever' kid somebody had. That musta broke their mama's an' daddy's hearts."

"Well, ya know, Lora Lee," her mother explained, "they don't feel things like we do."

"They don't?"

"No, honey, they don't. If they did, they jus' wouldn' a been able to stand it."

"They don't feel things like we do?" Lora Lee wondered. She was silent for a moment before she asked, "Do you know any Nigras, Mama?"

"No, honey, I don't," Ruth replied.

Lora Lee didn't say anything.

"You know," Ruth said, "when I wuz little, two of my . . ."

"Miz Baker," the receptionist called, "you can come in now."

They were only a couple of blocks away from the dime store, and Lora Lee asked if she could go there.

"You can go," Ruth answered, "but go straight there an' be careful. An' if you leave there, wait for me in the park."

"I will."

"All right," Ruth said. "I'll come when I'm done here."

As she walked along, Lora Lee thought about the little Negro children, and she remembered something Dinah, one of Missy's friends, had told her. Dinah was in Missy's class at school and she lived in Pierce, another phosphate town. She said at supper one night, she asked her daddy, "How come the Nigra children hafta stand out in the cold an' rain ta catch a school bus ta Bartow, when there's a school right here? How come they don't jus' go ta school in Pierce with us?"

She said her father hollered, "Dinah, are you outta yore mind?" and he got up from the table and stormed out of the room. She said she never brought the subject up again. She also told Lora Lee that at work, even though her father was a good Christian man, he made his Negro helper ride in the back of the truck, even when it was raining and he was alone in the front. Lora Lee thought that seemed mean, but she didn't know what he should have done. She didn't think she'd want a Negro sitting next to her.

"Oh, I almost stepped on a crack," she thought, looking down. "I gotta be careful, by cracky. Hee, hee. 'Step on a crack, break yore mama's back.'"

Half a block from the store, she could smell the popcorn, and by the time she got there, her mouth was watering. The popcorn stand was right at the front of the store, and she stopped for a moment, watching the popping corn, and listening to it. "That smells so good," she thought. "Oh! I wish I had a nickel." She looked at some what-nots, and picked up a hen and rooster set of salt and pepper shakers. "Ain't they cute," she smiled. Then she went straight to the back of the store to get a drink of water. She paused and looked at the "Colored" and "White" signs over the fountains and drank from the "white" fountain.

When she left the fountain, she passed a little Negro girl who had a bag of popcorn. "That little colored girl's got some popcorn," she thought. "I wish I had a nickel ta buy me some." She assumed the Negro woman nearby was the little girl's mother and had bought it. Lora Lee noticed the little girl's dress, and cute shoes. They were much nicer than hers, and something about that just didn't seem right to her. "A colored girl with a purty dress an' shoes, an' popcorn!"

"Judge not, lest ye be judged," flashed in her mind. "I wuz judgin'," she thought, feeling a little guilty. When the little girl looked at her, Lora Lee smiled, and the girl smiled at her. Then Lora Lee felt better, and thought, "She seems nice."

She stood for a moment looking around the store, wondering what she wanted to look at. "I could go downstairs to look at the funny books," she thought, but knew she could get comic books in the Brewster drug store. When she saw the jewelry counter, she thought, "I can look at the rings an' stuff," and rushed over to it. The clerk wasn't there, so she just took her time. She looked at the necklaces and earrings first. She thought a heart set with rhinestones on a silver chain was just beautiful. "If I had a lot a money, I'd buy me that necklace," she thought. "That's my favorite, a heart wi' diamonds."

Next, she moved over to the rings. She was admiring the ones that had stone settings, when she saw a ruby stone. "Oh, I wont that ring," she thought. "The red ruby one. It's so purty."

As she looked around for the clerk, she saw the little girl getting a drink from the "Colored" fountain. Then the girl went back to her mother.

When the clerk returned to the counter, Lora Lee noticed that her dress looked at least as faded as hers did. "She's got a job, but she must not have much money," she thought. "Oh, I'm judgin' ag'in."

"Can I he'p you wi' sumpin?" the clerk asked.

"How much are the rings?" she asked in a low voice.

"Thirty-five cents fer them in that case," the clerk replied. "Would ya like ta try one on?"

"No, ma'am, I'm jus' lookin'."

"That's all right," the clerk said softly. "Jus' take yore time."

"Might as well be a dollar, by cracky," Lora Lee thought, "'cause I ain't got thirty-five cents, either."

She stayed there for a couple more minutes. Then she said, "Thank you," and went to the toy counter. She picked up a little doll that had on a cute dress. "Aah! What a purty face this doll has," she thought. "I'd love ta have a doll like this. Course, Marie is a real purty doll." Although Lora Lee didn't have many toys, Santa Claus had brought her four dolls over the years, and when she was eight, she got Marie, her last doll.

Marie's face, arms, and legs were wooden, but she had a cloth body. She was her favorite doll.

Lora Lee hugged the doll and put her down. Then she moved over to the marbles. She loved marbles. "Boy, if I had some money, there are so many things I'd buy," she thought. "I shouldn' even come ta town 'cause I always see things I wont. But if I had some money, I'd buy the doll or the marbles, one." She thought for a minute. "Or maybe both."

Tired of looking around, she decided to go out to the park to wait for her mother. She noticed that the bench closest to the store was shaded by an oak tree, so she sat there. She knew it would be easy for her mother to see her so near the store.

♥   ♥   ♥

LORA LEE'S EYES FOLLOWED THE SIDEWALK to the middle of the park and the statue of a Confederate soldier, which stood on a tall, white marble pillar. She remembered the time she and her mother had walked through the park and stopped to look at the statue and read that it was put there in 1910. That's when she first found out that her grandfather had fought in "the War Between the States," as her mother called it.

She saw a little girl in a frilly dress, and watched as she headed straight for the pool around the fountain. Her mother yelled, running toward her, and grabbed her just in time. Lora Lee laughed, but the little girl cried. The tall fountain with water cascading over its tiers was Lora Lee's favorite thing in the park. "No wonder that little gal wanted to go in it," she thought. She wished she could go swimming. She felt like going and dipping her hands in the water, but she was concerned that her mother would come and wouldn't see her there. "I wish we lived close to the beach. Maybe I'd git ta go there sometime."

There were colorful flowers scattered about the park, but Lora Lee didn't know the names of many of them. She saw some yellow marigolds and noticed there was a rose garden with red roses; she knew her mother would like that. She also noticed some kind of small palm trees.

As she waited, she watched the people and squirrels and birds. Some of the birds were singing, and the squirrels were chattering to each other, but when a train passed nearby, that was all she heard. Most people were just walking through the park on their way somewhere, but a few sat on benches talking, or looking around. After the train passed, Lora Lee heard a mockingbird and she looked, but couldn't see it. She was fascinated by all the different sounds mockingbirds make.

"This place is noisy," she thought as a car with no muffler drove by. She was used to the bird and squirrel sounds, but she wasn't used to the chattering people and the train and automobile sounds.

Across the park, the little girl was chasing a squirrel. The squirrel would run far enough to get away from her, and sit and wait until she chased it again. Finally, it went up a tree. The little girl ran back to her mother, waving her arms, and Lora Lee imagined she was complaining about the squirrel quitting the game.

She heard two Negro men talking as they passed her, but she couldn't understand them. "What are they sayin'?" she wondered. "I cain't understand the way they talk." She'd only heard Negroes talking a few times at the grocery store in Bradley, and she often didn't understand them. The only thing they said to her or her parents was, "Good mornin'," or "Good evenin'." She was fascinated by the way they spoke. "I wish I could see what they're sayin' wrote down," she thought. "Then, maybe I could understand it."

When she saw her mother approaching, Lora Lee went to meet her at the dime store. Two Negro women were walking behind Ruth with parasols, shading themselves from the sun. "I wish I had a umbrella," she thought. "We ain't even got one for the rain."

"Let's git some popcorn, Lora Lee," Ruth said. "I could smell it a block away."

"Oh goodie. It's been makin' my mouth water."

Ruth bought the popcorn, took a handful, and handed the bag to Lora Lee. "I need some water," she said, wiping her brow. They went to the back of the store and drank from the "White" fountain.

"Let's look around a little bit," Ruth suggested.

"Come look at the ring I wont, Mama," Lora Lee said. "It's got a ruby."

They went to the jewelry counter, and the clerk asked, "Can I he'p ya?"

"No, thank you," Lora Lee answered. "I'm jus' showin' my mama the ring I like."

"That is a purty ring," Ruth agreed when Lora Lee pointed at it.

"It costs thirty-five cents. An' lookie here, Mama." She pointed to the heart with diamonds. "Ain't this a purty necklace!"

"Oh, that is purty," Ruth declared. "How much is that?"

"It's $2.99," the clerk answered. "Would ya like ta see it?"

"She's got enough money to buy it," Lora Lee thought hopefully.

"No, thank you," Ruth answered. "I wuz jus' curious." She turned away from the counter. "Let's look at the cloth, Lora Lee. I might buy some material an' make myself a dress."

Lora Lee was certainly not interested in cloth, and she was glad she had the popcorn to munch on. She saw two boys come up from downstairs and the taller one had a comic book in his hand, which the shorter boy reached for. The taller boy held it over his head, and the shorter one was jumping, trying to reach it as they left the store. "They prob'ly gonna git in a fight," she thought.

As they approached the dry goods counter, Ruth said, "Well, hello, Anna. How nice to see you."

"Wow," Lora Lee thought, looking at the clerk who was smiling at her mother. "Mama knows her an' she's purty. She's got purty blue eyes."

"Nice to see you, Miz Baker," the clerk said, smiling. "An' who's this cute little girl?"

"This is Lora Lee," Ruth informed her. "Lora Lee, do you remember Anna Love? Her family lives next to Miz Stamps." Mrs. Stamps had lived next to the Bakers.

Lora Lee didn't remember her, and she didn't say anything.

"Oh my goodness. This can't be Lora Lee," Anna exclaimed, smiling. "You've gotten a lot bigger since I saw you."

"She is growin'," Ruth said. "How's your mama, Anna?"

"Mama's doin' fine, Miz Baker. You should go see her sometime. I know she'd love to see you."

"I'd love ta see her, too. We jus' stay so busy on the farm."

"I'm sure it's a lot of work," Anna said, nodding her head. "Well, is there somethin' you were lookin' for today?"

"I'm lookin' for some cloth to make a dress," Ruth replied, touching a piece of fabric. "Somethin' not too expensive."

Anna helped her with the material, and Ruth found some she thought would make a nice dress. "I like this here. What do you think, Lora Lee?"

Lora Lee, who'd been munching on the popcorn, staring at Anna, and hoping she looked like her when she grew up, looked at the material and nodded her head. "It's nice. I like it."

"I do, too. I should git some cloth to make a dress for you, too. Do you see somethin' you like?"

Lora Lee got interested in the cloth. She looked at the selections Anna put out, and chose one. "I like that one, Mama." It had a red background with little blue and yellow butterflies on it.

Ruth liked it, too. "I guess this is the one, Anna."

Lora Lee smiled. "I'm gonna have a new dress," she thought.

"Good choice," Anna said. "How old are you now, Lora Lee?"

"I'm eleven, an' I'm in the sixth grade. I belong ta be in the fifth grade, but I took a test an' I got to go ahead when we changed from summer school to winter school." Until they changed, the "strawberry schools" had the winter months off so the farm children could pick the strawberries.

"That's just incredible. You're growin' up so fast, Lora Lee," Anna said, smiling. "How's Linda, Miz Baker?"

"She's doin' very well," Ruth replied. "She an' her husband have a little girl."

"Oh, that's great. I always thought she wuz so nice."

"Well, bless your heart. That's sweet of you to say," Ruth said.

She bought enough material to make the dresses. "Well, we should git goin'. Caleb will be back before long. Nice to see you, Anna. Give your mama my regards."

"I sure will. Nice to see you, Miz Baker, an' you, Lora Lee. Mama will be pleased to hear from you. Why don't you call her sometime?" she suggested, and hastily scribbled her telephone number on a scrap of paper.

"We don't have telephones out in the country," Ruth said, "but I can call her sometime when we're at Linda's house. Thank you."

"It wuz so nice ta see her," Ruth said as they walked across the street. "She's always so pleasant."

"She's purty," Lora Lee declared.

"An' she's not the least bit stuck up."

"I like her. Is she kin ta us, Mama?" She was hoping someone so pretty and nice was related.

"No, she wuz just a neighbor," Ruth replied. "You know, her mama came from the same part of Georgie that I did. I didn' know her then, but she only lived about eight miles away from where I grew up."

"That's sumpin," Lora Lee said. "Mama, do ya wont some more popcorn? I almost ate it all."

Ruth took the bag. "Let's take a look-see at the beautiful red roses," she said, and they walked over to the rose garden. As they neared the flowers, she took a deep breath. "Oh, smell that. Don't they smell good!"

Lora Lee agreed, "Shore do." She went close to one and breathed deeply.

As they walked to the bench that Lora Lee had sat on, Ruth said, "I remember now what I wuz fixin' to tell you about before they called me in to see the dentist. I had two little sisters that died one year. I must've been about your age then. Charlotte—we called her Charlie—was two, an' she died of pneumonia. Ethel was four, an' she died of typhoid fever."

"At the same time?" Lora Lee asked.

Neither of them noticed the sparrows chirping near their bench. However, Lora Lee did notice a boy riding a bicycle around the park.

"No, sugar. Charlie died the first of April, an' Ethel died the last of May. Ethel was sick for a month. Mama killed most of our chickens makin' soup for her, an' Daddy held her when Mama wuz busy. Daddy went for the doctor for both girls, but it didn' help; he did all he could, but they died anyway. I remember Daddy sittin' on the front porch after the second one died. He wuz cryin' so hard you could've heard 'im a mile away. It scared me because I hadn' ever seen anybody cry like that, an' certainly not a man. Of course, I know my poor mama wuz grievin', but it's my daddy I remember. That like to killed him. His poor ole heart wuz jus' broke."

"That's so sad, Mama," Lora Lee said, wiping away a tear. She noticed her mother wiping her eyes, as well. That made a big impression on her because her mother hardly ever cried. Caleb was sentimental and would shed a few tears when he heard a sad story, or saw something touching on television, like the reunion of family members who hadn't seen each other for many years. But Ruth didn't cry.

Lora Lee knew that Ruth had had a special relationship with her father. She remembered when she was younger asking Ruth for a box in her closet that she thought would be just the right size for some of her things. Ruth said she was keeping it because it was a box her daddy sent her with pecans from the trees in their yard in Georgia. "Look at this," she said, pointing at the top of the box. "That's my daddy's handwritin'." Lora Lee had looked at it and looked at her mother and saw that her eyes were moist.

"My daddy didn' do anything for a long time after that," Ruth continued, and Lora Lee noticed how sad her voice sounded. "He'd jus' sit, not say a word, an' jus' study. He'd already broke the land before Charlie died, an' neighbors had planted the seeds for 'im. I felt so helpless. There wadn' anything I could do to make him or Mama feel any better. Poor ole things. I wuz doin' all the cookin' for the fam'ly on our ole wood stove. It wuz time to cultivate the crops, but Daddy jus' couldn' bring himse'f to do the work. One mornin', neighbors an' church members came in their buggies with their families an' their mules, an' they brought food for ever'body, already cooked. I didn' have to cook that day. They harrowed and hoed an' that's the way our crops got done that spring. An' while the men were workin' in the field, the women cleaned up the house an' yard, an' planted some flower seeds. An' us kids got to play."

"That wuz real nice a them," Lora Lee said.

"Well, that's the way people did things back then. People helped each other out. My daddy used to do the same thing for other people when they went through hard times. An' ever'body did at one time or another."

They were both sitting quietly, lost in thought when they heard the car horn. And as they crossed the street and walked to the car, Lora Lee held her mother's hand.

♥   ♥   ♥

THE REVEREND BOOKER STOOD IN FRONT of the right row of pews. He did not use the pulpit for prayer meetings. Not as many people attended as regularly attended Sunday services, and everybody, except Mr. Cochoran, sat on the right side. Lora Lee's family sat in their usual place.

As soon as she sat down, Lora Lee reached for a fan. The evening was hot, and most people were fanning themselves. She looked at the picture of the Lord's Supper. She was hoping to trade it for one with Jesus holding a little lamb, but Ruth already had that one, and she didn't like the one with Jesus praying in the Garden of Gethsemane any better, so she just kept the one she had.

This was the night for the monthly business meeting, so after a prayer, the Reverend Booker called the meeting to order. As usual, Lora Lee found it boring, and she hoped for something to make it more interesting, something funny like what happened one Sunday night when she was sitting with Ben and Hannah. Just thinking about it almost made her giggle out loud, and she had to remind herself where she was. "How come things seem so much funnier when yo're not s'posed ta laugh?" she wondered.

After dinner one Sunday, Ben and Hannah had decided to go to the Bradley church that evening to see old friends. Luckily, Lora Lee sat with them on the other side of the church and further back than her parents, so she had a good view of what happened. She was just sitting there, waiting for Caleb to call a hymn number, when old Mr. Cochoran strolled in, late, as usual. "He's always late," she whispered to Hannah.

"I know," Hannah said, shaking her head.

Mr. and Mrs. Cochoran lived close to the church and walked there, but even though *she* was always on time, *he* was almost always late. Mr. Cochoran was a little pompous and Lora Lee could not understand why. "He ain't got nothin' ta be high-falutin' about, but he acts like he does," she thought. He had an air about him, and he kind of looked down his bulbous nose at other people.

That night, he plopped down five rows from the front, and, without looking, threw his arm around his wife—or so he thought. There was a collective, quiet gasp in the sanctuary. Lora Lee could feel the laughter in her throat, and she almost laughed out loud, but she waited, wide-eyed and breathless, afraid she'd miss something if she started laughing.

Mrs. Whitaker, whose husband wasn't there that night, was sitting where Mr. Cochoran thought his wife was. She'd looked up at him before he sat down, but didn't say anything as he sat down and put his arm around her. The people in the choir were watching and smiling broadly at her.

Lora Lee's eyes were glued to Mr. Cochoran; she was so determined not to miss a thing that she hardly blinked. Everyone just stared in anticipation, anxious to see what would happen next. It was a good thing it took Caleb a minute to find the hymn number because nobody was going to take their eyes off Mr. Cochoran. Although it was usually quiet in the church, that night, there wasn't a sound. No one coughed, and no one moved.

At first, Mr. Cochoran was looking at Caleb, but then he looked at the choir and noticed that people were staring and smiling. About that time, Mrs. Whitaker's shoulders started shaking as she gave in to laughter, and Mr. Cochoran jerked his head around and looked at her. He leaned forward a little, his eyes wide with surprise, and then puzzlement, as he looked down his nose at her as if to say, "What in the world are *you* doin' here?" Then he yanked his arm away, and turned bright red.

The choir and the congregation roared, and the preacher, who'd clearly been struggling to contain himself, could no longer stifle his laughter. Lora Lee wondered how he'd be able to preach without laughing.

Mr. Cochoran jumped up and meekly moved up two pews to where Mrs. Cochoran sat, but he didn't put his arm around her. Mrs. Cochoran looked all around, obviously wondering why people were laughing. When she saw her husband's red face, she had a questioning look in her eyes. He whispered to her, and then she burst out laughing so loudly Lora Lee could hear her over everybody else. Mr. Cochoran's shoulders seemed to shrink as he just sat there with a stern look on his face, the only one not amused.

Lora Lee was so tickled, she thought she might never stop laughing. After a little while, Caleb called a number and people started singing, but she continued laughing. She had a hard time not making any noise and she held her nose part of the time. Hannah was also having a hard time, mostly because of her. Lora Lee tried really hard, but she'd catch the eye of someone in the choir, and they'd both start, and when Lora Lee laughed, Hannah laughed. Ben was looking at them with a question in his eyes. When Lora Lee saw her father looking at her, she stopped for a while. It was a little easier not to laugh after the choir returned to their pews, but occasionally, she and Hannah would see Mrs. Whitaker's, or someone else's shoulders shaking, and they'd start laughing again.

Ben was getting mad and giving them dirty looks. He had his arm around Hannah, and once he thumped Lora Lee on the back of her head. That stopped her for a little while. She tried hard not to laugh, but when she remembered the sight of old Mr. Cochoran's face when he realized what he'd done, the need for the laughter to get out was stronger than the fear of getting thumped again. Lora Lee thought that if Mr. Cochoran hadn't been so serious about it, and had just laughed, and maybe said something to Mrs. Whitaker, it wouldn't have been so funny. But he was too embarrassed to find it funny. Lora Lee pressed her body as close to the back of the pew as she could so Ben couldn't see her unless he looked around Hannah. And Hannah had managed to stop laughing, perhaps listening to the sermon.

Lora Lee wondered if Mr. Cochoran would stay around to talk to people after the service, or if he'd scoot out the side door and go straight home. When the last prayer ended, she kept her eyes on him. He was moving quickly, and she laughed as out the side door he went!

Lora Lee had thought about that incident many times, and she laughed every time. It made going to church more entertaining, and she thought if something like that happened more often, she wouldn't ever mind going.

As she shifted from that memory to thinking about the ruby ring and picturing it on her finger, she heard the Rev. Booker talking about the cost of constructing a new Sunday school building. They'd talked before about the need for more space, and had decided to see how much it would cost.

"New Sunday school rooms?" she wondered, paying attention. Rev. Booker had figured out the amount of concrete that would be needed for the building, and the cost for the concrete. He was holding a sheet of paper with his math on it.

Shortly after he announced how many cubic feet of concrete would be needed, Caleb said, "Brother Booker, I b'lieve yore figgers are wrong." And he told him how much he thought would be needed. Caleb had worked as a mason for a while and knew how to figure concrete, and he'd just done the calculation in his head.

The Rev. Booker said he thought Caleb was wrong, but he stood there for a moment checking his figures. "Oh," he said, turning bright red. "I seem to have made a mistake. You're right, Brother Baker."

Lora Lee felt proud of her father. To her, he was a mathematical genius, and he'd had to quit school in the fourth grade to work on the family farm. "Brother Booker thinks he's so smart, an' he made a mistake with a pencil an' paper, an' Daddy did the figgers in his head," she thought. "Jus' like he figgers out how much we're makin' for the yearlin's we sell at the auction. Almost as soon as he knows the weight an' the price per pound, he knows how much they'll bring." Lora Lee had tried figuring it out in her head a few times, and she'd given up.

Lora Lee didn't get to go every time they had yearlings to sell because the auction was only held on Tuesdays, but she liked to go. She and Caleb, and sometimes Ruth, would go in the back and walk on the elevated walkways and look down on the cows that were waiting in stalls to be sold, looking for the ones they'd brought earlier in the day. She didn't like the mixed smells of sawdust and fresh manure, or the sounds of the cows lowing, and she didn't like to see the cattle prod being used on them, but she enjoyed sitting in the auction and watching the process.

The cows were driven into an enclosed scale, and then were run through a semi-circle on a sawdust floor, one at a time or in a group, as the owner desired. There was a wooden wall about six feet tall around the space, with horizontal iron railings above it. Tiered seats, for the cattlemen and others, looked down on the space. The auctioneer, and the woman who recorded the sales, sat up high above the danger zone behind the semi-circle. Occasionally, a cow or bull that was scared or violent would charge the young man who opened the metal gates to let them in. The man would quickly hop up on the wall out of the way, but the show was exciting for the onlookers. If a cow acted up while it was on the scale, the man would get on the wall and open the gate with a pole.

Lora Lee felt an addictive combination of emotions: excitement, fear, and sympathy. She felt excited when a cow was violent; she felt afraid that the young man or the cow would get hurt; but her main feeling was sympathy for the cows, especially when they tried to jump out of the ring, and they hit the metal posts or rails. She knew they were frightened, and that had to hurt. She watched, fascinated, when a cow jumped up, and the cattlemen in the front row barely moved their feet, which were propped on the wall. They acted like it was nothing to be concerned about, just a minor nuisance. The auctioneer would occasionally make a comment, especially when a cow was rambunctious. But when he was auctioneering, Lora Lee couldn't understand him, even when she listened closely.

The thing she really hated happened after they got home from the auction if they'd taken off some yearlings. Their mothers would low all night calling for them, and the sound broke her heart.

Lora Lee heard the Rev. Booker say, "That concludes the business from the deacons. Is there any new business?"

She was about to stand up when Mr. Ford stood up and said, "We oughta be serving wine for the Lord's Supper instead a grape juice, an' we need ta change it."

"Oh good gravy!" she thought. "Mr. Ford's gotta put his two cents in. Now they're gonna talk about this, by cracky! Shoot! I hope we don't miss the beginnin' a 'The Millionaire'."

Their church, like most Southern Baptist churches, served grape juice when they had the Lord's Supper. Mr. Ford had said before that he believed they should serve wine—as the Bible says—but others thought people shouldn't drink wine—as the Bible says.

Caleb spoke in favor of continuing to serve grape juice. He very eloquently explained that there couldn't be any harm in serving grape juice. "But if we serve wine and somebody, who's never even tasted wine before, develops a taste for 'Demon Wine' at our church, that would be unforgivable."

"But the Bible sez . . ." countered by, "Yes, an' the Bible sez . . ." continued for a while, with no resolution. Strong feelings provoked quite a hot debate. Lora Lee wasn't bored anymore.

They finally adjourned after the minister announced that the Lord's Supper would not be served the next Sunday night as scheduled, and that they'd take up the question again at the next business meeting. After they sang "Amazing Grace," the Rev. Booker gave a closing prayer asking God to guide them in deciding the right thing to do.

As the preacher prayed, Lora Lee thought about what he'd said Sunday night about Noah. "Noah was drunk!" she thought. "We don't even b'lieve in drinkin', an' he shouldn' a been drinkin'. Why would he blame Ham for seein' him naked, when *he* was the one that was drunk? I don't know if Nigras came from Ham or not, but it don't seem right ta have a curse on 'im for somethin' that was Noah's own fault. Anyhow, this is thousands a years later, an' they s'pose' ta still have a curse on 'em? I don't know much 'bout Nigras, but that ain't fair, period. I know *that*!" She heard the preacher say, "Amen," and she happily went outside.

On the way home, Caleb said, "Brother Booker sure thought he wuz right about that concrete. That got his goat when he figgered out he wuz wrong."

"It sure did," Ruth said, laughing. "That wuz some business meetin'."

Lora Lee saw a star and realized it was the first one she'd seen that night. She thought, "Star light, star bright, The first star I see tonight. I wish I may, I wish I might, Have the wish I wish tonight." And she closed her eyes, pictured the ruby ring, and wished as hard as she could.

"It beats me how anybody could think it's all right ta serve wine in the church," Caleb said. "B'lieve you me, that young whippersnapper's got some crazy idees."

"It's certainly not right," Ruth said. "If we shouldn' drink wine, we certainly should not serve it in the church."

"Well, I guess it takes all kinds," Caleb said.

Lora Lee sat between them listening. She knew that her father had never tasted any kind of alcohol. "Maybe I won't drink any alcohol when I grow up, either," she decided. But a moment later, she thought, "Or maybe I will. Wonder what wine tastes like."

Thursday

WHEN LORA LEE WOKE UP, SHE HEARD HER MOTHER in the kitchen and she heard the rooster crowing, so she figured it was probably time for her to get up. She went to the bathroom and washed her face. Then she dressed, put on her sweater because the morning was cool, and dragged herself to the kitchen.

"I'm surprised to see you up so early," Ruth said, looking at her. "Did you sleep all right? You look like your git-up-an'-go's done got up an' gone."

"Yes, ma'am," she replied. "I'll be glad when school's out." She sat down at the table. "Daddy already go to the field?"

"Yes, he's already down there. He got out early this mornin'." Ruth put her hand under Lora Lee's chin and looked at her closely. "I think you need to take some Carter's Little Liver pills when school's out."

"Oh, Mama," Lora Lee whined. "Do I have to?"

"Yes, you do, girl," Ruth said.

"Oh shoot!" Lora Lee thought. "I cain't even jus' look forward ta school gittin' out."

Ruth believed the laxative should be administered a few times a year. And Lora Lee knew from experience that she'd have to stay near the bathroom the day after she took the pills. At least the pills were more pleasant to take than the castor oil Ruth had given her when she was younger, and the results were the same.

"It's cloudy an' cool today," Ruth said. "I thought it wuz gonna start rainin' while I wuz down yonder milkin'."

Lora Lee thought about the quarter she'd get from Rita. In another week, she could have thirty-five cents saved. Of course, she didn't know when she'd get to go to Lakeland again, but she wanted to get the money for the ring as soon as possible, so when they did go, she'd be ready.

"Mama, do you have a nickel I can have?" she asked. "You'd prob'ly let me have the two bottles we got yesterday, an' that would be four cents. A nickel's just a penny more."

If she'd asked for more money, Ruth probably would've asked what she needed it for. "I don't believe I've got a nickel, but I'll see."

When she returned from her bedroom, she held four pennies in her hand. "Would you believe, this is all the change I have, Lora Lee," she apologized. "Four pennies! Do you wont them?"

"Yes, ma'am," Lora Lee said, taking the pennies. "Thank you, Mama."

Lora Lee was able to walk casually to the bus, thinking all the way about the problems she had at school with Lola and Herman. She went over things that had happened in her mind, trying to think of how she could have handled them differently, but she couldn't think of anything. She thought about the ruby ring and imagined that she wouldn't say anything about it, and Lola would notice it on her finger. Finally, she'd have a ring, too. She imagined that would, somehow, make her more acceptable to Lola.

When Lora Lee got on the bus, Rita noticed that she looked a little down. "Ever'thing all right?" she asked.

"Yes, ma'am," she said. "I'm jus' tired."

"Well, school's almost over, an' then you can sleep late."

"Yep. Course, Mama said she's gonna give me some Carter's Little Liver pills when we git out."

Rita laughed. "Well, that'll only be bad for one day. Then, maybe you'll have more energy."

Lora Lee was tempted to tell her about the ruby ring, but she didn't know when she'd be able to get it, so she decided to wait. Rita always wore rings, but they didn't have the big, pretty stones that Lora Lee liked. They were mostly just gold and silver bands with different shapes.

When she and Leroy got off the bus, they went straight to Mr. Docker's room. They didn't want to be outside in the cool weather, and Lora Lee certainly didn't feel like dealing with Herman that morning.

In fact, most of the bused kids ended up in Mr. Docker's room, including Herman. When Lora Lee saw him, she was glad she was sitting in the front row. "I hope he sits in the back so I don't hafta look at his ugly face," she thought.

And he did, but as he passed her desk, he said in a low voice, "Is it caaaaaaandy?" and chuckled.

Lora Lee didn't even look at him. She kept her eyes on the desk.

While the kids were sitting at the desks, some talking quietly, Mr. Docker asked Herman if he'd done his arithmetic homework.

"I did it," Herman said. "But I didn' understand ever'thang."

"La-de-da! I'm so surprised!" Lora Lee thought. "An' you think yo're so smart! Well, by cracky, I'm surprised ya understood anything."

Mr. Docker went to the blackboard and picked up a piece of chalk. "Tell me a problem you didn' understand," he said.

Herman looked in the arithmetic book and told him a problem. Mr. Docker wrote it on the board. Lora Lee watched closely because she wanted to see if she could figure it out.

Mr. Docker began explaining the problem to Herman. Then he asked Herman a question, which she could have answered, but Herman didn't say anything.

Lora Lee noticed that Mr. Docker was wearing a pair of light green cotton pants, which he wore occasionally. They had elastic in the waist, and Lora Lee thought they were weird because she'd never seen men's pants with an elastic band, and no belt.

As he waited for Herman's answer, Mr. Docker distractedly looked down and stretched the elastic out so that he was looking down his pants. As the kids sat silently and intently watching him, he just stood there for a moment looking.

Lora Lee noticed that Levi, who was sitting next to her, was reading a book, so she reached over and poked him gently. He looked at her and she pointed at Mr. Docker. Levi looked at him, and Lora Lee saw him smile.

"What is he doin'?" she wondered. "Did he forgit we're sittin' here? He's so crazy they oughta send him to Chattahoochee."

He let the elastic go when several of the kids, including Lora Lee, burst out laughing. Then he turned red and tried to cover his embarrassment by tapping the chalk on the board and repeating the question to Herman.

However, Herman did not hear the question over all the laughter, including his, and Mr. Docker got angry. He picked up his wooden yardstick and hit the desk with it.

"We're workin' on a problem," he said. "Let's have a little quiet."

Lora Lee was hoping Herman would get in trouble for laughing, but he didn't. However, he couldn't follow the logic path Mr. Docker was trying to lead him down, and Mr. Docker got impatient with him.

She felt very grateful to Mr. Docker. If he was going to look down his pants, he chose the best day and best time to do it—while she was in the room. He gave her a badly needed laugh, took her mind off her worries, and gave her the opportunity to see Herman in an awkward situation. Her mood improved, and now she had another funny incident involving Mr. Docker that she could replay and tell throughout the day.

As Lora Lee got near the house school, she could see her classmates standing outside in a circle, and she forgot about Mr. Docker. Somebody's fightin'," she thought. "Maybe somebody's beatin' up Lola." She giggled. She was surprised to see Arnold watching since he was the classmate most likely to be in a fight. "Who is it?" she wondered.

When she saw Perry and Lawrence wallowing in the grass, she was amazed. "Them two never fight," she thought. They were probably the shyest boys in the class, and she'd never seen either of them in a fight before, but they were both clearly mad now. Their faces were red and their squinty eyes were shooting daggers. Each was holding onto the other so tightly about all they could do was roll over. Mrs. Hoffman arrived right after Lora Lee, and she jumped out of her car and ran over to the circle.

"Stop it you two," she commanded. "Perry, Lawrence, I want you to stop it right now!" She grabbed Lawrence by the collar.

Lora Lee was amazed that they stopped. As mad as they appeared to be, she thought it would take two adults to separate them, but Mrs. Hoffman's voice worked magic.

"Everybody go on inside now, except Perry an' Lawrence," she said, unlocking the door. "Look at you two!" she exclaimed. Rolling in the dew-covered grass had allowed dirt to stick to their clothes, faces, and arms.

Lora Lee and some of the others watched from the windows. She heard Mrs. Hoffman tell them to give her their shirts. They took them off and handed them to her. Jimmy was standing at the door, and Mrs. Hoffman told him to get the whiskbroom from the kitchen closet. When he gave it to her, she used it to sweep off the boys' dungarees and shoes. She told them to bend over and shake the dirt out of their hair, and brush as much as possible off their arms. Then they went inside.

Mrs. Hoffman went in the bathroom and got two washrags for them, and told them to go in there one at a time—Lawrence first—and clean themselves up. She took a comb from her pocketbook and gave it to them to comb their hair. Then she put their dirty shirts in the washing machine in the kitchen to wash.

Lawrence and Perry sat shirtless in the class, both of them looking a little chagrined. As soon as the washer stopped, Mrs. Hoffman put their shirts in the dryer. When they were dry, she quickly pressed them while the class worked on an assignment. By the time they had to go to the schoolhouse for their arithmetic class, the boys had on neat, clean shirts, and they looked like they'd just arrived at school. No evidence of the fight remained.

Mrs. Hoffman never said anything about them fighting. Lora Lee figured she'd have been embarrassed to take them to see Mr. Docker since she'd already taken Arnold that week. Besides, Lawrence and Perry never fought, so Mrs. Hoffman probably assumed it wouldn't happen again.

Throughout the day, any time there was a break, Lora Lee, Grace, and Jimmy competed for the chance to tell the kids who weren't there that morning what happened with Mr. Docker—on the way to the schoolhouse, lunch period, and back to the house school. Lora Lee told Emily, and she felt fortunate to reach Lola and her three companions before Jimmy, who was telling one of the boys.

As they walked to the schoolhouse for lunch, Lora Lee caught up with the four of them. "Hey," she said, "y'all 'member what happened wi' Mr. Docker yesterday thinkin' Deborah fell off the roof?"

"Yeah," Lola answered coldly, not even looking at her.

"Well, guess what he did this mornin'."

Lola looked at her then, and her face showed interest.

As she relayed the story, she could see reactions in the listeners' eyes. She thought she also saw, at the end of the tale, disappointment that they weren't there to see Mr. Docker looking down his pants. She was so happy that she saw him. She lived for those kinds of things at school and at church.

Unfortunately, Herman and Bruce walked by her as she was leaving the lunchroom, and taunted her again with, "Is it caaaaaaandy?"

She looked at Herman with pure hatred as she felt the blood rush to her face, and immediately looked around to see who else might have heard them. Fortunately, there was no one nearby. She wished she had the nerve to say something to Herman like, "You cain't even do a simple arithmetic problem, an' you expect me ta know what's in yore stupid pocket!" But she was afraid he'd get mad. He seemed like a big hulk to her, and she didn't want to make him angry. "I shoulda tol' Billy. Maybe he woulda beat the livin' daylights outta him, or at least scared 'im so he'd leave me alone! I cain't wait till school's out. Next year, he'll go to the high school."

During the last class, just before time for physical education, Mrs. Hoffman made an announcement. Lora Lee wondered why she was speaking slowly and enunciating every word. "Okay now, listen to what I have to tell you. Each of you must take this form home an' give it to your parents. It's important that they read the form an' sign it. An' you need to bring it back. Please give it to them tonight, an' bring it back tomorrow. This is very important, Ladies an' Gentlemen."

Lora Lee wondered what could be so important, so as soon as she received the form, she looked at it. It said there was a possibility the school would be integrated, and asked whether the parents would still send their child there. "If they say 'no,' does that mean I hafta quit school?" she wondered.

On the bus that afternoon, as soon as the high school kids got off, she had the pleasure of telling Rita about Mr. Docker. Of course, Leroy had seen the whole thing, so he chimed in with comments, and the three of them had some good laughs.

Rita reacted the way Lora Lee hoped she would. Sometimes she seemed more like one of the kids about things like that than like an adult, and this was one of those times. As she laughed, she said, "I can jus' picture him doin' that. That man's jus' plain touched in the head!"

For a minute, everything was quiet. Then she said, "Wonder what he wuz lookin' at in his britches." And the laughter started again.

Lora Lee wondered, too.

♥ ♥ ♥

WHEN SHE GOT THE MAIL FROM THE MAILBOX, Lora Lee noticed something from her dentist, Dr. Spear. She didn't remember ever seeing any mail from him. "Maybe he wants to go quail huntin' wi' Daddy." She thought about what Dr. Spear had told Caleb right in front of her and wondered if it was true; he said she'd have false teeth by the time she was fourteen. "That's only three years from now." Then she started thinking about the form from school. She assumed her parents would say "yes" that she could continue going to school if the school were integrated, since they'd want her to get an education. However, she knew her father didn't approve of "race mixin'." She remembered a conversation at the house between him and her uncle Roger. They were talking about Negroes and how the "boys" just wanted to marry the white girls, and Roger got mad and used some harsh words, as he usually did when they talked about racial issues.

When she got home, she changed into her everyday clothes and took the mail and the form into the kitchen and put them both on the table, so she wouldn't forget to have the form signed. Then she looked on the stove to see what was left from the noon meal. In pots, were turnip greens and salt pork, and chicken and rice; and on a plate, some fried corn bread.

"Oh boy!" she said. She turned on the radio and Guy Mitchell's "Singing the Blues" was playing. She sang along with it as she fixed herself a plate full of food, put some ice in a glass, and poured herself some tea. When she sat down to eat, she saw a note from Ruth saying that her Aunt Rose's family was coming for supper, and for Lora Lee to wash the dishes, and churn. The churn was on the table with cream already in it.

"Oh, goodie, goodie!" she yelled, whirling around. "I cain't b'lieve it! P. J.'s comin', an' little Lucy."

P. J. Dobbin, who Lora Lee sometimes called "Dirt Dauber," was her nine-year old cousin and good friend. She was also very fond of her mother's sister, Rose, and her little cousin, Lucy. She wished they lived closer, but they lived in Lakeland and she didn't get to see them often. She wasn't quite so fond of her uncle Roger. When he laughed, his eyes opened wide and they looked scary to her, like they might pop out. That, and his talk about the "Commies," and how they were taking over the world and trying to destroy the United States, scared her. In addition, he smoked cigars, which Lora Lee thought smelled terrible. He smelled like them, and so did anyone else who rode in his car, or was in a room where he was smoking. Her mother didn't like the smell either and she'd air out the house as much as possible after he left. He always smoked at least one cigar while he was there. Caleb had smoked cigarettes when he was younger, but he'd quit when Lora Lee was little.

Just after she finished eating, Lora Lee heard Billy's car in the driveway. She was washing the dishes when he entered the kitchen. "Hey gal young'un," he said, picking up the form from the table. "What's this here?"

He studied the form. "You know good an' well what Daddy's gonna say. He ain't gonna let you go ta school wi' no Nigras."

"I know it," Lora Lee said.

Billy started fixing himself a plate. "You know, before you came along, there wuz a Nigra preacher that worked for us on Combee Road. We called 'im 'Nigger John.'"

"Really? To his face?" Lora Lee asked in disbelief.

"Yep. That's what we called 'im. We didn' know no better," he said as he put some ice in a glass.

"Did he mind?" she asked.

"Well, seein' as how he never said nothin' about it, I wouldn' know. He mighta wonted ta knock us up side the head."

"He worked on our farm?"

"Yeah, he did. An' he had a little girl that wuz with 'im part a the time. She wuz my first playmate. I guess I was around five." Billy sat down at the table with a plate full of food and a glass of tea.

"Really? You had a Nigra girl you played with?"

"Yep."

"I wish I did," she said. "I ain't ever even knew a Nigra."

"That's the only two I ever knew, 'cept for them I met when I wuz sellin' rabbits in the Quarters."

That gave Lora Lee something to think about. She had no idea that her father had employed a Negro man, or that Billy had played with a little Negro girl. She found that amazing. The only people who'd worked on the farm during her life were white people from the country.

"Billy," she said. "Do you reckon Nigras feel things the same way that we do?"

"What kinda things?" he asked between mouthfuls.

"Like in slavery when their kids got sold. Mama said they don't feel things like us, or they wouldn' a been able ta stand it. You reckon they did?"

"Lots a people like ta think that," he replied. "But I think they feel things jus' like us."

Lora Lee felt sad. She'd hoped her mother was right, that they didn't feel things like she would. Now, she needed to think about that. Nevertheless, she knew she didn't want to mix with Negroes. "They're diff'runt," she thought.

"I gotta go to the field now," Billy said, putting his empty glass and plate by the sink for her to wash. "I been workin' over at the other place, now I gotta work here, an' then I gotta go to my payin' job. I'm on the midnight shift. By the way, Mama an' Daddy'll be home soon."

She got serious about washing dishes. "You got a date tonight?"

"Nope. Patty cain't go out on a school night. But I'm goin' somewhere wi' Joe before I go ta work."

"Aunt Rose is comin' for supper."

"Mama tol' me," he said on his way out. "That's nice."

Lora Lee had thought a lot about Billy lately. She was aware that when he got married, she would miss him, and she'd be alone with her parents. Now, she thought about him being around a Negro man when he was small. "That mus' be how come he ain't afraid ta go in the Nigra Quarters." She remembered the time she went there with him.

During the previous year, before he had the job with the phosphate company, Billy would kill rabbits, and catch possums and gopher tortoises to sell to the Negroes. He needed money for dating, and Caleb didn't pay him for working on the farm, although he'd occasionally give him a few dollars, if Billy asked for money. One afternoon late, Billy took Lora Lee with him across the railroad tracks to the Negro Quarters in Brewster. She was nervous about going, but she was also excited. She'd been *through* the Quarters, but never *to* the Quarters.

When they got there, Lora Lee looked at the houses, which were basically the same as the wooden company houses in the white section. Some of the yards didn't look quite as neat—some didn't even have lawns, but they didn't have a lawn on the farm, either—and some were nice, with pretty flowers. Some had lawn chairs.

Lora Lee saw four little kids playing in the sand with spoons and a little tea set. "I never had a tea set," she thought. "I useta love to play wi' Sandra's, an' I always wonted one." Sandra had been Lora Lee's friend when they lived on Combee Road.

They passed by a house that had a lawn and some beautiful flowers. "That's a purty place," she said. "They got a nice lawn."

"Yep," Billy said, and he laughed. "You know my friend, Dwayne. He mows the lawn for a Nigra woman in Bradley. He says she sells bolita an' she's got money."

"What's bolita?" Lora Lee asked.

"That's that Cuban numbers gamblin' thing. You heard a that."

"Yeah. I heard Daddy talkin' 'bout it. He says it like it's a dirty word."

"Well, ya know we don't b'lieve in gamblin'," Billy said, "an' the mob's mixed up in it, too. Anyhow, Dwayne mows her lawn. He says it takes him fifteen minutes an' she pays him ten dollars an' gives him a five dollar tip."

"A dollar a minute!" Lora Lee exclaimed. "Boy! I'd like that job."

"An' when he's through, she gives him a big glass a milk an' a piece a fresh pie or cake. Plus, Dwayne says she's got a big Cadillac an' she picks him up. They put his lawn mower in the trunk, an' he sits in the front seat, an' when they drive through Bradley, he waves at ever'body he sees like a big shot. He thinks that Nigra woman gits a big kick outta that. An' she prob'ly does, but he does, too. I can jus' see 'im sittin' up there in that Cadillac with a big ole grin on his face."

They laughed. "A Nigra woman with all that money," she said. "I ain't never heard a that!"

"That's sumpin, all right!"

Billy stopped the truck and turned it off. "You stay here," he told her. "I'll be back directly."

Billy had four skinned and dressed rabbits in a light blue enamel pan. Lora Lee had seen that each of them had one hind foot still attached. She knew Billy always left one foot on because the first time he went to sell rabbits, a woman asked him how she could be sure it was a rabbit. She said some ole white boys had sold her a cat. After that, Billy provided proof that he was selling rabbits.

Lora Lee was happy to stay in the truck and watch him as he went to a few houses. She could hear a radio in somebody's house playing Little Richard's "Long Tall Sally," and she sang the words she knew, bouncing around on the seat to the rhythm. She liked the part where Uncle John was out with Long Tall Sally, and when he saw his wife coming, he jumped back in the alley. Then she could hear the Platters singing "The Great Pretender." She liked the "Oh-oh-oh yes" part.

She watched Billy as he went to several houses. He sold three of the rabbits for fifty cents each. Then he went back to the truck and got the bushel basket with the live possum in it.

As he started to walk down a dirt road that had high weeds and brush on each side, Lora Lee called, "Where you goin'?"

"Jus' down this road," he replied. "The ole man down there'll prob'ly buy the possum. You stay here in the truck. I'll be back directly."

Lora Lee watched him walk down the winding dirt road that went through the vacant lot beside the truck, until she couldn't see him anymore for the tall brush. She hadn't quite realized that she wouldn't be able to see him, and she felt anxious when he disappeared. She was distracted for a little while by the sound of Fats Domino singing "Blueberry Hill," and watching a robin tugging on an earthworm. After the struggle, the robin flew off with the worm.

She looked at the rabbit that was left and hoped they'd take it home. She loved fried rabbit and knew her mother would fry it, and make some grits for breakfast.

When she looked up, she saw a Negro man walking toward the truck. "Oh my Lord," she muttered, her heart pounding. She slid off the seat onto the floor and curled up, barely breathing, her mind busy with possible scenarios. She wanted to look out the window to see where he was, but she was afraid to. She didn't even hear the music anymore, although the radio was still playing.

Lora Lee was probably safer there than most anywhere else she could have been, but she didn't know that, and she was terrified. After a little while, when no one approached the truck and she thought enough time had passed, she slowly counted to ten, and then straightened up enough to look out. There was no one in sight, so she got back up on the seat. She looked back and saw the man over a block away.

"How come Billy ain't comin back?" she wondered. "By cracky, he said he'd be right back. What could he be doin' all this time?"

She looked for the robin again, but it hadn't returned. She did see a male cardinal on the ground under a pine tree.

She waited a little longer until she couldn't stand it anymore. "Oh, goodness gracious!" she exclaimed. "I waited long enough. He said he'd be right back, an' he ain't." And she got out of the truck, watching the cardinal fly away. Then she went down the dirt road.

There was one house at the end of the road, and Billy was standing in the yard talking to a white-haired old man, who was sitting on the porch slowly rocking. He saw Lora Lee first.

"Well, well. Who dis we got here?" he asked.

Billy looked at Lora Lee. "This is my sister, Mr. Hart."

"Well, howdy do, Ma'am," he said. "Please ta make yo' acquaintance."

"Hello," Lora Lee replied. No one had ever called her "ma'am," and she was impressed.

"Ya got a purty lil sistah dere," Mr. Hart said, and Lora Lee smiled. "Yassuh, a purty lil sistah."

"Thank you," Billy said, looking at Lora Lee who was glowing. He thought she did look pretty cute. "Well, I guess we better git goin'."

Lora Lee wasn't ready to leave. She wasn't used to compliments, and she was feeling good. She liked Mr. Hart.

"Thank ya fuh comin' by. Ah's gon clean dat possum an' bake me some sweet taters wit' it. Dat some good eatin'."

"I hope it's a good un," Billy said. "You take care a yoreself, Mr. Hart."

"Ah does my best. Nice ta meet ya, lil lady."

"Thank you," Lora Lee said, smiling broadly.

"See ya nex' time," Billy said.

"Awright then," Mr. Hart replied. "Y'all be careful."

When they were away from the house, Lora Lee scolded, "You said you'd be right back, Billy."

"No, I didn', gal young'un," he corrected. "I said I'd be back *directly*."

"Well," she started.

"That's a deep subject for such a shallow mind," he teased.

"Billy!" she said impatiently. "You know that's the same thing, an' you didn' come back."

"We got ta talkin'," he said, "but I wuz fixin' ta leave when you came. I reckon the ole man's lonely back there all by hisself."

"He ain't married?"

"His wife died a couple years ago," Billy told her, "but his kids come ta visit 'im regularly."

"Well, that's good." Lora Lee had started to feel a little sorry for Mr. Hart, her new admirer.

As she thought about those experiences, she thought again about never having had the opportunity to know a Negro. She thought of them as being so different, yet Mr. Hart had seemed like the old white men she knew, except they didn't call her "ma'am." "He seemed nice," she thought. "He sure wuz nice ta me."

♥　♥　♥

Lora Lee had finished washing the dishes and was getting ready to churn when her parents arrived. "Y'all are home already," she said, greeting them on the porch. "I wuz jus' fixin' ta churn."

"Well, we finished what we were doin', an' decided to come on home instead of startin' another project," Ruth said. "Besides, I thought we'd go to the field an' pick some pole beans for supper, an' some for your aunt Rose to take home with her." Since the season was almost over, the beans were not producing much, so they weren't trying to sell them, but there were plenty for their use.

Caleb was carrying a watermelon, which he put down on the porch. Lora Lee felt a lump in her throat as she looked at the long, light green melon. She thought, "Well, la-de-da, he wouldn' pick a watermelon for me, but he picked one for Aunt Rose an' them."

He looked at her and said, "You wanted a watermelon. Here it is."

She made herself smile at him, but she did not believe that he had her in mind at all when he picked it.

They went in the kitchen and Caleb and Ruth sat down at the table to look at the mail. "Well, I declare!" he said. "I got a dun from Dr. Spear for Lora Lee's last visit! How come he's dunnin' me? He knows I'll pay 'im what I owe sometime when I'm in Lakeland, like I always do. He mus' not trust me—dunnin' me like that." The postmark on the bill was from the day before Ruth's visit. "After all the times we went quail huntin' together! Well, that's it! We'll jus' git a new dentist." Caleb had false teeth, so he didn't go to him anymore, but Ruth, Billy, and Lora Lee did. Lora Lee hoped they did get a new dentist because she didn't like Dr. Spear.

She picked up the form from school and gave it to Ruth, who looked at it briefly and handed it to Caleb. He read it, made a check mark, signed it, and gave it to Lora Lee. "They're thinkin' 'bout integratin' yore school, now, you know."

Lora Lee looked at the form and saw that he'd checked the box saying she would not be attending the school if it were integrated.

"Will I hafta quit school if Nigras go there?" she asked.

"You'll go to a private school," he said.

Lora Lee thought, "I never even heard a no private school. I don't wanna go ta school wi' Nigras, but it shore wouldn' be fair if I had ta quit school. How come they wanna go ta school with us, anyhow? They got their own schools."

"Lora Lee," Ruth said. "Put some shoes on an' come help me pick beans. Rose an' them'll prob'ly be here before long."

"Okay, Mama," she said, "I gotta put this form in my pocketbook so I won't forgit it. I hafta take it back tomorrah."

As Lora Lee stepped off the bottom porch step, King appeared from nowhere and jumped up on her. "King, git down," she said sternly. "That dog drives me crazy."

"He is a pain," Ruth agreed. "At least, he's not as bad as he wuz when he wuz young. Eight years old—that's fifty-six in dog years."

As they walked through the grove on the little dirt road that went from the house to the field, Lora Lee heard a hawk's call and looked up to see two hawks circling overhead. "Mama, look at the hawks," she said. "Ain't they purty!"

Ruth answered, "They are, but if your daddy sees 'em, they'll be purty *dead* hawks."

Caleb killed hawks because he liked to hunt quail, as did hawks, and he wasn't interested in sharing with them. All of the family liked fried quail, and they were unaware, or unconcerned, about the place of hawks in the natural order of things.

As they neared the creek, Lora Lee looked at the water just in time to see a huge bullfrog jump in. "That wuz a big one," she said. "What a loud splash."

Ruth laughed. "That ole frog reminds me of what happened once when I wuz young. Daddy an' me were fishin' an' Daddy caught a great big ole frog. He wuz goin' to throw him back, but I said, 'I ain't ever had frog legs. Let's keep him.' Daddy said, 'All right, but you hafta clean 'im.' I said I would, not thinkin' about what all that meant. Well, I wadn' about to cut his hind legs off before he wuz dead, an' I decided the only way I could kill 'im wuz ta hit 'im on the head with a hammer."

"You were gonna kill 'im with a hammer?"

"I couldn' think of any other way to kill 'im. So I wuz holdin' onto him with one hand an' had the hammer in the other hand. I hit 'im—hard, I thought—but it didn' kill 'im. I had ta hit that poor ole frog several times with that hammer. I would've quit after I hit 'im the first time, 'cause I wuz feelin' sick on my stomach, but I knew good an' well I'd injured 'im. So Daddy and I each had one frog leg that night, but I didn' enjoy mine one bit, an' that wuz the last one I ate. Poor ole frog. I'd hafta be about to starve to death before I'd do that ag'in. And there's so much waste—all you eat's the hind legs."

Lora Lee was picturing her mother trying to kill the frog. She knew she didn't have any problem at all wringing a chicken's neck, but a frog would be different.

Before they got to the field, Ruth and Lora Lee heard the tractor. "Guess Billy's picking up the pipe from the field," Ruth said.

The cows and Denny Boy were standing near the barbed wire fence at the edge of the pasture. Lora Lee went over there and Denny Boy moved closer and she patted his head. She knew the cows had come because Billy was down there, and they were looking for something to eat besides grass. He was on the tractor, hauling a trailer full of pipe behind it.

Ruth and Lora Lee picked the pole beans together, Lora Lee on one side and Ruth on the other side of a double row. Lora Lee didn't mind picking pole beans; they were big enough that it was easy to know which ones were ready, and she didn't have to bend over much. At the end of the season, they usually left a few rows unpicked for a while so the beans could develop. Then they'd pick the ones that were ready to shell and add them to the snaps. Lora Lee loved that mixture.

As they picked, they listened to the crows that were in the back part of the field. "Caw, caw, caw."

"Them crows are loud," Lora Lee said. "I wish they'd go somewhere else."

She reached for a bean and her hand brushed something furry. "Oh!" she shrieked, jerking her hand away.

"What is it?" Ruth asked.

"An ole caterpillar." Lora Lee used a bean to knock it off the vine, and she stepped on it.

They picked in silence for a little while, with only the sound of the crows. Lora Lee looked up and saw some of their black shapes against the blue sky. She watched them for a moment.

"You know, Lora Lee," Ruth began, "I wuz thinkin' about your grandpa jus' now—my daddy. I wish he could've lived long enough for you to git to know 'im better. You were eight when he died, an' he couldn' talk for the last year after his stroke. I remember, musta been nineteen aught nine, when Halley's comet came—no, I wuz six, so it musta been nineteen an' ten. My daddy woke me up one night and we went outside so I could see it. He told me it wouldn' come 'round ag'in till I wuz eighty-four. Wonder if I'll live to see it ag'in."

Lora Lee had heard that story before, and she said the same thing she'd said the last time, "I hope so, Mama."

"I do, too. Of course, your daddy's daddy died before me an' your daddy were even married. Your grandpa wuz in the War Between the States, you know."

"Yes, ma'am, you tol' me."

"He wuz a young man an' he wuz one of the ones who'd shimmy up a pine saplin' to look for the Union soldiers. One time, he went up a little tree an' he jus' dropped right to the ground. By the time he hit the ground, a cannon ball took off the top of the tree where he'd jus' been."

"Good thing he dropped," Lora Lee commented, "or I wouldn' be here. An' neither would Daddy."

"That's the truth," Ruth agreed. "You know, your grandpa wuz never wounded, but lots of his friends were, or killed. Your daddy said he told him about a friend of his that wuz shot in the leg. When they headed back to their camp, your grandpa toted 'im for a long ways before he got so tired he jus' couldn' carry 'im anymore. His buddy said, 'Jus' leave me here. I'll be all right.' Your grandpa didn' have any choice; he hated to leave him, but he had to go on. An' you know, when he got back to camp, his buddy wuz the first person he saw."

"How'd he git back?" Lora Lee asked. She put the handful of beans she'd just picked in her bucket, and stopped for a minute.

"He drug hisself through the swamp that the others had to walk around."

"Through the swamp, Mama? With all the snakes? I'd a been scared a moccasin would bite me, or a 'gator might git me."

"I would, too," Ruth agreed. "But he wuz prob'ly more afraid of the Yankees."

Again, they both stayed quiet for a while as they worked, each lost in her own thoughts. Lora Lee wished she could have known her grandfather. She would've liked to hear him tell the stories. However, she knew that he was born in 1845, so he would be 112 if he had lived.

"We better git these beans to the house an' git 'em ready to cook," Ruth said. "I've got to fix supper."

♥   ♥   ♥

THEY WERE SITTING ON THE BACK PORCH, and had just finished snapping the beans, when Lora Lee said, "I hear their car. They jus' turned on the dirt road." She felt excitement rising in her chest. She and Ruth were standing on the porch waiting for them when the car pulled up at the back of the house. Lora Lee hopped off the porch.

Caleb came from the barn, where he'd been emptying a bag of cow feed into a metal barrel so the rats couldn't get into it. Ruth walked to the edge of the porch and called, "Y'all git out an' come on in."

P. J. bounded out of the car. His father, Roger, got out and spit on the ground. Lora Lee figured he was trying to get the cigar taste out of his mouth.

King suddenly appeared and jumped up on P. J., who tried to push the dog away. Roger yelled at King and kicked him, and Caleb yelled at King, who went slinking away with his tail between his legs.

Lora Lee was watching the process with the dog, thinking Roger didn't have to kick him, and her daddy didn't have to yell at him after Roger did, when she heard her mother's excited voice, "Mama! Oh my goodness!" She looked on the other side of the car, and there was her grandmother.

"Oh, Grandma!" she said with delight.

Ruth flew down the porch steps and hugged her mother.

Rose was laughing. "Quite a surprise, huh?"

"It surely is," Ruth said. "Why, you could've knocked me over with a toothpick!"

Lora Lee hugged her grandmother, noticing that she smelled of cigar smoke. Normally, when Lora Lee hugged her, she got a slight hint of baby powder and she liked that. She asked, "Are ya gonna stay with us for a while, Grandma?"

"For a little while," she answered. "But I hafta go stay wi' my sister, Bessie. She broke her ankle an' she's in the hospital. She's goin' home on Saturday, an' she'll be laid up for a while, so I hafta go to her house Saturday."

Her grandmother, Clara, was seventy-five, and Clara's sister Bessie was eighty-four. Bessie only had one child, a son, so Clara felt responsible for helping with her care. It also was an opportunity for them to spend some time together. Clara had stayed in Georgia, but Bessie moved to Lakeland, so they didn't see each other often.

Little Lucy threw her arms around Lora Lee's waist, and Lora Lee hugged her, a big smile on her face. "Hi, Lucy."

"Hi, Lor' Lee." Lucy also had a big smile. "I'm four," she said, holding up four fingers.

"You had a birthday last week, didn' you?"

"Uh-huh."

Lora Lee kissed her on the cheek. "Happy birthday, Lucy!"

Lucy smiled with pride.

P. J. saw the watermelon on the porch. And he asked, "Are we havin' watermelon, Uncle Caleb?"

"Yes, we are," he said proudly. "It's the first one a the season—not many ripe yet."

Lucy went over and tried to thump the melon as she'd seen adults do to test for ripeness.

"When can we cut it?" P. J. asked.

"Well, I guess now's as good a time as any," Caleb said. "Go git a knife, Lora Lee."

She went in the house and brought out a big butcher knife. Caleb cut the melon in half lengthwise, and then cut lengthwise slices. He handed the first one to P. J., then noticed little Lucy's big eyes looking up at him, so he cut the next slice for her.

"Oh Lord," Rose said. "She's gonna git that all over her. Come 'ere, Lucy." Ruth held the slice of watermelon while Rose took Lucy's pretty little dress off. "You be careful, P. J., not to git that all over yore clothes. Maybe you oughta take yore shirt off."

"Too late," he said. "I done got some on it." Juice was running down his chin, and down his arms.

P. J. was ready for a second slice by the time everybody else got their first one. Lora Lee had another one, too, and then P. J. said, "Let's go play, Lora Lee."

"I hafta churn first, Dirt Dauber, but I can prob'ly play after that. It won't take me long."

"I can churn for you, Lora Lee," her grandmother said.

"Can she, Mama?" Lora Lee pleaded.

Lora Lee saw a look pass between Clara and Ruth.

"All right, Lora Lee," she conceded. "Jus' this once. But I need you to git me some water for tea before you go runnin' off."

"Thank you, Mama," Lora Lee said, and hugged Clara. "Thank you, Grandma." She ran to the kitchen and got the bucket.

"You kids don't git around no moss," Rose said. "I don't want you comin' back covered with red-bugs, P. J."

The tiny, almost invisible red bugs (chiggers) got in the creases under arms and by crotches, and made a red bump, which itched for days, and many people thought they lived in Spanish moss. Rose didn't want to hear P. J. whining and complaining about itching. Nor, when she put alcohol on the scratched bumps by his crotch to prevent infection, did she want him screeching like he was dying, or dancing around all over the place.

P. J. ran to the pump ahead of Lora Lee and had it primed and the jar refilled by the time she got there, so she quickly pumped the bucket about three-fourths full. "It'll jus' take me a minute ta tote this to the house, an' then we'll go," she said, and she walked quickly to the house with only a little splashing.

When she went back outside, she saw P. J. throwing some of the little yellow oranges from the ground. There were some yellow ones under the trees, from marble-size to golf ball-size, premature ones that had fallen off.

"Le's go, P. J.," she said, and they took off for their secret place in the woods. King followed them.

For a year, the two of them had been working on a fort in a tree-sheltered area on the edge of the swamp, near where the creek ran through. P. J.'s father was a carpenter and he gave them a few pieces of scrap lumber and plywood. They'd managed to construct three makeshift walls and put some plywood over them so there was a semblance of a building. Of course, P. J. wasn't there often, so they didn't have much opportunity to work on it. When P. J.'s father took some stuff down there for them after they'd almost finished the structure, he said, "I see you kids have nigger-rigged this place."

Lora Lee hadn't heard that term before, but she could tell by his condescending tone that it wasn't complimentary. She and P. J. didn't care, though. They wanted a place they could work on if they wanted to, or they could just sit and talk, away from the adults.

When they were younger, they had often played "Red Rider and Little Beaver," or "The Lone Ranger and Tonto," but Lora Lee didn't like to play those games anymore. She told P. J. to play cowboys and Indians with his friends.

As they neared the creek, he said, "Aw, fiddlesticks," stopped, and bent over, and Lora Lee could see that his socks were down in his shoes. "These blamed ole shoes keep eatin' my socks."

"I hate that!" she replied, still walking.

"Wait on me, Lora Lee," he said, and she stopped and watched him pull up his socks. As she stood there waiting, she heard the crows.

"Jumpin' Jehosaphat!" P. J. exclaimed. "Listen to them ole crows."

"There was a slue of 'em down in the field squawkin' when me an' Mama went down there to pick beans," she complained.

"Crows are loud. Caw, caw, caw." He pointed at the ground near where he stood. "Lookie here!" he said excitedly. "A snake track."

"Oh shoot," she thought, looking at the smooth place where a snake had crossed the dirt road. She couldn't understand why P. J. always got so excited about snakes. "I don't like snakes," she said.

"Boy, I do," he declared. "Snakes are great. I caught a grass snake the other day, but Mama made me turn 'im loose." He spit near the snake track, and Lora Lee watched the spittle disappear, leaving a wet spot in the sand.

"Hey, Lora Lee," he said.

"What is it?"

"Wanna kill a chicken?"

They both laughed as they remembered the day P. J.'s father accepted the task of catching and killing a chicken for supper. Ruth pointed out the one she wanted, and she and Rose went in the house. Ruth would snatch a chicken up, hold it by the head, and swing it around a couple of times. When she put it down, it had a broken neck, and after a minute of frantic flapping around, it was dead. Roger was sure he could do that.

He recruited Lora Lee and P. J. to help him catch the chicken. The chickens weren't penned up and they scattered and ran around frantically as Roger and the kids chased the chosen one. Every now and then, some of them would try to fly, and squawk loudly. They almost had it a few times, but Roger seemed tentative, and it would get away each time. They were tired by the time they finally got it cornered, and Roger had the determination necessary to grab it.

Lora Lee started to walk away, but something told her to turn around, so she watched him wring the chicken's neck and put it down. And she watched the chicken get up and run off. And, she watched Roger just stand there with his mouth open and his hands hanging by his sides, staring in disbelief at the squawking chicken running for its life.

She and P. J. practically rolled on the ground laughing. They were both concerned that Roger would get mad at them, but their laughter just erupted. After that, when they were together, one of them would usually say, "Wanna kill a chicken?" and they'd remember that scene and laugh hysterically. For a while right after it happened, they'd just look at each other and start laughing.

When they got to their hideaway, the two of them sat down on a low makeshift bench they had painstakingly put together, and Lora Lee recounted in vivid detail what happened on Sunday. "You know how Howlie May's always pickin' on me."

P. J. nodded, listening intently.

"Sunday mornin', I wuz gittin' a drink a water from the water fountain, an' she came up behine me an' pushed my face in the water. An' she said sumpin 'bout washin' my freckles off."

"By cracky! she makes me so mad," he said. "I wish somebody would beat the stew outta her."

"Me, too," Lora Lee agreed. "I'd like ta see that."

"That girl's crazy," he said softly. "You oughta ask her if she excaped from Chattachoochee."

"You said a mouthful," she replied, nodding her head.

"Know what she is? She's a 'flibbertigibbet'!"

Lora Lee laughed. "A what?"

"A flibbertigibbet. Miz Smith said it's a ole word an' she likes it, so she taught it to us. It means somebody that's silly an' don't act their age."

"Well, that's her, all right. Maybe I'll call 'er that."

They sat quietly for a minute, just looking around. "Look at the magnolia bay trees," she said, pointing to the sweet bay trees at the edge of the swamp. "They're bloomin'." The white blooms were just beginning to open.

"Yep," P. J. said as he took a box from his shirt pocket. "They're purty." He handed Lora Lee a candy cigarette and put one in his mouth.

"Thanks, P. J.," she said, looking at his mouth with the red-tipped cigarette sticking out. "I like these."

"I know it," he said. "I do, too."

"Sunday night," she continued, "I wrote a note ta Missy tellin' 'er 'bout Howlie May an' she wrote me. She said if she wuz there, she'd double-dog-dare 'er ta push my face in the water. I wuz writin' back ta 'er, an' the preacher slammed his stupid hand down, an' I 'bout jumped off the bench."

P. J. started to laugh, but when he saw her face, he stopped. "What happened?"

After Lora Lee told him, he asked sympathetically, "Did ya git a whippin'?"

"Nuh-uh," she said, "but I wuz scared I would. Mama an' Daddy were mad. An' I cain't sit wi' Missy no more."

"La-de-da. You knew that'd happen."

Lora Lee told him about Missy going behind the car after the service to talk to her. "I don't know if Daddy saw 'er or not, but if he did, he didn' say nothin'."

"I don't think he did," P. J. offered. "I think he'd a said sumpin. Anyway, he knew it wadn' yore fault if Missy wuz there, nohow. The whole thing wuz her fault."

"She couldn' help laughin'," Lora Lee said. "She jus' don't understand how serious my parents are 'bout bein' quiet durin' preachin'."

"Ya tol' her before, Lora Lee. She jus' don't listen."

"I know it," she admitted. "I'm kinda mad at 'er."

"Me, too!" he exclaimed. He didn't even know Missy, but he didn't like to see his cousin in trouble. P. J. understood that Lora Lee's parents were strict and he felt sorry for her. He thought his own father was strict, but he knew hers was much stricter.

A couple of minutes passed in silence. Suddenly, he said, "I know what. You can tell yore Mama you won't hang aroun' wi' Missy no more."

Lora Lee knew that P. J. was a little jealous of her friendship with Missy, and her voice had an edge when she responded. "Nuh-uh, I cain't, P. J. She's my only frien'. 'Sides, they won't let me sit with 'er no more, an' she prob'ly won't go ta church no more, so I won't even see her."

P. J.'s face was solemn. He waited a moment before saying quietly, "I thought I wuz yore frien'."

"Oh shoot!" she thought. "Me an' my big mouth!" Her heart sank when she realized she'd hurt his feelings. She loved her cousin, but he was a boy and two years younger than her. "You are, P. J.," she said tenderly. "But yo're my cousin. 'Sides, I really meant my only girl friend."

"Oh," he said, not quite convinced.

"P. J., you been my frien' forever. Ever since we were little, we always played together. You'll always be my frien'. Ya know I tell you all my secrets."

As soon as she said that, she was sorry. She and Missy had shared secrets that she didn't share with P. J. "Unless it's girl stuff," she added to clear her conscience.

"What kind a girl stuff?" he asked innocently.

"You know. Stuff like about periods an' stuff like that."

"What are periods?"

"You know—girl's periods. When they fall off the roof."

For the second time that week, Lora Lee saw a male's mouth fall open when he heard those words. P. J. looked quizzically at her. She was beginning to realize that he didn't know anything about periods. And why would he? She only knew because Missy had told her.

"Forgit about it, P. J.," she said, standing up. "You'll understand when ya git older."

P. J. looked like she'd slapped him.

"Goodness gracious!" she exclaimed. "That's what Mama tells me. I'm so sorry, P. J."

"Okay," he said, but his face still had the hurt look.

"It's girl stuff," she said. "I cain't tell ya about it 'cause yore mama'd git mad at me. Maybe you can ask her, or yore daddy, sometime what periods are, but don't tell 'er I said it. Tell 'er you heard it at school."

Lora Lee felt guilt in the pit of her stomach that she knew she would carry for the rest of the day. "Shoot," she thought. "I'm the one who wuz in trouble an' losin' my frien', an' now I gotta try ta make *him* feel better."

"I tell you what!" she exclaimed, "let's play 'doctor'."

"Naw," he said.

They'd played "doctor" when they were younger. Their needles were orange thorns over an inch long that they cut off orange trees; their pretend "pills" from a wild vine were little hard, shiny red seeds with one black dot, which they called black-eyed suzies; their cotton was from their mothers' aspirin bottles, and they had an aspirin bottle and aspirin tin, which held the black-eyed suzies; and they found an empty nose-drops bottle with a dropper, which they filled with water. P. J. was the doctor since he was male, Lora Lee was the nurse, and if Lucy played with them, she was the patient. Ruth had a spindly green and white houseplant on the front porch that was often a patient. It bled a white milky substance when broken, and they gave the plant shots with the orange thorns, watched it bleed, and wiped it with the cotton. Of course, Ruth didn't know that.

Lora Lee had gotten tired of playing "doctor" because they did it for a while every time they got together. However, P. J. still liked to play, and he was disappointed that Lora Lee didn't want to. So, when he didn't jump at the chance, she knew how upset he was.

"I hafta be excused," he said.

"Number one or number two?" she asked. She knew he could do number one in the woods, as he usually did.

"Number two. I gotta go to the house."

"Okay," she said. "We can play Chinese checkers." P. J. liked to play Chinese checkers, and Lora Lee didn't like to play with him because she was much better than he was, and she felt like she had to let him win part of the time so he wouldn't feel bad; consequently, she seldom played with him. Linda had given her the marbles after she and Tim got tired of playing.

"Okay." He brightened a little. Lora Lee could tell that he saw through her, and she wasn't sure whether he wanted to play, or he was just accommodating her.

"I'll make sure he beats me," she thought, "like Grandma does me when we play regular checkers at her house." When they played, Clara would cheat so that Lora Lee would win one game, and she'd win the next game. Always. Lora Lee knew she could win without Clara cheating, but she thought it was funny how she'd cheat and be so obvious about it. And Clara never played fewer than, or more than, two games.

As they left the fort, Lora Lee stopped and whispered, "Look at King. He's pointing." The dog was standing like a statue at the edge of the orange grove about forty feet away, one front foot lifted, staring straight ahead. "There mus' be some quail. Let's go see." As they slowly and quietly approached the area, a covey flew, and the sound scared both of them.

"Dad-gummit!" she said. "Quail make so much noise when they fly an' they always scare me. Good dog, King!"

Excited, King ran over to them and jumped up on her. "Git down, King," she yelled. P. J. picked up a stick and threw it and King ran after it, but he didn't know that game. After a minute, he fell in with them.

♥ ♥ ♥

As soon as they neared the house, Lucy ran out to meet them. "Play wi' me, Lor' Lee," she said. "Play wi' me."

"I will," Lora Lee said. "We're gonna play wi' the marbles, an' you can play with 'em, too."

While P. J. was in the bathroom, Lora Lee got the marbles and checkerboard, and then she went to the kitchen and got two pie pans. Ruth saw her and asked, "Where are you goin' with my pans?"

"P. J. an' me are playin' marbles, an' I got these for Lucy so she can play. I'll bring 'em back."

"All right," Ruth said. "See that you do. An' y'all don't go off ag'in, Lora Lee; supper'll be ready before long."

"Yes, ma'am." The smell of frying chicken made her mouth water.

They went on the front porch and sat on the floor with the checkerboard between her and P. J. Lucy sat close to her. As they played, Lora Lee gave part of her attention to Lucy, who had the extra marbles in the two pans. Lucy put the yellow and red marbles in one pan, and the green and purple in the other pan. P. J. and Lora Lee were using the blue and white ones. Lora Lee preferred to play with the red, but she knew Lucy liked them, so she used the white ones. Lucy dumped them back into the old metal coffee can they were kept in, and arranged them differently. Lora Lee commented on what she was doing and made enough suggestions to keep her happy.

"Look, Lor' Lee, a dirt dob," Lucy said. "Jumpin' Joe's fat."

"Jumpin' Jehosaphat," Lora Lee thought, smiling at Lucy's pronunciation. A dirt dauber was building little clay tunnels to lay her eggs in where the wall met the ceiling. "It's okay," she said. There were several there.

She did a good enough job losing to P. J. that he didn't seem to notice that she wasn't playing her best. Clearly, he felt good about beating her. She wasn't happy when he asked, "Wanna play ag'in?" but she agreed.

"Lor' Lee, I tell you what!" Lucy exclaimed. "Le's look fer doo'bugs." She always wanted to look for doodlebugs.

"Okay," Lora Lee said. "As soon as we finish this game, we will."

Lucy left the marbles and climbed onto a rocking chair, which she managed to rock a little by moving the top part of her body forward and backward. "P. J., we hafta do the rhyme."

He sighed. "Oh yeah. Lora Lee, how does that rhyme go? You know, the one that starts, 'One bright day.'"

"You know that by heart, P. J.," she said.

"I forgot part of it, an' Lucy likes it. Say it for 'er."

"Well, say it wi' me," she said, and they said it together while Lucy listened, fascinated.

One bright day in the middle of the night,
Two dead boys got up ta fight.
Back ta back they faced each other,
Drew their swords an' shot each other.
A deaf policeman heard the noise
An' came an' killed the two dead boys.
If ya don't believe this story's true,
Ask the blind man. He saw it, too.

"I forgot the policeman," P. J. said. "Let's say it again."

Lora Lee watched Lucy as they said it, and she thought Lucy looked so cute sitting still and staring at them with her little mouth open.

Lora Lee gave P. J. a little more of a challenge in the second game, but she let him win again, which wasn't easy for her. She thought he seemed all right after that, and she relaxed a little.

"They're havin' a short revival at our church, an' I've got to go to church tomorrah night an' Saturday night, plus Sunday," she said. "I'm gonna miss my TV shows."

"I'm glad we don't go ta church at night," P. J. said. "Daddy says Sunday mornin's enough."

Lora Lee knew his family often went to the drive-in theater on Sunday evening, and she was jealous. Her family didn't go to movies, but a few times they'd passed the Lakeland Drive-in at night, and she'd glimpsed the screen and was dying to go. However, she knew she'd feel guilty if she went there instead of church.

"I made up a joke, P. J.," Lora Lee said. "What do ya call a cow all by itself?"

"A lone cow? I don't know," he replied.

"That's good. Alone cow. But I thought of 'a cow wi' no udders.'"

"What? I don't git it."

"You know. A cow has 'udders' an' it sounds like 'others,'" she explained.

P. J. looked at her with a blank stare.

"Jus' forget it," she said, feeling let down that he didn't understand her joke. She thought it was really clever. "I'll tell Grandma later," she thought.

After Lora Lee took the pans back to the kitchen, they went to the side of the house where she'd taken her little niece Hope on Sunday. She and P. J. called the little doodlebug homes under the house, "Doodlebug Village." They found sticks about three inches long, squatted down by the house, twirled them in the little sandy homes, and chanted:

> Doodlebug, doodlebug,
> Fly away home.
> Ya house is on fire,
> An' ya children are gone.

Lucy mostly watched, but she loved the chant. On the third one, Lora Lee turned up a doodlebug, which immediately scooted backwards under the sand, sand flying.

"Oh!" Lucy exclaimed, "you got one, Lor' Lee! You got one!"

Lora Lee was pleased that she got one for Lucy to see. "Did you git one, P. J.?" she asked.

"Nuh-uh," he said, "but I don't care, nohow. Let's make frog houses."

"Okay! Le's make frog houses," Lucy said. She liked making frog houses.

P. J. went ahead of Lora Lee and Lucy. He spit on the trunk of an orange tree as he passed it.

Just as they got to the back where they were planning to make frog houses, Rose called, "You young'uns come on in an' wash up for supper."

"Shoot," Lucy whined, and poked out her lower lip.

"Oh, yore lip's all pooched out," Lora Lee said. "Don't be poutin' or you'll git in trouble." She went behind Lucy, picked her up from behind under her arms, and spun her around several times while she giggled. After Lora Lee put her down, Lucy tried to walk and fell down in the sand, still giggling. "You're drunk, Lucy," Lora Lee said, helping her up, and she and P. J. held her hands and swung her between them part of the way, as they walked into the house. She arrived smiling, instead of pouting. Lora Lee felt pleased, and wished she had a little sister.

Ruth had made fried chicken, a small pork roast, rice, pole beans, and biscuits. And while Ruth cooked, Rose had made a potato salad with celery, onion, sweet pickles, boiled eggs, apple, and mayonnaise, the same way Ruth made it, except Ruth added some bell pepper. And of course, they had extra-sweet iced tea.

As little Lucy ate the pole beans, she asked, "Did I have this before? 'Cause if I did, Aaaaah like it!"

Everybody laughed, and Rose said, "Know what she said the other day? I'd stripped the beds to wash the sheets, an' she wuz gittin' dressed. She cain't buckle her sandals, so I told her to git up on her bed so I could buckle 'em for 'er. Well, she looked at the bed with no sheets on it, an' said, 'I ain't sittin' on that nekkid bed.' An' I had ta put her on that bed."

As before, they all laughed and little Lucy was grinning from ear to ear as though she'd done something wonderful. Clara hugged her, kissed her on the cheek, and said, "Lucy, you're just a little bundle of amusement." Lucy smiled contentedly.

Lora Lee felt her heart swell with the memories of visits to Georgia when she was little, and her grandmother hugging her tight and saying that to her. She'd always felt safe and at peace with the world in her grandmother's arms.

Caleb rattled the ice in his glass. Lora Lee knew that was a command to get him more tea and was about to get up when Ruth said, "Lora Lee, git ever'body some more tea."

She grabbed Roger's and Caleb's glasses and filled them with ice and tea. Then she filled the women's glasses, Billy's, P. J.'s, and hers. Little Lucy had a glass of milk.

They were just finishing supper when Caleb told them about the integration form Lora Lee had brought home. "I'll be John Brown if I'd let my daughter go ta school wi' colereds," he said.

Lora Lee looked across the table at Billy and he raised his eyebrows. She shrugged her shoulders.

Roger exclaimed loudly, "B'lieve you me, I'd never send my kids ta school wi' no dadblamed niggers, 'specially my daughter. They got their own schools, an' ya know all they wont is fer them blamed nigger boys ta marry our white girls."

"That's exactly what would happen, too," Caleb said.

"Yep, it shore would," Roger agreed. "An' we'd have all kinds a mixed young'uns aroun'."

Lora Lee looked at P. J. and they both got up from the table. In the hallway, she said, "I gotta go to the bathroom, an' then I'll meet you out back." She could still hear the men talking.

"Caleb, I know y'all don't git the paper out here," Roger said. "Did ya hear about that nigger boy in north Florida that raped that white girl?"

"No, I didn'," Caleb replied, interested.

"Happened jus' the other day. She wuz walkin' home from school an' he grabbed her. That boy wuz forty-two, an' she wuz only sixteen."

Ruth said, "My goodness!"

Lora Lee had stopped in the hallway listening. "Walkin' home from school," she thought, picturing herself on the dirt road, and feeling a moment of panic. Then she realized that she'd never seen a Negro anywhere around there.

"They oughta jus' go in there an' kill a bunch a 'em!" Roger asserted, angrily. "Teach 'em a lesson."

That scared Lora Lee. "Would they do that?" she wondered. "I ain't a nigger-lover, but that wouldn' be right. Miz Hoffman says one a the things that makes America great is that we treat people like they're innocent, an' we hafta prove they're guilty. That'd jus' be murder. I wouldn' care if they killed the one that raped her, but ya cain't jus' kill people, even Nigras, 'cause somebody else did sumpin wrong."

They were still talking about it when Lora Lee left the bathroom, and she heard Clara say, "Well, ya cain't kill people jus' because they're colored, Roger. Not all colored people are bad, an' that wouldn' be at all Christian." She looked at Lora Lee as she passed by the door.

They were through eating and Roger lit up one of his cigars and started talking about Communism. Billy said he had to go see a friend, and he hugged his grandmother, Rose, and Lucy. Lora Lee was glad she was going outside. She certainly didn't want to hear any of her uncle Roger's scary talk that would give her more nightmares, and she didn't want to smell the cigar.

P. J. was sitting on the edge of the porch with his feet dangling over the side. Lora Lee remembered to tell him about Mr. Cooper laughing Sunday morning. When she told him the joke the preacher had told, he thought it was funny. Then she told him about Mr. Cooper laughing with the book bouncing on his belly. P. J.'s family had been at the church one Sunday night when Mr. Cooper was laughing, so he knew how he looked. The memory was enough to set him off. Pretty soon, he and Lora Lee were both laughing hysterically.

When they stopped laughing and she could talk, Lora Lee told him about Mr. Docker looking down his britches, and they laughed again. She was so glad she'd thought about the two incidents because the laughter was like the final healing of the breach between them.

After they were done laughing, they went to the orange tree in the back yard and pulled themselves up on one of the limbs and skinned the cat a few times. P. J. was better at it than her, and she told him so and watched him swell with pride. Lora Lee thought he seemed more relaxed, and she hoped his feelings weren't hurt anymore.

They were in the tree when Rose called from the porch. "What are you young'uns doin'?" She could see Lora Lee hanging from a branch. "Ya just ate supper, an' now yo're hangin' upside down?" She laughed. "We're fixin' ta go, Lora Lee. Where's P. J. at?"

"Aw, Mama," he whined. He was standing on the limb and Rose couldn't see him. "Do we hafta go now?"

"P. J. Dobbin, don't you dare complain! You know you have school tomorrah, an' yes, we do hafta go now," Rose scolded.

They both did their final skin-the-cat, and Lora Lee almost landed on Lucy who had run under the tree. "Lucy," she said, "I didn' even see you."

Rose and Roger headed to the car, and the kids followed reluctantly. Lucy sat between her parents, and P. J. sat behind Rose. Lora Lee went to his side of the car where Ruth stood talking to Rose. Caleb was on the other side talking to Roger. She could smell the stale cigar scent that lingered in the car even though the windows were left open.

P. J. put his hand on top of the open window, and Lora Lee tried to hit it before he could move it. "You cain't do it," he taunted.

"Use'ly I do do it," she retorted.

"Oh, you said 'do do,'" he snickered, and Lora Lee remembered that he was a nine-year-old boy. However, she noticed that he was getting faster at the game and she only got him once.

When Roger started the car, P. J. said, "See ya later, Alligator."

"After while, Crocodile," she responded.

Rose said, "Toodle-oo, Lora Lee."

"Toodle-oo, Aunt Rose," she answered. "Toodle-oo, Lucy."

Lucy said, "Too-doo, Lor' Lee."

Lora Lee smiled. She wished her mother could be more like Rose. After all, they were sisters. Her aunt Rose seemed like she'd be more fun as a mother. Of course, she didn't have to work on a farm the way Ruth did. Roger made good money as a carpenter, and Rose was a housewife.

They all waved as the car pulled out of the driveway.

♥ ♥ ♥

They'd just gone back into the house when the rain started. They sat in the living room talking and listening to the sound of the rain and the occasional clap of thunder.

"I'm glad y'all have lightnin' rods," Clara said after a flash of lightning lit up the room and was followed immediately by a loud burst of thunder. "I know most that was right here."

Lora Lee thought she sounded scared.

"Prob'ly was," Ruth said. "It hits 'round here all the time."

The lights flickered and went out. "Oh my. I guess we'll be without electricity for a while," Ruth said, and she got up and moved slowly to the kitchen, feeling her way in the dark. In a minute, she returned with a kerosene lamp. It wasn't very bright, but at least they weren't in the dark anymore.

"We lost electricity last November after we'd butchered a hog," Caleb said. "I wuz still cuttin' it up when it went off, so we had a whole heap of meat that hadn' been wrapped an' put in the freezer. It wadn' a hot day, but I tell you, we were worried it wuz gonna spoil. I wuz thinkin' about takin' it to cold storage, but the power came back on after a couple a hours, so it wuz all right."

Lora Lee remembered that day. It was the first time she'd had to help with scraping the hair off the hog after Caleb slid it into the kettle of hot water to scald it. Billy was supposed to help, but he was late getting home from work, so Lora Lee had to. She had trouble holding the knife blade the right way, and she didn't like doing it. However, what bothered her more was the task her mother was doing after the pig was dressed, cleaning the intestines for chitterlings.

Ruth would cut off a piece of intestine about three feet long, hold one end, and drain the contents into a hole in the ground. Then she'd dip it in a pan of water, holding one end open so water would go in it, and empty that in the hole. Lora Lee knew it wouldn't be long before she'd have to help with that chore and she wasn't looking forward to it.

Of course, she had to admit that she did like "chit'lins." Ruth put them through a few more cleanings, including turning them inside out and soaking them in a pan with salt and dried cornhusks. When she was satisfied that they were clean, she looped them so they looked plaited, then boiled, floured, and fried them. Caleb loved "chit'lins." Billy and Lora Lee liked them, too, but Ruth barely ate them.

When it was time for bed, Ruth got a lamp for Lora Lee's bedroom. "Grandma, you gonna sleep wi' me?" Lora Lee asked.

"I shore am, honey," she replied.

"Goodie, goodie."

Lora Lee hated having to do things by lamplight, but she felt better about it with her grandmother in her room. She got into her shorty pajamas quickly and climbed into bed. Then she thought about telling Clara her joke.

"Grandma, I made up a joke. What do you call a cow by itself?"

"I don't know," Clara answered as she slowly changed into her nightgown, with her back to Lora Lee. "What?"

"A cow wi' no udders."

Clara laughed. That's a good one, Lora Lee. "I like that. Can I tell it to my friends?"

Lora Lee glowed. "Yes, ma'am. You can tell it to anybody."

"Your aunt Esther'll like that." The youngest child, Esther never married, and had always lived with her parents.. "You know, sugar, Esther wuz born on the day that women got the right to vote, August 26, 1920. Ain't that somethin'?"

"Women couldn' vote?" Lora Lee asked in disbelief, her eyes wide.

"No, sugar, they couldn'. I wadn' able to vote till I wuz thirty-eight years old." She smiled at Lora Lee.

Clara had a gold tooth near the front of her mouth, and Lora Lee loved to see it when she smiled. Lora Lee didn't know anyone else who had a gold tooth that could be seen. She had a gold filling in one of her upper molars, but it didn't show.

"That's awful," Lora Lee said. She thought for a minute. "That was jus' thirty-seven years ago."

Lora Lee told Clara things she wouldn't think about telling her parents. She told her about the ruby ring and her plan to save her money until she had thirty-five cents. She told her about Rita paying her and Leroy a quarter a week to pick up trash and put up the windows on the bus, and going by the drugstore on Fridays.

"Well, bless her heart," Clara said, "That's real sweet of her givin' you a chance to make a little money."

"I use'ly buy sumpin at the drug store on Friday," Lora Lee said, "but this week, I'm savin' my money. Mama gave me four pennies, so I'll jus' need six more cents."

Clara undid the bun at the back of her neck and combed her hair. Her straight gray hair was almost halfway down her back. Lora Lee forgot how long it was because Clara always wore it up, but she left it down for sleeping. Lora Lee loved to watch her comb and fix her hair.

"I wish you could come see us more often, Grandma," she said.

"I wish I could, too, sugar, but it's a right far piece from my house."

Later, when they were lying in bed, listening to the rain, Clara said, "Ya know, Lora Lee, I don't know much about colored people, but I wuz thinkin' 'bout what Roger said, an' I do know that God made us, an' He made them. I don't think they're like us, but I shore do think it would be a sin ta kill anybody, white or colored. An' all that talk comin' from Roger wuz just wrong. Why, if we did things like that, we'd be worse 'an them."

After a moment, Lora Lee asked, "Grandma, do ya think they feel things like we do? Like when they were slaves an' their kids got sold?"

"I've studied about that a lot, Lora Lee, honey, an' I don't know the answer. I reckon they prob'ly don't, 'cause they ain't really like us. They don't act like we do, nohow."

Lora Lee thought that was true. She was quiet for a little while before asking softly, "Do you know any Nigras, Grandma?"

"No, honey, I don't really," Clara said.

"I don't, either," Lora Lee admitted. "We saw a fam'ly at the grocery store an' they had two cute little kids. An' Daddy said they beat their kids."

"Well, I don't know about that—prob'ly some do, but I know for shore that some white people do, too."

"I know it, too."

"You know, my grandpa had some slaves. My mama tol' me that when she wuz a girl if anything happened to her clothes, if they got a little tear or something, she had to give them to the slave children. She said she had one dress that wuz her favorite, an' when it got a little tear, she didn't tell her mama. But her mama saw it the next time she wore it, and she made her give it away." She paused. "Sometimes I wish I could ask my mama some questions, but now she's dead an' gone."

Lora Lee was deep in thought, picturing a sad little white girl handing her beautiful dress to a smiling little Negro girl.

"Oh, listen," Clara said. "I hear a whippoorwill."

"Yeah, that ole thing's always soundin' sad out there."

They listened for a moment: "Whippoor-will, whippoor-will, whippoor-will."

"You know, sugar, while we were eatin' supper, I remembered somethin' that happened a few years ago when my cousin's daughter Hazel wuz visitin' us. Your grandpa wuz still alive then," she said softly. "Well, Hazel married a man from up the country somewhere an' moved up there, an' they had a little girl three years old. That child wuz the spittin' image of her mama. Well, we were sittin' 'roun' the table talkin' an' I wuz sittin' close to Hazel. Somebody said somethin' about colored people, an' I heard her little girl ask, 'Mama, what color are they?'"

Lora Lee said, "That's so sweet!"

"Idn't it cute!" Clara replied.

Neither spoke for a little while.

"Whippoor-will, whippoor-will." No more sound.

Lora Lee thought, "He musta flew." And after a little more silence, she said, "I love you, Grandma."

"I love you, too, sugar."

As Lora Lee lay peacefully next to her grandmother, she thought about what her uncle Roger had said, and what her grandmother had said. But as she fell asleep with a smile on her face, she was picturing what she thought that little girl her grandmother told her about had seen: a rainbow of "colored" people.

Friday

Lora Lee woke up with the bed shaking. Her immediate reaction was fear, but she quickly realized that her grandmother was getting out of bed.

"Is it time ta git up?" she asked sleepily, relieved that it had been her grandmother shaking the bed. In her dream, the Russians were storming the house as bombs fell.

"I'm gittin' up 'cause I hear your mama in the kitchen," Clara replied. "I'll ask her if you gotta git up now."

Clara opened the door and called, "Ruth, does Lora Lee need ta git up now?"

"She'll have to in five minutes," she replied.

"Might as well git up," Lora Lee thought. "Mama'd be callin' me 'bout the time I got back ta sleep."

She sat up in bed so she could watch her grandmother comb her hair and put it in a bun. She thought her long, straight hair was beautiful. She would've been surprised to know that Clara's hair was straight because Clara's grandmother was a Cherokee Indian.

As Lora Lee watched her, she remembered something. "You know what, Grandma? Lucy an' P. J. stayed with us one weekend while Aunt Rose an' Uncle Roger went to Miami. Well, Lucy was in the bedroom wi' Mama an' Mama rolled her hair around that rat thing she uses, an' then she put hairspray on. An' Lucy said, 'What ya doin', Aunt Ruth?' An' Mama said, 'I'm sprayin' my hair. Don't yore mama spray her hair?' An' Lucy said, 'My mama don't have bugs in her hair.'"

Clara laughed. "That chile don't miss a thing!"

Lora Lee continued, "Aunt Rose said she don't spray her hair while Lucy's in the room 'cause she don't want her breathin' in the spray, so Lucy don't see her sprayin' it."

"She hadn' ever seen her mama sprayin' her hair?"

"No, ma'am."

"What must go on in that little head!" Clara exclaimed, shaking her head. She finished fixing her hair and was about to leave the room.

"I wish I could stay home today, Grandma," Lora Lee said.

"I wish you could, too, sugar pie," Clara replied.

"I'm gonna ask Mama," Lora Lee said, jumping out of bed.

However, her feet had barely hit the floor when she heard Ruth say, "School's almost over, Lora Lee. You have to go."

"Oh shoot!" Lora Lee complained. "I never git ta see Grandma."

"I'll tell you what, Lora Lee." Clara was thinking out loud. "Why don't you come an' spend a week or two wi' me this summer?"

"Can I, Mama?" she asked excitedly. "Please, can I?"

"Well, we'd have to figure out how to git you there an' back," Ruth said, not wanting to make a promise she couldn't keep. "We could take you one way, but I doubt if your daddy would wont to go twice. But we'll see."

"Well," Clara said, "depending on when I go back, she might be able to go on the bus with me."

"That would be fun," Lora Lee said, brightening. Oh, I hope I can go. I never got ta stay wi' Grandma, ever!"

The possibility that she could visit Clara that summer made going to school a lot easier. Nevertheless, Lora Lee knew how her father could be and she knew not to get her hopes up too high.

After all, he wouldn't even let her go to the beach one day the previous summer with Ben and Hannah. And the only reason he gave her was, "Because I said so."

Ruth cut the leftover biscuits in half and fried them to go with the grits, eggs, and bacon. Clara liked fried biscuits and Lora Lee did, too.

She left the house happy and arrived at the bus stop early enough to hear the bus leaving Rita's place. As she waited, she thought about the possibility of going to stay with her grandmother.

"Mornin', honey," Rita said as Lora Lee climbed the bus steps. "Not many more days before you'll be out for the summer."

"I cain't wait," Lora Lee exclaimed. "An' I might git ta go stay for a week or two wi' my grandma, if Daddy'll let me. She came yesterday with Aunt Rose."

"Wouldn' that be nice!" Rita said. "I hope ya can."

The ditches on each side of the road had water in them, and Lora Lee watched some of those big, long-legged white birds wading and looking for food. "Birds can be big like them birds, or tiny like hummin'birds," she thought. "Boy, I'm glad people ain't like that. There'd be giants bigger 'an buildin's."

When Leroy got on the bus, he asked Lora Lee to help him with an arithmetic problem. They worked on math until they arrived at the school.

Once there, Lora Lee decided she wanted to play hopscotch, so she drew the squares in a sandy place behind the school. She hoped someone would play with her, but if they didn't, she'd play alone. Leroy didn't want to play. But when the station wagon arrived, Julie ran over to play with her. Lora Lee kept her eyes on Herman until she saw him headed for the swings.

"Who's goin' first?" Lora Lee asked.

"Let's do eeny, meeny, miney, moe," Julie suggested.

"Okay, you do it," Lora Lee said, knowing that Julie liked to.

Julie pointed to Lora Lee first as she started:

> Eeny, meeny, miney, moe,
> Catch a nigger by the toe.
> If he hollers, make 'im pay
> Fifty dollars ever' day.
> My mama tol' me to pick
> The very best one,
> An' that is y-o-u.

She ended the rhyme pointing to herself. "I'm first," she said.

Although Julie was only eight, she was almost as good as Lora Lee at hopscotch. Lora Lee looked around for something to use for a marker, found three things, and decided on a small flat stick. Julie took a shell from her pocketbook.

Julie got almost all the way through before her marker went into the wrong square when she threw it. Lora Lee was one square ahead of her when Julie said, with a smile, "You stepped on a line."

Lora Lee looked behind her and saw the slight footprint. "Oh shoot," she said, leaving the square. "Yore turn."

When they were in the third game, it was Lora Lee's turn, and she'd gone through the squares and was on her way back. Her stick was in the square below the one Julie's shell was in, so she had to stand on one foot and lean over Julie's square to pick up her stick. As she stretched to reach it, she felt her sandal give. She picked up the stick, but then threw it down, walked off, and sat down on the grass with her head down.

Julie sat down beside her. She knew a broken sandal strap could be a problem. It meant a trip to Lakeland and parents having the time to take you, and having the money to buy new shoes.

"Durn it!" Lora Lee said. Then she realized that Julie was three years younger than her. "Sorry, Julie. I shouldn' a said that."

"I don't care," Julie said. "I sometimes say it, too."

Lora Lee looked at Julie's beautiful blue eyes with the blond hair framing her cute face. She had a hard time imagining "durn it" coming out of that angelic little face. She smiled.

"No more hopscotch today," Julie said. "Reckon yore parents'll take ya ta git some new shoes?"

Suddenly, Lora Lee thought about her grandmother. "Oh yeah, we hafta go ta Lakeland. My grandma came yesterday, an' we hafta take her ta Lakeland tomorrah. I can git some new shoes tomorrah." She breathed a sigh of relief. Those sandals were her only shoes, except for the high top tennis shoes she used for phys. ed., and her old everyday shoes.

Lora Lee stood up. "I'm gonna go on over to the house school now 'fore the Brewster kids git here so they don't see me walkin' wi' my broke strap." Julie knew exactly what she meant.

The house wasn't open yet, so Lora Lee sat on the doorstep and read her library book until Mrs. Hoffman arrived, just before the other kids.

Right after she called the roll, Mrs. Hoffman said, "Please turn in the forms I gave you yesterday." She was rather pleased when she collected sixteen. Only five hadn't remembered. Lora Lee was glad she had hers. Of course, Mrs. Hoffman was the only one who knew they weren't due until Tuesday. "Okay, you five," she said, "have your parents sign the forms tonight and put them with your school things so you'll remember to bring them in on Monday. This is important."

In the English class that morning, Mrs. Hoffman gave the children something to think about, "What language do you speak?" she asked.

Lora Lee thought, "What language do we speak?"

She and most of the others answered, "American."

"American?" Mrs. Hoffman asked. "Do you think that's the language the Indians were speakin' when the Pilgrims got here?"

They sat quietly, thinking.

"English," Jimmy blurted out. "We speak English."

"Oh la-de-da," Lora Lee thought. "Course, we speak English."

"That's right, Jimmy," Mrs. Hoffman said. She hesitated for a minute. "What language do they speak in England?"

Everyone laughed and said, "English."

"What is your ethnic heritage?" she continued. "What countries did your ancestors come from?"

Mrs. Hoffman knew, from her years of teaching, that the children often did not connect their own past with the immigration into this country, even when they studied about the Pilgrims. Most of their ancestors' immigration was early on, and many families didn't even think about it.

A few people said, "We're American," but without the confidence of the answer to the first question.

"Are you an Indian?" Mrs. Hoffman asked.

"I'm part Indian," Lawrence said.

"That's good, Lawrence," she responded. "What are the other parts?"

"I don't know," he shrugged.

"Well, I want you all to talk to your families about this," she said. "Your ancestors came from other countries, and it's important for you to know where they came from. Some day, you might want to learn about those countries and even visit them. As for me, I know that some of my ancestors came from England, some from France, an' some from Russia."

"Russia," Lora Lee thought, and she was confused. "How could part a her be Russian?" Lora Lee was afraid of Russians, but she loved Mrs. Hoffman. "I wonder if any a my ancestors came from Russia. I'll havta ask Mama."

As soon as the class was over, Lora Lee started dreading the walk to the schoolhouse for the arithmetic class, and she forgot about the assignment Mrs. Hoffman had given them. She knew she couldn't walk without the kids noticing her shoe so she decided to walk behind them, but pretty soon she was way behind and Arnold noticed.

"Lora Lee's shoe's broke," he announced, and everybody turned around to look at her. Several of them laughed, including Lola, who seemed to be enjoying the situation. She was pointing at Lora Lee and saying something to her group. Cynthia laughed really loud, and Lora Lee figured she did it to please Lola.

During arithmetic class, Lora Lee realized she could wear her tennis shoes, so when it was over, she went to the bathroom and put them on. "I wish I thought about these this mornin'," she thought. "They might look stupid wi' my dress, but at least they ain't broke."

Lola said, "New style, Lora Lee?" but Lora Lee ignored her. No one else said anything.

"Just a few more days, Miss Priss," she said to herself, "an' I won't hafta put up wi' you no more for three whole months."

Later, when she was walking past Lola's seat to go to the pencil sharpener, Lola held up her pencil and said, "Sharpen mine." Lora Lee took the pencil reflexively—it was something she did for everybody—and she immediately regretted it. Lola never sharpened her own pencil, and seemed to expect anyone passing to sharpen hers.

"Next year, I ain't sharpenin' her pencils no more," she thought. "If she says, 'Sharpen mine,' I'm gonna say, 'Sharpen it yoreself.' It's jus' plain stupid ta sharpen her pencil the way she treats me. Miss High Falutin'."

At the end of the school day, Lora Lee left her tennis shoes in her locker in the bathroom. She knew she'd need them at school the next week. She went barefoot until it was time for the bus, and then, she put the sandals on. She noticed Rita looking at her sandal when she got on the bus.

When they stopped at the drugstore, she stayed in her seat. "You not gittin' anything, Lora Lee?" Leroy asked, looking at her.

"Not today," she answered, shaking her head.

Rita gave him a dime and said, "Git me a vanilla Coke, please, sir." And after he left she looked in her rearview mirror at Lora Lee. She wondered if the broken sandal strap was the reason she wasn't going to the drug store. "Are you feelin' bad?" she asked.

"No, I'm jus' savin' my money."

"Oh, I see," Rita said, uncertain about whether that was the truth. "There sumpin ya wanna buy?"

"Yep," Lora Lee said, smiling. "I wuz in the dime store, an' I saw a ruby ring. It costs thirty-five cents. Mama gave me four pennies, so I got four cents, plus my quarter for today. So I jus' need six more cents."

"I could pay you for next week now. Give you an advance," Rita suggested, feeling sorry for the child.

"No, thank ya," Lora Lee replied. She'd already thought about asking Rita to give her a loan, but she didn't like the idea. Leroy would know, and somehow, it just didn't feel right. She really wanted to take the money so she could get the ring on Saturday, but she told herself she oughta wait.

On the way home, they passed by a group of convicts working on the side of the road. Some were using slings to cut the tall grass, and some were digging in the ditch. Two guards stood nearby with shotguns. They all stopped working and watched the bus pass. Lora Lee was staring at one guy, who was also looking at her. "That convict's cute," she thought. "Wonder what he did. He's too cute to be a criminal."

After Leroy was dropped off, Rita asked, "How much did ya say you still need ta make thirty-five cents?"

"Six cents."

As Lora Lee got to the steps, Rita said, "Here, Lora Lee. I found this penny on the bus this mornin'. Take it an' you'll jus' need a nickel."

"Thank ya, Rita!" she exclaimed as though Rita had given her a wonderful gift.

♥   ♥   ♥

WHEN SHE GOT OFF THE BUS, she took her sandals off. She knew the sand would be hot, but she wasn't going to walk all the way home with a broken sandal. She walked faster than usual, anxious to get out of the hot sand. After a little while, her feet would feel hot, and she'd stop for a moment when she got to a patch of grass or some shade. However, in one patch of grass, she stepped on some sandspurs.

"Ow!" she said, and hopped on one foot to a place where she could sit down. "Shoot! Stupid ole sandspurs." She put her books down, and pulled the three sandspurs out one by one. "That's them ole Texas sandspurs," she said. Unlike the round ones she was used to, the Texas sandspurs were flatter and were shaped like the skull of a cow with horns. Of course, they both hurt, but she thought the Texas kind went deeper.

When she started walking again, she remembered that her grandmother was at the house. Lora Lee loved having company, especially her grandmother. "I wish Grandma lived close ta us," she thought. "Georgia's so far away an' I only git ta see her 'bout once a year."

Clara was sitting on the front porch waiting for her. She greeted her with a big hug. "Did you have a good day?" she asked.

"'Cept for breakin' my sandal," she said, "an' the kids makin' fun a me."

"They made fun of you 'cause your sandal wuz broke?" Clara asked.

"Yes, ma'am. But they make fun a me for other things, too, like my freckles an' my clothes."

"Oh, Lora Lee, I'm so sorry," Clara said, hugging her again and holding her close. "That is jus' naughty. What kind of parents do those children have, anyway? Jus' naughty! Bless your little heart."

Lora Lee felt tears spring to her eyes. She was always touched when her grandmother said, "Bless your little heart."

After a moment, Clara released her and said, "Guess what I did today, sugar. Somethin' extry special."

"What, Grandma?"

"I made us some peanut candy. You like it, don't you?"

"Yes-siree bob!" she grinned, forgetting the broken sandal and everything else. "Does a pig like . . . slop?" As she spoke, she remembered what her mother said about that expression, but decided to finish it, anyway.

Clara laughed. "You cain't eat too much now though, 'cause we hafta have a soon supper. We belong to go to church tonight."

"That's right," Lora Lee said, with a frown. "I forgot all about that."

Ruth was in the kitchen. When she saw Lora Lee holding her sandals, she moaned, "Oh Lord, did you break your sandal?"

"Yes, ma'am. Can we git me some new ones tomorrah?"

"I guess we'll have to," Ruth replied. "But you'll have to wear those to church tonight."

"I know it," Lora Lee said resignedly.

As she munched on peanut candy, she looked at the big bowl in Ruth's hand. "Mama, you makin' a coconut cake?" she asked expectantly.

"Yes, I am. I wish I'd had time to make one for las' night."

"Oh boy!" Lora Lee exclaimed, dancing around the kitchen. "Hot diggety dog! We ain't had a cake in a long time." She looked at Clara. "Must be for you, Grandma."

Clara smiled. "May be. But I reckon I know good an' well who's gonna enjoy it the most."

"You're prob'ly right about that," Ruth said, smiling.

Clara put her arm around Lora Lee. "You're still a little bundle of amusement," she said lovingly, with a smile.

Lora Lee saw her gold tooth and smiled. She was happy that her grandmother had something different from everybody else she knew.

"Mama, how's Miz Mary Sue Murphy doin?" Ruth asked.

"Well, she's deaf as a doorknob, for one thing," Clara answered. "My neighbor, Miz Andrews—you know she's Catholic an' she don't visit much— well, she said Mary Sue told her she's got kidney trouble, but I think there's somethin' else wrong wi' her 'cause she's fell off a lot—she musta lost twenty pounds. An' she takes on so, sounds like she's about to die, but she won't go to the doctor. If I felt as bad as she says she feels, I'd shore be gittin' myse'f to a doctor. But I b'lieve she went through somethin' like this last year for a spell, so maybe she'll snap out of it sometime soon."

"Is Mr. Murphy all right?"

"He said he wuz havin' sick headaches ever' now an' then, but he's some better now. They're both on up in eighty, you know. He's still a mess!

I saw 'im downtown last month in his overalls. You know he always wears overalls, even to church."

"I remember that," Ruth said, nodding.

"We were havin' a real dry spell," Clara continued. "I mean farmers were really startin' to worry about their crops. I asked 'im how things were, an' he said they shore needed some rain. Said it wuz dry as a bone at their place." She laughed. "Then he grinned an' said, 'It's so dry, we hafta prime ourselves to spit!'"

They all laughed. "That really tickled me," Clara said.

"He's a mess, all right," Ruth said, with a smile.

"I saw his sister, Minnie Smith, downtown one day, an' she jus' went to tellin' me things about 'im, an' I hafta say, they're not all so funny, least not for him," Clara continued. "She said a bunch of the family wuz at her house for dinner one Sunday, an' somebody made a fruit salad. Well, he ate a bate a that, like he was showin' off how much he could eat, an' it did not agree with him at all, an' he took sick. She said it tore up his stomach somethin' awful, an' he spent most of the night in the bathroom."

Ruth shook her head and laughed.

Lora Lee thought of something. "Mama, maybe I can eat some fruit salad instead a takin' them ole Carter's Little Liver pills."

Clara and Ruth looked at each other and chuckled. "I don't think so, Lora Lee," Ruth said.

Even though Lora Lee found the stories amusing, they were talking about people she didn't know, and she certainly wasn't interested in their health, so she went to her room to see if there was anything in there that interested her. She saw her button on a string—a whirlygig—lying on her dresser and picked it up.

Some of the kids at school were playing with them. They used a large, flat button with two holes, put a string about three feet long in one hole and out the other, and tied the string. Then each hand held the string stretched out horizontally in front of them with the button in the middle. They relaxed the string, whipped the button around a few times to twist the string, pulled it tight, and continuously moved their hands in and out a little to keep the button spinning. Lora Lee liked her new toy; for one thing it didn't cost a penny because they had buttons and string, so she could actually have one, just like the other kids. But she also enjoyed playing with it, and she could carry it in her pocket.

As she was leaving the porch, she heard her grandmother say, "You know, Minnie Smith goes to a lady doctor."

Lora Lee thought, "I never heard a no lady doctor. Didn' know ladies could even be doctors."

After she played with the button for a while, she saw the old metal barrel on its side near the driveway. Fortunately, it was under an orange tree so it wasn't hot. She pushed it away from the tree, got up on it, and walked on it, keeping her balance as it rolled under her until she fell off four times, landing on her feet. Then she looked for something else to do.

As she walked around in the grassless yard, she felt the warm sand under her feet, not too hot because the orange trees shaded it part of the time. However, she knew it would be really hot before many more days. She would still go barefoot when her mother let her, but she'd have to run from the shade of one tree to the next.

A few times, her brother Billy had gotten aggravated at her, and stood her in the hot sand, holding her shoulders so she couldn't get away. He was barefoot, too, but he was seven years older, and his feet were tougher than hers. Both of them would lift one foot, and when the one in the sand was on fire, they'd put the other one down, and lift it. However, the one that was up didn't have time to get cool before it went down again. After a little, both feet were burning like fire. She'd whine, "Turn me loose, Billy," but he'd laugh and hold on tight, his long fingers digging into her shoulders. Soon, she'd yell, "Ow, ow. Billy, let me go." When his feet got too hot, and Lora Lee was begging and near tears, he'd finally let her go. By then, her feet felt like they'd been heated on a stove, and it took a while for them to cool off. She'd sit on the porch and fan them until they stopped burning.

Lora Lee went to the side of the house, and as she disturbed a couple of doodlebug homes, she heard hammering. Just then, her father called, "Lora Lee, git me them nails in that poke on the porch."

"What's a *poke*?" she wondered. "I cain't remember." She looked at the three or four things on the porch, but she didn't see anything she thought would be called a "poke." She felt her heart beating faster, knowing her father would be expecting her to move quickly. "He's gonna git mad," she thought, "but maybe he won't yell at me since Grandma's here."

But he did. "Come on, Lora Lee," he yelled. "Come on!"

"Oh, it's a sack," she remembered, grabbing the small bag of nails.

She'd seen the bag sitting there, but had dismissed it as a possible poke. She'd only heard that word once or twice before, but she knew she'd remember it after that. She ran to give it to Caleb who was standing there glaring at her, making it obvious that she was keeping him waiting. Neither of them said anything. She wanted to explain why it took her so long, but she knew he didn't care, so she just gave him the nails. Then, she went to an old grapefruit tree out in the grove that was her favorite climbing tree.

There were a half dozen grapefruit trees scattered around in the orange grove; either the orange graft didn't take, or the grapefruit sprouts that came up from the bottom were not removed, and the grapefruit part took over. One tree in the grove had oranges and grapefruit on it.

The grapefruit tree was the place she went when she wanted to be alone, or needed a private place to think. Lately, she seemed to be thinking mostly about Herman or the girls at school who were mean to her. She went over situations in her mind trying to think of ways she could have handled things differently, or something she could have said, attempting to prepare herself for the next time something happened. However, it seemed to her that the next time was always different, or happened when she wasn't expecting it, so she was never prepared.

Lora Lee climbed onto her "sittin' branch," which was about six inches thick, and had a smaller one growing out of it. The two formed a "V," and a fairly comfortable seat. She sat there thinking about what had just happened, knowing she couldn't have gotten the nails any faster since she didn't know what she was looking for. "I shoulda asked 'im what a 'poke' is," she thought, "instead a jus' lookin'." She took a deep breath, sighed, and gradually began to relax.

After a little while, she picked a leaf, tore it, and put it to her nose for a few whiffs. When she heard, "bob-white," she whistled a response and the quail answered her. They went back and forth a few times. She watched a gray lizard run up the tree trunk and disappear. Then she sat in the tree listening to a mockingbird and watching a big black and yellow spider constructing its web, until she heard her mother call, "Lora Lee-eee."

♥   ♥   ♥

WHEN THEY GOT TO THE CHURCH THAT EVENING, Lora Lee went to the water fountain to get a drink, and was almost through drinking when she heard the voice behind her:

> Freckles on her nose,
> Freckles on her toes,
> Freckles on her face,
> Freckles ever' place.

Lora Lee scanned the area to see if anyone else might have heard that. Relieved that no one was around, she looked at Howlie May. "Yo're a poet, an' ya don't know it, but yore feet show it—they're long fellows."

That didn't seem to bother Howlie May. As Lora Lee left the water fountain, Howlie May asked sarcastically, "You makin' a new style in shoes, one reg'lar an' one broke?"

Lora Lee looked at her with disgust. "I ain't list'nin' to all yore jibber jabber, Howlie May." She remembered the word P. J. had used, or thought she did. "You're just a dadgum fibblegibble. Why don't you go pick on somebody yore own size?" She wondered if she had pronounced the word correctly, but she knew Howlie May wouldn't know, so she didn't care. Her stomach was churning and she was mad, but grateful that her grandmother didn't hear that rhyme.

She was about to go in the church when she saw Mr. Packer leaning against his car, smoking a cigarette. She stopped and watched him for a minute. She didn't like Mr. Packer. She felt guilty about that because the Bible says to love your neighbor, and she wasn't sure she could love someone she didn't like. And she didn't like Mrs. Packer, either. She remembered what Missy had said about her, "Miz Packer's awful uppity for somebody that ain't got no reason ta be."

As she watched Mr. Packer scratching his crotch, right in front of the church, she thought, "That's one reason I don't like him. He's always doin' that. If he's got ta scratch down there, how come he don't go 'round the corner where people cain't see 'im? Miz Goodie Two-Shoes oughta tell 'im how disgustin' that is. Boy! I'm glad I don't hafta shake his stupid hand." She watched him with a frown on her face. "An' he's always got his nose in the air, uppity, jus' like her."

She thought of the time she was pulling some low-hanging Spanish moss out of an oak tree on the side of the church where cars were parked. When Mr. Packer saw her, he asked, "What are you doin', Lora Lee?"

She thought it was perfectly obvious what she was doing. "Cain't you see?" she asked, knowing that was very fresh for her to say to an adult. "I'm pullin' moss outta this ole tree."

"Does yore daddy know you're doin' that?"

"No, he don't, but he wouldn' care, nohow," she said, feeling a little guilty for being disrespectful. "Ever'body knows too much moss'll kill a tree."

"Well, you better ask 'im if it's all right," he warned as he walked away.

"What could possibly be wrong wi' pullin' moss out of a tree?" she wondered with a big frown, pulling every bit she could reach. "Crazy ole man! Wish I had a rake so I could reach more of it. I'd like ta tell that ole busybody to mind his own business."

As Lora Lee turned to go into the church, she saw the tall, thin form of Mr. Tuttle walking down the street with his black hat on. "He's late tonight for him," she thought. "He's use'ly here 'fore us." Everyone thought of Mr. Tuttle as a true gentleman, polite and dignified. He was also rather shy and reserved. "He ain't like Mr. Packer. He don't stick his nose in my business."

Lora Lee sat next to her grandmother on the pew, happy and proud. Since Clara seldom visited them, she'd only been to their church once. It was hot in there, even though the ceiling fans were on, and Lora Lee handed her a fan, and got one for herself with the picture of Jesus and the lamb from the pew behind them. She decided she'd keep that fan in her pew and return the one Clara was using to the pew behind.

Lora Lee checked Mr. Cooper's pew to see if there might be any entertainment that night. She was sorry to see that he wasn't there, but she figured the night would be better, anyway, with her grandmother there.

When Caleb stood up, Ruth and others started going up to the choir loft. Lora Lee saw Billy and his fiancée going up, as they usually did. She wished she could sing in the choir, and look out at the congregation.

Mr. Tuttle passed by holding his hat, and she thought, "He's so tall an' skinny. An' he's late goin' to the choir. Wonder what's goin' on wi' him." Most people were already up there and seated.

Howlie May passed by right behind him. Lora Lee was amazed to see that she had on high heels and wondered when she'd started wearing them. She hadn't looked at her long enough outside to notice her shoes. "She's goin' up after ever'body else so she can show off in them high heels," she thought. "She thinks she's sumpin in them shoes." Howlie May gave her a condescending look, and Lora Lee watched her with contempt as she clunked along.

When Howlie May was right in the front, in clear view of everyone, one of her feet suddenly slid on the terrazzo floor. Lora Lee snapped to attention, her eyes glued to Howlie May whose body was bent forward. When her other foot hit the floor, it slid also. She kept moving forward, her feet hitting the floor like a drum beat as she attempted to regain her footing. Lora Lee stared in disbelief, her eyes wide and her mouth hanging open. Finally, one of Howlie May's feet flew up into the air behind her and she lunged forward. Lora Lee gasped as her dress flounced up, exposing her white panties.

Mr. Tuttle was on the steps leading to the choir loft, in front of Howlie May. He stopped when he heard the commotion behind him, but before he could turn around, Howlie May landed head first on him. Her head went between his legs and her arms wrapped around his knees.

The blow knocked Mr. Tuttle forward, and he landed facedown on the lap of the preacher's wife, who was sitting in the first seat. His left hand was grasping one of her knees, and his right arm was resting on her breast with his hand on her neck, still holding his hat.

Lora Lee could not believe her eyes. Happening right in front of her was some kind of justice, and it was funny justice, and she knew she'd remember it and replay it over and over in her mind, just like when Mr. Cochoran sat down by Mrs. Whitaker. The laughter just burst out of her. She would've laughed even if she knew she'd receive a whipping every day for a week. Most of the congregation held their laughter until they saw that Howlie May and Mr. Tuttle were all right, and then they laughed

"I cain't b'lieve this is happ'nin'," Lora Lee thought as she laughed. "By cracky, she's fin'ly gittin' what she deserves!"

The evangelist saw the whole thing and he started laughing. The pastor, who did not see Howlie May fall, jumped up and looked at his wife and Mr. Tuttle. Mr. Tuttle had immediately removed his head from her lap and his hands from her neck and knee. He was holding himself up and away from her with one hand on the floor, and the other one on her chair. Nevertheless, his face was near her breast, and he was obviously uncomfortable. His face was crimson as he looked at the preacher who was glaring at him. Clearly mortified, he was trying desperately to stand up, but Howlie May, apparently in shock, still had a vise grip on his legs.

Mr. Tuttle looked around at her and barked, "Let go of me, girl! Turn me loose!" When she finally let go and stood up, Mr. Tuttle bounced up, glanced at the preacher, and then at the preacher's wife.

Lora Lee could hear her grandmother laughing beside her. She looked at her and saw tears making tracks through her makeup.

Mr. Tuttle's face was still red, and his head, which he slapped his hat on, was down. Lora Lee was feeling sorry for him, even as she laughed. "Pore ole Mr. Tuttle," she thought. He whirled around, pushed past Howlie May, and rushed out the side door. Howlie May watched him with a confused look on her face.

Lora Lee fell over on the pew, holding her stomach. She listened to make sure she could hear laughter because she knew she had to stop laughing when everyone else did; then she was expected to sit quietly and be a little lady. Her parents were still laughing, so Lora Lee relaxed and laughed. She was surprised that her father was still laughing—she guessed what happened to the proper Mr. Tuttle was too much for him.

She would've laughed even if it had happened to someone else, but the fact that it happened to Howlie May seemed too good to be true. And right after Howlie May's rhyme about her freckles! Lora Lee sat up in time to see the preacher motion for the pianist to start playing, but she had her head down laughing and didn't see him.

Howlie May went up the steps to the choir loft and took a seat in the back row. Her red face was glowing. She looked sheepishly at Lora Lee, who fell over laughing, again.

After a couple of minutes, people were starting to settle down, except for Lora Lee. Caleb had managed to stop laughing and Lora Lee knew she had to, as well. Clara had stopped. "Course," Lora Lee thought, "they don't know how she is, or they'd still be laughin'." She sat up, but couldn't stop. She saw Caleb look at her and she knew drastic measures were called for. She pinched her leg until it hurt, and that was enough to stop her for a while, and singing helped, too. However, her leg hadn't stopped smarting before she felt another laughter attack coming. "What can I do that really hurts?" she wondered. Then she remembered how badly it had hurt when she was younger and her mother combed her hair. So she put her hand under her hair so people wouldn't see what she was doing, and pulled the hair in the back where she was most tender-headed. That hurt. When the need to laugh was more powerful than the music, she pulled it again. "Ow," she thought. "At least that makes me think a sumpin else."

"What am I gonna do?" she wondered. "I gotta stop laughin'."

She managed to do all right until the singing was over and the choir went back to their seats. When Ruth sat down by her, she knew she had to be quiet, but when Howlie May went by the pew and just glanced quickly at her, she almost laughed out loud. As her body shook with laughter, she thought, "I bet my broke sandal don't look so bad ta ya now, Miss Priss. That's what happens when ya git too big for yore britches! Maybe now you'll stop some a yore shenanigans!"

She had a hard time quieting down, and she didn't want to inflict more pain on herself, so she decided she had to do something else. She leaned next to Ruth and whispered, "Mama, I hafta be excused."

"All right, Lora Lee," Ruth whispered. "But you come right back."

She stood in the bathroom studying her face in the mirror. As she looked at the freckles she hated, she remembered what her grandmother had told her when she was little: "Lora Lee, you have the cutest freckles. Did you know that in some countries, freckles are thought ta be angels' kisses?"

"More like the devil's kisses," Lora Lee said out loud. She had believed her grandmother until Howlie May moved to Bradley and started going to the church. Right away, she started making fun of her freckles when no one else was around. "Did you forgit ta wash yore face this morning?" she'd ask, or, "Is that chicken doodoo on yore face? You musta slept in the hen house."

She washed her hands and thought about how much fun she'd have telling Missy and P. J. about Howlie May falling on Mr. Tuttle, and making him fall on the preacher's wife. She imagined their reactions, and started laughing again. She was sorry they hadn't been there to see it happen. "Boy howdy! So many things happened this week at church an' at school. I wish ever' week wuz like this one."

Suddenly, she remembered why she was in the bathroom and knew she'd better get back to the sanctuary. The fear of her father made the whole incident seem less funny. "I'll havta think about somethin' else," she thought, "like Daddy not lettin' me keep Whitey." As she walked back to the sanctuary, she suddenly remembered the dog in *The Call of the Wild*. "I'll think about Buck. That oughta keep me from laughin'." And it did. She kept picturing poor Buck stolen and taken from his comfortable, loving home to an unknown, cruel world, and the awful things that happened to him there.

Every now and then, she'd tune in to what the evangelist was saying, especially when he got loud, or slammed his hand down on the pulpit. He read a passage from the Book of Revelation and he was talking about Jesus coming again and how nobody knows when, but it won't be long.

First, Lora Lee pondered over the discrepancy: nobody knows when, but it won't be long. "How does he know it won't be long if nobody knows when? I might be dead 'fore He comes." But then, she started thinking about what it might be like if it happened soon, like the preacher said. She was feeling anxious, thinking that Jesus might come before she had time to grow up and get married and have children. She pictured herself at sixteen on a date with a cute boy having her first kiss, and all of a sudden, there's Jesus in the sky.

"Will you be ready?" the minister asked.

"No," Lora Lee thought. "It wouldn' be fair if he came 'fore I git to grow up an' git married an' be my own boss for a while."

Soon she forgot about that and went back to thinking about the book, and she was deep in thought about Buck when Caleb stood up to lead the invitational hymn. She was pleased and surprised that it got over so fast, and that she made it through without getting in trouble. She found the page number and shared the hymnal with her grandmother.

No one went forward when they sang two verses of the invitational hymn, so the evangelist had a few more things to say. When no one went forward after two more verses of the hymn, he said the closing prayer. It wasn't as short as Lora Lee would've liked, but it wasn't like Mr. Cooper's. During the prayer, the image of Howlie May falling flashed in her mind, and she had a really hard time being quiet. She pinched her arm so hard she made a blood blister. It hurt, but she figured that pain was nothing compared to what she'd get if she didn't stay quiet.

Lora Lee knew they'd be around the church for a while after the service because people would want to meet her grandmother. Clara was a Primitive, or Hard Shell, Baptist. Lora Lee's family had gone with her to church one time when they were visiting on the Fourth Sunday. There wasn't any Sunday school, but the service lasted for hours. After that experience, she felt lucky that her church had an hour service, although it was every Sunday morning and night, and Clara only had church on fourth Sundays. However, when there was a fifth Sunday in the month, they had a Sacred Harp sing.

When they started home, Caleb asked, "What in the world happened ta Howlie May tonight?"

They laughed for a while before Ruth said, "Well, that terrazzo floor can be quite slippery, an' it wuz prob'ly the first time she ever wore any high heel shoes."

"Well, she oughta broke 'em in a little—walked aroun' the house for a few days, or sumpin," Caleb said. "B'lieve you me, Double L, when you start wearin' high heels, ya gonna hafta practice in the house. We cain't have you flyin' through the air without a trapeze."

Lora Lee thought that was clever and funny.

"Poor ole Mr. Tuttle," Ruth said, laughing. "He wuz mighty embarrassed. We may have seen the last of him."

"I know it," Caleb said. "The pore old fella couldn' git outta there fast enough."

"I declare, that wuz one a the funniest things I ever saw," Clara said. "I didn' know y'all provided a show durin' the service. We don't do that in our church."

"I liked ta died laughin'," Lora Lee announced. "That was soooo funny. I couldn' hardly quit laughin'."

"We noticed," Caleb said. "Truth is, I had trouble myse'f. I thought about it while the preacher wuz preachin', an' it wuz all I could do to keep from laughin' out loud. I tell you, I had to jus' make myself think about sumpin else."

"You shoulda pinched yoreself," Lora Lee said. "That's what I did."

They chuckled.

"It sure wuz funny," Ruth said.

"Howlie May's jus' plain mean," Lora Lee said. "She's always makin' fun a my freckles, an' pesterin' me. Tonight, before the service, she made fun a my freckles, an' my shoe."

"I declare!" Clara said. "Well then, maybe she got exactly what she deserved."

"That's all well an' good," Caleb agreed, "but what 'id pore ole Mr. Tuttle ever do to anybody?"

They laughed off and on all the way home.

As they went into the house, Lora Lee said, "Mama, can I have another piece a coconut cake?"

"Sure," Ruth replied. "Put out the milk, and I'll cut the cake. Maybe ever'body would like some."

They put the cake, milk, and some ice water on the table, and they all ate cake as they sat around talking. From time to time, one of them would mention something about Howlie May's fall or Mr. Tuttle's rapid exit, and they'd all break out laughing again.

Ruth said, "I'm so glad you're here, Mama. I wish you could come more often."

"Well, Ruth," Clara replied. "You know how much I hate ta leave home."

Once when they were visiting Clara, Lora Lee had asked her why she didn't like to leave home. "My dear sweet husband died in this house," Clara had replied, "an' this is where I wanna die. If I go off, I might die some place else."

Although Lora Lee understood her grandmother's thinking, she felt deprived that Clara didn't visit them more. She didn't have anything else tying her down, and she could have visited a lot. Of course, it was a long way to her house.

♥　♥　♥

WHEN THEY WERE ALONE IN THE BEDROOM, Clara said, "I been thinkin' 'bout that ruby ring you wont, Lora Lee. Did you save your quarter today?"

"Yes, ma'am, I did, an' Mama give me four pennies, an' Rita give me one more, so now I got thirty cents."

Clara took out her change purse. "Well, next week you won't hafta save your money, an' you can git somethin' from the drugstore." She held out her hand with a nickel in it.

"Oh, thank you, Grandma!" Lora Lee exclaimed, hugging her. "I can prob'ly git the ring tomorrah when we take you to Lakeland."

As Lora Lee was opening her pocketbook, it fell out of her hands and onto the floor. The drawing Lola did fell out, and it opened up enough for Clara to see the word, "freckles."

"What is this?" she asked, picking up the paper they both reached for, and opening it. "Lora Lee," she said with concern, but when she saw the tears in Lora Lee's eyes, she stopped talking and put her arms around her.

"Who did this, sugar?" she asked after a little while.

"Lola," Lora Lee answered softly.

"Did you tell your parents about this?"

"No, ma'am, but I told 'em she wuz always makin' fun a me."

"An' did they do anything?"

"Daddy tol' me I oughta give her candy an' chewin' gum. I ain't even got none for myself, an' she's already got all she wonts."

"Well, if that don't beat all! I'm sorry, Lora Lee. I think your daddy wuz really tryin' to help. Anyway, that little girl's too big for her britches, an' somebody needs to talk to her. You know, some people are just unkind, an' I really think people like that are unhappy. They've got somethin' in their lives causin' them to need to put other people down. That girl's got somethin' that's not right in her life, or she's jus' plain mean, one."

Lora Lee was thinking about all of that. She couldn't imagine that there was anything wrong in Lola's perfect life. She thought she must be just plain mean.

"Lora Lee, what's that place on your arm?" Clara asked.

Lora Lee looked at it. "Oh, that's just a blood blister. That's where I wuz pinchin' myself to keep from laughin' while the preacher wuz prayin'."

Clara laughed. "Well, honey. You shore musta pinched your pore little arm mighty hard!"

Lora Lee climbed into bed and watched her grandmother take her hair down and comb it. "Grandma, do you comb yore hair ever' night?" she asked.

"Yes I do. I always take it down at night, so it seems like a good time to comb it."

"I jus' comb mine in the mornin'," Lora Lee said, but thought that she might start combing hers at night, too. "Or maybe I'll brush it," she thought. "Missy says you're s'posed to brush yore hair a hundred strokes ever' night."

"Oh Grandma!" Lora Lee exclaimed. "There's that big ole spider right over the door!"

Clara looked up.

"I hate that spider, but Daddy won't kill it 'cause he says it eats roaches an' mosquitoes."

"Well, it could eat roaches somewhere else besides your bedroom," Clara said, slipping on her shoes. She went to the kitchen and returned with the fly swatter.

"I don't think the fly swatter'll kill that big ole thing," Lora Lee said.

Clara didn't reply as she eyed the spider. She hit it with the swatter and when it fell to the floor, she stepped on it before it had a chance to scurry away. "I'll flush him when I go to the bathroom," she said.

Lora Lee laughed. "Thank you, Grandma. Daddy'll never know."

"An' what he don't know won't hurt 'im," Clara said, and flashed her gold tooth.

"One afternoon, I wuz readin' in here an' I lay down on the bed wi' my book. I felt somethin' pullin' my hair an' I jumped up, an' a big spider went runnin' off. I screamed an' Mama came an' killed that one. It gives me the shivers jus' thinkin' about it in my hair." She shivered.

"I guess so," Clara said, picking up her comb.

"An' you know what happened to Hannah, Grandma? A big spider lived in their bathroom before her an' Ben got married, an' her daddy wouldn' kill it. One night, she washed her face after a date, an' when she grabbed the towel with her eyes closed, that spider was on it an' it got on her face. Well, she fainted dead away, an' then her daddy killed that ole spider.

"Huh! Well, I'm not scared of spiders, but I shore wouldn' want one on my face."

"Me, neither. It wuz bad enough havin' that one in my hair." She shivered again. "Oooh!"

After a moment, Clara asked, "Do you remember what I tol' ya before, Lora Lee? How in Mali, I b'lieve it was—Mali's a country in Africa—freckles are considered wonderful. They call 'em 'angels' kisses.'"

"I 'member, Grandma," she whimpered. "But they're more like the devil's kisses ta me."

"Oh, sugar," Clara said tenderly. "I wont you ta know, I think your freckles are real cute."

After Clara got in bed, Lora Lee said, "I love you so much, Grandma."

"An' I love you so much, Lora Lee." Clara patted her arm, and after a moment, she said, "There's that ole whippoorwill ag'in."

They lay there quietly, listening to it. "Whippoor-will, whippoor-will, whippoor-will."

Clara was trying to think of something that would help Lora Lee feel better. She was glad she'd remembered about Mali and freckles. And she remembered a story that she thought might help.

"Whippoor-will, whippoor-will."

"Lora Lee, do you know the story about the pine tree in the forest?" she asked in her quiet night voice.

"I think so," Lora Lee answered with her quiet voice. "Mama useta tell it to me when I wuz little."

"Well, it reminds me of what you're goin' through wi' the freckles. 'Member how the pine tree wadn' happy with her plain ole green needles?"

"Yes, ma'am."

"Whippoor-will, whippoor-will."

"An' one day she wuz crying, an' the good fairy heard her an' asked what wuz wrong. The pine tree tol' her it didn' like its plain ole needles, an' the fairy said the tree could have three wishes. So, the pine tree said, 'I wish to have shiny glass needles.' An' the next mornin' when she woke up, the green needles had been replaced with beautiful, shiny glass needles. The pine tree wuz so happy. She jus' stood there shimmerin' an' glowin' all day long, thinkin' she wuz the prettiest tree in the forest. She wuz so happy with her glass needles. However, the next day wuz awf'ly windy, an' the little tree stood there helpless as her beautiful glass needles shattered with the wind blowing them against each other until they were all broken."

"Whippoor-will, whippoor-will, whippoor-will."

"Do you remember what happened next, Lora Lee?"

"She got another wish."

"That's right. The tree wuz brokenhearted an' she started weeping. An' the good fairy heard her an' asked her what wuz wrong now. She said, 'My beautiful glass needles are all broke, an' now I don't have any needles.' So the fairy asked her if she had another wish. 'I wish,' she said, 'that I had beautiful gold needles.' An' the next mornin' when she woke up, she wuz covered wi' golden needles. 'Oh, look at me!' she said. 'I'm truly the most beautiful tree in this forest, or in any forest. Look how I shine!'"

"Whippoor-will, whippoor-will."

"An' she wuz beautiful, an' she did shine. All day, she jus' felt so proud of her gold needles. 'All the other trees must be envious of me,' she thought. 'I'm so beautiful!' However, the next day, some men were in the forest an' they saw the tree wi' the gold needles. An' what 'id they do?" she asked.

"They stole all the needles," Lora Lee replied.

"That's right," Clara said. "They picked ever' last one of her shiny gold needles. Course, the tree wuz brokenhearted ag'in, an' soon she wuz weepin' ag'in. When the good fairy appeared, she wuz rather stern wi' the tree. 'You asked for glass needles an' I gave 'em to you, an' they got broken. Then you asked for gold needles an' I gave them to you an' they got stolen. Now, you only have one wish left, so you should give this one a lot a thought.'"

"'I already did,' the tree said. 'I wont my beautiful green needles back."

"Whippoor-will, whippoor-will, whippoor-will."

"You still awake, Lora Lee?"

"Yes, ma'am, I'm listenin'."

"All right. I thought you mighta gone ta sleep. The fairy said she should give her wish a lot a thought, an' the tree said, 'I already did. I wish to have my beautiful green needles back.' 'Are you sure?' the fairy asked, 'because this is your last wish.' 'Oh yes, ma'am, I'm sure,' the pine tree said. An' the next mornin' when she woke up, she had her beautiful green needles. An' she felt like the luckiest tree in the forest. From then on, she stood there, holdin' her limbs up, proud as a peacock. An' she never got tired of her plain ole green needles ag'in."

"Whippoor-will, whippoor-will, whippoor-will. Whippoor-will, whippoor-will, whippoor-will."

After a few moments, Clara said, "You're a purty girl just as you are, Lora Lee. An' remember: you're still my little bundle of amusement. Good night, sugar."

"Good night, Grandma." Lora Lee said softly, with a big smile on her face.

And she went to sleep thinking about a pine tree standing tall and proud. And in the whole forest, it was the only one glowing.

Saturday

Lᴏʀᴀ Lᴇᴇ ᴛʀɪᴇᴅ ᴛᴏ ᴛᴜʀɴ ᴏᴠᴇʀ, but she felt something blocking her. When she actually woke up, she realized that her back was against her grandmother's back. She scooted over on the bed and turned over. Clara also turned over and looked at Lora Lee. "Mornin', sugar pie," she said sweetly, and smiled.

"Mornin', Grandma." Lora Lee seldom smiled the first thing in the morning, but she had no trouble returning Clara's smile, especially when she saw the gold filling. "I like sleepin' wi' you," she said. She had slept alone since Linda got married.

"I like sleepin' wi' you, too, sugar. Reckon we oughta git up now?"

Lora Lee could tell by the brightness of the room that it was later than when she got up for school. Normally, she would've stayed in bed longer, but normally her grandmother wasn't there. Besides, school would be out in a few days, and she could sleep late a lot. "When yo're ready to, Grandma."

"I'm gonna see if your Mama's up," Clara said, sitting up. She got up and took a light housecoat from her suitcase. In a moment, Lora Lee heard her talking to Ruth.

Lora Lee had been sure her mother was up because she smelled coffee and something cooking. And, she'd never been up before her mother. "Guess I should git up," she thought.

When Clara returned to the room to dress, she said, "Your mama's makin' us some pancakes an' fried ham for breakfast."

"Boy howdy!" Lora Lee exclaimed. "I love pancakes." That gave her the boost she needed to get up and dress and go to the kitchen with a spring in her step.

"When do ya hafta leave, Grandma?" she asked.

"Not till after dinner. We'll have a soon dinner, an' prob'ly go right after that 'cause y'all hafta git back in time for church tonight."

"Oh shoot," Lora Lee thought. "I forgot about church tonight."

"Lora Lee," Ruth said, "remember it's Saturday. You have to take a bath before we go to Lakeland."

"Yes, ma'am."

"It's hot this mornin'," Clara said.

"It shore is," Ruth replied. "It's goin' to be a scorcher."

The white enamel bucket with the red rim that was used as a milk pail was sitting on the kitchen counter, and Clara asked, "Ruth, did you already milk this mornin'?"

"Yes, ma'am," she replied. "I milk ever' mornin' an' evenin', unless Billy does it for me."

"Well, bless your heart," Clara said. "An' I hear the washing machine runnin'. You shore do work hard."

"Jus' like you, Mama," Ruth said. "Jus' like you. You used to do the same things I do. An' you had to use the ole washboard to wash all of our clothes. Not to mention havin' a wood stove to cook on."

"Well, that's true," Clara affirmed. "But I always hoped my daughters wouldn' hafta work so extry hard, an' Rose don't."

"I'm used to it," Ruth assured her. "It's jus' what I do."

Ruth and Clara started talking about people they knew in Georgia, and as soon as Lora Lee finished her pancakes, which were smothered in cane syrup, she went to her room and looked for something to do. She had dolls, marbles, jacks, and fiddlestix (pick-up sticks). She grabbed the can of fiddlestix, sat down on the floor, and played with them for a while. She loved the colorful wooden sticks, and was pretty good at picking them up without moving any. When she was tired of them, she got her jacks.

"Same thing," she thought. "Pick 'em up without touchin' the others. I need some more things to play with."

She flipped the jacks without dropping any, and she got through the "onesies" without missing. Next, she did the "Double bounces," and got through that. "Eggs in the basket" usually gave her more trouble, but she got all the way through without missing. She didn't really like "Around the world," and it was the one that gave her the most trouble. When the image of Howlie May falling popped into her mind, she started laughing and missed. Then she put the jacks away and went outside.

While she was on the porch, she looked around quickly for King. She could hear the tractor way down in the field and hoped he went down there with her father.

She knew that Ruth and Clara had gone outside while she was playing, and she followed their voices to the back of the house and the washing machine, which was behind the older part of the house. Ruth was taking clothes from the machine and running them through the wringer into a rinse tub full of water.

"Rinse these for me, Lora Lee," she said, "while I show Mama my gardenia bush."

As Ruth and Clara walked off, she heard Ruth say, "I don't know why that bush has got so many flowers on it this year, an' some years it won't have hardly any."

"Do you give it any cow manure?" Clara asked.

Lora Lee didn't hear the answer as she swished the clothes around and up and down in the tub. She was disappointed that the wash contained mostly Caleb's work clothes because they were harder to put through the wringer. Ruth worked in dresses and they were easy. Towels were also easy to run through the ringer, so they were her favorite things, but there were no towels in the wash, just clothes.

She remembered how happy her mother had been to get the washing machine and the two aluminum rinse tubs—no more having to use the old scrub board and heating water in the big old kettle to boil the work clothes. And the rinse tubs were on a stand, so she didn't have to bend over. Of course, she did heat water on the stove and add it to the machine for clothes that needed warm water, since they had to use the hose to fill the machine. "Havin' this machine will make washin' clothes so much faster an' easier," Ruth had said. "If somethin's not too dirty, it'll wash fast, an' if things are real dirty, like Caleb's work clothes, I can go do somethin' else while they wash longer." Caleb built a roof over the area, so she'd be out of the sun.

Lora Lee had heard her aunt Rose tell Ruth that she needed to get an automatic washing machine instead of that "ole-fashioned thing." "All you hafta do is throw the clothes an' washin' powder in, an' turn it on," she said. And she heard Ruth's reply, "They don't git the clothes as clean as that 'ole-fashioned thing' does. Caleb's clothes git awf'ly dirty." And even though the machine was a lot more work than an automatic would've been, it was a lot less work than the old washboard Ruth had to use before, and she was happy with it.

Lora Lee had been fascinated with the washing process, and she still liked to watch the machine when her mother put the clothes in. Ruth would put in water from the hose, add soap powder and start the washer. When she'd add a piece of laundry, it would immediately get pulled down and swished around, and she'd keep adding pieces until the tub was full.

Also, Lora Lee, who was ten when they got the machine, was fascinated with the wringer and begged her mother to let her use it. At first, Ruth had been concerned that she might get her fingers caught in it, and would only let her run towels through, watching her and cautioning her when she thought her fingers were too close. But now, she often had to help, and it wasn't fun anymore.

When the clothes were in the second rinse tub, Lora Lee positioned the wringer so they'd fall in the big aluminum pan her mother used as a clothesbasket. She ran Ruth's clothes through the wringer first, one piece at a time, because they usually went through without any trouble. However, one dress started wrapping around the wringer, and she had to stop it and reverse it. When it got back to the beginning, she stopped the wringer, reached over it and held onto the dress so it couldn't wrap around again, turned the wringer back on, and let the dress go when she knew it was all right. She folded her father's shirts so that the buttons were inside and wouldn't get popped off by the wringer, and she saved his work pants for last. She folded the pants so that the zipper was inside, but just as she expected, they got stuck. So she stopped the wringer, reversed it until the pants backed up about half way. Then she spread the material out more, turned the wringer on again, and they went through.

By the time she finished, Ruth and Clara were back, and Ruth took the pan of clothes to the clothesline. Lora Lee went with her, expecting to hand the clothes to Ruth as she hung them, but Clara told her she'd help. Ruth had folded the bottom of an apron up so it met the top, sewed the sides together, and tacked it in the middle, making a pouch. She used it to hold her clothespins, and wore it while she was hanging the wash.

"You can empty the tubs, Lora Lee," Ruth said.

She wouldn't tell her mother, but she enjoyed that job, especially on a hot day when some of the cleaner water just happened to splash on her. She emptied the washing machine by unhooking the rubber hose and laying it on the ground so the water would drain out. As she worked, she sang Guy Mitchell's "Singing the Blues," moving her feet to the beat. While the first rinse tub emptied, she took the bucket that Ruth kept nearby, dipped some water from the second rinse tub, and poured it into the washing machine, splashing it around the edges, to rinse it out. She did that until the machine looked clean; she repeated that routine with the first rinse tub, and then, she drained the second one.

"Mama, can I go play now?" she asked as Ruth and Clara returned.

"Yes, you can," Ruth replied.

She thought about throwing the ball on the old kitchen roof and catching it when it rolled off, but she decided the noise might bother Ruth and Clara. "I'll play hopscotch," she thought.

She got a big stick and drew a hopscotch court in the sand. She looked for something to use for a marker, and picked up a marble-sized yellow orange from the ground. She got through the first five squares, but when she threw the orange into the sixth square, it rolled out.

"I shoulda known it would roll," she thought. She looked around for something else that wouldn't roll, but didn't see anything.

An image of Howlie May hanging onto Mr. Tuttle's knees flashed in her mind, and she laughed out loud. "That wuz so funny," she thought.

She went out to the front area away from the house, and looked at the woodpile. In the winter, it was her job to get wood in when there was some already cut; her parents thought she was too young to chop wood. She'd take in some oak pieces and some aged pine, "lighter." The lighter, which they called "lighterd," was full of resin and burned hot. They'd start the fire with that and add oak, which burned slower. Lora Lee looked at some long, narrow pieces. "I can chop them little pieces," she thought, and she got the axe and chopped a few pieces, feeling satisfaction that she could do it. Then, one piece flew up and almost hit her in the head. "Maybe that's why they tol' me not ta chop it," she thought, dropping the axe, and looking around to make sure no one had seen her.

It was also her job to pick some oranges and grapefruit in the winter, and put them in the living room. After supper, they'd sit around the fire eating them. She didn't pick many grapefruit because they didn't eat them every night. The smell of oranges would permeate the air, mixing with the smell of the fat sap from the burning lighter. As they peeled the fruit, they threw the peels in the fire, or saved them for the milk cow when they had her in the small front pasture near the house.

Lora Lee got her jump rope from the back porch and jumped rope for a little while. Then, she went to the bathroom.

As she looked out, she saw a little green frog on the outside of the window. "Oh, what a cute little rain frog," she thought. "I know what I can do. I can make frog houses."

She went back outside and found a place at the back of the house where no one walked. She squatted down, brushed the dry sand back with her hands, and put one foot in front of her. Then she pulled the damp earth up until she had enough covering her foot. She patted it down gently, and slowly and carefully withdrew her foot.

"That's a good one," she said. And she made another one. She was working on a third one when she heard a car turn from the paved road onto their dirt road. "That sounds like Aunt Rose's car," she thought. She jumped up, not caring about the frog house, and ran to the front yard to see who was coming.

"It is them," she said when she saw the car. She yelled, "Mama, Aunt Rose is here."

♥ ♥ ♥

Ruth and Clara were on the front porch before Rose and her family had time to get out. As she stepped out of the car, Rose said, "We're just here for a few minutes. We're goin' down ta Wachula to visit Roger's daddy."

Ruth said, "Well, y'all come on in."

Lora Lee looked in the car and saw Lucy sleeping on the back seat. She smelled cigar. The car was parked in the shade and they left Lucy there with the windows down. When P. J. started off with Lora Lee, Rose said, "P. J., don't git dirty, an' you stay here so you can hear Lucy if she wakes up. 'Member we're jus' stayin' for a few minutes. You young'uns don't go gallivantin' aroun'." Roger went in the house with the women.

P. J. and Lora Lee sat down on a grassy spot near the car. "There's a ant bed by yore foot," he warned.

"I know it. One a 'em bit me the other day," she said, moving her foot and watching the tiny ants running around excitedly. "Look at 'em go. Oh, them two got a dead cricket." She and P. J. watched the two ants struggle to pull the cricket over a half-inch rise in the ground. "That cricket weighs so much more 'an they do. How can they be so strong?"

"Beats me. Is that a grasshopper over there?" he asked, pointing to a weed near the fence.

"Looks like it," she replied. She was conscious of everything she said, remembering the last time P. J. was there, when her comment about Missy being her only friend had made him feel bad.

He got up and went over to check it out.

"You better be careful," Lora Lee warned just as he touched it, and the three-inch-long green and brown grasshopper spit some brown goo right in his face.

"Aw, heck!" he exclaimed, wiping his face with the back of his hand. He spit on the ground.

Lora Lee really wanted to laugh, but she could tell P. J. was angry and she couldn't afford to upset him. He sat back down near her.

"You still got tobacco juice on yore cheek," she said.

"Aw, heck!" Disgustedly, he wiped at his face. "Blamed ole thing!"

"Well, you know they spit."

"Yeah, I know. I jus' wadn' thinkin' 'bout it." He wiped his face again.

"We almost had a wreck comin' here," he said.

"Really? What happened?"

"Some ole Yankee pulled out right in front a us. Had a Massatusetts tag on his car. We'd a hit 'im if Daddy hadn' slammed on brakes."

"Good gravy!" Lora Lee exclaimed. She moved the sand a little on one side of the anthill and watched as the ants scurried around frantically.

"Oh, P. J.," she said, with her eyes lighting up and a grin from ear to ear. "You'll never guess what happened at church last night."

"What?" he asked, shifting his gaze from the ants to her.

"First, Howlie May said this poem she made up about my freckles, 'bout havin' freckles on my face an' ever' place, which I don't, nohow."

"That girl ain't right in the head," he said, shaking his head. "She's ugly as homemade sin. And she's so dumb, she couldn' count to twenty without takin' off her shoes."

Lora Lee laughed, amused at the worst things he could think of to say about Howlie May, and appreciating his attempt to make her feel better. She continued, "She wuz all dolled up, an' she wuz stompin' aroun' in high heel shoes."

"No kiddin'?" he said. "She ain't old enough for any high heels. Hey, Lora Lee, did you call her a 'flibbertigibbet'?"

"Yeah, I did. She jus' looked at me like I wuz crazy." She put a small stick in the path of the ants so they'd have to go over or around it. "An' I wuz eyein' her while she wuz struttin' her prissy self up to the choir. All of a sudden—an' I couldn' b'lieve this happened—her foot slid, an' she went flyin' through the air. An' she fell on Mr. Tuttle who wuz goin' up the steps, an' he fell on the preacher's wife's lap."

P. J. was bending over, holding his sides as he laughed. Lora Lee laughed, too. When she could talk, she continued, "I just about died laughin'. The preacher jumped up an' gave Mr. Tuttle a dirty look. Mr. Tuttle wuz tryin' ta git up, but Howlie May still had ahold of 'im. An' as soon as she got up, pore ole Mr. Tuttle put his hat on an' practic'ly pushed her outta the way, an' almos' ran out the side door. Daddy said he couldn' git outta there fast enough."

P. J. lay down on the grass howling, and Lora Lee was laughing and holding her sides. When he could talk, he said, "I bet she had a hissy fit when she got home, by cracky."

"She prob'ly did," Lora Lee agreed, nodding her head. "I wuz laughin' so much, I had ta go to the bathroom ta keep from gittin' in trouble. I got a place on my arm where I pinched myself ta keep from laughin'. Look at it." She showed him the blood blister.

"Wow, Lora Lee!" he said with admiration. "You didn' wanna go ta church last night, but I bet yo're glad you went."

"I shore am!" she exclaimed. "I wouldn' a wanted ta miss that."

They sat quietly for a minute, both of them watching the ants, which had calmed down some. She moved the stick just a little, and they got frantic again.

All of a sudden, Lora Lee started laughing. "P. J., you 'member when we had that mean ole rooster that useta chase us?"

"I shore do!" he exclaimed. "I won't ever forgit that mean ole thing."

"'Member that time y'all got here 'fore I got home from school, an' that rooster was chasin' you 'roun' the house. Aunt Rose said you went aroun' the house a couple a times, an' when you saw her standin' in the doorway, you yelled while you were runnin', 'When I come aroun' ag'in, open the door!'"

They laughed.

"Yeah, I 'member," he replied. "Whatever happened to that ole rooster?"

"He made the mistake of jumpin' up on Daddy one day. Daddy jus' grabbed ahold of 'im, an' wrung his mean ole neck. Then we had chicken an' dumplin's. Daddy said he was gonna kill him, anyway, since he wuz always chasin' us kids."

They'd just stopped talking when they heard Lucy say, "Hey, Lor' Lee, we di'n't make froggie houses."

"Hey, Lucy. Yo're awake," Lora Lee said, quickly removing the stick from the ants' path. "I wuz jus' makin' frog houses when ya'll came." She got Lucy out of the car. "I can show ya what I made, but we cain't make no more 'cause yore mama said y'all cain't git dirty."

They went to the back of the house. "I jus' started makin' 'em, an' I only made two. I cain't make 'em as good as P. J. can," she told Lucy. That was almost the truth, and it seemed to make P. J. feel good.

He smiled. "They're purty good."

Lora Lee thought they were very good. "Lucy, ya wanna git some grass to make a yard?"

Lucy's eyes lit up. The three of them broke off pieces of tall grass that was growing between the orange trees. Then they scattered it around the little houses. "It's a pretend yard," Lora Lee said. "Do ya like it?"

Lucy nodded her head, smiling, her eyes shining as she looked at what they'd created. "When will the froggies come?" she asked.

Lora Lee smiled as she thought, "She thinks frogs are gonna live there. How cute."

"They'll prob'ly come later, after we leave," she said.

Lucy's eyes were moving back and forth like she was deep in thought. She smiled, and after a moment, she tugged on Lora Lee's skirt and said, "Lor' Lee, Lor' Lee, I tell you what! Le's do the clappin' game."

"Okay," she said, "hold yore hands up in front a you."

Lucy held her little hands up, and Lora Lee knelt down in front of her. Lora Lee clapped her hands together, and then alternated clapping one of Lucy's hands with one of hers to the rhythm of the rhyme. She chanted:

> My boyfriend gave me peaches,
> My boyfriend gave me pears,
> My boyfriend gave me fifteen cents,
> An' kissed me up the stairs.
>
> I gave him back his peaches,
> I gave him back his pears,
> I gave him back his fifteen cents,
> An' kicked him down the stairs.

Lucy was smiling. Lora Lee knew she wanted to do it again, but P. J. was spinning round and round with his arms outstretched. She knew he was bored, and she watched as he got dizzy and started stumbling around. Lora Lee had tried a few times to do the clapping game with him, but he hadn't been able to get the knack of clapping correctly, so she didn't ask him to do it anymore. At some point, he always hit the wrong hand. She'd noticed that only the girls did the clapping game at school. They did it a lot and they had a few different rhymes they used. She figured the boys probably thought it was sissy. She was about to suggest that they do something else when Rose called.

"P. J., where are you? We're fixin' ta go now."

"Oh," Lucy said, and pushed out her lower lip.

"It's okay, Lucy," Lora Lee said as they went to the front of the house. "You'll come back soon, an' we'll all make frog houses."

That seemed to make her feel better. She said, "Okay, Lor' Lee."

"You woke up, baby," Rose said when she saw Lucy.

"Lor' Lee made froggie houses, an' we put grass," she told her mother.

"That's nice," Rose said. "I bet they look purty."

"Uh-huh," Lucy replied, nodding her head.

Lora Lee hugged Lucy and her aunt Rose, and said goodbye to P.J. Roger basically ignored her, and she, him. When the family was in the car, P.J. leaned out the back window, "See you later, Alligator."

"After while, Crocodile," Lora Lee answered.

Rose said, "Toodle-oo, Lora Lee."

"Toodle-oo, Aunt Rose."

"Toodoo, Lor' Lee," Lucy said, sitting between her parents.

Lora Lee smiled and replied, "Toodle-oo, Lucy."

♥ ♥ ♥

AFTER HER BATH, LORA LEE PUT ON A SUNDRESS Ruth had made for her from a feedsack. She put on the sandals with the broken strap, and grumbled to her grandmother. "I hate ta wear these ole broke sandals."

"You'll git some new ones soon," Clara reminded her.

"Yes'm," Lora Lee said. "I know it; I just hate wearin' these."

Lora Lee checked her pocketbook before she left the bedroom. "I got ta be sure I got the right amount a change," she thought. "If I don't git that ring today, no tellin' when I'll be in Lakeland ag'in. Thirty-five cents," she said, satisfied.

Billy got up just before they left. He usually slept until mid-afternoon when he was on the midnight shift. Lora Lee figured he got up early because he wanted to see Clara. He gave her a big hug and told her he'd go to see her while she was in Lakeland.

Ruth told him there was a plate for him on the stove, which she fixed before she put the leftovers away. "And there's some iced tea in the icebox."

When they went outside, King came running up, but Caleb snapped, "Git on," and he slinked off, with his tail between his legs.

After they got in the car, Clara said, "I shore do like this car. The colors are so purty."

That reminded Lora Lee of Grace calling it a "nigger" car. "That Grace's family's jus' stupid," she thought, and she decided not to mention that remark to Clara. She didn't want her grandmother to have any bad feelings about the car.

When they passed Rita's house, Lora Lee pointed at the school bus. "That's my bus an' that's Rita's house. She's my bus driver."

"She shore has some purty zinnias," Clara said.

"Yes, she does," Ruth agreed. "I enjoy 'em ever' time we pass by here."

Lora Lee wondered if she was going to say anything about wanting a flower garden, but she didn't. Lora Lee had heard her tell Caleb, the previous year and a few weeks earlier, that she wanted him to use the tractor to cut down the weeds on the far side of the house, and fix a place for her to plant some flowers, but he didn't say anything and he didn't do anything. And Lora Lee didn't expect him to. She wished he would, though; she wanted some pretty flowers, too.

As they passed through Bradley Junction on the way to Lakeland, they saw an old man with a long beard walking by the side of the road. "There's Mr. Gleason," Caleb said. "I declare, I don't know why he's got that ole beard. Mus' be hot as Hades this time a year."

"Prob'ly is," Clara said. "But you remember, Caleb, in the olden days, lots of men had long beards like that. I remember my grandfather's beard. It was snow white, and it went all the way down his chest. I mean to tell ya that wuz one fine beard. I wuz just a little girl when Grandma died, an' he came to live with us, an' I thought his beard wuz the most beautiful thing. Course, in that day an' time, most a the men had beards, but Grandpa's wuz diff'runt, an' he wuz so proud a that beard. He told ever'body he wuz never goin' to cut it; he wonted to lie in his casket with that beard displayed on his chest for all to see."

"Look at those cows out there," Caleb said. "Ain't they purty."

"They shore are," Ruth agreed. "Nice an' healthy lookin'."

"Y'all's cows are purty, too, Caleb," Clara said.

Lora Lee was impatient. "Is there more about the beard, Grandma?"

"Oh yes," Clara said. "Well, the pore ole soul got pneumonia, an' the doctor tol' the family to cut his beard off an' put a plaster on his chest. They didn' wont to cut it, but they were worried that he'd die, so they cut it, an' put the plaster on."

Clara stopped talking for a minute and wiped her eyes.

"What happened, Grandma?" Lora Lee asked, anxious to hear.

"The pore ole thing only lived for a few days, bless his heart. An' then he died without his beard. That jus' broke my little heart."

She wiped her eyes again, and Lora Lee wiped hers. "That's so sad."

"I know it, sugar. I felt so bad about that. That beard meant so much to him. I've often wondered if that didn' make him die sooner. It seemed like he jus' gave up."

She stopped for a minute. "I thought maybe he lost *his* strength like Samson in the Bible when they cut his hair."

Lora Lee knew she would look at beards differently from then on, especially Mr. Gleason's long one. However, his was not snow white, and she didn't think it was anywhere near as long as her great-great-grandfather's. She wished she could have seen his beard.

After a moment, Ruth said, "Caleb, I wuz tellin' Lora Lee a little bit about your daddy's time in the War Between the States. I told her about the pine saplin' an' his buddy gittin' shot. Seems like there wuz somethin' else, but I cain't remember."

Caleb didn't say anything for a minute. "I ain't thought about any a that in a coon's age. I do remember sumpin that happened after the war, though. My daddy said the soldiers were all walkin' home, an' when they got close to a settlement, the people would go out to meet 'em, an' sometimes the people would call out names of their loved ones, hoping they'd be amongst them, or the soldiers would know somethin' about 'em. He said they were goin' slow 'cause they were helpin' the cripples; some a 'em had lost a leg, or still had wounds that hadn' healed up."

"Daddy said there wuz a river by the ole dirt road, an' sometimes families would be walkin' along on the other side a the river. His friend—the one that he toted after he got shot—saw his wife on the other side, an' he jus' couldn' wait ta git to 'er. So, he started walkin' down the riverbank, an' he told 'em, 'I'm gonna swim it, Boys!' They told him not ta do it 'cause the current wuz really strong there."

A phosphate train with three engines was just starting to cross the road at the edge of Mulberry, and they had to stop for it. Lora Lee knew her father would be counting the railroad cars. "Shoot!" she thought. "He won't finish the story till that train's gone." She thought it might be one of the really long trains, so she decided to count with him. They counted 107 cars.

"That mighta been the longest one I ever counted," Caleb said.

Lora Lee figured he wouldn't get back to the story for a little while, so she started talking to Clara. "See that ole mulberry tree, Grandma? Missy's friend said Dinah—she lives in Pierce—tol' her they used ta hang Nigras from that tree. Dinah tol' her one Sund'y mornin' they were goin' ta church, an' Dinah wuz seven. She wuz sittin' in the front seat an' when they got close ta here, her mama pushed her head down, but she'd already seen a Nigra man hangin' from that mulberry tree."

"Oh my," Clara said.

"I'll be goin' to high school here in Mulberry," Lora Lee continued. "Missy comes skatin' here. Her mama brings her."

"Really?" Clara asked. "Where's the skatin' rink?"

"There ain't a reg'lar one here," Lora Lee said. "There's one that's here for a month in the summer, an' they move it. Missy said it goes ta Bartow, an' Fort Meade, an' Mulberry. I ain't ever been skatin'."

"I ain't either," Clara said. "I'd be afraid to git on skates."

Lora Lee looked at her grandmother quizzically as she thought, "Well, la-de-da, course you would! Look how ole you are."

"Skatin's for kids, Grandma," she said.

"I guess it is," Clara replied.

When she noticed that the front seat was quiet, Lora Lee asked, "What happened ta that man, Daddy? Did he die?"

"Oh yeah," Caleb said. "He went down to the water an' said, 'I'm swimmin' it, Boys!' An' some of 'em said, 'Don't do it. There's a bridge about a mile on up the road, an' that current's too strong to swim. Jus' wait.'"

Lora Lee leaned forward, folded her arms on the top of the front seat, and rested her chin on her arms. "Did he swim it?" she asked.

"Well, he tried to," Caleb said. "Nohow he wuz gonna wait any longer. He walked right out inta that rushin' river an' that water jus' took 'im, an' they never saw 'im again." He paused. "After all that time, he couldn' wait just a few more minutes ta be with his wife, an' that cost 'im his life."

"That's sad," Lora Lee said, "but he wuz stupid."

"It shore wadn' smart," Caleb replied.

"I bet there's a lotta stories like that," Clara said. "Young people can be awf'ly impatient."

Lora Lee thought, "I wouldn' do sumpin stupid like that."

"Ya know," Caleb said, "when I wuz young, I useta wonder why they called it the Civil War. There wadn't nothin' civil about it."

"That's the truth!" Ruth said.

Everyone was quiet for a moment before Clara pointed at a man who was hitchhiking. "Look at that man," she said. "He reminds me a little of Mr. Murphy when he was young. He's a character, that man. One Sunday at church, he told me that his son had a cow he'd been milkin' an' he thought she was bred, and he asked Mr. Murphy how long he could milk her after she wuz bred. Mr. Murphy said he told him, 'Well, we always jus' milk 'em till they start goin' dry, an' we don't ask 'em nothin' about their social life.'"

Clara, Caleb, and Ruth laughed, and Lora Lee joined in, but she didn't quite understand the joke.

"Mr. Murphy's a mess," Ruth said.

As they neared Lakeland, Lora Lee asked, "Where does Aunt Bessie live?" She noticed the drive-in theater and wished she could go there like her classmates and her sister, Linda. Caleb and Ruth didn't approve of going to the movies, so they didn't go, but Lora Lee intended to go when she got older.

"You've been to Aunt Bessie's," Ruth said. "But we're not goin' to her house. Rose came by today to tell us that she took pneumonia, an' she's still in the hospital. Rose said she's in an oxygen tent."

"That means Grandma's goin' back with us," Lora Lee thought, feeling happy. Then she asked, "What's an oxygen tent?"

"It's like a tent made outta plastic that they put over the patient, an' oxygen's pumped into it, so it's easier for patients to git the oxygen they need," Ruth explained.

"I wanna see that," Lora Lee said.

"She'll prob'ly be in a rollin' chair when she gits outta there," Clara remarked. "At least for a while."

"I'd like ta try a rollin' chair!" Lora Lee exclaimed.

"You know, I hadn' thought about this," Ruth said, "but Lora Lee cain't go in the hospital."

"That's right," Caleb agreed.

"How come, Mama?" she asked, disappointed. She wanted to see the oxygen tent, and maybe get a chance to sit in a wheel chair.

"Yo're too young, Double L," Caleb replied. "They don't let children go in."

She was quiet for a minute, and then she realized that might be a good thing. "Daddy, can I go to the dime store while y'all go to the hospital?"

"You got any money?" Caleb asked.

"A little bit." Lora Lee figured he was just curious, and not intending to give her any.

"I don't know how long we'll be," Ruth said. "It might be too long."

"Well Mama, I can sit in the park if I git tired a bein' in there," she pleaded. "I can watch the birds an' the people, an' I can wait there so we can go buy me some new sandals."

"Well, I'll be John Brown!" Caleb said. "I forgot about havin' ta git her new sandals. That's gonna be five or six dollars. I tell you, it's jus' one thing after another."

Lora Lee knew when it was time to keep quiet, and she did.

Clara suggested, "Maybe Lora Lee could go to the shoe store before she goes to the dime store. She could try on some sandals, so all y'all'd havta do is pay for 'em. She'd have plenty a time ta do that."

Lora Lee felt hope rising in her chest.

"That's a good idee, Miz Hall," Caleb said. "Double L, you go to the shoe store an' try on some sandals, an' tell the man to put 'em aside for ya. Tell 'im we'll be in later. Then go to the dime store, an' then wait for us in the park."

"Try on sandals about like those you've got on," Ruth said.

"Yes, ma'am," Lora Lee said as she smiled at her grandmother, who was smiling at her.

When they passed the Polk Theatre on Florida Avenue, again Lora Lee thought, "I wish I could go to the movies."

"An' give Mama a hug," Ruth added. "She won't be comin' back with us, you know."

"But Aunt Bessie's still in the hospital," she protested.

"Your grandma's goin' to stay with Rose. They don't know when Aunt Bessie'll git out. It could be any day."

"I wish you could stay with us, Grandma," Lora Lee said, hugging her.

"You'll hafta come see me while I'm at Bessie's," Clara replied.

"Can we, Daddy?" she asked.

"I spec' so," he said.

The car stopped by the park and Caleb pointed. "All right, Lora Lee," he said. "The shoe store's right down yonder. Ya know where it is?"

"Yes, sir, I know."

"Well, don't git lost here in the big city," he teased. "The dime store's right there, on the other side of the park. An' wait for us on that bench over yonder. It's the closest one to the shoe store."

"I will," she said.

She kissed her grandmother's cheek before she got out of the car. "Bye, Grandma."

"Bye, sugar," Clara said. "I hope you git that purty ring."

Lora Lee felt the blood rise to her face. "Daddy's prob'ly gonna say sumpin," she thought. She hadn't told her parents she was planning to buy a ring, although she did show it to her mother, and would've preferred that they not know until she had it on her finger. She figured Caleb would have an opinion about how she spent her money, even though they didn't give any of it to her, except the four cents from her mother. But she instantly forgave her grandmother. "She don't know how Daddy is," she thought. "He don't yell at Grandma."

In fact, Lora Lee was well aware of the respect he showed to Ruth's mother. He never argued with her, even when he wanted something a different way. She remembered the previous summer when they spent a week in Georgia. Clara still had a hired hand who grew tobacco for her, and some of it was ready for harvesting. They had a "puttin'-in" day while they were there, and of course, Caleb offered to help, which meant Lora Lee had to help, too. Clara no longer worked in the fields since she'd developed a heart condition, and she stayed at the house.

Lora Lee had never worked in tobacco before. She knew that people grew it in north Florida because she'd seen the fields and the tobacco barns, but they didn't grow it in central Florida. The tobacco leaves were cropped and taken to the tobacco barn, and her job was to put about three leaves together and hand them to Ruth, who'd wrap string around the stems and string them on a stick about an inch thick and about four and a half feet long. They were then hung in the tobacco barn where the tobacco was cured. It wasn't a hard job, but she was doing it for hours. They quit to eat, and then went back to work more in the afternoon.

She remembered that Caleb had thrown a big green tobacco worm at Ruth that day. "Mama said that ole worm wuz almost three inches long," Lora Lee thought. Even though Ruth had lived and worked on a farm almost her whole life, she didn't like worms. Even the earthworms they used for fishing made her shiver. Ruth screamed when the tobacco worm hit her, and unfortunately for her, Caleb's aim was better than he'd planned, and the worm went down the front of her dress.

"Caleb!" she screamed. She was dancing around hysterically, trying to get it out. "Oh my Lord. Caleb!"

Of course, he was laughing the whole time, but Lora Lee could tell that he didn't enjoy it as much as he would have if it hadn't gone down her dress. He hadn't meant for it to go there, and he knew she was really distressed.

When they went back to the house after they finished, Clara handed Lora Lee a fifty-cent piece. Her eyes lit up and she grinned—she hadn't expected to be paid. "Thank you, Grandma!" she exclaimed, hugging her.

Caleb said, "Oh no, Miz Hall, you don't hafta pay her."

Lora Lee felt her heart sink, and her smile vanished. She held her hand out with the money in it.

"I know I don't hafta pay her, Caleb," Clara said. "I'm payin' her 'cause I know good an' well she worked hard. It ain't much, but she deserves a little somethin' for her work."

Caleb didn't say anything else, and Lora Lee kept the money. It was the first time she remembered seeing her father give in, and she was impressed and pleased. It was also the first time she'd been paid for anything, except what Rita gave her on the bus. She'd asked Caleb to pay her a little bit for picking strawberries, but he replied, "You git paid. You git food to eat an' a bed ta sleep in."

She didn't think that was fair at all. The other pickers got paid, and she didn't even expect him to pay her as much as they got. However, he'd never paid her sister and brothers, so she knew she had no reason to expect that he'd pay her, but she'd had hope.

♥   ♥   ♥

As Lora Lee walked slowly past the park, she tried to hide the fact that her sandal strap was broken. She found it wasn't so obvious if she walked slowly and kind of dragged her foot instead of picking it up. When she noticed that no one was staring at her, she relaxed a little.

There were squirrels all around, and a few, along with some pigeons and sparrows, were gathered around a bench where an old man was giving them popcorn. She saw two sparrows in a puddle taking a bath, and she stopped in the shade for a moment to watch. Several people were sitting on the park benches, and a few were strolling through the park. A little girl was standing on tiptoes trying to reach a red rose. "There's thorns on there," Lora Lee thought. "Better not do that, little girl."

"I like it here," she decided. "There's so much ta see."

She took a minute to study the statue of the Confederate soldier, thinking, "That man's shore up high." She heard water falling, turned to look at the fountain, and watched the water cascading over its tiers.

After a moment, she decided to go to the shoe store so she'd be sure to have plenty of time in the dime store. Once there, she was all business, anxious to get to the dime store. The salesman brought her a pair of sandals a half size larger than hers, which she tried on and said she'd take. She explained that she'd be back later with her parents, and he said he'd hold the shoes for her. She thanked him and headed for the dime store.

On her way, she remembered to walk slowly and kind of drag her foot, hoping people wouldn't notice the sandal. The delicious aroma of popcorn met her outside the store, and she wondered, momentarily, if maybe she should spend her money on other things. She'd eaten at the lunch counter one time with her mother. "I could git some popcorn an' a cherry coke. Or I could sit down an' have a piece a pie or a doughnut." But in the store, she went straight to the jewelry counter.

Unfortunately, the clerk was not there. When Lora Lee looked around to see if she might be nearby, she saw Anna, the clerk her mother had talked to on Wednesday. Lora Lee decided she'd speak to her, but it would have to be later because Anna had a customer. So after confirming that the ruby ring was still there, Lora Lee went to the back of the store to get a drink of water. "Grandma said it wuz hot today, an' it shore is."

She was drinking absentmindedly when the clerk from the jewelry counter leaned near her ear and whispered, "Honey, this is the colored fountain."

Lora Lee stopped drinking, looked at the clerk and thought, "That's the clerk from the jewelry counter. How come she don't go back ta her counter instead a watchin' me?" Then she looked up at the "Colored" sign. She was surprised that she hadn't noticed it because she knew the signs were there. They'd always been there.

She whispered, "Oh, I'm sorry." She knew her face was probably red because she felt humiliated. She wished the clerk had just left her alone. "What's the diff'runce?" she wondered. "Is my hand gonna fall off now? Does she think it'll turn black? Anyhow, I wuz almost done drinkin'."

"That's all right," the clerk whispered. "Jus' be careful."

Lora Lee was more embarrassed by the clerk's attention than she was about drinking from the colored fountain, and she thought the clerk probably drew attention to her. Glancing around to see if anyone else had seen her, she noticed a Negro man across the room, and was grateful that he wasn't looking at her.

She decided to wait a little while before she went back to the jewelry counter. She didn't want to have to face that clerk yet. As she walked slowly, with her shoe scraping the floor, she thought about going to Anna's counter, but a customer went there, so she stopped at the toys. She noticed that the Negro man was drinking from the fountain where she'd just been, and she felt self-conscious.

Lora Lee picked up the same doll she'd held on Wednesday. "She's so cute," she thought, her face lighting up, and the recent embarrassment momentarily forgotten. "An' she's got a beautiful pink dress." She put the doll down. "No sense in wishin'."

Anna was still busy, so she walked slowly to the jewelry counter. She glanced at the clerk and saw her wipe her eyes. "Is she cryin'?" she wondered, but assumed she wasn't. "She cain't be cryin' at work."

Lora Lee knew she wanted to buy the ring, but when the clerk didn't go right over to her, she pretended she was trying to make up her mind.

"Can I he'p ya wi' sumpin, honey?" the clerk asked, walking over to her.

"I wanna buy that ruby ring, please," she said softly, pointing at the rings.

"Sure," the clerk said, and put the rings on the counter.

Lora Lee stared at the ruby ring for a moment. "I wont that one," she said, pointing. "The ruby one."

As the clerk took the ring out, she said, "Try it on."

Lora Lee's eyes lit up as she slipped the ring on her finger. "It fits," she said, smiling. "I'll take it." She put her money on the counter, thrilled that she was going to have the ring she liked so much.

"It's adjustable," the clerk said, and silently counted the change. She looked at Lora Lee and stated, "You owe another penny. It's thirty-six cents."

Lora Lee could feel her heart beating faster. She thought she must not have heard right. "Did you say 'thirty-six'?" she asked, her eyes wide.

"Yes, honey. It's thirty-six cents," the clerk responded. "You need another penny."

"You tol' me thirty-five cents the other day," Lora Lee said.

"Well, there's a penny tax," the clerk explained.

"Oh." Lora Lee felt her heart sink. Her enthusiasm was gone, as was the sparkle in her eyes. She was beginning to feel embarrassed again, and she knew she was sweating.

"I only got thirty-five cents," she said, hoping and thinking the clerk would give her a penny. She stood there breathing fast, looking at the clerk. "Goodness gracious!" she thought. "She could give me a penny. If she tol' me the right price the other day, Grandma woulda gave me a penny." She glanced around to see if anyone was staring at her.

The clerk also looked around the store, and then at Lora Lee, who thought she looked very uncomfortable. Finally, she said, "I'm sorry," but Lora Lee didn't think she sounded sorry.

"How come she won't jus' give me a penny?" Lora Lee wondered. She was staring at the clerk, who was looking around the store again. Lora Lee felt tears sting her eyes, and knew she was on the verge of crying. She dug her fingernails into her palms.

She was about to pick up her money and leave when she heard a man's voice behind her say, "Ah got a penny."

She turned to see who had said that, who was maybe going to save her from further embarrassment, and make it possible for her to buy the ring she craved. She was surprised to see the Negro man she'd seen at the water fountain. "Oh my goodness!" she thought. "That Nigra man's gonna give me a penny."

For the first time, she noticed that he was wearing a pretty blue shirt, which had a couple of water spots on it. And, for the first time, she looked into his warm, sympathetic eyes, and she liked him. Then she looked at the hand he was holding out and saw the penny.

An overwhelming sense of relief and gratitude descended on her. "Oh, thank you," she said, her voice full of emotion, as he placed the penny on the counter. And yet, she felt a little uncomfortable that a Negro had seen her in that humiliating situation.

"You welcome, Miss," he said as he stepped back.

She took a deep breath and sighed. "Imagine that," she thought. "He seems nice. That clerk wouldn' give me a penny, an' he gave me one. An' he called me 'Miss,' an' that ole Nigra man in the Quarters called me 'ma'am.'" She felt a couple of inches taller; no one had ever called her "Miss" before.

The clerk asked, "Ya wanna wear it?"

"Yes, ma'am," she said happily, and slipped the ring on her finger. She turned slightly to look behind her at the Negro man. She smiled shyly, and he smiled at her.

She sighed, and thought, "I'm glad that's over. I thought I wadn' goin' ta git my ring."

She noticed that no one was at Anna's counter, so she slowly went over there, sliding her feet on the floor. Anna was folding and straightening the cloth.

"Hi Anna," Lora Lee said.

"Well, hi, Lora Lee," she said warmly. "What a pleasant surprise! Are you shoppin' today?"

Lora Lee held out her hand. "I bought me a ring."

"Oh how pretty!" Anna exclaimed. "And it looks so good on you."

Lora Lee's face flushed, and she smiled. "Mama an' Daddy'll be back in a little while," she said. "I gotta go wait for 'em in the park. Bye, bye."

"Wait," Anna said, reaching for her pocketbook. "If you're goin' to the park, git some popcorn for yourself, an' you can give some to the birds an' squirrels. Here's a nickel."

"Thank you, Anna," she exclaimed, her eyes lighting up. "She woulda give me a penny," she thought. "She ain't like that mean ole woman."

"You're welcome, Lora Lee," Anna said.

Lora Lee walked carefully to the popcorn stand. When she got the popcorn, she felt so happy that she forgot about her shoe and started to skip. Of course, the sandal with the broken strap came off, and she had to stop and put the shoe back on, her momentary happiness replaced by embarrassment. She quickly looked around the store to see if anyone had seen her. The girl at the popcorn machine was adding corn to the popper, Anna had her back to her, and the jewelry clerk and the Negro man were looking at each other. She was relieved.

"I wonder how come that Nigra man's still there," she thought. "That clerk must notta waited on 'im yet, but he wuz right behine me." She watched the clerk go to the other side of the counter to wait on a white woman. "She's jus' plain mean. Boy howdy! I'm glad that's over."

As she waited for some cars to go by, a sheriff's car passed in front of her, and she remembered the day the sheriff had gone to their house a year earlier. An old friend, he drove all the way to the farm to tell Caleb that he'd busted up a still south of Lakeland, and they could have the corn mash for the hogs if they wanted to go get it. So Caleb and Billy went and got three barrels of mash.

When Lora Lee stepped off the curb to cross the street, her sandal came off again. "Shoot," she thought, "I wish I could jus' go barefoot."

She passed the bench where she'd sat Wednesday, and noticed a man and woman sitting there. The man was mostly bald and he had a paunch, and the woman had on too much makeup and too little dress; it was low cut and a few inches above her knees. "That's a short dress!" Lora Lee thought. They were sitting close together, talking and laughing, and Lora Lee noticed that their legs were touching. And although she felt uncomfortable, she couldn't help staring at the woman. "I know what Mama would call *her*," she thought. "Mama ain't got no use for 'painted women', 'speshly one with a dress like that."

She walked slowly and carefully on the sidewalk until she reached the bench Caleb had pointed out under an oak tree with Spanish moss. She'd barely gotten settled there before two squirrels appeared in front of her, and five sparrows lit on the grass beside the bench. "Hey," she said. "I gotta have some popcorn, too. Y'all don't be greedy. It ain't all for y'all."

She ate some of the popcorn as the squirrels watched her and the sparrows twittered and scratched in the sand nearby. Occasionally, she threw them a small handful. She was in a good spot to see the statue and the fountain, which was bathed in sunlight. Lora Lee was mesmerized by the glittering water, bejeweled by a small rainbow. When there were no cars passing, she could hear the water, and she imagined that it sounded like a waterfall. "I'd like ta see a waterfall," she thought.

She looked to her left to see if that couple was still sitting on the bench where she and her mother had sat on Wednesday. They were. She frowned as she looked at them. "I hope they leave before Mama and Daddy come," she thought, "or Mama'll be talkin' 'bout 'em all the way ta Bradley. I guess women didn't dress like that when she wuz growin' up. Things musta been real diff'runt then."

She thought about her mother's story of the first time she ever saw a car. Ruth said she was in town with her cousin, and she went home and told her daddy, "I saw a buggy runnin' without any horses." He explained that it was an automobile and it had a motor. "'Magine not knowin' 'bout cars!" she thought. "Mama's old."

As she ate her popcorn, more sparrows landed around her, and pretty soon some pigeons arrived. "All right," she said, "there's too many a y'all now. Shoo away. I ain't givin' ya no more. It's almost gone an' I'm eatin' the rest. Y'all git a lot more popcorn 'an me. Shoo, shoo." She put her hand down as though pushing them away.

Neither the squirrels nor the birds paid any attention to the shooing, so she just ignored them. She put some popcorn in her mouth and looked at her ring, happiness bubbling inside her. "I wish Grandma could see my ring," she thought, "but I can show it to Rita Monday mornin'. She'll like it. An' I'll show it to Grace an' Emily, an' Lola'll prob'ly want ta see what I'm showin' 'em."

Lora Lee didn't feel special very often, but she felt special now. The Negro man had given her a penny, Anna had given her a nickel to buy popcorn, and she had a shiny new ring on her finger.

Suddenly, she thought, "Oh my goodness! I got my wish. I wished on a star Wednesday night, an' I got my wish."

When she looked up, she saw a Negro man walking across the park. "That's the man that gave me the penny," she thought. "That wuz so nice a him! That mean ole woman wouldn' give me a penny, but he did, by cracky." She smiled, raised her hand a little, and waved at him shyly. And he smiled and waved back at her.

She felt drawn to his beautiful smile and warm, friendly eyes, but knew she'd probably never see him again. "Looks to me like he feels things," she thought. "I think Mama's wrong. He cared enough to give me a penny, an' I could see in his eyes he felt sorry for me. Mama said she don't know no Nigras, an' I don't either, but I know he's nice, an' I wish I knew him. I wish he could be my frien'." She remembered the preacher's words about the curse on Ham and his descendants. "I shore hope he ain't got no curse on him. He's real nice."

Lora Lee listened to cars going by, birds singing, and people chatting. She looked at the water fountain, the flowers, and up through the branches of the oak tree at the bright blue sky. She didn't care about her freckles, or Howlie May, or any of the kids at school. With her face turned up, she said a silent prayer: "Thank you, God, for my ruby ring. An' please bless that nice Nigra man that gave me a penny."

"Huh!" she thought. "That's the first time I ever prayed for a Nigra." She remembered the story she heard Billy tell about his friends throwing rocks at two Negro kids and thought, "I oughta say some prayers for that Nigra girl an' boy ta help 'em forget about that. That wuz a really mean thing to do. That'd be like me an' P. J. bein' close to the Nigra Quarters, an' two big Nigra boys chasin' us an' throwin' rocks at us. That'd scare me half ta death, not ta mention how much them rocks would hurt! Them two kids might still be scared a white boys. But that was a few years ago—they mus' be big by now."

A pigeon lit on the bench, and she shooed it away. She sat still for a while, just listening to all the sounds around her. Then she thought, "This was a good week. Funny things happened with Mr. Docker and at church, Grandma an' P. J. came, an' I got my ring. I wish all my weeks could be like this one."

As she looked around the park, she thought, "Miz Hoffman said we got five senses. Seein', hearin', smellin', tastin', an', . . . what else? Oh yeah, feelin'. I always forget *feelin'*. An' I'm doin' all five a 'em right now. I see the sky an' ever'thing in the park, an' my ring; I hear the birds an' cars, an' people talkin'; I smell the popcorn an' the stink from that ole truck that jus' went by; I'm tastin' popcorn an' butter an' salt; an' I'm feelin' my new ring on my finger, an' the bench on my backside." She smiled.

She threw some popcorn into her mouth, looked in the bag, and emptied out the last few kernels for the sparrows. She watched them for a moment as they pecked at the popcorn. Then, she took a deep breath and sighed, leaned back on the bench, and smiled contentedly, gazing at her very own ruby ring.

Book II

James
A Heart with Diamonds

◊ ◊

Like a diamond uncut, his brilliance could only be seen
by those who looked with clear eyes.

Cast of Characters
appearing more than once

James Thomas Cleveland, 19

Family:
Pearl (Jackson), 57, mother
Pearson, 58, father
Martha, 21, sister; husband Jasper, 21
Freeman Jackson, 69, uncle (Pearl's brother); wife Drusilla
Ruby, 22, cousin (Freeman's daughter); husband Harley, 23;
    son Rubin, 10 months
Junior, 33, cousin (Freeman's son)
Rosella, 38, cousin (Freeman's daughter); husband Brook, 40
Jacob Jackson, 60 (Freeman and Pearl's cousin)
Charity, 67, aunt (Freeman and Pearl's sister)
Pearl, 35, cousin (Charity's daughter)
Kizzy, 17, 2nd cousin (cousin Pearl's daughter)

Friends:
Saleena, 17, girlfriend
Maggie McClellan (Mis' Mac), 70, neighbor
Emmy, companion for Maggie

Church:
Mardella, 16
Rev. Johnson, minister

Other:
J. B. Hatchett, wife Sophie, daughter Carla (Jacob's friends)
Tom Hiers (the farmer Harley sharecrops for)
Mabel, secretary, phosphate company
Carl Roberts, Head of Personnel, phosphate company
Dr. Stone, family doctor
Mr. Wilson (farmer Pearson works for occasionally)

Sunday

JAMES WOKE TO THE SOUND OF A CROWING ROOSTER much earlier than he wanted to be awake on a Sunday morning. He rolled onto his side, put the pillow over his head, and tried to go back to sleep. However, when the image of Saleena appeared, he knew his sleep was finished.

"Oh Lawd!" he thought. "Hi she got dat sweet lil waist an' dem fine curvy hips! No mo' sleep fuh me now. Jes' keep crowin', ole roostah."

He sat up and positioned his pillow against the bedstead so that he could sit comfortably, and his mind went right back to Saleena. "Ah loves Sund'ys," he thought, "'cause Ah gits ta see dat fine thang at church." He pictured the way her nose wrinkled just a little when she laughed—he liked to tease her about that. And he remembered her lovely brown eyes looking up at him, and the feel of her fingers entwined in his. "Lawd have mercy on me!" he thought. He whispered her name, "Saleena," loving the sound. "Saleena, Saleena."

At nineteen, James was an attractive young man, lean and muscular from farm work. His smooth, dark brown skin complimented a nicely-shaped face, and his brown eyes revealed a confidence and calmness not usually found in one so young. He'd considered straightening his short black hair, but none of his friends had straightened theirs, and he knew his parents wouldn't approve. With his good looks and warm, playful personality, he was popular with the girls. Dating since he was sixteen, he'd slept with one girl a few times and he carried guilt about that, and occasionally thought about the possibility of burning in hell. But with Saleena, it was the first time he'd actually felt the magic.

James had known Saleena since they were small and had thought of her as just a friend until three months earlier. He wondered how he'd failed to notice sooner how beautiful she'd become. Closing his eyes for a moment, he thought about that night.

At a church party for the young people, he and Saleena had ended up as partners in a Bible challenge. Bible questions were asked, and partners who answered incorrectly were dropped from the game. Soon, Saleena and James were one of the two couples left. In her excitement, she took his hand, and energy surged through his body. He was so distracted that Saleena had to answer all the questions. They came in second when she couldn't think of the name of David's wayward son, and James couldn't think at all. Later, remembering the game, he couldn't believe what had happened—he'd known the story of David and Absalom since he was a child, and he realized that something different was happening to him.

After that night, James had started sitting with her in church, holding her hand. And when he had enough money, he'd taken her to see Elvis Presley in *Love Me Tender* at the Roxy Theatre in Lakeland with his cousin Ruby and her husband, Harley. Saleena had snuggled up close to him during the movie, and he'd kissed her in the dark theatre, which had no light except for what came from the movie screen. After that, he barely heard any more of the movie. He just kept thinking about that incredible kiss, and looking for the right moment to kiss her again.

Negroes were not allowed to go to the lovely Polk Theatre in downtown Lakeland; they went to the Roxy Theatre in the Negro section. James never saw any rodents in the Roxy, but adults told the kids to hold their feet up because there were mice and rats in there. Saleena kept her feet on her seat, sometimes sitting on them, but James decided to be brave and keep his on the floor. He understood that he was risking his strong male image and reputation, because he knew if a rat ran across his feet, he'd yell and probably jump up on the seat.

After the movie, they went to a restaurant to get a hamburger and a soda. James put a quarter in the jukebox and chose three slow songs. Harley and Ruby and he and Saleena danced, and he was struck by how perfectly her body fit his and how wonderful she felt in his arms.

He thought Saleena felt about him the same way he felt about her, but he was so much in love that he was afraid he was imagining it. It seemed too good to be true. At seventeen, she had another year of high school and was planning to go to college because she wanted to be a teacher.

Sitting in bed wide awake, James was ready to get up, but he didn't want to disturb his parents. He knew they needed the rest they got by sleeping a little late on Sunday. The only work they did Sundays was feeding the animals, cooking, and washing dishes. Pearson not only worked their twenty-acre farm, he sometimes worked for a white farmer, Mr. Wilson. And Pearl took care of their house and yard and chickens, canned and froze some of the vegetables they grew, made her own clothes, and occasionally made a little money sewing for other people and helping a neighbor with big household projects.

When he heard his German shepherd stirring in the kitchen, he knew his parents would be awake soon. If Shep didn't wake them up, James getting up to let him out probably would.

Through his front bedroom window, his mother's flowerbed caught his eye as the morning sunshine highlighted the flowers that were blooming. He noticed how she'd planted three rows close together, with the tallest plants in back, so that there were three layers of color. "Oughta tell huh how good dey look," he thought. He often noticed them, but didn't think about saying anything to her.

Pearl also had some hibiscus, gardenias, and hydrangeas next to the house, and she added plants when someone gave her a plant or a cutting. About ten feet away from one side of the house was a pink oleander. In the back yard were a few citrus trees: oranges, grapefruit, tangerines, and lemons. Their barn was behind the citrus trees, and behind the barn and to the right of the house was land they farmed. To the left of the citrus trees was a pasture. Near the back porch in front of their clothesline, a six-foot tall kumquat tree was loaded with kumquats. They ate them ripe off the tree, and Pearl made kumquat preserves, mostly for James.

Like most other houses in the area, the house was made of hard southern pine, and sat on large pine blocks. One summer, Pearson and James had painted the house white while Pearl was at their son's house in north Florida helping to care for his new baby daughter. Their other son had two boys she adored, but she was thrilled to have a granddaughter. Pearl had wanted the house painted for years, but Pearson never seemed to have the time. They weren't very busy while she was away, and James suggested that they paint it and surprise her.

When she saw the house, she carried on pretty much the way she had when she saw her new grandbaby. James and Pearson looked at each other and smiled. "Lawd a mercy!" she said, hugging both of them. "Fust Ah got me a granddaughter, an' now mah house is painted. Oh Lawd!" For days, she talked about how much she liked the house, and even two years later, she still mentioned it occasionally. James noticed that she'd planted even more flowers near the house after it was painted, and put potted plants on both porches. Pearl loved living on a farm, and though she didn't work in the fields, she enjoyed working with her flowers.

The kitchen and living room were on one side of the house, a hall ran down the middle for airflow, and three small bedrooms were on the other side of the hall. The bathroom, which they'd added three years earlier, was on the back porch, which was screened in, but the front porch was open.

When James heard Pearl in the kitchen, he pulled on his slacks and joined her. "Mornin' Mama," he said as he went up behind her and kissed her on the cheek. "Yo' flow'rs look real purty. Ah wuz lookin' at 'em out da windah dis mornin'."

"Thank ya, son," she said, pleased that he'd noticed.

Pearl was one of those women who'd managed to bear four children and reach her mid-fifties without putting on much weight. James was proud of her, and she was proud of him. Since her three older children had gotten married, she and James had developed a close relationship. Pearl knew other women whose teenage sons gave them lots of heartache, and she was grateful that James didn't cause her any worry. "Hi ya feelin' dis mornin', baby?" she asked, wiping her hands on her apron.

James noticed that she had on her warm housecoat. It was cool out, and she didn't like to be cold.

"Jes' fine, Mama," he answered. "Lookin' for'd ta church today. Preacher Brown 'pose' ta be good. Ah likes havin' vis'tin' preachers."

"Unh, unh, unh." Pearl looked at James with a smile on her face and a twinkle in her eye. "Well, James Thomas Cleveland, dat da onliest reason ya lookin' for'd to it?" She liked Saleena and enjoyed teasing him about her.

Pearson entered the kitchen in time to hear Pearl's question. "Whut us lookin' for'd to?"

"James lookin' for'd ta church today. Ah'm jes' tryin' ta figger out how come."

"Ah see," Pearson grinned and winked at Pearl. "He sho do like church now, don' he?"

James looked at the two of them and shook his head. He left the room, with the sound of their laughter in his ears, and he smiled, in spite of himself.

"Breakfas' be ready 'bout five minute," Pearl called.

♥   ♥   ♥

WHEN THEY ARRIVED AT THE CHURCH, James did a quick scan of the parked vehicles. There were a lot of pick-up trucks there, but his heart sank when he didn't see the one he was looking for. Saleena wasn't there.

People greeted each other as they arrived, and went inside to get out of the cool air. James was glad that the teenagers were about the only ones who stayed outside.

The church was typical of small country churches. It was a simple, white wooden building with three tall windows on each side, and it had a small steeple. On the left was a huge old oak tree with Spanish moss decorating its branches, and behind the church was one fairly new, small bathroom with concrete-block walls. There was also an old well at the back that was covered with a screen to catch the falling oak leaves.

James walked back to the well, removed the screen, and held the rope so that he could let the bucket go slowly down into the water. When it was full, he pulled on the rope, hand over hand, until he could reach the bucket. Although there was now an electric pump in the well and a water tank with a spigot beside it, James liked to draw the water. It was the only old-fashioned well he knew of in the area, and he thought the water he drew was cooler and tasted better than that from the spigot.

He set the bucket on the ledge that was built for that purpose, took the dipper off the post, filled it with the fresh, cool water, and drank deeply. He threw the remaining water from the dipper on the sandy ground, hung the dipper on the post, and put the screen back over the well.

As he walked to the front of the church, he saw the blue pick-up truck he'd been waiting for, and his spirits lifted just as quickly as they'd fallen. He restrained himself from running to the truck and opening the door, and patiently waited for her to go to him.

Saleena got out of the truck as soon as it stopped, but her parents stayed as though they were finishing a conversation. As she approached, James looked at her shapely legs, warm brown eyes, and lovely smile, and his heart skipped a beat.

"Ah t'ought you wadn' e'em comin'," he said as he took her hand, wishing he could kiss her and hold her in his arms. Holding hands was about the only form of affection acceptable at the church.

"Stupid ole pigs got out," Saleena said, frowning.

James laughed. "So ya been chasin' ole pigs, huh?"

"Yeah, an' it ain't funny," she said, the frown still there until she gave in to laughter.

James touched the laugh wrinkle on her nose and pulled one of her short tight curls.

Saleena's parents passed by and gave her a look.

"Time ta go in," she said to James.

As they went into the church, Saleena said, "When Mama wuz young, she worked fuh a white lady went ta a diff'unt church. She say dey jes' go ta sumpin like Sund'y school till dey fo'teen. Den dey quit goin'."

"Huh!" James exclaimed. "Onliest way us git ta quit goin' is ta quit church . . . or die."

They both laughed. And they both thought about how it might be nice not to have Sunday school, and they both felt a little guilty for having the thought. After all, they learned a lot about the Bible in Sunday school, and they liked their teacher. But James pictured himself sitting under the oak tree with Saleena instead of going to Sunday school, and thought that would be wonderful. The church could not afford to build Sunday school rooms without borrowing a lot of money—although many of the members tithed their ten percent—so they only had four classes, which met in the four corners of the building. That worked fairly well because there were only fifty-two members, plus the children, and they were never all there. The teachers spoke softly, so the sound didn't disturb the other groups. When it wasn't raining, the teacher would often take the little children outside for a while.

James and Saleena sat down in the section where the young people had their Sunday school class. Before the teacher arrived, two of the boys were talking about the Nat King Cole show they'd seen Monday night. He had a fifteen-minute show, which had started the previous November. James and his parents had gone to his aunt Charity's house in Lakeland a couple of times to see the show. He remembered how strange and wonderful it seemed to see a Negro man on television—that was amazing, but that it was *his* show was even more amazing.

For years, the young people had talked about Jackie Robinson and what a brave man he was to be playing baseball on a "white" team. They knew about the names he was called, the hate mail, and death threats; they knew about pitchers throwing at his legs and head, and catchers spitting on his shoes. And they knew that he'd held his tongue until he proved himself to be a great player and won the respect and support of his team, and that when he started speaking out about things, he was called an "uppity nigger." They were so proud of his amazing accomplishments and how he'd handled everything, but since his retirement in January, they seldom mentioned him, and they mostly talked about Nat King Cole and the guests on his show.

During the church service, James and Saleena sat about two-thirds of the way back in the church. Their parents wouldn't approve of them sitting on the back seat, the way some of their peers did. They were expected to participate in the service, to pay attention and to sing the hymns. Of course, James was old enough now that he wouldn't have gotten in trouble with his parents if he didn't do what they wished, but he didn't want to disappoint them, especially since he still lived with them. Also, he wanted Saleena's parents to approve of him.

Neither James nor Saleena sang in the choir, but they both liked to sing and they loved the old hymns. They sang "Nearer My God to Thee," "In the Garden," and "Amazing Grace" that morning. For James, the music both lifted his spirit and brought him peace. And he loved to hear Saleena's sweet, soprano voice.

When they sat down for the sermon, James took the fan from the hymnal rack in front of him, and gently fanned himself and Saleena. The fan had a picture of Jesus with the little lost lamb in his arms on one side and "Lincoln Funeral Home" on the other side.

The preacher hadn't been preaching long before James decided he liked him. He would've preferred a different topic, however. The preacher's sermon was about fornication—both adultery, and sex before marriage. James was in complete agreement about adultery. He believed that his father had always been faithful to his mother, partly because he was still alive. James had heard conversations between his parents about people who cheated and he knew they both felt strongly about it. And he had strong feelings about it himself.

During the service, James would sit as close to Saleena as she'd let him, and he tried to sit close enough that their thighs were touching. They held hands, and he'd pull her hand into his lap and play with her fingers for a minute, then interlock their hands and put them on her thigh, making sure that the back of her hand rested on her thigh, so his fingers were touching it. He usually missed a lot of what the preacher said.

They'd squeeze each other's hands when the preacher said something that they agreed with, and James was disappointed when she squeezed his hand while the preacher was talking about sex before marriage being a sin. He heard that! The preacher warned the young people to beware of Satan's temptations, and about how easy it was to fall into sin; he said young people have lots of temptations put before them and they need to be strong. He also warned them about the dangers of drinking, saying that alcohol makes it harder to think straight and people are more likely to give in to temptation after a few drinks. James agreed with the drinking part, and even though he had friends who drank, he didn't.

He did believe that sex before marriage was a sin—that's why he felt guilty about what he'd already done—but his desire for Saleena was stronger every day, and seemed to be always on his mind. He hoped she was feeling the same way. He'd think about her tiny waist and curvy hips, and forget completely about the sin part. Or, he'd think that, since he was in love with her, maybe it wouldn't be a sin. But now that the preacher was preaching sin, James thought he'd probably have to give up hope, at least for a while. "Saleena ain't gon' lay down wit' me 'less we's married," he thought.

And marriage was something that James had already thought about, much to his surprise. One day while he was helping his father pick lima beans, he found his mind on Saleena and realized that he'd just pictured himself going home from work and entering a kitchen where she was cooking supper. "Oh Lawd," he thought. "Ah'm thankin' 'bout gittin' married."

As the pianist began playing "Just As I Am," James turned to look at Saleena's lovely face, and she looked up at him with a smile. As his heart beat faster, he wondered if she had any idea how much power she could have over him.

♥　♥　♥

Pearl and Pearson had four children; the two older boys had married girls from north Florida and moved up there. Their daughter Martha, who was twenty-one, married a local boy, Jasper, and they lived with his parents.

Jasper, also twenty-one, had bought two acres of land about three miles from Pearl and Pearson, and he was building a house on it. He worked at a sawmill and the owner told Jasper he was the best worker he'd ever had. He let Jasper have the boards that were discards, some of which were only fit for burning, but some had a few feet of good lumber. Jasper would cut off the bad ends for firewood, and save the good pieces to use in building the house. He'd bought some lumber from the owner at a discount, and with that and the pieces he'd salvaged, he and his brother had the shell of the house almost finished. He worked on it after he got off from work, and all day Saturday when he didn't have to work at the sawmill. He was trying hard to get it to a point where they could move in because Martha was three months pregnant and they wanted to be in their own place when the baby was born.

The Clevelands had known Jasper's family for many years and they were pleased when Martha married him. They were proud of his work ethic and the way he provided for their daughter. They saw them at church every

Sunday morning, and had them over for Sunday dinner a couple of times a month.

Pearl always cooked a meal for them like those she cooked for other company—plenty of fresh vegetables, one or two kinds of pork, beef, or chicken, and fresh-baked biscuits or corn bread. Today, the table was spread with a pork roast, baked sweet potatoes, black-eyed peas cooked with ham, corn on the cob, sliced cucumbers, and corn bread fresh from the oven. A banana pudding cooled in the refrigerator for dessert.

After Pearson finished saying grace, Pearl said, "Ah aks Freeman ta come fuh dinner, but he say he busy. Whut could he be doin'?" Pearl had talked with her brother Freeman at church that morning.

"Dat's a good question," Pearson said.

"Ah 'on't know 'bout him," Pearl sighed. "James, he say Mis' Mac need some mo' wood cut. She wond'rin' kin ya go ovah dere dis week. She 'on't wanna wait till fall. Freeman say she been walkin' in dem ole piney woods an' dere's a bunch a fat pine on da groun'."

Pearl's and Freeman's father, Mr. Jackson, had been a sharecropper for the McClellan family and all his children were born in the sharecropper's house. When she was young, Pearl had worked some for Mrs. McClellan, occasionally filling in for her mother, who worked for her. Pearl mostly did their weekly laundry, which, with no electricity, had to be done on a washboard. Freeman had worked with his father on the farm when he was young, and after his father died, he'd become the sharecropper and he still worked for Miss Maggie McClellan.

"Mis' Mac doin' awright?" Martha asked. "She gittin' ole, ain't she?"

"Sebenny," Pearl replied. "Jes' like yo' Unc' Freeman. He be sebenny dis nex' Friday. But she keep huh head up an' she still movin'."

Maggie, whom the local whites called "Aunt Maggie," and the Negroes called "Mis' Mac," lived about half a mile down the road from the Clevelands. She still lived in the old white farmhouse where she was born, which, although large, was unpretentious. Everyone knew how Maggie had left her job as a teacher to stay home and care for her parents when they were elderly and sick, and how she tended the 150-acre farm after they died, and they all spoke highly of her. James had known her and worked for her off and on since he was a child, and he knew she was fair and honest, and open with her opinions. They'd developed a fondness for each other when he was little, which had lasted through the years. He looked forward to seeing her, and hoped to go Monday.

"Ya needs me in da mornin', Daddy?" James asked.

"Naw," Pearson replied. "Mr. Wilson wont me ta cut dat cover crop in dat Ah planted in da grove. Diskin' dat'll take da whole mornin' an' some a da aftanoon."

"Why ya do dat?" Martha asked. "Ain't dey 'nough ta do 'thout workin' fuh dat ole cracker?" She knew her father worked hard on the farm and thought he should be slowing down. "Ya almos' sixty, ya know."

"Ah see," Pearson replied, with a grin. "Well, le's 'on't push it now. Fifty-eight ain't sixty, an Ah ain't been put out ta pasture yet."

They all laughed.

"Well, it's true, Pearson," Pearl joined in. "Ya has a lotta work. Martha worries 'bout ya an' Ah does, too."

"Ah knows it, an' Ah knows whut Ah'm doin', too," Pearson said. "An' we kin use da money."

"His ole tractor e'em runnin'?" Pearl asked.

"Said 'tis," he replied. "He say da mechanic come out an' fix it."

"Well, Ah sho hope he fix it good," Pearl said. "Ya 'on't need ta spen' half yo' time messin' wit' dat sorry ole tractor."

As soon as James heard that Mis' Mac had work for him, he started thinking about money. "If Ah gits enough, Ah kin git sumpin nice fuh Saleena. Maybe git huh a purty necklace." He wanted to get back to the subject of going to Mis' Mac's.

"Well," he said. "Ah'm goin' ovah ta Mis' Mac's tomorrah mornin'. Me an' Harley talkin' 'bout goin' ta town Sadday an' Ah needs some money."

He knew if he worked four hours for Mis' Mac, she'd pay him $2.80. He hoped she'd need him to work more than four hours, which he'd do another day that week, so he'd be sure to have enough money. He had $2.00. He'd need to give Harley 25 cents for gas, and he'd like to get a haircut, which would be 50 cents. If he had enough, he might even buy some popcorn and a soda—maybe an orange Nehi.

Pearl noticed the smile on James's face. "Ya lookin' right pleased wit' yo'se'f," she said. "Looka him. Dat chile got sumpin up his sleeve."

Martha leaned against her mother laughing.

Jasper looked at James. "Yassuh! Ah seen dat look befo'."

"Dat his bran' new look," Pearson said.

"It ain't nuttin'," James protested. "Ah jes' likes goin' ta town."

Pearson chuckled low. "Ah see," he said. Then to Pearl, "Yep. Sumpin's up."

Pearl was smiling. "Uh-huh," she said in her knowing way.

"Anybody else ready fuh some 'nana puddin'?" James asked, standing up, and hoping to change the subject.

After a chorus of enthusiastic responses, Pearl said, "Brang it here ta da table," and they all forgot about him and Saleena.

♥   ♥   ♥

AFTER CHURCH THAT NIGHT AND A SNACK from the leftovers, including the banana pudding, James grabbed his cap from a nail on the porch wall and started for Harley's house. He wasn't even out of the yard when Shep joined him.

When James was little, he'd heard Red Foley singing "Old Shep," and had cried as he pictured a little boy kneeling beside a lifeless dog. He decided when he got a dog, he'd name him "Shep." When he heard Elvis Presley's version, he cried again, this time thinking of his own Shep.

They walked the mile along the straight dirt road that led to Harley's place—Shep often sniffing the ground, and James listening to birds and watching them fly around in the remaining daylight. Harley's father, who'd been a sharecropper, had died four years earlier, and his mother had died soon after. Harley and his wife, Ruby, had been living with his parents. Since he liked farming, he'd taken over as Mr. Hiers' sharecropper, and they'd remained in the house.

Mr. Hiers owned the land and paid the bills, Harley did the work, and they split the profits. Harley enjoyed planting seeds and watching them grow, and he enjoyed the work, even though it was hard and he didn't make much money. He also did other work for Mr. Hiers—repairing fences, doing carpentry, painting, or cutting wood—when he had time. That wasn't expected of a sharecropper, so he got paid for that work. And Harley always had some of his own vegetables growing in a garden behind the house.

As James approached, he saw him and Ruby sitting in the old wooden swing on their open front porch. Neither the swing nor the house had ever been painted and they were both the gray color of aged southern pine. Their house also sat on big blocks of pine.

Ruby was Freeman's daughter, so she and James were first cousins and they'd spent a lot of time together as they were growing up. She was three years older than James, and Harley was four years older. They'd been ahead of him in school, but Piney Woods was a small community and, with 115 children in the George Washington Carver School in grades 1–12, they all knew each other and didn't pay much attention to age. Ruby and Harley had been married for five years and had a ten-month-old son.

James saw their gray cat run around the corner of the house. Shep had never bothered her, but she had been chased by another dog and didn't trust Shep. She was due to have kittens soon, and James' mother had told Ruby she wanted one to replace their old cat, which had died a couple of months earlier.

James could hear their voices in casual conversation. The swing creaked, continuing its back and forth beat as he and Shep walked up the dirt path and up the three wooden steps with a blue hydrangea on each side. Shep went over to Harley and Ruby, wagging his tail, and they stopped swinging and patted him. After the greeting was over, he stretched out on the floor. Harley and Ruby just looked at James as he sat down in a rocking chair. Their friendship was as easy as the rhythm of the swing.

"Harley, you still plannin' on goin' ta town dis Sadday?"

"Hey ta you, too, James," Harley responded, grinning. "Sho, we goin'."

Ruby laughed. "Ya sho anxious ta git ta town. Ya afta sumpin, or somebody?" Harley laughed and Ruby laughed again as she leaned towards Harley and brushed his shoulder with hers.

James studied the floor. "Well, Ah . . . uhh . . . Ah . . ."

"Looka him, Harley," Ruby giggled. "Ya ever see James tongue-tied?"

Harley chuckled, stretched out one leg, and pushed the rocker with his bare foot. "Ain't nuttin' but a gal make a boy look like dat dere! Ya got it bad, boy!"

James nodded his head slowly. "You right, Harley," he admitted. "Ah cain't har'ly thank a nuttin' else no mo'."

"Do Saleena know ya done gon' crazy ovah huh?" Ruby asked.

"Prob'ly," James acknowledged. "Ah ain't hid nuttin' from 'er."

Ruby persisted, "Dat ain't whut Ah aks ya. Do she know hi ya feel?"

"Naw. Ah'm 'fraid she 'on't like me da same," James replied softly.

"Yeah, Ah 'member dat feelin'," Ruby said. She knew Saleena liked James. She could tell by the way she looked at him, and she was amazed that James didn't see it.

"Ah thank dat gal like ya, James. She sit right by ya at church, an' she wouldn' do dat if she ain't like ya."

James thought about that for a minute. "She so purty," he said. "All da boys likes huh." He studied the floorboards as though he might find something helpful there. "All dem boys at school wonts huh."

"Who she sit wit', James? YOU!" Ruby said, exasperated. "Ah done tol' ya befo', she wouldn' sit wit' ya if she ain't like ya. G'wan now an' tell dat gal hi ya feelin'."

"Mebbe Ah will," James said. He was thinking that she'd know how he felt if he gave her a necklace, so maybe he'd tell her then. It seemed like the perfect time.

"Us went ovah ta Daddy's yestiddy," Ruby said. "Ah'm gon' have a party fuh 'im on Friday. Tell Aunt Pearl an' Unc' Pearson. He 'on't go out at night, so us gon' have a dinner. Rosella an' Junior cain't e'em come 'cause dey workin'."

"Ah could git 'im an' take 'im home," James offered.

"Naw, it ain't dat. He say he go ta bed early 'cause he be ti'ed," Ruby said. "Ah thank he sick."

"Might be," James said, shaking his head. "A party be nice. Jes' might make 'im feel better."

Harley sat quietly, listening to the two of them talking. He waited until they both fell silent before he spoke.

"Abraham say dey hirin' at da mine."

James' head jerked up. "Fuh real?" he asked, with a broad smile.

He'd been hoping to get a job with the phosphate company ever since he graduated from high school the previous year. It was about the only opportunity in the area for employment and they hadn't hired for a couple of years. Harley had told James he'd ask his sister's husband, who worked at the mine, to let him know if they started hiring.

"Yeah, fuh real. He jes' tol' me today," Harley answered. They sometimes went to his sister's church and spent the day with her family. "Ah wuz gon' go ta y'all house ta let ya know if ya didn' come ovah here. Job prob'ly start in a couple weeks. Ya wanna go out dere?"

"Ah sho do," James responded immediately. "Whut Ah got ta do?"

"Go see boss man. He in da big office up dere," Harley said. "He name Mr. Roberts."

"Sho will," James said. "Soon's Ah can. Ah'm goin' ta Mis' Mac's tomorrah, an' Daddy gon' have da truck—he workin' at Mr. Wilson's—so Ah kin go Tuesday. Ah sho will. Been waitin' a long time fuh dis."

"Ah knows," Harley said. "Now, wanna play some checkahs?"

"Ya knows Ah always wants ta play checkahs," James responded. "Ya better git yo' head on straight 'cause Ah'm gon' whip yo' butt. Jes' got time fuh two games, 'cause Ah'm goin' ta Mis' Mac's early."

Harley went to get the checkerboard.

"Hi lil junior doin'?" James asked Ruby about their ten-month-old son.

"Dat boy inta mo' stuff ever'day," Ruby complained. "But he fun. Wish he wadn' sleepin' so ya could see 'im."

"Me, too," James responded. "Seem like he been sleepin' ever time Ah'm here. Only see 'im at church."

"Y'all wont some lemonade?" Ruby asked. "Ah'm gon' look in on 'im."

Harley had insisted on naming the baby after Ruby. She'd had two miscarriages, and the pregnancy had not been easy, and he said she deserved that, at least. So they named him Rubin.

Shep followed her and she gave him some water and a leftover biscuit. He'd learned that Ruby was good for a handout, and he dogged her steps.

Ruby gave the men the lemonade, and sat in the swing looking at a *Companion* magazine from January of 1942 that her friend Sadie had given her. Sadie said the white woman she worked for must have thought she could part with it since it was fifteen years old. Ruby cut out recipes and put them in a drawer, but most called for ingredients she didn't have. Flipping the pages, she occasionally commented on a picture.

Shep resumed his position on the floor and settled down for a nap. James and Harley sat on the floor with the checkerboard between them, each with a leg dangling over the edge of the porch. They usually played quietly until one of them made a really smart move; then they made enough noise to make the sleeping dog open his eyes. To them, playing checkers was serious business.

Suddenly, James burst out laughing. "Awright, Ah'm in da kingdom, Harley. Now put a crown on 'im."

Harley moaned.

"Y'all know whut?" Ruby closed the magazine. "Dere mus' be hun'erds a pitchas in dis magazine, an' dey's only two coloreds. A man carryin' suitcases an' a lil boy look like he leadin' a band a white boys." She thumbed through the magazine. "Looka dis pitcha here."

"Looka dat boy standin' on a stack a books," Harley said, with a big smile on his face, "an' leadin' dem white boys."

"Where dat at?" James asked.

Ruby looked at the caption. "New York," she said. "No wondah. Ah knowed it wadn' here."

"Dat fuh sho," James said as he turned back to the checkerboard. "Thangs diff'unt dere."

"Thank thangs ever be like dat here?" Harley asked.

"'On't look like it," James said, shaking his head. "But Rev'ren' King doin' his best, an' udder peoples, too."

Ruby closed the magazine again. "Looka da back a dis magazine," she said, holding it up.

James and Harley both looked, but saw nothing interesting, so they turned back to their game.

"See dat white woman. Say she a 'charmin' member of a fine ole Southern fam'ly.' She 'pose' ta be rich, an' look, she talkin' 'bout cigarettes. Looka huh, dressed ta kill, dat blon' hair all done up fine, an' smokin' a cigarette."

They both looked again briefly.

"Preacher say smokin' a sin," James said.

"Dat whut mah daddy said," Harley added.

"An' dey put da names a fifteen high-class womens from all ovah da country. Say 'A few a da many udder distinguish' women who prefer Camel cigarettes.' Ain't dat sumpin!"

"Ain't very high class!" Harley said. "Dey jes' sinnin' 'gainst God."

"Mah frien' Sadie say Miz Jones smoke," Ruby said, "Dat da white woman Sadie work fuh. She hide huh smokin'—'on't wont nobody ta know 'bout it. She leave huh cigarettes home when she go out."

"Preacher say it's a sin," James said again.

"Prob'ly is," Ruby said.

"Oh no, you cain't do dat now!" James exclaimed as Harley burst into laughter. "Ruby, he done took mah king." He playfully punched Harley on the arm, and noticed that Shep had opened his eyes.

Harley clapped his hands. "Ya been payin' too much 'tention ta huh," he teased.

James rubbed the back of his neck. "Awright, Ruby," James warned. "Ah'm playin' checkahs now. Dis boy gon' tear me up if Ah 'on't keep mah eye on dis checkahboard."

Ruby laughed, resting her hand on his shoulder. Then she took her magazine into the house.

"Brang us some mo' lemonade," Harley called. She took the pitcher to the porch, filled their glasses, and went back inside.

James beat Harley in both games. They were actually evenly matched, so James was pleased. Harley said love must be making James' brain work better, or maybe just being around Saleena was having a good effect on him.

He said being in love might help James with Mr. Roberts at the mine, and he added that James would need all the help he could get. "Mr. Roberts 'on't take ta coloreds much," Harley said. "Only hire one a us if dey needs somebody fuh da jobs whites 'on't want."

"Ain't no s'prise dere. Ah'm gon' ack right," James assured him. "Whut Ah oughta wear? My Sund'y-go-ta-meetin' clothes?"

"Jes' wear reg'lar stuff," Harley said.

"Okeedokee." They were silent for a minute before James added, "Well, guess Ah bes' git goin'," and they both stood up.

"Awright," Harley said, and he picked up the checkerboard and took it inside.

James stuck his head in and called, "Thanks fuh da lemonade, Ruby."

"Any time, James. Any time," she responded.

James heard her say, "Ah'm goin' ta bed Harley; Ah'm ti'ed."

Shep jumped in the back of Harley's pick-up truck as soon as the two men started down the porch steps.

"Ole Shep know da drill," Harley said.

"Yep," James replied.

As they drove along, James asked, "Hi many times you seen whites on dis here road, Harley?"

"'On't take but one time wit' da wrong ones," Harley answered.

"Dat da truf," James replied. "Ah knows dat fuh sho." He hesitated. "But Ah been thankin'. Now on, Ah'm gon' be walkin' home 'less it's col' or rainin'. Ah got Shep wit' me an' Ah knows ta be careful."

"Ah 'on't know, James," Harley said.

"Ah knows," James replied. "Ain't gon' let da white man change mah life no mo'. Ah got me a good flashlight an' Ah got my dog Shep. Got me some good ears, too. An' ya know ya kin hear a car comin' a mile away out here. Now on, Ah be walkin' home."

"Awright," Harley agreed reluctantly. "But Ah be watchin' an' if a car or strange truck dat 'on't live 'roun' here come down dis here road, Ah be comin', too'."

"Okeedokee," James agreed. "But whut ya gon' do?"

"Ah 'on't know, but Ah be dere."

"Dat make ya feel better, Shep?" he asked, looking back at his dog.

Harley smiled, and shook his head. "Git on now."

"Harley," James said softly, "dey's only 'bout a hun'erd yards on dis here road dat ain't got no trees, an' if Ah hears a car, Ah kin run dat far 'fore anybody see me. Ain't worryin' 'bout it no mo'." Then he added, "An' Ah got Shep."

Harley smiled. "Yeah," he said with doubt in his voice, "'less he smell a rabbit. Den he gon' take care a him."

James laughed. "Dat fuh sho!"

As they stopped at the house, Harley asked, "Whut yo' Mama an' Daddy gon' say 'bout dat?"

"Ain't tellin' 'em," James said. "Jes' doin' it." He knew well what they would say.

When he went to bed, he didn't think he'd ever fall asleep. He'd seen Saleena that day, he'd won both checker games with Harley, the mine was finally hiring, he was going to work for Mis' Mac the next morning, and he was going to Lakeland on Saturday to buy a necklace for Saleena.

He thought briefly about his conversation with Harley and then thought about what had happened on the road that Sunday night almost a year earlier. "Gotta git past dat," he thought. "Ah has ta trust God an' Shep an' mahse'f."

Eventually, his thoughts shifted to Saleena and what he'd buy for her on Saturday. He wanted to buy her a nice necklace, but had no idea what was available in the dime store. When he realized he'd be near Lakeland when he applied for the job on Tuesday, he decided he'd go to the store then to see if he could find something special for her. He might even buy it if he had enough money—then he wouldn't have to go Saturday, unless he wanted to.

He pictured Saleena seeing the necklace and looking at him with her beautiful smile and shining eyes. She'd be so happy. She'd kiss him and tell him how much she liked the necklace . . . and him. And he finally went to sleep, with a smile in his heart.

Monday

JAMES WAS UP BEFORE SUNRISE, even before the rooster crowed. He took time to eat a big bowl of cereal, though, because Maggie McClellan did not like to be awakened by the sound of an axe striking wood. James knew that from experience. He heard movement in his parents' bedroom, called to them that he was going to Mis' Mac's, and left without seeing them.

Shep was asleep on his blanket when his master entered the kitchen, but he hopped up, wagging his tail, and licked his hand. James knew he wanted to go with him, but sometimes Shep ran off at Maggie's, just as he did at home, and James didn't want to have to think about him.

James went to the backyard and picked an orange to eat on his walk to Maggie's. They had a Hamlin tree, an early orange, so its fruit was gone, and a Valencia tree, a late orange, which he knew would still be nice and juicy. He stopped for a moment and watched a big black and yellow spider working on a web. A moth carcass dangled from the edge. "Bad luck, Mr. Moth," he said. He took out his pocketknife and peeled the orange as he walked. He stopped when a droplet of acid flew into his eye. "Damn," he said, rubbing his eye. "Ah hate dat." He carefully removed the white pulp, put the knife back in his pocket, and ate the orange slice by slice. "Dis good," he thought. "Shoulda got me two a 'em."

By the time he walked the half-mile to her house, the sun was up and so was Maggie. She opened the screen door and walked onto the back porch, which wasn't screened in. Her back was straight and her steps perky. She had on a plain, lavender dress and her gray hair was braided and wrapped neatly around her head, her face radiant, ready for the day.

Maggie liked to have a colorful yard. She had a row of red hibiscus by the side of the house, which was painted white, and she'd planted some yellow marigolds in front of them. And to keep the grass out, in front of the flowers was a row of red bricks, standing on their corners. Her small lawn consisted of Bermuda grass, which had planted itself there; of course, like a weed, it came up all over, but the lawn was mowed and neat.

In the front yard, there was a large oak tree with Spanish moss hanging from its limbs, and in the back yard stood three tall longleaf pines. Maggie had scattered some pink and white azaleas amongst the pine trees, and they bloomed beautifully in the spring, but were through blooming before May. She also had some fruit trees in the back yard: two Florida cherries which had ripe red fruit on them, a red guava and a white guava, each with some ripe fruit, and a persimmon tree with green fruit. Behind the shorter cherry and guavas were two loquat trees with only a smattering of orange loquats left. A six-foot tall lemon tree, covered with green and yellow fruit, stood with drooping branches by the woodshed near the back porch. Freeman, Maggie's sharecropper, had built the woodshed when he was eighteen. It had three sides and a roof, but the front was open so the wood was easily accessible.

By the garage were some pineapple plants, three of which were adorned with green pineapples, and a tangerine tree with tiny green tangerines and a smattering of ripe ones. Behind the garage was a large avocado tree her father had planted, hoping to protect it from any cold winter wind. Every time Maggie picked an avocado, she remembered how pleased he'd been when he picked the first one. She loved having such a variety of fruit, and thought everybody who lived in Florida should have some fruit trees—at least an orange tree.

The driveway by the lawn led to a garage with no door, which was set back from the house. The little dirt road that went past the garage and to the sharecropper's house separated the yard from the orange grove. Near the road was a small pile of cut oak wood that was waiting to be split.

James took his cap off when he saw Maggie and held it in his hands in front of him as he'd learned long ago from watching his father and his uncle Freeman. "She a good-lookin' ole white woman," he thought.

She greeted him warmly, her green eyes sparkling, "James, you're a sight for sore eyes! I was hopin' you'd come today. How are you doin'?"

"Fine, Mis' Mac. How you doin'?"

"I'm just fine, James. Just fine. How are your mama an' daddy?"

"Dey doin' fine, too, Mis' Mac."

"I'm glad," she said. "I haven't seen Pearl since March when she came to help me with spring cleanin'. After all the washin' of screens an' windows an' floors, she probably hasn't wanted to come back here." She laughed. "Well, isn't it a beautiful day?"

"Sho is," he agreed. "Ah wuz jes' thankin' dat on da walk over." He was, part of the time, but most of the time he was thinking about Saleena.

He thought of her smile, and how her nose wrinkled a little when she smiled; he always had an urge to kiss that spot. "She a fine mama," he'd thought as he visualized the body that he longed to run his fingers over and explore. "Ah cain't har'ly thank a nuttin' else but huh." But he did notice that it was a beautiful day. The morning air was cool and refreshing—not hot yet—and the blue sky was clear and massive looking.

"I had half a grapefruit with some honey on it with my breakfast, an' there's still a half left," Maggie said. "Do you want it?"

"No, thank ya, ma'am" he replied. "Ah done awready ate."

She pointed to her wood shed. "You know my woodpile got mighty low this past winter."

"Ah'll soon fix dat," James assured her.

"I know you will. An' after you've worked for a while, we'll have a watermelon break. Freeman will pick one for us.

"Ah sho 'preciate it," James said, smiling. He'd wondered if it was too early for the melons to be ripe. Maggie was the only person James knew who still grew strawberry watermelons. The basketball sized, dark green balls of fruit had deep red flesh that was flavorful and sweet, sweet, sweet. Most people had stopped growing them because they were too breakable to be shipped, and they had to be handled so carefully the farmers could hardly get them to the local farmers' market in one piece. But Freeman always planted some for Maggie from seeds he saved every year.

"James," she said, "I think you'll find more lighter in the middle part of the woods. I know it's further to have to haul it out, but we need to get it out of there sometime."

Maggie was the only person James knew who called it "lighter." He figured since she called it that, it was probably the proper word. Everybody else he knew called the aged Southern pinewood that was full of sap "lighterd."

"Yes'm, dat ain't nuttin' but da truf. Well, Mis' Mac, Ah be back here in a while," he said, and Maggie went back into the house.

James went to the shed to get her axe and wheelbarrow. He put the axe in the wheelbarrow and pushed it into the nearby longleaf pine forest. He was cautious around the clumps of saw palmettos that grew on the edge of the woods. "Any a you rattlesnakes in dere?" he asked, smiling mischieviously as he skirted around the palmettos.

In the woods, the forest was still and quiet except for the birds singing their salutations to the new day. The pines provided a carpet of long light-brown needles, which kept out most undergrowth except for a few low-growing plants here and there, and the needles were littered with large pine cones. Most of the limbs were on the top part of the trees, so there were none to impede walking. James loved the tall, stately trees: the smell of the sap, the long green needles, the pine cones, and the reddish-brown scaly bark. He often felt awed by the majestic trees, some of which were almost a hundred feet tall.

He began picking up the pieces of wood, limbs which had fallen from the trees, and with time had turned into lighter. Full of resin, the wood made starting a fire easy. It must have got its name from its fire starting capability, certainly not its weight; it was heavy wood. Lighter burned fast and hot, and oak burned slowly, so the mix made a great fire.

James found some lighter knots and other short pieces that wouldn't need to be chopped, and he chopped some longer ones so they wouldn't fall off the wheelbarrow. When it was as full as he could get it, with pieces of wood hanging over the edges, he sat down to rest next to one of the big old pines. He picked up some of the brown needles, which were almost a foot long, and just held them, running his fingers along them. He took his cap off, leaned back against the tree, and looked up at the brown limbs, green needles, and small patches of blue sky visible through the trees.

After a little while, a pair of cardinals lit in a tree near him and he watched them without moving a muscle. He loved their bright red color against the dark green of the pine needles. He whistled softly the cardinal's song, which reminded him of the whistle he used to call Shep. The cardinals turned their heads from side-to-side looking for the source of the whistle. After a little while, the male cardinal answered him, still looking around. He and James whistled back and forth a few times before James threw the pine needles into the air and watched the cardinals fly away. Then he put his cap on and went back to work.

It was not easy pushing the heavy load through the forest, but it was much easier than carrying the wood. The trees were too close together in some places to drive a vehicle through, so the wheelbarrow was the only way to get the wood out. He emptied it and looked on the back porch to see if Maggie had left a glass for him. She'd usually leave either lemonade, iced tea, or water when he was working with the wood. She knew it was a hard job that made him sweaty and thirsty. Sure enough, a glass of cool lemonade was waiting and James drank it happily before going back for another load.

Maggie still had a lot of oak left that James and Harley had sold her. The two of them had permission to cut trees from Mr. Hiers' land beside Harley's house, and they usually cut enough wood for their own use and for Maggie, using an axe and an old, two-person cross-cut saw. All of them still used a fireplace or wood stove to heat their homes, but Maggie also had a small electric heater that she used in her bedroom on the really cold mornings. Like her neighbors, she was sensitive to the cold. She would dress for bed in the living room in front of her fireplace, and then go get into her quilt-covered bed. In the morning, the house would be about the same temperature as it was outside, and she would get up and turn on the heater, climb back into the warm bed, and let the bedroom get warm before getting up, dressing, and building a fire in the fireplace. Fortunately, Florida winters are short and mild.

Freeman would help James cut the longer pieces of oak with the two-person saw when Harley was busy. He could only pull the saw for a little while before he had to stop and rest. James would have pushed the saw while Freeman was pulling it if the saw would have allowed it, but the long blade would bend. James would use the axe to split the large oak pieces until Freeman said he was ready to go again. He didn't like to work that way, but he was concerned about his uncle. After a while, he'd figure Freeman had probably had enough and James would say he had other work to do, or make up some other excuse to go home. Freeman's expression wouldn't change, but James could hear him breathe a sigh of relief.

When he returned with the second load, James started chopping the long pieces. Most of what he'd got was small enough to be chopped easily with an axe. After he cut some, he loaded a mixture of oak and pine onto the wheelbarrow and pushed it to the woodshed.

He was not surprised to see Maggie's orange cat lying on top of the little bit of wood that remained in the shed. "'Lo, Tommy," James said, "ya takin' care a da rats 'roun' here?" The big, eight-year-old tomcat flopped over on his back and purred, waiting for James to rub his belly. Tommy was the son of a cat that Maggie had for sixteen years and Maggie said Tommy was the best mouser she'd ever had. After James petted the cat for a little while, he took him off the woodpile and tried to shoo him away. "Scat, Tommy," he said a few times. However, Tommy did not leave, but rubbed against James' legs, purring.

James moved the old wood to one side of the shed, and piled the wood from the wheelbarrow where it had been. It would've been easier to work without Tommy at his feet, but he was patient with the cat.

He was thirsty again, and as he worked, he was feeling ready for a watermelon break. He wondered if Mis' Mac knew he was back from the woods and he stacked the wood a little more noisily than usual hoping she would hear him and cut the melon. It must have worked because when he got to the shed with the second load, the melon, two spoons, and a large knife lay on the table on the back porch.

When James was almost through unloading the wheelbarrow, Maggie called, "Ready for a break, James?"

"Yes'm, Ah sho is," he replied. He threw the last pieces on the pile, and removed his cap as he walked to the porch.

"Well, just wash up an' we'll sit a spell an' have the first melon of the year," Maggie said as he went up the steps and to the hand pump on the side of the porch.

♥   ♥   ♥

A WHITE ENAMEL WASH PAN WITH A RED RIM, and a matching enamel bucket half full of water, sat on a stand at the edge of the porch. Maggie had indoor plumbing, but she left the pump there because it had always been there, and it was handy. James took the dipper from the nail where it hung next to the bucket and poured some water into the pan. A bar of soap was in a dish next to the pan, and he washed his hands and arms and rinsed the sweat from his face and neck. He felt cooled and refreshed.

After he dried himself with the line-dried, fresh-smelling towel, he threw the dirty water into the back yard near where three Rhode Island Red chickens were scratching in the sand. James smiled as they scurried away squawking loudly, as he knew they would. He put a little more water in the pan, swished it around, and threw it out. Then he poured a dipper full of water into the old pump to prime it, and pumped the bucket full. He liked to do little things like that for Maggie, and she appreciated it.

On the porch were four straight back chairs, a table, and three rocking chairs. Maggie sat waiting in the rocker with a leather seat and back. Two spoons rested on her apron.

"I saved the honor for you, James," she told him.

"Thank ya, ma'am." he said, and smiled. She knew he loved cutting the strawberry melons. He'd stick the knife in gently and try to cut some before the melon burst. Often it would split in front of the knife as soon as he stuck it into the melon. Today was no exception. As soon as the knife was in, it split enough that he could see the beautiful red flesh and smell the heavenly aroma. His mouth watered so much he had to swallow.

"Hurry up, James," Maggie teased. "My mouth's waterin'."

"Mine, too," he said as he finished cutting it. They both laughed.

"Smells like a good one," Maggie observed, as she moved to the table.

"I noticed old Tommiecat was helpin' you with the wood," she said.

James laughed. "He's a mighty big he'p, awright."

They each took a half of the melon and ate it with a spoon. The table was near the edge of the porch, and as they ate, they spit the seeds into the yard. The three Rhode Island Red chickens had returned and were now joined by a big shiny black rooster, two white hens, and three black pullets. Maggie kept enough chickens to provide eggs for herself and Freeman.

As she and James spit the seeds, the chickens would run from one seed to the next, trying to get it before another one did. The rooster was quite aggressive, so James would spit his seed away from the bunch so all of the chickens had a chance.

Maggie had taught James, when he was little, how to hold a seed between his thumb and index finger and squeeze it so that it would shoot. When he was younger, they'd have contests to see who could make them go further. Now, as Maggie watched, James shot a couple. One hit the rooster, and he jumped and squawked.

"That was a good one, James!" Maggie exclaimed, laughing.

James was always pleased at the way she enjoyed simple things like that, and he did things that he thought would amuse her. She was the only older person he knew who played like that.

"Dere wuz a bunch a lighterd out dere, Mis' Mac," he said. He looked at Maggie, who had a line of watermelon juice running down her chin.

"I thought you'd find a lot," she said as she wiped her chin with the back of her hand. "Freeman picked a good melon, didn't he?"

"He sho did!" James exclaimed. "Ah wuz lookin' for'd ta dis while Ah wuz workin' out dere, an' it wuz worf all da waitin'."

"It sure is sweet," she said.

Maggie looked at the chickens running around after the seeds. "Look at the little black pullets shining in the sun. They're just like the rooster."

"Dey sho purty. Are dey layin' yet?" James asked.

"Not yet. But it's just as well because we don't need the eggs right now," she replied.

For a couple of minutes, neither of them spoke. They just enjoyed the sweet, juicy melon. Then he broke the silence.

"Dey's hirin' out at da mine,"

"That's great, James," she said enthusiastically. "I'm sure you're plannin' to apply for a job."

"Yes'm. Ah been waitin' fuh dis. Ah'm goin' out dere tomorrah."

"Well, let me know how you make out. I know Carl Roberts, an' he can be a difficult man." she warned, "Be extra careful with him."

"Ah done heared ever' word dat ya say," James assured her. "Ah'm gon' be careful. Ya needn' worry 'bout dat."

"If you get that job, James, you'll have a regular income then, an' you'll have money to manage. Be sure you spend it wisely an' save some," she advised. "You always need some for a rainy day."

She paused and shot a seed at a chicken that was chasing another one away. She missed it. "There's a funny thing about money," she said. "Just like time, it comes an' it goes. Money's hard to come by, but easy to go through." She shot another seed past the chickens, and they ran after it.

James nodded. "Ah done learnt dat. You right." He shot a couple of seeds just to see how far they'd go.

When they finished eating the melon, they scraped the rind with their spoons. After they ate the scrapings, they picked up the fleshless rinds and drank the remaining juice. Neither of them cared if they got some on their chins; they'd just go to the water stand and wash it off.

When they were through eating, after Maggie washed her hands and chin, she said, as she always did, "I think I won the contest today, James."

"Ah 'on't know now, Mis' Mac," he said challengingly.

"Do you want to measure?" she asked, and they both laughed, looking at the ground and the chickens that had eaten all of the evidence.

Maggie started the routine when James was seven. Pearl had been sewing for her for several years and she usually had James with her. They'd shared watermelons before, but Maggie had waited until she thought James was old enough to either spit the seeds or shoot them before she started the routine. At first, he couldn't shoot them, so they'd spit them as far as possible. Maggie thought he was so cute trying to spit the seeds further than her. And Pearl, refusing to join in the silliness, would laugh at the two of them.

There were always chickens in the yard eating the seeds, but the first time she said she thought she won the contest, James scared the chickens away and looked for some seeds. Maggie figured, as he got older, that if she wasn't too big to do it, James wasn't either and they both enjoyed the game. Of course, if anyone else was there, it was either Pearl or Freeman. Neither James nor Maggie was embarrassed to act childish in front of them.

When James was nine, Maggie began paying him to do simple work for her when he was with Pearl, like pulling weeds from her vegetable and flower gardens and raking the yard. He was thrilled; at nine, he was no stranger to work, but he'd never been paid for it. He worked with his dad and brothers on their farm, but Pearson had never paid any of them for work they did. He and Pearl figured, as the other farmers did and as their parents had, that it was the children's responsibility. So James was happy to be able to do the same kind of work he did at home and get paid.

Then as Freeman got older, Maggie could tell he was slowing down and she wanted to lighten his workload, so she talked to Pearl about James doing more. He was fourteen. Pearl was enthusiastic—she knew he'd be treated well by Maggie, who'd let them know when she had work for him. His agreement with his parents was that they got half of the money he made, and he had to save half of his, but he didn't mind. He felt good having a little money in his pocket and a little saved. When he graduated from high school at eighteen, they told him he could keep all of the money he made, provided he saved at least half for his future; however, as long as he lived at home, he'd be expected to work on the farm.

After James threw the empty rinds to the chickens and washed his hands and chin, he went back to work. He hauled out another load of wood, chopped and split some more, and put it in the woodshed. He put the axe and wheelbarrow back in the tool shed, and went to the house to tell Maggie that he was finished. He called her and waited in the yard with his cap in his hand. "Mis' Mac, Ah finished fuh today."

"I'll be right there, James," she called and soon appeared on the porch with her pocketbook in her hand. James had been there four hours, and Maggie never deducted anything for the break time. So he figured he'd get $2.80.

"James, I'm sorry," she said, "but I don't have the right change. I don't suppose you'd have change for a five in your work clothes."

"No, ma'am," he said, but thought, "Wish Ah did. Ah ain't got change nowhere fuh no five." He didn't even think about his savings because he couldn't touch that. "But Ah kin prob'ly come back here on Wednesday," he said. "Da shed be 'bout half full."

He thought, "If Ah gits dat job, Ah might start nex' week, so Ah needs ta git huh wood ready."

"That would be good, James," she said. "I do have a dollar bill. Let me give you that."

"Dat's awright Mis' Mac, ma'am. Ah'll jes' wait till Wednesday."

"All right then. Tell your mama I have some sewin' for her, if she's interested, but I'd like her to come visit me, anyway. I haven't seen her in weeks."

"Yes'm, Ah sho will, but she purty busy doin' cannin' an' puttin' stuff in da freezer right now."

"Maybe later, then. Is your daddy still workin' in Mr. Wilson's grove?"

"Off an' on, but not a awful lot," he answered. "He got plenty ta do right dere on da farm."

"Here comes Freeman now to drive you home," she said. And as James started to protest, she added, "It's too hot for you to walk all that way. Besides, there's a melon for your mama an' daddy. You wouldn't want to have to tote that all the way home."

"Ruby be plannin' a party for Unc' Freeman on his birfday," James said.

"Yes, he told me," Maggie replied. "I'm so glad. He'll enjoy that."

Freeman pulled up in the noisy old Model A Ford truck and the few chickens scattered that had wandered into the driveway. "Looks like I'll have to buy a new truck soon," Maggie said. "That thing's fallin' apart."

James stood thinking for a moment. "Lemme know if ya gon' buy one. Ah might wanna buy dat ole one," he said, amazed at the words coming out of his mouth.

"You'll be the first to know, James," she said. "Don't worry."

James loved that old truck. He remembered riding around the farm in it when he was little. His uncle Freeman held him on his lap and let him hold the steering wheel, and when he got bigger, he taught him how to shift the gears. "Unc' Freeman learnt me ta drive in dat truck," he thought. Nevertheless, he was wondering how he could afford to buy even an old rattletrap like that. If he got the job at the phosphate mine, which was twenty miles away, he'd need transportation. To afford transportation, he needed a job. He hoped Mis' Mac would let him make monthly payments on the truck, which would be no problem if he got the job.

As he opened the truck door, he smiled and called, "Thank ya fuh da bes' watermelon in da whole worl'."

Maggie laughed and waved. "Remember to tell Pearl I'd like to see her." She could hear Freeman laughing, too. She stood on the porch and watched them drive away before going back into the house. It was a simple, childlike tradition she and James had had for twelve years, and it still brought her joy. She loved James and always looked forward to his coming. She'd actually waited until Freeman told her some of the melons were ripe before asking him to tell Pearl about the work.

Sometimes she'd give James work that she knew Freeman could still do, but she figured with that one stone, she was killing three birds:

Freeman didn't have to do the work, James could use the money, and it was a good deed on her part. She wasn't rich, but she had more than most, and even though Maggie didn't go to church—and considered a lot of people who did hypocrites—she did believe in the principles of Christianity and she thought it her duty to share what she had.

She'd put Freeman on a monthly salary a few years earlier when she thought he was no longer capable of sharecropping. Now, he looked after the cows, took care of the orange grove, and planted a vegetable garden large enough for her and him every spring and fall. There wasn't much to do with the cows, and the orange grove just required fertilizing and disking. When it needed to be sprayed, Maggie would get someone else to come and do that. Freeman had usually been able to handle the work, but James took care of the wood, and anything extra. Whenever she thought Freeman needed help, she called on James.

"No sense in waitin'," Maggie said to herself. "We'll go to town this week—maybe Thursday—and I'll buy a new truck. Then James can have that old one. Bless his heart, I don't know how much longer that old thing will run, but he probably knows how to fix it." She smiled. "And if he doesn't, no doubt he'll learn."

The old truck rattled more than usual with the bumps in the dirt road. James took the watermelon off the seat and held it in his lap, making sure that it would survive the trip. After their initial greeting, he and his Uncle Freeman rode without speaking, each of them deep in thought.

James hadn't seen Freeman for over a month except at church, and that was a fast greeting because he was so intent on spending every minute with Saleena. As he looked at him now, he was thinking about how he seemed to be slipping. For a long time, hard work had made Freeman short of breath, and James noticed as Freeman drove the truck that he seemed to shift the gears more slowly. More importantly, he seemed to have lost his enthusiasm. James studied his face as he drove. "Use'ly he be talkin'," he thought. And he realized something else: "An' da light done gon' outta his eyes."

Finally, he asked, "How ya gittin' 'long, Unc' Freeman?"

"Well, awright, Ah guess," Freeman replied.

James frowned. "Jes' doin' awright?"

"Well, Ah ain't been feelin' good as usual, but it prob'ly ain't nuttin'," Freeman assured him.

"Ya go ta see da doctor?"

"Naw. It ain't dat bad."

As they arrived at the house, James said, "Ah bet ya anythang Mama's 'spectin' you ta come fuh dinner. Come on in da house, Unc' Freeman, an' sit down at da table wit' us."

"Ah cain't do it today, but mebbe one day later on dis week. Ah'd like ta sit fer a spell."

"Wednesday Ah'm goin' back ta Mis' Mac's ta work. Ah'm gon' tell Mama you be comin' Wednesday."

"Awright," Freeman agreed.

"Awright, den. Take care a yo'se'f, Unc' Freeman," James said solicitously, as he got out of the truck.

"Ah be awright," Freeman replied. "Tell ya Mama Ah see huh Wednesday."

James found his mother in the kitchen. "Hey, Mama," he said.

"Hey, baby," Pearl said, with a smile. "Hi Mis' Mac?"

"She fine. She sent ya dis here watermelon," he said as he gently put the melon on the floor.

"Oh! dat's a purty one!" Pearl said. "You an' huh have one?"

"Yes'm," James said, smiling.

"You two!" Pearl laughed. "Whut a pair!"

"Dat whut me an' Mis' Mac does. We eats da watermelon, an' da chickens eats da seeds an' da rine. An' Ah won today! Mis' Mac 'on't thank so, but Ah outspit an' outshot huh today."

"An' ya proud a dat, e'em though you's a lot younger, an' ya got a lot mo' wind," Pearl said, poking him in the belly. "Unh, unh, unh."

He grinned. "Mis' Mac 'on't thank so."

"Bof y'all crazy!" she laughed.

James' face turned serious. "Mama, ya thank sumpin wrong wit' Unc' Freeman?"

"Well," Pearl replied. "He ain't no spring chicken no mo'. He done slowed down now. Ain't nuttin' like he use' ta be."

"He sho ain't. Ah thank sumpin wrong wit' 'im."

"Well, dere might be," Pearl said. "Ever'thang in da worl' changes when ya git ole."

James went to the bathroom to wash off the remaining dirt from the morning's work. He was still thinking about Freeman, and when he looked in the mirror, he was surprised to see tears in his eyes. Freeman had lived on Maggie's place James' whole life, and James had spent a lot of time with him—visiting with him and working with him. He couldn't imagine not having his uncle Freeman around. That would change everything if he were no longer at Mis' Mac's.

And as Freeman drove the truck back, he thought about James' question. "Mebbe dey is sumpin wrong wit' me. But ain't nuttin' ta do 'bout it if dey is. A body git ole an' a body die. Whut diffunce do it make? Ah ain't got nuttin' ta live fuh, nohow."

♥ ♥ ♥

WHEN FREEMAN GOT BACK TO MAGGIE'S, he stopped to see if she had any work in mind for him to do. As he walked up to the porch he saw Maggie sitting in her rocking chair. He could tell she'd been crying, but he pretended not to notice.

"Ya got anythang fuh me ta do now, Mis' Maggie?" he asked, holding his cap in his hands.

"Come an' sit with me for a while," she said.

Freeman climbed the three steps to the porch and sat down at the top with his feet resting on the steps.

"You look tired, Freeman. Let me get you a cool drink of water," she said as she walked to the bucket.

She was surprised that he didn't object to her getting the water for him. Normally, he would not allow her to do even simple things like that for him. After all these years, he still was always careful to act "appropriately." So that reinforced what she already knew: he was not well.

"Well, mah ole clock might not be tickin' on time no mo'," he said, nodding his head.

Maggie laughed, glad that he injected a little lightness into the moment. "I'm afraid neither of us is as young as we used to be, Freeman. I'm older than you are, you know."

"Dat's right," he chuckled, "you sho is."

Busily pumping, she let the first water run into the wash pan; that water would sit there until she needed to wash her hands—Maggie McClellan didn't believe in wasting water or anything else. She lived, as her parents had, by the slogan, "Waste not, want not."

"James filled the bucket for me," she said as she filled the dipper with the cool water and took it to Freeman. "He always does that for me. He's such a sweetheart."

"He a good boy, dat James," Freeman agreed.

"He sure is." Maggie said.

He thanked her for the water, and he drank about half of it before tossing the rest in the yard. "Dat hit da spot," he said, handing her the dipper.

"I've got some soup on the stove that's ready to eat and I've got some cornbread fresh from the oven," she said. "I know you like my chicken an' rice soup, and I'll get us some. You just sit there, and I'll bring it right out."

Freeman stayed where he was mostly because he didn't feel like moving. Maggie often offered him lunch, but he seldom accepted. He was afraid the wrong people would find out and it might mean trouble for him—even though he was almost seventy years old—and it might hurt Maggie's reputation, even though she was seventy. He knew she wasn't concerned about herself, but he was concerned about her. He certainly didn't want her to have any trouble because of him.

When she brought the food out on a tray, he got up and sat at the table with her. Once, when he'd expressed concern about eating with her, Maggie said, "We're sittin' out here in the open. If anyone comes, it will be obvious that we're not hidin' anything. Everybody knows you work for me, Freeman." Nevertheless, Freeman continued to feel a little nervous about what might happen if a white person saw them eating together—a Negro man and a white woman. However, he was feeling bad enough then that he didn't even think about it.

When Freeman was born on the McClellan farm, his father was a sharecropper with Maggie's father. His mother worked in the field with his father, when she wasn't in the late stages of pregnancy, until their children got old enough to help him. Freeman was the first of eight, all of whom were born in the sharecropper's house, and Pearl, James' mother, was the last, thirteen years younger than Freeman.

Right after Mr. McClellan bought the farm, and before he hired Freeman's father, he fixed up the sharecropper's shack, which was about two hundred feet behind the McClellan's house. He knew other farmers who never made any improvements or repairs on their sharecroppers' houses, but he wanted his workers to have a decent house; he thought everyone deserved a decent place to live. He had walls put in what had been a one-room house so that there was a living room, kitchen, and bedroom, and he added a second bedroom. Freeman had two brothers who shared that bedroom with him. When a little girl was born, Mr. McClellan hired a carpenter to work with Freeman's father to add another bedroom, which they made large enough to fit two double beds.

The family eventually had five boys and three girls. The two older boys slept in one bed and the three younger boys slept in the other one. The three girls also slept in one bed. When they were short enough, they slept crossways on the beds so they had more space. But as the older ones got taller, they insisted on sleeping the right way on the bed, and the youngest one, who was in the middle, complained that there wasn't enough room. There wasn't, but nobody's feet were hanging over the side of the bed.

When the oldest boy got married, the three youngest celebrated because one of them could move into the other bed. Since Pearl was the youngest child and the last one at home, her sisters would tease her, "Gal, you git lost in dat big bed all by yo'se'f?"

As Freeman and the others were growing up, they noticed that other sharecropper's houses weren't as nice as theirs. And their parents commented frequently about what a good and honest man Mr. Mac was. He made out statements for Mr. Jackson itemizing expenses and sales of the produce. Then he subtracted the expenses and split the profits equally. None of the other farmers that they knew showed their sharecroppers any statements.

In addition to washing clothes for Mrs. McClellan, Freeman's mother also helped her when there was extra work to do, like canning or cooking for company; she'd help with the preparation and cooking on the wood stove, but Mrs. McClellan felt responsible for her own daily cooking and housekeeping. Twice a year, however, she'd ask Mrs. Jackson to help her clean the house from top to bottom. Maggie liked her, and she liked having her around, especially when she had one of her little ones with her. Mrs. McClellan let Mrs. Jackson use her treadle Singer sewing machine to make clothes for her children, but Mrs. McClellan did the sewing for her own family.

Freeman and Maggie were both born in 1887. When they were small, they played together, and as Freeman's siblings got old enough, they joined them. Mrs. McClellan began to notice that Maggie was using the same speech pattern as her playmates. She was amused by her speech and assumed it would change as she aged. Once, when Maggie was talking to her dolls, her mother heard her say, "Look at yo' dress. Whut you done did ta git dat so dirty? You chilluns gon' be da de'f a me." Later, when she told Mr. McClellan about it, he didn't seem amused.

When Maggie and Freeman were six and Maggie was in the first grade, she arrived home one day as Freeman was walking toward the house in his play clothes. "Are you sick today, Freeman?" she asked.

"Naw," he replied.

"Well, why didn't you go to school?"

"Ah 'on't go ta school."

"Why not?"

"We ain't got no school. Wanna play?"

"Soon as I change my clothes," she answered, running up the porch steps.

Her mother had overheard the conversation, so she was waiting for the questions she knew would be coming from Maggie. As soon as Maggie saw her, they started. Mrs. McClellan explained that there weren't many Negroes in the country around there, so there weren't enough children for a Negro school. She didn't tell her that most of the children had to work on farms and wouldn't have been able to go, anyway.

"Well, Freeman can go to my school!" Maggie exclaimed, wide-eyed.

"The Negro children can't go to the white school. It's against the law."

"Why?"

Their conversation continued while Maggie changed her clothes. When she went outside, she asked Freeman, "Do you know your letters?"

"What's letters?" he asked.

"The ABCs."

He looked at her with questions in his eyes.

"I know what," Maggie said. "We can play school and I can teach you. Want to do that?"

Freeman normally agreed to do whatever Maggie suggested, so he readily agreed to that without realizing that there would be some work involved on his part. Maggie ran into the house and got some paper and pencils, and class was in session. From then on, when they played together, at least some of the playtime was devoted to learning. And she was also teaching Freeman's five-year old brother when he played with them. Within a few months both of the boys knew the alphabet, could count to a hundred, could do a fair job of writing the numbers and letters, and Freeman could write "Freeman Jackson." Maggie loved teaching them and they were proud to be learning. Their parents were also proud.

One afternoon, when Freeman and Maggie were seven and she was in the second grade, they were playing "house" with Freeman's little brothers. Their fathers walked up as Freeman sat next to Maggie with his arm around her. Maggie was looking at him adoringly.

The two men stopped in their tracks, looked at each other, and then back at the children. After a moment, Freeman's father said, "Freeman, ya take yo' brot'ers home now, an' den ya come wit' me."

After that, Freeman worked in the field with his father, or stayed at home. Maggie complained to her father about losing her playmate and student, and he told her it was Mr. Jackson's decision. So Maggie approached Mr. Jackson at the first opportunity to ask him if Freeman could play with her. Freeman was standing a few feet behind his father. Mr. McClellan overheard the question and waited to hear what Mr. Jackson would say. He hadn't expected his precocious daughter to say anything to him.

"Mis' Maggie," he said, "Freeman gittin' big, an' Ah needs 'im ta he'p me in da fiel's."

"But he's my favorite playmate, an' I'm teachin' him how to read," Maggie pleaded.

"Yes'm, Ah knows dat fuh sho," Mr. Jackson replied softly, nodding his head.

"Maggie," Mr. McClellan called. "You heard what he said. Now you go in the house." Later, he told Maggie that she was not to speak of it again.

And she didn't, but her little heart was broken. She would see Freeman coming and going, but he barely looked at her. She noticed that even when he wasn't working with his father, he didn't go to play with her anymore. She asked her mother about it, but she simply replied, "Maggie, my dear, that's just the way things are."

She didn't ask her mother any more questions, but she wondered. There was something the adults seemed to know that they were not explaining to her. "What does 'The way things are' mean? You can change the way things are," she thought.

As they passed their mid-teens, Maggie felt as though she hardly knew the good-looking young man Freeman had become. Sometimes when she was working in the yard or sitting on the porch and he was in the yard with his father, she would catch him sneaking glances at her, and sometimes they'd smile at each other. Maggie didn't always sneak glances; sometimes she just stared at him. About the only thing he ever said to her was, "Mornin', Mis' Maggie," or "'Lo, Mis' Maggie."

She also asked her mother why he called her "Mis'." Again, her mother replied, "That's the way things are, Maggie." But this time, she added, "Negroes have to be respectful of white people." Freeman continued to call her Mis' Maggie as an adult, even though the other Negroes called her Mis' Mac.

When she was eighteen, Maggie's parents sent her to Tallahassee to a school for teachers. She stayed there with her father's sister, and after she finished her training, which only lasted a few months, she stayed on and taught school in Tallahassee for four years. She enjoyed living in town after all her years on the farm. Maggie observed that the Negroes were completely segregated in town. In the country, most of their neighbors were Negroes, but she knew that wasn't true in many farming communities. Of course, most of the Negroes who lived among the whites in the country worked as sharecroppers or laborers. And she understood that even though they lived near each other, their lives were basically segregated.

Maggie was twenty-three when her parents wrote her about a new teaching position at the local school. They wanted her back home, and when she got the position, she returned to the farm.

A pretty young woman, she had several suitors, and more than one of them asked her to marry him. The last one asked her just before he was sent to France to fight in World War I. Maggie knew he loved her, but although she was fond of him, she knew she did not love him, and she was beginning to think that she'd never find a man to love. She seriously considered accepting his marriage proposal, but decided she didn't want to make a decision until after he came back from the war. She said they might change their minds after being apart for a while. When he was killed in the war, she decided she just wouldn't get married, but would continue to live with her parents, and she decided she didn't care if people called her an "old maid school teacher," which they did.

About a year after Maggie left the farm, Freeman married a local girl, Drusilla, and moved away. He'd signed on as a sharecropper with a farmer north of there and he worked for him for over twenty years. By then, one of Freeman's brothers had started working for a phosphate company, and he talked Freeman into going to work there. Freeman moved his family to Mulberry and worked for the company for ten years. He didn't mind the work, but he had trouble breathing with all the phosphate dust around the mine, and he arrived home from work covered with it. He felt tired a lot and wondered if the job was affecting his health.

Also, although he was pleased with the steady income, he soon realized that he missed farming. For the first time in his life, he didn't grow anything he ate, and he didn't like having to buy the types of vegetables that he'd always grown. They weren't fresh enough to suit him, and he was bothered by the price, which he knew was much more than the farmer got paid. And he missed planting the seeds and watching the plants grow. He missed living in the quiet of the country and the stillness it brought to his spirit. The farm work was about as hard as the work at the phosphate company, but he had always felt rewarded by it—he planted the seeds, took care of the plants, and then harvested the produce. Where they lived in Mulberry, he didn't have space in the yard for anything but a couple of tomato plants. And with the phosphate job, he did the same work every day just to get a paycheck, and changing shifts almost every week left him feeling tired most of the time.

He had a lot of daydreams about being back on the McClellan farm. When he visited his family, Freeman could tell that his father was no longer capable of doing the hard work, and he started thinking about sharecropping there. He knew it wouldn't be long before Mr. McClellan would want somebody else to take over for his father. "Ah needs my hands in da dirt," he thought. And he had another reason to want to go back there—a longing that he wouldn't admit, even to himself.

When his father died in 1937, Freeman was fifty, and he saw the opportunity he'd been hoping for. The McClellans attended his father's funeral, and after the graveside service, Freeman asked Mr. McClellan if he could have his father's job. Mr. McClellan was enthusiastic about it, so Freeman quit his job with the phosphate company, and moved his wife and three children who were still at home—the two older ones were married—to the farm. Freeman's mother, who still lived in the sharecropper's house, thought the house was too small for her and Freeman's family, particularly Drusilla, her daughter-in-law, so she went to live with a daughter in Lakeland.

Freeman was amazed at how large the little three-bedroom house seemed with three children in it instead of eight. He and his siblings had shared beds for a long time, two or three to a bed, and his children had a bed apiece. However, neither Drusilla nor the children were happy there. They said the only good thing about it was getting away from the sulfur water they had in Mulberry. The town water had a high sulfur content, and the kids thought it smelled like rotten eggs. They complained when they drank it and washed their faces in it first thing in the morning.

And Freeman's friends told him he was crazy—they all thought working for the phosphate company was the best job around and he should be happy to have that job. They couldn't believe he'd give it up to return to a life of sharecropping, which they looked down on. But Freeman was happy!

The children were fifteen, twelve, and two. They'd always had chores to do around the house, but they weren't pleased about having to do farm work. They weren't happy about leaving the small town environment where they had friends living nearby and always something to do, they weren't happy with their new school, and they weren't happy with the work. Their complaints were in vain, but the two boys informed Freeman that they would not be farmers. However, the younger boy and Ruby actually learned to enjoy some aspects of farming, and Ruby married a farmer, Harley.

Mr. McClellan was happy to have Freeman working for him. Freeman's dad had been too feeble to do all of the work for a few years before he died, but Mr. McClellan didn't have the heart to let him go, so he hired a young man, on a part-time basis, to help Mr. Jackson. Mr. McClellan knew that farming was too hard for men their age, and he knew the farm would bring in more money with someone younger working it, and it did after Freeman took over.

When Freeman had been back sharecropping for five years, Mr. McClellan died. Maggie was so grateful to have Freeman to take care of the farm for her and her mother. She often said she didn't know what they would've done without him.

After her father died, Maggie, who was fifty-five, quit her job and stayed home with her mother. Mrs. McClellan had heart trouble and was under doctor's orders not to do any work. Maggie missed teaching and the children, but she didn't resent her mother; she was happy to take care of her, and considered it her duty as the only child.

One afternoon, the two of them were sitting on the back porch and Freeman, who'd finished work for the day, told them what he'd done, and asked if there was anything else he needed to do. Mrs. McClellan told him that anything else could certainly wait until another day.

Then Freeman asked Maggie a question she'd never expected to hear: "Mis' Maggie, ma'am, would ya be willin' ta teach me an Drusilla ta read? I done taught her da numbers an' letters. An' Ah could pay ya."

"Oh my goodness, Freeman!" Maggie exclaimed, with tears in her eyes. "I would certainly love to teach you an' Drusilla to read, and I would not accept any payment from you. We'll start tomorrow."

When their children started going to school, Freeman had felt ashamed that he couldn't read or write, but he was happy that they were learning. Fortunately, a Negro school had opened in the country, and the children were able to continue going when they moved there.

After Freeman left, Maggie said, "You know, Mama, for years I thought about the fact that I couldn't keep teaching him when we were little. That bothered me so much. But after a while I stopped thinking about it, and I'm ashamed to say, I'd forgotten that he couldn't read."

Freeman and Drusilla met with her three times a week for a year. They sat on the porch and worked on the table there. Maggie pushed them the same way she had her students, always giving them homework assignments and deserved praise, and by the end of the year, they were reading and writing well. Freeman already knew how to calculate some problems in his head, but Drusilla didn't understand much about math, so she taught them basic math skills.

They were so proud of their accomplishments and so grateful to Maggie. She wouldn't accept pay, but Drusilla would make her a cake or pie, and she'd just appear when she knew they were preparing vegetables for canning or freezing. And if Freeman noticed that the flower garden needed weeding, he'd quietly do it.

Maggie gave Drusilla all of her magazines when she finished reading them to be sure they had something to keep them reading, and something she thought they'd enjoy. When she learned that they were planning to read the Bible, she told them to let her know if they needed help with some of the words, and they did.

Maggie's mother died three years after her father. She had been in poor health for a long time, so Maggie thought it was a blessing, but she missed her. After her death, Maggie assumed complete responsibility for the farm. She'd already been doing it since her father's death, but out of respect for her mother, she always asked her opinion before making any decisions.

She did not have to worry about money. Her father had inherited a good amount, which had enabled him to buy the large property, and he made a good salary as a supervisor at the phosphate company. Maggie had saved most of her salary over her thirty-five years of teaching since she had few expenses living with her parents, and when they died, she inherited everything. The orange grove provided enough income to pay all of her expenses, including a generous salary for Freeman, and she sold a few yearlings each year, so she seldom touched the money she inherited, except for charitable purposes.

Unfortunately, only a couple of years after Maggie's mother died, Drusilla was bitten by a rattlesnake one morning while picking huckleberries in the woods behind the house. She was able to get back to the house and lie down on the bed. When Freeman went home at noon, he became concerned when he saw her half-full pail of huckleberries on the kitchen table. He glanced at the stove and saw that no cooking had been done. He called her and immediately went to their bedroom looking for her. When he saw her body on the bed, the first thing he noticed were the fang marks on her leg. He knew immediately what had happened. He knelt beside the bed and held her face tenderly as he wept.

Ruby, who was twelve and the only child still living at home, had spent the night at a friend's house. Drusilla had taught her how to cook and do housework and she lived with her father until she married Harley at seventeen. When Ruby got married, Maggie and Freeman were both sixty-five and the only ones left on the farm.

As they sat on the porch eating their soup, Maggie didn't try to talk to Freeman. She thought he seemed too tired, or too ill, to both eat and talk. He'd moved very slowly from the porch steps to the table, and she knew he needed to eat, so she didn't want to distract him by talking. She thought, "Normally, I would have mentioned that it's cloudin' up, and lookin' like we might have a thunderstorm. Lord, I dread lightnin'."

She was glad she'd made the soup. She planned to freeze most of what was left in jars just the right size for her, and when she felt like eating soup, or didn't feel like cooking, she'd defrost a container.

When they finished eating, he thanked her and asked if she had any work for him that afternoon. She simply said, "No, Freeman," and wondered how he thought he could work, given the way he clearly felt. She noticed the flicker of relief on his face.

"You go home an' rest," she said. "You look like you don't feel well. Do you think you caught a cold or the flu? I could get the doctor to come out an' give you a penicillin shot."

"Ah'm fine," he said. "Jes' ti'ed."

"Freeman," Maggie said. "You need to take care of yourself. Rest, an' if you want some more soup, come back for supper. Or you could take some home with you. Do you want some to take home?"

"No, ma'am, Mis' Maggie," he replied as he struggled to stand up. "Thank ya fuh aksin'."

Maggie thought he just seemed too tired to think about taking any soup home. "Well, come back if you want some for supper," she continued. "And sleep late tomorrow morning, an' get some good rest. There's nothin' needin' to be done right now. Not even any watermelons that need to be picked. Don't forget to eat yours, by the way."

"Ah sho won't," he replied.

"I'll see you tomorrow," she said.

"Awright den," he said, and turned and walked down the steps, holding on to the handrail.

"He is not well," Maggie thought. "He's just not himself."

And she sat in a rocking chair and watched the old truck until she could no longer see it through her tears.

Tuesday

JAMES HAD TROUBLE SLEEPING. He kept waking up all through the night thinking about the job at the mine and wondering how he could make the right impression to get hired. He went through a make-believe interview several times, each time telling himself that he might not even have an interview, that he'd probably fill out an application and leave. He tried to think of Saleena so that he could remove the worry from his mind, but that didn't work.

When his father knocked on his bedroom door, James thought he'd just fallen asleep. "James, ya woke up yet?"

"Yassuh," he replied, wondering why his father was calling him in the middle of the night. However, when he opened his eyes, he was surprised by the brightness of his room and the deliciously mingled smells of coffee and bacon.

"Lawd a mercy," he said as he quickly dressed in his work clothes, not taking time to put on his shoes. After a quick stop to use the bathroom and wash his face, he went into the kitchen and found his parents already eating breakfast. That had only happened a few times in his life; he was an early riser and was usually up before his mother finished making breakfast, and often before she started. He walked into the kitchen, rubbing his eyes.

"Mornin' Sunshine," Pearl said.

"Mornin' Mama. Mornin' Daddy," he said, and yawned.

"Mornin'," Pearson said. "Ya didn' sleep good, huh?"

"Nawsuh. Ah'm worried 'bout dat job," James replied.

"Ah see," Pearson said. "Well, ya know worryin' won't do ya no good atall."

"Yassuh, Ah knows it," he said. "But Ah couldn' quit thankin' 'bout thangs."

"Fix ya plate, baby," Pearl said. "Ah lef' it on da stove fuh ya."

She got up to get more coffee for her and Pearson, and while she was up, she poured a cup for James.

"Mama, ya made biscuits," James said. She seldom took the time to make them for breakfast, and when she did, they were greatly appreciated.

"Ya needs a good breakfas'," she said. "Dis gon' be a big day fuh ya."

James loaded his plate with grits, eggs, bacon, and a couple of biscuits. When he got to the table, he buttered his grits and biscuits, and took some sliced tomatoes from a small dish on the table. James was the only one in the family who ate tomatoes with breakfast, but Pearl would slice one for him when they had some.

"Dis a good way ta start it off," he said, looking at the strawberry jam and guava jelly sitting on the table and wondering which one he'd put on his second biscuit.

He ate fast. He knew his father had orders from three stores, and he wanted to get the black-eyed peas picked and delivered as soon as possible. He and Pearson were leaving the house just minutes after he got out of bed. He walked out with his third biscuit, loaded with butter and strawberry jam. He'd decided on guava jelly for his second one.

"Ain't many peas lef'," Pearson said as they walked to the barn behind the house. "I needs eight hampers fuh da sto's. Ya mama say if dey mo' dan dat, she put da rest in da freezer. Ah spec' dey's less 'an ten hampers."

"Ought not take us long ta pick 'em," James said. "Ah'll git da hampers."

The morning was cool and pleasant. James enjoyed the morning air before the sun heated everything up. He got ten hampers and ten lids, put them in the back of the truck, and drove it to the field where the peas were, and where Pearson was waiting.

The pea plants were still damp with dew. Sometimes in the spring, James' fingers would get cold from the dew when he picked peas and other produce. But strawberries were the worst because they got ripe in the winter, and on cold mornings, his fingers felt like they were freezing. Fortunately for James, they'd stopped growing strawberries when the school department changed the school year in 1950. Until then, the school year for some schools in farming areas ran through the summer, with the winter months off so the farmers' children were available to pick strawberries. Pearson figured he wouldn't make much money if he had to pay people to pick the berries, so he stopped growing them.

James unloaded the hampers, and was at the end of a pea row when he stepped on some sandspurs. "Ow," he said. "Blamed ole sandspurs!" He would've said something else, but he thought his father might hear him. He pulled the thorny offenders from his toe, said, "Guess Ah shoulda put some shoes on," and started picking peas.

After they picked in silence for a few minutes, Pearson said, "Ah's dreamin' 'bout Mr. McClellan las' night."

"Fuh real?"

"Ya know if dat man hadn' sol' us dis lan', us prob'ly wouldn' have no lan'."

James had heard the story many times before, but he knew his father liked to tell it. "Dat right?" he asked as though he'd never heard it.

"Yep," Pearson continued as they picked the peas. "Me an' yo' unc' Joseph worked hard an' saved ever' penny us could. Ah's 'bout ta aks yo' mama ta marry me. An' Joseph an' me went ta see Mr. McClellan—course he knowed yo' mama—an' us aks 'im ta sell us some lan'. Joseph handed 'im all our money, an' he say, 'You each plannin' ta build a house?' An' us say 'Yassuh.' An' he say, 'Well, y'all keep yo' money fuh dat. Ah'll draw up a mortgage an' ya kin pay me by da month.' Me an' Joseph wadn' e'em thankin' 'bout how much a house 'ud cost. An' he sol' us twenty acres apiece, an' us paid 'im ever' month. One year, it wuz so dry, da crops didn' do nuttin', an' he tol' me don' worry 'bout payin' dat year. Ah tell ya, Mr. McClellan wuz a good ole white man," he said, nodding his head. "An' Mis' Mac's a good white woman, too."

"Sho is," James agreed. "Ah 'on't 'member Mr. McClellan. Ah wuz jes' lil when he died." He took his full hamper to the truck, and then took Pearson's.

"Dis a good year fuh sellin' peas," Pearson said. "Price wuz awright."

"Yassuh," James said. "Ah 'membah da bad year." James was at school one day when Pearson needed the peas picked, and he hired a man to help him. When he took the peas to the farmers' market where corporate buyers bid on the produce for their companies, the price offered was fifty cents a hamper. The hampers had cost forty cents each, so that left him ten cents. By the time he discounted labor and the cost of growing them, he was in debt. He decided very quickly to take them home and feed them to their hogs. "Off'rin' us farmers a dime fuh a hamper a peas!" he exclaimed over supper. "Mos' da farmers didn' sell 'em."

"Wadn' bad fuh da *whole* year," Pearson admitted. "Jes' da las' part. Dey said dey wuz too many peas growed."

They bent over the vines picking the peas, and straightened up when they needed to move their hampers further down the rows.

"Ah been thankin' 'bout sellin' da cows, 'cept Holstein an' Polly an' maybe a couple others, an' plantin' 'bout ten acres in orange trees," Pearson said. They normally milked Holstein, but she was due to have a calf soon, and her milk had dried up.

"Dat dere's a good ideal, Daddy," James replied enthusiastically. He figured with Pearson getting older, having a grove would be a lot easier for him than farming, and would pay more than raising a small number of cattle. "A real good ideal." He'd have to keep farming until the grove started to produce income, and then he could plant more trees if he wanted to.

After a while, Pearson straightened up, stretched, and rubbed his back. "Da raccoons done been in da corn." He looked at the rows of corn on the other side of the peas and noticed some half-eaten ears on the ground.

"If dey's one a mile away, dey gon' smell da corn," James said, and he and Pearson laughed.

"Sho seem like it," Pearson agreed. "Ole Shep sleepin' on da job. He ain't earnin' his keep."

"Nawsuh, he ain't," James said. "He too lazy. We oughta leave 'im out at night." But as the words were coming out of his mouth, James knew they wouldn't.

Pearson was right about the amount of peas. After they picked nine and a half hampers, they put lids on eight, and took the rest to the house for Pearl. She went out on the porch to see how many peas they had.

James put the hamper full on the porch. As Pearson put down the half hamper, he told her, "Ah he'p ya shell 'em when Ah gits back."

"Awright," Pearl replied. "Ah'm gon' wait fuh ya."

She called to James, who'd gotten back in the truck, "James, dinner be ready when ya git back. Ya needs ta eat befo' ya go ta da phosphate comp'ny."

"Yes, ma'am," James replied. He wasn't thinking about eating, he was thinking about getting a job. But he knew his mother was right and he'd humor her. He had to take a bath and change clothes, anyway, and he knew he'd be hungry by then.

♥ ♥ ♥

As James drove down the highway on his way to the phosphate company, the phosphate pits he saw along the way looked different to him. Now that he was thinking of working for a mine, he wasn't as critical. Before, he thought what a shame it was that the company had mined there, ruining the natural beauty of the landscape. The pits were full of water, of course, and many of them had been there long enough that trees were growing around them, but James didn't like the unnatural-looking mounds of dirt that surrounded them.

After the company finished digging with their draglines, the pits would fill with water and the company would stock some of them with fish. Many people fished in the pits, but they could be very dangerous. The shallow part was only a few feet wide at the edge; then, there was a sharp drop-off of around twenty feet or more. Occasionally, people drowned in the pits. James had been fishing in a couple with his dad and Harley. And one day, when he was eight, he went with his Uncle Freeman to visit some old friends in Brewster, and afterwards, the two of them went fishing in the Number 4 pit nearby.

James remembered standing on the bank with Freeman, both of them holding fishing poles. Four white teenage boys in a boat went near them, and one asked, "Y'all catchin' anythang, boy?"

James thought he was talking to him, and he was about to answer when Freeman said, "Nawsuh. Dey ain't bitin' today."

"Dat boy called Unc' Freeman '*boy*,'" James thought. He looked at Freeman, but Freeman lowered his head, and didn't return the look. James never mentioned it, and he never forgot it. And, he never forgot the feelings of shame and humiliation he felt for his uncle. He'd peeked into the grown-ups' world that day, and a spark of anger was lit in his heart.

By the time he got to the phosphate plant, it was almost three o'clock and time for a shift change. Before he left the truck, James drank about half of the ice water from the quart jar that his mother had fixed for him. As he approached the building, he saw a young white man, who was smoking a cigarette and leaning against the building. James asked him where the boss man's office was.

The man looked at him and pointed at a door. "It's in there," he said. Then he added, "Lotsa luck."

James went through the door into a hallway that had a few doors and one water fountain, which he knew was not for colored, and he went through the first door on the right with a sign that said, "Personnel Office." The secretary, an attractive blond young woman about James' age, handed him a form. The plaque on her desk said "Mabel."

"Just fill out this form an' give it back to me," she said, smiling at James.

Since he had no work experience except on the farm, he filled it out quickly and was handing the form to Mabel, when a gray-haired man came out of a door that had a small sign, "Mr. Roberts."

James stepped away from Mabel's desk and nodded.

"You lookin' fer a job?" he asked James.

"Yassuh," James replied, bowing his head as he spoke.

"Well, we ain't got many jobs," he said as he turned to face Mabel.

James felt his heart drop. He remembered the interviews he had imagined during the night. He'd thought about the proper English that he learned in school. He waited until Mr. Roberts finished talking to Mabel before he spoke.

"Mr. Roberts, sir," he said as the man started toward his office. "Ah'm a good worker. Used ta workin' hard on the farm."

"Well, this is different," Mr. Roberts said without turning to face him. "You young bucks come in here thinkin' you gonna git hired 'cause you young an' strong. Well, there's more to it 'an that, boy."

James' head dropped almost to his chest. He didn't always feel like a man. At nineteen, he was still getting used to the word applying to him. However, he knew that when a white man called him "boy," it wasn't because of his age. He felt all of the hope drain out of him.

"Yes, sir," he said, "Thank you, sir."

"Whut da hell Ah'm sayin' 'thank you' fuh?" he wondered. He rubbed the back of his neck. "He ain't done nuttin' fuh me." James felt disdain for himself and a flash of hatred for the cold-hearted man who'd humiliated him. And although his body was filled with adrenaline, he could neither fight nor run.

He knew he was sweating. When he looked at Mabel, she was looking at him with sympathetic eyes. He thought he saw pity.

James felt the blood rush into his face. It would've been bad enough if no one had witnessed the situation, but he'd been shamed in front of this nice young white woman who'd treated him with respect.

"Thank ya, ma'am," he said, lowering his head again.

As he walked away with his head hung down, he heard her say, "You're welcome," and then add softly, "Good luck to you."

Back in the hot truck, he drank the rest of the cool water. Then he sat there going over and over the short exchange, asking himself if he could have done anything differently. He knew he'd been respectful. He knew he said the important things. He knew he used pretty good English. He thought his clothes were all right; he hadn't worn a suit or tie or anything real dressy, but he had worn his nice gray slacks and green shirt. He thought maybe he should have worn his old work clothes, but that seemed disrespectful to him. Harley told him not to dress up and he didn't, but he didn't dress down either.

After going over the same details again and again, he always came to the same conclusion: He was simply the wrong color. Harley had told him Mr. Roberts didn't like coloreds, and Mis' Mac said he was difficult. "Ah cain't change nuttin' now," he thought. "Whut's done's done."

Nevertheless, he felt like crying. He'd gone in there full of hope, and come out drained, an empty shell. He slammed his hands down on the steering wheel three times and hurt his hands. "Ah run inta da wall," he thought, rubbing his hands together. "Da wall Ah cain't go thu."

He wanted to scream at the top of his lungs, but there was a lot of activity in the parking lot, men coming and going. So he just sat there. He wanted to go home. He almost decided to just go, but then he thought about how that would allow some old cracker to ruin his day; it was bad enough that he probably wouldn't get the job. He wanted to go to Lakeland to look for a necklace for Saleena, and if he didn't do it, Mr. Roberts would be ruining something else for him. He set his jaw in determination: he was going to Lakeland.

The end of the 7:00–3:00 shift kept him moving slowly for a while. It seemed that everybody was leaving at once, as they basically were. His family had been caught in this afternoon traffic a few times over the years when they were on the road between three and three thirty, and they avoided being on the road then, if possible.

As he sat in the slow traffic, he obsessed about what had happened. The process always ended with the same thought: "Ah won't git dat job."

The traffic was starting to move at a good rate of speed when he came to a railroad crossing. The lights were flashing and the stop gate was across the lane. "Lawd have mercy on me!" he moaned. "Now Ah has ta wait on a phosphate train. An' it hot as hell." He took a freshly-ironed handkerchief from his pocket and wiped the sweat off his face. He looked in the glove compartment and found a piece of cardboard to use as a fan.

James often enjoyed waiting for the trains so he could count the railroad cars. Several times, he'd counted over a hundred before the caboose finally appeared. Today, he was not in the mood for counting, but he soon found himself counting, in spite of himself. "Sebenny-three," he said, disappointed. "Only sebenny-three. Wadn' e'em worf countin'."

The train stopped, and as it started backing up, James realized that his bladder was feeling full and he knew he'd have to pee before long. "Oh Lawd," he thought, "ain't no bathrooms downtown fuh coloreds." He thought about going to the Negro section of town—maybe to his cousin's house—but he was hot and it was out of his way, and he knew he couldn't just run in and use the bathroom and leave, and he was in no mood for socializing. Normally, he would stop and go behind a tree, but with all the traffic, he didn't feel comfortable doing that. After his experiences at the phosphate company, he didn't want to go into the woods with a bunch of white men around.

He looked at the empty quart jar beside him. "Ah drunk too much water," he thought, and he remembered the three glasses of iced tea he'd had at the house. And he remembered being so excited about the job that he didn't think to go to the bathroom before he left. He looked at the train, which had stopped, and knew it would soon be moving again. "Ah kin pee in dat jar," he said.

James remembered being in Lakeland with his mother one time when he was seven years old. She'd reminded him to use the bathroom before they left the house, but he didn't feel like he needed to, so he didn't. However, while they were downtown, he had to go. Pearl gave him the look he dreaded before taking him down an alley and standing in front of him, holding her skirt out while he peed, and fussing at him the whole time because she knew he hadn't peed at home.

On the way to Lakeland, he saw another phosphate pit. Just looking at it disgusted him and he quickly looked away.

When he finally got downtown, he found a parking place near the dime store where he really wanted to park, but there was a parking meter. James Thomas Cleveland wasn't about to spend a nickel for parking. He pictured things he could buy with a nickel, like a candy bar, a bag of popcorn, or a soda. So he drove two blocks down and parked in front of a restaurant-supply store where there were no meters. Walking along and sweating in the heat, he thought if he got the job, he might spend a nickel to park on a hot day. Soon, he was convinced that he would.

Walking past the park, he glanced at the tall white column with the statue of a Confederate soldier on top, and he looked away. "Dat dere man a big hero 'round here," he thought. "Dat ole rebel soldier from the Freedom War."

As he entered the dime store, his focus shifted from his experience at the phosphate company to Saleena and what kind of necklace he might buy for her. But before he even looked at the necklaces, he went to the back of the store and got a drink of water from the "Colored" fountain. He noticed the fountain looked dirty, and he looked at the "White" fountain, which looked clean. "No s'prise dere," he thought.

He smiled when he remembered being in the store once with his father, whom he idolized, and hoped to be like. That day, Pearson turned on the water in the "White" fountain and looked at it. James stared at him with his mouth hanging open and his heart racing, wondering if he'd lost his mind. Pearson moved to the "Colored" fountain next, turned on the water, and looked at it. "Bof a dem looks da same ta me!" he announced. "Dat one clear an' dis one clear." Then they laughed together. James had been amazed that his father would do that, and he was afraid he'd get in trouble, but if anyone saw him, they didn't say anything. James heard later that it was a common game. However, even though they turned the water on at the white fountain, they wouldn't dare drink from it.

As James looked around the store, he saw, as he expected, that he was the only Negro there. Usually, when he'd been in the dime store, he was with his mother. They'd been in there several times, so he knew where things were. He remembered being a little boy and spending time looking at the toys and dreaming. Occasionally, his mother would buy him some little toy, a car, some marbles, or something else inexpensive. James would feel so grateful when she bought him something. He remembered how happy he felt. It didn't matter what it was or what it cost; he'd play with it and love having it.

Of course, there were certain things that he really wanted. If they were within her budget, Pearl would buy them for him, but often they cost too much—like the cowboy outfit, and especially the belt with the silver buckle. He always wanted that and Pearl always shook her head. However, when he was nine, the outfit with the belt, and the cap gun, were under the tree on Christmas morning, and his little body wasn't big enough to contain his joy. After that, he often got more caps when they were in the store.

James remembered, when he was seven, asking to eat at the lunch counter. Pearl was embarrassed because a white clerk heard him, but she simply said, "No baby, dey 'on't serve coloreds. We cain't do dat." That was the day he got the jackknife he'd been coveting, even though Pearl thought he was too young to have it, and it was not in her budget.

As he neared the toy counter, he saw a little white girl looking at the toys. She was a cute little girl with blond hair and blue eyes, and she had on a frilly pink dress and white shoes, and socks trimmed with lace. "Huh daddy got money," James thought.

He watched her for a minute, noticing how she was picking up toys and putting them down in different places. Then, as her mother walked up, the little girl started whining for her to buy something. The mother suggested one toy, but that didn't satisfy her. When he left the area, her mother was agreeing to buy three toys.

"Not like whut happened wit' me," James thought. "Dat lil white gal need a better Mama, one like mine. If Ah done dat, mah mama woulda to'e up mah behine."

Approaching the counter where the necklaces were, James noticed that the clerk was busy straightening the earrings, so he stopped a few feet from the counter and waited for her to finish. He stood patiently waiting, studying the necklaces. He glanced at the clerk a few times. "She one skinny white woman, an' *huh* daddy ain't got no money," he thought facetiously as he looked at her well-worn dress.

After a little while, he saw her looking at his clothes, and when their eyes met, he saw disdain. He immediately looked back at the necklaces.

"Did ya wanna see sumpin?" she asked in a monotone.

"Ah like ta see ya looka me like Ah'm a person an' not a piece a trash," James thought.

"Yes, ma'am," he said softly, moving a couple of steps closer to the counter. "Some a dem necklaces, please."

The clerk took out the display case that James pointed at. He remained about three feet from the counter, knowing the clerk didn't want to wait on him. He'd heard that white women were afraid of Negro men—afraid they'd rape them. He knew she couldn't be afraid of that in the store, but she was clearly uncomfortable.

The instant he saw the necklace, he knew it was the one. He didn't need to be any closer or see any other necklaces. There it was: a rhinestone heart on a silver-colored chain. That would be perfect for Saleena.

"Hi much dat heart wit' di'mon's cost?" he asked.

"All them in this case is $2.99," she answered.

The frilly little white girl and her mother went to the counter, and the little girl went right in front of him and stood staring at the necklaces.

James took a step backwards. "Looka dat lil snot-nose gal walk right in front a me," he thought. "Why huh mama 'on't teach huh how ta ack?"

She picked up one necklace, but put it down and picked up the heart. "I wont this one," she demanded, looking at her mother. "This one—the heart wi' diamonds."

"Oh Lawd," James thought, and his hand went to his mouth. "If Ah had da money, Ah coulda done bought dat necklace. Now dat lil brat gal prob'ly gon' buy it. If Mis' Mac had da right change, Ah coulda bought it." For the first time in his life, he felt a little angry at her.

"Excuse me," the clerk said, "that boy wuz here before you an' he wuz lookin' at that necklace."

"Damn! Ah guess she 'on't like huh eit'er," he thought. "She sayin' Ah'm lookin' at dat necklace, an' Ah knows she 'on't like me."

The little girl turned around, looked at James, and frowned. Her squinched-up blue eyes looked angry. If an adult had looked at him like that, he would've felt threatened.

"E'em at dat lil, dey 'on't like us," James thought. "Lawd a mercy."

He was afraid she'd buy the necklace, but he didn't have enough money to buy it, so there was nothing he could do. Looking at the back of her head, he thought, "Oh no! Please 'on't buy dat necklace, lil gal." He'd just have to return on Saturday, and he hoped there'd be another necklace worthy of Saleena, if the heart with diamonds was gone.

James nodded his head to the clerk and said, "Dat's awright—Ah'll come back. Thank ya, ma'am." And he turned and walked out of the store, his eyes on the floor. He could feel eyes on his back as he left, but he didn't care. He'd felt happy before that little girl went to the counter, but now he wasn't sure he'd be able to get that "perfect" necklace for Saleena. He'd have to wait until Saturday to see if it was still there. "E'em if she 'on't buy it, somebody else might," he thought. "Hit so purty."

As soon as he left Lakeland and the truck picked up speed, James let out a heavy, manly scream. And then he silently apologized to Maggie for feeling angry at her, scolding himself for taking his anger out on her. "She da one gon' gimme da money in da fust place," he said to himself. "Ah couldn' e'em buy it 'thout huh."

As he drove along, he realized he hadn't even had the radio on that day, and he turned it on. He was ready for some music. As he listened to his favorite station, his spirits began to lift. When Little Richard's "Long Tall Sally" came on, he found himself singing along and even drumming on the steering wheel.

James thought about talking to Harley as he rode along in the truck. He needed to tell someone about his experiences and he didn't want to burden his parents. He'd simply tell them that he filled out an application, but he didn't have an interview. That was the truth and that was all he wanted them to know.

Just before he got to Harley's, James stopped the truck and emptied the jar. When he arrived, he took it to the back of the house to the hand pump, and rinsed the jar thoroughly before taking the dipper from the post and drinking a couple of dippers full of water. Then, he stuck his head under the pump and pumped the cool water on his head.

Unfortunately, as James expected, Harley wasn't at home. It was only four-thirty, and Harley usually worked until five. However, James did get to see little Rubin.

Rubin was beginning to walk and James squatted down about three feet from him and called him. Rubin took a couple of steps and fell into James outstretched arms. James hugged him and kissed the little chubby face, then held him over his head a few times, with Rubin laughing his sweet baby laugh. Then he played peek-a-boo and pat-a-cake with him.

Ruby asked about the job, but he didn't want to talk about it without Harley there. James mentioned Freeman's health. "Ya's right 'bout yo' daddy, Ruby. He 'on't look good, an' he say he ain't been feelin' good." James was careful not to mention his observation that the light was gone from his eyes.

"Ah knows it. When Junior come two weeks ago, an' us went ovah dere, he look bad den," she replied. "An' Ah saw 'im today an' he still look bad. But he comin' Friday fuh his birfday."

"Dat's right," James said. "He gon' be sebenny."

When James left, he felt much better. Being with the child had worked wonders on him. As he drove away, Ruby was holding Rubin and waving his chubby little hand, and Rubin had a big smile on his little face.

♥   ♥   ♥

AFTER SUPPER, JAMES WALKED BACK TO HARLEY's with Shep by his side. Just as before, Harley and Ruby were sitting on the porch swing, gently gliding back and forth. Harley knew as soon as he saw James that the day hadn't gone well. Of course, Ruby had told him that James didn't look happy when he stopped by. There'd be no joking around this night.

Shep walked over to the swing, and both of them patted him for a moment. Then, he lay down beside the rocking chair where James sat.

"Ya git ta see da boss man?" Harley asked.

"He come outta his office an' seen me an' he aks, 'Ya lookin' fuh a job?' An' Ah say, 'Yassuh.' An' he tell me, 'Ain't many jobs.'" James paused.

"'Ain't many jobs! Ah jes' needs one," he said, and slammed his fist into his hand.

"Absalom say he 'on't like us, James," Harley said.

"Ah knows it. But ya know hi it feels."

"Ah sho do."

They sat silently for a moment. Ruby was leaning forward in the swing with her elbows on her knees.

"Den he talk ta da woman, name Mabel, an' when he start ta leave, Ah tell 'im Ah works hard on da farm. An' he say, 'You young bucks thank ya kin jes' come in here an' git a job 'cause ya strong.' An' Ah feels 'bout knee-high ta a grasshopper. An' dat gal Mabel lookin' at me like she feel sorry fuh me. An' Ah say 'Thank ya, suh,' an' 'Thank ya,' ta huh, an' Ah wonts ta go thu da flo'."

"Whut dey lookin' fuh if not strong mens?" Ruby asked.

"White mens," Harley answered with anger in his voice. "An' we jes' boys."

"Dat's right," James said, nodding his head.

Ruby leaned back. "No man kin keep from ya what da Lawd got fuh ya," she said. Then, she added softly, "Jes' stay on yo' knees, boy. Tell Him all 'bout it."

"Ya right, Ruby," James agreed.

"He aks ya anythang 'bout yo'se'f?" she asked.

"He knowed ever'thang he need ta know," James said bitterly.

"Ah'm sorry, James," Ruby said. "Lawd, mebbe one day thangs be diff'unt."

"Afta us dead an' gone," Harley said. "But us got ta live now, an' work now."

James sat quietly. He felt a little better after confiding in his friends.

After a little while, he said, "Mis' Mac gon' buy a new truck an' sell me da ole one. Kin ya he'p me fix up dat truck, Harley?"

"Sho, James," Harley said, glad to talk about something more pleasant. "Us make dat baby purr."

James laughed. "Ah'm talkin' 'bout dat *ole* truck, Harley. Ah thank it purrin' days be ovah. Ah jes' wonts hit ta stop rattlin' like hit 'bout ta fall ta pieces."

"Us fix huh, James," Harley assured him. "Might hafta buy some mo' parts, but us fix huh up."

James was silent again. He knew there was one more person that he had to tell how things had gone for him at the phosphate company, and he wasn't sure how much he'd tell her. He couldn't lie to her—that he knew. Mis' Mac would see right through him, even better than his parents, whom he told that he'd just filled out an application. He told them he was tired, which was true—he felt exhausted, drained—and they seemed to believe him. He knew Mis' Mac wanted the best for him, but she *was* white, after all. He would have to see how things went with her, how much she asked him, and he would decide at the time how much to tell her.

He stayed for a while with Harley and Ruby, but there were no checker games and not much conversation. Ruby served some lemonade, but James only drank half of his. Harley and Ruby exchanged a glance when he got up, said he had to go, and handed Ruby his glass. James always finished Ruby's lemonade, usually had seconds, and often, thirds.

Harley got up to take him home, but James said, "Ah tol' ya Ah'm walkin' from now on, less hit's col' or rainin. Hit ain't col', an' it ain't rainin', so Ah'm walkin'. Le's go, Shep."

Shep stood up. Normally, he did not stand up unless he was pretty sure they were leaving. The men usually played checkers and moved around some, so Shep waited for a signal—no use wasting energy getting up and down. Of course, he did get up if Ruby went in the house; that was a gamble worth expending energy for.

"Ah knows whut ya tol' me, but Ah wonts ta drive ya home tonight," Harley said gently.

"Ah'm walkin'," James said. "Ah needs ta walk now. An' da night air feel good." He and Shep went down the steps.

The air had cooled several degrees after the sun went down. The moon was bright and the sky was clear.

"Thanks fuh da lemonade, Ruby," he called.

"Ya welcome, James. Any time," she said.

"Ya still might git da job," Harley said tenderly. "Dey is some a us workin' dere, doin' jobs white folks ain't gon' do. Ya jes' 'on't know."

"Dat da truf, awright," James said, nodding. "Dat ain't nuttin' but da truf."

Walking along the dirt road, he thought how silly it would've been to have Harley drive him home when it wasn't even that dark. With the moon out, there was plenty of light.

Shep walked beside him for quite a while before venturing off to follow a scent. James smiled. "Guess Harley right 'bout Shep. He smell a rabbit, an' he done gon'."

James hadn't told Harley and Ruby about his experience in the dime store because he didn't want them to know that he was planning to buy a necklace for Saleena. He thought about it and wanted to tell them, but he thought Saleena should be the first one to know that he was buying her a necklace. He was also concerned that Ruby might let it slip if she happened to see Saleena, and he wanted it to be a surprise.

As he walked along, he thought about the dime store, and the way the clerk looked at him. And he thought about how that bratty little white girl walked right in front of him as though he weren't even there. And he thought of how the clerk had referred to him as 'boy.' He felt helpless and frustrated having to endure that kind of treatment. He tried to think of Saleena, but that made him feel worse. How could he be the kind of strong man he thought she wanted when he had to act like a bump on a log, and not say anything even when a little girl stepped right in front of him?

"Damn dem," he said loudly, "Ah'm a man. No matter who call me a boy, Ah'm still a man!" Some of his frustration left with the outburst, but he still had an overwhelming sense of sadness.

When James got to *the place*, he stopped. In the moonlight he could see it clearly. "Dis is it," he said. "Dis is where it happen' at." It was the first time he'd walked there in the dark since that awful night. "One mo' thang ta make me feel bad."

It was a hot Sunday night in July, almost a year earlier, and he'd been visiting with Harley and Ruby. Shep wasn't with him that night; he'd somehow managed to cut his leg, possibly going through a barbed wire fence, and James thought he should stay off the leg as much as possible, so he'd left him in the house.

James was walking home, occasionally shining his flashlight in the woods to see if he could see a rabbit or some other animal. The moon was just a few days past full so there was enough light that he didn't need a flashlight, but Pearl always insisted that he carry one, just in case. He thought he saw something move in the light and he stopped to watch, but saw nothing, so he went on. He didn't have his gun, anyway, so he couldn't shoot a rabbit even if he saw one.

He'd just passed Maggie McClellan's piney woods and the road to her house, and was beside her orange grove when he heard a pick-up truck coming. "Unc' Joseph," he thought, wiping the sweat from his brow with the back of his hand. Pearson's brother Joseph lived on down the road, and his was the only family that lived past James' family on the dead-end dirt road.

He stepped off the road, turned off his flashlight, and stood facing the road ready to greet his uncle. As the truck approached, however, he realized it sounded different, and was newer than his uncle's. Then, he saw a white boy leaning out the window.

James got an immediate shot of adrenaline, and he took a couple of steps back. "Oh Lawd!" he thought. "Boys out ta have a good time. Bad time fuh me."

When the truck stopped, he saw three white boys that he thought looked about sixteen. He took his cap off and waited, trying his best to appear respectful and calm.

The boy leaning out of the window asked, "Whatcha doin' out here, Nigger?"

"Ah lives out here, suh," James said as respectfully as he would have to their fathers.

"Where you live at?" the boy asked.

"Down da road yonder," James replied, pointing down the road, aware of the sweat from his underarms running down his ribs. He was immediately sorry that he'd told them that, and he was glad there were trees hiding the light from the house.

James had no idea what the boys had in mind, but he knew it couldn't be good. "I knows whut kin happen to coloreds caught by da white man out in da country like dis," he thought. Images flashed through his mind from some of the horror stories he and his family often discussed.

"I thank you better git in the back a the truck an' show us," the boy said.

James looked at the back of the truck, and he could see a piece of rope hanging from the tailgate. "Oh Lawd, he'p me," he silently prayed, feeling terrified. He stood there trying to think of something to say. He was definitely not going to get his parents involved. He wanted to ask why they wanted to go to his house, but he knew he couldn't do that.

"Dey 'on't wont ta go ta da house," he realized. "Dey jes' wont me ta git in da truck."

"He said 'Git in the truck,'" another boy commanded.

James' mind was racing. Scenes of him being dragged behind the truck, and hanging from a tree flashed before him. "Thank 'bout whut ya gon' do," he commanded himself.

"Ah could run in Mis' Mac's grove," he thought, looking across the back of the pickup at the orange trees. But then he realized that the boys could drive the truck in there. "Ah knows Mis' Mac's woods."

"Yassuh," he said, and started walking toward the back of the truck.

When he got to the back, he hit the tailgate and pushed down on it, so it sounded and felt like he was getting in, and he took off. He was forty feet away before the gloating, snickering boys realized he was gone.

James heard one of them say, "Where the hell did he go? Stinkin' Nigger!"

Someone else said, "Le's git 'im!"

And somebody said, "Git the flashlight, Ray."

By the time they started after him, he was in the woods, and his mind was racing as fast as his feet. The woods were dark even though it was fairly light out, and he wanted to turn on his flashlight, but he knew they'd see the light. He knew they could hear him running, even though they probably couldn't see him for all the trees. He stumbled a couple of times, and almost fell once when he tripped on a fallen limb. He was really glad he'd worn his tennis shoes; sometimes when it was hot, he went to Harley's barefoot. After a little, he stopped running and he could see their flashlight and hear them. He tried not to make any noise breathing, even though he was gasping for breath.

"Ah has ta git outta here," he thought, and he turned right and started walking as quietly as he could toward the edge of the woods and toward Maggie's grove. When they were near where he'd been, he went behind a big tree and stopped. He could hear them running deeper into the woods. Occasionally, one of them would say something, but he couldn't understand what they were saying.

James started walking again and he heard a noise and a yell. One of them had run into a tree or tripped over something. He walked faster. When he reached the clearing, he saw Mis' Mac's orange grove across the dirt road that led to her place, and he ran into the grove and stopped behind an orange tree to think. He knew that his tracks could be seen in the dirt road, but the orange grove had grass in it, so he wouldn't leave any more tracks. "Mebbe Ah oughta go ta huh place," he thought. "Ah'm closer ta huh house. But Ah won't bot'er huh, jes' hide dere. If dey go dere, dey won't bot'er a ole white woman."

He probably could have walked there before the three boys got back in the truck and drove there, but his feet wouldn't let him. They were running. Once he was near the end of the grove, he started to relax a little, and began walking. He was still panting, and he noticed that his clothes were soaked with sweat. He realized that, if he hadn't run, they might be soaked with blood.

He was already near her house when he heard the truck start. He hadn't actually expected them to go down Mis' Mac's road, but he wasn't surprised when they did; they probably didn't know the area and had no idea where the road went. He was glad they hadn't gone toward his house; he didn't want to think what might have happened with his parents.

James decided to stay in the orange grove, which stopped about thirty feet from her house. He climbed onto a low limb, and felt a spider web across his face. Normally, that would've caused him a lot of anxiety, but he just brushed it away, reflexively. Trembling, he stood facing the house with his left arm around the trunk of the tree. He knew no one could see him there unless they walked out into the grove with a light.

As he waited, he saw Mis' Mac go to her living room window, look out, and walk away. "She mus' a heared da truck." In a minute, he saw two lights come on in the back of the house. "Whut she doin'?" he wondered. "She gittin' a gun?" Just before the truck pulled up, he saw her turn the outside light on, walk out onto the screened-in front porch, and latch the screen door. "She ain't got no gun, thank ya Jesus," James breathed in relief.

Suddenly, he became afraid for her. "Whut if dem boys does do sumpin ta Mis' Mac?" he worried. "Whut kin Ah do?"

He wondered if she had a tool that he might be able to use as a weapon. He could run to save himself, but if they did something to Mis' Mac, he knew he would have to do something to help her. The only tools he thought he could use were the shovel and the axe. "Lawd, Ah hope Ah 'on't havta use 'em," he thought. He knew Mis' Mac had a gun in her house somewhere, probably in the bedroom, but he'd never been in that part of her house. He wasn't about to use a gun, anyway; he figured if he shot a white boy, even to save Mis' Mac, he'd end up swinging from a tree.

"Ah'm sweatin' buckets," he thought. He pulled the front of his wet shirt away from his chest.

The truck pulled into the driveway beside her house and stopped. She was standing on the side of the porch near the driveway. "She so thin," James thought. "Little, but brave." James noticed that her hair was down. She'd undone the braids and combed it. He'd never seen her hair hanging loose and was surprised that it hung halfway down her back. Some other time, that would've made a big impression on him.

"You boys lost?" she asked. "Or rabbit huntin'?"

"No, ma'am, we coon huntin'," the driver said, and they laughed.

James' heart skipped a beat. He wanted to make sure his silhouette couldn't be seen through the tree leaves, and he instinctively moved closer to the tree trunk, and wrapped his arm tighter around it. He put his right hand on a limb and a thorn pricked his finger. He didn't make a sound, but moved his hand slowly, and felt carefully before wrapping his hand around the limb.

He wondered if Mis' Mac knew what they meant by "coon." He certainly had never heard her use any such language.

"Huntin' coons?" she asked. She glanced at the back of the truck. She didn't think they were hunting coons, and when she saw a rope, but no dog, she knew what they were after. Nobody hunted coons without a good coon dog.

"Yes, ma'am. We seen one down the road," he answered. "Thought he might a come up here. You seen one?"

James heard them laughing. And he felt himself shaking. He was unaware of placing his right hand over his heart. "Oh Lawd," he whispered, and it became a prayer. "Please he'p us. Please keep Mis' Mac safe from dese boys. Please, Jesus. Dey only here 'cause a me. Please 'on't let 'em hurt Mis' Mac." Sweat was dripping off his face.

Maggie knew exactly what they meant, and suddenly, she felt afraid. Not for herself, but for whomever they'd seen. Her mind went first to Freeman, her sharecropper and friend, but she realized immediately that he wouldn't be out after nine o'clock. Then she thought of James. She knew that he often went to Harley's on Sunday evenings and he was probably walking home.

"Oh dear God," she thought, "they must be after James." She worked hard to keep her face from showing any of the emotion that was surging through her body.

"Look," she said. "I have animals on this property, so I don't allow any hunting. But there are a lot of woods around that you can hunt in. If you go back down this lane an' turn right, you'll come to the highway in a couple of miles. If you go straight across, there's a big field an' some woods there where you can hunt. Good night now. You boys be careful now."

With that, she turned and started walking toward the door.

"Hey, lady," one of the boys called.

She stopped and turned to face them.

"That coon wuz headed in this direction. He might be dangerous, so you better lock yore doors," he said sarcastically. Then he asked, "Ain't you scared livin' out here all by yoreself?"

James could feel his heart thumping against his chest. Sweat was running into his eyes, but he didn't dare move to wipe them. "Whut dey gon' do?" he wondered. "Dat soun' like a threat." He imagined all kinds of scenarios while he held his breath waiting for her answer.

"Who said I live by myself?" she asked. "Everybody else is gittin' ready for bed." And she opened the door, went in the house, and turned off the porch light.

"Dat's why she turned dem lights on in da back," he thought, "so dey thank dey's somebody else in da house." James admired her more in that moment than he ever had before, and he'd always greatly admired her.

From where he stood, still hardly breathing, he saw her lock the door, and then stand with her back against it. He saw her put both hands over her heart and look toward the ceiling. When the truck backed up, she sat down in a chair away from the window, but looking out. Clearly, she didn't want to be seen, but she wanted to see the truck leave.

James stayed where he was for a few minutes to make sure the boys were really gone. When Maggie got up and turned the light off in the living room, he figured she was all right and she was going to bed. He could go home. He took a deep breath and sighed.

Suddenly, he heard a choir of crickets chirping and realized they must have been chirping the whole time he'd been there. He was amazed that he hadn't heard them.

He jumped down from the limb he'd stood on, and when his feet hit the ground, his weak knees almost buckled under him. He wasn't sure he could walk, so he sat down on the limb and leaned against the tree trunk. He closed his eyes, and just breathed, saying a silent prayer of thanks. Then he looked at the house again and saw that Maggie only had one light on in the back of the house. "Thank ya, Lawd Jesus," he said, thinking she was getting ready for bed.

On his way home, James thought about telling his parents how Maggie had handled the boys, but he didn't want them to know about the danger he'd been in, so he decided not to say anything about it. When he undressed for bed, he saw a cut on his leg, and blood on his pant leg. He was glad it didn't get on his tennis shoe. He washed the pant leg in the sink because he didn't want his mother to see the blood, even though he knew it was just a scratch. And he washed the wound.

The next night when they were having supper, his mother said, "Freeman wuz here dis e'enin'. Seems dere wuz some white boys coon huntin' out here las' night. Dey went up ta Mis' Mac's an' she say dey had a rope in da back a da truck."

James and Pearson had been busily eating, but Pearl's tone made them both stop and look at her. She was watching James, and he knew by her expression that she'd found out what she wanted to know.

"She wuz sk'ed hit wuz you," Pearl said. "Why didn' ya tell us, baby?"

"Didn' wont ta worry ya," James said.

"Son, whut in da worl' happened?" Pearson asked.

"Ah's walkin' home from Harley's an' dis truck come 'long. Ah t'ought it wuz Unc' Joseph, an' Ah's standin' dere by da side a da road. When is dey ever any white folks on dis road?" He paused.

"Dey tol' me ta git in da truck, an' Ah went behine it an' knocked on da tail gate like Ah wuz gittin' in, an' tuk off in da woods. Ah's gon' 'fore dey e'em knowed it," James said, studying his parents' faces.

After a few questions and much expressed concern, James told them about Maggie and how she handled the situation. "Ah's sk'ed dey might hurt huh, an' Ah woulda had ta he'p huh, but ya shoulda saw huh."

"Ah'm glad dey didn' bot'er Mis' Mac," Pearson said. "Ya done da right thang, Son."

"Freeman wuz upset dat he didn' e'em hear da truck," Pearl said. She didn't tell them the rest of what Freeman said because she thought he'd spoken to her in confidence. He said he felt like he let Maggie down. It really bothered him that she might have needed him, and he didn't even know it, and he didn't take care of her. "Dat's mah job," he said, with moist eyes. He said five years earlier, he would've heard the truck and gone over there with his shotgun. Pearl didn't tell him, but she was relieved for him, James, and Maggie that he didn't hear the truck.

James and his parents were afraid for a while. Pearl and Pearson made James promise that he'd either drive to Harley's after that, or get Harley to drive him home. James drove for a while because he was too afraid to even walk over there in the daylight. But it had been almost a year, no one had seen those boys again, and James was not afraid anymore. He had Shep with him and he liked to walk. He knew if he heard someone coming, he could go in the woods or the orange grove and they wouldn't see him. He'd have plenty of time before they got to where he was because he could hear a vehicle coming a long way off.

Standing alone at the site, and feeling his body tensing, James asked out loud, "Why dey come in threes?" He paused. "Damn cowards, dat's why. Ah bet none a dem ole scared asses would come out here by demse'f. Ah bet ya dat. Naw, dey ain't got da nerve ta face me like a man." His voice was getting louder. "Ah swear, if Ah could jes' git my hands on one a dem, dey wouldn' never bot'er none a us ag'in. When Ah git thu wit' dem, dey wish dey never wuz born. Dem damn crackers!"

He remained silent and watched the big full moon for a while as he walked along the little country road, catching occasional whiffs of orange blossoms on some late-blooming trees, and feeling more peaceful as he walked. He looked at the night sky, full of glittering diamonds, and wondered how many thousands of stars there were.

Suddenly, he stopped. He thought about some of the things he had to be grateful for, and he was overwhelmed with joy, as though it had descended on him from the stars. Looking up at the twinkling sky, he said, "Life ain't always easy, but it mostly good. Thank ya, Lawd Jesus. Thank ya, Suh."

As he started walking again, he looked at the big moon and declared, "Ah'm gon' fine a nice necklace fuh huh, da purtiest one Ah gots da money fuh. If da heart wit' diamonds ain't dere, Ah'm still gon' fine a good un. Dey cost three dollars, an' it take me ovah fo' hours a work fuh dat, but Ah 'on't care. Ah'm gon' buy a nice necklace fuh mah Saleena!"

Wednesday

Sometime during the night, James decided that he'd stop trying to go to sleep since his mind kept hopping from the encounter with Mr. Roberts at the phosphate company, to the clerk and the little girl in the dime store. He was afraid the girl had bought the necklace that he wanted so badly for Saleena. And he was afraid that he had no chance of getting a job at the phosphate company. However, his tired body eventually overpowered his brain, and he drifted off. Then he slept so well, he was surprised when he woke up to find that it was full daylight.

He immediately sprang out of bed. "Ah'm awready 'pose' ta be at Mis' Mac's," he thought. Nevertheless, he took time to eat the breakfast that his mother had prepared for him: half a grapefruit covered with honey, eggs, grits, sausage links, and fried biscuits.

"You up late yestiddy an' today," Pearl observed, as she sat across from him, sipping her second cup of coffee. Pearson had already left for the field.

"Ah knows," James replied. "Ah got a lot on mah mind."

"Ya gon' git dat job, son," Pearl said. "Jes talk ta da Lawd 'bout it."

"Ah sho hopes so," he said, and then changed the subject. "Ya'll git all dem peas shelled an' put up?"

"Sho we did," Pearl laughed. "Ya knows Ah'm a good pea sheller, an' yo' daddy he'ped me, too."

"You a good pea sheller, awright." He looked at a piece of sausage link dangling from his fork. "Dese sausage is good."

"Dey is, ain't dey?" Pearl said. "Ya daddy make good sausage, dat da truf, an' we ain't got many lef'. Time ta git us anot'er pig."

They'd raised hogs for several years, but their last bunch rooted their way under the American-wire fence so many times Pearson decided they weren't worth the trouble. Now, they'd occasionally buy a small pig from one of their neighbors and raise it to butcher.

"Saleena's daddy got pigs," James reminded her. "Us could prob'ly git one from him."

"Yeah, he do," Pearl agreed. "Dat dere's a good ideal."

"Ah got ta go," James said after he put the last bite in his mouth. "Mis' Mac gon' thank Ah ain't comin', fuh sho."

"She sho will. Ya ain't never been dis late."

James put some kumquat preserves on the last piece of fried biscuit, kissed his mother's cheek, and walked onto the porch.

"Tell Mis' Mac Ah see huh soon," Pearl said, wiping her hands on her apron. "An' thank huh fuh da watermelon. Don' tell huh we ain't et it yet."

"Ah won't," James assured her. "We oughta cut it dis aftanoon." He took his cap off the nail on the porch, and put it on.

"Oh, an' remin' yo' unc' Freeman he comin' ta dinner," Pearl added.

"Yes, ma'am," he called, as he went down the porch steps.

The morning air was still nice, but James could tell it was going to be a hot day. The sun was higher than it normally was when he went to Maggie's. "Ah hates ta start late," he thought. "Da mornin' done gone befo' ya e'em knows it."

He looked around for Shep, but didn't see him anywhere. "Mus' be out wit' Daddy," he thought. He walked along in the right rut of the dirt road. If he walked on the left, he felt like he was on the wrong side of the road, the way it would feel if he were driving. The sand in the road was packed down hard in the ruts, so walking was pretty easy.

"Ah done been rushin' so much dis mornin', Ah ain't e'em t'ought nuttin' 'bout Saleena," he said. "Dat ain't happen' fuh a while." Thinking of her made energy surge through his body, and at the same time, made him feel weak in the pit of his stomach. "Lawd, she fine! Ah sho hopes she come ta church tonight."

He looked to the left, and he saw his father on the tractor way out in the field. "Mus' be diskin' up where dem taters wuz at," he thought. "We dug da las' a dem las' week."

Shep ran up to James, who bent over and patted his head. "Ya awready out here, an' Mis' Mac like ya, Shep, so you kin come. Ah be e'em later if Ah tuk ya back ta da house."

As they approached Maggie's orange grove and *the place*, James thought about that hot July night. Any time he thought about it, he could feel his energy change; he started to feel nervous the way he had that night, and he started sweating. The morning was warm, but not that warm. "Ah oughta talk ta Mis' Mac 'bout dat night. Ah never e'em tole huh Ah wuz watchin' huh an' dem boys. Ah's so sk'ed dey'd hurt huh." He'd worked for her one day about a month after the incident, but Harley was with him, and neither she nor James mentioned it. A few months later, he'd worked for her again, but by then, he just wanted to forget about it. On the rest of the walk to her place, he went over different ways he might tell her, but by the time he got there, he still hadn't decided when or how.

She didn't come out when he arrived. "Mis' Mac," he called loudly, wondering if she was in the house.

He was standing in the yard near the back porch, cap in hand, when she walked out on the porch. Salty tracks of dried tears made lines down her cheeks.

"James," she said. "When you weren't here earlier, I didn't think you were comin' today."

"Could she be cryin' 'bout dat?" James wondered.

"Ah'm sorry," he said. "Ah wuz mighty ti'ed an' Ah slept late. You awright, Mis' Mac?"

"Yes, I'm fine," she said. "Come sit with me. I'm anxious to hear about what happened at the phosphate company."

Maggie sat down in a rocking chair, and James went on the porch, followed by Shep, and sat down in a rocker near her. He noticed a basket on the table with some guavas in it, and he breathed deeply to savor the aroma. Shep walked over to her.

"Well, hello there, Shep," she said, patting his head and rubbing his ears. "Haven't seen you for a while."

Shep showed his feelings with a fiercely wagging tail, but when she stopped petting him, he lay down beside the chair James was sitting in. With his head resting on his front paws, he was soon asleep.

The chickens gathered in the yard in front of them, just in case watermelon seeds should start descending. But they didn't stand and wait; they were busily scratching and pecking. And three of them went running off after a big grasshopper.

James and Maggie sat and rocked as they talked. He found the back-and-forth motion of the rocking chair soothing. He repeated his experience at the mine word for word as well as he remembered it, which was pretty well—it was vivid in his mind. Every now and then, the scent of the guavas reached him and relaxed him a little.

When James told her that Mr. Roberts said, "You young bucks come in here an' thank ya jes' gonna git hired 'cause ya young an' strong," she exclaimed, "Oh my Lord! I can't believe he said that!"

"Yes, ma'am," James replied, nodding his head. "Dat whut he tol' me."

"Well, I've known Carl Roberts for many years—decades, in fact," she said. "My daddy was his boss for a long time an' I heard quite a bit about him. I knew he wouldn't treat you really well, but that was just crude. Completely uncalled for."

They were both silent for a couple of minutes. "I'm so sorry that happened to you, James. A good worker like you should be able to apply for a job an' just be treated decently. Anybody should." She sat, just thinking, for a moment before saying again, "I'm so sorry."

James didn't know what to say. He was touched by what she said. "Thank you, Mis' Mac," he replied.

He thought of Maggie differently than he did other white people. However, from the time he was small, he'd been trained to show deference to her that he didn't have to show to any other adults he knew, except whites. And he saw his dad and Freeman do the same. *She* didn't demand it, but the culture did.

Again they remained silent for a little while, both gently rocking back and forth. The aroma from the guavas made his mouth water. She took her handkerchief out of her apron pocket, and he saw in his peripheral vision that she wiped her eyes.

The chickens were giving up hope of food descending on them, and they gradually drifted off to other parts of the yard and into the grove, stopping to scratch here and there as they went.

James stopped rocking and shifted in his chair. "Ya know, Mis' Mac," he said hesitantly, "We ain't talked about dat night when dem boys wuz afta me."

"Oh James," she said. "I was scared to death. I saw the rope in the back of their truck, and I hardly slept at all that night, wondering where you were, if you were at home, . . ." and her voice trembled as she added, "an' listenin' for a gun shot."

James had never considered what she might have gone through. He was surprised that she had lost sleep worrying about him. "Ah shoulda said sumpin dat night ta let huh know Ah's here," he thought.

"Ah never tol' ya 'bout it," he said. "Ah wuz sk'ed fuh you. Ah wuz in a orange tree right out dere when dey come ta da house." He pointed at the tree. "Ah woulda said sumpin to ya afta dey lef', but Ah t'ought you went ta bed, an' Ah didn' wont ta scare ya no mo'."

"Freeman told me you were in the grove. An' you were right there!"

"Ah never t'ought dey'd come on up here, Mis' Mac. Ah sho wouldn' never put you in no danger."

"I was a little scared," she admitted. "You just never know what a bunch of crazy boys might do. I surely didn't want anybody to think I was here alone, so I turned the lights on in the back rooms when I heard the truck comin', just in case it was somebody I didn't know. You know, I thought someone was comin' to tell me that somebody had died; it's times like that I wish we had telephones out here."

"Sho would be nice," James said. "Ya sho wuz brave, Mis' Mac. Da way dem boys wuz talkin', Ah wuz scared dey wuz gon' hurt ya."

"Well, don't you worry about it. Everything turned out all right."

"Ah'm sorry Ah didn' say nuttin'," James said, his head hung down. "Ah t'ought ya went ta bed."

"Yes, of course, you would think that," she said softly.

"At firs', Ah went in da woods, but Ah couldn' git away from dem boys," James explained, "so Ah went in da grove. Ah knowed dey'd see mah tracks in da road, but not in da grove. Dey didn' know Ah come dis way, an' Ah never t'ought dey'd come dis way. Den, when Ah heared da truck comin' up here, Ah went in dat dere tree."

"Well, did they say somethin' to you at first, or did you just run right away?" she asked.

"Ah's goin' home from Harley's," James explained. "Ah t'ought it were Unc' Joseph comin', so Ah jes' stood dere waitin' ta talk ta 'im, but it wuz dem dere boys. Dey aks me whut Ah wuz doin' out here in da woods," James said, "an' tol' me ta git in da back a da truck. Ah's tryin' ta thank a whut ta do, an' dey's gittin' mad, an' Ah saw a rope in da back a da truck, so Ah hit da tailgate like Ah's gittin' in, an' Ah tuk off in da woods."

"You must have been really scared, James," she said.

"Ah sho wuz, Mis' Mac," he admitted. "'Ah's sc'ed ta def. 'Bout da worse in mah life."

"You could have called me an' come in the house when you got here," she said. "I would've hidden you in the back room."

"Ah never t'ought a dat," he said. "But dey mighta seen mah tracks in da sandy driveway, an' dey'd know Ah's in da house."

"You're right, James," she agreed, nodding her head. Then, her voice rising, "It makes me so angry that white boys do things like that. I don't understand them at all. It's just terrible that you can't even feel safe out here in the country right near your own home." She paused, and her voice returned to normal. "I sure hope things will be different soon."

"Ah sho do, too, Mis' Mac," he said softly. "Ah sho do, too. An' Ah'm sorry dat happen' ta you."

"Well, I was mostly just worried about *you*," she said.

James thought he needed to get busy with the wood, but he stayed where he was because Maggie seemed to have something else on her mind.

"You know, I've been wantin' to ask you somethin', James," she said.

"Yes'm," he replied, wondering what it could be.

She hesitated for a moment, thinking about how to say it. "Now that Freeman is older an' not able to do as much around here, I've been thinkin' about hirin' someone to do sharecroppin'. Of course, I'd still keep Freeman on for the kinds of things he does now, an' he can stay in the sharecropper's house."

She hesitated again. "I was wonderin' if you would be interested. You could live with your parents, or we could arrange somethin' else for you." She added softly, "I want your honest feelings, James."

James was surprised by the offer; he had actually thought a few times about the possibility of doing it after Freeman died. He knew he'd have no problem working for Maggie.

"Ah 'preciate dat, Mis' Mac," he replied. "Ah likes workin' fuh ya, but Ah wonts ta work somewhere else fuh a while if Ah kin—do sumpin 'sides farmin'. Ah wonts ta work at da mines."

"That's what I thought, James, but I wanted to offer you the job before I talked to anyone else, just in case you were interested. I know we could work well together."

"Dat ain't nuttin' but da truf," he said.

Maggie stopped rocking, took her glasses off, put them on her lap, and rubbed her eyes with the back of her hand. She put the glasses back on and started rocking again.

"I haven't made any decisions about this," she went on. "I haven't even talked to Freeman about it, so please don't say anything to him, or to anyone else."

"Ah sho won't say nuttin', Mis' Mac," he replied.

As much as she disliked having to do it, she'd started thinking about finding someone who could replace Freeman. She had to have someone to run the farm when he was no longer able to. She sort of hoped James wouldn't take the offer because she didn't think he'd be satisfied for long. And, she had someone in mind that she thought would be perfect.

"Well, I've talked your ear off, James." She smiled. "Were you expectin' to work today? Unfortunately, it's getting' late an' warm now."

James stood up and so did Shep. "Ah'll work fuh a lil while—till dinner time," he answered. "Mine if Ah gits some water, ma'am?"

"Help yourself. An' I bet Shep would like some, too."

James took a little bowl from beside the wall and put a dipper full in it. Mis' Mac kept the bowl there for Tommiecat and for Shep's visits even though he was only there a few times a year.

"James, would you like some guavas?" she asked, knowing the answer.

"Sho would, Mis' Mac. Thank ya, ma'am." He took two, put one in his pocket, and started munching on the other one. "Ah'm gon' go git da wheelbarrow."

"All right, then," she said. "Let me know when you finish."

James was looking forward to being in the woods. He was already hot and he knew it would be a little cooler in there. And his conversation with Maggie had been unsettling to him.

"Po' Mis' Mac—worryin' 'bout me afta Ah's done home in bed." He tried to think of some way he could make it up to her, but he knew there was nothing he could do. "Mebbe Ah oughta be huh sharecropper," he thought, but he knew he wouldn't be happy doing that. He was tired of farm work. But he decided that in the future, he'd try extra hard not to cause her any worry of any kind. If she needed him to work, he'd be there as soon as he could, even if he did get the job at the phosphate company.

♥   ♥   ♥

SHEP WAS RIGHT BESIDE JAMES AS THEY STARTED for the woods, but he soon ran ahead. As they neared the woods, James was still deep in thought. He was almost through eating the guava, and he breathed in its unique aroma. He heard the rattle the first time, but he was so preoccupied with his thoughts and the guava that it didn't register. The second rattle stopped him in his tracks. Because he'd been distracted, he hadn't even noticed when Shep stopped near the palmettos.

He saw him instantly. "Shep!" he exclaimed. "Oh sweet Jesus." Fortunately, Shep did not move.

James was nine when his Aunt Drusilla died from a rattlesnake bite, so he remembered it well. The fear that was instilled in him made him afraid of all snakes; even if a harmless snake startled him, his heart would race for several minutes.

One day when he was twelve, he was walking to the field with his father, and he stepped over a grass snake. He knew, instantly, that it was a grass snake, but his heart reacted faster than his brain. Pearson was about to laugh as James yelled and jumped, but when he saw the fear on the boy's face, he realized it wasn't funny. He assured him that grass snakes were harmless, but James already knew that.

Around the same time, a kingsnake was living in their barn. James knew it was there, but every time he saw it, it scared him. He asked Pearson to kill it, but Pearson explained how beneficial kingsnakes were, and that they eat rattlesnakes. When James heard that, he was content to let the snake live there even though it still scared him.

But this *was* a rattlesnake. The axe was in the wheelbarrow, but it wasn't long enough to use. He knew if he used the axe, he'd be within striking distance of the snake. And he knew that if Shep moved, he could easily get bit. James thought about throwing the axe at the snake, but he was afraid he'd miss and the snake would bite Shep.

He stood still. "Oh Lawd, please he'p me," he prayed in earnest.

He wanted to go back to the house and ask Mis' Mac for her gun, but he was afraid that if he left, Shep would move and the snake would bite him. Shep was still as a statue, just looking at the snake. James couldn't see it, and that scared him more. If he could see it, he'd know how close it was to Shep. He knew the snake could strike faster than the eye could see; he knew it could bite Shep before he even saw it. As he strained to see the snake, he suddenly realized that he wasn't hearing any more rattles, and Shep started moving forward. James finally saw it as it slithered away. It looked about five feet long.

"Shep, no!" he commanded. "Come 'ere." Shep looked at him as if to say, "Do I have to?" and James repeated, "Come 'ere."

As the dog approached him, James fell on his knees and threw his arms around him. "Oh Shep, Ah t'ought ya wuz a goner." After a moment, he added, "Dat's why you 'on't always git ta come wit' me. But ya ain't done nuttin' wrong. Good dog, Shep. Good dog."

"Oh Lawd," he said as he stood up, "Ah wuz sk'ed. Thank you, Lawd Jesus, fuh savin' mah Shep. Thank ya Suh, thank ya."

He knew he ought to kill the snake, and he thought about trying to hit it with the axe as it crawled away, but he was too scared. It wasn't as dangerous then, not coiled; it could still strike, it just couldn't leap as far. And he knew the snake would be gone before he could go back to Mis' Mac's and get her gun. So he just continued on his way, being careful to keep Shep near him. "At least, dey eats rats," he thought. But he knew they also ate birds, squirrels, and rabbits.

In the piney woods, everything was still and quiet, except for an occasional birdcall. It seemed to James that he could hear the silence. As he absorbed the peacefulness of the forest, he gradually began to relax. He took some long, slow breaths as he pushed the wheelbarrow deep into the woods, breathing in the pungent smell of pinesap. He'd forgotten all his worries with the rattlesnake giving him something different to worry about, but in the woods, he stopped thinking about the snake. Once he was working, he stayed focused on getting the pieces of lighter. Of course, that didn't prevent images of Saleena from popping into his mind.

Shep walked alongside him as he worked, and James would make comments sporadically. "It's a bunch a lighterd ovah dere, Shep," he teased. "Git it an' put it in da wheelbarrow." Shep looked at him with a puzzled expression, and James laughed.

It didn't take him long to fill the wheelbarrow, and he decided that, instead of sitting down to rest, he'd go to the pond. He munched on the other guava as he walked. The pond had always been one of his favorite places. He'd fished there since he was a little boy, usually with his father or Freeman, and, occasionally, with his mother and Maggie.

As he stood in the sunshine, he thought about how nice it would be to go swimming. James had been to Walker Lake in Tampa a few times with his family or some of his friends. There were only a few places where Negroes were allowed to go in the water, or even be on the beach. When they went, they'd pack a picnic lunch—usually some sandwiches, fried chicken, potato salad, and iced tea. Once, James and his sister went with their parents up to Butler Beach, near St. Augustine. His brothers, who lived in north Florida, met them at the beach and they spent the day together. James loved the ocean and wanted to go back, but they hadn't made the trip again. When he went to the lake with his friends, they played on the sandy shore most of the day, usually staying until dark. He wanted to take Saleena there, but her parents wouldn't allow her to go.

James looked at the area around the pond. For years, it had been the main pasture for most of the McClellans' cows. Mr. McClellan had the pond dug so the cows would have water, and he had it stocked with fish because he liked to fish. Maggie had left the cows in that area until Freeman got older. Then, she'd sold several cows to reduce the size of her herd, and moved the rest to a smaller pasture behind her house to make things easier for Freeman. Now, the grass was tall and young oaks were scattered about. Over near the fence where the grass was thin, James could see yellow blooms on some prickly pear cactuses.

For a few years, Freeman had cut the grass for hay, but Maggie knew that loading the hay onto a truck and unloading it into the barn was too hard for him, even though she hired someone to help him. She thought about getting someone else to do the whole process, but thought that would embarrass Freeman, so she told him that hay was too much trouble, she didn't want to fool with it anymore, and she'd just buy it.

James stood under a big oak tree near the pond and leaned with his back against the trunk, and one foot propped on it. Shep got a drink from the pond and then walked around the edge, checking to see if anything needed attention. When he was certain that everything was in order, he went over to James and lay down beside him. James sat down, put his hand on the dog's side, and closed his eyes, feeling the connection.

As he relaxed, he thought about fishing, and remembered one day when he and his dad went fishing in a phosphate pit. They went to Pierce to go with Pearson's friend Sam, who had a boat. James ran off with Sam's two sons to play hide-and-seek while the two men talked, and he hid fairly near to where they were talking, and overheard the end of their conversation.

"Ah tell you Pearson," Sam said, "dey ain't no way dey looked at dat woman wrong. Dey woulda been too sc'ed ta do sumpin dat stupid. Man, dey tried ta say dat dem boys wuz comin' on ta huh. Ah knowed dem like Ah know da back a my han', an' dey wouldn' never e'em thank 'bout nuttin' dat stupid." Sam shook his head.

"Sho 'on't seem like it," Pearson said.

"Lemuel saw 'em dere, bof a 'em tied ta a pine tree wit' dey throats slit wide open. Man, Lemuel say it's da worse thang he ever laid his ole eyes on. All 'cause dey say dey looked at a white woman. All 'cause of a lie, dem boys los' dey lifes. Dem crackers done killed 'em dead fuh no reason."

Sam didn't feel like going fishing that day; he said he was sticking close to home for a while. So Pearson and James went to a pit between Lakeland and Mulberry and fished from the bank. They stood right by Highway 37 in plain view of people passing by. James knew that his father was nervous, and he saw him look at the road any time a car drove by slowly.

Pearson didn't mention the incident to James because he was only nine, and James didn't mention it because he didn't want Pearson to think he'd been eavesdropping on him and Sam, but James noticed his father was jumpy, and that made him uneasy. They didn't fish long. Luckily, the fish were biting, and when they had six fish, Pearson said they had enough for supper and they were going home. Normally, James would've begged to stay longer, but that day, he was actually relieved to be going home. Even as a boy, he understood the danger, and he was afraid he might do something that would get him tied to a tree.

James realized, as he sat in the safe, isolated place, that he was feeling that old fear and that he was now an age when he always had to be extra careful and always on guard. "Lawd, Lawd, Lawd," he thought. "Am Ah gon' hafta be sc'ed all mah life?"

He opened his eyes just a second too late to see a large bass reenter the water, but he heard the splash. "Oh no," he said, seeing the wake in the water. "Ah sho woulda like ta seen dat." He kept his eyes open then, and pretty soon he was rewarded with another splash. "Ah got ta come fishin' here," he said. "Me an' Harley."

He felt energized thinking about catching that big bass. When he returned to work, he pushed the wheelbarrow out of the woods more easily than usual even though it was a long trip. He was anxious to tell Maggie about the fish and the snake, but she was in the yard on the other side of the house in her flower garden. He finished chopping the lighter and some oak from the woodpile, and piling it in the shed, and she appeared with a big smile and a handful of colorful zinnias.

"It's eleven-thirty," she said. "Are you plannin' to go for another load?"

"No, ma'am," he answered, removing his cap.

"I made some lemonade," Maggie said. "I'll get it."

She went in the house, and James walked over to the porch and sat down on the steps. Shep sat at his feet. Maggie returned with two glasses of lemonade, and handed James one.

"Me an' Shep done had quite a mornin'," he said, leaning over and patting Shep on the head.

"Is that so?" she asked, sitting down in the rocking chair nearest James. "What happened?"

James told her about the rattlesnake, and she expressed concern for Shep and said she was glad James hadn't tried to kill it. "That scares me just thinkin' about it," she said, shaking her head. "There are plenty of rattlesnakes; one more won't matter. You surely did have quite a mornin'."

He told her about the bass. "Ah'd like ta go fishin', if dat's awright."

"Of course," she responded. "Maybe you an' Freeman can go. That would probably do him good. Don't you think so, James?"

"Prob'ly would, Mis' Mac," he said. He wanted to go with Harley, but he realized that he probably wouldn't be doing much more fishing with his uncle Freeman. "Prob'ly do us bof some good."

James was still sitting on the step when they heard Freeman coming in the old truck. "Here he come now," James said. "Mus' be gittin' hongry. He 'pose' ta come ta da house fuh dinner wit' us."

"He is?" she asked, surprised. "That's good. Maybe your mama can talk some sense into him. He hasn't been feelin' well, and I'm really concerned about his health. I tried to get him to go to a doctor, but he won't even consider it. Sometimes he is so stubborn!"

"Yes'm," he agreed. "Ah 'on't thank Unc' Freeman listen ta nobody, but she kin try. Ah knows she worried, too."

"I hope she will," Maggie said. "I'm afraid he has somethin' wrong with him."

James was struck by her concern for his uncle. He knew Mis' Mac and Freeman were old friends and he knew that she depended on him to take care of the place, but he was surprised at the depth of her concern. "Mebbe dat's why she wuz cryin'," he thought.

"By the way, if he feels up to it, we're goin' to go look at trucks tomorrow," Maggie said, and waved at Freeman, who was sitting in the truck.

"Oh no!" James thought. "If Ah 'on't get da job, Ah cain't buy da ole truck. Course, if Ah 'on't git da job, Ah won't need it. But Ah sho wonts it. Mebbe Ah kin work fuh huh 'nough ta buy it."

"I believe you worked for almost two hours, James," Maggie said. "I'll add that to the $2.80 I owe you from Monday. I haven't been anywhere to get change, but I'll have it for you tomorrow."

James responded. "Ah b'lieve Ah jes' worked a hour an' a half today. Ah tuk some time goin' down ta da pond."

"All right, James if that's what you think," she said. "It's always a pleasure doin' business with you, not to mention that I enjoy your company, as well."

"Thank ya, Mis' Mac," he replied.

"That's $1.05, plus $2.80. How much is that, James?" She knew very well how much it was, but the teacher in her liked to give him problems to figure out.

"Le's see." He rubbed the back of his neck and smiled, knowing he was being tested. "Three dollars an' eighty-five cent'."

"Thank you, James," she said. "If you want to come over tomorrow afternoon, I should have the right change for you then."

As he turned to leave, Maggie remembered the guavas. "Here James, take these guavas. I've got plenty more."

He smiled as he stuffed four guavas in his pockets and kept one out to eat. "Thank ya, Mis' Mac."

As James started for the truck, Shep ran ahead of him and jumped in the back. James looked at Freeman's face through the open window and was glad to see that his uncle looked better than he had on Monday.

"Freeman," Maggie called. "Relax and enjoy your dinner with Pearl, and don't hurry back. There's nothin' to do today. And if you can get some rest, maybe you'll feel like goin' to town tomorrow."

Freeman thought there were things to do. All he'd done that week was pick three watermelons and drive James home on Monday. But he didn't feel like doing anything. He hoped he'd feel better the next week and he could do everything then. Of course, there was nothing very important to do, just keeping up with things—probably picking some peas or tomatoes, and Maggie would do that if it needed to be done, but he didn't like for her to have to do it. He thought of that as his responsibility.

"Yes'm," he answered. "Ah will, Mis' Maggie."

As they pulled out of the driveway, James asked, "Wanna guava, Unc' Freeman?"

"No, thank ya. She done awready give me some."

"Ya look better today, Unc' Freeman," James said, studying the older man. "Ya feelin' better?"

"Yep, Ah is, James," he replied. "Praise da Lawd fuh dat."

"Dat's good," James said. "Us been worried 'bout you."

"Felt bad Monday, but Ah's feelin' better now," Freeman said. "Maggie worryin', too. She got ta stop all dat worryin' 'bout me. Ah kin take care a mahse'f."

James was surprised to hear him say her name without the "Mis'." Freeman always called her "Mis' Maggie." James had asked him why one time, because all the other Negroes called her "Mis' Mac." Freeman told him that his father told him to call her "Mis' Maggie" when he was a little boy, and he'd always called her that. Pearl had called her that, too, until she was grown and heard others calling her "Mis' Mac."

"Ah knows," James said. "Ah jes' foun' out she wuz worried 'bout me dat night when dem crazy white boys wuz out here."

"She sho wuz," Freeman said. "She's still upset da nex' day. Made me go ovah ta ya mama's ta fine out if ya's awright."

They were silent for a minute while James felt even worse about worrying her. He rubbed his head as though trying to move the thoughts in his brain. Apparently, it worked.

"Ah seen a nice bass in da pond today," he said. "Mis' Mac say you an' me oughta go fishin'."

"Ya know, James," Freeman said in a serious tone. "Ah been thankin' 'bout whut gon' happen ta huh when Ah dies."

"Whut *will* happen to huh when he dies?" James wondered.

"Ah wont ya ta give me yo' word dat you gon' see ta huh," he said, and looked at James. "Not da farm, jes' huh. She like ya, an' she trust ya, boy. Ya got ta be dere fuh huh. Ya hear whut Ah say?"

James nodded. "Yessuh. Ah'll do dat," he said, thinking he wanted him to check on her occasionally, but he wasn't sure how often, nor did he ask. "Ah likes huh, too." He wanted to give his uncle some peace of mind. Obviously, Freeman was worried about it. James made a mental note to talk to his mother about this conversation.

He didn't tell Freeman about the snake, and he didn't mention the fish again. He decided to save those stories to tell over dinner.

Pearl was still busy cooking when they arrived at the house, so they went to the kitchen to be with her. James kissed her on the cheek, and then watched as she hugged her brother. When Freeman went to the bathroom, James took the opportunity to tell her what Maggie had requested.

"She wont me ta tell 'im ta go to da doctor?" Pearl asked. "Unh, unh, unh. Don' dat woman know dat man? He ain't gon' listen ta nobody 'bout no doctor."

"Ah tol' huh he wouldn' do it. She say he stubborn," James paused. "An' she thank he got sumpin wrong wit' 'im."

"She do? She mus' thank he really sick," Pearl said, concerned. "She know 'im right good."

"He look better today," James said, hoping to allay his mother's concern.

"Yeah, he do," Pearl agreed. "But Ah'm gon' talk ta 'im. If Mis' Mac dat worried, mus' be a problem."

When he returned to the kitchen, she asked, "Freeman, hi ya feelin'?"

"Awright," he replied.

"Ya lookin' better today, but ya been lookin' sick lately," Pearl said, "kinda like ya lost yo' bes' frien'."

"Ah knows. Ah been feelin' kinda porely."

"Mebbe you oughta see Doc Stone. He might fine out whut's troublin' you."

"Naw, Ah 'on't need no doctor. Ah'm on my knees ever night ta da good Lawd."

"Ya 'pose' ta pray, but da Lawd done give ya good sense an' spec' fuh ya ta use it an' 'on't be stupid," Pearl continued. "Dey might be sumpin wrong dat Doc Stone could fine."

"Ya been talkin' ta Maggie?" he asked suspiciously.

Pearl was able to answer honestly, "No, Ah ain't." Then she asked, "She worried 'bout you, too?"

"Yeah," he admitted. "She say da same thang."

They heard the tractor drive up and Freeman escaped to the porch to wait for Pearson. Pearl looked at James and shook her head. "Jes' whut Ah spected," she said, and they laughed. "He jes' 'bout hopeless."

She brought up the subject again after dinner when he was leaving. He was already in his truck, and she stood beside it talking to him, with one hand on the open window. Pearson and James had gone to the field.

"Whut Ah got ta live fuh?" he asked. "Da Lawd done gi' me three score an' ten. No sense tryin' ta be greedy."

"Freeman," Pearl said, somewhat dismayed. "Da Lawd ain't say ya kin *jes'* live three score an' ten. Ya cain't figger out whut He wont. Look whut happen wit' Drusilla; she went way befo' sebenny. Mebbe ya 'pose' ta live ten mo' years."

"Well, if Ah is, Ah will," he declared. "Don' ya worry 'bout me, an' tell Maggie don' be worryin' herse'f 'bout me." He started the truck. "Ya fixed a good dinner, Pearl. Ya always been a good cook. You a good sistah, too." He patted her hand. "Ah see ya soon," he said as he drove off.

Freeman had eaten with them many times during the ten years since Drusilla died, and many times over the years with Drusilla, and he'd never told her before that she was a good cook. And he'd never told her she was a good sister. After that, Pearl was even more concerned about him.

♥   ♥   ♥

Prayer meeting was a weekly event for the Cleveland family. Every Wednesday night. James had always liked going, but lately he looked forward to it even more because Saleena was usually there. Most weeks, he only saw her at church. Since she was still in school, her parents didn't allow her to go out much, and never on a school night. Besides, James didn't make any money unless he worked for Maggie, so he could only afford an occasional hamburger or movie. After the Elvis movie, they'd been to a western, and they both wanted to see more movies.

His family was the first to arrive at the church; Pearl and Pearson didn't like to be late, which meant they were often early. Consequently, James had to wait for Saleena to arrive. He hated the waiting, and was always disappointed if she wasn't there. His parents got out and went into the church, but he waited in the truck.

He sat and watched anxiously as the others arrived, occasionally wiping sweat from his brow. Most of them were in pick-up trucks because they were farmers, sharecroppers, or farm workers. A few stopped to speak to him before going on into the church.

Mardella didn't go right in. She was a pretty sixteen-year-old girl, who had a crush on James, and she sashayed over to the truck to talk to him. Since she was fairly obvious with her flirtation, James knew that Saleena was aware of her interest in him. As he waited for her, he talked to Mardella, but he was hoping she'd leave before Saleena got there. However, she was still leaning on the truck door when Saleena arrived.

"Ah got ta go," James said as he gently pushed the truck door open, forcing her to move. "Dere Saleena."

Saleena took in the scene in a glance, and she approached with a big smile on her face. Mardella stood right beside James. He took Saleena's hand and said, "'Scuse us, Mardella," and he and Saleena went under the big oak tree by the side of the church. He kissed her on the cheek.

"Ah see yo' frien' wuz keepin' you comp'ny," Saleena teased.

"Somebody need to. It take you so long ta git here," James teased back.

He got serious quickly, though. "Ah got a lotta thangs ta tell ya."

He figured he had about four minutes to talk to her. He started with the phosphate company, but first he had to tell her about going to Harley's Sunday night and Harley informing him that the mine was hiring. He managed to finish telling her about the phosphate company experience, but he knew he'd have to wait until after the service to tell her about the snake and Mis' Mac's truck and Freeman asking him to see to Mis' Mac.

The two of them went into the church and sat down in their usual pew just before the service started. James held her hand, as usual, and sat close enough to her that his leg was touching hers. She took a fan from the hymnal rack and fanned the two of them. James noticed the picture on the fan of Jesus holding a lamb. "Lil los' lamb," he thought.

The Rev. Johnson stood in front of the congregation. He didn't use the pulpit for the prayer meetings; his message was shorter than the Sunday services and the service was informal.

"Ah'm led ta read Matthew 5:44 an' 45 tonight." He waited for the people to find the passage in their Bibles.

James turned loose of Saleena's hand, and the two of them opened their Bibles and quickly flipped through the pages, trying to be the first to find Matthew and the verses. Saleena won.

"'But Ah say unto you, Love yo' enemies, bless dem dat curse you, do good ta dem dat hate you, an' pray fuh dem which despitefully use you, an' persecute you;

"Dat ye may be da children a yo' Father which is in heaven, fuh he maketh his sun ta rise on da evil an' on da good, an' sendeth rain on da jus' an' on da unjus'.'"

"Praise da Lawd God," an old man in the front row said.

James wondered about loving Mr. Roberts at the phosphate company, and the white boys who chased him. "Dat sho hard," he thought.

"Ah'm thankin' tonight 'bout da late Harry Moore," Rev. Johnson continued. "Mr. Moore wuz a brave man, an' he did all he could ta he'p us colored people. Ah wish Ah coulda knowed 'im." He paused.

"He started da firs' Flor'da branch of da NAACP, an' it spread all ovah da state. In da forties, he worked ta git equal teacher salaries fuh our people wit' da whites, an' he got 'em—he got equal salaries fuh our people! 'Magine dat! An' he registered folks ta vote. An' dat brave man investigated all da lynchin's dat happen' in dis state. How could one man—a colored man in Flor'da—do all dat? But den we know, in 1951, his house wuz bombed on Christmas day, an' him an' his wife wuz killed. Christmas day!" He paused, took out his handkerchief, and wiped his face.

James was thirteen when that happened. He remembered his family sitting around the kitchen table grieving, and talking about what a brave man Mr. Moore was. He still thought about him occasionally.

"Lovin' our enemies might be a full-time job fuh some a us," Rev. Johnson said. "Ah ain't sayin' it easy. Ah ain't sayin' Ah kin do it. But it whut da Master tol' us ta do, an' we has ta try."

"Dat's right," someone said. "Dat's right, Preacher."

"It's whut we has ta try ta do," Preacher Johnson went on. "We all knows 'bout dem. Dey hate us an' cuss us an' persecute us jus' 'cause a da color of our skin. An' Jesus tells us ta love dem peoples."

"We knows," some echoed.

"Ya know, he wadn' some white man sittin' on a throne givin' out advice. Nawsuh. He knowed from experience whut he was talkin' 'bout."

"Dat's right."

His voice was rising. "Lot a people hated Jesus."

"Yes, Lawd."

James sat still, looking at Rev. Johnson. "Ah needs ta hear dis," he thought. "Mebbe Ah kin 'membah dis when Ah needs it. Jesus wuz hated, too." Of course, James had heard it several times before, but it was particularly relevant to him now. He was out in the world more as he was becoming an adult, and he was aware of more hostile stares and hateful looks, like the ones from Mr. Roberts and the clerk in the dime store.

Beside him, Saleena was also attentive. James was still holding his open Bible, too focused on the message to even think about holding her hand.

"Ah thank offen 'bout dat po' Willie Edwards in Alabama, only twenty-five years ole," Rev. Johnson continued.

"Yes, Lawd."

"Da Klan kilt dat man 'cause dey t'ought he said sumpin ta a white woman, made 'remarks' ta huh. Mind you, dey *t'ought*. E'em if he had a done it, whut kine a remark deserve def? Ah aks ya."

James thought, "Jes' like po' Emmett Till, but he wuz only fo'teen."

"It wuz his fust day on da job drivin' a truck. His fust day. An' dey 'on't e'em know if he wuz da one dat made remarks. 'On't look like he wuz e'em da one. But da Klan 'on't care."

"Nawsuh." People were shaking their heads.

"Hel' guns on 'im an' made 'im jump off a big bridge. Dey foun' his body on down da river two months later."

James could see moisture in Rev. Johnson's eyes, and he could feel it in his. Rev. Johnson used his handkerchief to wipe his face again.

"An' mah frien's, we has ta love dem people under dem sheets."

"Preach it, Brot'er."

"Jesus say love our enemies, an' dey are our enemies."

"Yeah, dey are."

"An' we know lots a udder examples where our people been persecuted," he continued. "Even afta we wuz freed from slav'ry, dey arrested innocent mens, an' some womens, an' hired 'em out ta farmers an' comp'nies fuh years. Sometimes dem po' peoples wuz beat, ha'f starved, an' didn' have no place ta sleep. An' sometimes dey wuz worked ta def. We been hunted down, dragged behine trucks, beat ta def, worked ta def, hung from trees . . ." He paused. "No justice, no trials, an' no punishment fuh dem dat does it."

When the preacher said, "dragged behine trucks," the hairs on the back of James' neck stood up. He pictured himself being dragged behind a truck with the three white boys sitting in it laughing.

"Look whut dey done ta Jesus," Rev. Johnson said. "Gave 'im thirty-nine lashes like a common criminal, an' den crucified 'im on da cross." His voice got quieter. "Whut did he ever do ta anybody, 'cept good?"

"Yeah, Lawd."

"An' he prayed ta God, 'Father, fuhgive dem, fuh dey know not whut dey do,' Luke 23:34. We has ta fuhgive dem dat persecute us; dey 'on't understan' whut dey doin'. An' God give dem souls, jus' like us. Jus' like us." Then he spoke softly, "'Membah whut Jesus said when you feelin' persecuted."

People were nodding their heads, and some were wiping their eyes.

Rev. Johnson paused, and rubbed his forehead with his handkerchief. "Ah could g'wan all night 'bout dis," he said, "but we has da udder readin'."

"Yeah, we do."

"Thank 'bout dese thangs. It ain't easy, but we has ta try ta love dem dat 'on't love us, dat hates us."

"Amen."

He moved a little closer. "Now befo' we move on to da nex' readin', Sista Rawlins, will ya play 'Whut a Friend We Have in Jesus.' Page 160."

They stood and sang the old well-loved hymn, grateful for the transition, and grateful for the reminder of the words that they could take their troubles to Jesus in prayer. The preacher's talk had aroused a lot of emotion in them, and the song helped them feel calmer.

Rev. Johnson read another passage from the Bible and talked about that one as well. James had a little trouble concentrating because he was still thinking about the reading from Matthew and trying to figure out how to love people who hated him.

After the meeting let out, people stood around in front of the church in clusters talking about the service in the "after meetin'." The children were playing tag and running all around. The young people had their own cluster, but they talked about topics they were more interested in, like whether the school's baseball team would win the next week. Mardella made sure she was standing by James, but his focus was on Saleena, whose hand he was holding. He noticed that the adults were preoccupied with their conversations and he whispered to Saleena, "Le's go ovah ta da dark side a da church." She smiled, and they quietly slipped away.

As soon as they got around the corner, James said, "Fine'ly," and he pulled her to him and gave her a long kiss.

"How ya been?" he asked.

Saleena told him about a couple of things that had happened at school, including that Jonas Smith had been asking her to go on a date with him.

James was surprised at how nervous he felt suddenly. He held his breath after he asked, "You goin'?"

"Naw," she replied, and smiled.

"Dat da right answer," James said, and kissed her again.

Every now and then, he'd peek around the corner of the building to make sure his and Saleena's parents were still engrossed in conversation.

"He won't let me alone," Saleena continued. "Keep aksin' me, an' tryin' ta hol' my han'."

James frowned. "Whut ya say ta 'im?"

"Ah tol' 'im ta let me alone. Ah reckon Ah'm gon' havta hit 'im ovah da head."

"Sound like a good ideal," James said. "Else Ah'm gon' havta beat 'im up." But he thought, "School be almos' ovah, but mebbe Ah be talkin' ta dat crazy boy! An' Sadday, Ah'm gon' aks huh ta be mah gal."

"Hey," Saleena said, hitting him on the arm. "Ah takes care a myse'f."

"Ow!" James said in mock pain. "Why 'on't ya hit *him* like dat?"

She laughed. "Ah'm tryin' ta be peaceful."

James ran his fingers down the side of her face and under her chin. He tilted her face up and kissed her again. He had a hard time deciding whether to keep kissing her, or tell her the things he wanted to tell her. But he didn't have to decide because she gently pulled away.

"Tell me da res' a whut ya havta tell me," she said.

"Awright. But Ah's wonderin' if ya wants ta go out Sadday night."

She said she did. He wasn't sure what they'd do, but he would definitely arrange to do something special so he could give her the necklace he'd get for her that day. He'd have to have a plan by Saturday because her parents would ask him what they were going to do.

Then he told her about the rattlesnake, the chance he might have to buy Mis' Mac's truck, and the request of Freeman that he "see ta huh." Then, there was another kiss.

When he looked again, he noticed that his parents were walking toward the truck. "Dey goin'." He and Saleena walked back into the light, holding hands. "Ah see ya Sadday," he said, squeezing her hand.

On the way home, Pearl and Pearson talked about the service. James remained silent most of the time, hoping to hear something that would help him find some way to love those who wanted to hurt him, those who looked at him like he was garbage, and those who just looked through him.

Later, when James went into his bedroom, he saw the big gray spider that lived in his room. It was usually on the wall above his dresser, but it was on the ceiling over his bed. "Dat da wrong place tuh be, spider," he said. "Ah ain't waitin' fuh ya tuh fall on me durin' da night. Nawsuh." He stood on the bed and killed the spider with his shoe.

When he went to bed a little later, he was thinking about those Bible verses the preacher had read. Then he thought about Mr. Roberts and wondered, "How could da Lawd expect a colored ta love somebody like dat? Ah sho cain't figger dat out, so Ah jes' havta pray ta overcome." And he went to sleep with a very earnest prayer on his lips.

Thursday

At breakfast, Pearson asked James to go to the pasture to see if he could locate their good Holstein milk cow. Pearson was going to spend the day working for Mr. Wilson, and he was concerned about "Holstein," who was ready to calve. He wanted to be sure she was all right.

James was pleased to have that project. He enjoyed walking around the pasture among the cows while the air was still cool, and he hoped it would keep his mind off his job situation. He knew that cows often chose to calve in palmetto patches, but he figured the cow would be smart enough not to choose one with a rattlesnake. As soon as they finished eating, James threw a long-sleeved shirt over his t-shirt and headed for the door with Shep at his heels.

"Dere's some peas lef' ovah us gon' have fuh dinner," Pearl said. "Pick a few ears a dat corn, an' see if sumpin else need pickin'. We needs some mo' tomaters, too. An' Ah reckon dey mus' be some mo' okra ready ta pick. Dat sho would be good."

"Dat sho *would* be good," James thought. He loved okra. Pearl often threw some pods in with the black-eyed peas just before the peas were done. He loved the flavor and the slimy texture that some people detested. He also loved it fried. "Ah'm gon' aks huh ta drop dem okras in some hot grease, if dey's any ready. Ain't nuttin' like some fried okras."

James grabbed his cap from the nail on the porch, and went out back. He knew the tangerines were about half dry, but he didn't care—as long as they had any juice, he'd eat them. He picked a tangerine and an orange and put them in his pockets. He looked for the black and yellow spider on the orange tree and saw two bug skeletons in its web. A few feet away, another spider had a web. Both webs still had some dewdrops on them, which glistened in the sunlight.

As he passed the barn, he picked up two buckets, which he put down at the edge of the field where the peas, corn, string beans, okra, tomatoes, yellow squash, pepper, and cucumbers were. A quick inspection told him that the tomatoes, okra, squash, and cucumbers all needed to be picked. "Ah'm gon' be pickin' fuh a while," he thought.

He opened the gate to the pasture and saw Shep running toward him, so he waited for him to catch up before he closed it. "Cloudy day," he said to Shep, as he patted his head and looked at the sunless sky. "Where ya been at, boy?" He peeled the tangerine as he walked along, breathing in the smell. He bit the slices in half and threw the dried ends on the ground.

James strolled casually in the pasture savoring the early morning coolness with Shep by his side. As the dew from the grass soaked through his tennis shoes, he could feel the dampness on his feet. He glanced at the ground periodically to make sure he stepped over any droppings, occasionally getting a whiff of some fresh manure. He noted the general location of a cow lowing down by the swamp.

Their land ended halfway through the swamp, where Pearson's brother's began. Since Joseph didn't have any cows, he allowed them to put their fence on the other side of the swamp, so their cows had plenty of access to water. He'd planted an orange grove on his property, rather than farming or raising cattle. After working for the phosphate company for thirty years, he retired and just took care of his grove, which brought in a nice income. Pearson loved working with the land and the cows, so he'd chosen a farmer's life.

When James reached the trail that the cows had made walking behind each other, he walked on it. It always pleased him to see the cow trails cutting through the grass and winding around the pasture. He couldn't understand how they decided to curve here and there rather than just walking straight, but once they did, they followed the trail.

James could hear a blue jay and assumed it was in one of the big old oak trees in the pasture that provided shade under their broad umbrella of leaves. He looked forward to sitting next to one of the magnificent trees for a little while after he found Holstein. The cows ate the oak leaves as high up as they could reach, and the trees looked like someone had pruned the bottoms, which were straight across. They also ate the abundant Spanish moss when it got within their reach.

Although it was likely that Holstein was fine, some cows did have problems calving. James remembered one time when a calf was coming out with its hind feet first, and the cow was having a terrible time. They didn't want the expense of a veterinarian and, fortunately, Pearson could usually take care of the problems. James watched as his father put his hand and most of his arm into the cow and spent nearly half an hour working to turn the calf around. It was finally born healthy. The cow was fine, Pearson was exhausted, and James was impressed.

James heard a few cows mooing and he saw the multi-colored herd, most of which were lying under a big oak tree chewing their cuds. There were eleven calves and twenty-three cows: the one Holstein, some Jerseys, one Guernsey, some mixed breeds, and a Black Angus bull. The Clevelands kept the calves for several months until they were big enough to sell, and James hated the days when they took them to the auction. It seemed as though the mother cows lowed all night long, calling their babies. He felt bad for them and their calves, which he imagined were bleating for their mothers, and it was often the middle of the night before he got so tired he could go to sleep, in spite of the mournful sound.

By the time they reached the herd, Shep was walking with his nose near the ground, and he followed the scent into the swampy area. He didn't pay any attention to the cows, but took off into the swamp.

A couple of the cows walked over to James, sniffing for food. He patted them and pushed by them. He didn't see the bull, which was tame, but James had been taught to always keep an eye on him; he didn't want an encounter with a bull. He scanned the pasture looking for him. "Mebbe he in da swamp," he thought.

James walked on down nearer the swamp looking for Holstein. He quickly spotted her black and white coloring among some palmetto bushes, as he'd expected, a spot off the beaten path. Beside Holstein stood a little black calf. James knew not to get too near to them, because many new mothers were protective of their babies and would attack, or at least run at, anyone who got too close. Holstein was tame, but she was a new mother, so James respected the boundary.

"Hi ya doin', girl?" he cooed. "Dat's a mighty fine baby ya done got dere. Look like his daddy. When he git older, we be milkin' ya, ole girl. Ya sho gives a lotta good milk."

He could tell by the looks of her calf that it was probably a day old. Unfortunately, Holstein had some afterbirth hanging from her that she hadn't been able to pass. That kind of problem was the reason Pearson wanted him to check on her.

As he walked back through the pasture, James looked up into the oak trees, hoping to find some mistletoe, which lived as a parasite on some trees. He remembered his father having him climb a tree to get mistletoe for a cow with the same problem a few years earlier. Pearson said it would clean her out. James couldn't remember where he'd gotten it the last time until he finally found some in the last tree he looked at, right at the end of the pasture. He could have seen the mistletoe if it had been on the side closer to him, but it was on the opposite side of the tree. As he climbed, he realized that climbing had been easier a few years earlier when he was younger and smaller.

He took a couple of big handfuls of mistletoe to Holstein, holding it out in front of him as he walked slowly and spoke softly to her. She studied him for a moment, and then started walking toward him. He put the mistletoe on the ground and backed away, watching her as she munched, and making a mental note to ask Pearson about it later to see if he gave her enough.

James was feeling thirsty after his trek through the pasture, and he reached in his pocket for the orange. He took out his pocketknife and peeled it carefully so that he left plenty of the white part, and he tossed the peel near Holstein. Walking away, he breathed in the aroma as he cut a round plug out of the top of the orange. He popped it in his mouth, ran the knife around inside the orange, spit out the chewed pulp, squeezed the orange gently, and began sucking out the cool, sweet juice. When he reached the oaks, he sat down under one, stretched out his legs, and leaned against the tree.

As he sucked the orange, he looked up at the oak leaves and moss and got an occasional glimpse of the blue sky. He could see a deserted bird nest and wondered what kind of bird had made it. His peace was interrupted when one of the Jersey cows approached about the time he finished sucking the orange. He'd planned to tear it open and eat the remaining pulp, but instead, he tore it open and handed it to her, one half at a time. "Dere ya go, Polly," he said. "Ya done walked a long ways fuh dat, gal." He patted the cow's leg. "When ya gon' have *yo'* baby? Holstein done had huhs."

James thought Polly was their prettiest cow. He liked her face; there was something about the Jersey cows' eyes that was different from other cows and he thought that was what made them pretty. He had observed that cows were a lot like people in their appearance; some were just more pleasing to look at than others.

He saw old Bossy, who was a mixed breed and brindled with brown and black, walking toward him on the cow trail. "Ah'm not feedin' all a y'all," he complained.

Polly stood around waiting for James to give her something else to eat, but he didn't have anything else. "G'on now," he said, but she lingered. "Guess Ah ain't gon' have no peace, so Ah might's well git busy."

He stood up, reached into the tree, and pulled some Spanish moss for her, which she immediately started munching on. He gave her a couple of handfuls, some of which he had to jump up to reach, and a couple to Bossy, who'd tried to get some of Polly's.

When he whistled for Shep, the dog quickly appeared and they started on their way. "Did ya fine anythang int'restin' out dere in da swamp, Shep?" Shep responded by wagging his tail, and James stopped for a moment and patted his head.

As he and Shep walked along, he noticed a circle of buzzards off in the distance. "Look like dey ovah at Mr. Hiers' place," he said to Shep. "Wonder if dey got a dead cow ovah dere or sumpin." He made a mental note to ask Harley about it when he saw him.

In the garden, James quickly filled one bucket with ripe tomatoes. He took out his pocketknife, cut three handfuls of okra, and put it on top of the tomatoes. In the other bucket, he put the cucumbers, squash, and a half dozen ears of corn.

"Oh mah," Pearl said when he took the buckets into the kitchen. "Look like we gon' have some corn an' okra an' squash an' cucumbers an' tomaters fuh dinner. Dey any mo' tomaters 'bout ripe? Ah done canned all Ah wonts to, so if dey's too many, look like da chickens gon' git dem some ta eat."

"Not too many out dere," James replied. "Ah kin aks Mis' Mac if she need some mo' cucumbers an' tomaters."

"Dat dere's a good ideal," Pearl said. "But she prob'ly got 'em comin' out bof huh ears, too."

"Prob'ly do," James said, laughing.

♥ ♥ ♥

Maggie was very business-like when she got up that morning. She'd taken a bath the night before and laid out her clothes. She washed her face and put some coffee on the stove to perk. Then she quickly dressed and returned to the kitchen.

It was a simple kitchen, pastel green walls, white refrigerator and electric stove, and pine cabinets that were painted white. In the corner stood a round wooden table covered with a yellow cloth and surrounded by four chairs. Two leaves were attached to the underside of the table, and four more chairs were in other rooms of the house. Maggie kept her kitchen neat—everything was where it belonged unless she was using it, and as she cooked, when possible, she washed the dishes she'd used.

She poured herself a cup of coffee. Then she fried an egg and made a piece of toast. After she ate, she quickly washed her dishes, took a quick shower, brushed her teeth, combed her hair, plaited it and wrapped it around her head, dressed, put on some lipstick, got her pocketbook, and went and sat on the porch waiting for Freeman.

She only had to wait about five minutes before he arrived in the truck wearing his Panama hat. He wore the straw hat to keep the sun off his face, and he liked the way it looked. Freeman knew Maggie liked to get an early start when she had business to take care of; he quickly parked the truck and got the car from the garage. He drove, and she sat in the back seat.

Maggie would've sat in the front, but she'd learned years earlier that Freeman wouldn't drive if she sat in the front seat. "Somebody got ta be in da back," he told her very respectfully. "Ya got ta sit in da back, Mis' Maggie, an' Ah got ta drive." And against her will, she had ever since, but she didn't like it. Of course, she often went places by herself, but she always wanted Freeman with her when she went to buy a new vehicle.

They went first to look at trucks. When the owner saw that Maggie was there, he told the salesman that *he* would wait on her.

"Aunt Maggie," John said. "Good to see you."

"Hello, John," she responded warmly. "How have you been? An' how's the family, an' your daddy?"

"Fair to middlin'," he replied. "Ever'body's doin' awright, I guess, 'cept we've all had bad colds this spring. Daddy's doin' awright—got a little arthritis. How 'bout yourself?" He did not look at or speak to Freeman.

Freeman shifted from one foot to the other. "Ah guess Ah done got invisible," he thought. But he knew why John ignored him.

"I'm doin' fine," Maggie said, "but Freeman's been feelin' rather poorly."

John had to acknowledge Freeman then. "Sorry to hear that, Freeman," he said, looking at him.

Freeman nodded, "Thank ya, suh." But he thought, "Dat man young 'nough ta be mah son. Be nice ta hear 'Mr. Jackson,' but dat ain't 'bout ta happen."

"Are you lookin' for a truck, Aunt Maggie?" John asked. "I know yores is gittin' old."

"Yes, we are," she replied. "When we pick one out, I'd like for Freeman to take it for a drive."

John had been through this routine before. Maggie McClellan was the only white person that went into his place with a Negro, and always sought his approval before she bought anything. He didn't like it much, but he liked Maggie's business. He sold cars and trucks, and he had some tractors on an adjoining lot. He and his father had sold vehicles to Maggie's family and serviced them for many years, and he wanted to keep it that way, so he swallowed his pride and went along with Maggie's wishes. He'd stopped trying to figure her out many years earlier.

They looked at the 1957 trucks, but those didn't have any running boards. "Ah'm too old ta git in a truck dat ain't got no runnin' board," Freeman said. "Ah needs dat extry step." Maggie agreed that it was a necessity.

"Ford stopped puttin' runnin' boards on their trucks this year," John said. "But I still got three '56 trucks left an' they got 'em. They're a little cheaper, too, since they're last year's models." They walked over to look at those trucks.

Freeman was pleased. He knew Maggie was buying the truck mostly for him, and he was glad it would cost her less money.

"The '57s look more modern," Maggie said. "However, I agree with Freeman; we both need a runnin' board."

John got a key for one of the trucks, and the two men took it for a drive. When they returned, Maggie could tell by looking at Freeman's face that he didn't like it. "Do you want to try another one, Freeman?" she asked.

"Yes'm," he answered softly, "Ah b'lieves so."

"What was wrong with that one?" John asked. "They're all the same basically, just a different color."

"We'll try another one," Maggie replied. "That is, unless you're too busy."

"Oh, no, ma'am," John said quickly. "Take your time."

And they did. Freeman drove the other two '56 trucks. When they returned after the last one, he had a smile on his face. "Dat da one, Mis' Maggie," he said, nodding his head. "Dat da one."

"We'll take the blue one," Maggie said to John.

Freeman sat in the car while Maggie took care of the purchase. John told her the truck would be delivered the next day. "Terrific," she replied. "Tomorrow's Freeman's birthday, and it'll be a present to him not to have to drive that old rattletrap anymore."

"Do you want to trade in that ole truck?" he asked. "I can give you $20 for it, sight unseen." Since his dealership serviced the truck, he knew exactly what it was like.

"No, thank you," Maggie answered. "I've promised it to a young friend."

John was disappointed. "A nigger, no doubt," he thought. "I can give you twenty-five," he said.

"No, thank you, John," Maggie said, standing up. "Tell Mary an' your daddy I said hello. I never see Mary anymore."

"Well, you're not around much, Aunt Maggie," he replied.

"I guess that's true," she said. "I'm content just stayin' at home an' takin' care of the place."

Maggie hurried out because she knew the car was in the sun, and even though it was only 9 o'clock, it would be getting warm. She was concerned about Freeman. And he'd thought she might sit inside and talk for a while, so he was relieved to see her.

"Next I want to go to the dime store," she said. "We're not that far away, an' I need a few things."

"Yes'm," Freeman replied.

"Do you need anything, Freeman?" she asked, knowing that he would probably say "No," even if he did.

"No, ma'am, Mis' Maggie," he replied. "Cain't say as Ah do."

Freeman found a parking place right in front of the dime store.

"Well, Freeman, I guess I won't have to walk far today."

"Ah got jes' as close as Ah could," he chuckled.

"Are you comin' in?" she asked, again knowing the answer.

"Ah'm gon' wait in da park."

Maggie went first to the jewelry counter to look at the clocks. She noticed the clerk had a small stain on the front of her dress, which looked almost threadbare, and her face looked sad. Maggie immediately felt sorry for her. "You never know what people's lives are like," she thought, "or what goes on in their homes."

"Can I he'p you, ma'am?" the clerk asked.

Maggie smiled. "I'm lookin' for a good alarm clock," she said in the up-beat tone she'd used with her students when they appeared to be feeling down. "A nice-lookin' little clock."

The clerk pointed out some, and Maggie chose one similar to her own. She watched her wrap it in paper and put it in a paper bag. The clerk smiled as she handed it to Maggie. "I'm sorry we don't have a sack the right size. We got big ones an' little ones, but we're outta the right size."

"That's quite all right," Maggie said.

The clerk handed her the change, and said, "Thank you, ma'am."

As Maggie took the money, she noticed a slight change in the clerk's demeanor. She seemed a little less troubled. "Thank you," she replied, with a smile. "I'm buyin' this for a friend an' I think he'll like it. Thank you for showin' me this one."

Next, she went to the counter with the pocketbooks. "Well, this clerk looks a little happier," she thought.

"What can I help you with today?" the clerk asked.

"I need a new change purse," Maggie replied. "My old one is pretty well worn."

"That selection's all we got," the clerk said as Maggie looked at the ones on the counter.

Maggie quickly picked one, paid for it, and moved to the counter with the cloth. She didn't want to keep Freeman waiting any longer than she had to.

"Good morning, ma'am. Is there somethin' I can help you with today?" the clerk asked.

"Good morning, dear. I need some new dishrags," Maggie replied.

The clerk showed her the selection. "Aren't you Miss McClellan?" she asked.

"Yes, I am," Maggie replied. "Do I know you?"

"No, ma'am, but my daddy was one of your students—Daniel Love."

"Oh my," she smiled. "I remember Daniel. He was one of the best students I ever had. How is he?"

"He's fine," the clerk said. "He'll be thrilled when I tell him I saw you today. I remember you from a few years ago, Miss McClellan. I was with Daddy when we saw you somewhere."

"I'm sorry I don't remember," Maggie said.

"Oh, I wouldn't expect you to. I was just so impressed to meet one of Daddy's teachers, an' he said such nice things about you. You were his favorite teacher."

"Well, isn't that nice," Maggie said, smiling again. "What is your name, honey?"

"Anna," she replied. "Anna Love."

"I'll remember that. What a beautiful name!"

Maggie chose the dishrags she wanted and said, "I believe I have the exact change."

"And so you do," Anna said, taking the money. As she put the dishrags in a paper bag, she said, "Thank you, Miss McClellan. It was nice to see you again."

"Thank you, Anna. It was nice talkin' to you, an' next time, I'll remember you. Please give your daddy my best."

On her way out, Maggie stopped at the popcorn counter and bought a bag of popcorn, mostly for Freeman. When she left the store, she quickly spotted him sitting on the ground, leaning against the trunk of an oak tree. "Oh my!" she thought. "I forgot he won't sit on a park bench. I've kept him waitin' too long." Maggie normally drove herself to Lakeland, and only had Freeman take her because they'd gone to the car dealer and were close by. She didn't know whether or not Negroes were allowed to sit on the park benches, but she'd seen a few sitting on them recently. However, Freeman wouldn't.

When he saw her, he slowly got to his feet, and ambled over to the car. "Ya all done now, Mis' Maggie?" he asked.

"Yes, I am, I'm glad to say. Are you feelin' all right?" She noticed that he walked slower than usual and was worried that he might be tired already.

"Yes'm, Mis' Maggie," he replied. "Whut we doin' next?"

When they got in the car and Maggie could put her bags down, she took a handful of popcorn and handed the bag to Freeman. "Thank ya, Mis' Maggie," he said. "Ah kin use dis."

"Let's swing by Cash Feed store an' get some citrus pulp for the cows. I think they're about out." That was a quick stop. Maggie paid for it while Freeman put the sacks of pulp in the trunk.

As they got in the car, Maggie said, "Look at the lake, Freeman, an' the cute little ducks swimmin' by the edge. I've always loved Lake Mirror, an' especially at Christmas time when they put the tree in the middle."

"Yes'm, it sho purty, an' Ah likes da Christmas tree, too." He started the car, and glanced at the gas gauge. "Dis car need some gas, Mis' Maggie."

"Well, it's just a few blocks on down East Main Street to Selph's station. Let's go there before we head out of town."

The attendant filled the tank, washed the windshield and back glass, and would've swept out the car, but Maggie told him the car didn't need sweeping because Freeman kept it clean. Once, she made the mistake of having it swept, and she listened to Freeman grumble all the way home.

♥ ♥ ♥

WHEN THEY GOT TO THE PHOSPHATE PLANT, Freeman said he'd stay in the car, but Maggie objected. "You would die of heat stroke sittin' in the car. It's hot just ridin' around with the air blowin' in. Come on in with me."

They left the windows open and the keys in the ignition. And they left the car unlocked.

Maggie knew right where to find Carl Roberts. She walked along with Freeman behind her; she'd learned long ago from Freeman that it had to be that way. "Ah'm gon' wait right out here," he said when they got to the door of the building.

"Oh no, Freeman," she insisted. "Please come in an' sit down in a chair while I go to his office." Since he was beginning to feel tired, he did as she requested.

Maggie went to the secretary's desk and looked at her name. "Hello, Mabel," she said, looking at the pleasant young face. "I'm Maggie McClellan and I'd like to see Carl."

Mabel said, "Oh, Miss McClellan, I've heard of you." She buzzed Carl, told him Miss McClellan wanted to see him, and then told her that she could go right in.

"Well, Aunt Maggie, I'm surprised to see you," he said. "It's been years." He stood up, reached across his desk, and shook her hand.

"I guess it has, Carl," she replied. "How have you been?"

"Doin' awright, Aunt Maggie. Have a seat." He pointed to a chair in front of the desk. "How've you been?"

"I've been just fine. Not as young as I used to be, but thank God, I'm still feelin' fine." She paused. "I was sorry to hear about your sister passin', Carl. I didn't know about it until after the funeral. As you know, we still don't have telephones out my way."

"Well, thank you, ma'am. Actually, her passin' was a blessin'; she had cancer, you know, an' was in a lotta pain near the end."

"I'm sorry, Carl. That must've been hard for your family."

"Yes, it was," he said, and paused. "Well, what brings you here today? This a social visit?" he asked, knowing it wasn't.

"I came to talk to you about a young man who has applied for a job here," she said. "His name is James Cleveland, an' he was here Tuesday."

"A Nigra boy," he replied. "I saw him."

Maggie figured he said "Nigra" for her benefit. She suspected he normally used a different word.

"James has worked for me since he was seven years old." She continued, emphasizing the adjectives, "He's a *fine* young man, comes from a *good* family, an' he's a *hard* worker."

"Well, I'll see what I can do," he said half-heartedly.

"James will be a good worker for this company," she insisted, even though she knew Carl's last statement was dismissive. "He'll give you a hundred percent, an' you won't find anybody better. So, what I'd like, and what I think is the right thing for you to do is to give me a letter, addressed to him, offerin' him a job."

"Well, now," he said, looking down at his desk. "You're askin' a lot."

"I don't think so, Carl," she replied emphatically. "I think I'm askin' for what's right. I'm tellin' you that this young man will be a good employee for this company, an' he deserves a job. I'm not askin' you to hire somebody who's a *relative of mine*." She stopped, and waited for him to look her in the eye. When he did, he saw steel. "I'm not asking you to hire somebody who's not going to be worth their pay. I know you get that kind of request."

Carl looked down at the desk and shifted in his chair.

Maggie had intended to stop there; she didn't want to say any more. However, Carl had not made her the offer she went there for.

"My father got those requests, too, Carl. In fact, I seem to remember somethin' about you askin' him to hire your brother." She paused until he looked at her again. "Do you happen to remember that?"

"That boy must mean a lot to you, Maggie," he said. "Sounds like you're callin' in yore chips."

She noticed that he'd dropped the "aunt" from in front of her name, and she didn't care one bit. "Well, I may not have much longer to call them in, you know. And he *does* mean a lot to me. As I said, he has been workin' for me since he was seven."

"All right, Maggie," he said. "I'll hire 'im."

He stood up, but Maggie remained in her chair. "I said I'll hire him," he repeated.

"First of all, don't think for a minute that I think this favor evens the score; it's not such a big favor to hire a man who'll be an asset to this company. In contrast, I remember hearing about the glowing recommendation you gave for your brother. My father found out the hard way that you left out a couple of very important details. An' second, I would like to leave here with a letter."

"All right, all right," he said impatiently. "I'll write you a damn letter."

"Oh my," she said, surprised that he'd swear in front of a lady. "Make it a *nice* letter."

He buzzed Mabel, and when she opened the door, Maggie stood up. "I'll be right back," she said. "Thank you, Carl."

Freeman wasn't in the waiting room, and Maggie had to go outside to find him. He'd squatted down in the shade of the building, and was leaning against it.

"Are you all right, Freeman?" she asked.

"Yes'm, Mis' Maggie."

"Why don't you come back in an' get some water."

"Dey's only one water fountain in dere," he replied.

Maggie had seen the fountain in the hallway, but hadn't noticed that there was only one. She felt bad that she hadn't noticed. "I should have gotten him some water earlier," she thought. "The things we take for granted!"

"Well, you come in, and I'll get you some water," she insisted. And Freeman was thirsty enough that he went.

"How you gon' git me some water?" he asked softly, as they went back into the building. He waited in the hallway while she went in the office.

By then, the secretary had returned, and was typing. When Maggie, went to the desk, she noticed the letterhead in the typewriter. "Excuse me, Mabel," she said, "do you have somethin' I can get some water in?"

"To drink?" the secretary asked.

"Yes, honey," Maggie replied.

Mabel opened one of her desk drawers and took out a coffee cup. "This is all I have," she said.

"That'll do," Maggie said. "Thank you, dear."

When Freeman saw the coffee cup, he asked, "Dis dat lady cup?"

Maggie lied. "I don't know, but this is what we have," and she filled it with water and handed it to him.

He hesitated for a second before drinking the water. After he drank it, he handed the cup to Maggie.

"Do you want some more?" she asked.

"Please," he replied. He'd just finished it when Carl Roberts opened the door, stepped out into the hall, and saw him hand Maggie the cup. Carl stopped and stared at Maggie.

She filled the cup again. She knew what Carl was thinking as she drank the water from the cup.

He glanced at Freeman, and then just stood there looking at her like she'd lost her mind. And she just stood there looking at him as though she had no idea why he was looking at her. And Freeman looked from one to the other, and wished he were somewhere else.

"Have you ever noticed that you only have one water fountain in here?" she asked, looking Carl straight in the eye. "You need to get a 'Colored' fountain." He didn't say anything, and she added, "Maybe that should be another one of my chips."

Carl shook his head, said, "Yore letter's ready," and walked on down the hall.

"Thank you, Carl," Maggie called, and turned to Freeman. "I'll be right back. We're almost done here."

She went to Mabel's desk. "I should tell you, Miss Mabel, that my Negro friend drank from your cup, as did I. I expect Carl will inform you of that. You know, there's no 'Colored' fountain in the hall. Would you like me to wash your cup for you?"

"Oh, no, ma'am," Mabel replied. "That's all right." She took the letter from the typewriter and handed it to Maggie. "Mr. Roberts said for you to look at the letter an' make sure it meets your approval."

Maggie smiled and took the letter. After a quick read, she said, "It's fine," and returned it to Mabel, who folded it, put it in an envelope, and gave it to Maggie.

"I'm glad he's gittin' a job," Mabel said. "There was somethin' about him that impressed me, an' I cain't say that about many people who come in here, colored or white. He just seemed so pleasant." She lowered her voice, "An' I'm afraid Mr. Roberts wasn't nice to 'im."

"I heard," Maggie said softly. "I've known James his whole life, an' he's a good friend of mine. Thank you, Mabel, for your kindness."

As she and Freeman walked to the car, Maggie breathed a sigh of relief. "Well, I'm glad that's over," she said.

"Whut we doin' here?" Freeman asked gently. He'd wondered the whole time, but wouldn't ask. Now, however, he felt that she'd given him an opening, and he felt comfortable asking.

"We came here for James, Freeman," Maggie replied, and smiled. "James has got a job."

"Dat right?" Freeman asked. "Oh Lawd, Mis' Maggie! You done dat?"

"I guess you could say that," she said. "Next an' last stop, the grocery store, unless you're too tired. I can come back later."

"No, ma'am," he said. "Ah needs some groceries, too." He paused for a moment. "Ah cain't b'lieve you done dat."

When they got to her house, Maggie got out of the car with her small bag of groceries and other bags, and said, "If I don't see you tomorrow morning, I hope you have a really good time at your party, Freeman."

He smiled. "Thank ya, Mis' Maggie, but Ah be by."

♥   ♥   ♥

AFTER MAGGIE ATE SOME LEFTOVERS FROM Wednesday night's supper, she got busy. She knew Ruby would have a birthday cake for Freeman, and she knew he preferred pie. It would have been less work for her to make just one pie, but she wanted to do something special for him. This was a big birthday. He loved both coconut cream and lemon meringue pies, so she made one of each for him.

She was just taking the pies from the oven when James arrived. She had the radio on and he could hear Tony Bennett singing "Don't Get Around Much Anymore," and he had to call her three times. When she went out on the porch, James was standing there, cap in hand, and the chickens were headed in his direction.

"Afternoon, James," she said. "I'm glad you came over."

"Mis' Mac," James smiled. "Ah could smell dat pie way back yonder. Ah bet Unc' Freeman kin smell it, too."

"Well, I hope not. I made two of Freeman's favorite pies, and I want him to be surprised."

"Mama wontin' ta know if ya needs some mo' cucumbers or tomaters."

"Tell her I'd be happy to send her some of ours," Maggie said, laughing.

"Dat whut we spected." James grinned.

"Come sit with me for a while, James. I'll get us some iced tea, if you want some."

"Oh, dat do sound mighty good," James said, walking onto the porch.

The chickens had congregated and most were half-heartedly scratching in the sand, obviously expecting food to start raining down on them.

When Maggie returned with the iced tea and a white envelope, James was still standing. "Have a seat," she said, and they sat in the rocking chairs.

She saw the chickens congregated in the yard. "Why, there those chickens are again. They're certainly optimistic."

"Dey 'on't wont ta miss no food," he said.

"That's for sure," she said, looking around. "I don't see Shep. Did he decide to stay home?"

"Didn' see 'im anywhere when Ah lef'. Guess he done run off huntin' sumpin."

"Probably," Maggie nodded and smiled. She put the envelope on her lap and reached in her apron pocket. "I've got the money I owe you," she said, handing James $3.85.

"Thank ya, Mis' Mac."

"Freeman and I had a busy morning," she announced. "We had a few errands to run."

James sat quietly, rocking slowly and listening. He wanted to ask her if she bought a truck, but he thought that would be disrespectful. However, he was feeling excitement rising in his chest at the thought that he might soon have a truck to drive—his very own truck—even if it was an *old* one.

"First we went to look at trucks," she continued. "Then we made a little stop at the phosphate company."

James turned his head sharply to look at her. "Why she go out dere?" he wondered.

"This is for you," she said as she gave him the envelope.

He saw the name of the company on the envelope and slowly opened it, unaware that he had stopped breathing. He unfolded the nice company stationery inside, and his heart raced as he read the job offer. He bounded from his chair and let out a yell. The chickens squawked and scattered, running in all directions.

James remembered where he was and restrained himself a little, although he felt as though he might burst. He immediately turned to Maggie, who sat watching him with a big smile on her face.

"Congratulations, James," she said.

"Oh, Mis' Mac." He bent toward her with his hand outstretched, and she took his hand. "Thank ya, thank ya, thank ya!" he exclaimed, shaking her hand vigorously.

"Well, James," she said. "It isn't often that a person has the opportunity to help someone. Indeed, it was *my* pleasure to be able to do this for you. Of course, you may have gotten the job, anyway."

"Ah 'on't thank so, Mis' Mac," he replied, sitting back down. "Sho didn' look like it. Dat man didn' like me atall." James knew there were certain jobs that only Negroes were hired for, but he didn't think Mr. Roberts would hire him for anything.

"Well, Carl Roberts is a hard man, and he's set in some old-fashioned ways. But now you are a young man with a job. I believe the letter says you start Monday week."

"Dat right? Oh Lawd, Ah cain't b'lieve it."

"Of course, you know you'll be working as a laborer, and it's hard work. You may be working with the 'float pipe,' but you probably know that."

The phosphate companies used pipe to pump the phosphate rock, sand, and water from the pits they dug to the "float plant." A plant would be set up in the area where they'd be digging, and pipes would be laid and moved by the Negro employees when digging finished in one place and began in another.

"Ah done knows it," James said, "an' dat ain't nuttin' but da truf. Ah ain't 'fraid a no hard work."

"That's for sure, James," Maggie said. "I know you're used to hard work an' you'll do a good job."

"Ah sho do 'preciate you goin' an' doin' dis fuh me!" he exclaimed, smiling again. "Ya musta sho sk'ed dat Mr. Roberts."

"I don't think he was too scared," she said, smiling. "My daddy was his supervisor at the company many years ago. Let's just say that I reminded him of somethin' he requested and Daddy did for him. I just had to jog his memory a little bit."

James laughed.

"I'm sure you know it's important that you arrive on time, an' don't do anything to call attention to yourself, because he may be resentful. Of course, I know he doesn't want to see me in there again, but I have to say, I don't trust him one bit."

"Ah'm gon' do mah bes'," he said. "Ah'm gon' buy me a bran' new alarm clock Sadday when me an' Harley goin' ta Lakelan'."

"That's a good idea, James," she said. "You'll be workin' different shifts, an' sometimes, you may have trouble wakin' up when you need to. You know," she said, her brow wrinkled like she was trying to remember something. "I think I have an extra clock. Let me look."

James stood up when Maggie stood. He went to the pump and got a drink of water and filled her bucket.

She came back out holding a paper bag and a clock. "I was right, James. This one's never even been used." Maggie wound the clock she'd bought that morning, and handed it to him. They both heard it ticking. "If you want it, you can set it when you get home."

"Thank ya, Mis' Mac," he said, taking the clock. "Dis look like a real nice clock. Thank ya, ma'am."

"Consider it your 'Congratulations-on-your-new-job' clock. An' take the sack to carry it in," she offered, handing it to him.

They both sat down, and James put the clock back in the bag.

"The new truck's comin' tomorrow, James, so you can take the old one then. I have no idea what it's worth, but the dealer offered me $20 for it, so you can have it for that if it sounds fair to you."

He'd expected it to cost a lot more than that. "Sho do, Mis' Mac!" he exclaimed. "Hi kin Ah ever thank ya?" Again, he had trouble containing himself. He was so happy he could hardly stay in the chair. "A job an' a truck," he thought, grinning from ear to ear, his heart thumping, and his brain busy. If he worked five mornings the following week, he'd make $14, and two afternoons would make $20. He could do all that and have it paid for before he started working at the mine. Of course, he could just pay for it after he started the job, but he knew he wouldn't get paid for a while, and he didn't want to owe money, even for a little while. And he wanted to help her and do most of the jobs she needed done before he started his new job.

"'Sides gittin' in da wood, you got udder thangs ya wonts me ta do fuh ya?" he asked. "Ah could pay off da truck wit' mah work, if dat's awright."

"Of course, that's fine, if that's what you'd like. You can spend several more hours bringin' lighter out of the woods, even if it doesn't all fit in the shed. I know there are other things that need to be done around here, an' Freeman's not feelin' that well. I'll think about it and I'll ask him what he thinks is a priority."

"Awright, den," James said, standing up. He hesitated for a minute, thinking. "Ah b'lieve Ah kin put in some hours in da mornin', if dat's awright. Ah'd havta come early 'cause Ruby's havin' da birfday party fuh Unc' Freeman."

"That would be fine," she said. "I don't have anything tomorrow until my friend Etta comes for dinner at noon."

When he left, he thanked Maggie again for getting him the job. He felt like hugging her, but that was something he hadn't done since he was a little boy. "Mis' Mac went to da comp'ny an' talked wit' dat ole Mr. Roberts ta git me dat job," he thought. "Ain't dat sumpin!" He laughed with sheer joy. "She always been a good frien'."

♥ ♥ ♥

JAMES CHOSE TO WALK FOR A WHILE THROUGH Maggie's orange grove. He was hoping to find some orange blossoms to smell, and he did find a limb that had a few on it. He stood for a minute just inhaling the aroma. He'd heard that brides carried bouquets of orange blossoms in some fancy weddings; he thought that must be for the smell.

As he walked through the grove, he saw some small yellow oranges that had fallen from the trees. He walked past several trees with little ones underneath them, feeling kind of silly that he wanted to throw some the way he had when he was a child. He was so happy he finally gave in and picked up a handful.

He put the bag with the clock in it on the ground and started throwing the oranges. As he threw them one at a time, a scene flashed in his mind of white boys throwing rocks. "Oh Lawd," he said, wishing he hadn't picked up the little oranges.

When James was ten years old, he went to Lakeland with his parents to visit his grandmother, who was living with Pearl's sister, Charity. Normally, the whole family went, but that day the older kids were at a picnic for their Sunday school class. Pearl's niece, who was named after Pearl, and her little girl Kizzie were also visiting. Kizzie was eight.

Charity lived in the Negro section of town, which was often referred to as "the Quarters," in a wooden house much like the other houses around it. Most of the houses were close together, but Charity's house, which had a fresh coat of white paint, had a nice-sized yard. The lawn was bordered by flowering shrubs on each side, and a row of red petunias bloomed along the front of the house.

After the family had been there for a little while, Pearson left to go visit a friend. He asked James if he wanted to go, but James chose to stay and play with Kizzie. He could tell by the shy way she looked at him that she liked him, and he thought she was cute. She had a hint of the devil in her dark brown eyes. Just like his sister's, her hair was tightly braided in pigtails all over her head, and tied with blue ribbons that matched her blue dress.

When he felt that he'd visited long enough with his grandmother, James got permission from both Pearls for him and Kizzie to go outside, and they went in the back yard. He suggested that they walk on the railroad tracks behind the house, and Kizzie agreed. They'd done that before with his siblings.

James noticed the rocks that covered the ground by the rails. He had an urge to throw some, but knew his mother wouldn't approve.

"Ah kin stay on here longer'n you can," he teased.

"Bet ya cain't, eit'er," she shot back.

He walked on one rail and she walked on the other one. They stared down at the rails and held their arms straight out to the side to keep their balance.

"Ah knows Kizzie gon' lose," James sang. "Ah knows Kizzie gon' lose."

"Ah knows James gon' lose," Kizzie sang. "Ah knows James gon' lose."

Every now and then one of them would step off the rail and the other one would laugh and sing their little ditty. Having fun and immersed in the game, they didn't notice how far they'd gone until they heard laughter. Three white boys, eleven or twelve years old, were standing about thirty feet away watching them.

James and Kizzie froze. He was hardly breathing, and he could feel his heart pounding against his chest.

And as James stood in Mis' Mac's grove thinking about it, his heart was pounding furiously as anger rose in him. His face was stern, his back was straight, and his hands had become fists.

He remembered Kizzie whispering, "Us ain't 'pose' ta go dis far, James. Us gotta go back now." They stepped off the rails, and started walking back.

"Mama tol' me not ta ever come down here," Kizzie said. And James could hear the fear in her voice.

The only thing that made James control the impulse to run was the fear that the boys would chase them. Two of them were bigger than him, and when he glanced back, he didn't like the way they were looking at him. The urge to run was powerful. He kept repeating softly, mostly for himself, "Jes' walk! Don' be runnin'! Jes' walk! Don' be runnin'!"

Suddenly he felt a pain in his leg and realized he'd been hit by a rock. "Le's run, Kizzie," he whispered urgently. "Dey's th'owin' dem rocks."

He grabbed her hand and pulled her along as they ran. They heard loud pings as rocks hit the rails. The boys ran, too, stopping occasionally to pick up more rocks from the tracks. Fortunately, they couldn't throw quite as accurately while they were running, but they managed to hit James several times; they were only throwing at him.

James noticed that the boys stayed about the same distance behind them; stopping to pick up more rocks slowed them down. James wanted to run faster, but Kizzie couldn't run as fast as he could. He kept telling her to hurry, but she was running as fast as her little legs could move. And it was not easy running on the railroad bed. She was as scared as James was of the boys, and she was afraid of what her mother would do if she found out they'd gone into forbidden territory. James didn't know the area well, but she did. She'd been there many times.

When they were getting near the house, she stumbled and fell, and James stopped with her. As he stood there helping her up, rocks were hitting him, and one hit him in the back of the head, hurting worse than any of the others had. "Ow," he said. He didn't wait for Kizzie, but ran to the house as fast as he could, rocks flying at him. He flew up the back steps, through the screen door, and onto the porch.

With James gone, they started pelting Kizzie. He stood on the screened-in porch anxiously waiting for her. As he watched her trying to get away, and saw the terror on her face, he felt ashamed for leaving her, ashamed for being so afraid of getting hurt. The boys stopped chasing her, but continued throwing rocks, except for one boy. James noticed that he was standing behind the other two, just watching. He had his hands in his pockets, and when he saw James looking at him, he looked down.

"Dat boy ain't th'owin' rocks," James thought. "Ah 'on't thank he like it. He look kinda sad."

By the time Kizzie reached the house, she was crying. James held the screen door open for her, relieved that they were both safe inside.

The two Pearls heard her and went to see what the trouble was. "Dem white boys been th'owin' rocks at us," James said.

The boys were walking away by then, but Kizzie's mother went out in the yard and yelled, her fist in the air, "Bunch a cowards! Why 'on't y'all pick on somebody yo' own size? Or mebbe y'all like ta try me. Y'all come on back 'ere; Ah take ya all three on."

The boys walked along casually, but looked behind them every now and then to make sure no one was after them. James believed that if they had accepted her challenge, Kizzie's mother would've beaten all three of them; she was that mad.

The next moment, she was holding Kizzie in her arms, soothing her. Kizzie's knee was skinned and bloody from her fall. Pearl looked James over and found a knot on his head. Kizzie didn't tell them that James had left her. He was grateful to her for that because he figured he'd be in trouble if Pearl knew.

Kizzie's mother didn't ask them anything about where they'd been and James hoped she hadn't asked Kizzie later. The day was bad enough without poor little Kizzie getting punished, as well.

Now, nine years later, James still felt guilty. He knew that if he'd stayed with her, the boys would've thrown rocks at him instead of her. He'd told himself before that he was just a child and he ran because he was hurt and afraid. Nevertheless, he still felt ashamed when he thought about it and he felt ashamed that he hadn't mentioned anything about it to Kizzie the few times he'd seen her. Of course, she hadn't mentioned it either, but James didn't let that make him feel any better. He decided he'd apologize to Kizzie the next time he saw her—in private, of course. He still didn't want his mother to know; he knew the look she'd give him.

He realized, as he thought about the whole scene, that he was feeling the same fear he'd felt that day, the same sense of helplessness, and the same anger. He scrounged around for a handful of fallen oranges and started throwing them one by one as hard as he could throw, visualizing a target of the two boys who were throwing rocks at them.

"Ah like ta see you cowards now," he yelled. "Ah beat da hell outta bof a ya at da same time. No-good white trash! Wha' kine a people th'ows rocks at a lil gal?"

After he threw the last orange, James dropped to his knees in the grove and sobbed. "Oh Lawd Jesus, why wuz Ah so sc'ed?" He started wringing his hands. "Ah wuz jes' a coward. How could Ah ever leave po' lil Kizzie all 'lone like dat? Ah'm so sorry. . . . Ah'm so sorry."

When he stopped weeping, he stayed where he was for a while, sitting on his heels. With his eyes glazed over, he stared at nothing in particular, no longer having any feelings about the truck or his new job.

It took him a while to realize that it was raining. The envelope was stuffed in his jeans, so he figured it would stay dry. He took the clock out of the bag, which was already damp, and carefully tucked it under his arm. Then he trudged home slowly, feeling beat down by the rain, and not caring that he was soaking wet.

Friday

JAMES WAS UP AND DRESSED BEFORE HE HEARD any sounds from his parents' bedroom. He let Shep out, and was in the kitchen with cereal and milk on the table when his mother walked in wearing her housecoat.

"Ya up early dis mornin', baby," Pearl said, giving him a hug.

"'Member? Ah wonts ta git ta Mis' Mac's early an' work a few hours befo' da party," he said. "Ah needs ta pay fuh huh truck."

"Dat's right," Pearl said. "Ah forgot. An' Ah still cain't b'lieve she got dat job fuh you, baby. Dat sho wuz nice a huh."

"Ah cain't b'lieve it neit'er, Mama. Ain't she sumpin!"

During supper Thursday evening, James had told his parents about his depressing experience with Mr. Roberts, and Maggie getting him the job. They were as pleased about the job as he was.

"How come *you* up so early?" James asked as he poured milk on his cereal.

"Ah jes' woke up an' couldn' git back ta sleep," she said. "Guess Ah's thankin' 'bout da party. Ah tol' Ruby Ah'd do some cookin'."

"Daddy still sleepin'?"

"Yep, he still sawin' logs in dere."

"You reckon Unc' Freeman gon' like da party?"

"Ah hope so. Ah'm takin' some a our records dat Ah knows got some a da music dat he like," Pearl said. "Dat man useta cut a rug. When dere wuz a party, all dem girls wanted ta dance wit' 'im. Course, it wadn' jes' 'cause a his dancin'; Freeman wuz some kinda *fine lookin' man!*"

"Ain't bad now," James said.

"Fuh real! But you shoulda seen 'im. He sho could turn da heads. An' he wuz built mighty fine, too. Ah was lil, but Ah 'member Daddy tellin' 'im ta watch out fuh da white womens. He said if he wadn' careful, he wuz gon' fine hisse'f hangin' from a tree somewhere."

James was quiet for a moment, imagining the young Freeman. "He musta really been sumpin," he said softly.

"Sho was," Pearl replied, nodding her head. "Dat sc'ed me, whut Daddy said, 'cause Ah loved mah big brot'er. He wuz always teasin' me, an' he'd pick me up an' spin me 'roun' till Ah couldn' stand up. Ah didn' know whut Daddy meant, but he sho sc'ed me. Guess dat's why Ah 'members it."

Pearl thought for a minute. "It's a good thang he was 'umble, an' not one a dem ole cocky, uppity boys."

"Sho is," James said as he stood up with his empty cereal bowl in his hand. He was anxious to get going.

"Us 'pose' ta be dere at noon, an' Ah wonts ta be a bit early ta he'p Ruby," Pearl said.

"Awright," James replied. "Ah be back by den."

Shep was waiting outside for James as though he knew he could go. He fell into step with him as soon as James put on his cap and stepped off the porch.

When they got to Maggie's, everything was quiet and still. The rooster wasn't even crowing. James got the wheelbarrow and axe very quietly, and walked slowly so the wheelbarrow didn't make any racket. It was 6:30, and he didn't want to wake Maggie. He planned to work four hours—that would give him a good start toward paying off the truck the next week.

As he thought about that, a big smile spread across his face. "Ah'm gon' be workin' at da phosphate mine," he said. A surge of elation spread through his body. He pictured Maggie talking to Mr. Roberts. "She sho brave," he thought, "standin' up ta a tough ole man like dat. Wish Ah coulda been a fly on da wall ta hear whut she say ta 'im wit' his ole prejudice se'f."

When they got to the forest, James made sure that he and Shep skirted the palmettos where the snake was the last time they were there. Pushing the wheelbarrow across the brown pine needles, James was smelling the pines, and thinking about how his life would change. "Ah'm gon' have set hours ever' week. Not like here, where Ah kin come when Ah feels like it. But a reg'lar paycheck ever' week. Thank ya, Lawd! Ooo wee! Ah likes dat!"

In one section deep in the woods, he quickly filled the wheelbarrow. "It's a bunch a lighterd here, Shep," he said. He knew he could get another load from the same area. He decided he'd push the wheelbarrow for a while before stopping to rest, because he had quite a ways to push it. He was at the edge of the forest when he stopped. He could see an oak tree as he looked down the line of trees, and he decided to go sit under it.

James put his hand on the tree—almost as though asking permission to sit under it—and he felt something rough. Looking carefully at the tree, he saw that someone had carved initials in the bark many years earlier. He had to look closely to make out the letters because the bark had spread over the edges of them. He was sure that the top letters were "F. J." "Dat's Unc' Freeman," he thought, getting excited by his discovery. "Freeman Jackson. He musta been real young when he done dat." James noticed that the carving was on the side least likely to be seen.

The plus sign was still clear, but the lower letters were hard to make out. "Look like 'M. M.,'" he thought. "M. M. Who could dat be?" Right away, he thought of Maggie McClellan, but he dismissed that thought. "It cain't be Mis' Mac 'cause she white. Could be Sistah Mavis Sharp. Ah 'on't know whut huh name wuz 'fore she married. Ah havta aks Mama who dat is. It sho 'on't stan' fuh Drusilla. Dat fuh sho. An' it might not e'em be 'M. M.,' but it sho do look like it."

As he sat under the tree, leaning against the trunk, he was thinking of all the older Negro women he knew. He even tried to remember those who'd died. He thought of a woman he knew named "Mary," but her name was "Black," and she wasn't married.

James saw a gopher tortoise slowly making its way toward the forest. "You better hide or somebody gon' be eatin' you." He laughed.

His family didn't eat gophers, but he knew people who did. The tortoise stopped and ate some grass. "Don' worry, Ah thanks ya safe here."

When he got the wheelbarrow full of wood back to the yard, Maggie was throwing some cracked corn to her chickens. "Well, good mornin' to you, James! You've already got a load of wood, an' I didn't even know you'd been here."

James released the wheelbarrow and removed his cap. "Mornin', Mis' Mac. Ah wanted ta git started early so Ah could work fuh fo' hours."

Maggie smiled. James was a good worker, but she'd never seen him quite so anxious to work. "You want to pay for the truck, don't you?"

"Yes'm, Ah sho do. Ah wonts it ta be mine."

"Well, Freeman hasn't picked any more watermelons yet, so we won't have any, but I'll make us some lemonade for later. There's still a lot of lemons on that ole tree," she said, pointing to the lemon tree near the garage. The tree had yellow and green lemons on it, and below it, a few lay rotting on the ground. "I'd like to know how many I've picked this year. I've made lemon pies an' lemonade for months."

"Dat's a good tree," James said.

"Yes, it is."

"Ruby got one like dat, too. She still makin' lemonade."

"You know, the new truck is supposed to arrive later this mornin'. Maybe it'll come while you're still here."

"Ah hope it do," he said. He wanted to see the new truck, and he hoped he'd be able to take his truck, even though it wouldn't be paid for. Just the thought of it made him happy, and a smile spread across his face.

And the new truck did come. When James got back with the second load of wood, Maggie and Freeman were sitting on the porch in the rocking chairs. "Come join us after you empty that wood, James," she called. He was planning to chop the long pieces of wood, but after he emptied the wheelbarrow, he went to sit with them. They were all three sitting there drinking lemonade and talking when the truck arrived. A car followed the truck to carry the truck driver back to the dealership. Maggie went out to get the keys and talk to John, the dealer, who drove the car.

He got out and leaned against the car, waiting for Maggie. The truck driver said, "You got a good truck here. Handles nice."

John was staring at James and Freeman who'd walked off the porch after Maggie, and stood waiting near the steps. "Them niggers sittin' on the porch wi' her jus' like reg'lar people," he thought. "What's she thinkin' sittin' there wi' them on her porch?"

Maggie noticed the look of disapproval on his face.

"Hello, John," she said, smiling.

"Aunt Maggie," he responded, nodding his head and standing up straight.

She answered the question she imagined was in his mind. "James is bringin' some wood in for me, and we were all just havin' a lemonade break. Would you fellows care for some lemonade?"

Maggie thought she heard the driver say, "Yes, ma'am." But John said, "No, thank you," and the distasteful look remained on his face as he thought, "I ain't drinkin' outta no glass a nigger mighta drunk out of."

"We got your truck all ready," he said. "I hope you'll be happy with it."

"I'm sure we will, John," she responded. "Thank you for bringin' it out."

The truck driver handed Maggie two keys.

"Well, we got to git back," John said, opening the car door. "Let me know if you have any problems with that truck. Nice doin' business wi' you, Aunt Maggie."

"And with you, John," she replied.

Maggie dropped a key in her apron pocket, and handed Freeman the other key as the car left the driveway. "Here's the key to your new truck, Freeman," she said.

He smiled and said, "Thank ya, ma'am."

And she reached in her other apron pocket, and handed James the key to the old truck. "And here's the key to *your* truck, James," she said.

Freeman added, "Da udder key in da truck."

"Thank ya, Mis' Mac," James said, grinning. He couldn't wait to drive it, and he couldn't have been much happier if she'd given him the key to the new truck.

Freeman and James spent some time looking over the new truck while Maggie sat on the porch watching them. She had the satisfaction of knowing she'd made those two men happy that day.

After Freeman left in the new truck, James told Maggie he should leave, too. "Ah chop dat wood some udder time," he said. "But Ah might not work tomorrah 'cause Ah'm goin' ta Lakelan' wit' Ruby an' Harley."

"All right," she said. "By the way, James, when you see Harley, please tell him I'd like to talk to him sometime."

"Yes'm, Ah will," he said. "Ah see ya on Monday."

"See you Monday. Have a good time at the party."

Maggie went in the kitchen to finish preparing dinner for her friend, Etta. As she worked, she was listening to the "William Tell Overture" on her record player. It always made her think of the *Lone Ranger*, which she'd listened to on the radio until it went off the air in 1954. Deeply engrossed in the music, she didn't hear the truck come, but she did hear a man's voice calling her. She was surprised to see Harley when she went on the porch.

"Hello, Harley. I didn't expect to see you so soon," she said, wiping her hands on her apron.

"Mornin', Mis' Mac," he replied. "James came by. Say ya wonts ta talk ta me, an' Ah thank he wuz wantin' to show off his truck."

Maggie laughed, nodding her head. "He is quite pleased to have it."

"He sho is," Harley agreed. "He cain't wait fuh us ta start workin' on dat truck."

"I'm glad you'll be helpin' him with it. I know it needs an awful lot of work."

"It do, Mis' Mac, but it worf mo' 'an twenty dollars."

"I hope so," she said. "Please come an' sit down, Harley."

Harley went on the porch and Maggie shook his hand. "I didn't mean to drag you away from the party preparations. I thought James would tell you later."

"Dat's awright. Ruby got it 'bout done."

They sat down in the rocking chairs. "How have y'all been?" she asked.

"Us fine, Mis' Mac," Harley said. "Hi you been doin'?"

"I've been fine, too," Maggie replied. "How's Rubin? He must be quite active now."

"He sho is," Harley heartily agreed, smiling. "He inta ever'thang, dat boy."

Maggie knew he was curious, so she didn't keep him waiting. "I've been wantin' to talk to you about Freeman," she said, "and about the farm. You know he hasn't been feelin' well lately."

"Yes'm," Harley said.

"I'm afraid for him to continue workin' the way he looks. He doesn't have much to do, but I think he's probably doin' more than he should." She paused. "It reminds me of the way things were twenty years ago when Freeman's daddy was startin' to get feeble. My daddy hired a man to do most of the work for Mr. Jackson."

"Sound da same," Harley said.

"The thing is, I'd really like to have this farm producin' again. You know we haven't been sharecroppin' for a long time now, and I haven't grown my own hay for years. Right now, Freeman's not doin' well, the farm's not doin' well, and some days I'm not doin' well, either. I need to have activity here the way it used to be—more to think about and more to keep me busy."

"Oh, Mis' Mac," Harley said with sympathy in his voice.

She took her glasses off, put them in her lap, wiped tears from each cheek, and rubbed her eyes. Harley shifted in his chair, and looked away.

Maggie put her glasses back on and continued. "Freeman has been a wonderful worker and he's my dear, dear friend. Of course, I'd continue to pay him the same, and he can stay in the sharecropper's house, but I want him to mostly retire. The new man can take over some of what he does now. And I'll arrange some other place for the sharecropper to live."

Harley just nodded his head. He wondered where Mis' Mac would put a sharecropper. He wouldn't have imagined it, but she was sitting there wondering, too, and thinking she might have to build a new house.

"The reason I wanted to talk to you, Harley, was to see if you know anyone who's a good honest worker who might be interested in sharecroppin' with me. I want you to know that I didn't think James would be, but I asked him, just in case."

"Dat's real good," Harley said, nodding. He paused for a moment, thinking. "Ah cain't thank a nobody offhand, Mis' Mac."

"Well, that's all right, Harley," Maggie replied. "I just wanted to let you know so you could think about it. Let me know if you think of somebody."

She stood up and Harley did, too. "I've got to finish preparin' dinner for my friend, Etta."

"Awright den. Ah sho will thank 'bout it, Mis' Mac," he said.

"Thank you for comin' by, Harley. I trust your judgment," she said. "An' ask Ruby if she's heard of anyone, but please don't mention it in front of Freeman because I'm not goin' to say anything to him until I know for sure that I have somebody. If I don't find anybody, I don't want him to know about it. He'd probably feel bad."

"Ah sho wont."

As he walked to the truck, she called, "You and Ruby come visit some time, and bring Rubin."

Maggie was in the yard greeting her friend when Freeman drove by slowly in the new truck on his way to his party. As they all waved, Maggie saw that he was wearing the sporty gray hat that made her knees weak. "Oh my Lord," she thought. "He wears that fedoro set jauntily at just the right angle for his handsome face. Thank God he doesn't know the effect it has on me."

♥   ♥   ♥

JAMES WAS THE FIRST TO ARRIVE AT RUBY'S, proudly driving his truck. As soon as he pulled up, Harley bounded out of the house to take a closer look at it. He was excited, too, because he was looking forward to working on it with James. James raced the engine a few times so they could listen to it, and Harley looked under the hood and tinkered with the carburetor until they agreed that it sounded better.

James got out of the truck. "Dat sound good," he said coolly, looking at the engine. "Might make it ta da phosphate comp'ny, now dat Ah got me a job."

Harley's head jerked up. "Ya done got yo'se'f a job?"

James just grinned, and Harley slapped him on the back and they both laughed happily. When they calmed down a little, James told him about Maggie talking to Mr. Roberts.

Pearl and Pearson arrived while they were still talking and tinkering. They hugged Harley, and he and James helped them take the food they'd brought into the house. Pearl, Pearson, and James hugged Ruby, who was holding Rubin, and kissed him on his pudgy cheek, and James tickled him and laughed along with him. They spent a few minutes exclaiming over how cute he was and playing with him.

They oooed and aaaahed as he took a few steps. Of course, the attention he received brought out his best performance and kept a smile on his chubby little face. He was a beautiful baby and generous with his smiles. James picked him up and swung him around, and Rubin's laugh made the adults laugh.

"Rubin look mo' like Harley ever' day," Pearl said.

"Yeah, he sho do," Ruby agreed, looking at him.

"He ten months ole now?" Pearl asked.

"Yes'm," Ruby replied.

The men went back to the truck, taking Rubin with them. He liked the truck, too. Harley sat him behind the steering wheel and let him tug on it. Harley made engine sounds, and Rubin stuck out his little lips and blew. He didn't produce much sound, but he blew a lot of bubbles.

When Freeman arrived in the new truck, all of the attention went to it. Pearl and Ruby took a break from the kitchen so Ruby could nurse Rubin, and they sat on the porch in the swing, watching the men. They found it amusing how interested the men were in the new truck, looking under the hood and inside the cab, and letting down the tailgate and checking out the back.

"Thank dey missed anythang?" Ruby asked, chuckling.

"Unh, unh, unh," Pearl shook her head. "If dey did, dey'll go back over it ag'in," she said, and she leaned against Ruby as they laughed.

After Rubin stopped nursing, Ruby took him back into the house and she and Pearl finished getting the meal ready. When Ruby announced that it was time to eat, the men suddenly lost interest in the new truck, and headed for the house.

Ruby and Pearl hugged Freeman and wished him a happy birthday. He played with Rubin while Ruby and Pearl put ice in the glasses and poured the iced tea, and the other men went to wash their greasy hands. Freeman hadn't gotten his hands greasy.

"Dis look like a feast ta me," he said, looking at the table full of food. Pearl had cooked a pork shoulder, and cooked rice in the broth; a big pot of black-eyed peas, which she'd shelled that morning after Pearson picked them for her; and some macaroni and cheese. Ruby had made some creamed corn, collard greens, fried chicken, corn bread, and a birthday cake. They'd both contributed sliced tomatoes and cucumbers and iced tea.

Harley put Rubin in his high chair and everyone sat down around the table. When they got quiet, Ruby said, "Unc Pearson, please aks da blessin'."

Pearson prayed: "Oh Lawd, we come ta ya wit' rejoicin' fuh our brot'er who sebenny years ole today. We aks ya ta bless 'im on his birfday, dear Lawd. An' be wit' us as we all git togather today, an' he'p us always ta do yo' will. An' thank ya Lawd fuh dis good meal here befo' us, an' please bless dis food. We thank ya fuh dis an' fuh all our blessin's. In Jesus' name we pray. Amen."

Everyone got busy passing food and fixing their plates. Ruby put some small bits of chicken and some black-eyed peas on Rubin's tray, and he stayed busy picking them up with his little fingers one by one. Some of the peas were a little mashed by the time they got to his mouth, and a few fell to the floor, but no one minded.

"You eatin' yo' peas?" Ruby asked, wiping his chin.

"Ya doin' a good job, Rubin," Pearl said, looking at his sweet little face. Her reward for the compliment was a smile showing his cute little baby teeth and some partially-chewed peas.

"Ah seen a big bass jump in Mis' Mac's pond da udder day," James said. "Unc' Freeman, ya wanna go fishin' wit' me late dis aftanoon? Ah'm 'termin' dat Ah'm gon' git dat fish."

"Sho, le's go fishin'. Ain't been fishin' fuh a long time," Freeman replied. "Dat be real nice."

"Well, awright, den," James said. "Us goin' fishin'."

Pearl said, "Ya lookin' better today, Freeman, now dat you sebenny. Hi ya feelin'?"

Freeman replied, "Ah'm doin' good," and returned his attention to his food. "Ah needs some mo' peas, an' some mo' cream' corn. Ruby, Pearl, y'all kin cook yo' butts off. Dis here is some good ole food."

"Sho is," James, Harley, and Pearson said in unison.

"Do taste purty good," Ruby said, smiling.

James was near the peas and the corn, so he passed them both. "Harley, Mr. Hiers done lost a cow?" he asked. "Ah seen a big bunch a ole buzzards over dat way yestiddy."

"Yep, one a dem ole cows," Harley said. "She been sick fuh couple a days, so we figgered she wuz gon' die."

"Dey sho wuz a bunch a dem ole buzzards circlin' 'round out dere," James said.

"Sho wuz," Harley agreed. "Ah seen 'em."

"Anybody want mo' chicken or pork?" Ruby asked, passing both. "James, Aunt Pearl told me dat Mis' Mac got ya hired at da phosphate company. Dat sho is good."

Harley slapped him on the back again. "Ah still cain't b'lieve dat."

"Dat ole white cracker didn' stan' a chance wit' huh. Ah like ta been in dat room wit' 'em," Freeman said. "Dey wadn' no colored fountain an' Mis' Maggie wuz gittin' me some water in da lady dat work dere cup from da white fountain, an' she drunk outta dat cup behine me. Ya shoulda saw huh. Dat cracker seen huh an' she stan' dere right in fron' a him drinkin', an' she wadn' carin' nuttin' 'bout him, an' he lookin' at huh like him saw a ghos'." They all roared.

"Ah sho like ta seen dat," James said.

"Ah's wishin' Ah coulda went thu da flo'," Freeman said, and they laughed some more.

"An' den she tell dat man," he continued, "dey need ta git a 'colored' fountain."

"Fuh real!" Pearl exclaimed. "Dat woman sumpin."

"Ah'm sho grateful ta huh," James said. "Ah wouldn' a got dat job. Dat man didn' like me e'em a lil bit."

When they were done eating, Ruby and Pearl cleared the table and Rubin's tray, and Ruby put a couple of toys on the tray for him to play with. Then she brought out the birthday cake. She'd bought some red food coloring, colored some of the frosting, and put little pink dots and squiggles on the white frosting. Freeman was obviously pleased that she made such a pretty cake for him.

The cake had seven candles on it. "One candle fuh each decade," Ruby announced.

Harley lit the candles as Rubin watched with wide eyes. After they sang "Happy Birthday" to Freeman, Pearl said, "Well, you sebenny now, Freeman."

"Guess Ah is," he replied. "Dat's hard ta b'lieve. Never t'ought Ah be sebenny."

"Ah made a devil's food cake wit' white frostin' an' coconut on da top fuh you, Daddy," Ruby said, "'cause Ah know dat's yo' favorite." And she kissed him on the cheek.

Freeman put his arm around her. "Thank ya, baby." He looked at little Rubin and said, "Dis *mah* baby." Rubin sat staring with wide eyes at the two of them. And Pearl put her arm around James and said, "An' dis *mah* baby." Rubin let out a little squeal and they laughed. Ruby took him out of his high chair so he could play on the floor.

Everyone exclaimed about how delicious the cake was. "Oh man," James said, rubbing his stomach. "Ah'm full as a tick on a fat hound dawg."

Again, Harley slapped him on the back. "Ah's thankin', James. Now dat ya got a truck, Ah ain't gon' havta haul yo' sorry se'f 'roun' no mo'." They all laughed.

"Dat da truf," James said. "Ah got mah own ride now, an' Ah 'on't need ya no mo'."

"Dat's a good truck, James," Freeman stated. "Ah been drivin' dat truck fuh twen'y years, an' dat baby 'on't play. It ain't nuttin' but da truf. Ah didn' e'em care 'bout gittin' a new one."

"Well, Unc' Freeman," James said, "Ah be glad ta trade wit' ya." They laughed again.

"Bet ya would," Freeman quipped. "Ah 'on't thank Mis' Maggie be too happy wit' dat deal."

"Good thang she cain't hear us," Pearl said. "She thank we's crazy."

They laughed and nodded their heads.

"Ya know, James," Ruby said, "ya gon' havta beat dem gals off wit' a stick when dey see you in dat fancy truck. Us all noticin' how pop'lar you is now. Saleena hangin' on yo' arm, an' Mardella waitin' in line." And laughing, she leaned towards Pearl until their shoulders touched.

Everybody laughed, except James. He just shook his head, grinning. He tried to think of a good retort, but he was too embarrassed, which was exactly what Ruby was hoping for.

Finally, he said, "Ah knows it a beat-up ole truck, but it *mah* truck. An' Harley an' me gon' fix huh up. Ain't we Harley?"

"Yassuh," Harley said, saluting James.

Rubin started crying and everybody's attention shifted to him. "He ti'ed," Ruby said, and she took him to his room for a nap.

"He been good fuh a long time," Pearl said.

Pearl cleared the dessert dishes with the help of James and Harley. When Ruby returned, Pearson asked, "You womens able ta do dis work yo'selves, or does us mens havta he'p y'all?"

"Dat'll be da day!" Pearl said, and she and Ruby laughed.

"Sho will," Ruby said, nodding. "Sho will."

The men sat in the living room and talked while the women washed the dishes and cleaned up the kitchen. They'd spent a long time at the dinner table, and Pearl knew that Pearson was planning to leave kind of early, so she was business-like with the cleaning.

"Ah brought us some records ta play fuh ya daddy," she told Ruby. "He gon' dance on his birfday."

"Oh, dat be good fuh him," Ruby said.

"Oughta be," Pearl agreed.

After they finished in the kitchen, they joined the men in the living room. "Y'all had yo' rest," Pearl declared. "Now, time ta dance. Ah brought some records Ah knows ya like, Freeman." She sat down and thumbed through a small stack of 78s, and put one on.

When Nat King Cole's "Unforgettable" began, Pearl didn't even have to ask him to dance. She just started walking toward him, and he got right up to dance with her. The others sat smiling, watching them.

"Way ta go, Daddy," Ruby said when he twirled Pearl around. "Ya still got da moves."

Freeman laughed. "Ah might still got 'em, but dey ain't doin' me no good no mo'."

Pearl put on some faster songs after that and the others took turns dancing while Freeman rested. James danced with Ruby and Pearl. "Us gon' git down on some Little Richard," Pearl said as she picked up a 45, and put on "Tutti Frutti." Harley and Ruby hopped right up, and everybody sang along with the "whop bops" and "bam boos," and laughed.

When Pearl put on "All Shook Up" by Elvis Presley, they laughed at her. "Go'n an' laugh all ya want to. Ah 'on't care 'cause Ah likes dis song," she said, laughing. Harley and Ruby danced again, but when Pearson and Pearl started dancing, they had the floor. The two of them anticipated each other's moves, and moved together as one.

"Dat's a thang a beauty," James said as he watched them. "Ya'll still got it, too."

"An' Ah intends ta keep it," Pearson grinned. "Dere might be snow on da roof, but dere's still fire in da furnace."

Pearl had chosen Freeman's favorite for the last dance, Duke Ellington's "Don't Get Around Much Anymore." He danced with her again.

"Lookin' good, Unc' Freeman," James said.

"Yeah, you is," Pearson agreed.

Freeman smiled. "Ah might be ole, but Ah's good as gol'." He was clearly enjoying himself. After a little while, he let go of Pearl and danced some with Ruby. However, as soon as the song ended, he announced that Rubin was not the only one who needed a nap. "Da young an' da ole got ta have dere naps."

Then Pearson said, "Ah tol' Mr. Wilson Ah's gon' check on his sprayer fuh 'im today. Ole thang ain't workin' right. So, us got ta go, too. An' James, ya need ta check on Holstein an' see how she doin'. If she ain't cleared up, give huh some mo' mistletoe."

"Yassuh," James said.

And, just like that, the party was over. James hung around talking to Harley and Ruby for a little while after the others left, but then he went home to check on Holstein.

♥　♥　♥

Maggie's friend had gone and she was sitting at the table on the porch eating a grapefruit. She liked to peel the grapefruit, remove the pulp, pull it apart, and then remove the skin on the slices, so that all she was eating was the fruit, which she salted. Eating a grapefruit was an enjoyable process for her and it took a while. She was on her last slice when Harley and Ruby arrived. She hurriedly popped it in her mouth and went to the washstand to wash her hands, as they got out of their truck. Harley and Ruby each held one of Rubin's hands, letting him walk between them.

"Come an' sit down!" Maggie exclaimed, pleased to see them.

They picked Rubin up by his hands so that he hopped up the steps. He started laughing and continued until they were on the porch and he looked at Maggie; then his face went serious. Harley picked him up as Maggie hugged Ruby, and Rubin watched her. Then she shook Harley's hand and asked Rubin if she could have a kiss. He just looked at her.

"Perhaps I should wait until he gets a little more used to me," she said. "Have a seat, you two."

"My," she said after they were seated in the rocking chairs. "Twice in one day, Harley."

Harley scratched his head and smiled. "When it rains, it po's."

"Did you think of someone?" Maggie asked, hoping she knew the answer.

"Well, Mis' Mac," he replied, "Ruby an' me wuz talkin' 'bout it. Ah might wont da job myse'f, if dat's awright wit' you."

Maggie could tell that he was anxious to hear her response. "Are you unhappy with Tom Hiers, Harley?"

"Some ways," he said. "An' Ah thank a change be good fuh me an' Ruby, Mis' Mac."

Maggie took her glasses off, put them in her lap, and rubbed her eyes with the backs of her hands. Then she put her glasses back on.

She looked into his eyes. "I'll tell you this, Harley: nothin' would make me happier than havin' you as a sharecropper. However, I don't want to come between you an' Tom."

"It da end a da season," Harley said as though thinking it through. "Ain't much lef' ta do in da fiel's now wit' summer comin'. An' Mr. Hiers have a few months ta fine somebody else ta work fuh 'im. Ah sho would like ta work fuh you."

Ruby couldn't contain herself. "An' us could live wit' Daddy. Ah knows us all like dat. Ah could cook fuh 'im all da time, an' he'p 'im out. He like dat. An' Mis' Mac, Ah could work fuh you, too, if ya wonts me to."

Maggie felt so happy, and her face felt so warm, she thought she must be glowing. "I was hopin' you'd both feel that way!" she exclaimed. "I didn't want to make things awkward for you, Harley, by askin' you, in case you didn't want the job. But I would love to have you work with me. An' you too, Ruby; I could use some help around the house, now that I'm gettin' older. And I think you're right about Freeman. I think he'd love to have you with him, and it would do him good to have Rubin around. An' Lord knows, it will sure make it easier for me to tell him."

Maggie knew Harley was a pleasant, hard-working, honest man, and she liked him and Ruby a lot. She hadn't wanted to ask him directly because she was afraid he might agree without giving it enough thought, or because he felt put on the spot. And she wanted Harley and Ruby to come to that decision together. Now, she could see that they were as pleased as she was. Ruby's eyes were shining, and none of them could stop smiling.

"I haven't been to your father's house for a long time," she said to Ruby. "Why don't you look around and tell me if there are things that need to be done to make it more comfortable."

"Oh Mis' Mac," Ruby said, "dey's mo' room, an' it much nicer dan where we live at now."

"I'd like you to look, anyway, Ruby," she said, "to see if any of the rooms need to be painted, or anything needs to be repaired. I know Freeman has kept it nice, so it's probably in good shape, but I want you to be sure."

"Yes'm, Ah sho will."

"When ya wonts me ta start?" Harley asked.

"Yesterday," Maggie quipped, and they all laughed. "You'll need to give Tom notice, and work somethin' out with him. As for me, the sooner, the better. There are a lot of things that could be done now which aren't part of sharecropping, and of course, I'll pay you separately for those."

"Ah'm sho gon' talk ta 'im, an' Ah'll let ya know," Harley said. "Ah'm gon' talk ta 'im tomorrah if Ah sees 'im."

"That's fine," said Maggie. "I'm so pleased that you're goin' to work with me. I know we're goin' to have a great partnership."

"Mis' Mac," Ruby said hesitantly, "dey is one thang Ah jes' 'membered. Could us have a porch swing on da front porch? Ah always wonted a swing when Ah's lil, an' Daddy wouldn' buy one or aks fuh one."

"Of course, Ruby," Maggie said. "I'll get a swing right away, and I'm sorry I didn't know you wanted one when you were little. You certainly would've had it if I'd known."

Maggie felt bad. She knew how important things like that were to children, especially children who have very little. "I should have thought of a swing," she thought. She felt a little better when she remembered that the children did, at least, have a tire swing hanging from an oak tree.

"By the way, please don't say anything about this to Freeman yet," Maggie requested. "I'd like to wait until we know when you'll be startin' before I tell him."

After they left and Maggie went in to take her nap, she thought about how nice it would be to have a young couple around, and little Rubin. She knew it would be good for her and for Freeman. "I should have put a swing on that porch a long time ago," she thought. "Freeman probably would've liked that." Of course, she knew Freeman would've bought one if he wanted one. Nevertheless, it bothered her.

She'd just gotten up from her nap when she heard a truck and went out barefoot in time to see Freeman getting out of the new one. "I have to get used to the sound of that truck," she thought. "I didn't even know it was him."

Maggie was happy to see him; her favorite part of the day was sitting and talking with Freeman. They sat comfortably together, rocking, and drinking their iced tea—two old friends.

"Did you have a chance for a nap?" Maggie asked, thinking he'd be tired after the party.

"Yes'm, Ah sho did."

"How's the new truck? Do you like it?"

"Yes'm, Mis' Maggie. Seem like a good truck."

The cat went on the porch, brushed against Freeman's legs, and then hers. "Hello, Tommy," she said, "I saw the present you left me this mornin'." She smiled. "Freeman, Tommy brought me a dead mouse and left it right outside the kitchen door so I'd be sure to see it."

Freeman laughed. "Tommy sho a good mouser."

"He sure is. I couldn't ask for a better cat." She scratched his head.

Tommy saw a blue jay light in the crape myrtle bush near the porch and he went to the edge of the porch and assumed his waiting-to-pounce pose. The bird flew, and Tommy left to go pursue it. "Of course, I'd choose different prey for him sometimes," she lamented.

"Cats 'on't care 'bout birds atall."

"No, they don't, or little bunnies either."

They rocked in silence for a moment.

"Did you enjoy the party?" Maggie asked.

"Yes'm, Mis' Maggie. Us had a ball. Ruby an' Pearl bof cooked, an' Ruby made a devil's food cake. Pearl brought some good ole records an' Ah e'em danced a lil to a couple a Nat King Cole an' Duke Ellington songs."

"That's wonderful," she said. "I wish I could have seen you. Did you dance with Pearl?"

"Yes'm, Ah sho did."

"I would dearly love to dance with you," she thought, studying the face that was so dear to her.

"You know Freeman," she said, "until you were seven years old and your father sent you to the field, you called me 'Maggie.' Now, that you're seventy, I think it's high time you called me that again."

"Awright, Maggie," he said softly. Her name without the "Mis'" sounded a little familiar, and he liked it.

Tears formed in her eyes. "Thank you, Freeman. That sounds so much better to my old ears."

He decided he'd say it that way from then on when they were alone. After all, they'd known each other their whole lives, and it was what she wanted. He liked the thought of it, too.

They rocked for a while in silence, each of them looking across the driveway at the orange grove, deep in their own thoughts. Maggie looked at the tree where James had hid that awful night, and she thought about that. Freeman thought about all the work he'd done in that grove, and of his father before him, who planted the grove. "Da years go by," he thought.

"Da years go by," he said resignedly, and added, "Maggie."

"Yes, they do, Freeman. Where does the time go?"

"Fuh sho, Ah 'on't know.

"Nor do I," she said sadly. And she thought, "All the lonely years."

They sat quietly again. Maggie realized she was feeling melancholy, and she didn't like that feeling.

"Want to take the truck for a drive around the farm?" she asked. "You know that truck is sort of a birthday present for you."

"Ah 'preciate it!" he exclaimed, and smiled. "Le's go, Maggie."

"Lord, that smile!" she thought, but responded, "Music to my ears!"

They both stood up. "I'll be right back," she said, and went into the house. Freeman got a drink of water from the pump.

Maggie returned with her shoes on, a long-sleeved shirt draped over her arm, and a hat in her hand. She was prepared to protect herself from the sun in case they decided to get out of the truck.

They drove through the grove, then around the back of Freeman's house by the pasture that the cows were in. They saw three calves frolicking together, running and leaping into the air, as well as they could for very young calves. Two of them were brown and one was black.

"Aah! Look at the little calves. Stop for a minute, Freeman, so we can watch them. Aren't they precious?"

"Dey purty," he said. "Ah likes ta watch 'em." The sharecropper's house was right by the pasture, and Freeman could see the cows from his back porch and from the windows in the back of the house.

Maggie looked at the house. Drusilla had planted some kumquats and Florida cherries, and several flowering bushes in the yard, and some of them were blooming. Obviously, Freeman had taken care of them after her death. Maggie thought it was a cute little place, and she decided she'd get a swing for the back porch also. She thought Harley and Ruby might like to sit there and watch the cows, especially with Rubin. And she thought Freeman might like it, too; she pictured him sitting in a swing with Rubin by his side. She knew he often sat in a rocking chair on the back porch.

The cows started gathering by the fence as the truck sat there. "They're hopin' we brought some feed," Maggie said, laughing. "I guess that beautiful pasture isn't enough for them."

"Mebbe dey wants dessert," he suggested, and they laughed.

They drove on past the pine forest and through the unused back pasture. As they passed the pond, Maggie said, "I hope you'll go fishin' with James one day soon."

"Us plannin' ta go dis aftanoon," he said. "Sho is."

"That's great, Freeman! I think that would be good for you. Maybe we can have a fish fry for supper. Wouldn't that be nice?"

"Dat do sound good," he agreed.

"You an' James catch the fish, an' I'll cook them for the three of us." She remembered, and quickly added, "And we'll eat on the porch."

As they drove back to the house, Maggie said, "This has been so enjoyable. We should do this more often, Freeman, now that we have this nice truck. I wish I'd bought a new truck a long time ago. I don't know why I waited so long."

The only rides they'd taken in the old truck were so Freeman could show her a problem she needed to solve, or occasionally, to look at the cows. However, she normally walked back to the pasture if she just wanted to see the cows up close; part of the pasture was only fifty yards from her house.

When they got back to the house, she asked Freeman if he thought he could eat a piece of pie. He said it had been long enough since dinner, and he'd love to have some.

Maggie put some water and ice in a pitcher and took it and a pie to the table on the porch.

"Ah coulda he'ped ya," Freeman said as he went to the table.

"It's your birthday," Maggie said playfully. "You just sit down, and I'll wait on you."

His eyes got big when she brought out the second pie and two glasses, dishes, and forks. "Maggie, ya made two?"

"Just for you, my friend," she said, looking at him. "Just for you. An' when you turn seventy-five, I'll make you three."

"If Ah lives ta be seventy-five, Ah'm gon' make you a pie," he replied.

"I'm goin' to remember that, Mr. Jackson," Maggie said, nodding her head and smiling. "Now, which do you want? Coconut cream, lemon meringue, or both? I cut the lemon at dinner so Etta could have a piece."

"Ya knows me, Maggie, an' ya knows Ah'm greedy 'bout pies. Ah'm gon' have a lil piece a bof."

"I do know you, Freeman," she replied. "And I believe you know me."

"Yes, ma'am, Ah b'lieves Ah do. An' Ah know you is gon' have a lil piece a bof, too."

She chuckled. "You are correct, my friend."

As she cut herself a small piece of each, she thought how nice it would be if he'd stop saying "ma'am" to her, but she knew that was out of the question. She wouldn't even mention that.

"This has been a good day for me," she said. "I enjoyed visitin' with Etta and talkin' about old times. And I enjoyed ridin' around the farm with you. That was special. Don't you think we should do that more?"

"Yes'm, Ah do. Ah had a good time, too," he said. "An' dis pie is 'bout da bes' Ah ever had in my life. Thank ya, Maggie."

"You're welcome, Freeman," she said, loving the sound of him finally calling her "Maggie."

When he stood up to go, she stood also, and she said, "You know, Freeman, you've been my best friend for a long time."

"Ah knows, Maggie. An' you been mine."

"An' I believe we've only had two hugs since we've been adults: one when I left home, and one when your father died."

He nodded, staring at her intently.

"I think turnin' seventy calls for another hug, don't you?"

Freeman didn't speak, but his eyes were full of emotion. He opened his arms, and she walked into them as though that was where she belonged. They stood there holding each other for several seconds—eyes closed, cheeks pressed together—savoring the moment, before letting go. Maggie knew she had tears in her eyes, and was only a little surprised to see some in his.

Neither of them spoke. They looked in each other's eyes for a moment before Freeman walked off the porch, got in the truck, and drove away.

Maggie sat down in the rocker and watched him go, tears streaming down her face. She sat there until she heard the truck engine die. Then she got up and washed her face, and went in the yard and watered the marigolds by the side of the house.

♥   ♥   ♥

FREEMAN HAD ONLY BEEN GONE FOR A FEW MINUTES, and Maggie was sitting barefoot on her front porch swing reading Charles Dickens' *Great Expectations* for the third time, when she heard her old truck. Her first thought was that Freeman had returned, but then she remembered that James had the truck. She waved as he drove by the house. "Must be goin' to get Freeman to go fishin'," she thought.

And he was. He'd checked Holstein, gone for more mistletoe, and fed her. Now, he was ready to go fishing. He thought it was great that Freeman was going fishing on his birthday.

He got out and leaned against the truck, waiting for his uncle to walk out onto the porch. When Freeman didn't appear, James went on the back porch and knocked on the door.

"It James, Unc' Freeman."

"Come in," Freeman called.

James thought his voice sounded strange, like something was wrong. He went in, but didn't see him until he stuck his head in the bedroom.

Freeman was sitting on the edge of the bed grimacing and clutching his chest. He reached one hand out toward James.

"Unc' Freeman," James cried. "Ya havin' a heart-ertack?"

Freeman nodded his head.

James went to his uncle and put his hand on his shoulder. "Whut in da worl' kin Ah do?" he wondered.

His first impulse was to get Maggie. She'd know what to do.

"Ah'm gon' go an' git Mis' Mac," James said.

Freeman shook his head. He didn't want to make her responsible for his care. He pointed toward a bottle of aspirin that was on the nightstand by his bed. He hoped some aspirin might relieve some of the intense pain that gripped his heart.

"Ya wont some aspirin?" James asked, and Freeman nodded his head.

"Ya needs some water," James said, and quickly got some. Freeman threw three aspirin in his mouth and washed them down. James wondered how often he'd done that. The aspirin and an empty glass were by his bed.

"He need ta go to da hospital," James thought.

"Us goin' ta da hospital, Unc' Freeman," he said.

And even though Freeman shook his head, James bent over and picked up his uncle. Freeman was not light, but James didn't even think about whether or not he could carry him—he just did it. He managed to get him to the new truck and put him on the seat. Then he went back in the house and grabbed the two pillows from the bed and fixed them so that Freeman could rest more comfortably.

When James got in the truck, Freeman muttered, "Go ta Doc Stone's." Dr. Stone was the local Negro doctor, well-loved by the community, and all of James' family went to him.

Freeman did not want to go to Lakeland, which had the nearest hospital. Negroes were housed behind the hospital in a set of barracks—the "Colored Division." Another set of barracks was used for obstetrics for white women and their babies. The barracks had been moved from Lodwick Airfield in 1949 and were connected to the hospital by a canopy. If Negro patients needed surgery, they were moved to the hospital for the surgery and returned to the barracks afterward. There weren't many Negro doctors, and their barracks lacked facilities and equipment.

"Awright," James agreed. He didn't care where they went as long as there was a doctor there.

"Tell Maggie," Freeman said. James didn't say anything, but he was already planning to tell her. He started blowing the horn so that Maggie would go in the yard, and they could save time.

When she heard the horn, fear gripped her heart. "Must be Freeman," she thought. She ran, barefoot, into the yard, her hands over her heart, with a silent prayer: "Please God, not Freeman. Not now. Not now!"

"Unc' Freeman havin' a heart-ertack!" James yelled. "Us goin' ta Doc Stone's."

Maggie wasn't surprised that Freeman wanted to go to Dr. Stone. She knew he had a good reputation.

"All right," she said. "I'll tell Ruby and Pearl and I'll come."

She saw Freeman's head on a pillow, and she saw his twisted features and knew he was in pain. His eyes were tightly closed.

"Awright" James said, and he sped away.

"Oh Lord, please don't let him die," she pleaded, as she ran into her bedroom, slipped on the shoes she'd worn earlier, grabbed her pocketbook, and rushed out the door and down the steps. She stumbled on the bottom step and almost fell.

"I have to be careful," she thought. "Can't have two of us needin' a doctor."

She went to Pearl's first, wondering on the way what she'd do if Pearl wasn't at home. Fortunately she was, and had heard the car and was waiting on the porch. She knew as soon as she saw Maggie's face that something was terribly wrong.

Maggie just stood in the yard, not wanting to take the time to go on the porch. "Oh Pearl," she said. "Freeman's havin' a heart attack, and James is takin' him to Dr. Stone's office."

"Oh Lawd," Pearl said, collapsing onto a chair.

"Do you want to come with me?" Maggie asked.

"No'm, Mis' Mac, you go on," Pearl said. "Ah havta change mah clothes, an' Pearson be home any minute."

"All right. I'm stoppin' at Ruby's to tell her. I'm so sorry, Pearl."

Ruby was sitting on the porch swing with Rubin beside her. Maggie quickly told her the situation and that she'd told Pearl. Ruby calmly said that Harley was in the garden out back, and they'd drop Rubin off with somebody and be there as soon as possible. As Maggie pulled off, she saw Harley walking toward the house, and Ruby—still sitting in the swing—with her head down, sobbing. Maggie gasped when Ruby's gray cat dashed across the road several yards in front of the car.

Maggie drove faster than normal, and then she sat in the waiting room, waiting. It was late in the afternoon, but there were still a few people there. No one said a word, not even the children, who looked at Maggie and then at their parents with questions in their eyes.

She sat, impatiently, waiting for information. "I wish I had my knitting," she thought, "or somethin' to do with my hands."

She was relieved to see James after a few minutes. "I knew there was somethin' bad wrong with him. What did the doctor say, James?"

"Nuttin' yet," he answered, "but Doc Stone say he be right out. Ah has ta move da truck." He'd parked right in front of the office.

Maggie could not sit still. She crossed her legs and uncrossed them. She finally crossed her arms over her chest and gently rocked back and forth.

When James returned, he sat down by Maggie. He decided not to mention the aspirin bottle by Freeman's bed, but he decided if Freeman didn't die, he'd tell her and his mother. He'd already told the doctor.

"I'm goin' out of my mind," she said.

"Ah hates waitin', too," James replied.

After a little while, she went to the receptionist's desk. "What's your name, honey?" she asked. She didn't see a nameplate.

"Miracell," the receptionist replied.

"Well, Miracell, can you please find out what's happenin' with Mr. Jackson?" Maggie pleaded.

"Ah'm sho da doctor be right out ta tell ya," Miracell answered. "You wanna drink a water?"

"Water?" Maggie asked, and realized that she was thirsty. "That would be nice. An' some for my friend, as well, please."

She gave Maggie two glasses full, and she and James had just finished drinking the water when the doctor appeared. Maggie knew Dr. Stone, and they greeted each other and shook hands. "Come with me," he said, and they went into his office.

Dr. Stone went behind his desk, motioned to two straight-back chairs, and waited for them to sit. "Mr. Jackson did have a heart attack, an' I'm quite sure he's had others. An' frankly, this one was a bad one." He paused for a moment as they looked at him expectantly, and then said softly, "I'm sorry to say I don't believe he'll make it through the night."

"Oh no," Maggie moaned. She bent over sobbing, her head in her hands, oblivious to the presence of James and the doctor.

Neither man said anything. They looked at Maggie and then, with questions in their eyes, at each other. James had tears running down his cheeks, affected as much by Maggie as by the doctor's pronouncement.

After a few moments, Dr. Stone said softly, "Miss McClellan."

Maggie straightened up, took a deep breath, and wiped her eyes with the back of her hand. She looked at the doctor.

"He's sleepin' right now, but you're welcome to stay with 'im as long as you wont to. And if you'd like to lie down, there's a couch ovah there where I sleep sometimes if fam'lies stay with a patient who's here overnight. James, you need ta let his children know so they can come. You can use the telephone at the desk."

"Yassuh," James replied.

Dr. Stone stood up. "I'll show you where he's at. An' he may wake up an' talk to ya. You jus' never know."

James went to make the phone calls and Maggie went to the room with the doctor. Freeman was lying, propped up, in a hospital bed. A nurse stood at his side. The doctor placed his stethoscope over Freeman's heart and whispered, "He's a little more stable now. Jus' call me if there's a problem. I have to see the rest of my patients." The nurse left with him.

Maggie sat by Freeman's bed, holding his hand. She knew he was dying, so nobody could hurt him, and she didn't care one bit what anyone thought of her. She realized that she had very little time, and she was determined to spend it the way a woman should spend the last hours with the man she loves. She tried not to cry, but frequently, tears would roll down her cheeks. When she started sobbing, Freeman stirred.

She quickly wiped her face with her handkerchief. "Are you awake, Freeman?" she asked softly.

"Maggie, dat you?" he whispered, without opening his eyes.

"Yes, Freeman, it's me." She stood up so that she could see his face better. "You had a heart attack and you're in Dr. Stone's office."

"Ah 'members," he whispered.

"Your family will be comin' soon," Maggie said.

He opened his eyes and looked around the room, and then at Maggie. "Ah knows Ah'm dyin'," he said, "an' Ah'm mighty glad you's here." He took a deep breath.

She put one hand on his face, and the other one held his hand. "Oh Freeman," she said, "all these wasted years, and now you're goin' to leave me."

"Ah 'on't wanna leave ya," he said with much effort.

Neither of them heard James enter the room. He didn't want to disturb them, so he sat down in a chair by the wall.

"I'm so sorry this is happenin' to you," Maggie said.

They were quiet for a little while. "Do you remember when we were little, Freeman—when we used to play house?" she asked. "You were the daddy an' I was the mama, an' your little brothers were our children. Do you remember?"

He grunted. She was stroking his face.

"I loved that game and it broke my heart when you had to go work in the field. Oh Freeman, I missed you so much."

"Whut she talkin' 'bout?" James wondered. "Huh an' Unc' Freeman played toget'er? Ah ain't never knowed dat."

Again, they were quiet for a little while. Maggie was still holding his hand with her right hand, and she pulled it over her heart. She put her left hand on his shoulder.

"I have things I need to tell you that I've never said before," she said with determination. He nodded his head slightly.

"Freeman, I've loved you as long as I can remember. I know I wanted to marry you when I was seven. And I regret with all my bein' that things are the way they are."

James thought he should leave the room, but he was afraid if he moved that he'd interrupt their conversation. They didn't seem to know he was there.

"Ah love you, Maggie," Freeman said, his voice weak and low. "You always had mah heart."

She could feel her heart swelling as she heard the words she thought she'd never hear. "Oh Freeman, my heart fills with joy hearin' you say those words. I've waited a lifetime."

James was fighting back the tears.

"Ah loved Drusilla," Freeman said. "But Ah longed fuh you. Ah had ta come back ta da farm."

James lost his battle with the tears.

"See mah pants?" Freeman looked at them hanging from a hook on the wall.

"You want somethin' from them?" she asked.

"Front pocket," he replied.

Maggie noticed James when she got the pants, but she was so focused on what was going on with Freeman that his presence didn't even register in her mind. She put her hand in the pants pocket, and pulled out a small piece of wood shaped like half a heart. "Is this what you wanted?" she asked, giving it to Freeman.

"Dis fuh you," he said slowly, looking at her with eyes full of love. "Da udder piece at da top da lef' post in da front a da woodshed." He stopped to breathe for a minute.

"Oh my love," she moaned, and she took the half of a heart. Even though the piece was small, she could see the grain of the wood. He had put shellac on it, and it was beautiful. She looked at it for a moment, and then held it tightly in her hand and put her closed hand over her heart. "It's beautiful, Freeman."

He put his hand up in the air and Maggie thought he wanted her to take it, but he put it on her face. She put her hand over his and turned her head slightly and kissed his hand. When she felt his hand sag a little, she held it there for him, savoring the feeling of his touch—something she'd dreamed of, but thought she would never experience.

"Ah carved it out a piece a lighterd knot when Ah wuz eighteen an' Ah builded da shed. Den Ah cut it in half."

"Oh, Freeman," she murmured.

"Ah put it dere den. Ya always had mah heart, Maggie."

"Have you carried this with you all these years, Freeman?"

"No, Maggie," he replied so softly she had to strain to hear his voice. "Ah put it on da post by yo' piece when Ah married Drusilla. Den, a few years after she died, Ah got dem bof down an' fixed 'em up nice." He paused and she waited patiently. "Been carryin' mine since den."

A moment later, the door to the room opened and Pearl saw Maggie leaning over Freeman with her lips pressed lightly against his. Pearl stopped in her tracks and said nothing. She also saw James sitting by the wall watching them, with tears running down his face. Her own eyes full of tears, Pearl stepped back, gently closed the door, and put her finger to her lips. "Mis' Mac wit' 'im," she whispered to the others. She wiped her eyes, waited several seconds, and opened the door again. Maggie was just standing by the bed then, gazing at Freeman, with one hand on his face.

James saw his mother and said, "Hey, Mama," so Freeman and Maggie would know others were there. Freeman looked at Pearl, and Maggie turned and looked at her and Pearson and Ruby and Harley.

"Please come on in," Maggie said when she noticed their hesitation.

Pearl wasn't surprised by what she saw. She'd seen the love in their eyes when they looked at each other, and felt the electricity between them for years, but had never mentioned it to anyone. She sometimes wondered if they were even aware of it—it had been a part of them for so long.

The others didn't see them kissing; however, they were surprised to see Maggie with her hand on Freeman's face. But no one said a word.

"Your family's here," Maggie told Freeman, and she moved away from the bed. She knew his sister and daughter needed time with him.

James got up from his chair so that Maggie and Pearson could sit in the two available chairs. He stood beside Maggie, wishing he could do something for her.

Pearl asked him if the rest of the family had been told, and he said that he'd called Rosella, Freeman's daughter, and she was going to call everyone else. Two of his brothers and one sister had died. Two brothers and two of Freeman's children had moved to Washington, D. C. James had also called his own sister, Martha, and one of his brothers in north Florida, who said he'd tell their other brother.

Several minutes after Pearl and the others arrived, Dr. Stone went in to check on Freeman. He listened to his heart and said, "I think y'all need to let Mr. Jackson rest for a while. Ever'one's gone from the waitin' room, so you're welcome ta sit in there. I'll stay with 'im, so you won't have to worry about 'im."

As they started filing out, Freeman said, "Maggie."

"Yes, Freeman," she said, going to the bed.

"Kin ya stay, or is ya ti'ed?"

"I can stay, Freeman," she assured him. Then she lied, "I'm not tired." She felt exhausted, but she didn't care.

Dr. Stone stayed also. After a while, he said, "My nurse has gone home. If you're goin' ta stay, Miss McClellan, I'm goin' ta my office. Jus' call me if there's any problem."

Maggie sat by Freeman's bed holding his hand while he slept, still holding the piece of heart in her other hand, and occasionally looking at it. She kept hearing his voice over and over saying he loved her, wondering in amazement about the other piece of heart and knowing that she'd be looking for that when she got home. And she thought, as she had so many times, about how things might have been different in another place or time. "John Greenleaf Whittier was right," she whispered.

> For of all sad words of tongue or pen,
> The saddest are these: 'It might have been!'

She sighed. She always knew the odds were that he'd die before her, and she had dreaded this day. However, she was grateful that she was there with him, and they were finally declaring their love for each other.

After a while, emotional exhaustion made her lay her head down on the bed beside him. In no time, she was asleep. When the doctor returned, that's the way he found her. She sat up the instant she heard him and said, "Oh, I didn't mean to go to sleep. I guess I'm tired."

"It would be a miracle if you weren't," Dr. Stone said softly. "This is a hard thing ta go through." He paused. "I'm sorry to bother you, but some more of the fam'ly jus' came, an' I'm goin' ta let them come in now. Would you like ta lie down in my office for a while?"

"Thank you, Doctor, but I'd rather stay here," Maggie replied. "Freeman asked me to stay."

Pearl's daughter Martha, and other family members had gathered in the waiting room. They wanted to know what had happened, and since James was the one who found Freeman having the heart attack, he told them how he'd found him and got him to the doctor. He told them about the aspirin and water glass by Freeman's bed. He thought about telling them what he'd seen and heard that evening, but he couldn't. He felt as though he'd shared something sacred, and he couldn't talk about it.

"Mis' Mac's in dere wit' 'im," Pearl said.

Her sister Charity asked, "Who's in dere?"

"Mis' Maggie McClellan," Pearl answered.

"Ah knows who she is. Ah jes' wonted ta make sho mah ears wuz hearin' ya right," Charity said. "What da heck she doin' in dere?"

"Freeman aks huh ta stay," Pearl said.

James was pleased that his mother had told them that Maggie was in there. He didn't know that Pearl had seen them kissing, and thought she'd told them everything she knew.

Charity and Rosella were each about to ask another question when Dr. Stone appeared and told them they could go in.

As they filed in, they quietly greeted Maggie. Since Freeman was sleeping, they just looked at him and then talked softly amongst themselves. After a while, he heard them and woke up.

"Ya here, Maggie?" he whispered with his eyes still closed.

"Yes, Freeman, I'm here, but your family's here now, so I'll be back in a little while."

The family gathered around him then, and Maggie went to the bathroom. "Oh my goodness! I'm a mess," she said to her reflection in the mirror. She let her hands fill with water, drank some, and splashed some on her face. "Well, I don't *look* any better, but I *feel* a little better."

She went to the open window in the bathroom and stood for a moment feeling the cool night air. "I don't know how I'm goin' to get through this," she said. "If you're listenin', God, I sure do need your help."

When she started back to the room where Freeman lay, the doctor and James were rushing toward it. "Doctor," she called.

"He may be dying," Dr. Stone said without slowing his pace. James had gone after him and was right behind him.

When Dr. Stone entered the room, he asked everyone to step back from the bed. He spent a minute with Freeman, who had his right hand over his chest and was clearly in pain. Maggie went to stand with the family.

After a moment, Freeman looked at them, and motioned to Ruby and Rosella. And when he saw Maggie, he motioned to her, too.

When they looked at Dr. Stone, he nodded, and they went to the bed. Maggie held his hand. Ruby stood across from Maggie with her hand on his shoulder, and Rosella stood next to Ruby and held his other hand.

Freeman looked at his daughters and said, "Ah love you gals."

Both of them responded, "Ah love you, Daddy."

And Freeman said, still looking at them, "An' Ah love Maggie."

Even though she was filled with sadness, when she heard those words, her heart sang. She was overjoyed that he confessed his love for her to his daughters. "Oh my love," she said as they gazed at each other.

The doctor walked over to the rest of the family and announced softly to the others that he was dying. Maggie heard crying and moaning, but she never took her eyes off Freeman's.

She felt like she could hardly get enough air into her lungs, her knees were weak, and she was fighting back the tears, but she knew she had to be strong. She wanted to experience every precious second she had left with him.

His sister Pearl went to stand beside her, and she put one hand on Maggie's shoulder and the other one on Freeman's leg; his sister Charity stood on the other side of the bed with her hand on his other leg. Dr. Stone stood at the foot of the bed and watched Freeman. The rest of the family gathered near the doctor.

Suddenly, Freeman grimaced, his eyes shut tight, and groaned. They all looked at the doctor, who simply nodded.

Maggie and Ruby exchanged glances, with tear-filled eyes.

Freeman moaned, "Hol' me, Maggie, Ah'm dyin'."

The thought flashed in her mind, "He wants me to hold him right in front of his family," and she was thinking particularly of his sister Charity. "Oh, my darlin'," she whispered, tears streaming down her face.

And she did.

Saturday

It was almost two o'clock when James finally got to bed. Freeman had died at 11:55, just barely on his birthday. The family stayed at the doctor's office for a long time seeking comfort from each other, and talking to Freeman's body the way mourners often do, as though it's their last chance to tell the person things that are important to them. Then they stayed in the room and talked about funeral arrangements. Freeman's daughter Rosella wanted his body to lie in rest at her house, and no one objected. They decided to have his funeral on Monday morning; his children in Washington, D. C. were already making plans, so they'd arrive in plenty of time.

After the others left, James and Maggie sat silently in the waiting room for a few moments. James was about to ask her what she wanted to do, when she got up, and without a word, went back into the room where Freeman was.

Unfortunately, the undertaker arrived to get the body before Maggie had come out. Mr. Solomon Lincoln was the only Negro undertaker in the area, so everybody knew him. James stood up as he and Dr. Stone approached. Mr. Lincoln shook his hand, expressed his condolences, and then told James he needed to move the body, and asked if he thought Miss McClellan would be leaving soon.

James dreaded the thought of disturbing her and practically begged Mr. Lincoln to wait a few more minutes. He was aware that she'd waited a lifetime to tell Freeman how she felt, and he knew there must be things she needed to say to him. Mr. Lincoln agreed to wait five minutes, and James said he'd get her if she hadn't come out. He stood outside the door, and he could hear her weeping and talking and weeping. He was glad he couldn't hear what she was saying.

Maggie had a hard time pulling herself away from Freeman's side. She appeared after about ten minutes, just as the undertaker and doctor returned. James was very grateful that he hadn't had to disturb her. Dr. Stone offered her something to help her sleep, and much to James' surprise, she accepted.

She asked Mr. Lincoln when Freeman's body would be at Rosella's house, and he said it would be there right after noon. She thanked him, and after Dr. Stone gave her the sedative, they left.

As they walked out, Maggie said, "Oh, I don't feel like drivin' home."

"Ah'm gon' be drivin' ya home, Mis' Mac," James said. "Harley done drove yo' new truck that Ah brought Unc' Freeman in, so Ah could drive ya home in yo' car."

"That is so thoughtful," Maggie said with relief in her voice. "Your mama must've thought of that."

"Yes'm," James replied. "It wuz huh, awright."

"Bless her heart. Even in her time of grief, she's thinkin' about other people," she said. "Your mama's got the right name, James—she is a pearl."

Maggie got in the back seat as she was used to doing. "Thank you, James," she said, "for all you've done, and especially for stayin' with me tonight. It was comforting having you by my side."

"You welcome, Mis' Mac," he said earnestly.

On the way home, they didn't say much. Once, she said, "It was his birthday. Who knew it would also be . . . ?"

He responded, "At least, it wuz a good day fuh 'im. All us had fun at da party, wit' good food an' dancin'. Unc' Freeman danced wit' Mama an' wit' Ruby. Ya shoulda seen 'im, Mis' Mac; he still had da moves."

"I wish I could have," Maggie said. "He really seemed happy today." She sat silent for a moment before adding, "And I'll forever be grateful that we had such a wonderful afternoon. We talked, and we rode around the farm in the new truck. I'm just sorry I didn't get it sooner."

"Unc' Freeman like dat ole truck," James replied. "He say he wouldn' mine keepin' it."

When they arrived at her house, she was surprised to see a car parked in front, and the house lit up. "What in the world?" she asked.

"Oh," James said, "Mama call Miss Emmy an' aks huh ta come stay wit' ya tonight. Look like she done awready got here."

"Oh my goodness," she said. "I don't need anyone. I'll just send her home." Pearl had told Maggie about Emmy before, but Maggie had never met her. Emmy had a reputation for helping people out in times of need, having the gift of knowing just what needed to be done, and taking control of situations. She was a widow whose husband had paid for their home before he died, and she worked to cover her food and other expenses.

She stayed busy more than she needed to for her finances, working mostly for white people.

"Mis' Mac, Emmy kin cook fuh ya, an' drive ya places. You won't hafta thank 'bout nuttin'. She here ta he'p ya out; she do dis fuh udder peoples, too."

"That does sound good, James," she admitted. "I guess she can stay tonight. Tell your mama I sure appreciate all her thoughtfulness."

When the car stopped, Maggie said, "I want to see if I can find the piece of heart that Freeman told me about." She knew James overheard him. "Please get the flashlight out of the glove compartment for me."

James was curious, too. He'd been in the woodshed many times, and hadn't noticed it. "Unc' Freeman said it wuz at da top a da lef' post."

"That's right, James." Maggie shined the flashlight up, and they saw a small piece of wood sticking out over the post. "There it is!" she exclaimed.

"Oh my Lord," she said softly, barely able to talk. She could see the tall, handsome young man putting the piece of heart up there, and her knees got weak, just as they had so many times when she looked at him. She put her hand out, and James took her arm. She leaned against the woodpile.

"Ya awright, Mis' Mac?" he asked, his voice full of concern.

"No James, I'm not. I don't know if I'll ever be all right again." She paused. "I just keep thinkin' of all those years I was longin' for him, and I never knew he was longin' for me the same way. I guess it's a good thing I didn't know because it would've been even worse."

She moved close to the post and reached up, but couldn't quite touch the piece of heart. "Just imagine," she said. "All these years and I never knew it was there."

"Want me ta take it down?" James asked.

"No, James. Freeman put it there, and it will stay there as long as I live. I decided to put the piece he gave me last night over his heart." She stopped for a moment and wiped her eyes. "And when I die, I hope someone will place this piece in my casket over my heart. Would you do that for me, James?" she asked, looking up at him.

"Ah sho will, Mis' Mac," he said, unashamed of the tears running down his face. "Don' worry 'bout dat atall. Ah'm sho gon' do it."

When they went to the house, they found Emmy waiting on the porch. James was really happy she was there because he didn't know how he could have left Maggie there alone.

Emmy was in her mid-forties and she had a build and demeanor that said she could handle anything. At the moment, she was sympathetic with James and Maggie. And after expressing her condolences, she said, "Dere's some hot tea made. Ya wonts some, or some milk an' pie?" She'd obviously seen the leftovers in Maggie's refrigerator.

Maggie suddenly realized that it was past midnight, and she hadn't had anything to eat since the pie with Freeman. She didn't feel hungry, but thought maybe she should eat something. "Maybe a cup of tea and a little bit of that chicken salad," she said. There was some left from the dinner she'd made for her friend Etta.

"You want somethin' to eat, James?" she offered.

"No, ma'am. Thank ya, Mis' Mac," he said, feeling exhausted. "Ah'm gon' git me sumpin at home. Mama prob'ly be waitin' up fuh me."

"Oh, she probably will be," Maggie said. "I didn't think of that." She hugged James, thanked him for staying with her the whole evening, and went in the house with Emmy.

James walked down to the sharecropper's house and got his truck. When he got home, Shep was in the yard barking. When James stopped and got out, Shep put his tail between his legs, apparently ashamed that he'd barked at his master. James just patted him on the head, and the two of them went into the house.

He found his mother sitting at the kitchen table eating a cup of saltine crackers crumbled in milk. She always ate that when she was upset.

"Wont some?" she asked James.

He got a cup and spoon and sat down with her, but the cup sat empty for a long time while James told Pearl what he'd witnessed and heard that evening. When he finished, they were silent for a moment. Then, he concluded, "Mis' Mac an' Unc' Freeman really loved each udder."

"Ah knows it, baby," Pearl said. "Ah's too little ta notice much when dey wuz young, but one thang Ah do 'membah. Da day befo' she went ta Tallahassee, Ah seen dem talkin' behine da garage. Dey wuz lookin' real serious like. An' den, Mis' Mac hug Freeman an' he hug huh, an' it were a long hug. An' she lay huh head on his chest. Ah wuz prob'ly five or six—ole 'nough ta be s'prised. Den she turn an' run in da house."

"Ah jes' t'ought dey wuz good friends," James said.

"Dey wuz, 'cause dat's all dey could be. But dey felt lots mo'," she said, shaking her head. "Lots mo'. Ah seen dem soon as Freeman come back ta da farm when dey wuz bof fifty. Da sparks jes' flew 'tween 'em."

"It so sad, Mama," James said, his eyes full of tears. He wondered how he'd missed the sparks flying between them, and thought maybe they weren't so bright after the two got older.

"Sho is, baby. It sho is. Freeman knowed dat Ah knowed 'bout it. He tol' me she aksed him ta go in da house ta eat wit' huh afta Drusilla wuz dead, but he wouldn'. He wuz sk'ed he'd git hisse'f in big trouble. He 'on't thank she . . ." She remembered and paused, wiped away tears with the back of her hand, and continued, "*didn'* thank she knew how bad thangs coulda been if dey got caught."

"Ah couldn' hardly stand it," James told her. "Dey wuz talkin' an' dey didn' e'em know Ah wuz in dere. Jes' break my heart, da pore ole thangs." The tears ran down his face.

"Ah knows," Pearl said. "Ah seen it fuh years. Dey hearts broke fuh life when dey's young."

"Dat remin' me," he said. "Jes' yestiddy mornin', Ah found some 'nitials carved in a ole oak tree in Mis' Mac's woods. Say F. J. plus M. M. Ah t'ought it couldn' be Mis' Mac, but mebbe it were. Ah forgot ta tell huh 'bout dat."

"Ah seen dat tree, when Ah were 'bout fifteen an' Ah never tol' nobody."

"'Magine dem lovin' each udder all dis time, an' couldn' git married or . . ." He paused. "It ain't right. It jes' ain't right."

"Ah knows it, baby," Pearl agreed. "But ain't nuttin' us kin do."

"Mebbe not, Mama. But Ah hopes thangs change 'fore Ah sebenny."

James noticed the bottle on the table. "Doc Stone give ya sumpin ta take? He give Mis' Mac sumpin, too."

She nodded her head. "Good. She need it. Ah does, too, an' Ah tuk it. Ah 'on't thank Ah could sleep wit'out it. An' Ah'm goin' ta bed now."

"Mr. Lincoln say da body be at Rosella's right after noon."

"Awright," Pearl said, shaking her head in grief.

James gave his mother a comforting hug and a kiss on the cheek. Then he ate some milk and crackers. He thought about his feelings for Saleena and how miserable he'd be if he couldn't have a relationship with her. And he thought about how much he had to tell her. "Dis awready Sadday," he thought. "Ah 'on't know if Ah kin e'em see huh tonight, since Unc' Freeman done died."

When he started to bed, he got the old blanket that Shep slept on near the kitchen door, and put it on the floor next to his bed. James needed some company. He closed the shades on the two bedroom windows so the sun wouldn't wake him.

Even though he felt exhausted, he lay in bed sleepless for a long time, and he thought he should have taken one of his mother's pills. He kept seeing the image of Freeman lying in the bed with his hand on Maggie's face, and Maggie kissing his hand and holding it up, and he knew that would be in his mind forever. He thought about how he could just touch Saleena's face, and his uncle Freeman didn't touch the face of the woman he loved until he was seventy years old, and only then because he was on his deathbed. "Color keep peoples apart," he thought, "but it 'on't keep 'em from lovin' each udder."

Eventually, James let his arm hang off the bed with his hand resting on Shep's back. With that connection, and the sound of Shep's even breathing, he finally fell asleep.

♥ ♥ ♥

SHEP HELPED HIM GET TO SLEEP, and Shep woke him up in the morning. James was pleased to see that he'd slept until eight-thirty.

He heard his parents stirring. "Dat whut woke ya up, huh Shep? Ya hears 'em, too."

James put Shep out and went back to his room and pulled on a pair of pants over the underwear he'd slept in. He left his undershirt on, went barefoot into the kitchen, and put some coffee on the stove so Pearl wouldn't have to. He was taking the bacon and eggs out of the refrigerator when she entered the kitchen.

"Mornin', baby," she said. "Ya sleep awright?"

"Tuk me a while ta git ta sleep." James kissed her on the cheek. "Ya sleep awright?"

"Dat pill done he'ped me."

"Ah'm makin' da breakfast fuh ya dis mornin'," James announced.

"Thank ya, baby," Pearl said as she sat down. "Ah sho 'preciate dat."

"Whut us gon' do today?" he asked.

"Us goin' ta Rosella's late dis mornin'."

"Guess Mis' Mac goin' ta Rosella's."

"Sho, she goin'. She spen' all da time she kin wit' 'im."

And when they arrived, Maggie and Emmy were already there, still sitting in Emmy's car. Emmy had prepared a nice breakfast for her, which she said Maggie barely touched. Actually, Emmy knew Freeman and his family, so would've been there even without Maggie.

Rosella and Brook had one of the few houses in the Negro section that was made of cement blocks instead of wood. It was painted a pale yellow with white trim. The lawn was green and healthy, and some red and white hibiscus were blooming by the house. There was an oak tree that looked about ten years old on one side of the yard.

Maggie noticed how attractive the house and yard looked when she got out of the car. She and Pearl hugged and cried together. Maggie told her how sorry she was for her loss, and then added, "Pearl, that was so thoughtful and kind of you to get Emmy for me. I never would've thought of it, and it was comforting to me to know that she was there."

"Ah knowed ya needed somebody," Pearl said.

"I didn't know it," Maggie acknowledged. "But she has been such a big help. In fact, I've asked her to stay for a few more days."

"Dat's good," Pearl said. "Oh Mis' Mac, us so grateful to ya fuh gittin' dat dere job fuh James."

"It was my pleasure, Pearl," Maggie replied. "I know he'll be a good worker and the company will be fortunate to have him."

Maggie shook Pearson's hand and hugged James. Pearl, Pearson, and Emmy went into the house, so Maggie had a moment alone with James.

"I asked Harley yesterday if he knew of a sharecropper for me and he said he'd like the job," she said.

"Dat's great!" James exclaimed. "Dat be good fuh you an' him."

"I'm happy about it, especially now that . . ." She couldn't say the words. "However, I don't know when he'll be able to start because he has to give Tom Hiers notice and see what he needs. In the meantime, I'd really like to have someone in the sharecropper's house. I don't like the idea of bein' out there all by myself, and even though it's a good distance from my house, it's comforting to know someone's there. So, I was wonderin' if you'd live there until Harley and Ruby can move in."

"Ah sho kin do dat," he agreed, nodding his head. Then he remembered Freeman asking him to "see ta huh," and his eyes moistened. He had two thoughts right together. The first one was that, by moving into the house, he was kind of looking after her. The second one was that Freeman knew he was going to die. James felt a chill run down his spine.

They were just about to go into the house when Ruby and Harley arrived. Ruby's eyes were swollen, and Maggie felt an instant empathy for her—she knew that Ruby and Freeman had a special bond. She hugged her and Harley warmly and tried to comfort her a little: "Your daddy really loved you, Ruby. You were there with him after your mama died—just the two of you."

"Yes'm, Mis' Mac," Ruby said. "Dat ain't nuttin' but da truf."

"He was so happy that you stayed close by after you and Harley married. I know you're goin' to miss him, and I'm glad you have some wonderful memories."

"Ah sho do, Mis' Mac. Thank da Lawd."

Maggie took a clean white handkerchief—with an embroidered pink rose in one corner, and light blue crocheted trim around the edges—from her pocketbook, one of six that Emmy had put in. She wiped Ruby's tears, and put the handkerchief in her hand.

"Who's keepin' Rubin?" she asked.

"My sistah got 'im," Harley said. "He use' ta huh."

"Oh, that's good," Maggie replied.

"Mis' Mac," Harley said. "Ah seen Mr. Hiers dis mornin' an' Ah tol' 'im 'bout da sharecroppin', an' he say since Freeman gon', Ah oughta jes' g'wan ovah dere. Say he 'on't need me none now, an' you prob'ly do. So us awready plannin' ta move nex' week, if dat's awright."

Freeman's death made it easier for Harley to tell Mr. Hiers. If Mr. Hiers knew that Maggie had asked Harley to take the job before Freeman died, he might have responded differently.

"Oh Harley, that's wonderful!" she exclaimed. "I'm so glad to hear that." She looked at James, "Did you hear that, James?"

"Ah sho did. Ain't dat good."

"It's wonderful," she said, looking at Harley and Ruby. "That just puts my mind at ease. I'm so glad you and Ruby will be livin' there and workin' with me. And I'm lookin' forward to getting to know Rubin better and watchin' him grow. It will be nice to have a child around again." She smiled. "Maybe *children*. There haven't been any there since you, Ruby."

Pearl and Pearson had greeted Rosella and her husband, Brook, when they went into the house, and they were talking to Pearl's cousin Jacob, who had a shoeshine stand on North Florida Avenue. For years, his stand had been in a barbershop, but when the barber retired and sold the shop, the new owner didn't want him there. Jacob went three blocks down the street and asked the owner of Hatchett's garage if he could set up beside his shop. He told him he could, and if Jacob would bring him some new customers, he'd build a lean-to for him to provide shade and protection from the rain. Of course, Jacob told all his old customers where he'd be and most of them went there for shines, and some of them started using the garage. So he got his lean-to. During his twelve years there, he'd developed a friendship with Mr. J. B. Hatchett, his wife, Sophie, and sixteen-year-old daughter, Carla, and occasionally went fishing with them.

"Been fishin' lately?" Brook asked him.

"Couple weeks ago," Jacob replied. "Caught five a da bigges' speckle perch ya ever laid yo' eyes on, an' dey caught nine a 'em."

"Who all went wit' ya dis time?" Brook asked. He was curious about Jacob's relationship with the white family and always asked him questions.

"Miz Hatchett didn' go—jes' Mr. J. B. an' Mis' Carla. Dat gal sho do like ta fish. She da one always aksin' ta go."

"Ah b'lieve you like ta fish, too," Brook declared. "Ah tell ya, Jacob, one day ya gon' look at dat gal a lil too long an' dat man gone leave yo' behind out dere in da woods, all by yo'se'f."

"Dey ain't like dat, Brook. Ah done tol' ya dat dey fine white folks. Ya ought not speak bad 'bout dem."

When Maggie and the others went in the house, Jacob greeted them and started talking to Ruby. "What wuz wrong wit' yo' daddy? Ah didn' e'em know he wuz sick. Jes' saw 'im 'bout two months ago."

Ruby was telling him about how sudden Freeman's heart problem seemed to come on, when they heard the hearse arrive. Everyone stopped talking. Mr. Lincoln asked the women to go into another room, and the men to help him. The women went into the kitchen and closed the door. Mr. Lincoln only had one man with him, so Pearson, James, Harley, Brook, and Jacob helped them carry the casket into the house. Mr. Lincoln asked the men to give him a moment, and they joined the ladies in the kitchen.

"Y'all done got a TV," James said to Brook, noticing one that was sitting on a table in the corner.

"Yeah, but da antenna ain't hooked up in here," Brook said. "We moved it out da livin' room ta make room fuh da casket."

"When Ah starts workin', Ah'm gon' git us a TV," James announced.

"Oh my goodness," Pearl said. "Boy, you gon' be sumpin den."

"Sho is," Pearson agreed. "He gon' be smilin' from ear ta ear. Ain't gon' be able ta tell dat boy nuttin'." They all laughed.

James laughed, too, but he had the look of someone who was the butt of the joke. "Mis' Mac, ya oughta git you one," he said. "It keep ya comp'ny."

"I guess I should," she replied, thinking more about what was going on in the other room.

Mr. Lincoln announced that everything was ready. The women went in first, and when they saw the open casket, all of them started crying.

About the time they settled down, Freeman's sister Charity arrived with her daughter Pearl and granddaughter Kizzie. Then the grieving started all over again. James observed how contagious it was. Every time someone started crying, he felt like crying, too, and the women did cry.

James and Kizzie felt a little awkward together because they hadn't seen each other for three years, since her family moved to Gainesville. After a little while, he asked her if she'd like to go outside.

They found a grassy spot under a tree and sat down in the shade. James noticed that Kizzie's pigtails didn't stick out anymore, but were larger and braided close to her head. He also noticed that she was an attractive girl.

"Dis so hard fuh Mama an' Grandma," Kizzie said.

"Yeah," he said, "dis hard for mah mama, too."

"Ah's s'prised ta see Mis' Mac," Kizzie said.

"Well," James paused. He didn't know how much he should tell Kizzie. "Ever'body prob'ly gon' fine out Unc' Freeman an' Mis' Mac loved each udder from when dey's little, an' never done nuttin' 'bout it. Dey didn' e'em say it till las' night."

"Fuh real?" she asked in disbelief.

"Fuh real. Ah wuz cryin' jes' lis'nin' ta 'em talk."

"Dat so sad," Kizzie said, and James saw tears in her eyes.

They were silent for a few moments.

"Kizzie," James said, "you 'membah dat day when us wuz on da tracks, and dem white boys th'owed rocks at us?"

"Sho, Ah 'membah."

"Ah's thankin' 'bout it jes' da udder day."

"Whut you's thankin'?" she asked.

"Thankin' Ah never tol' ya Ah'm sorry fuh leavin' ya behine. Ah got hit in da head wit' a rock, an' Ah tuk off, but Ah didn' know dey's gon' th'ow rocks at you, at a lil gal. Ah'm so sorry Ah lef' ya, Kizzie."

"Dat's awright, James. Ah 'on't blame ya fuh protectin' yo'se'f."

"Ah shouldn' a lef' ya," he said, "an' Ah still feels bad 'bout it."

She put her hand on James' arm. "Dat 'on't matter no mo'. Never did matter ta me—you didn' th'ow rocks at me."

"Ah didn' he'p ya none, eit'er."

"Ya did he'p me. Till Ah fell down, ya he'ped me run faster. James, us wuz bof sc'ed ta def." Her hand moved to his shoulder. "Forgit 'bout dat day, James. Ya didn' do nuttin' wrong."

"Thank ya, Kizzie," James said, a solemn expression on his face. He took a deep breath and sighed, finally feeling relief.

They both sat silently for a while. When the sound of grieving began spilling from the house, James tried to block it out. He heard some crows cawing way off in the distance, and tried to focus on them.

"Ya got a gal, James?" Kizzie asked.

"Ah got a gal Ah likes. Ah b'lieve she like me. How 'bout you?"

"Ah likes dis boy, but he like some udder gal," she said, looking down at her lap.

James watched two pigeons light on the lawn a few feet in front of them. He moved his foot and they flew to the other side of the lawn.

"Kizzie, ya nice an' ya purty," he said. "Gon' be lots a boys likin' ya."

She giggled. "Thank ya, James."

Freeman's son Junior arrived a little later, and James and Kizzie hugged him and went inside with him. James had seen Junior often a few years earlier. After he came home from the war in 1945, he lived with Freeman and the family for a while.

Maggie was sitting by the casket alone, talking to Freeman, and she didn't hear them enter. Junior didn't go near the casket, but he stopped and looked at his father for a moment, careful not to disturb Maggie.

The family was in the kitchen eating some of the food friends and neighbors had brought over. Everybody greeted Junior.

"Ya'll wont sumpin ta eat?" Pearl asked.

"Dat chocolate cake look good," James said.

"Mis' Mac doin' awright, James?" Ruby asked.

"She talkin' ta Unc' Freeman," he replied.

"Pore thang," Ruby said.

James guessed that Pearl had told all the adults about Mis' Mac and Freeman, because no one asked any questions, or seemed surprised at her being there. Rosella had called Junior the night before and told him what she'd learned, and he'd been thinking about it. He hadn't gone to Dr. Stone's office because he hadn't been at home when Rosella called to tell him about Freeman's condition, and he was upset that he wasn't at his father's side when he died.

After he fixed a plate and sat down at the table, he asked, "If Daddy loved Mis' Mac, whut dat say 'bout Mama?"

"He loved Mama, too, an' ya know fuh sho he wuz good to huh," Rosella said. "But he couldn' he'p lovin' Mis' Mac. He loved huh fust, from when dey wuz lil toget'er. Least he didn' do nuttin' stupid, which is mo' dan ya kin say 'bout some people."

Junior, who was recently divorced, didn't respond to the veiled accusation. He knew he'd done some stupid things, like running around on his wife, and not spending enough time with his children, and his heart ached often because of his mistakes.

He'd had problems ever since the war. He thought it was his duty and an honor to fight in World War II to defend his country. Although he was never injured, his Negro unit was full of courageous men who were wounded, and many who died serving their country. When he returned, he'd expected things to be different than they were before the war. However, when his unit was discharged from a base in South Carolina and he went to the Greyhound bus station for a ticket home, he found the same "Colored" waiting room, and hateful and condescending attitudes. His uniform made little or no difference.

The white man behind the ticket counter looked at his uniform with disgust in his eyes. "Where you goin', boy?" he growled.

"Lakeland, Florida, sir," Junior answered respectfully, like a soldier.

On the bus, Junior walked past the rows of white people and sat on the last seat. When he got off at the bus station in Lakeland, he saw a taxi waiting on the street, walked over expectantly, and told the driver his sister's address. The man looked at him with some sympathy, possibly for the uniform, and said, "Sorry, we don't drive coloreds. I cain't take you nowhere." So he walked in the heat, hauling his duffle bag, the mile and a half to Rosella's house.

But what made Junior even angrier than what happened to him was what happened to his best friend Charlie. Charlie joined the Army Air Corp and became a Tuskegee Airman. He was put in the 332nd Fighter Group and sent to Italy, where he flew many dangerous missions protecting the big, slow-moving American bombers from the Nazi planes. The Tuskegee Airmen painted the tails of their planes red, and were called "Red Tail Angels." They became known for their skill and courage as pilots, and many white pilots, who didn't want them at first, would later request them. Charlie returned home knowing he had served his country well.

The first week he was home, he and Junior were together in a town in north Florida one day. In Italy, Charlie had dated some Italian women, and as he and Junior walked past a store, Charlie smiled at an attractive young white woman, and grunted softly in appreciation. A white man inside the store saw him, yelled something, and he and three others ran out of the store. The four of them hustled him into an alley kicking and beating him. Junior knew he couldn't help him, and if he intervened, he'd receive the same treatment, so he went quickly around the block and cautiously approached the alley from the other side. By the time he got there, the men were gone, and Charlie was unconscious. Junior managed to get him to a doctor, but he died a few hours later without regaining consciousness.

Junior never got over that or the transition from the battlefield, where the white foreigners greeted the Negro soldiers with open arms and gratitude in their eyes, to his country, where he was often greeted with contempt and hatred in white Americans' eyes. He felt like his "brothers" had died in vain, and he knew Charlie would not have flirted with a white woman if he hadn't been away for two years and forgot. Junior often thought about moving to Europe, but he didn't want to leave his father.

He sat quietly at the table with his head slightly bowed. He had a defeated look on his face.

Pearl looked at him and could see that he was in pain. She went behind him and put her hands on his shoulders. "Dey was kids toget'er, an' dey cain't he'p hi dey feel," she said softly. "One thang ya know fuh sho—yo' daddy loved ya an' wuz proud a ya, an' Ah is, too."

Junior's eyes moistened, and he put his head down. He didn't say anything about it after that. Rosella figured he must have been satisfied, or felt—as she did—that he had no right to judge Freeman.

"Does ya thank they done anythang?" Brook asked.

Pearl answered that question with no hesitation. "No, dey didn'! Dey jes' tol' each udder hi dey feels yestiddy evenin'."

After a moment, Pearl said, "Thank Ah check on Mis' Mac," and she went into the other room. She was about to speak to Maggie when she heard her talking and she stopped near the door.

" . . . my sharecropper, and he and Ruby will live in your house. I talked to them about it just yesterday afternoon—they were plannin' to live with you, an' I would've kept payin' you, but Harley was goin' to take over the hard work. I knew you'd be glad about that. Now little Rubin will grow up where his grandfather and his mother did."

Pearl didn't know that, and she was pleased. She'd wondered what Maggie would do about replacing Freeman.

"An', remember I told you I was thinkin' about what to do with the farm if you went before me. You know you're the one in my will. Well, I'm thinkin' I'll probably leave it to James and Ruby. They can divide it, or do whatever they want to with it. James is so good to me, and now Harley and Ruby are goin' to be livin' there. You know I've always loved Ruby an' James—they've both grown up around me—an' it seems like the right thing to do."

Pearl stopped in her tracks. "Whut she say?" she thought. "She was gon' leave da farm ta Freeman. Now, she prob'ly gon' leave it ta James an' Ruby? Oh mah goodness! Oh Lawd have mercy on mah baby! Oh Lawd bless Mis' Mac. Lawd have mercy!" Her knees felt weak and she needed to sit down, but she didn't want to make any noise, so she just leaned against the wall.

"My five cousins are the closest relatives I have left, an' they don't really know me," Maggie went on. "Anyway, they'd probably fight over it if I left it to them. An' they wouldn't want anything to do with me if they knew how I've always felt about you, so I don't want any of them to have the place that I love, an' that you loved. James an' Ruby are the only logical people, an' I feel good about them havin' it. They'll love it, too, an' take care of it." Maggie bent down and picked up her pocketbook.

"She leavin' James and Ruby da farm," Pearl repeated to herself. "Lawd have mercy. Ah cain't b'lieve dis." She didn't want Maggie to know she'd overheard that, so she quietly went back into the kitchen. She would like to have been alone to absorb that news, but the kitchen was full of people.

Pearl left just before Maggie took the wooden piece of heart from her pocketbook and slipped it under his hand, over his heart, "I'm givin' you my heart, Freeman. I saw the piece you left for me, and I'll have that to look at, an' feel your love, any time I want to. An' when I die, James will place it on my heart. I want this piece to stay with you. You always had my heart, Freeman. Always, my love."

In the kitchen, Pearl felt happy about what she'd overheard, and then she felt nervous about it, first happy, then nervous. She knew she shouldn't know that. She decided she'd try to forget it, but even as she thought about forgetting it, she asked herself, "How kin Ah ever forgit dat?"

"One thang fuh sho," she thought, "Ah ain't tellin' nobody. Ah ain't 'pose' ta know it, an' Ah ain't tellin' nary a soul, jes' like Ah didn' tell a single soul, not e'em Pearson, 'bout da two a dem."

Then she thought, "Mebbe Mis' Mac gon' tell me if Ah goes over ta sew fuh huh. Mebbe us talk 'bout it. Ah oughta go over dere, anyhow. She gon' need some comp'ny now."

She made up her mind about another thing, too. She would be sure that James was good to Mis' Mac. Freeman had requested that James look after her, and Pearl would make sure that he didn't get too busy and forget about her. And she would do her best to make sure that he stayed in the area, and didn't put roots down somewhere else like her two older sons had.

"Mis' Mac doin' awright?" Ruby asked.

"Yeah, she busy jes' talkin' ta yo' daddy," Pearl replied.

"Oh my lawdy, it so sad," Ruby said. "Sad 'nough Daddy done died, but ta fine out him an' Mis' Mac . . ."

Ruby had always loved Maggie, and she got very close to her after her mother died. She was at Maggie's every day, doing her homework, watching Maggie doing housework, cooking, and gardening, and helping her. Of course, Maggie paid her, and Ruby liked that, too. Freeman noticed how much time she was spending there and told her not to bother Maggie, but when Ruby didn't go over for two days, Maggie asked him why. When he told her, she let him know, in no uncertain terms, that Ruby was welcome there any time, and if she needed some time to herself, she knew how to send her home. Maggie enjoyed her company, and she secretly hoped the smart and serene young girl would be a teacher. And although she was disappointed when Ruby got married, she heartily approved of Harley. And she looked forward to having Ruby next door again.

♥   ♥   ♥

JAMES HAD EATEN SOME CHOCOLATE CAKE, and was working on some chicken and dumplings when Maggie entered the kitchen. Everyone was sitting around the table except him and Kizzie, who were leaning against the kitchen counter. Some were eating and some were just sitting. The food was on the stove and counter, except for the chocolate cake and pecan pie, which were on the table, and each was missing several pieces.

Everyone got quiet, and the men stood up. James put his plate down and went over to her. "Kin Ah git ya sumpin ta eat, Mis' Mac?" he asked solicitously.

She put her hand on his arm. "What were you eating, James?"

"Some chicken an' dumplin's. Dey make ya lick ya fingers, dey so good."

"Well, they do sound good," she said, smiling. "I'll have a small servin', please."

"An' ya jes' got ta have some ice tea an' a biscuit ta top it off," he said.

She smiled again. "Thank you, James."

Pearl stood up and she and Maggie had a long hug. "Ah know dis is a tryin' time fuh you," Pearl said.

"It sure is. An' I know it's hard for you," Maggie responded. "We all loved him an' we're all goin' to miss him."

Maggie noticed that Junior was there. "Well, hello, Junior. I didn't see you come in. Are you doin' all right?"

"Yes'm," he replied. "Good as 'spected, Ah reckon."

"You know, your father talked about you so much, especially during the war. He worried about you, and was so proud of you. Of course, he was relieved when you came home." Maggie felt sorry for Junior. Freeman had talked to her often about him, and she knew he'd had a rough time since the war. And she knew how close he was to his father.

He was clearly hurting, and she felt like putting her arms around him, but his demeanor was not welcoming. She made a mental note to send him a letter and a check; she'd say that she owed Freeman a week's pay and she knew his father would want him to have it.

"Come sit down, Mis' Mac," Harley said, offering her his chair.

"Thank you, Harley. I wouldn't take your seat, but I'm awf'ly tired," she said as she sat down. "Did you tell them that you're goin' to be workin' with me? I just asked him yesterday before Freeman . . ." Just mentioning his name sent her into a little crying spell. Ruby, who had tears streaming down her face, put her arm around Maggie's shoulder.

"Of course," Maggie continued, when she could speak, "they were goin' to share the house with him."

"Daddy 'preciated dat ya kept 'im on," Rosella said. "He knowed he wadn' able ta work much no mo', an' he hated dat. He said you wuz a special lady."

"Your daddy was a special man, and I would've kept him on until he was a hundred years old. He was a wonderful friend to me." She remembered the words they'd exchanged the day before, each saying that the other was their best friend. She felt so grateful for that.

"Dat whut he said 'bout you, dat you wuz a won'erful frien'," Rosella said. "An' he said you wuz da bes' boss anybody could ever have."

Maggie smiled and reflexively placed her hand over her heart. "Thank you for tellin' me that, Rosella. That means so much to me. I never thought of myself as his boss, just his friend."

After she finished the chicken and dumplings, which were as good as James said they were, she said, "I'd like to come back tomorrow if that's all right. Is there a time that would be better for you all?"

"Mis' Mac," Rosella said, "ya welcome ta come whenever's best fuh you. It 'on't matter atall."

"Thank you," Maggie said. "That's very kind. An' thank you for your hospitality." She looked at Emmy. "Are you about ready to go, Emmy?"

"Any time you is, Mis' Mac."

"You need ta take some a dis here food home fuh you an' Emmy," Pearl said, getting up.

"Thank you, but that's not necessary," Maggie said, "unless Emmy wants some."

Pearl and Rosella fixed them plenty of food for supper and some for the next day. Emmy took it out to the car.

James walked out with Maggie. "James, I was goin' to thank Pearl again for getting Emmy for me," she said. "Please tell her she's just a lifesaver. She got the eggs for me this mornin' an' fed the chickens an' Tommiecat. I wasn't even thinkin' about the poor animals."

"Ah will, Mis' Mac. An' Ah'll be over Tuesday an' Ah'll work da rest a da week. Whutever ya needs me ta do, stuff like Unc' Freeman did fuh ya."

"All right, but I'm not really worried about any of that now."

"Ah knows it. But Ah'm gon' be dere fuh ya, anyhow. Harley say dey prob'ly gon' move Friday or Sadday, an' Ah be he'pin' dem."

"Thank you, James. I appreciate your concern and your help. You're a good friend, a special friend."

"Ya welcome, Mis' Mac," he said. "Ya wonts me ta stay in da sharecropper house till dey moves?"

"I don't think so. I thought it would be a lot longer before they'd move in, an' Emmy will be with me for a few more days."

"Awright den."

"I'll probably see you here tomorrow."

"Yes'm, Mis' Mac. Ah spec' so."

♥ ♥ ♥

JAMES WANTED TO BE OUTSIDE FOR A WHILE, so he walked the two blocks to the main street. He saw a barbershop and remembered he had intended to get a haircut, so he went in.

He'd smelled the straightening solution from the outside, and inside, it almost took his breath away. A young man was sitting in a chair squirming, the lye seeping into his scalp. His whole body seemed to be moving. "How long Ah has ta sit here?" he asked.

The barber grinned and pointed at James. "Ya be dere till Ah gits dis boy's hair cut."

"Oh Lawd," the young man moaned. "Cut fas', man, cut fas'."

"Ya wont yo's straighten'?" the barber asked, grinning. "Ah kin have ya lookin' like Nat King Cole."

James laughed. "Nawsuh. Ah gits mine done, Ah'll have two fires, fust da lye, den mah mama. She kill me."

The barber laughed, but the young man with the lye on his head didn't. Every now and then, James would hear him moaning. James was also wishing the barber would cut his hair fast and give that poor man some relief. When James finally stood up, the man's face looked like pure misery: there were tears running down his cheeks, and he was writhing in the chair. After seeing that, James knew he'd never get his hair straightened.

On his way back to the house, he walked slowly, studying the houses he passed. He noticed that some houses were nicely painted and neat, and others were unkempt; some had trees and bushes and flowers in their yards, and some didn't. "People diff'unt," he thought. Then he remembered when he first began to notice the houses of white people. He'd been surprised. He'd assumed that all white people lived in nicely painted houses with nice yards, like Mis' Mac's place, but he saw that there were the same differences in their places. "An' people da same."

When he got back, he found the family gathered in the living room. A few more relatives had come, and the women were huddled around the casket weeping. "Ah cain't take dis," James thought. He'd been wondering all day if he'd go to the dime store to buy the necklace for Saleena. Since that would get him out of the house, he decided to go. He was still planning to see her that night, provided her family didn't go to Rosella's after he left. He hoped they planned to go on Sunday.

James motioned to Harley and the two of them stepped outside. "Ya still plannin' on goin' downtown today?"

"Ah's thankin' 'bout it. Mr. Hiers aks me ta git some stuff at da feed sto' since Ah wuz gon' be in town."

"Ah got ta git outta here," James said. "Ah'm goin' ta da dime sto'."

"Well, le's go den," Harley agreed. "Ah'll tell Ruby."

James felt more alive when he knew he was going to the store to buy a necklace for Saleena. "Ah sho hopes dat one Ah likes still dere."

Pearl watched them go outside, and when Harley went back in the house, she went out. "Whut y'all doin'?" she asked James.

"Goin' downtown," he replied.

"Well, be sho you 'membah where you at down dere, son. You know whut happen ta dat pore ole Willie Edwards in Alabama, and Junior's frien' Charlie. E'em bein' a hero didn' he'p him."

"Ah 'membah, Mama, an' Ah knows how ta ack. Don' worry none."

She looked at him. "You looks like ya ready ta take on da worl' now. Jes' be careful, an' always 'membah where you at," she said again. She knew James was responsible, but he didn't go to town often and she was concerned that he might forget. And the weight of Freeman's death made her feel more protective of him.

"Yes'm," he said, and gave her a reassuring hug.

On the way downtown, Harley told James that he had to go to Selph's service station to get some gas after he went to the feed store. They had a discussion about who might be through first, and Harley said he'd wait for James if he got there first.

James said, "Ah could ride da bus back, if we could e'em ride da bus. In Montgomery, mus' be da city owns dem buses 'cause dey lets coloreds ride 'em—course, dey hasta sit in da back, so dey 'on't touch no whites."

"Mebbe dey sc'ed dey gon' turn black," Harley said, and they laughed.

James slapped his leg. "Dat be good, wouldn' it? Let dem walk in colored skin fuh a lil while."

Harley dropped him off on the corner by the park. James took his time walking past the park, looking at the fountain, the white people sitting on the benches and the white children running around playing. One little boy tried to climb into the fountain, but his mother caught him. "Dat water look good ta me, too, lil boy," he thought.

He saw some sparrows on the ground where no grass was growing and he stopped and watched them for a minute; some were scratching in the sand, and some were taking a dust bath. One flew up and landed on the statue of the Confederate soldier. "Dat man still standin' dere," he thought facetiously. "Guess he gone be standin' dere fuh a long time."

A few squirrels were gathered around an old white man, who was sitting on a bench, a cane propped against it, giving them popcorn. James watched as he emptied the bag, and said, "That's all for today, little buddies."

He watched a squirrel chase another squirrel up a tree, around the tree, out on a limb, and onto another tree. He noticed the flowers, but thought his mother's were just as pretty. He saw a blue jay sitting in a tree and noticed the cloudless, bright blue sky like a giant umbrella overhead. "Unc' Freeman done dead, but life goin' on, anyhow," he thought, feeling serene. "An' still purty." He heard the blue jay screech just as he left the park.

♥ ♥ ♥

As James entered the store, he felt a moment of dread, "Ah hopes dat same white woman ain't gon' be here today." And when he saw her at the jewelry counter, some of his enthusiasm slipped away. He'd have to deal with her attitude and the way she looked at him, again.

He went to the counter, and as before, stood a few feet away. When he saw the necklace, his spirits lifted and he could hardly keep from smiling, but he knew people would stare at him suspiciously if he just stood there smiling. He put his hand over his mouth. He was anxious to buy it, but the clerk was busily waiting on an elderly white woman. James waited until the woman left, and he was just about to go to the counter when the clerk glanced at him, and left. "Lawd have mercy on me! Lawd Jesus, gimme strength! She ack like she ain't e'em see me."

He looked at the other clerks, whose counters were close by, to see if one of them would help him, but they were busy. He decided to get a drink of water, but the clerk was at the white fountain, so he stood across the store trying to be invisible. He watched her go to the stairs before he went to get a drink. "Dis fountain still dirty," he thought, looking at the fountain under the "Colored" sign. "It wuz done dirty Tuesd'y." He looked at the one under the "White" sign and saw that it was clean. "Guess da water's clean, anyhow," he thought, taking a drink.

James walked around the store looking at different things, trying to look inconspicuous. "Ah be glad ta git mahse'f home," he thought. He noticed that there was a Negro woman with a little girl in the section where the kitchen stuff was, and he felt relieved that he wasn't the only Negro in the store. When he passed the counter with the thread, he remembered his mother mentioning that she was almost out of white thread, and he decided to buy some for her, even though he dreaded having to deal with another clerk. However, the young white woman greeted him with a smile.

James smiled shyly, looking at the counter.

"Can I help you with somethin'?" she asked.

He noticed her warm blue eyes and bright smile, and felt his heart skip a beat. "Some white thread, please."

He breathed a sigh of relief and looked away, afraid he'd stare at her. He glanced around the store to see if the jewelry clerk had returned.

"Must be for your wife," the clerk said.

"Oh, no, ma'am," James replied. "It fuh mah mama. Ah ain't got married."

"Oh," she said. "Well, it's nice of you to buy it for your mama."

"Thank ya, ma'am," he said, handing her a coin for the thread.

"I'll just put this in a little sack for you." When she handed him the little bag and his change, she said, "Thank you."

James said, "Thank ya, ma'am," and felt a little foolish for saying it after she said it to him, but he was struck by her looks and grateful that she'd been nice to him, and it just came out.

"She a nice white woman," he thought. "An' she purty, too. Wish huh da one sol' da jew'ry."

He returned to the back of the store to wait for the jewelry clerk, just looking around the store while he waited. He was debating going back and asking the clerk if she could help him with the jewelry, when a white woman went to her counter.

James noticed a little white girl going to the colored fountain. He watched in awe. "Lawd have mercy! She drinkin' from dat dirty ole fountain," he thought. "Mus' not a seen da sign up dere. Po' lil thang." From thirty feet away, he could tell that her dress was made out of feedsack cloth. "Us had a feedsack jes' like dat wit' cow feed. Ah ain't never seen no white gal wear feedsack—jes' coloreds. She a farm gal."

The jewelry clerk came back downstairs and said something to the little girl, who stopped drinking, looked at the clerk, looked up at the sign, and then said something to the clerk. James realized that he was sweating. "She gon' git in trouble fuh drinkin' from dat colored fountain?" he wondered.

He turned his head a little so he wouldn't get caught looking, and stepped closer to a counter so it seemed that he was interested in something, but he kept his eyes on them. The clerk looked in his direction and he quickly diverted his eyes. "Good thang Ah done turned mah head," he thought. When the clerk left, his eyes went back to the little girl and shifted away again when he saw her looking to see if anyone was watching her.

It was hot in the store, as well as outside, and after she left, James went to the fountain for another drink. After he drank, he noticed that a couple of drops of water had splattered on his blue shirt. He wore the same grey slacks that he'd worn on Tuesday, but he had on a light blue shirt, his favorite. His mother had pressed it nicely, and he knew it looked good. Now it had two water spots on it—he hoped no one would think it was dirty.

He saw the little white girl at the toy counter, and he noticed the sprinkling of freckles on her nose and cheeks. "She cute," he thought. He remembered the other little white girl he'd seen there on Tuesday. "Dem two gals is diffunt. Dis po' lil ole gal got a po' fam'ly." He watched her walk away from the toys and he noticed that she was walking funny. Then he saw that one sandal strap was broken. "Ah, dat's too bad." he thought.

He was surprised when she went to the jewelry counter. "She got some money?" There weren't any customers at the counter, so the clerk was just standing there, and James saw her wipe her eyes.

"Whut in da worl'?" he wondered. "Look like dat crazy thang cryin'. Why she cryin'?"

The clerk just waited while the little girl looked at the jewelry. After a couple of minutes, James went to the usual spot a few feet behind her.

"Can I he'p ya wi' sumpin, honey?" the clerk asked as she went over to the girl.

"I wanna buy that ruby ring, please," she said softly. James noticed that she pointed at the rings.

"She got 'nough money ta buy a ring?" he wondered.

"Sure," the clerk said.

James looked at her eyes, which were a little red. "She *wuz* cryin'," he thought. "Ah knowed she wuz cryin', right here in da sto'. Wonder if somebody in huh fam'ly died, too."

She put the rings on the counter.

After a moment, the girl said, "I wont that one. The ruby one."

"She wont da ruby one. Ain't dat cute," he thought.

The clerk took the ring out for her. "Try it on."

The girl put it on her finger. "It fits," she said happily. "I'll take it." And she put a quarter, a nickel, and five pennies on the counter.

"She happy now," James thought. "She gon' git a ring an' she happy. Ah gon' be happy, too, when Ah gits my girl dat dere necklace."

The clerk said, "It's adjustable," and silently counted the money. She looked at the girl and said, "You owe another penny. It's thirty-six cents."

"Did you say 'thirty-six'?" the girl asked.

"Yes, honey. It's thirty-six cents," the clerk replied. "You need another penny."

"You tol' me thirty-five cents the other day," the girl said.

"Well, there's a penny tax," the clerk said.

"Oh," the little girl said softly, sounding deflated. "I only got thirty-five cents." Then she just stood there looking at the clerk.

"She jes' need one mo' penny," James thought. "One mo' penny. Dat dere woman gon' give huh a penny."

"I'm sorry," the clerk said.

"She 'on't sound sorry atall," he thought. "She sound like she thu wit' huh an' jes' wont huh ta go away." He was looking at the clerk, who looked at him. He looked down.

They all just stood there. "Dat crazy woman ain't gon' give huh a penny?" James wondered. "Good Lawd! Jes' a penny!"

He felt in his pocket for his change. He spread it out on his hand and was pleased to see that he had a penny. He put the rest of the change back in his pocket.

James looked at the clerk, who was looking around the store. Then she looked back at the little girl. "She ain't gon' e'em he'p huh," he thought. "Ah cain't b'lieve dat ole white woman ain't gon' he'p dat po' chile."

He stepped forward. "Ah got a penny," he said, holding out his hand.

The little girl turned and looked up at him. "Oh, thank you," she said, clearly relieved and grateful, as he placed the penny on the counter.

James noticed that she had tears in her eyes. "She wuz 'bout ta cry," he thought. "Po' lil ole thang." His heart felt full.

"You welcome, Miss," he said tenderly, as he stepped back.

"Ya wanna wear it?" the clerk asked.

"Yes, ma'am," the little girl said. She slipped the ring on her finger, turned slightly, shyly looked up at James, and smiled.

He smiled at her. Because she was a child, James was able to really look into her eyes, and he could see beyond her color. He thought he saw pain, relief, and gratitude. He felt sorry for her, but he also felt hopeful—there was something in those eyes that held promise.

Mis' Mac was the only white person that he could really look at and he loved her, but she had privilege—she belonged. This child did not—not yet, anyway.

"Ah'm glad Ah's here, or she wouldn' a got dat ring," he thought. Being able to help her and seeing her so happy made him feel better. He actually felt good inside. "Since Ah been big, she prob'ly da onliest white person dat Ah looked right in dere eyes, 'cept fuh Mis' Mac."

He took a deep breath and sighed as he watched her going to the counter with the thread, sliding her feet on the floor. "She tryin' ta keep huh shoe on," he thought. He saw her talking to the clerk and showing her the ring. "She know dat nice white woman dat sol' me da thread." And again, he felt pleased knowing he helped her buy the ring.

He stepped closer to the jewelry counter. He noticed that the jewelry clerk was also watching the little girl. He looked at the girl again just as the clerk handed her something, and she said, "Thank you, Anna."

"Dat nice woman name Anna," he thought. "Ah likes dat name."

"You're welcome, Lora Lee," the clerk said.

"An' huh name Lora Lee. Dat's a cute lil name fuh huh." James watched her as she walked slowly to the popcorn stand. "She gon' git huh some popcorn," he thought, and he felt pleased. "Dat Anna done give huh some money." Holding her popcorn, she apparently forgot that her sandal was broken and she started skipping. Her shoe fell off immediately, and she had to stop and put it back on. "Ahhhhh," he thought. She looked around to see if anyone had seen her, and James quickly looked at the jewelry clerk, who turned her head and looked at him. "She wuz watchin' huh, too."

He thought the clerk was going to help him then, but a white woman walked up to the clocks on the other side of the counter. Right away, she went to help her as though she'd been waiting for her.

"Oh Lawd!" James thought. "Ag'in she ain't gon' wait on me. Damn huh! Dat white woman jes' come here, an' she gon' wait on huh, an' Ah awready been standin' here waitin'." He stepped back and rubbed his stiff, tense neck.

James could feel himself sweating, and although it was hot, he knew that wasn't the reason. "If Ah 'on't git closer, dat crazy ole woman ain't never gon' wait on me," he thought, and he moved two steps forward. He watched the clerk and the woman, who had no idea what kind of clock she wanted. "Ah could done bought dat necklace while dat ole white woman jes' lookin'." He closed his eyes and took a long, deep breath.

"Ah guess dat crazy woman happy," he thought. "She makin' me stan' here an' wait. Dat whut Ah gits, e'em though Ah give dat lil gal a penny." He thought about taking another stroll around the store, but he didn't feel like it. And he didn't feel like standing there. He felt like going home.

He moved one step closer to the counter. Now he was only about one step away, and as close as he thought he should go. "Ah goes too close, dat mean ole thang ain't never gon' wait on me. Good thang Mis' Mac give me dat clock, or Ah'd havta buy a clock from dat mean ole thang, too. Ah'd be here till supper time."

He studied the necklaces. The heart with diamonds was the only one he liked. He thought some of the others were nice necklaces for somebody, but that was the only necklace worthy of his Saleena. "Ah'm only waitin' 'cause a you, Saleena," he thought.

James looked at the clerk. He hadn't noticed before what she was wearing, but he could study her with her back turned. Her dress was faded a little in places, and her sandals looked kind of shabby. James thought she needed a new dress and new shoes. He felt his attitude toward her shift a little. "She jes' a po' ole white woman havin' ta work," he thought, "an' she mad at da worl'. An' sumpin bad 'nough in huh life dat she cryin' on da job."

The customer finally left, and James thought, "Fine'ly she gon' come." However, another clerk walked over and started talking to her. The other clerk knew James was waiting because she looked right at him, though James thought she looked right through him. He took a deep breath. He was already sweating, and he could feel the anger rising in him. "Lawd, ya really be tryin' mah patience, now." He swallowed. His stomach churning, he wanted to scream at the clerk. He wanted to scream at the world.

"Ah cain't git mad now," he thought. "An' Ah cain't leave wit'out dat necklace. Ah done waited dis long." He forced himself to take another deep breath, and he tried to keep his face neutral, while inside several different feelings were competing. Humiliation was winning. He took his nicely ironed white handkerchief from his back pocket and wiped the sweat from his face. "Now, Ah gon' hafta wait longer," he thought, but much to his surprise, the jewelry clerk turned around and went to wait on him.

"She lef' dat udder woman jes' standin' dere," he thought, "an' neit'er a dem looks happy."

"Did ya wanna see sumpin?" she asked James.

"Yes, ma'am," he said, looking at the counter. "Ah'd like ta see dem necklaces, please."

She took the display case out and put it on the counter. "Ah'd like da heart wit' di'mon's, please," he said softly.

He glanced at the clerk. She had a pained expression on her face and James thought she was going to cry again.

"Dere sumpin wrong, ma'am?" he asked.

"Oh no," she responded. He saw her swallow, and her face returned to normal. "You know they ain't real di'mon's, don't ya?"

"Yes'm," he said, and he wondered if there was something about him that made her think he was an idiot. "Mus' be mah skin," he thought. "Guess dat make me look dumb ta huh. Wrong color skin."

"Is it fer yore wife?" she asked, picking up the necklace. She put the others back under the counter.

"It fuh mah girlfrien'. Ah ain't got married," he replied. "Dis woman nice all a sudden," he thought.

"Is it her birthday?" she asked.

"No, ma'am. It jes' a present," he answered, but he wondered, "Why she wanna know 'bout dat?"

"It's a nice present. When ya git married, keep givin' her nice thangs," she said.

"Yes, ma'am, Ah sho will," he said. "Dat one weird woman," James thought. "Firs', she won't wait on me. Den she aks me all dem questions like she mah frien'."

He was relieved when he finally stepped outside the store. He had the necklace, and he was through dealing with that clerk.

As he entered the park, he saw a white couple sitting on a bench under an oak tree. He thought they looked about fifty. He heard the woman ask, "How long we gotta wait?" and the man answer, "Not that long. She gits off at five."

"Mus' be waitin' on somebody," James thought. He saw, with just a glance, that the woman had on too much makeup, and revealing clothes. "She look like a ole floozy. An' he look like a ole bum."

He saw the little white girl on a bench, holding the bag of popcorn and looking at the ruby ring on her finger. There were birds and squirrels on the ground, and she dropped a few pieces of popcorn. "Dere dat lil Lora Lee," he thought. He took a deep breath and smiled. "Ah he'ped huh buy dat dere ring, an' she happy now. She wouldn' e'em have it if Ah wadn' dere, an' huh be cryin' huh eyes out." She looked up as he was looking at her, and she smiled and raised her hand in a small wave.

"She a cute lil ole thang!" he thought, and he smiled and raised his hand as inconspicuously as possible. As he passed the rose garden, he had a strong desire to pick one of the beautiful red roses and give it to her. He walked on through the park with a spring in his step, feeling more hopeful about the whole human race. "Ah didn' thank Ah wuz gon' git dat dere necklace fuh Saleena, but Ah got it, an' Ah he'ped dat lil gal. An' Mama gon' be happy Ah bought dat thread."

James was in such a good mood that he even felt like saluting the statue of the Confederate soldier as he passed it. He smiled and kept his hands by his side. He walked slowly past the fountain, feeling the cool mist on his face and arms.

After he left the park, he walked on the sidewalk, feeling good—confident and smiling. He felt like dancing, but he confined himself to long strides, swinging his arms in step with his feet. His head held high, he looked straight ahead as though headed for a destination.

He remembered looking into the little girl's eyes, and his heart swelled as he recalled the gratitude he saw there. James said her name, letting it roll slowly off his tongue, "Lil Lora Lee." And he remembered the clerk who sold him the thread, "Anna. She wuz nice ta me."

Then he thought about the jewelry clerk—that woman who had tortured him by avoiding him and making him wait for no reason. He wondered what her name was and wished he knew. And he wished he knew what was so terrible in her life that she was crying at work. When he'd been able to really look at her, he'd seen her differently, and he'd even felt a little sorry for her.

James felt like he'd been to church—like his heart had opened a little, and he didn't even know it was closed. And he knew that once a heart opens, if only a crack, it can open wider.

As he walked along deep in thought, a car approached with two white teenage boys in it. He noticed it, but he was feeling good and it didn't actually register until he heard, "Hey, Nigger."

A shock went through his body. His smile faded. His heart seemed to stop for a moment, and the air he breathed seemed devoid of oxygen. A vision of Junior's murdered friend flashed before his eyes.

He stopped swinging his arms and slowed his step. As he glanced at the car, he saw the driver, and a boy on the passenger side, who was leaning out the window with a bottle in his hand. Thinking that the boy was planning to throw the bottle at him, James' immediate impulse was to run. But he pictured himself being chased, and he was in the city, rather than the woods that he knew.

"Git back to the Quarters!" the boy growled.

The driver glared at James and yelled, "You don't b'long here, boy!"

James became aware of the cold pangs of fear that were running through his body, and the thumping heart that seemed to be trying to burst out of his chest, but he was unaware of the sweat running down his ribs, wetting the shirt his mother had so lovingly ironed for him. Suddenly, he could see her caring face, and hear her voice saying, "Always 'membah where you at."

"Ah forgot," he thought. "Ah's too happy."

For a little while, he'd forgotten about color, and about the lines he couldn't cross, and he'd felt relaxed and carefree. Now, with the different feelings, and his slowed pace, he simply put one foot in front of the other. Automatically, he lowered his head and let his shoulders slump, assuming the posture his body knew so well.

As the car went on down the street, he took a deep breath and emitted a sigh of relief. But he felt disappointed in himself that he could forget what he'd known since he was a child.

With his subservient posture, the good things that had happened were no longer in his mind, and he started thinking again about his uncle Freeman and the sad house he was going back to. And in that moment, he felt more comfortable with the grief.

Book III

Hattie
A Heart with Hope

◊ ◊ ◊

Poor Hattie. All the beauty seemed to have drained from her body, and passion, from her spirit. But even a shattered diamond shines.

Cast of Characters
appearing more than once

Hattie, 42

Horace, 48, husband
Francis Bridges, 40, brother; wife Susan, 38
Walter Bridges, father
Essie Bridges, mother
Darrell, 47, brother-in-law (Horace's brother); wife Shirley, 45
Sophie, 42, cousin; husband J. B. Hatchett, 44
Grandma Springer

Neighbors:
Mr. & Mrs. Wutherton, retired

Work:
Anna Love, clerk
Carolyn Peabody, clerk
Mr. Simmons, boss

Sunday

"Thank God fer Sundays" was Hattie's first thought as she opened her eyes. "Otherwise, I'd hafta work ever' blessed day a the week." She quickly turned her head to see if Horace was awake and was relieved to see his eyes still closed.

"He looks so peaceful," she thought. "Looks like the man I thought I wuz marryin', 'cept now he's mostly bald an' got a big belly." She wanted to stay in bed a little longer, but knew if she hadn't started cooking by the time he got up, he'd start yelling, "Where's my breakfast at, woman?"

Hattie put her feet on the unfinished wood floor, pulled her long cotton gown up over her head, took her housedress from a straight-back chair, and put it on. "At least it's a blessin' not ta hafta wake up ta that ole alarm clock," she thought. "An' thank God I don't hafta wear no ole brassiere or stockin's today."

As she was about to get her shoes, she stopped briefly to observe the tired blue eyes staring back at her from the mirror above the dresser, the only piece of furniture in the room besides the chair and the bed. She smoothed her slightly wavy, light brown hair, which almost reached her shoulders, noticing that it looked dry and unhealthy. "Look at the split ends," she thought, pulling at them. "I need ta git my hair cut when I can ever afford to. It's too long now, but I ain't had no money to git it cut. I got more waves when it's shorter, an' it don't look so stringy."

In the corner of the room was a small, door-less closet, which had a long piece of dark gray cloth hanging in front of it. Hattie took her old white sandals—one of which had a strap that was almost broken—from the closet, sat on the chair, and put them on. Then she took the old metal slop jar she'd peed in during the night from under the bed. The enamel pot was white with a narrow red strip around it. It was shaped like a bucket with a lip around the top, and it had a matching lid.

"An' thank God fer toilet paper, too," she thought, remembering the years of using pages from Sears and Roebuck catalogs. She looked at Horace again because the bedsprings had squeaked when she stood up, but he was still sleeping.

The bed had an old iron frame that had been white originally, but much of the paint had flaked off, showing the dark iron underneath. It wasn't one of those beautiful iron beds with all the fancy curlicues, but an inexpensive, plain iron bed. Hattie liked it. She kept intending to paint it, but she never had enough money to justify spending it on paint and a paintbrush. The mattress was about five inches thick and it had a set of bare springs under it, the sides of which were visible when the bed was stripped. There were three wooden slats under the springs that held them and the mattress up. Over the years the slats would move a little and the springs and mattress had fallen a couple of times.

The last time they fell was late one night when Horace had come in drunk just after they'd moved, and before they had a slop jar under the bed. Hattie woke up when he slammed the screen door. The moon was bright and she watched him stagger into the bedroom, mumbling to himself. He staggered over to the bed, turned around ever so slowly and carefully, hesitated a moment while his body swayed back and forth, and then plopped down. The bed crashed to the floor and Hattie burst out laughing. Horace, however, did not laugh. He got mad and refused her pleas to fix it, and they spent the rest of the night with it on the floor.

A white crocheted bedspread with popcorn stitches that Hattie had made during her senior year in high school covered the bed, but was too warm to leave on at night, except during cold weather. The spread had a small stain where Horace had sat on it in his greasy pants. When they got married, she'd been proud to contribute it to their meager belongings. It seemed to Hattie that he didn't care about the intricacy of the work or the beauty of it; it was just one thing they didn't have to buy. She would've been surprised to know that when they were first married, he'd taken his brother Darrell into their bedroom and proudly showed him the bedspread.

Hattie saw a big cockroach (palmetto bug) scamper behind the sink as she went through the kitchen. "Oh my goodness!" she thought. "Guess I'll hafta put out some more poison."

As she opened the back door, she remembered how cool it had been the night before, and there was still a bit of a chill in the air. "We don't use'ly hafta close the doors at night in May," she thought, "but it musta been in the sixties last night. This is prob'ly the last time I'll hafta open the door fer a while." Neither of the doors was ever locked—there were no house keys, but the doors had flimsy latches on the inside. She tiptoed back into the bedroom and put on her old sweater. "I know most it's gon' be hot today. An' I'm shore it'll be hot soon."

On her way to the outhouse to empty the slop jar, Hattie passed by a deserted chicken pen, surrounded by six-feet-high chicken wire. Tall weeds were growing in the pen now, but Hattie saw no reason to pull them. Beyond the pen was a grassy field with a few tall pine trees and small pines and scrub oaks scattered about. On the other side of her yard was the yard of her neighbors, the Wuthertons. They were a quiet, older retired couple. So with no neighbors on one side or in front, and just trees in the back, it was a very quiet neighborhood. The main sounds came from the birds, and Hattie liked it like that.

As she walked along, she looked down at the light gray sand in the narrow, sandy path and saw several anthills. She stopped to watch three ants that were slowly moving a beetle. "How do y'all do that?" she asked in amazement. "That beetle's twenty times yore size. If we could do that, we could pick up cows."

The outhouse was located about fifty feet from the back porch behind an old fence at the back of the yard with an opening where a gate had been. On the other side of the fence, the path turned sharply to the right, facing the outhouse, which was mostly hidden from the house by the fence and some wild plants, including what Hattie thought was dog fennel, and an oak tree which shaded the outhouse. Spanish moss hung from the tree and some of it touched the outhouse roof.

She looked at the Bermuda grass by the path, about the only thing besides sandspurs that would grow in that dry, sandy soil, and she stooped to pull a couple of weeds. She watched a spider scurry away with a white egg sack on its back. "You better move on away from them ants 'fore yore babies hatch out," she said.

The outhouse was a one-seater, which suited Hattie just fine. She wanted to be alone in there. There were times when the outhouse was a sanctuary for her; when Horace got to be too much, she could escape for a few minutes.

Hattie studied the maggots wiggling in the waste for a moment, then she emptied the slop jar, and sat on the seat. She left the door open because it was cooler, and no one was ever back there except Horace, and he didn't go if he knew she was out there. The only opening, besides the door, was a small heart-shaped hole behind and high above the seat, which let in some light and allowed a little air circulation.

On the way back to the house, she glanced at the empty chicken pen. "I wish I didn' hafta see that empty pen ever' day," she mumbled. Her brother Francis had given her a dozen biddies three years before so she could have fresh eggs. Knowing that Horace wouldn't lift a finger, Francis had brought supplies and helped her put up the posts and chicken wire, and build a small coop where the chickens could lay eggs and roost.

Seven of the chicks were roosters, so that only left five hens. She and Horace had eaten six of the roosters, and early one Sunday morning when the crowing of the last one woke Horace up, he went out to the pen and wrung its neck. Hattie was yelling at him the whole time, trying to get him to stop; she was hoping to set one of the hens so they'd have more chickens to eat and to lay eggs. She wanted to have enough that she could even sell a few eggs and bring in a little more money. She'd been grateful that it was a Sunday morning, though; at least she had time to pluck and dress it, so the rooster didn't go to waste. She made chicken and dumplings, which she couldn't enjoy at all. But Horace did.

He killed the remaining chickens, one by one, except the one that he said must have gotten out, until they were gone. Hattie kept reminding him of the eggs they were getting, but he'd respond with how much chicken feed cost. She saved all of their food scraps for the chickens and even got some from their neighbor, Mrs. Wutherton, in exchange for a few eggs, so she didn't have to buy much food, but Horace insisted they cost too much money.

She had loved those chickens—partly because her brother gave them to her—and tears of frustration still stung her eyes when she thought about them, and about all the eggs that she didn't get. And she knew that Horace's motivation for killing them, besides wanting to eat them, was that Francis had given them to her, and she loved them. Horace was not fond of Francis, and Francis didn't like Horace enough to even care what Horace thought of him.

Hattie rinsed the slop jar under their outside faucet beside the small back porch, set it on the bottom doorstep to dry, and rinsed her hands under the faucet. She'd given up on having an indoor bathroom long ago. Horace wouldn't ask their landlord to put one in because he thought the rent would go up. Hattie didn't make enough money to put one in, and Horace seldom made any money. Occasionally, he would work on someone's car or get an old one and fix it up and sell it. But he used much of what he made going to juke joints with his brother Darrell, and lately, he had not made anything.

The house did have running water in the kitchen—another thing Hattie regularly thanked God for. She still had to heat water on the old kerosene kitchen stove for taking baths and washing dishes, but turning on the tap was a lot easier and quicker than pumping and hauling water.

The kitchen was simple: it had white walls, which were badly in need of repainting, and a floor covered with well-worn brown and white linoleum. There was a curtain-less window in each sidewall. One faced the driveway, and the other faced the Wuthertons' house. Hattie kept her dishes in the only wall cabinet. Under it, next to the sink, was a small counter with a drawer and a small cabinet. There was a kerosene stove and an old refrigerator, one shelf over the sink, and a metal cabinet. Four chairs sat around a small wooden table, which was covered with an oilcloth that had little red, yellow, and white squares. She'd bought the tablecloth on sale at S. H. Kress and Company, the five-and-dime store where she worked, and which she referred to as "Kresses," or more often, "the dime store."

Hattie had breakfast almost ready when Horace got up. She heard him and thought how wonderful it would be to wake up again, just once, with breakfast ready and the smell of coffee in the air. "Nobody's made breakfast fer me since Mama moved to Georgia. A course, that makes me jus' like other women. Who ever made breakfast fer Mama?" Of course, her mother had also prepared the other meals, sometimes with Hattie's help. Many evenings, however, her mother would have supper on the table when Hattie got home from work.

Hattie liked to have coffee for breakfast, but she doctored it up with lots of milk and sugar. Horace drank his black, and he raised cane if they ran out. When she heard him coming, she took the pot off the kerosene stove, filled a coffee-stained white cup, set it on a matching saucer, and put it at his place. Neither of them said anything.

He sat down and started his morning ritual: he poured a little coffee into the saucer, picked it up, blew on it, and then slowly slurped it. Then he poured a little more, blew on it, and slurped it—slurp . . . slurp . . . slurp. The sound bothered Hattie, as did many things about Horace. She did not mention it to him, though, because she knew if she did he would probably slurp all his drinks.

She put a plate in front of him with scrambled eggs—from store-bought eggs, she reminded herself—and fried biscuits. She didn't like biscuits reheated, but she did like them when she split them in half and fried them just as her mother and grandmother had done. Her grandmother would say, "No sense in wastin' perfectly good food."

"Ain't we got no bacon?" Horace growled.

"I couldn't afford ta buy no bacon, Horace," she replied. "I bought groceries fer the week, a little kerosene fer the stove, an' I finished payin' what we owed on the rent. I paid some a the rent an' the light bill last week. I only had twenty cents left Friday after I paid the bills, an' I gave it ta you. Next week, maybe I can buy some bacon."

Horace started eating and didn't respond, so Hattie went out to the front yard. She was hungry, but she didn't want to eat with him because of his table manners, and he didn't seem to care if he ate alone.

When they'd moved to the house seven years earlier, the only plant in the yard was a small guava bush, which was killed one winter during a hard freeze. But Hattie had been busy planting in the small front yard. There was a little grass, mostly Bermuda, which *she* usually had to cut with the push mower.

The flowers were blooming and she felt herself begin to relax. She took a deep breath and sighed. Hattie loved her flowers like they were the children she never had. She would've preferred to spend more time with them, but she seldom had time to give them much attention, except on Sundays. After she got home from work, cooked supper, and cleaned up the kitchen, she felt like resting. She might go out and pick off some spent blooms, but often she just sat in her porch swing looking at the flowers.

Beside the front porch were six large hibiscus bushes, three on each side of the wooden steps—one yellow, one red, and one white. Hattie had started them from cuttings she got from her sister-in-law, and put them in front of the porch. The house was on concrete blocks and she wanted to hide the open space underneath, and have more privacy when she sat on the porch. She kept the plants trimmed so that they were bushy and only grew about three feet higher than the porch floor so she could see the road and anybody who passed by.

A dirt road ran in front of the house. Beside it, Hattie had planted a row of mixed zinnias—pink, red, yellow, orange, and white. Across the road was an open field of grass. Their landlord, who lived a quarter of a mile down the dirt road, owned it and the vacant land beside the house. He cut the grass a few times a year for hay, which he sold. Hattie thought he'd intended to build more houses to rent when he built theirs, but he never did.

There were two houses between Hattie's place and the main road that were owned by the people who lived in them. She almost never saw the neighbors who lived near the main road, but the Wuthertons, who lived next to her, would often walk by while she was outside and tell her the flowers looked beautiful or what a wonderful gardener she was.

Hattie had asked Horace to dig up the grass so she could plant the zinnias, but he'd looked at her like she was crazy. So, as with many other chores around the house, she did it herself. She dug up the grass, turned and enriched the soil, and sowed the seeds while Horace sat in the house listening to the radio. She kept them watered and weeded, and they were rewarding her with their beautiful blooms.

On the left side of the yard by the driveway, she'd planted three crape myrtle bushes. One day during the previous year, she'd come home from the grocery store to find three little twigs growing in tin cans on her doorsteps, and she'd planted them and cared for them like they were orphans. She had no idea who left them for her, and that bothered her because she felt grateful and wanted to thank them.

Although Hattie talked to all of her plants, she talked to the crape myrtles most of all. And this morning was no exception. "Well, good mornin'. An' how y'all doin' today? Ya growin' so good, an' I cain't wait ta see what color y'all'll be. Ya know I'm partial ta white crape myrtles. It'd shore be nice if y'all were all white, or at least some a ya." She touched a flower bud. "An' we'll know purty soon, won't we?"

She moved over to the zinnias, pulled a few weeds, and pulled off the spent blooms. "Y'all are lookin' plum purty. I b'lieve I'll pick some a you an' make a bouquet for the house. I can look at you instiddy a Horace while I eat breakfast," she said, laughing.

When she went into the house to get a knife, she was glad to see that Horace had finished eating and had left the kitchen. His empty dish, fork, and coffee cup sat on the table. Hattie didn't think he had ever put a dish in the sink. She sighed, and picked up a small piece of egg that was on the floor in plain sight.

Since she didn't have any vases, she took a quart canning jar from the shelf over the sink, put some water in it, got a knife, and went back outside. She was engrossed in cutting the flowers when Horace yelled, "Hattie, where you at?"

"Oh Lord!" she muttered. "What's he wont wi' me now?" She called, "I'm in the front yard, Horace."

"Whacha doin' piddlin' 'round out here, woman?" he asked as he walked out onto the porch. "Oh, you an' them dad-blamed flow'rs! You ain't even ate yore breakfast yet, an' ya already messin' wi' them flow'rs. I wish ya tuk as good a care a me as ya do them."

"Don't ya thank they're purty?" she asked, resigned to his jealousy of anything that brought her pleasure.

"Purty? They oughta be as much time as ya spend on 'em." He turned to go back into the house. "I'm goin' down ta Darrell's."

"Horace, you know there ain't much gas in the car," Hattie pleaded, "an' I don't have no money, so I cain't put none in. You still got that twenty cents I give you yestiddy? I gotta git ta work all next week." Horace's brother lived about twelve miles away in Mulberry. Hattie figured she could go to work the whole week with the amount of gas that trip would take, and that's what she'd planned.

The screen door slammed before she finished talking and she heard him mumbling to himself. A minute later she heard the back door slam, and then she heard the car start.

"Goodness gracious!" she moaned. "How come he has ta ruin ever'thang? He'd as lief use all the gas as not, an' he prob'ly will. An' I'm gittin' too ole ta walk two miles ta work an' back home."

In five minutes she'd gone from happy and peaceful to resentful and worried. "How in tarnation does he thank I'm gon' git ta work? I reckon I'll hafta borry money from somebody," she thought. "Prob'ly that stuck-up ole Carolyn, and she takes on so." Carolyn Peabody, who worked with Hattie, had loaned her money twice before. But Carolyn would assume a superior attitude and ask her why she needed it, and shake her head and make tsking sounds. Hattie felt ashamed just thinking of having to ask her.

As Horace backed out of the driveway, Hattie called, "Git Darrell to give ya some money fer gas," and knew immediately that he wouldn't even ask. "Sorry ole buzzard!" she said under her breath even though no one was around. "I know most he's gonna brang it back sittin' on empty."

"Ole buzzard" was the worst name Hattie had for anyone. She was offended at Horace's use of "cuss words," and she didn't use them; however, once when he referred to someone as a "bastard," she heard "buzzard." And after that, she said it when she needed a negative word for someone.

Hattie took the flowers she'd picked into the kitchen, but even her beautiful zinnias couldn't cheer her up now. She set the bouquet on the table distractedly, and cleared Horace's breakfast dishes.

"Seems like all I do is pick up after that man," she said out loud as she threw a dishtowel down on the table. "A course, that's after workin' my fingers ta the bone puttin' food on the table fer 'im. An' him too lazy ta work hisse'f! It'd be diff'runt if he wuz sick, but there ain't nothin' much wrong wi' him. An' I ain't got nobody ta blame but me. I knew his fam'ly wuz sorry 'fore I married 'im. Whole fam'ly's a no-count sorry bunch! His mama an' daddy, Darrell, Sam, Becky an' Horace! Ain't a one a 'em ever done a honest day's work in their life! I oughta jus' quit 'im! I'd be better off shed a him. I don't know how come I don't jus' quit 'im."

Hattie knew that wasn't quite true. Horace had worked hard as a mechanic for several years before and after they were married, but in the last few years, he hadn't held a job. And his brother Sam, who'd moved to Miami, had a good job. Hattie thought he probably moved to get away from the family. The rest, including their father, acted like they were allergic to work.

She sat down at the table, placed her folded arms on it, put her head down, and cried. After a few minutes, she picked her head up and blew her nose on a soiled handkerchief she kept in the pocket of her housedress. "Lord, ain't I a mess," she said. "A miserable, hopeless mess jus' sittin' here squallin'. I don't know how come I don't jus' leave 'im."

She did know why. She had nowhere to go. And she knew Horace wouldn't leave. He had nowhere to go either, and he wasn't about to look for a job. Hattie figured he was satisfied with his life, but she was absolutely *not* satisfied with hers.

♥ ♥ ♥

Hattie had lived in Mulberry on the opposite side of town from where Horace's family lived. Although Mulberry was a small town, she hadn't met him in the four years her family had lived there. He was six years older than her, and his siblings were older than him, so none of them were in school with her. Her cousin, Sophie, had introduced her to Horace when she was eighteen. He was working as a mechanic at her father's garage, as was Sophie's boyfriend, J. B. Hatchett.

Sophie felt sorry for Hattie because her father was an alcoholic and when he was drunk, he beat Hattie, her brother Francis, who was two years younger than Hattie, and their mother. Their fathers were brothers and Sophie and Hattie could not understand how they could be so different. Sophie's father was a God-fearing man and he would talk to his brother about his "wicked ways," but nothing ever changed.

Hattie's father worked at a lumberyard Monday through Saturday. And every Saturday night after he got paid, he went to the County Line liquor joint and got drunk. Polk County was dry and beer wasn't even sold, but Hillsborough County was wet and the county line was only a few miles away. He'd be drunk when he got home, and usually somebody would get a beating.

For almost two years, Hattie and Francis had taken turns making themselves available to protect their mother, who'd had a heart attack after a beating. He beat her with his fists, but he took his belt off and whipped Hattie and Francis. When Hattie was getting a whipping, she would wish that his pants would fall down, but they never did. She dreaded Saturdays. She hated the whippings, but knowing Francis was getting whipped was almost as bad as being whipped. Whipping the kids exhausted him and he would fall on the bed and go right to sleep.

When Francis was sixteen, one Saturday night while he and Hattie were sitting on the front steps looking at the stars and waiting for their father to come home, he announced that he was leaving. "It's my turn fer a beatin'," he said, "but this is my last one. I cain't do it no more. I hate him so much I could kill 'im, an' if I stay here, I prob'ly will."

Hattie was shocked. "Oh Francis, where ya gon' go? What ya gon' do?"

"You know how I been the one goin' to git the mail lately?" he asked. "I wrote Grandma Springer an' asked her if I could stay wi' her an' git me a job. Well, I got a letter from her today an' she sent me a bus ticket, so I'm a goin' back to Georgia an' stay wi' her."

"You goin' ta school up there?"

"Nope. I don't like school, nohow. I'm gonna drop out on Monday."

"I wish I could go wi' you, Francis, I'd love ta stay wi' Grandma."

Hattie had spent a lot of time with her grandmother when they lived in Georgia. Her house was only a mile from theirs, and Hattie would often walk over after school or on Saturday.

Hattie's family had lived in a small town right beside the railroad tracks. The white people lived on one side of the tracks, and the Negroes lived on the other side. Of course, only white children went to Hattie's school, and they'd tease Hattie about where she lived. Almost everyday, as they were leaving the school, somebody would call, "Hey, Hattie, don't fergit which side a the tracks you live on," and the kids would laugh. Francis would get mad if he heard them but he was much smaller than the ones who taunted Hattie, so he couldn't do anything. Hattie couldn't understand why it bothered her so much, but it embarrassed her, so she'd been glad to move away, but sorry to leave her grandmother. Her family had moved to Florida when Hattie was fourteen and Francis was twelve.

"You almost thu wi' school, Hattie," Francis said. "You need to stay here. But don't worry 'bout the whippin's. I talked to Mr. Smith yesterd'y an' he's gonna git the Klan after Daddy. When I told 'im 'bout his drinkin' an' how he beat Mama, he said they'd heard sumpin 'bout that before, an' they'll put the fear a God in 'im. Maybe they will an' he'll quit drinkin'."

And they did. On Monday night, the Klan burned a cross in the front yard, and they nailed a note on the front door saying, "Walter Bridges, we don't hold with getting drunk and wife beating. Quit it now or what ye sow, that shall ye also reap."

For a few months, he didn't even drink and Hattie had begun to relax about Saturdays. Her father was grouchy, but she was used to that. Her graduation was only two weeks away when he got drunk one Saturday night.

Sophie had talked Hattie into going out with Horace that night on a double date with her and J. B. Hattie went mostly because Sophie said she and J. B. were going to Lakeland to the Polk Theatre to see a movie. She had never been to a movie and she felt awkward when the girls at school talked about the ones they'd seen. She always stayed quiet and placed herself in the background. If someone asked her if she'd seen a particular movie, she'd say, "No, I didn' see that one," or "I didn' see it yet," ashamed to admit that she couldn't go to the movies. Her father considered them a waste of money and wouldn't take her or give her money to go.

It was Hattie's first real date. The two boyfriends she'd had were still students and they'd meet her at school dances and ballgames, but they never went on what she thought of as a real date. She'd been kissed twice by one of them.

Hattie was an attractive girl. She had light blue eyes and long brown hair with gold highlights from the sun. At five and a half feet, she was tall for a girl born in 1915, and she had a nice figure. She did not see herself as attractive, however. No one had ever told her she was pretty, and she was not one of the popular girls at school.

That Saturday night, J. B. and Sophie picked her up in J. B.'s car. Horace was already with them. When Hattie saw him, she immediately liked his curly, sandy brown hair, hazel eyes, and broad smile. He was four inches taller than her, and he had a good build. He wore a nice green shirt that brought out the green in his eyes and went well with his slacks, and Hattie sensed that he was trying to make a good impression. Her father was not at home, but she was pleased to introduce him to her mother who was clearly impressed with him.

In the car, they sat in the back seat, but most of their conversation was with Sophie and J. B. Yet, Hattie was acutely aware of the man beside her. She felt intoxicated by his Old Spice aftershave. Once, he leaned close to her and said, "That's a really nice dress an' you look real purty."

"Thank you," Hattie replied, all warm inside. "You look nice, too."

They got to the theatre a few minutes late and headed for the balcony. As they walked up the staircase, Hattie noticed the beautiful tiles. In the mezzanine lobby, she wanted to look at the intricate moldings, cornices, and twisted columns, but the others wanted to go right in to the movie. Hattie had never been in such an ornate building, and she was feeling happy and full of wonder. When they entered the balcony, she was even more amazed. "It's like a fairyland," she thought. "How beautiful! I never saw anythang like this."

When they found four seats together, Sophie, J.B., and Horace lowered their seats and sat down. Hattie, never having been in the theatre, and distracted by the movie and the theatre, started to sit, not noticing that the seat was up, and she sat on the raised seat. She quickly lowered it, trying to avoid embarrassment, but Horace burst out laughing. She sat down, annoyed that he'd laughed at her, and grateful that it was too dark for anyone to see her red face.

She hardly looked at the screen for the first few minutes. She couldn't believe that no one had mentioned how beautiful the theatre was. Of course, since she'd never been in a theater, she assumed they must all be similar. She stared at the high rounded ceiling, which was like the night sky with twinkling stars, and she stared at the building facades complete with balconies and lighted windows with curtains. She sat in amazement with a big smile and eyes wide with wonder. She'd passed the theatre many times, never dreaming what was inside.

An Italian immigrant, J. E. Casale, had designed the Polk Theatre in the style of a Mediterranean village. The movie screen was set in a beautiful facade with an archway over the screen.

Hattie also noticed that the theatre was nice and cool and wondered what made it that way when it was so hot outside. In fact, the theatre had a pump that used artesian well water in an "air wash system" that chilled the air. When it was too cool, an usher would go to the basement and inform the operator, who would shut it down. In the early years of operation, the system drew so much energy that when it was turned on, lights in downtown Lakeland would dim.

As she looked around, Hattie felt gratitude toward Sophie and Horace. She was surrounded by beauty. So, when Horace put his arm around her, she was comfortable and happy, enjoying the feel of his arm on her shoulders.

She could smell his Old Spice, and she closed her eyes and took some long, slow breaths. The smell and his closeness made her feel even giddier than she was already feeling. She quickly forgave him for laughing at her, realizing it probably had been funny. Here she was watching a movie in the most beautiful building she'd ever seen, on a real date with a cute guy, who had told her she looked pretty and had his arm around her.

"So this is what it's like," she thought. "I'm finally at a picture show." She relaxed into the chair, feeling happy and contented. Finally at eighteen, she felt the way she'd imagined the other girls felt.

Unfortunately, it didn't last long. Soon, Horace turned her face toward him, pulled her close, and kissed her. Not only did she feel it was too soon for a kiss, but she was interested in the movie then, and just wanted to watch. She noticed that J. B. and Sophie were just watching the movie. Horace looked at the screen for a few minutes and then kissed her again. A little later, he kissed her again and Hattie felt his hand slide down her back and move to the side of her breast. She quickly moved his hand. "Quit it," she whispered. He stopped for a little while, but soon she felt his hand again.

She decided that allowing him to kiss her had encouraged him; of course, he had not asked permission. Actually, she enjoyed it, even though she thought it was too soon, but she did not like the wandering hands. Several times, she'd heard girls at school talking about boys being fresh, and they said they'd just start talking and the boy would stop and talk to them. But in the theater, she couldn't just start talking.

When Sophie asked her if she wanted to go to the bathroom, she jumped at the chance. Hattie had never seen a bathroom like that one. "Look at this," she said to Sophie, "a whole room with a settee and chairs outside the bathroom. This theatre's the most beautiful place I ever saw. It's like a fairyland."

"It is beautiful," Sophie agreed, but she'd been there several times and was no longer impressed. "Do you like 'im?" she asked hopefully. "Don't you think he's cute?"

"He's kindly cute, but he's fresh," Hattie confided. "He keeps tryin' ta feel me up."

"He's older," Sophie replied. "He's twenty-four. He prob'ly has a lot of experience. Just hold his hand so he cain't do it," Sophie suggested.

"I'll try that. I tell 'im ta quit, but he won't. I don't like it."

Hattie did try holding his hand. It would stop him for a little while, but then he'd get his hand away and start again. She noticed Sophie and J. B. kissing, but J. B. was not trying to feel Sophie up. Hattie kept saying,

"Quit it!" but he didn't stop and she felt frustrated and embarrassed. Her hands were so busy trying to stop his that she couldn't enjoy the movie, and she was glad when it ended.

Afterwards, they went to a restaurant for hamburgers and drinks. Hattie was relieved that Horace wasn't bothering her there. He and J. B. talked about how much they loved working on cars, and they both said they planned to have their own garages one day. Horace told Hattie that he almost had enough money saved to buy a car. He said he could buy a used one with the money he had, but he was waiting until he could buy a really good one, maybe a new one.

When Horace and J. B. went to the jukebox to play a few songs, Sophie told Hattie they were planning to go bowling the next Saturday night. Hattie immediately said, "I don't wanna go."

"Why not?" Sophie asked.

"I don't like him, Sophie," Hattie answered. "He's too fresh."

"Yeah, but bowlin' will be fun. He cain't be fresh with people all around. Come on Hattie. Please go; it'll be fun," Sophie pleaded.

"Okay," Hattie agreed. "But if he's fresh, it'll be the last time."

"I'll git J. B. to talk to 'im," Sophie promised. "He'll tell 'im you're a nice girl an' you don't like that stuff."

"He is kindly cute," Hattie admitted. "If he wadn' fresh, he'd be great."

"I'll git J. B. ta talk to 'im," Sophie repeated. "He'll be better."

On the drive home, Horace started trying to fondle her again, and Hattie thought about what the girls had said about talking. She asked him about his family and he told her a little. Then he kissed her and started again. Sophie asked him about his sister who'd married a man she knew and moved up north somewhere, and that kept him talking for a little while. Then he started again. As soon as the car stopped at her house, Hattie jumped out and closed the car door behind her. "Night, J. B. See you tomorrah, Sophie," she said through Sophie's open window, and ran into the house. Horace had opened his door, but he didn't get out.

Hattie stopped in the kitchen and looked in the refrigerator for something to drink. She had a choice of milk or water and she poured herself a small glass of milk. She breathed a sigh of relief and was surprised to see the glass of milk shaking in her hands. Now that she was free of Horace's groping hands, a feeling of humiliation overwhelmed her.

When she heard her mother's footsteps, she tried to look cheerful. "Couldn' sleep?"

"Yore daddy ain't home yet," she answered with pain in her voice.

Hattie knew what that meant. "I'm sorry, Mama," she said softly, "but I'm real tired an' I'm goin' ta bed." She felt guilty leaving her mother to face her father, but she just couldn't stand the thought of a beating after what she'd been through that evening.

The next morning, Hattie was surprised to learn that her father had not come home. They didn't have a telephone, so her mother asked her to go to a neighbor's house to call Sophie's father; she thought he might know something, or could find out what happened to him.

Hattie picked up the earpiece of the old candlestick phone. When the operator asked for a name, she said her uncle's name, and the operator placed the call. Her uncle said he was about to leave for church, but he'd look into it. Hattie felt a little shame because her family didn't go to church.

Hattie's mother had taken her and Francis to church for a while when they lived in Georgia. The church was only four blocks from their house, so they could walk there—her father would not have driven them, and her mother couldn't drive. Hattie didn't know why they stopped going, and she asked her mother, but she wouldn't say. However, Hattie overheard her saying something to her grandmother about not being able to hold her head up because everybody knew about his drinking.

Later that Sunday, Hattie's uncle dropped by the house and told them that her dad had been arrested for public drunkenness and was in jail. He added that he was certainly not going to bail him out—he could rot in jail for all he cared. Hattie was glad. Her father was in jail for three weeks.

Hattie and her mother had three weeks of complete peace during which they spent a lot of time talking. Hattie had built up resentment at her mother for several years for staying with her father, and even though she couldn't let go of all of it during those three weeks, they did get closer. She began to understand her better and was amazed at how different her mother seemed without her father around—relaxed and even a little silly. When her father got home, however, everything changed again and he was in an even worse temper than usual. The time in jail had cost him his job.

♥   ♥   ♥

Hattie was still sitting at the kitchen table when she heard a knock on the front door. She hastily wiped her eyes and went to the door. When she saw her brother standing there, she was concerned that her face still showed the evidence of her tears, and she quickly wiped it with her hands. Francis was standing with his back to the door looking at the yard.

As usual, he was dressed nicely in a striped shirt and neat slacks. Francis was a good-looking man. Like Hattie, he had inherited their mother's blue eyes, and he also had her blond hair, which had darkened some over the years. Hattie noticed that his hair already had some blond highlights from the sun, as it normally did in the summertime. She looked at his broad shoulders, which hard work had developed.

"Hey, Francis," Hattie said, happy to see him.

"Hey, gal," he said, using the same greeting he'd used since his return from Georgia when he was twenty. While he was with their grandmother and could easily have gotten away with all kinds of things, he was serious and motivated and didn't even drink, mostly because of his father's alcohol abuse. He stayed with her for over four years and he managed to give her money, buy a car, and save enough so that when he returned to Florida, he could buy an old house to live in.

He worked in a small grocery store, and when the owner retired, Francis had enough money saved to buy it and the one-bedroom house behind it—a package deal—and only have a small mortgage. He sold his other house, lived in the house behind the store, and when the mortgage was paid off, he expanded the store, which was doing well. The customers liked the handsome young man who'd worked hard and had been able to buy the store, and Francis treated them well. When someone asked for a particular item, it would usually be there the next time they were in the store.

Hattie was happy for him. However, every time she saw him, she was intensely aware of her own situation and felt overwhelmed with shame.

"Your flowers look great," he said as he turned.

Before Hattie could reply, he said, "My goodness, Hattie. What's happened now?" He only knew part of what went on in Hattie's life, but he understood a lot more than she wanted him to.

"Come in an' let me make you a cup a coffee," she responded.

Francis had not intended to stay, but when he saw Hattie's face, he changed his mind. He picked up a box from the porch swing. He knew how much Hattie had liked sitting in the swing on their grandmother's front porch, so he bought the swing for her and hung it one Christmas Eve while she was at work. He knew she had little enough pleasure in her life and he hoped the swing would add a little. Horace wasn't home, so Francis waited for her to get home so he could see her reaction, and he was sitting in the swing when she pulled into the driveway. She burst into tears when she saw him and the swing, and she sat in the car for a while crying. He just continued swinging, waiting for her. By the time she got out of the car, she was laughing at him sitting there swinging as though he didn't even see her. She sat down beside him, hugged him, and thanked him profusely. His was the only present she received that Christmas.

Hattie glanced at the box Francis carried.

"I brought you a few things," he said.

When he visited her, he almost always had a box with items from his store—bent cans, and fruit and vegetables that were starting to deteriorate—all things that he knew she liked and could use. Occasionally, he'd throw in other things, like a can of peaches or shredded coconut, just because she liked them.

"Oh Francis," she responded, and said the same words she always said. "You don't hafta do that. Didn' Susan wont this stuff?" Of course, he had a constant supply of things that he took home for his family.

"We don't need it, an' I know I don't have to, Hattie, but I wont to. I worry 'bout you," he replied softly.

"I wish you wouldn', Francis. I'm okay," Hattie said as she lit the burner under the coffee pot. "How are the kids?"

He ignored her question and asked, "Well, if you're okay, then how come ya been cryin'?"

She'd almost forgotten about her tear-stained face, but his question brought her back to her situation. "I'm too ashamed ta tell ya, Francis," she replied, with her head down.

His voice had an edge when he asked, "Did he hit you?"

"No, no," she quickly responded. "Nothin' like that."

Horace had never hit her, but he had pushed her a couple of times, and scared her. She had started to believe that he would hit her and she had begun to have an underlying fear when he was at home. She was grateful that Francis didn't know about those times. She was afraid of what he might do if he found out, and the last thing she wanted was for her brother to get in trouble, especially because of her. He was the only person that she truly loved, and she knew he loved her. "It's . . . well, he jus' uses money without thankin' 'bout how much we have an' will it last 'til payday."

"For him, it's like it grows on trees," he said angrily. "He can jus' loaf an' the money still comes in. But for you, it means workin' six days a week. There are lots a ways to abuse people, ya know." He studied the face of his forty-two-year-old sister, thinking that she looked ten years older.

"Why don't you leave 'im, Hattie?" he asked. "We can work somethin' out for you." He hesitated for a minute—he hadn't made this offer before, but he'd thought about it a lot and he felt that the time might be right.

"You know that little yeller house I own behine the store? It ain't rented now. You could live there an' pay me rent an' work at the store."

Hattie surprised him and herself when she blurted out, "But what would Horace do?"

Francis studied his sister as she moved about the kitchen and he felt intense anger rising inside him. His back straightened and his hands curled into fists. He realized that her response was the reason he didn't talk to her about her situation. He never could understand what there was about Horace that had attracted her or why she'd married him. It seemed to him that her life with Horace had been miserable from the start, and now that he was offering her a way out, she was thinking about that bum.

Hattie poured two cups of coffee. She took a can of evaporated milk from the refrigerator and put it, the sugar bowl, and a couple of spoons on the table.

Francis looked at the cup she put in front of him. "I'm offerin' you a way out, Hattie," he said with the edge back in his voice. He looked at her, "You don't hafta decide right now, but I'm not sure how long the offer will stand. I need to rent the place, so you think about it."

He knew he couldn't drink the coffee feeling the way he did—just sit there and act like everything was fine. As he got to his feet, he thought, "I know most she needs some money," but he asked, "You need some money?" Normally, he would have put a couple of dollars down on the table before he left, but he was too angry now. If she got it, she'd have to ask for it.

"No," Hattie answered, too proud to ask. "I'll be okay."

Francis turned to leave, "Think about my offer, Hattie," he said, softly now. "I'd really like to see you happy before one of us dies."

When he was gone, Hattie sat down at the table and wept.

Monday

HATTIE WOKE UP SOMETIME DURING THE NIGHT when Horace stumbled in. He made no attempt to be quiet and Hattie could tell by the way he clomped around that he'd been drinking. She lay completely still with her eyes closed, hoping he wouldn't notice her, and if he did, he wouldn't bother her. She wondered where he got alcohol since everything was closed on Sunday. "I bet that Darrell's runnin' a still ag'in," she thought. "The sheriff busted up the last one. He wuz jus' lucky he didn' git caught. I shore wish he hadda, an' they put that sorry thang in jail."

Horace plopped down on the edge of the bed and slid off onto the floor. "Damn it!" he muttered. Hattie almost burst out laughing, but she clamped her hand over her mouth, and tried not to move. She could hear him taking off his shoes while he sat on the floor. When he accomplished that task, which took a while, he climbed onto the bed in his clothes. His body pulled the sheet down tight over her and she needed to shift to make herself comfortable, but she didn't dare move. The last thing she wanted was for him to start pawing her.

After a couple of minutes, he was snoring and Hattie shifted herself. However, she could not go back to sleep; her brain was awake and she had a lot of things on her mind. "It's a good thing I taken my bath Saturd'y night, 'cause I shore didn' feel like doin' it tonight," she thought. Taking her weekly bath meant bringing in her metal washtub from outside, repeatedly filling a pot with water and emptying it into the tub, and heating water on the stove to add, so the water would be at least lukewarm. Afterwards, she had to use a pot to dip the water out of the tub because it was too heavy for her to pick up. She didn't even bother to ask Horace to help her anymore; she'd learned that was a waste of her breath. She'd often carry a bucketful to the front yard, water some flowers, and go back for more.

Hattie was thinking about how little gas must be in the car, her conversation with Francis, how she'd approach Carolyn for a loan, and wishing she'd just asked Francis for a dollar. She could have bought fifty cents worth of gas and hidden fifty cents for the next time she needed it. And she was sure there'd be a next time.

She thought about how wonderful it would be to live by herself in that little yellow house Francis owned. She'd always thought it was a cute little house. There weren't many plants in the yard, but she knew there was enough space in the front yard for a nice flower garden, and space in the back yard for some chickens and a small vegetable garden—at least some tomatoes and a row of green beans.

"That'd be wonderful," she thought. "I could run some cucumbers up on the fence an' I could stick some pepper plants in with my flow'rs. An' I thank there's a orange tree on the side." She had all kinds of images flashing in her mind. "I could move the crape myrtles 'cause they little enough, an' take cuttin's from my hibiscus plants, an' plant some zinnias over on the side a the yard, an' maybe there's room fer a gardenia. I jus' love the way they smell. An' I already tol' Miz Wutherton I wont a cuttin' from her bush. An' I'm sure it's got runnin' water an' a bathroom inside."

Her heart was beating fast as her mind raced. She found herself feeling excited at the mere thought of it. "No Horace ta hafta pick up after, ta spend the money I make, or ta sleep with. I shore wouldn' miss none a that." Then she felt guilty just for thinking it. After all, he was her husband. Nevertheless, she lay awake for another hour daydreaming.

She woke up about a minute before the alarm was set to ring and quickly turned it off, wishing she could go back to sleep. She needed to pee, but she didn't want to chance waking Horace by using the slop jar. So she went to the hole-in-the-wall closet and quietly put on her housecoat, which had a couple of holes in it and was usually too warm for May, but felt good in the cool morning air. The closet had been built after the house was finished; it protruded into the living room, and the front door opened against the back of it. She had arranged the little bit of living room furniture they had so that the closet was not in the way.

Hattie put on her old sandals, even though she'd have preferred to go barefoot, because sandspurs appeared, in spite of her vigilance. She took the slop jar from under the bed, and headed for the outhouse. As she passed the chicken pen, she averted her eyes and watched a squirrel run across the path in front of her, jump on the fence, then onto the oak tree, and scurry up it.

After she used the toilet, she emptied the slop jar, and took it back to the house. She rinsed the pot under the outside faucet, set it on the bottom step to dry, and rinsed her hands under the faucet.

When she tiptoed back into the bedroom, Hattie saw something shiny on the bed half under Horace. She tiptoed closer, and could hardly believe her eyes when she realized it was a quarter. "Must a fell outta his pocket durin' the night," she thought. "But where did he git a quarter from?" She stood staring at the coin, tempted to try to get it, but afraid she'd wake him. After she'd changed her panties and put the dirty ones in the dirty clothes hamper in the closet, she put on her brassiere, stockings and garters, and her slip. As she reached for her dress, she thought, "I shore wish I knew how to sew. I could make me some more dresses. Course I ain't got no sewin' machine." Her dress buttoned, she put on her white sweater—her only good sweater—and her good white sandals, and then looked again. Horace hadn't moved. She decided to look later to see if he might have rolled over, and off the quarter.

Hattie put some water and coffee in the coffee pot and put it on the stove. She always made enough for Horace; he just had to heat it when he got up. She didn't usually make breakfast for him on the days she had to work, though.

She got two eggs from the refrigerator and put one on to boil. As she scrambled the other egg, she thought of nothing but that quarter on the bed and how she could get it. She put the egg on a plate and then buttered a piece of lightbread—the sliced white loaf bread she bought at the grocery store—to brown in the frying pan. As the bread browned, she went to the sink, took the washcloth off the nail beside it, wet it in the cold water, and washed her face and arms. She unbuttoned the front of her dress and wiped under each arm before rinsing the cloth and hanging it back on the nail. Then she turned the bread. As the other side browned, she took her jar of Mum deodorant from the top of the refrigerator, rubbed some of the cream under both arms, and put the jar back on the refrigerator.

She washed the deodorant off her fingers, and went to the bedroom door to look at Horace again before she sat down to eat. He still hadn't moved. She removed the boiled egg from the hot water and put it in a small bowl of cold water. She ate her breakfast, thinking about how she could buy over a gallon of gas with that quarter and she wouldn't have to ask Carolyn to loan her any money, at least not until later in the week.

She quickly washed her dishes without heating any water and left them in the dish drainer. Then she took her toothbrush and toothpaste from a cup on the shelf over the sink, put some toothpaste on the toothbrush, put some water in a glass, and went on the back porch to brush her teeth. She did not approve of spitting in the kitchen sink, and insisted that Horace go on the porch, also. Hattie tried to take care of her teeth, partly because she didn't have enough money to go to the dentist.

While she made a sandwich for work with bread, mayonnaise, and cheese, she made up her mind to just take the quarter. If he woke up and realized she'd taken it, she'd be on her way out and she'd say she needed it to buy gas. "There," she thought, "that's the way it oughta be. What can he say? After all, he used the gas I need an' I'm the one who made that money, anyhow. I wouldn' a give him the two dimes I had left after payin' the bills if I knew he wuz gon' use all that gas." But she felt herself getting nervous, knowing that Horace could always say something—could always get fighting mad over things she thought were insignificant.

Hattie filled her thermos with iced tea left from Sunday night. She dried the boiled egg and put it and her sandwich in her pocketbook. Then she took a small square of waxed paper, put some salt in it, and folded the paper carefully into a smaller square. As she got the scissors, cut a small piece off one corner of the waxed paper, and folded the paper over so the salt wouldn't spill, she thought about the first time she'd seen salt like that; it was at the picnic she went on with Horace in June of 1933.

♥   ♥   ♥

Hattie had continued going out with Horace, Sophie, and J. B. for a couple of months, and was starting to like Horace. J. B. had told him that Hattie wouldn't go out with him anymore if he didn't stop getting fresh with her. Apparently, he liked Hattie enough to want to be with her, and he did change some of his behavior. The four of them had fun, with lots of talking and laughing. And when Horace would kiss her goodnight, her body had feelings it had never had before.

She remembered him picking her up in his "new" car. "He wuz so proud a that car," she thought. "Prouder a it than any other one we ever had. An' it wuz the best. Nary a one came close to it." They'd had several over the years, since Horace had kept some of the ones he fixed for a while before selling them.

"I wore my blue dress that day," Hattie remembered, "the one Horace said matched my eyes. Now I ain't even got a blue dress. Oh, I 'member that like it wuz yestiddy. I 'member my hair wuz long an' Horace said it wuz shinin' in the sunlight. He ran his fingers through it an' said it wuz soft as silk. I bet he never even touched no silk. We went fer a drive 'roun' Mulberry, which didn't take long in that little town. Then we took Highway 37 north towards Lakeland. I asked Horace where we were goin' an' he said, 'to the hills.' I said, 'Hills?' I didn' even know there wuz any hills in Lakeland."

"My uncle's got a orange grove south a Lakeland a few miles right a Highway 37," Horace had told her. "There's a open field next to the grove that oughta be a nice place fer a picnic, an' we can sit in the shade of a orange tree. That ole sun's mighty hot."

Even though the hills were not very high, Hattie loved them. "Reminds me a Georgia," she said.

The orange grove was on a gently sloping hill. As they looked over the open grassy field, they saw some woods, other orange groves, and a couple of houses in the distance. Horace had chosen a good place.

Little white and yellow wildflowers, with honeybees buzzing around them, were scattered about the field. "Listen ta them bees," Hattie said, tilting her head.

"My uncle's got some hives," Horace said. "He's got lots a bees."

As they walked along beside the orange grove, Hattie noticed that the trees were covered with golf-ball sized green oranges. "Look at all the oranges," she exclaimed. "They're so cute." She wouldn't have admitted it to Horace, but it was the first time she'd been in an orange grove. Horace, who was carrying an old quilt and the bag of food, handed Hattie the quilt. He picked up a little yellow orange off the ground and handed it to her.

"How come it's yeller?" she asked.

"It's no good; it fell off the tree." He picked up another one and threw it out into the field. "Let me see ya beat that."

"I cain't throw that far," she said, and quickly slipped the little orange into her pocket to show to her mother later.

Horace picked some of the wildflowers as they walked along. He put together a nice little bouquet.

"Don't mash one a them bees," Hattie warned, "or you'll be sorry."

When they found a place Horace liked in the shade of an orange tree, they spread the quilt on the ground and Hattie sat down. He put the food bag on the edge of the quilt and sat down beside her. "I bought these beautiful flow'rs fer you," he said, handing them to her with a smile, and a twinkle in his eyes.

"Oh, how thoughtful of you," she said, laughing. She took the bouquet, sniffed it, and sneezed. They both laughed.

He put the bouquet on the edge of the quilt and they watched as a bee lit on it briefly. "Good thang I put it there," Horace said, "or that ole bee might a lit on yore nose."

Hattie thought that was really funny. She fell back on the quilt laughing.

Horace, who'd been laughing also, saw an opportunity and lay down beside her. She stopped laughing. As he kissed her passionately, she suddenly realized she was alone with him out in the middle of nowhere, and she pulled away from him.

"What's wrong, Hattie?" he asked innocently.

"I'm hungry," she declared, not about to explain her concern to him. "We oughta eat."

Horace said he was hungry, too, and he unpacked the sandwiches. He'd made two bologna and two peanut butter on lightbread. Hattie had never had bologna or peanut butter, and her family didn't buy bread very often. She was impressed and she expressed her enthusiasm to Horace, who was pleased with her reaction. She was so grateful to him for making those sandwiches that she welcomed his kiss.

In her house, they almost never had sandwiches. Her father sometimes took them to work, but he preferred biscuits with pieces of meat, and that's what he normally had. Sometimes her mother would put leftover vegetables in a pint jar and send them with him. He said he'd rather have cold string beans cooked with ham, or pork and beans, than sandwiches. As Hattie ate, she couldn't imagine why her father felt that way. "He must notta had baloney," she thought.

Horace apologized that he only had water in his thermos. "That's all right," Hattie assured him. "I don't mind water."

When they finished eating, he asked, "Wont a orange?"

"Them oranges are little an' green," she said, looking at the trees.

"Thank so?" He went to a tree, climbed up on a limb, pulled a regular sized yellowish-green orange, and threw it to her. Then he moved to another tree, reached up and picked another orange.

"How come these are so big?" she asked, looking at the oranges.

"They're from last season," Horace explained. "Some a the oranges that don't git picked stay on the tree an' turn green ag'in. They gradually dry up, but there'll be some juice in the bottom a these."

Hattie watched in amazement as Horace took out his pocketknife and peeled one of the oranges without breaking the peel. He dropped the orange spiral in her lap. "If you say the alphabet while ya spin that aroun', you'll know what letter yore boyfriend's name starts with when the peel breaks."

She spun the peel around gently until she got to "H," and then she did it hard and the peel broke. "H," she said. "Guess yo're my boyfriend."

He cut the top half off the orange, threw it out into the field, and handed her the bottom, which she ate. "It's nice an' sweet," she said, surprised.

"Wont another one?" he asked, before shoving the remainder of his in his mouth.

"No, thank you. I'm full. That wuz a great dinner! Thank you."

Horace went to a tree and picked up a little yellow orange from the ground. Hattie watched as he cut it in two, cut a slice off, and scooped out the middle of the slice, just leaving the rind.

He looked at Hattie sitting on the quilt looking relaxed and pretty. "You look really nice," he said. "You know I like you in that dress."

"That's how come I wore it," Hattie replied, smiling. She was glad she'd worn it for him. He'd shown her hills she didn't know existed, made delicious sandwiches for her, picked flowers for her, and taught her some things about oranges. She was feeling satisfied and happy.

Horace knelt down in front of her. "I been thankin', Hattie," he said and cleared his throat. "Maybe we oughta git married."

Hattie couldn't believe that someone she found so cute and so much fun and whose touch warmed her blood was actually asking her to marry him. "Really, Horace?" she asked in earnest.

"Really!" he replied, and pushed the little yellow ring he'd just made onto her finger.

"Oh, Horace," she said, and threw her arms around his neck. "That is so sweet."

He kissed her hungrily.

Hattie felt desire rising in her, but she wasn't ready for what came next as his kisses became more passionate. She wanted him to continue, and she wanted him to stop. As she thought about it later, she couldn't remember exactly how it happened.

She knew she'd been excited about the picnic, happy with the food, pleased to be experiencing the area and other new things, and happy to be with Horace. And he'd asked her to marry him. It was perfect. But she had not agreed to anything else.

Horace adjusted the quilt, gently pushed her down, and lay beside her, holding her close and kissing her. She thought he was a little too close, but she thought, "We're gon' git married," and she didn't object. She was feeling happy and enjoying her body's sensations.

Soon, however, Horace pushed her onto her back, got on top of her, and one hand went to her breast. Suddenly, Hattie remembered again that she was in the middle of nowhere, alone with this man—this man who'd been fresh with her on their very first date.

She asked him to stop and get off her. Instead, he unzipped his pants. She tried to get up, but he held her down. "What are you doin'?" she shrieked. She asked him to stop—begged him to stop.

"I cain't stop," he said. "You got me so turned on."

With Hattie's lack of experience, she believed him. She was trying to think, but everything was happening so fast. She had a mixture of desire and fear, but the desire disappeared as the fear increased. "Please, Horace," she pleaded, "We ain't married."

"Jus' relax," he said impatiently. "I'm too excited. It's all right 'cause we gon' git married. We ain't gon' do the real thang, nohow. It won't hurt."

"No, Horace. We hafta wait," Hattie pleaded. "Stop."

But he didn't stop. And as she lay under him, unable to move, she focused on the thrusting between her legs, her initial stimulation replaced by repulsion. When he finally finished, she felt furious that her first sexual experience was completely against her will, and relieved that he hadn't penetrated her; she'd been afraid that he would.

As Horace lay still on top of her, he felt wetness on his face. He lifted his head and looked at Hattie, whose face was wet with tears.

"We'll git married right away," he said.

"I don't wonna marry you now," she wailed. "I ain't gon' marry you!"

Horace moved off her. "Durn it all, Hattie! I wouldn' a done it if I didn' love you. You git me so excited."

When Hattie sat up, she tore the orange ring from her finger and threw it on the blanket. "I don't wont that thang," she shrieked, as she went behind an orange tree. "Is there any water left?"

Horace took her the thermos. "Look at this slimy stuff on me," she whined, showing him her leg.

"It'll come right off," he said as he knelt to help her.

"No!" she cried. "Don't you dare touch me an' don't look at me. Look at my dress; it's ruint, jus' like me!"

"You ain't ruint, Hattie. Yo're still a virgin, ya know. You can wash yore dress, an' I'm gon' marry you."

"You *gon'* marry me? You done put the cart before the horse, Mister," she said with the same angry tone. "All I wont *you* ta do is take me home."

Neither of them said a single word on the way home. Horace looked at her occasionally, and each time she was looking straight ahead with tears streaming down her face.

When he stopped the car at her house, he took her hand, "I'm sorry. I jus' couldn' stop. It don't mean nothin'. An' I wanna marry you, Hattie."

Hattie didn't look at him. She pulled her hand away and jumped out, leaving the car door open. He watched her run into the house.

When Sophie went by later to ask her how the picnic went, Hattie told her everything. When she told her about the proposal and the orange ring, Sophie said, "That's so sweet." But when Hattie told her about the rest, she said, "I cain't b'lieve he'd do that. What are ya gonna do?"

"I gotta marry 'im now. I ain't got no choice."

"Why not?" Sophie asked, knowing the answer.

"I'm ruint," Hattie answered with tears in her voice. "I been used, Sophie. I'm soiled. No other man's gon' marry me now."

"But how would they even know, Hattie?"

"Well, *I* know. An' I did kindly go along with it fer a while. He jus' didn' stop when I wonted 'im to."

"Did ya tell 'im to stop?"

"I told 'im several times, but he said I got 'im too excited an' he couldn'."

"That ain't true, Hattie. J. B. gits real excited an' he always stops when I tell 'im to," Sophie said emphatically.

"Well, I'm ruint now. I don't know what I'm gon' do. Daddy's like a stick a dynamite jus' waitin' to explode. Thangs were goin' good wi' Horace till this an' I thought maybe we'd git married an' I could git away from this crazy house."

Hattie had started working at Badcock's Furniture Store in Mulberry the week after she graduated. She wanted to get an apartment, but her father wasn't working, so she said she'd live at home and use what she made on household expenses until he found a job. However, she barely made enough to pay the bills. She wouldn't give him any money because she was afraid he'd get drunk, but she did put gas in his car so he could look for work.

He seemed resigned and defeated, and Hattie felt sorry for him. After a couple of months, he got drunk one night, drove his car into a tree, and died instantly. She knew he'd felt hopeless, and she worried about whether she could've done more to help him.

"I wuz so young," she thought, suddenly realizing she'd been daydreaming. Annoyed with herself, she tiptoed into the bedroom. "Lord! Why do I even thank about that ole stuff?" she wondered.

She combed her hair and put on some lipstick. Then she tiptoed up to the bed, but before she even reached it, she realized she couldn't see the quarter. Horace was still asleep, but he'd turned over. Hattie looked beside his still form, and then she knelt down beside the bed and looked under the bed. She tiptoed to the other side of the bed, hoping it would be on the other side of him. It wasn't. "He must be lyin' on it," she thought.

She tried to feel better by telling herself that she hadn't even known the quarter existed an hour earlier, but that didn't help. She could hear Carolyn's words: "Yo're too nice for yore own good, Hattie. You let that man git away wi' murder."

"Maybe I am too nice, or too timid," she thought. "I should a jus' tuk it when I seen it. Why in tarnation didn' I jus' take it? But, ain't nothin' I can do now, but jus' go ta work." She knew she'd been afraid Horace would wake up, and that could have been awful.

When Hattie turned the key in the car, she asked, "Are you gon' crank, Ole Car?" When it started, she looked at the gas gauge, but she couldn't tell if it'd moved off empty. She said a prayer that she'd make it to work and she did. She was grateful for the old Chevrolet, which they'd had for several years. It was one thing Horace was responsible for; he'd gotten it from somebody to fix up and sell, but he kept it, and sold their other car. It was a black '42 Chevrolet with running boards, which Hattie really liked. She thought the more modern cars looked strange without them.

Hattie liked to get to work a few minutes earlier than she had to so she could enjoy the quiet time before the customers arrived. She worked at the jewelry counter with the jewelry, clocks, and watches. She didn't care much about the clocks, but she liked arranging the pretty jewelry for display, and she enjoyed looking at it during the day. She cleaned her counters, put out new jewelry in the glass display cases, and rearranged a few necklaces that hung from small racks on the counters. Then she worked with the clocks and watches to make a nice display, frequently changing them around.

Before the store opened to customers, she went to the water fountain to get a drink. There were two fountains in the back of the store: "Colored" and "White." In the front was a popcorn stand, and a lunch counter was on the same side. Hattie had eaten there a few times when she first started working at the store, but she couldn't afford to anymore.

When she went back to her counter, she noticed a necklace in the glass case, which she'd been attracted to since she first saw it a few days earlier. On a silver chain was a silver heart with little rhinestones on it. "That is so purty. I wish Horace would buy it fer me," she thought. "A long time ago he might have, but not now, even if he had the money. A long time ago, like when he first came back from Miami."

After the picnic, she told him she never wanted to see him again, and she meant it. He'd gone by her house a few times, and her mother, who always went to the door, finally told him not to go there anymore. Sophie said he asked her to put in a good word for him, and she told him she didn't *have* a good word for him. Eventually, he gave up, and soon after, he left Mulberry. Sophie told her he'd gone to Miami to work with his brother.

He was gone for four years. A couple of months before he returned, Hattie got a letter from him apologizing. He said he realized he'd taken advantage of her and he was real sorry. Then, when he got home, he went to see her. In spite of herself, she was happy to see him and felt some of the old stirrings. She went out with him a few times and when he asked her to marry him, she agreed. Her mother was planning to move to Georgia to live with her own mother and Hattie was already feeling lonely. And she didn't feel right going out with other men after the picnic because she felt dirty. At twenty-two, she was starting to think of herself as an old maid. She knew that Horace wasn't the kind of man she'd hoped to marry, but she told herself he'd changed, and in some ways, he had. He was considerate and thoughtful—for a while.

♥   ♥   ♥

ALL MORNING, HATTIE WORRIED ABOUT HOW she'd get some money. Carolyn wasn't at work, and there was no one else she wanted to ask. She really liked Anna, who'd only worked at the store for a year, and thought she'd loan her the money, but Hattie was too ashamed to ask her. She didn't want her to know that she needed money, especially so soon after payday. Anna and most of the other clerks were much younger than Carolyn and her, and she would've felt even more humiliated asking them for money than asking Carolyn.

She hoped Carolyn would appear after lunch. She thought maybe she'd gone to the dentist that morning and would show up later, but she didn't.

When Hattie saw the manager, Mr. Simmons, coming down the stairs, she decided to ask him if Carolyn was sick. Mr. Simmons almost always had a pencil stuck behind his ear, but Hattie never saw him use it. She assumed he kept it there to look more business-like, but she thought it looked stupid. When she asked him about Carolyn, he simply said that she wouldn't be in that day or the next. He left the odor of stale cigarette smoke behind him, and Hattie walked to the other side of her counter trying to escape it. Horace had smoked when they got married, and she'd gone from liking the smell on his breath to being repulsed by it. Fortunately, he quit when they had no money.

Hattie felt desperate. She began hoping that someone she knew would come in and she could borrow a quarter; she'd make up some excuse, like she forgot her pocketbook that morning. She watched the doors and the sidewalk for an acquaintance going by outside—the double doors were left open, except when it was cold, and she could see the passers-by.

All afternoon, she debated with herself the pluses and minuses of asking Mr. Simmons for an advance on her salary. She'd gotten an advance a couple of times and he'd seemed displeased when she asked. Between customers, and there were not many, Hattie would imagine scenarios and she'd think about Horace and his lack of consideration for her until the tears sprang to her eyes. Then she'd stop herself for fear of being seen crying. "Forgit Horace an' thank about how ya gon' git gas ta git home on," she'd say to herself. She could feel a headache coming on.

It was nearly closing time when she decided to take a quarter from her cash register. She'd never done that before, but she was desperate. "After all, I'll jus' borry it till tomorrah," she thought. "I gotta git some gas. An' Horace wuz prob'ly too drunk ta remember that he even had a quarter an' he prob'ly didn' see it on the bed. God knows he never bothers ta make the bed when he gits up. I can brang it in tomorrah and tell Mr. Simmons I musta dropped it 'cause I found it on the floor. What can he say? Anybody can drop a quarter. It can slip right through yore fingers."

She looked around to see if anyone was looking at her. She wished she'd thought about taking the quarter sooner so she could've taken it when she had a customer. She thought that would've been easier. When she took the money from the register to give to Mr. Simmons, she looked around once more, and quickly dropped a quarter into a pocket on the front of her dress. "Thank God I wore a dress with pockets," she thought, and immediately felt guilty for thanking God for helping her steal money.

When she gave Mr. Simmons her cash, she tried to act natural, but she felt like a thief. She went upstairs with the other women to the employees' room to get her sweater. She sat down and waited until everyone left before opening her pocketbook and taking the quarter from her pocket. "Oh Lord, I got such a headache," she thought, rubbing the back of her neck.

"Hattie, do you need a ride?" Anna asked from the doorway.

Hattie jumped and dropped the quarter. "I'll git it," Anna said as she walked into the room. "I just realized you didn't leave with the rest of us an' I thought maybe you needed a ride."

"Thank you," Hattie said, "but I got my car. I got a headache an' I wuz jus' restin'."

"Oh, I'm sorry," Anna replied, handing her the quarter. "I've got some aspirin." She took an aspirin tin out of her purse and handed it to Hattie. "Just keep it, Hattie, and you take it easy. I hope you feel better."

"Thank you, Anna."

Anna felt sorry for Hattie. Her mother was just two years older than her, and she'd never had to get a job outside the home. Anna had heard stories about her situation, mostly from Carolyn. She'd noticed that Hattie often looked tired and that she only wore six dresses, alternating them with the days of the week. Anna had watched what she wore, trying to figure out how she alternated the dresses. She finally realized that she switched the previous Tuesday dress to Monday, and wore the rest in order starting over again the following week.

Anna liked Hattie and she talked to her mother about her. Her mother told her that she should be extra nice to her—she probably felt trapped and didn't have any way to change her life. So when Anna noticed she hadn't left with her and the others, she went back to check on her.

When she got to the doorway, she saw Hattie take the quarter from her pocket. She acted as though nothing had happened, but she'd seen the frightened and guilty look on Hattie's face when she spoke to her. She wished she hadn't seen that. She thought Hattie had probably stolen the quarter, and wondered if she regularly stole from the store. There was certainly nothing about her appearance that made it look like she spent any money on herself. Anna thought about reporting what she had seen to Mr. Simmons, but she wondered if she should talk to Hattie about it instead. She decided to confide in her mother that evening before making a decision about what to do.

Hattie remained in her chair after Anna left. Her knees felt weak and she realized she was trembling slightly. She wondered if Anna had seen her take the quarter from her pocket. If not, she probably thought she'd taken it from her pocketbook. What if she had seen her? If she told on her, would Mr. Simmons fire her? Hattie thought that would be the one excuse he needed; he didn't seem to like her.

She slowly got to her feet, went to the bathroom, and took an aspirin. When she went downstairs, Mr. Simmons observed that everyone else had left already and asked why she was late leaving. Hattie told him she was just resting because she was tired and had a headache, and she quickly went to the door.

Before she got outside, she saw the rain. "Oh Lord," she thought. "Jus' what I need!" She would have waited to see if the rain would let up, but she didn't want to be there with Mr. Simmons, even though she saw lightning flashing in the distance. She took the little plastic rain bonnet—folded neatly into a tiny package—from her pocketbook, put it on her head, and added an umbrella to her mental list of things she wanted. By the time she got to her car, she was completely drenched, except for her hair.

When she started the car, she knew the gas gauge did not move. She tried to remember which station was closest, and decided to go to Selph's Texaco on East Main Street. She knew she'd be lucky to make it, and she didn't. She'd gone only a few blocks when the car died in an intersection. She felt completely humiliated, and she felt exhausted, but she did the only thing she knew to do; she got out and started trying to push it—in the rain. A man in a store saw her plight and immediately went to help her push. Another man stopped his car and got out and helped. He told Hattie to get back in the car so she could steer it while they pushed. Fortunately, there was an empty parking place that she could steer right into.

She got out of the car and profusely thanked the two men, who were now soaking wet, as was she. The man with the car asked if she needed a ride and she meekly admitted that she needed to get some gas. He and Hattie got in his car, and as he drove the few blocks to Selph's Texaco, he commented on her bad luck, having this happen while it was pouring rain. "Thank God it's not lightnin' now," he said. He told her his name was Ray and he worked in Wilson's Grocery Store, and he just happened to be off that day. Hattie almost told him about her brother's store, but she realized that he might know Francis, and she didn't want him to know about her running out of gas. He would have too many questions.

"It's good ya come along when you did," she said. "I shore do thank you."

Ray was planning to get the gas for her, but she said, "No, sir. You already done enough fer me. You jus' stay in the car outta the rain." And he did, but she could tell it was hard for him.

Hattie was embarrassed when she asked the attendant for a quarter's worth of gas; she'd have been even more embarrassed if Ray had been there. He drove her back to her car, and said he'd put the gas in for her. Hattie insisted that she could do it, but this time, he insisted that she stay in his car while he put the gas in hers. She felt grateful that he did those things for her, mentally comparing him to Horace.

Hattie couldn't remember when Horace had gone out of his way to help her with anything. He certainly wouldn't go out in the rain for her.

And he was the one who'd used the gas she needed to get to work and brought the car home with an empty gas tank.

When Ray gave her the gas can to return to the station, he said, "You know, yore right rear tire looks a little low an' you should prob'ly ask 'em to check it at the station."

Hattie thanked him again enthusiastically, and thought how nice he was to be concerned about her tire. She wished Horace would be more like that—more of a gentleman, or, at least, some of a gentleman. She felt warm inside from receiving special attention, and she was well aware of that feeling; she hadn't felt it for a long time.

When the mechanic checked the tire, he couldn't see anything wrong with it, but it did need a little air. He put in some air, and Hattie left happy. It was a little while before she realized that her headache was gone.

Her mind was racing all the way home. She'd think about Anna and worry about whether Anna thought she'd stolen the quarter she dropped; she argued with herself that there was no reason she shouldn't have money in her pocket, but her argument didn't even convince her. Then she'd think about Ray and the embarrassment of running out of gas and how nice he was. And finally, she'd think about Horace and how different he was and how all of it was his fault.

♥ ♥ ♥

Horace was not home when Hattie arrived. Even though she was soaked and cold, she went straight to the bedroom, like a woman possessed, to look for the quarter. It occurred to her that, since he had a quarter, he might have other change also and she decided she'd do a thorough search of the room, looking everywhere change might be hidden.

First, she moved the pillow and straightened the rumpled sheet where Horace had slept; then, she pulled the top sheet back and looked under it, but the sheet did not hide the quarter. She looked carefully at the old pine boards beside the bed and under the bed, but she didn't see it. She looked on the dresser thinking Horace might have put it there and she looked under the dresser. She walked around the room looking at the floor.

"Where is that thang at?" she wondered. "There ain't nowhere else ta look. He taken it, an' he'll spend it. I know he will. An' here I am havin' ta take a quarter from the store. It's jus' one thang after another wi' him." And holding back the tears, she stripped off her wet clothes and put on her housedress. Then she sat down on the bed and cried.

After a little while, she got up and went to the kitchen. There, she saw the box of groceries that Francis had brought her sitting on the table. Normally she would have put them away Sunday evening, but she'd been too depressed to care about them. Now, as she looked to see if there was anything she might use for supper, she noticed that several things were missing. She assumed Horace might have eaten some of the bananas and carrots she knew were there, but not all of them, and some of the canned food was missing. She knew he couldn't possibly have eaten all of that. She looked in the metal cabinet, but it wasn't in there.

"What in tarnation did he do wi' all that food?" she asked out loud, her eyes busily looking all around the kitchen. She thought for a minute. "Why, I bet he tuk it ta Darrell's. That ole buzzard!" She went back to check the box again to confirm that the cans were really gone.

"Or maybe he tuk it ta sell," Hattie said in amazement at the thought. "Where'd he git a quarter from, anyway? An' he mighta had more money! Would he take food right off a our table? Why, that's jus' stealin'. Jus' plain stealin'! I cain't b'lieve Horace would actually stoop that low."

She considered another possibility: "Maybe somebody came in the house an' tuk stuff." She shook her head. "Nope, if somebody else did it, they'd a tuk the whole box. It wuz Horace; it had ta be *him*."

Hattie plopped down at the kitchen table. "Good gracious! I shorely picked a winner!" She stared at the zinnias, still perky in the jar she'd put them in on Sunday. In her mind, she was going over past times when food had disappeared. She always assumed that he'd eaten it, even though sometimes it had seemed like a lot to eat, but now that she knew he'd taken stuff Francis had brought on Sunday, she thought he must've taken things before.

Suddenly, she thought about the chicken that Horace said had gotten out of the pen. She'd gone around that pen, carefully checking the fence. There was no place she could see where that hen could have gotten out. And Hattie kept her wing feathers clipped, so she knew the hen couldn't fly out.

She put her hands over her heart. "Oh my Lord," she moaned, and stood up. She went to the back door and looked out at the chicken pen. "He musta stole my hen. I cain't b'lieve even Horace could stoop *that* low. He knew how much I counted on them eggs, an' he knew how much I loved my hens." However, as she thought about it, she knew he would. She admitted to herself that he actually would.

At first she was hurt. Then she began to get angry. She whirled around and put her hands on her hips. "I quit," she muttered; then, her voice rising more and more, "Ever'thang jus' keeps gittin' worser an' worser. Thangs've been bad fer a long time, but this is jus' crazy now. He done a good job a makin' it easy fer me ta leave. I cain't stay here no more! This is jus' crazy, him stealin' our food. I quit, I quit, I quit!"

She walked into the bedroom. "I'm gon' do it," she ranted. "I'm gon' leave 'im an' quit my job an' go live in Francis' house an' work in his store. That's what I'm gon' do. I don't care who likes it an' who don't. I cain't do this no more, nohow. It's about time, dad gummit! An' I'm gon' do it!"

She went back to the table and looked at the box. "An' I ain't tellin' Horace 'bout it till the day I leave. The day I leave. But when will I leave?" she wondered. "It's got ta be soon 'cause I cain't stand this no more. An' I gotta call Francis an' tell 'im, an' I'll need ta have some money. I ain't got a penny ta my name, so I better work the rest a this week. That way I'll have a full week's pay, an' I'll have my last check the next week. That's it," she said, nodding her head. "I'll quit on Saturd'y, an' go work fer Francis. I can stand ta stay here fer five more days, an' that'll give me plenty a time ta git ever'thang ready."

Feeling energized after her decision, she put the rest of the food away. She was thinking about how much of it she'd leave for Horace and decided she'd leave most of it, remembering that she'd get paid on Friday.

"An' when I git paid, I'll pay fer one more week a rent fer Horace, an' then he'll be on his own. If he's got any sense, he'll git hisse'f a job right away. I ain't payin' fer no more food an' no more 'lectricity. They can turn it off fer all I care. If he's too sorry ta work, he can sit in the dark."

Hattie put the empty box under the sink, knowing that she'd want a few boxes to pack her stuff in. As she did so, she thought about how she'd manage to call Francis. Her phone had been turned off for months because Horace had called his brother in Miami several times, and she didn't have enough money to pay the long distance charges and pay the electric bill, so she hadn't paid the phone company yet. Besides, Horace was the main one who used the telephone, so she figured he should make some money and pay off the bill if he wanted a phone. "Maybe Mr. Simmons will let me use the phone at work," she thought. And her mind went back to the borrowed quarter and her imaginings returned to haunt her again. "Oh, I hope Anna didn' see me take that quarter outta my pocket."

She decided to make macaroni and cheese for supper, and open a can of green beans to go with it. Her macaroni and cheese was simple; she cooked the macaroni and added a little milk and butter, and then cheese. When the cheese melted, it was done. As the macaroni cooked, she warmed the green beans and boiled some tea leaves, strained the tea into a pitcher, added some water from the tap, and then stirred in sugar until the tea was syrupy sweet the way her mother taught her to make it. "This pitcher wuz Mama's," she thought. "I'll be shore ta take it wi' me."

When she was almost through eating supper, Horace arrived. Hattie looked at the floor as he tracked dirt through the kitchen and into the bedroom. He took off his shoes and socks and went back into the kitchen barefoot to get his supper. "There's dirt on this floor," he complained.

"There is *now*," Hattie pointed out. "You jus' brung it in."

She got up and fixed him a plate with the remaining food. He sat down opposite her. "Why ain't you made no coffee?" he growled.

For the first time since he'd arrived, Hattie looked at him. He was shoveling food into his mouth and wasn't even looking at her. "I shore won't miss this," she thought as she silently fixed him a glass of iced tea. Hattie preferred iced tea with her meals, but Horace usually wanted coffee for supper. "I ain't fixin' ta make him no coffee tonight!" she thought, although she almost always made what he wanted. "No sir-eee, Bob!"

She'd decided to wait until he was done to ask him about the missing cans of food, but she was feeling too aggravated to wait. She sat back down and ate the last couple of bites of her supper. Then she asked, "Horace, what happened ta the bananas an' carrots an' the cans a food that Francis brought?"

"Oh Francis, Francis, Mister Francis. Ain't he jus' so wonderful!" he whined.

"What happened ta the food?" Hattie persisted.

"I figger half of it's mine, so what I do with it's my business!"

"Half of it's yores ta eat, Horace. Ta eat! Not ta take." She came as close to yelling at him as she ever had. "Now, we only got half as much fer both a us ta eat."

"We got food in the cabinet," he said, looking at her with contempt.

"Thanks ta Francis," she said.

"You better watch yore mouth, woman," he threatened.

Hattie knew he was getting mad when he called her "woman." Normally, she would have dropped the topic then, but with her decision to leave him, she was feeling more confident. She still went on, but instead of asking any more questions, she decided to ask for money. She figured if he'd sold the food, he should have some money.

"I need fifty cents ta buy gas," she said simply.

"Well, I ain't no money tree," he replied.

Hattie felt like laughing, but the urge to cry was just as strong. She fixed another glass of iced tea for herself and sat back down and watched him eat. She waited for him to finish his supper before asking, "What happened ta the quarter that wuz on the bed this mornin'?" She wanted to ask him where he got it and what he'd done to get it.

"What quarter?" he asked suspiciously.

Hattie could tell by the way he looked that he was serious. She wondered how he could have had that quarter that had obviously fallen out of his pocket, and not even know it. And, if he hadn't taken it off the bed, it had to still be in the room. So how had she missed it?

She knew she needed to pretend that she wasn't sure she'd seen a quarter. Since he thought she was stupid, that wasn't very hard. "Well, I saw sumpin on the bed. It musta been sumpin else."

Horace looked at her suspiciously. Then, he got up and went into the bedroom and Hattie followed him. She watched with dread as he turned back the sheet and looked around a little, but when he didn't see it, he looked at her and said, "You crazy, woman." Then he went back in the kitchen, poured himself more tea, and sat down at the table.

As she looked around a little more, she saw the dirt he'd tracked in. "It's gon' be so wonderful not ta have him aroun'," she thought. She took his shoes outside, knocked them together a few times, and left them on the porch. "I'm leavin' them dirty shoes on the porch," she announced.

Then she took the broom into the bedroom. As she swept, she caught a glint of something shiny on the floor near Horace's side of the bed. She got down on her knees and stared at the pine floorboards. She was about to give up and could not believe her eyes when she saw the barely visible quarter. It was wedged between two boards so that only the ridge was showing. "No wonder I didn' see it," she thought. "Thank you fer trackin' the dirt in, you ole goat. I guess it happened fer a good reason."

She knew she'd need something to pry it out with, probably a knife. Since both the knives and Horace were in the kitchen, she decided she'd wait until he went to the outhouse. If she tried to get it now and he walked in, he might take it away from her.

She decided not to say anything else about the missing food, knowing that his temper could erupt at any minute, and she'd be in trouble. But now, she felt happy. She finished sweeping the bedroom and then she swept the kitchen. Horace had gone into the living room and was listening to a country station on the radio.

As she washed the dishes, the mellow tones of Eddie Arnold singing and yodeling drifted in. Hattie dreamed about how things would be when she moved into Francis' little yellow house.

When she dried the dishes and put them away, she made a mental note of which dishes she'd take with her and that was almost all of them. Four pieces had belonged to Horace's mother. The rest had either belonged to her mother or Hattie had bought them. She'd leave his mother's dishes, the cup and saucer he always used, and the plate that he was responsible for chipping; one day he was mad and pushed her against the sink and that plate fell into the sink, and a chip came out. She didn't want it around reminding her of him.

Satisfied that she'd done all she could with the dishes, she decided to go to the outhouse since it wasn't quite dark. When she got back, she walked around the house to the front yard and spent a few minutes looking at and talking to her flowers. She went in the house just as Horace was coming in the back door. "He went ta the outhouse while I wuz in the front yard," she thought, disappointed, "an' I didn' get the quarter. Now, I'll hafta wait till mornin' an' get it while he's sleepin'."

Too tired to get ready for bed, she sat down on the couch in the living room and turned the radio dial to a station from Del Rio, Texas that played religious music. She found it soothing. Horace had gone in the bedroom and she was hoping he'd be asleep by the time she went to bed.

After a little while, she went on the back porch and brushed her teeth. She heard some crickets chirping, sat down on the steps, and stayed out there for a few minutes, just listening to them and the other night sounds.

Horace was in bed when she tiptoed into the bedroom and started changing her clothes. As she wound the alarm clock, he said, "Don't bother puttin' that gown on."

"Oh Lord, I jus' knew he was asleep," she thought as she lay down on the bed. "Please let this be the last time." She believed that the man was the head of the house—even if he didn't act like it—and if he wanted sex, unless she was sick, it was her duty. "I oughta tell 'im I'm leavin' 'im," she thought. "Maybe he wouldn' want to do it. But he prob'ly wouldn' care, knowin' him, an' then he'd know. Oh my! That'd complicate my life."

Hattie thought about how things were when they were first married. When Horace had looked at her with hunger in his eyes, she knew part of that was because of her; now when it happened, it was all about sex.

As Horace satisfied himself, Hattie thought about Ray, the nice man who helped push her car in the rain, took her to get gas, put it in the car, and warned her about the tire. Lying there under Horace, smelling his body odor and feeling his gruffness, she realized that she felt more warmth thinking about a stranger than she did from what Horace was doing.

Tuesday

Hattie woke to the sound of a blue jay screeching a half hour before she had to get up. "Dad-blamed ole blue bird!" she thought, wishing she could have slept longer. But there was no going back to sleep for her; she was already thinking about the quarter that was hidden so well in the floorboards. She figured she probably couldn't get it without making some noise that would wake Horace up, so she'd have to be completely ready to leave the house before she got it. Then she could get out the door before he realized what was happening.

She lay in bed for a little while, and then turned off the alarm ten minutes before it was due to ring. She went to the hole-in-the-wall closet and took down her "Tuesday dress" and the slip that was hanging on the nail. She quietly put them on the bed. Then she pulled off her gown and put on her brassiere. She'd washed herself the night before, as she always did after Horace used her for sex, and put on a clean pair of panties; she left those on and sprinkled some baby powder in them. Then she put on her stockings and garters, the slip, and the dress.

After she slipped on her old sandals and combed her hair, she took the slop jar past the chicken pen to the outhouse. She found it easier to look at the pen now because she knew she'd be able to have chickens again after she moved to Francis' cute little house. A blue jay sat on the far side of the fence and Hattie was surprised that it didn't fly as she passed by. "Are you the one that woke me up?" she asked. "You better move somewhere else, Mr. Bird, 'cause if you start wakin' Horace up, he'll be borryin' Darrell's shotgun." After she passed, she heard its screeching call again. "Don't say I didn' warn ya," she said, and smiled.

As she stepped into the outhouse, she felt a spider web on her face. She took a step back, brushed the web off her face, and used her hand to take down the rest of the web. "Sorry, spider," she said to a small gray spider on the wall, "but ole Hattie's gotta come in here an' you cain't have no web across the doorway."

When she went back to the house, the blue jay was no longer around. "Guess ya tuk my advice," she said, looking at the fence where it had been. "If yo're smart, you'll stay clear a Horace. That's what I plan ta do." She rinsed the slop jar, put it on the bottom step to dry, and rinsed her hands.

Since she was up a little early, Hattie took time to cook some grits for breakfast. She liked to have grits, but often just had an egg and the toast she made in the frying pan, since that was faster. Occasionally, she'd buy some cereal, but Horace didn't want cold cereal for breakfast, so she didn't buy it often. Sometimes though, they'd eat some before they went to bed.

She put some water and coffee in the coffee pot to boil, and she put the grits on. While they cooked, she went to the kitchen sink, took the washcloth off the nail beside it, wet it in the cold water, and washed her face and arms. Then she put the cloth down and stirred the grits. She went back to the sink, unbuttoned the front of her dress, and wiped under each arm before rinsing the cloth and hanging it back on the nail. She stirred the grits again, then took the deodorant from the top of the refrigerator and put some under each arm.

"That coffee's smellin' good," Hattie thought as she washed her hands and breathed in the aroma. "There ain't much that smells better'n coffee perkin'."

When Hattie took an egg from the refrigerator, she noticed there were six eggs left; if Horace didn't eat one for breakfast and if she didn't take any more to work, they could each have one for the next three days. She'd get paid on Friday, and she could buy eggs if she decided to leave some for Horace.

She quickly fried an egg and put it and some grits on her plate. After she put butter on the grits, she sat down to eat. Looking appreciatively at the jar of zinnias on the table, she thought, "I'm gon' have plenty of zinnias, an' other flow'rs, too. Maybe I'll git me some a them dinner plate dahlias like Grandma useta grow. But 'fore I do that, I hafta git outta here."

Hattie thought about how she was going to leave Horace. She decided that she had to make sure he didn't find out she was leaving; that would certainly save her a lot of trouble. She didn't think Horace cared about her, but she knew he cared about not having to work, and he wouldn't want her to leave. Also, it would hurt his pride for her to leave him. She knew that he'd want to be the one who left—not that he *would* leave. Of course, he'd tell everybody that he kicked her out, and she didn't care. She didn't care who he told or what he told them. Her freedom was all that mattered to her now. She looked forward to making a new life for herself, by herself.

She'd work the rest of the week so she'd have some money, and if it was all right with Francis, move Saturday after work, and start working at his store the next week. She knew she'd have to get her things organized and ready to pack quickly after work on Saturday, not that she had many things, but she did have some of her mother's dishes and a few other things she wanted to keep. She intended to take the couch and chair in the living room, both of which had belonged to her mother, although they weren't sentimental. "I don't want that ole kitchen table from the second-hand store. "I'll take the dresser an' maybe the bed," she thought. "But then Horace won't have nothin' to sleep on. Well, I'll decide. And, a course, I'll take the swing Francis give me. I hope that porch is wide enough fer it."

She remembered that she had to call Francis to tell him that she was accepting his offer to live in the little house and to work in his store. Also, she needed him to pick her up at the house on Saturday with her things. She hoped they could take everything in his truck with only one trip.

Hattie decided that she'd definitely wait until Saturday after work to tell Horace. He wouldn't make a fuss with Francis there. Of course, there was a possibility that he'd be off with Darrell. "It wouldn' be right ta jus' leave 'im a note," she thought. "If he ain't home, I'll hafta wait fer 'im, or leave an' come back later. But if he comes home an' the furniture's gone, he'll be madder'n a wet settin' hen. Well, I just hope he'll be home. If he ain't, I guess I'll hafta git Francis ta come back wi' me. A course," she realized, "he'll hafta brang me, if I leave the car."

Horace had bought the car and fixed it up, and although Hattie drove it much more than Horace, she considered it his and planned to leave it for him. She wondered, knowing him well, if it would soon become his home, or if he'd get a job.

When she finished eating, she washed her dishes in the cold tap water. Then she opened a can of tuna fish and made a sandwich to take to work. She put the rest of the tuna in the refrigerator for Horace and took out the iced tea that was left from Monday night's supper. She filled her thermos and put the rest back. Then she wrapped the sandwich in waxed paper and put it in her pocketbook.

After she brushed her teeth, she stood for a minute and went over details to be sure she was completely ready for work before going to get the quarter. "All right," she thought. She placed her pocketbook and her thermos on the kitchen table where she could grab them on her way out. Satisfied that she was ready, she took a dull knife from a drawer by the sink and tiptoed into the bedroom.

Horace was still sound asleep. "Good," Hattie thought, listening to his steady breathing. She tiptoed to the dresser and quickly put on some lipstick. Then she put on her good sandals, tiptoed to where the quarter was, and squatted down facing the bed so she could keep an eye on Horace. She quietly slid the knife blade behind the quarter and tried to get it a little under it, but the quarter did not move. She tried a few more times, but the knife wouldn't go under the quarter enough to move it. Finally, she decided she'd have to try the side closer to the bed. There seemed to be a little more space on that side.

She got up and moved so that her back was to Horace. She looked at him to be sure that he was still asleep. After she squatted down, she listened to his steady breathing as she pushed the blade under the quarter and lifted. To her amazement, it went flying a couple of feet into the air, spinning around. It landed with a clunk and rolled a few feet toward the door. "Uh-oh," she thought when she heard the noise it made. "Thank God it didn' go under the bed." She stood up, moved quickly to where the quarter landed, and glanced at Horace.

He was sitting up in bed, glaring at her. "What in the worl' . . . ?"

Hattie didn't give him time to think. She grabbed the quarter off the floor, put it in her pocket as she hurried into the kitchen, jerked her pocketbook and thermos off the kitchen table, and ran out of the house, letting the screen door slam behind her, something she never did.

The car was always left unlocked with the key in the ignition, so Hattie had it started by the time Horace got out the back door, letting the screen door slam behind him, something he *always* did. What *was* unusual though, even for him, was that he ran out in his underwear—no shirt or pants, just his old boxer shorts. "Hattie, you git on back here now!" he yelled. "Git back here, woman!"

Hattie, her heart beating furiously, already had the car in reverse and she quickly backed out of the driveway. As she stopped to put the car in first gear, Horace was running down the driveway toward her. She was afraid he'd catch the car and pull her out of it. But, as he neared the end of the driveway and she started driving away, he yelled, "Dammit," hobbled a couple of steps, and stopped.

She looked in the rearview mirror at Horace, who was bent over his foot, which was resting upside down on the other knee. "This is the first time I ever been glad fer sandspurs," she said, and smiled.

As she passed the Wuthertons' house, she saw Mr. Wutherton in the yard with a hose, watering their gardenia bush. He was looking at Horace.

When she reached the end of the dirt road, she looked in the mirror again. Horace was standing in the road in his boxers, and Mr. Wutherton was shaking his finger at him. She could tell that Mr. Wutherton was saying something and she saw him point at the house. Horace looked down at himself and started walking back up the driveway. Horace and Mr. Wutherton didn't like each other, but this time Horace couldn't say anything in his own defense.

Hattie laughed, but immediately began worrying about how she could go home that afternoon. There was no telling what Horace would do. "He's gon' still be mad," she thought. "I never guessed he'd git that mad. An' he'll be even madder 'cause Mr. Wutherton seen 'im makin' a fool outta hisse'f." She began to regret getting the quarter. "I coulda waited till this afternoon to git that quarter. I didn' even thank a that. I coulda waited till tomorrah ta give it ta Mr. Simmons. Horace prob'ly won't even be home this afternoon. Oh Lord! Now I got another mess ta deal with!"

♥   ♥   ♥

It was a slow morning in the store. Still, it was eleven o'clock before Hattie asked Anna to watch her counter, and went to Mr. Simmons' office. She dreaded going in there. She didn't think Mr. Simmons liked her any more than she liked him. She'd noticed the way he talked to the other clerks about ordinary things, but seldom said anything to her, and when he did, it was about business. She knocked tentatively on the door, but there was no response.

"I thank I'll go pee," Hattie thought, putting off what she dreaded doing. "I hate havin' ta ask him fer anythang."

In the bathroom, Hattie looked around. "I'm gon' have a real bathroom soon. Jus' like other people. Oh boy! That's gon' be so wonderful. Not to mention, I won't hafta work here no more."

Feeling a little more positive, she knocked again on Mr. Simmons' door, this time a little harder. And this time he said, "Come in."

He was sitting at his desk, with a pencil behind his ear, seriously poring over some papers. Hattie noticed the black and gold fountain pen and mechanical pencil set in a matching holder on his desk. That set was the only thing she liked in his office—in fact, she coveted it. She tried not to breathe because the air was heavy with the smell of smoke. A lit cigarette burned in the dirty ashtray on his desk. He looked at her, and she thought he looked disappointed to see her. "I found this on the floor, Mr. Simmons." She handed him the quarter. "I musta dropped it yestiddy."

"Uh-huh," he responded, nodding his head and taking the quarter. "You better be more careful, Hattie," he said sternly. He put it on his desk and looked back down at the papers while Hattie just stood there. After a moment, he looked back up at her. In an annoyed tone, he asked, "Was there somethin' else, Hattie?"

"Could I please use the telephone? I need ta make a call."

"You know I don't like people makin' personal calls durin' business hours," he grumbled, and frowned. "Whom do you need to call? Do you have an emergency?"

"I need ta call my brother," she said. "It's important." And she thought, "That's *whoooom* I need ta call."

"Well, I'm guessin' it'll wait until your lunch break. Come back then." He looked down at the papers on his desk.

Hattie turned and left the room. Feeling distracted and offended, she forgot to close the door.

"Shut the door, Hattie," he called in the same annoyed tone. "It was closed when you knocked."

She went back and gently closed the door even though she felt like slamming it. "I bet he woulda let Carolyn or Anna use the telephone," she thought. "He'll prob'ly be glad when I quit, but he won't be half as glad as I will, that's for shore. The ole buzzard! Now I gotta go back in that stinkin' office ag'in."

When Hattie got back to her counter, Anna was standing between her own counter, which had cloth, towels and dishcloths, and Hattie's counter. Anna told her she'd sold a clock while she was gone. "Is anything wrong, Hattie?" she asked.

Before Hattie thought, she said, "No, I jus' had ta give Mr. Simmons a quarter."

She realized what she'd said at the same time that Anna's face showed interest. "A quarter?" Anna asked.

The scene from the previous afternoon flashed into Hattie's mind. She could see herself taking the quarter from her pocket as Anna walked into the room. Suddenly, she saw an opportunity.

"I found a quarter on the floor yestiddy after I gave Mr. Simmons my cash an' I didn' feel like botherin' 'im with it then, so I jus' turned it in now."

Hattie thought, "That's a good explanation fer her if she wuz wonderin' 'bout it."

"Oh," Anna said. "Did he say anything to you about it?"

"No, he jus' tuk it," Hattie answered.

Anna turned and went back to her counter. She'd talked to her mother the previous evening about Hattie and the quarter. Her mother said, "Well, maybe it was *her* quarter."

Anna asked, "But why would she look so guilty, an' even scared, if it was hers?"

"Well, that's a good question, dear," her mother said, deep in thought. "Maybe you should speak to Mr. Simmons about it so he can keep an eye on her, just in case. You don't have to accuse her of stealing, or even suggest the possibility. Just tell him what happened—what you saw—and that Hattie looked startled an' frightened when she saw you."

And that morning, Anna had arrived a few minutes early and talked to Mr. Simmons. She noticed that he didn't seem surprised. He thanked her for telling him and said he'd keep an eye on Hattie and her receipts.

Anna thought he sounded kind of harsh when he said that, and she felt a need to protect Hattie a little. "I'm not sayin' she was stealin', Mr. Simmons. It jus' seemed kind of strange."

"Don't worry; I'll take care of it," he assured her.

She'd felt uncomfortable about Mr. Simmons' reaction, and now she felt guilty about telling him. Hattie said she found the quarter on the floor, so maybe she didn't take it, but she sure had looked guilty. But even if she did take it, she returned it. Maybe she needed it for something. Anna hoped she hadn't caused a problem for her.

As for Hattie, she felt relieved. She'd returned the quarter and told Anna she found it on the floor. That should take care of that. She didn't want Anna to think she stole it.

Hattie was busy the rest of the morning, so it went by rather quickly. Before she knew it, it was time for her lunch break, and she went straight to Mr. Simmons' office. This time, he had the door open. "Good," she thought. "Maybe some a that stinkin' smoke got outta there." Hattie thought he opened it when it was time for lunch so that he could see if anyone took too long. And she also suspected that he liked to watch the younger clerks, especially Anna, who was the most attractive. "He's always eyein' Anna," she thought.

Again, he reminded her that he did not approve of personal calls. "Don't you have a telephone at home?" he asked.

"No, sir," Hattie replied, without offering any excuses.

"Well, you ought to! Everybody has to use the telephone sometime. What if you had an emergency?"

Hattie just stood quietly and nodded her head. "Ever'body has ta use a pencil sometimes, too," she thought, "but we don't all walk aroun' with 'em stickin' behine our ears." She was not about to tell Mr. Simmons that she couldn't afford a phone because her husband called his brother in Miami a few times one month and they couldn't pay the phone bill, or that Horace spent too much of her hard-earned money on booze. Then she thought about the future and looked him straight in the eyes. "I'll be gittin' one soon," she said, and smiled.

"I should think so!" He replied. "It's the '50s; people have telephones in their houses."

"Yes, sir," she said. "Can I please use it now?"

"All right, but I hope this will be the last time."

Hattie thought, "I could already be through an' outta this stinkin' place if he jus' let me use it. I didn' need a sermon. You'd thank I wuz in here all the time askin' ta use the telephone."

The black, rotary-dial telephone was on Mr. Simmons desk. Hattie looked at him, hoping he'd leave, but he lit a cigarette and remained in his chair as she dialed the number, so she had no privacy. Francis' wife answered. "Hello, Susan," Hattie said. "This is Hattie. Is Francis there?"

"You jus' missed him, Hattie," Susan replied. "He went to pick up some produce."

"He jus' left?" Hattie asked, looking at Mr. Simmons, who picked up some papers from his desk and looked down at them.

"Just a minute ago. I heard the truck pulling out."

"Just a minute ago? Oh, I'm so sorry I missed 'im," she said. "I need ta talk to 'im. Do ya thank he could come by here later?"

"Not today," Susan said. "I know he'll be out the rest of the day, Hattie. He has a few things to do. By the way, he tol' me about your talk. Are you thinkin' about his offer?"

"Yes," Hattie said, being careful in front of Mr. Simmons.

"Oh, Hattie, I'm so glad! Francis will be so happy. Have you made up your mind?"

"Yes, I have."

"Is that what you need to talk to him about?"

"Yes, it is."

"Oh, Hattie! I know good an' well Francis will be thrilled!"

Hattie smiled. Now Mr. Simmons was watching her intently.

Susan continued, "I'll tell him as soon as he gits home. I know he'll want to talk to you, so why don't you call him tomorrah?"

"I cain't," Hattie said, looking at Mr. Simmons. "Mr. Simmons don't like me usin' the telephone. Please jus' tell 'im fer me, an' ask him ta come by here tomorrah."

As she hung up the phone, Mr. Simmons said, "You know how I feel about personal visits, Hattie."

Hattie looked him straight in the eye. "Well, if you hadn' spent so much time tellin' me how much you don't like personal telephone calls, I woulda caught my brother an' he wouldn' hafta come here tomorrah."

Mr. Simmons' jaw dropped and he looked at her in disbelief, and he watched her as she turned and left the room. He had never heard Hattie speak like that.

Hattie knew she'd lied because she'd planned to ask Francis to go to see her so they could talk; she couldn't say what she needed to with Mr. Simmons listening. And she knew she'd lied to Anna about the quarter. And even though she felt a little guilty about the lies, she felt proud that she'd said what she did to Mr. Simmons.

When Hattie entered the employees' room, Anna noticed that she was glowing, and wondered what was going on with her. Hattie didn't have much time left for lunch, so she went in there instead of going to the park, which she preferred. Anna's table was full, so Hattie sat with some women that she barely knew. As she looked around the room at the other women, who all seemed to be friends, she decided that she'd definitely eat by herself in the park for the rest of the week, unless it was raining.

Hattie was conscious of her clothes and financial situation, and so ashamed of Horace and embarrassed that she was married to him, that she hadn't made many friends. She expected people to judge her, and many did. She had a long relationship with Carolyn, but Anna was the only one at work that she really liked, and considered a friend.

She thought about what had happened with Mr. Simmons—how she'd stood up to him—and thought maybe she could stand up to Horace. Unfortunately, compared to Horace, Mr. Simmons was easy, especially now that she'd be leaving her job in a few days and felt that she had nothing to lose. She dreaded having to tell Horace she was leaving him; she had no idea how he'd react, but she knew how unpredictable he could be, and that scared her.

That was on her mind for much of the afternoon. Whenever she had no customers, she thought about how and when she'd tell him. She planned to tell him on Saturday, but she kept wondering if that was best, if it was fair to him.

She also thought about Francis and how he'd always been there for her, and how he'd encouraged her to leave Horace. Clearly, he'd seen right through Horace from the beginning. Hattie knew she hadn't wanted to see the truth. As she thought about Francis, she remembered how happy she'd been when he returned to Florida from their grandmother Springer's. Hattie's mood shifted a little and she smiled when she thought about what he'd told her about their grandmother when she was eighty-nine and getting a little senile.

Francis had taken her to town to visit her brother and his wife. Mrs. Springer lived in the country, and when she went to town, she always commented on how many cars there were. That day, she sat on the porch swing, watching the cars go by, while Francis was in the house talking to his great uncle. He heard Mrs. Springer yelling, so he went on the porch and asked her if there was something wrong.

"No, sir," she answered, "I'm advertising them cars when they go by."

"Well, don't do that, Grandma," Francis said. "I won't know when you need somethin'."

She thought for a moment and responded, "Well, who's gonna advertise them cars?"

Hattie smiled. "She was a mess, my grandma. I shore do miss 'er." She thought for a minute trying to remember sonething. "I know there was sumpin else Francis tol' me 'bout 'er." When she remembered, she almost laughed out loud.

Francis said they were eating dinner and her brother noticed that Mrs. Springer had a lot of food on her plate. Knowing she didn't normally eat very much, he said, "If you eat ever'thing on yore plate, I think it's gonna make you sick."

She looked at her plate, and at his plate, and again at her plate, and his plate. Then she replied, "Well, if what I got on *my* plate will make me *sick*, what you got on *yores* will *kill you*."

"She mighta been a little senile, but she still thought a funny thangs to say," Hattie thought. "A course, she prob'ly didn' thank it wuz funny."

Hattie was still deep in thought rearranging the earrings when she noticed a young Negro man standing off to the side looking at the necklaces. He had on a nice pair of dark gray slacks and a short-sleeve, nicely pressed, green shirt. Hattie thought Horace would look really nice in those clothes, especially the green shirt. Then she thought about the fact that Horace didn't even have any clothes that nice anymore. "It ain't fair," she thought, "It just ain't fair."

The young man glanced at Hattie, but immediately looked back at the necklaces. "Well, at least he don't look like a bum," she thought. "But how's he thank he's gon' see anythang standin' over there? Them people jus' cain't thank straight."

"Did ya wanna see sumpin?" she asked in a monotone.

"Yes, ma'am," he responded softly, moving closer to the counter. "Some a dem necklaces, please."

Hattie took the display case out. Still standing about three feet from the counter, the young man studied the jewelry for a moment.

"Hi much dat heart wit' di'mon's cost?" he asked.

"All them in this case is $2.99," Hattie answered.

All of a sudden, a little white girl and her mother walked over to the counter, and the little girl went right in front of the Negro man and stood staring at the necklaces. She picked up one necklace, but put it down and picked up the rhinestone heart. "I wont this one," she demanded, looking at her mother. "This one—the heart wi' diamonds."

"Of all the nerve!" Hattie thought. "What a little brat." "Excuse me," she said. "That boy wuz here before you an' he wuz lookin' at that necklace."

The little girl looked at the Negro man, and Hattie saw an angry frown on her face.

The young man just nodded his head and said, "Dat's awright—Ah'll come back. Thank ya, ma'am." And he left.

The mother pulled the girl away whining as Hattie watched the young man walk out of the store. "Why! I bet he ain't got a nickel to his name," she thought, disgusted. "So how come he made me take the necklaces out? How in tarnation does he thank he can buy one wi' no money? I jus' don't understan' them people."

Even though she'd lived just across the tracks from the Quarters in Georgia, she never had any communication with Negroes. Her father told her and Francis to stay away from them. "They all the same: sorry, ig'runt, an' no-count," he said. When Hattie was twelve, he told her, "A nigger man would jus' love ta git aholt a you, Hattie." She wondered what for, but she didn't dare ask; her father didn't particularly like questions.

He succeeded in scaring Hattie enough, though, that she avoided Negro men as much as possible. That was pretty easy, since their neighbors across the tracks were well aware of the lines that were not to be crossed. If a white girl didn't speak to a Negro man, he didn't speak to her. And, of course, he would just quickly glance at her. If he approached her on the sidewalk, he'd step off, tip his hat, and stare at the ground.

Her grandmother was also afraid of Negro men. She closed and locked all her windows, in summer as well as winter. She also closed the curtains even though she lived in the country, and her neighbors, all of whom were white, weren't close enough to see in. Hattie's mother was so concerned about her sleeping in that hot house that she got Hattie's father to install a small window at each end of the house up high, so that her mother could feel safe leaving them open and get a little bit of air on the hot nights. She had a pole to use for opening and closing them.

When Hattie asked her why she closed and locked the windows, she said, "You never know when there's a nigger out there in the woods lookin' in. An' if you don't lock the winders, he'll jus' come right in, an' you know what would happen then." Hattie didn't know, but it sounded so awful, she didn't dare ask. She looked at her eighty-year-old grandmother and wondered why *any* man would be waiting in the woods to get a peak at her.

Now, in the store, she was basically polite when she waited on Negro men, but she always felt a little uneasy and more alert. She studied the women carefully, and often they were better dressed than she was. She didn't think it was fair, and it always upset her. She thought, "I ain't even got no clothes like that, an' I'm white."

♥   ♥   ♥

As soon as Hattie opened the back door, she knew something was terribly wrong. There were grits scattered all over the kitchen floor and the empty grits bag was wadded up and lying under the edge of the table. The metal cabinet door was open and the cabinet was empty. She knew exactly what had been in there: enough tea leaves to make about four pitchers of tea, a little bit of coffee, three cans of soup, two cans of corn, two cans of beans, one can of fruit cocktail, about half a bag each of sugar and corn meal, half a box of elbow macaroni, a bag of dried black-eyed peas, about a fourth of a box of saltine crackers, a few slices of lightbread, and about a pound of grits left in the five-pound bag. Everything was gone except an almost-empty flour sack, and the grits. She *knew* where they were.

"Oh Lord," Hattie moaned. "Oh Lord, oh Lord. What in tarnation?" Her first thought was that Horace had done it. Then, for an instant, she thought someone else had gone in and stolen the food. But as she looked at the grits on the floor, she knew who did it. "What in tarnation did he do wi' my food?" She opened the refrigerator door and discovered that it was also empty. The only things left were the bottle they used for ice water, the mayonnaise jar, which had about a tablespoon of mayonnaise in it, and a broken egg lying on the bottom of the refrigerator in the front near the door. "I might be able ta eat that," she thought. "But if he dropped it a little further out, it woulda been on the floor."

"There wuz some pork chops, which I wuz gon' fry fer supper, a half a dozen eggs, some milk an' cheese, part of a can of evaporated milk, an' a stick an' a half a butter in here," Hattie moaned. "Oh Lord, oh Lord. This is jus' plum terrible. What am I gon' do fer food?"

"Maybe he didn' thank 'bout the freezer," she said. But when she opened it, she saw that the only things left in there were the two ice trays. "I had a chicken in here, an' two bags a strawberries Francis give me that I mashed an' sweetened an' froze so we could have a strawberry short cake some Sunday. I cain't b'lieve he'd take them strawberries I fixed."

Slowly, Hattie's feelings of fear, betrayal, and hurt turned to anger. "This is the stupidest thang you ever done, Horace," she said, "Takin' the food I bought wi' my hard-earned money, an' what my brother give me! An' you prob'ly thank you can jus' come back here now, an' go on like nothin' happened, but you got another thank comin', Mister!"

Her heart still racing, Hattie went on the front porch, sat in the swing, and looked at her flowers. She'd hoped that Horace wouldn't be home, and she could, at least, eat in peace. She knew there would be no peace if he were home. Now he wasn't home, but she didn't feel peaceful; he took the food and made a mess on the floor, and she had almost nothing to eat. And she was hungry.

"Okay Hattie," she said, taking a deep breath. "You gone hungry before, but I don't know if you can make it three whole days wi' no food. Right now, I don't even know if you can make it through tonight. What wuz he thankin', anyhow? Does he plan on comin' home wi' no food in the house?"

She thought for a minute. "A course not! There ain't no food here. He's gon' stay at Darrell's till Friday when I git paid. Then, he'll prob'ly come strollin' in here like nothin' even happened. Well, I hope he does stay down there. I might go hungry, but at least I'll have some peace." However, although she knew that her thinking made perfect sense, the knots in her stomach told her she was afraid he'd suddenly appear and she'd have to deal with him.

After a few minutes, she went back inside and looked around the kitchen. She noticed that Horace had left the almost-empty lard can on the counter by the stove, but the box of salt—which was at least half full—was gone. "Crazy ole buzzard! He must really be mad. It weren't nothin' but a quarter.

All that food he tuk's worth a lot more 'an a quarter." Hattie rubbed the back of her neck as tears trickled down her face. She could tell she'd have a headache soon.

She opened the cabinet door to see if he took the dishes. They were still there, as was the saltshaker, which was almost full, and the half-full sugar dish. "Aha," she said, "he forgot about the saltshaker." Also, much to her relief, the box of matches was still there. "He wuz prob'ly too lazy ta open the cabinet door."

Hattie got the aspirin tin from her purse, took a glass from the cabinet and went to the sink to get some water. "Thank God Anna give me them aspirin yestiddy, or I wouldn' have nothin' fer a headache."

The can of evaporated milk, which had been half full, was turned upside down over the sink drain. "Mean ole buzzard," she said. "Mean, mean ole buzzard." As she picked up the empty can, she noticed the remainder of the saltine crackers lay in a corner of the sink. They'd been dumped into the sink and crushed. Fortunately, they were dry. She swallowed an aspirin, and took a plate from the cabinet and carefully brushed the crumbs onto it. "How come he did that?" she asked. "He musta dropped 'em with sumpin heavy on top a 'em, an' wuz too lazy ta clean 'em up. Musta thought I wouldn' eat 'em or he wouldn' a left 'em. But, by golly, they shore look like food ta me. Thank ya, Lord."

After she cleaned up the crackers and rinsed the sink, she looked underneath it. The empty cardboard box she'd saved to use for packing was gone. "Guess he used that box to steal my food," she mumbled. "I'll hafta remember ta ask Francis ta brang some boxes on Saturd'y."

Hattie saw something under the sink. "Aha!" she said, smiling. "He didn' thank about my bottle a cane syrup!" The syrup bottle, which was too tall to fit in the cabinet, was next to the wall and didn't show up very well in the dim light under the sink. She chuckled. "He'd hafta bend way over to see it, an' he's too lazy fer that."

Hattie filled the glass almost full with water. She poured some syrup into the glass, took a spoon from the drawer, and stirred the syrup around until it was dissolved in the water. Then she took a long swig. "Ummm," she cooed. "I ain't had water an' syrup in a long time. I ain't got no bread ta put syrup on, but I can put it in my water. I wish I had some clabber ta put some in. I could make a meal outta that." She remembered how she and her mother used to have it. They'd get milk from her mother's brother, who had a milk cow, leave it out of the refrigerator for a few days so it would turn into clabber, put syrup in it, stir it around, and drink it.

Francis said it was disgusting. Neither he nor their father liked it, but she and her mother did.

The consistency of clabber was similar to yogurt. With syrup stirred in it, clabber resembled cottage cheese, but it was soft, like soft jello. Besides drinking it with syrup, they used it in place of buttermilk in biscuits.

Hattie looked at the crumbs sitting on the counter. "I can put some syrup in some a them cracker crumbs, too. An' I can put some mayonnaise in some. An' I can git most a them grits off the floor; most a 'em are in a pile. Anyhow, I swept this floor last night after Horace tracked in all that dirt. Wonder where he was at ta git his shoes so dirty. Lots a people would be happy ta have this much food. I jus' hafta thank how ta make it last till Saturd'y."

With her spirits lifted a little, she decided to change her clothes as she did every day after work. "'Fore I do anythang else," she thought, "I hafta hide this syrup in case Horace comes in. It'll prob'ly be okay under the sink till I thank of a better place." She put it away and put her unfinished glass in the refrigerator, thinking he wouldn't bother to look in there.

"I better hide them cracker crumbs, too. I can put 'em in a bag," she thought. Hattie had saved some paper bags, which she kept in a dresser drawer to keep Horace from throwing them out. She took the crumbs into the bedroom.

As she entered the room, she worried about what she might find. But Horace hadn't done anything to the bedroom; it was as untidy as he normally left it, but no worse. Hattie put the crumbs in the bag and put the bag in a dresser drawer. She didn't think Horace would even think about looking in her underwear drawer, but she carefully covered it with a slip. Then she quickly changed into her old faded everyday dress and took another bag to the kitchen.

Hattie took her dustpan, washed it in the kitchen sink, and dried it with a piece of an old sheet. Then she took up as many grits as she could that were in the pile and not touching the floor. She put them in a bowl. "I thank that's enough ta last all week," she thought. "But I'll take up the rest, in case I need 'em." She got the broom, carefully swept the rest into a pile, and swept them into the dustpan.

She got her pencil and made an X on the bag she put them in, so she was sure she wouldn't get them mixed up with the good grits. "An' I need ta put this in a diff'runt place," she muttered. She stood on a chair and put them in the back of the highest shelf, behind a bowl. "Horace is too lazy to get a chair and look up there."

She decided that she'd make some grits for her supper, and she'd rescue as much of the broken egg as possible. She took out about a quarter of a cup of grits from the bowl and then got a paper bag from her drawer. She put the rest of the grits from the bowl in the bag and put them in her underwear drawer next to the cracker crumbs. "At least I know I'll have me some grits ta eat, even if I ain't got nothin' ta go with 'em, an' they don't taste very good. At least I know I'll have some food, sech as it is. An' tonight, I might even have some egg."

Actually, she was able to salvage most of the egg, which she scrambled in some of the lard Horace had left, probably thinking there wasn't enough to bother taking and she wouldn't use it, with no food. Since the saltshaker was still there, she was able to salt the grits and the egg. As the egg cooked, the smell wafted up to Hattie. "Oh, my mouth's a waterin'," she said. "Thank you fer this food, God. I didn' thank I had any, an' now look at this. A scrambled egg an' grits. Plus I got more grits an' cracker crumbs an' syrup. I might not git full, or have what I'd like ta have, but at least I won't go hungry."

When she sat down at the table, she touched the petals on one of the red zinnias in the bouquet. "An' thank you fer my flow'rs," she said. "I'm gon' have lots a flow'rs when I move, an' nobody ta complain 'bout me spendin' time workin' in my own yard."

She stirred the scrambled egg into the grits to give them more flavor. With the food and her water and syrup, she was pleased with her supper. "I ain't had ta go hungry fer a long time," she said. "I oughta be more thankful fer all the food I use'ly have. An' after this, I will be."

As Hattie cleaned up the kitchen and put everything away so that Horace wouldn't be able to tell that she'd cooked and eaten, she thought about the early years of her marriage. Horace had discouraged her from getting a job. "I'm the head a the house, an' I'm s'posed to make the livin'," he declared. "You cook an' wash clothes, an' clean the house."

That had suited Hattie just fine until Horace lost his job and they had no income and no food. Horace told Hattie to get some money from her family. Francis had just got married and just bought the store, and he was sending money to their mother in Georgia every month, so Hattie knew he needed all he had. So the only person she could ask was her cousin Sophie. She and J. B. were married, had one child, and she was pregnant. "I cain't give you much, Hattie," Sophie told her. "Babies cost a lot."

"I'll pay you back," Hattie had promised. "I'm lookin' fer a job an' Horace is, too, an' I'll pay you back."

The money Sophie loaned her was gone long before Hattie landed a job as a waitress. Horace's father had died, and he borrowed a little money from his mother, but during the two-month period before they got evicted from their apartment and moved in with her, they often ran out of food. Hattie knew what it was like to be hungry.

With her supper dishes put away, she looked around the kitchen to see how much she would have to pack. "I won't hafta worry 'bout what food ta take wi' me, thanks ta you, Horace, you ole buzzard," she thought. "I wuz gon' buy some rice after I git paid on Friday an' make some dried black-eyed peas an' rice an' corn bread fer ya. That woulda lasted you a few days, ya know. Now, I don't care if ya starve ta death. That's what you'd let me do. Yo're jus' plain heartless!"

Hattie placed some of the things she wanted on a shelf together. She realized she was whistling and knew it had been a long time since she'd whistled. "I must be happy," she laughed. "I ain't got no food, but jus' knowin' I'm leavin' here's makin' me happy." She found an old napkin in the cabinet and threw it in the trash.

Suddenly, she thought, "If he comes here, he's prob'ly gon' look in the trash fer them grits an' cracker crumbs. I better burn this trash so he won't know I kep' 'em. She took the trash out back and burned it in their usual spot, standing nearby to monitor the fire. She loved watching the rising red sparks drift in the air until they blackened.

The sun was low on the horizon when she finished burning the trash, and went to the outhouse. She smiled as she heard the birds singing. "The birds don't have problems like we do," she said. "A course, they do hafta git their food ever' single day, an' we do, too. An' I feel sorry fer the birds if they have as much trouble findin' food as I'm havin' right now."

When she got back to the house, she took the slop jar into the bedroom and put it under the bed. Then she went to the front yard to check on the crape myrtle blooms. They were still tightly closed, so she couldn't tell what color they were. Again, she told them how much she loved white crape myrtles. After she admired the row of colorful zinnias, she moved to the hibiscus at the edge of the porch and admired them, especially the white ones, feeling truly grateful for all of her flowers.

She went on the porch and sat in the swing, listening to and watching some sparrows sitting in a row on the electric line across the dirt road. She watched the Wuthertons coming down the road on their afternoon walk. They waved at her and stopped.

"Hey, Hattie. Nice evenin'," Mrs. Wutherton said.

"Yes, ma'am, it is. A nice evenin' ta sit on the porch," Hattie responded. "Y'all are walkin' late today."

"Yeah. We had to go visit my brother in the ole folks' home," Mrs. Wutherton replied.

"Are you doin' all right, Hattie?" Mr. Wutherton asked.

Hattie knew he asked that because of what had happened that morning. She was embarrassed that he'd witnessed the shameful thing. "Yes, sir, I'm fine," she reassured him.

She wanted to say, "I'm fine. I ain't got no food, but I ain't got no Horace, either. An' that ain't a bad trade."

"Well, you take care a yoreself now," he said solicitously.

Hattie thought he probably wanted to ask her about what had happened—why Horace was acting like an escapee from Chattahoochee—and she was grateful that he hadn't mentioned the morning's events. She knew it was bad enough that she put up with Horace's treatment of her, but she could barely endure the shame of some of it having been played out in front of Mr. Wutherton.

As they walked away, Hattie swallowed and breathed a sigh of relief. And she remained there, in the swing, slowly moving back and forth, back and forth, back and forth, until the sun had set, the stars were shining, and the birds were no longer singing.

Wednesday

THE LITTLE HAND WAS ON ONE WHEN HATTIE WOKE UP. With the moon full only a few days earlier, the room was bright enough for her to see the clock well, but her tired body had already let her know that she hadn't been asleep long. When her head had hit the pillow, her anger had dissolved into hurt. "How could ya do this, Horace?" she'd asked, weeping. "If you hate me so much, how come you don't jus' leave?" Of course, she knew the reason: Without her financial support, he'd have to get a job.

"If only I'd listened to what my own heart wuz tellin' me! I knowed good an' well I shouldn' marry him. Land sakes! He showed me from the very first date that he didn' even respect me." Hattie had wanted to have a family and was afraid she wouldn't ever get married if she didn't marry Horace, the only man who had asked her.

They got married just a few weeks before Francis returned to Florida. He'd stayed in Georgia with their grandmother until their mother was settled in and able to take care of her. Hattie often thought that if Francis had been around to get to know Horace, she probably wouldn't have married him. She trusted Francis, and he figured Horace out pretty fast after he met him.

At one o'clock, Hattie knew that he wasn't coming home. "Thank God," she thought. She'd lain awake many nights wondering where he was, worrying about what he might be doing, and hoping he wasn't with a woman. This time, she breathed a sigh of relief, got up and peed, and went back to bed.

Very often when Horace got angry about something, even if it had nothing to do with Hattie, he'd use it as an excuse to be gone for two or three days. She hoped this would be one of those three-day absences; that would take her to Friday.

She knew he went down to his brother's in Mulberry. Horace, Darrell, and his wife, Shirley, would often get drunk together and Horace would spend the night on their couch. Hattie had asked him if he drank before they were married, and he said he didn't. But right after they got married, they were down there, and the three of them started drinking beer. Hattie could tell it wasn't the first time. They tried to get her to join them, but she remembered her father's drunkenness, and she wouldn't touch alcohol.

Hattie knew Shirley well. She'd hoped to have a friendship with her, thinking Shirley could be the sister she'd always wanted, but Shirley was more interested in being with Horace and Darrell, especially when they were drinking. Hattie soon began to consider her and Darrell bad influences on Horace. And she found their drunken behavior so disgusting she wouldn't go there anymore. She begged Horace not to go to their house, and suggested that they could get together somewhere else, but he wouldn't listen to her.

Horace's drinking was the first thing that made her feel betrayed by him after they got married. She thought she was marrying a man who didn't drink, a man different from her father. The first time he arrived home with beer, she put her foot down. "No alcohol in the house, Horace," she said.

"It's jus' beer," he sneered.

"I don't care," she countered. "It's alcohol, an' I won't have alcohol in the house. You know how my daddy was."

"Yeah, I know how yore daddy was, but I ain't yore daddy. Anyhow, it's my house, too."

"I mean it, Horace."

"Well, here it is, in the house," he challenged, holding it in front of him. "What ya gon' do about it?"

"I'll pour it out," she said.

Horace laughed. "I b'lieve I'm bigger an' stronger 'an you are, woman."

Hattie looked him straight in the eye. "I'll leave!" she said. "I will not live in a house with alcohol in it."

He must have believed her because he left with the beer, and Hattie never saw any alcohol in the house, even after they started having more problems. If he took any in, he hid it well.

Like Hattie, Francis didn't drink; he was afraid he might develop a taste for it like his father had. And he'd get furious when he thought about Horace drinking. Hattie had been married several years before he found out that Horace drank. At first, he tried to get Hattie to leave him. He already had a low opinion of him, and the drinking made it worse.

One day, when Horace was not at home, Hattie and Francis were sitting at her kitchen table. "Daddy wuz always bad to drink," he said, "an' now you're married to a man jus' like 'im."

"He ain't jus' like 'im!" Hattie protested. "He don't hit me!"

"He don't hit you," Francis said sarcastically. "Well, I guess there ain't no problem then! Hattie, for God's sake. Daddy didn' always hit Mama, either; Mama said that started after a few years. Who knows what'll happen in the future?"

Hattie sat quietly feeling shame, and trying not to let him see it.

"An' he lives off you, anyway," he continued. "He ain't even workin'. Think about how much better off you'd be without 'im. He's throwin' money away at jook joints jus' like Daddy used to do. But, Good Lord, Hattie! At least Daddy worked for the money he wasted. Horace ain't even got a job, an' he ain't had one for over a year. An' it don't look to me like he's even lookin' for one. He don't even have enough pride to be ashamed of livin' off a woman. He's jus' plain sorry! If you'll leave 'im Hattie, I'll he'p you."

By the time Francis stopped talking, Hattie was crying, and seeing her tears cooled his anger. They just sat there for a while. When she stopped crying, he said, "You're like Mama, Hattie."

"Well, I thank that's good," she replied defensively. "She wuz a good 'umble woman."

"She was 'umble, an' that's good. But, she took too much! She believed what she wuz taught that the man is the head a the house, no matter what kinda man he is. An' we both know that ain't right."

Hattie didn't say anything.

Francis knew he'd said enough. He stood up and put his hand on her shoulder. "It jus' gits my goat," he said gently. "'Member, Hattie, the offer stands . . . any time, I'll he'p you." Francis never spoke of Horace that way again until Sunday, and then he'd held back, and been careful not to say what he really felt.

Through the years, Hattie thought about what he'd said that day. For a long time it made her angry, but recently she'd begun to acknowledge to herself that it was all true. Consequently, she began to doubt her judgment, and she felt ashamed and trapped. "I shoulda listened ta Francis back then," she thought. "I coulda saved myse'f a lot a heartache, an' had a better life. That's what he wuz tryin' ta he'p me do, bless his heart."

After a while, Hattie went back to sleep, and when she woke up again, it was half an hour before the alarm was set to go off. She looked at Horace's side of the bed just to make sure he hadn't come in while she was sleeping. She breathed a sigh of relief and said, "Today's Wednesday. Carolyn oughta be there today. I'm prob'ly gon' need more gas 'fore I git paid, but Lord, I hate ta ask that woman ta borry a quarter." She had just finished the sentence when she realized she could have kept the quarter she took from the cash register. "I coulda saved myse'f a lot a trouble by waitin' till Friday ta give it to Mr. Simmons. That wuz jus' stupid, Hattie! Stupid!" She sighed. "Oh well, no sense cryin' over spilt milk. What's done's done. A course, I wuz afraid a what Anna thought, an' that Mr. Simmons would notice a quarter wuz missin'."

She stood up and stretched, and realized she seldom did that when Horace was there. She pulled the long gown over her head and put on her housedress and old sandals. Since she didn't have to be afraid of waking Horace, she could relax about spending more time in the bedroom. "I feel free," she thought as she took the slop jar from under the bed. "I don't hafta tippy-toe aroun'."

Walking through the kitchen, she thought about her options for food and decided she'd have crackers and syrup for breakfast. "Or actually, cracker crumbs an' syrup," she grinned. "What a ridiculous situation ta be in! But I'm glad this happened 'cause it jus' proves I wuz right ta decide ta leave 'im. I don't thank I'm gon' regret it. I jus' cain't figure out why in tarnation I waited so long. He's been a mean ole cuss an' a pain in the neck fer a long time now."

As she passed the chicken pen, she lamented, "I really don't know how come I waited so long. I coulda saved my chickens. They'd still be scratchin' an' cluckin' aroun', an' cacklin' when they laid a egg." The blue jay was on the fence singing its shrill song, but Hattie didn't even notice.

While she was in the outhouse, she remembered the orange tree behind it. Surrounded by tall weeds, the neglected tree was on the Wuthertons' property, but they used the fruit from a tree in their yard, and they didn't use that one. Hattie and Horace ate the oranges, but she hadn't gotten any from it for a few weeks because they'd eaten most of them, and the rest were starting to dry up. She knew they'd be half dry by now, but the bottom half would probably still be juicy.

"Huh, reminds me of the picnic," Hattie thought. "That wuz the first time I ever had a orange like that." She took a deep breath. "Good gracious! I don't wont ta thank about that picnic."

Two black birds flew from the top of the tree when she got near it. "Sorry ta bother y'all," she said halfheartedly.

A few oranges were rotting on the ground, and Hattie could see little flies buzzing around and crawling on them. And she could smell the rotten odor, but she didn't mind the smell.

The tree was full of little green oranges, but Hattie only saw three ripe ones. "Three's enough," she mumbled.

A big black and yellow spider worked busily on a web that stretched between two limbs, and was near the orange Hattie planned to pick. The orange was low enough that she could reach it by standing on her tiptoes. She stood still and studied the spider for a moment, then shuddered as she went near it, and hurriedly picked the orange.

The other two were higher in the tree and she'd have to stand on a limb to reach them. She only picked one because she wanted to be sure that, if Horace came home, he wouldn't eat them, or know that she had any food. "Thanks ta you, Horace, I know 'bout oranges like this, but I ain't willin' ta share 'em wi' ya. Not now." Clutching her orange, Hattie watched the spider for a minute as it wove its intricate design. Fascinated, she decided that both the web and the spider were actually quite interesting.

On her way back to the house, she remembered that Francis was supposed to go to see her at the store that day. "I'll tell 'im I need ta git gas an' ask *him* fer a quarter. He'll prob'ly give me a dollar," she thought. "I don't care now if he knows Horace used all the gas, but I don't wont 'im ta know that he tuk all the food. He'd git really mad."

Hattie rinsed the slop jar and put it on the bottom step, and she rinsed her hands and the orange. Back in the kitchen, she saw a cockroach on the table. She knocked it off with her hand, and stepped on it. "I killed you," she said as she swept it out, "but I ain't botherin' ta put out no poison. Horace can do that if he wants to or he can let y'all take over the place. I ain't doin' it, an' he prob'ly won't, either."

She went to the bedroom and got the bag of grits, measured a serving, and put them with some water and salt in a pot, and lit two burners. "Might as well have some hot water an' syrup since I ain't got no coffee or tea," she said, putting some water on the burner.

She took the washcloth off the nail by the sink. She washed her face, rinsed the washcloth, wiped under each arm, and rinsed it again, "Today's Wednesday. I washed Monday night after Horace *made love* ta me." She laughed derisively. "I guess I'd better wash downstairs, too." She did, and she washed the washcloth and hung it on the nail. After she stirred the grits, she took the Mum from the top of the refrigerator, put some under each arm, and washed her hands.

The orange was as she had anticipated. After she peeled it, she cut the top half off, and ate the bottom half. It was not very juicy, but it was sweet and flavorful. "Good," she said, licking her lips.

She also liked the hot water and syrup. "Wonder how come I never tried it hot before. We always drunk it cold."

She took the cracker crumbs from her dresser drawer, poured about a third of them into a small bowl, and poured some syrup on top. "Thank God I still got this syrup," she said, stirring the mixture.

They were not as satisfactory as the hot water and syrup; the crumbs were too salty to be good with the syrup's sweet flavor, but Hattie didn't complain. Instead, she thought, "Well, I'm tryin' sumpin new, thanks ta Horace." But she wished she had a nice biscuit instead of the cracker crumbs. "I love biscuits and syrup."

The grits were not satisfactory, either. With nothing to put on them for flavor, they were bland. But she knew she needed to eat them; otherwise, she'd be hungry all day. And she was grateful for them. "Lots a people ain't got *nothin'* ta eat, Hattie," she said. She thought about asking the Wuthertons to loan her some butter. She dreaded it, but decided she'd do it that afternoon. The thought of eating bland grits for two more days made her willing to ask.

She'd put off thinking about what she'd take to work to eat. She knew she'd take syrup and water to drink, so she mixed some ice water and syrup in a glass and put it in her thermos. She took the syrup into the bedroom and put it on the floor in the back of the closet. Then she took her Tuesday dress and draped it over the bottle as though it had fallen, knowing that Horace wouldn't pick it up.

Finally facing the issue about what to take for lunch, she decided her only option was cracker crumbs and mayonnaise. "Better save some fer tomorrah, too," she thought. She put half of the crumbs into a small bowl, put half of the mayonnaise in, and stirred it. She put the spoon in her mouth and closed her eyes, slowly savoring the mayonnaise. Then she cleaned the spoon and put it away, covered the crumb mixture with waxed paper, took a paper bag from her drawer, and put the bowl and spoon in the bag, and declared, "Okay, that's my pathetic dinner."

When she went on the back porch to brush her teeth, the blue jay was on the fence again. This time, she was aware of his shrill call. "I hear ya, Mister Jay," she thought. "Prob'ly the whole neighborhood hears ya." She brushed her teeth and put the toothbrush away.

In the bedroom, she hid the remaining cracker crumbs in her drawer. "Not much left," she thought, and wondered how she could get more food without any money. "If I git money from Francis today, I can buy gas an' food. I'll prob'ly hafta put gas in the car tomorrah."

Hattie quickly dressed for work, wearing the appropriate dress for Wednesday, and her good sandals. "When I git a little money together, I'm gon' buy me some more dresses an' git shed a this un. I'm so tired a this dress." It was a tan, short-sleeved cotton dress, and it showed some wear. She put on the matching belt and looked in the mirror. "I'm gon' git me one of them sacks women are wearin'. They look real comf'table." She combed her hair and put on some lipstick. "An' I'm gon' buy another pair a shoes! From now on, I'm gon' have at least two pair a good shoes."

She looked around the room to make sure that no food was visible. "I can make the bed!" she thought. "I almost never git to make the bed in the mornin' 'cause Horace is always in it." She made it and covered it with her crocheted bedspread. "There, that looks right purty," she said as she surveyed the room. "It's nice not havin' Horace 'round in the mornin'." She laughed, "Or in the daytime, or at night, 'specially at night. No Horace is almost worth no food."

She'd started to leave the bedroom, but she stopped. "I betcha he'll come here today. He prob'ly wonts ta see if I had anythang ta eat." She took the remaining cracker crumbs and grits out of her drawer, and stuffed them into her pocketbook. Hattie laughed. "The crackers are already crumbs, so I don't hafta worry 'bout breakin' 'em."

Knowing that Horace might come home while she was at work, Hattie decided to dry the dishes and put them away so there would be no evidence of eating, instead of leaving them, as she normally did, to dry in the dish drain on the sink. Then she got some toilet paper from the bedroom, wrapped the orange peel in it, and sniffed it a couple of times before squeezing it into her pocketbook. "I'll throw that in the trash can in the park," she thought. "I don't wont Horace ta even know I had that ole orange. Let 'im thank I ain't got nothin' atall ta eat."

As she drove to work, she thought about her cousin Sophie and how close they'd been as teenagers. "Has she got three or four children? Her youngest girl, Carla, mus' be 'bout grown," she said. "Well, Sophie, as you know, thangs *didn'* turn out good fer me. An' it's my own fault; I never shoulda married Horace. I shoulda knowed better."

Sophie and J. B. got married right after she graduated from high school. They had Hattie and her mother over for supper a few times, and Hattie had them over. And they talked on the phone a lot. However, things cooled between them when Hattie married Horace. Sophie didn't forget what Hattie had told her about the picnic and she didn't want to be around him. And Hattie resented Sophie's attitude; she figured if she could forgive Horace, Sophie should be able to. The friendship dissolved after Horace started drinking a lot, and even J. B. began to see his darker side.

"All that's water under the bridge now," Hattie thought. "Sophie wuz right about him and I wuz stupid ta marry him. Maybe now we can be friends ag'in. Francis said she goes in his store an' she asks about me. I wonder what he tells her. Oh, an' I thank she goes to his church. Maybe I'll start goin' ta church ag'in. I wonder if I'd like it."

♥   ♥   ♥

Carolyn was at work when Hattie arrived. As Hattie straightened up her counters and put out some new jewelry, Carolyn told her that her aunt in north Florida had died on Saturday. She'd driven up on Sunday, gone to the funeral on Monday, and driven back on Tuesday.

"Oh," Hattie said, "I'm sorry."

"Thanks," Carolyn replied. "It wuz for the best. She wuz eighty-five an' sick. I thought she wuz gonna die a few years ago, but she hung on." Carolyn kept talking about her until Hattie interrupted her.

"Well, good gracious!" she exclaimed. "How come Mr. Simmons couldn' tell me that? I asked 'im how come you were out."

Carolyn smiled. "He was prob'ly jus' bein' cautious. Maybe he thought it was personal."

"Personal?" Hattie looked at Carolyn closely to see if she was serious. She was. "A funeral? Personal? People die all the time," she thought. "Use'ly you wont people ta know. Them two ain't right in the head."

"I don't know. Anyway, it's all over," Carolyn said in an aggravated tone, and she turned away from Hattie and went back to her counter, which had pocketbooks, change purses, wallets, key rings, and a few other things.

Hattie thought, "Well, it might be over fer you, but it ain't over fer me. No sir-eee, Bob! Jus' 'cause you say it's over don't make it over, Miss Priss Peabody! That Mr. Simmons is a ole buzzard, an' you ain't much better."

She wished she could say what she was thinking, but she didn't talk to people that way even if she did feel like it. And besides, she was well aware that if Francis couldn't go to see her, she'd have to ask Carolyn to loan her a quarter. When he didn't arrive by the lunch break, she started worrying. Of course, he didn't know that she needed money; she'd told him on Sunday that she was fine.

Hattie didn't tell anyone she was going to the park across the street to eat. Normally, if someone was going to the park, and others on the same lunch break found out, they'd go with them, but she wanted to be alone. She didn't want anyone to see what she had to eat.

She took the orange peel from her pocketbook and threw it in a trash can near the bench, which was under a big oak tree. Hattie liked to sit under the tree, and the bench faced away from the store, so she could forget about work for a little while. She looked up at the Spanish moss hanging over her head. "I love this ole tree," she thought. "I'm gon' miss it. I don't know why I ain't eat out here more."

Hattie heard children laughing and looked across the park and saw a woman and a little boy and girl. As the woman sat on a bench watching them, they chased each other around the bench, and then ran over to the fountain. They ran around it a couple of times before stopping to dip their hands in the water. "I always wonted ta have children," she thought, "but now I guess it's better that I didn' since I ain't gon' have no husband. 'Sides, Horace would be a awful daddy."

She poured some water and syrup into the thermos cup and took a big swallow. She had forgotten that it wasn't iced tea, and she was surprised by the taste. Somehow it didn't taste as good as it had the night before, probably because she'd expected tea.

Hattie's gaze followed the paved walkway and stopped at the statue of the Confederate soldier on the other side of the park. She liked the tall white base under the statue. "Both my grandpas an' one a my great-grandpas wuz in the War of Northern Aggression, as Mama called it," she thought.

She looked around the park at the flowers that were blooming. She enjoyed all the flowers, but she'd decided that the red roses were her favorites.

When she took the bag out of her pocketbook, the odor of the orange peel that had been in there wafted up, and she closed her eyes and breathed it in. She took the spoon and the bowl of cracker crumbs out of the bag, took the waxed paper off the bowl, carefully folded it, put it in the bag, and put the bag back in her pocketbook. She was hungry. "This ain't much of a dinner," she thought. "An' I ain't got nothin' fer supper but a half-dried orange an' some grits with nothin' ta put on 'em but salt. But anyhow, I do have some food ta eat. I should be thankful."

As she ate, Hattie watched a couple of squirrels on an oak tree in front of her. She also watched people passing by, people who sat on other benches in the park, and the children. When the woman with the children stood up and said something, the little girl started to cry. "That's the other part a havin' children," Hattie thought. "It ain't all playin' an' laughin'."

She was almost done with the crumbs when she heard a familiar voice. "Hattie, mind if I join you? I had to go to the shoe store to return a pair of shoes for my mother." Anna stood at the end of the bench. She'd noticed Hattie going to the park and thought it would be a nice day to eat outside. It was sunny, but a little breezy, and not too warm.

Hattie said, "No, please sit down." But she thought, "I declare! She's gon' see me eatin' cracker crumbs," and she tried, without being obvious, to hold the bowl so Anna couldn't see in it.

"What are you eatin'?" Anna asked. She'd seen what looked to her like cracker crumbs in the bowl.

"Oh, nothin' much," Hattie replied, hoping she wouldn't ask anything else. While Anna was taking out her sandwich, Hattie stuffed the last spoonful in her mouth.

"Would you like to share my sandwich?" Anna offered, holding out half of what looked like a delicious sandwich.

"Oh no," Hattie answered. "That's yore dinner."

"My mama always makes more than I need, Hattie. An' I'm not that hungry today, anyway."

Anna's mother knew how much Anna would eat and Anna had intended to eat it all that day, as she always did. But she could tell that whatever Hattie had in that bowl was not a good meal. Anna had a lot of questions she would've liked to ask, but she knew it would only embarrass Hattie and they'd both be uncomfortable.

"Well, thank you," Hattie said as she put the bowl and spoon on the other side of her out of Anna's line-of-sight, and gratefully accepted the sandwich. "This is delicious, Anna," she said after her first bite. "Tastes like pork roast."

Anna smiled. "It is. Mama made pork for supper last night." She wondered when Hattie had last had a pork roast for supper, and if she actually was eating cracker crumbs.

"Well, tell yore Mama it's good," Hattie said.

"I will, Hattie. She'll be glad you enjoyed it."

"Ain't them roses purty," Hattie said. "I think they're the purtiest flowers in the park."

"Me too," Anna responded. "They're such a pretty red."

The little bowl of crumbs and mayonnaise had hardly dented Hattie's appetite. She ate the sandwich as though she hadn't eaten anything.

As Anna ate her sandwich and occasionally glanced at Hattie, tears filled her eyes. She didn't know why she felt so sorry for Hattie; Carolyn didn't seem to at all. But something about Hattie made Anna feel kind of motherly. She wiped one eye and waited before wiping the other one so that Hattie wouldn't notice. Neither of them said anything as they ate.

When they finished, Anna said, "It must be about time to get back to work."

"Anna," Hattie said, "before you go, I wanna tell you sumpin. I ain't tol' nobody else yet, but I'm leavin' Horace."

Anna studied her face. When she was sure that Hattie was pleased with her decision, she said, "Oh, Hattie, I'm so pleased for you. Where are you gonna live?"

"Don't tell nobody, but I'm gon' live in a house Francis has behine his store. An' I'm gon' quit this job an' work fer Francis."

"That's great, Hattie. Francis must be so pleased."

"He is. He's tried fer a long time ta git me ta do it."

"Well, don't you worry. Your secret's safe with me. When are you leaving?"

"Saturd'y."

"Of this week?" Anna asked. Hattie nodded her head. "Oh my goodness. I'm sorry you won't be here anymore. I'll miss you."

"I'll miss you, too, Anna," Hattie said, and she meant it. Anna was probably the only one at the store that she'd miss.

"But that should be really nice—working for your brother."

"It shore will be. An' livin' in that house all by myse'f. It's a nice little yeller house."

"I've seen that house on my way home from work. It's directly behind his store, right?"

"That's it," Hattie said, pleased that Anna knew where she'd be living. "I can walk ta work."

"You sure can," Anna said, standing up. "Well, I have to get back to my counter. I'll talk to you later, Hattie."

"I'll be there in a minute," she replied. "Thank you fer the san'wich. I hope you won't be hungry."

"You're more than welcome, Hattie," Anna said softly. "If I git hungry, I'll buy a bag of popcorn."

"Wouldn' that be nice," Hattie thought. "Jus' ta buy a bag a popcorn if you git hungry. It's been a while since I could do that."

She took the empty bag out of her pocketbook, took the waxed paper out of the bag, covered her bowl, put the bowl in the bag, and put it back in her pocketbook, carefully placing it between the grits and the crumbs. Then she started back to the store.

An old man with a cane limped across the street in front of her. He had one hand in his pocket and when he took it out, a nickel fell out. Hattie stooped over and picked it up.

"I can buy a bag a popcorn with this, or a candy bar," she thought excitedly. But her next thought was, "Hattie, what are you thankin'? This ain't yore nickel."

When they reached the sidewalk, she said, "Excuse me, sir. You dropped a nickel."

The old man reached out his hand. "Thank you, lady," was all he said, but Hattie could see the gratitude in his eyes.

"He prob'ly needs it more 'an I do," Hattie thought. "Anyhow, it wuz the right thang ta do. It weren't mine, nohow."

During the afternoon, Hattie felt nice and full. She hadn't liked accepting the sandwich from Anna, but she was happy that she had. She had a satisfied feeling she did not expect to have until Friday evening. She would've felt completely comfortable if it hadn't been so hot—her counter didn't get a lot of breeze from the ceiling fans, and she had to wipe the sweat off her face a few times. "That's one thang 'bout Francis' store," she thought. "It ain't that big an' the ceilin' fans really he'p a lot."

There were quite a few customers for a Wednesday afternoon and they kept her fairly busy. "It's a good thang some people have money," she thought. She forgot about Francis coming in and her need to put gas in her car.

Around three o'clock, Mr. Simmons went to her counter with the usual pencil behind his ear and the usual nauseating smell of stale smoke. "Hattie," he said. "Your brother called. He said he cain't come in today an' for you to go by the store tomorrow after work."

"Okay," Hattie replied. "Thank you."

"You know, Hattie," he continued, "I ain't a messenger boy. An' this makes two days in a row that you've had personal business durin' work hours. If this happens again, I'm goin' to deduct some time from your hours."

"He's mad," Hattie thought. "I ain't ever heard him say 'ain't.'" "It won't happen again," she said with certainty, but she thought, "I didn' even leave my counter, an' he's talkin' 'bout deductin' time."

Hattie looked at Anna, but she was busy with a customer. She was glad she didn't overhear that conversation. She looked at Carolyn, who clearly did hear it; although Carolyn wasn't looking at them, Hattie could tell she was listening. Hattie could see a faint smile. "Oh Lord," she thought, "now I'm gon' hafta ask her ta borry a quarter."

Mr. Simmons stopped at Carolyn's counter and leaned on the counter talking to her. Hattie wondered if he was telling her something about her and the phone calls. Whatever it was, they were soon laughing. She looked at Carolyn's low-cut dress and thought, "What a hussy ta wear a dress like that ta work. She's shore playin' up ta Mr. Simmons." Hattie looked at his pencil and wished it would fall down her dress. She smiled at the thought.

After she waited on two customers, Hattie saw that he was just leaving Carolyn's counter. "Musta been ten minutes," she thought. "An' he's talkin' 'bout deductin' *my* time! I guess his time an' Carolyn's time ain't the same as mine, but I knowed that fer a long time."

On her way to get a drink of water, she asked Carolyn, "What 'id Mr. Simmons say that wuz so funny?"

"Oh, nothin'," Carolyn replied. "He wuz jus' bein' silly."

"Oh." Hattie knew she could not afford to upset Carolyn or she wouldn't loan her a quarter. She also knew that she needed to wait a while before she asked her for the loan.

"Jus' bein' silly!" she thought. "He's gittin' a little ole fer silly, I thank. But he's silly, all right; both of 'em are. An' they're both sumpin else 'sides silly. I guess she don't mind how he smells. Maybe she likes it."

A little Negro girl, around eight years old, was getting a drink from the "Colored" fountain and holding a bag of popcorn. Hattie looked at her and thought, "That little nigger girl can afford popcorn, an' I ain't got a penny ta my name. It ain't right." The child's mother, who was shopping at a nearby counter, saw Hattie looking at the child, and called her. Hattie looked at the mother, who had on a pretty dress. The woman had a pleasant face, and she smiled at Hattie, who smiled, and immediately felt ashamed of what she'd just thought.

The little girl said "Yes, ma'am," and immediately went to her mother.

"She's just a little girl," Hattie thought. "She ain't responsible fer my problems. An' she's a lot nicer than that spoilt little white girl that was in here yestiddy. What a brat she wuz."

When she returned to her counter, a little white girl, who looked about ten, was standing there studying the rings. Hattie observed the well-worn dress the girl was wearing, thinking that it looked like something she might have worn when she was that age. Something about her touched Hattie's heart. She didn't look like she'd have enough money to buy anything, and Hattie wondered why she was even looking, and where her parents were. She looked around the store to see if anyone looked like they might be her parents, but no one did. Hattie saw the Negro girl again and noticed that her dress was much nicer than the white girl's. "It just ain't right," she thought, shaking her head.

"Can I he'p you wi' sumpin?" she asked.

"How much are the rings?" the girl asked tentatively.

"Thirty-five cents fer them in that case," Hattie replied. "Would ya like ta try one on?"

"No, ma'am. I'm jus' lookin'."

"That's all right," Hattie said softly. "Jus' take yore time."

The girl stayed there for a couple more minutes. Then she said, "Thank you," and went over to the toy counter and looked at the toys.

Hattie noticed her leaving the store a little later. After a couple of customers came and went, Hattie saw her return with a woman who bought a bag of popcorn. After they got water at the fountain, they went to her counter and the woman smiled at Hattie.

"Can I he'p ya?" Hattie asked.

"No, thank you," the woman said. "We're jus' lookin'."

"I'm showin' my mama the ring I like," the girl said, pointing at it.

Her mother said, "That is a purty ring."

"It costs thirty-five cents," the girl said, and pointed to the necklace Hattie liked, the rhinestone heart. "An' lookie here, Mama. Ain't this a purty necklace!"

"Oh, that is purty," her mother said. "How much is that?"

Hattie had been listening to them. "It's $2.99. Would ya like ta see it?" she asked, and thought, "That nigger boy liked it. Wonder if he'll be back."

"No, thank you," the woman answered. "I wuz jus' curious." She turned away from the counter. "Let's look at the cloth, Lora Lee. I might buy some material an' make myself a dress."

And they went over to Anna's counter. Hattie watched as the woman started talking to Anna. "Anna knows her," Hattie thought. "I'll hafta ask her who she is."

Hattie soon had customers to wait on. There were enough to keep her busy, and the rest of the afternoon went quickly. She forgot about the quarter, and had given her receipts to Mr. Simmons before she realized she hadn't talked to Carolyn about the loan.

When she went to the break room looking for Carolyn, she noticed that Carolyn and Anna were the only ones in there. Hattie didn't want Anna to know about her money situation, and she waited for her to leave; they were talking about an episode of "I Love Lucy."

"That woman's hilarious. She acts so dumb sometimes," Anna said, and they laughed. Hattie had seen "I Love Lucy" once at Francis' house, and she laughed, too.

The three of them walked out together. When Anna and Carolyn started in the opposite direction from Hattie, she said, "Carolyn, can I talk to ya fer a minute?"

Carolyn stopped, her shoulders stiffening. Hattie heard her mumble something, and hoped Anna didn't hear her.

Anna turned, smiled at Hattie, and said, "See you both tomorrow."

After a moment, Carolyn turned around. "Are you gonna ask me for money, Hattie?" she asked with disgust in her voice, "'Cause if you are, I don't have none. I had expenses goin' to my aunt's funeral, you know."

"Okay," Hattie said with resignation, and turned to leave. "Does she thank I jus' got outta Chattahoochee?" she wondered. "It don't take much gas ta go to north Florida, an' I know she's got kinfolks ta stay with."

"Hattie," Carolyn continued. "I ain't loanin' you no more money. I don't understand why you stay with Horace, but that's yore choice. If you wanna support that bum, that's yore choice, too, but I ain't gonna he'p you. If you wanna live like that, . . . I jus' don't understand how you can stay with him!"

"That there woman needs a good blessin' out," Hattie thought, but she simply said, "Maybe that's 'cause you ain't ever been married, *Miss* Peabody." As Carolyn started to walk away, Hattie added, "Anyhow, I won't be askin' you ag'in, nohow. 'Sides, I'm leavin' Horace."

Carolyn stopped and asked suspiciously, "Are you really? When?"

"Saturd'y," Hattie answered. But she thought, "Not that it's any a yore business," and left. "That witch thanks I'm lyin'." She immediately regretted telling Carolyn that she was leaving Horace. "He don't even know yet, an' I jus' tol' the biggest mouth aroun'. Good Lord."

She turned around and called, "Carolyn."

Carolyn was half a block away standing next to her car. She turned to face her.

Hattie saw Carolyn's light blue and white station wagon. "Why's she got that big ole car jus' fer her?" she wondered. "Maybe she did use a lot a gas in that heavy ole thang."

"I ain't tol' nobody at work yet," Hattie said, remembering that she'd told Anna, "so please don't say nothin'."

"All right," Carolyn responded.

Hattie didn't feel any better. She didn't believe Carolyn could keep any secret, especially one she'd consider so juicy. "I'd as lief trust the devil as her. An'," she wondered, "where in tarnation am I gon' git a quarter? For goodness sake! All I wanted to borry was a quarter."

She felt nervous as she walked to her car. "I ought not ta pay her no never mind," she thought. "I know she's always raisin' sand 'bout sumpin or other, anything that don't jus' suit her. But she still gits under my skin. An' she'll prob'ly tell ever'body I'm leavin' Horace."

"How will I git a quarter?" she wondered, as she slumped in the car. "I'd rather steal than git one from her." She felt a headache coming on.

♥ ♥ ♥

Hattie was right about Horace. He'd been home that day, and Hattie assumed Darrell was with him. There were two Coca-Cola bottles on the kitchen table, and wrappers from a bag of peanuts and a Baby Ruth candy bar. "Where did he git the money ta buy that from?" Hattie wondered. "Darrell musta bought it fer 'im."

When she picked up the wrappers, the smell of peanuts and chocolate made her mouth water. She knew Horace planned that because he thought she had no food. He knew she liked to put peanuts in her Coke, and that Baby Ruth was her favorite candy bar. One of the bottles was at her place and she noticed it had a little Coke left. She was considering drinking it, but when she picked the bottle up, she saw a cigarette butt in it. "It was just a smidgin, anyhow," she thought.

"Yo're jus' plain mean, Horace," she said. "You don't smoke no more, but Darrell does, so it musta been his cigarette." But Hattie knew that when Darrell was at the house, he always sat in the chair on the end. And the other bottle was at Horace's place. She wondered why Darrell would sit in her chair. "That don't make no sense," she thought, but she dismissed it from her mind. She threw the wrappers away, emptied the bottle with the butt in it, rinsed both bottles, and put them under the sink.

With the table cleared, she suddenly realized that her zinnias were gone. Even the jar they were in was gone. Hattie folded her hands over her chest as she felt the pain in her heart. "What would he even wont wi' my flow'rs," she wondered. "Maybe he sol' them, too. I never imagined Horace could be so mean!"

She stood there for a moment. "An' he even tuk my jar! Now I ain't got nothin' ta put my flow'rs in." Tears filled her eyes. "That's below the belt, Horace," she said. "Takin' my flow'rs, an' my jar!"

She sat down at the table and just looked at the empty place where her flowers had been. Then, she took a deep breath. "Oh my Lord, I shore picked a winner. Whoever heard a anybody actin' like that?"

She took an aspirin and went in the bedroom. Everything had been dumped out of her three dresser drawers. "There just ain't no reason for this kind of meanness," she moaned. The floor was littered with her underwear; her box of sanitary pads; a seldom-used jar of face cream she'd purchased from the dime store years ago; two cheap pins that were her mother's; three cheap necklaces with matching clip-on earrings, two of which were her mothers and one she'd bought at the dime store; some paper bags; some wrapping paper and ribbon from presents Francis and Susan had given her for Christmas; her scissors; two spools of thread—one black, one white; her little package of needles; some mail and other papers; her two books of S & H green stamps, plus a few loose ones; and the three drawers.

She lay down on the bed and put her hand on her aching head. A few tears rolled down her face, but as her weary body relaxed, she was soon asleep.

When she got up half an hour later, her headache was gone and she felt able to face the mess. "Ain't no surprise here," she said. "I wuz expectin' sumpin bad from you, Horace, 'cause yo're a mean ole man." She took a deep breath and started picking up her things. "Well, there is one surprise: ya didn' take these two books a green stamps. Ya mus' notta noticed 'em."

As she picked up the stamps, she started thinking about what she could get with them. Many stores were giving them out with purchases and Hattie had been saving them for quite some time. She'd traded some in once for the yellow basket-weave clothes hamper in her closet where she put her dirty clothes. "I got two books," she thought. "I'll hafta git a catalog ta see what I can git wi' two books. I wish I could git money. If I could, I'd cash 'em in now."

"What a mean thang ta do! Ya jus' git worser all the time," she said as she picked up her underwear, folded it, and put it back in the drawer. "Good thang I tuk the crackers an' grits wi' me or I wouldn' have one bit a food. It'd be jus' like he thanks. Course I ain't got enough now ta speak of, but I wouldn' have none if he saw it." She put the rest of her stuff in the drawers and put them away, and then took off her dress, slip, brassiere, sandals, and stockings, and put on her housedress and old sandals. "Just you wait, Mr. Horace," she said. "I wonder if yo're so stupid you thank you can jus' steal my food an' come in here an' dump out my thangs, an' then we'll jus' go on like nothin' happened. And steal my flow'rs." She nodded her head. "He prob'ly is that stupid."

Hattie felt a need to keep moving. She went outside and got the slop jar and put it under the bed. She also put her pocketbook under her side of the bed just in case Horace showed up during the night. "I don't wont ta lose what little food I got," she thought. "Oh, an' I better put them green stamps in my pocketbook, 'cause he'll prob'ly thank about takin' 'em. They're like money—I shore wouldn' wonta lose 'em."

When she finished in the bedroom, she decided to sweep the front porch. She wanted the house to look neat when Francis helped her move Saturday evening.

As she swept, she thought about what she could have for supper. She had to save the cracker crumbs to take to work. So the only thing she had was grits. Grits and not even any butter to go on them. "I hate to, but I'm gon' ask Miz Wutherton," she thought. She wondered how they'd taste if she melted some lard and put it on them. That didn't sound good. If she had an egg, she could fry it over easy, put it on the grits, and mix the yolk in to flavor them. Her mouth started watering just thinking about it.

"Thank God fer Anna," she thought. "I'm hungry, but I'd be starvin' if she hadn' shared her san'wich. I'll hafta find some way ta pay her back after I git on my feet. I know! I'll make her a coconut cake. She liked my coconut cake." Hattie had taken a cake to a Christmas party at the store the previous year. "Come ta thank of it, Anna's the one who suggested the party. We ain't ever had one before in the eight years I been workin' there."

Hattie had finished the porch and was sweeping the steps when the Wuthertons walked down the road. "Evenin', Hattie," Mrs. Wutherton called. "Yore flowers look real nice."

"Evenin'," Hattie replied. "I don't spend as much time on 'em as I ought to."

"Well, you stay busy with yore job, Hattie," Mr. Wutherton said.

Hattie put the broom down and walked out to the road where they were. "Would ya like ta have some zinnias?" she asked. The Wuthertons had several flowering shrubs in their yard, but they didn't plant annuals.

"Oh, you don't need to cut 'em for me," Mrs. Wutherton replied.

"I'd like to," Hattie assured her, knowing she'd be leaving them in a few days. "Y'all've always been so nice ta me. Jus' let me git a knife."

"Here," Mr. Wutherton offered, reaching into his pocket. "Use my pocket knife, Hattie."

"Looks like yore crape myrtles are 'bout to open," Mrs. Wutherton said.

"Yes, ma'am, they are," Hattie agreed. "Somebody left 'em fer me in little cans on my porch steps, so I don't know what color they are, an' I'm real anxious ta see. I'm hopin' they're white 'cause I like the white ones the best." She handed the small bunch of flowers she'd cut to Mrs. Wutherton.

"Well then, I hope they're white, too," Mrs. Wutherton said. She looked at the bouquet. "These are beautiful, Hattie. Thank you so much. You know, we were jus' talkin' 'bout havin' some coffee. Why don't you come over an' have a cup with us."

"Yeah, Hattie," Mr. Wutherton said. "Come have a cup with us."

That sounded wonderful to Hattie. With milk and sugar in it, that would help make up for the loss of food. "Thank you," Hattie said, her face lighting up. "That'd be real nice."

Hattie had only been in the Wuthertons' house twice in the six years they'd been her neighbors, both times to use their telephone. They'd never been in her house. And she knew that if Horace were home, they wouldn't have invited her over now. They wouldn't have taken the chance that he'd go over there.

"Maybe when I live at Francis' little yeller house, I can be friends wi' my neighbors," she thought. "I can go ta their houses an' they can come ta mine."

Hattie thought it was the best coffee she'd ever tasted, and she told them so with enthusiasm. The Wuthertons used *cream* in their coffee. She and Horace had never had cream; Hattie bought the canned evaporated milk for herself, and Horace took his black. She felt relaxed and comfortable as she sipped the coffee, and she decided that when she moved, she'd use cream in her coffee, too. She felt warm inside just thinking of doing something special for herself, with no one to object.

The Wuthertons made small talk for most of the time Hattie was there, part of the time just talking to each other. As Hattie listened to them, she thought how nice it would be to have a partner she could just talk to, and walk with, and feel comfortable with.

When she saw an egg carton on the kitchen counter, she thought, "I could borry an egg from them. Then I'd have an egg ta put in my grits. That'd be better 'an borryin' butter."

"What in the world wuz goin' on with Horace yesterday mornin'?" Mr. Wutherton asked.

He caught Hattie by surprise. She was lost in thought about the egg, and was stunned by the question. She just looked at him.

"He was out in the road in his underwear actin' like a madman," he continued. "I saw him runnin' after the car an' I was scared he was gonna hurt you."

Hattie could tell by the expression on Mr. Wutherton's face that he'd been afraid for her. She felt her eyes moisten and hoped he wouldn't notice.

"Well, it really weren't nothin'," she said. "He jus' got mad 'bout sumpin an' started actin' crazy."

"Well, he shore was mad. I never saw 'im like that before. Truth is, Hattie, the wife an' I worry 'bout you, an' what he might do when he acts like that. We worry 'bout yore safety."

"Oh my," Hattie said, visibly moved. "I don't wont y'all ta worry 'bout me. I'll be fine."

She wanted to tell them that she was going to leave Horace, but she regretted telling Carolyn, so she didn't. "Would you be willin' ta loan me one egg?" she asked, partly to change the subject.

"Of course, Hattie," Mrs. Wutherton said, and patted Hattie's shoulder. "Will one be enough?"

"Thank you," Hattie said, feeling grateful. "Actually, I could use two, if ya don't mind, ma'am. I'll pay ya back Friday."

"Oh no. Don't worry 'bout that. We jus' bought these today. I haven't even put 'em in the icebox yet. You know, on the farm, we didn' put eggs in the icebox except in the hottest part of summer. There was so many of us kids, eggs didn't last long, nohow, but we prob'ly kept some for a few weeks, an' they never spoilt. Would you like to have a cucumber, Hattie? My sister brought us some from her garden."

"Oh, thank you," Hattie replied. "That'd be real nice."

She went home happy. She had thoroughly enjoyed the coffee, and she had two eggs and a cucumber. She could have grits and an egg for supper and for breakfast, and she could take the cucumber to work. She was going to see Francis after work and he'd give her some money and maybe take her to supper.

After she ate and cleaned up the kitchen, she decided to wash her dirty clothes so they'd be clean when she moved. She put some water on the stove to heat, and went in the bedroom. She took all of the dirty clothes out of her clothes hamper, dumped them on the bed to sort them, and put Horace's clothes back in the hamper. "I ain't washin' nothin' a hissen," she declared. He had a filthy pair of jeans, a shirt, some underwear, and two pairs of socks. She laughed. "When I married 'im, he didn' even have no socks. After we bought some, he asked me how ta tell which sock went on which foot. Ain't that sumpin! What a fam'ly he's from."

Hattie took her clothes to the kitchen and put them on a chair. She had a dress, a slip, a brassiere, and two pairs of panties. "This won't take long," she said as she turned on the water. She added the hot water and some washing powder, which she had in a glass jar under the sink. Then she put the clothes in the sink, took a smooth stick from under the sink, and stirred the clothes around several times. She put a little washing powder on a spot on her dress and rubbed the cloth between her hands.

"Thank God I don't need ta use the washboard," she said. "I'm too tired ta scrub clothes. One thang I'm gon' do is save my money an' buy me a washin' machine." When they'd had a little money, Hattie would take the clothes to a laundromat, but it had been months since she was able to do that.

"I'm gon let these clothes soak an' go ta the outhouse while it's still daylight," she said. "An' I'm gon' take them grits I swept up out for the birds. I don't wont ta forgit 'em an' leave 'em here fer Horace, not after the way he's treated me. Anyhow, I'm gon' see Francis tomorrah, an' I git paid on Friday, so I'll have enough food. I'm keepin' the good grits in my pocketbook, so Horace cain't find 'em, nohow."

She got the grits from the cabinet, and on the way to the outhouse, scattered them beside the path. As she started back to the house, she was pleased to see the blue jay already pecking away at them. "I thought you'd be gone home an' ta bed, Mr. Blue Bird," she said, smiling. "I guess you oughta be grateful ta Horace fer yore supper. He stole mine." The blue jay flew when she got near, but she looked back when she got to the house, and it had returned. She stood there watching as four sparrows joined the blue jay, and two mourning doves lit on the fence, observing. She watched until the doves joined the other birds.

Back in the kitchen, Hattie stirred the clothes around again with the stick, and when she was satisfied that they were clean, she wrung them out and put them on the side of the sink. Then, she drained the soapy water, put more water in the sink, and rinsed everything. After wringing it all out, she hung it on the clothesline that was strung across the back porch.

When she went to bed, she remembered that she still needed a quarter for gas. She knew she had enough for the morning, but she didn't want to run out again, so she'd need to put some in before she went to see Francis. "Guess I'll jus' borry another one from the cash register," she thought. "Mr. Simmons is too grouchy ta ask him fer it, an' I don't care if he finds out I tuk it. I'm leavin' Saturd'y, anyhow."

Hattie wound the alarm clock, hoping she'd wake up before the alarm sounded; she didn't want to be startled awake by the loud ringing. As she lay there, she thought about Horace taking her flowers and dumping out her dresser drawers. "He mus' really hate me." After a little while, she thought, "I don't hafta thank about that ole bad stuff. I already know how mean Horace is. Startin' Saturd'y, I'm gon' have me a brand new life—a happy one, I b'lieve. I can thank 'bout that."

She thought about the little yellow house and wondered what it was like inside. Many years earlier, she'd been there once when Francis lived there. She thought about the yard and wished she had seen it recently so she could figure how much space she'd have for plants. And as she thought about locations for plants, and what kind of flowers she wanted in *her* yard, she drifted off into a beautiful garden.

Thursday

The alarm made Hattie jump. "Good gracious," she said. "I don't know when I slept till that ole alarm went off. An' I didn' even wake up all night ta pee." She got up and took the slop jar from under the bed. "An' since Horace ain't here, I can pee now without worryin' 'bout wakin' him up. When I move, I'll have a bathroom. Jus' thank how much time an' agg'avation I'm gon' save not havin' ta use the slop jar an' goin' to the outhouse, 'specially when it's rainin' or cold out."

She pulled the gown off over her head and put on her housedress and old sandals. "I thank I'll wait till later ta empty the pot. Then, if I hafta pee, I'll jus' hafta go to the outhouse one time. I'm so tired a walkin' that ole path ever' day."

As she went into the kitchen, she remembered the two oranges on the tree behind the outhouse. "Well, I'll jus' have 'em both tomorrah if I wont 'em. I got a egg fer this mornin', anyhow." She washed her hands in the sink, lit two burners, and put two pots on with water and salt in one and just water in the other. She went back to the bedroom and got her pocketbook and the bottle of syrup. She took the grits from her pocketbook and put some in the salted water, which was boiling. Hattie looked at the old stove. "I bet there's a 'lectric stove in Francis' house," she said. "I won't hafta mess with buyin' no ole stinkin' kerosene no more. That's one more thang ta be grateful fer."

She fixed a cup of hot water and syrup, stirred the grits, and went to the sink. After she unbuttoned her housedress, she took the washcloth from the nail, and washed her face. She rinsed the cloth and wiped under each arm. Then she rinsed it again and hung it back on the nail. She shivered. "It's kindly cool this mornin'," she said.

She stirred the grits, and went to the bedroom and got the egg and the cucumber out of her drawer. "Well, thank you fer bein' a cabinet an' a icebox," she chuckled. "I bet not many people keep their cucumbers in a dresser drawer. I'm prob'ly the only one."

As the egg fried, she took the deodorant from the top of the refrigerator and smeared some under each arm. Then she washed her hands and buttoned her dress. She left the egg yolk runny enough to mix into her grits and flavor them well, and she was quite happy with her breakfast. "Only three more days countin' today," she thought. "Three days an' I'll be free. Oh boy! I cain't wait. This evenin' I'm gon' see Francis an' I'll see the house an' what it's like inside. Boy! I don't 'member when I wuz so excited. I wish today wuz Saturd'y."

When she finished eating, she washed and dried her dishes and put them away. "There ya go, Mr. Horace," she said in a mocking tone. "Pore ole Hattie ain't got nothin' ta eat, ya know."

She took the cracker crumbs from her pocketbook, and put them in the same small bowl she'd used the day before. She scraped the mayonnaise jar, but didn't get as much as she'd have liked. She put a few of the crumbs in the jar and stirred them around the side of the jar to pick up any mayonnaise left there. She stirred it into the crackers, covered the bowl with waxed paper, and put it, the cucumber, a knife, and a spoon into the bag she'd used on Wednesday. Then she stirred some syrup into a glass of ice water and poured it into her thermos.

"Now I got a jar fer my flow'rs," she thought, looking at the mayonnaise jar, "but I ain't gon' pick no more fer Horace to steal. He's too lazy to pick 'em hisse'f."

"Salt fer my cucumber," she thought, and poured a little from the saltshaker into a piece of waxed paper and carefully folded the paper. She put the saltshaker back in the cabinet, got her scissors from the bedroom, and snipped a tiny piece off one corner of the folded waxed paper. Then she folded that piece over so the salt wouldn't spill, and put it in the bag. "Guess I'll always thank a the picnic when I fix salt like that," she thought. "A course, when I work at Francis' store, I can go home ta eat, so I won't need ta do it. That'll be so nice."

After she put the bag in her pocketbook, she put it and her thermos on the table. She took her toothbrush and toothpaste from the cup on top of the refrigerator, put some toothpaste on the toothbrush, put some water in a glass, and went on the back porch to brush her teeth. She saw Mrs. Wutherton pulling some weeds from around her plants, but she had her back to her, so Hattie didn't say anything.

She went to the bedroom to get the slop jar to take to the outhouse. "Cloudy today," she thought as she stepped off the porch. "An' cool." She rubbed her arms.

Hattie could see something red in the Wutherton's back yard. "I b'lieve that's them red hibiscus she planted a few months ago. They already bloomin'. I oughta ask her if she wants some cuttin's offa my white ones ta plant with 'em."

"Mornin', Miz Wutherton," she called.

"Good mornin', Hattie."

"I cain't b'lieve them hibiscus is already bloomin'. Would ya like ta have some white ones or yeller ones to plant with 'em?"

"That would be nice, Hattie. I think I'd like some white ones."

"I'll git ya some cuttin's tomorrah afternoon."

She sat in the outhouse, thinking about the little yellow house. "I cain't wait ta git outta work an' go see where I'm gon' live at," she said. She was picturing herself sitting in her swing on the front porch, looking at a yard with all kinds of beautiful flowers. "I hafta ask Francis ta move the swing over there fer me."

On her way back to the house, she saw the blue jay sitting on the chicken-pen fence. It just looked at her as she walked past, but it let out its shrill call a few times as she rinsed the pot, put it on the bottom step to dry, and rinsed her hands. She could still hear it when she went in the house to get dressed for work.

She changed her panties, put on her brassiere, her stockings and garters, her slip, her Thursday dress, and her good sandals. Then, she combed her hair and put on some lipstick. As she looked in the mirror, she saw a small stain on the front of her dress. "Well, there ain't nothin' I can do 'bout it now," she said. "I shore need me some new clothes." She thought for a minute, and put on her sweater.

She turned away from the mirror and looked at the bed. "I ain't useta makin' the bed 'fore I go ta work," she said, making it. "It shore is nice not havin' Horace in it."

"Okay," she thought. "Three more days ta work in that ole store." She picked up her pocketbook and thermos, and went to the car.

"Well ole car, you cranked fer me one more time," she said as the car started. "I jus' need ya fer two more days after today." She looked at the gas gauge. "Yep, I'm gon' hafta git gas 'fore I go ta see Francis. I'll hafta borry a quarter from the cash register ag'in. Miss smarty pants Carolyn ain't gon' let me borry one. Mean ole thang. She makes out like she ain't got no money. I hope she don't thank I b'lieve her nonsense."

When she got to work, Hattie noticed that Mr. Simmons was at Carolyn's counter. As she straightened up her counter and put out the new jewelry, she could hear them talking and laughing. Carolyn didn't seem to be doing anything but messing around with Mr. Simmons.

"I'm glad I'm leavin' here," she thought. "They make me sick. I'd go crazy if I had ta listen ta much a this. An' I can smell him from clear over here." She looked around the store and noticed that some of the other clerks were watching them, too. "Both a them's got a screw loose, actin' like that. Ever'body's gon' be talkin' 'bout 'em."

Hattie thought about the way Mr. Simmons had acted with her when she went to his office to call Francis. "He made me go back on my dinner break, but he wastes a lot a Carolyn's time. He's got his druthers 'bout how time's wasted, an' who's doin' it. He'd be raisin' sand if I wasted half the time he wastes wi' her. He give me such a hard time 'bout that telephone call." She was glad the store didn't have a party line or she might've had to wait for a line, and that would've caused more problems with him.

A picture suddenly flashed in her mind of a girl demonstrating how to use a rotary phone in an informational short before a movie. She was with Horace and they watched in fascination as the woman slowly dialed a number, and held up the receiver so they could hear how it sounded when the phone she dialed was ringing, and what it sounded like when it was busy. "That was a few years ago," she thought. "Funny how thangs change wi' time. Before that, the operator had to connect us, and we were glad to be able to even use a telephone. The first telephone I ever had wuz when Horace an' me lived in that apartment right after we got married."

"That was prob'ly our happiest time," she thought, "when we lived in that apartment." She remembered the Sunday morning when she and Horace woke up and were just lying in bed, lazily talking about having a baby. Suddenly, he said, "Look at that little bitty fly on the wall." It was close to the bed.

"Looks like a baby fly ta me," Hattie said. "Ain't it cute."

They watched it for a little while, and Hattie made up a little song. As she sang the little fly flew, so she added more words:

> There's a baby fly on the wall,
> There's a baby fly on the wall,
> It flew away. It flew away.
> Baby fly flew all away.

They laughed and both sang it. "I wish he'd come back," Horace said. "Maybe another one'll come," she said, and started singing again:

Maybe another fly'll come,
Maybe another fly'll come.
There must be a fly ta take its place.
We hope another fly'll come.

Hattie smiled as she remembered her little ditty. "I used ta sing that ever now an' then, but I ain't sung it fer a long time now," she thought. "It's stupid, anyhow. That's what Horace said 'bout it when he was mad 'cause I couldn' git pergnant."

She finished straightening her counter and watched the people walking by on the sidewalk. A young couple passed by holding hands. Then she saw a woman who looked a lot like the landlady at the apartment complex. "Well, ain't that sumpin! I wuz jus' thankin' 'bout that place."

The landlady's uncle owned the complex, which consisted of several two-story buildings, and she and her husband lived next to Horace and Hattie. A stairwell was between their apartments, but only a thin wall separated the kitchens, and sound went right through the wall. The couple drank and fought every weekend and Hattie and Horace would hear them. The man would call his wife "a drunk," and she'd respond, slurring her words, "Well, what are *you*?" Sometimes, Horace and Hattie would say, "Well, what are you?" to each other and laugh. In her current situation, however, she didn't see anything amusing about it, and she felt bad that she'd ever made fun of the miserable couple.

"It must be time to open up," Hattie thought, looking at the clock on the wall. Mr. Simmons finally pulled himself away from Carolyn's counter to let the customers in, six minutes late.

♥ ♥ ♥

Her first customer of the day was an older woman with her gray hair neatly braided and encircling her head. Hattie noticed her clear green eyes. "What a neat lookin' lady," she thought. "An' she's got purty eyes. Horace's hazel eyes have got a lot a green in 'em, but they ain't bright an' purty like hers. An' she looks like a nice lady."

"Can I he'p you, ma'am?" she asked.

"I'm lookin' for a good, dependable alarm clock. And I'd like it to be a really nice-lookin' little clock."

Hattie pointed out a couple of clocks, one that was her favorite of all the clocks. She was pleased when the woman chose that one. She wrapped it in some paper, and looking at the bags, she thought, "I tol' Mr. Simmons two weeks ago that I needed more a them medium sacks. An' I used the last one yestiddy."

"I'm sorry we don't have a sack the right size," she said. "We got big ones an' little ones, but we're outta the right size."

"That's quite all right," the woman said.

She put the clock in one of the larger bags. As she gave the woman her change, Hattie said, "Thank you, ma'am."

"Thank you," the woman replied, smiling. "I'm buyin' this for a young friend, an' I think he'll like it. Thank you for showing me this one."

Hattie wished the woman would stay a little longer. "Wadn' she nice!" she thought. She watched her as she went to Carolyn's counter.

"Oh, Carolyn's all peaches an' cream wi' her," she thought when she saw Carolyn smiling and asking, "What can I he'p you with today?"

Hattie heard the woman say, "I need a new change purse. My old one is pretty well worn." And she heard Carolyn tell her, "That selection's all we got." But Hattie had a customer, so she gave her attention to her, and when she saw the woman again, she was at Anna's counter talking to her.

She heard Anna say something about her daddy. She seemed to be having a nice conversation with the woman. "I'll hafta ask Anna who she is," she thought. She had another customer, and when she looked at Anna's counter again, the woman was gone, and another woman was there.

Hattie noticed that Mr. Simmons was not only spending a lot of time at Carolyn's counter, he was also spending a lot behind the lunch counter. Normally, he spent almost the whole day in his office. "What in tarnation is he doin'?" she wondered. All of a sudden, she thought, "He's watchin' me. I bet the ole buzzard figgered out I tuk that quarter." He made her nervous, and she didn't feel comfortable enough all morning to take the quarter she needed to buy gas.

One time, he went to her counter and started picking up clocks and looking at them. She watched him pick up a clock and put it down and pick up another one and put it down. After a minute, she asked, "Are you looking for sumpin, Mr. Simmons, or are you jus' piddlin' aroun'?"

Mr. Simmons just looked at her for a moment with expressionless eyes. Then he left and went back to the lunch counter.

As she was leaving for lunch, she stopped at Anna's counter to see if she was going to the park, hoping she wasn't because she didn't want Anna to see her lunch. Anna said she'd promised one of the new clerks she'd join her for lunch. Hattie asked her who the woman was she was talking to earlier.

"That's Miss Maggie McClellan," Anna said. "She used to be a school teacher, an' my daddy was in her class. She taught two grades together, so he had her for two years. I don't really know her, but I know who she is, an' she was my daddy's favorite teacher. He said she cared about all the kids, an' she was a really good teacher."

"She bought a clock," Hattie said. "She seemed real nice."

"She is," Anna replied enthusiastically. "She's as sweet as she can be, an' smart as a whip."

"Is she a widder woman?"

"No. Daddy said she's an old maid."

"Oh," Hattie was surprised. "By the way, who was that woman with the little girl yestiddy? She seemed to know you, too."

"Oh," Anna replied. "That was Miz Ruth Baker, an' her little girl, Lora Lee. They were our neighbors until they moved south of here to a big farm."

"The little girl was looking at a ring," Hattie said. "But she don't look like she's got no money."

"Well, the family probably has a lot of expenses with the new farm."

"Yo're prob'ly right," Hattie responded, glad to know that the family had a farm, which meant the girl would have plenty to eat. She wished she knew someone who had a farm, thinking maybe she could get some food for herself.

Hattie went to the park, hoping no one else would go over from the store. However, she'd just settled down and taken her bowl of cracker crumbs and mayonnaise out of her bag when Mr. Simmons walked past her. "Oh good gracious," Hattie thought. "What is he doin' out here? Is he plannin' ta watch me eat, too?" Fortunately, he didn't say anything to her or stop near her, but went to a bench across the park not far from the the statue of the Confederate soldier. "He's still got that ole pencil behind his ear," she thought. "It must be glued to his head."

As she ate her crumbs, she thought, "I'm grateful for this food, but I'd really ruther have a nice sandwich. I ain't picky, but I do have my druthers."

Five sparrows lit near Hattie's bench, and chirped hopefully. "Sorry," she said, "but I ain't even got enough crumbs fer me."

She'd almost finished her crumbs when Carolyn walked past. "Looks delicious," Carolyn mumbled.

"It is," Hattie responded, and smiled at her a smile of self-satisfaction, while thinking, "Who does she thank she is? Ole witch!"

Carolyn didn't bother to return the smile, but continued walking until she reached the bench where Mr. Simmons was. "Look at her sashaying her stuck-up se'f over to Mr. Simmons." She sat down with him. "Oh good gracious. I bet she's gon' tell 'im I'm leavin' Horace. I knew I shouldn' a tol' her nothin'."

She watched the two of them talking and laughing. "Why! Mr. Simmons is married," Hattie remembered. "I wonder what's goin' on with them two. Oh my goodness! Could they be havin' an affair? If they are, I guess they don't care who knows it, 'cause they're sittin' there fer all the world ta see."

Hattie was looking at the fountain and thinking of walking around it and going by the rose garden when she suddenly realized that they were both out of the store, and if she got back to the store before they did, she might have an opportunity to take the quarter she needed.

She hurriedly peeled her cucumber, cut it in half lengthwise, unfolded the corner of the square of waxed paper, and sprinkled salt on it. She ate it faster than she wanted to, put the bowl, knife, and spoon back in the paper bag, and put it in her pocketbook. Then she put the cucumber peels and the waxed paper square in a trash can and glanced across the park to make sure Mr. Simmons and Carolyn were still there. It seemed they were so interested in each other that they'd forgotten about her, so she hurried back to the store.

There was a customer at Hattie's counter, and the other clerks were busy, so no one was waiting on her. Hattie normally went to the bathroom before returning to work, but today she went straight to her counter. The woman was interested in buying a necklace and Hattie had to take a few out of the glass case. By the time the customer made up her mind, Mr. Simmons had entered the store.

"Now he's back, an' I didn' git the quarter or even go ta the bathroom," Hattie thought. However, he walked by just as she was ringing up the sale and when the drawer opened, he was past her counter. She glanced from side to side to see if anyone was looking at her. The customer was watching Mr. Simmons. As Hattie took her change from the drawer, she took out an extra quarter and quickly dropped it in her pocket. "Thank God that's over," she thought, and immediately felt guilty for thanking God.

"It wuz hard enough ta git," Hattie thought, "an' now that I got it, I'm gon' leave it in my pocket."

Not long before she got off from work, she saw flashes of lightning and heard thunder. Looking out the door, she could see the rain. "I'm glad I'm still in here," she thought, "an' I hope it quits 'fore I leave. I'm gon' git wet if it's still rainin'." Her car was parked a couple of blocks away in free parking, and luckily for her, it was a passing shower.

When she left the store, she saw some puddles in the park. "I didn' know it rained that much," she thought. "There's some standin' puddles." She remembered once in Georgia when they'd crossed a river just after a hard rain. "That water riz so fast. Sometimes rain don't seem like a lot when it is, an' sometimes it seems like a lot when it ain't."

♥   ♥   ♥

HATTIE STOPPED TO GET GAS AND WAS EMBARRASSED to tell the young man to just put in a quarter's worth, but at least that was a gallon. He washed her windshield, and would've swept out her car, but she thanked him and told him not to bother.

Her mind was busy on the way to Francis' store, wondering what she would have for lunch on Friday, hoping Francis would give her some money, and thinking about what it would be like to live alone, Then her thoughts shifted to the present. "It's nice ta have somethin' ta do after work. All I ever do is go ta work an' go home, 'cept when I go ta the grocery store."

She stopped at a red light. "A course, I'll walk ta work when I move. I won't even have a car. I'm gon' miss you, Ole Car," she said, patting the steering wheel. "Guess I won't be goin' nowhere fer a while, but I don't thank I'll mind since my house won't have Horace in it, nohow." Then she remembered the bus. "I can take a bus to go downtown; it goes right in front of Francis' store. Maybe I can buy a television set. Wouldn' that be nice! That'd be a good trade fer Horace." She laughed. "It'll talk to me more 'an he does."

Francis and Susan had bought a television four years before, and Hattie and Horace had been to their house twice for supper not long after they got it. They'd seen "The Lone Ranger" and "I Love Lucy." She knew Francis would've asked them over more if he liked Horace, but he only tolerated him because of her. The last time they were there, Francis' two teenage children were watching "The Lone Ranger" with them. When Tonto appeared on the screen, Horace called him a "dumb redskin." Francis told him not to say that, but after the program was over and they were talking about the show, he said it again.

Francis said, "Horace, you cain't be talkin' that way in my house an' in front of my children." He looked at Hattie, and she said it was time for them to go. She knew he was mad. Francis didn't want his children to hear that kind of talk, even if they weren't little anymore. Hattie didn't understand why Francis got so upset, but she never mentioned it to him.

"I'm sorry, Francis," she said as she hugged him goodnight.

"Me, too, Hattie."

They did not get invited back, but Hattie had been by the store a few times after work when Horace was down at Darrell's. Horace was still mad at Francis and she didn't tell him about going by the store.

Hattie yearned to see the programs she heard people talking about, especially Ed Sullivan, and anything Elvis Presley was on. She loved Elvis. He had performed in Lakeland at the Polk Theatre the previous August, but she didn't have enough money to buy a ticket. She listened to his radio interview and cried, mostly for her pathetic money situation, which prevented her from seeing him, even when he was so close.

When Hattie went in the store, she saw Susan behind the cash register, but she didn't see Francis. It was a small store, but very neat, and it contained lots of things that were usually only found in a larger grocery store. Francis and Susan had a lot of pride in the store, and they had a lot of customers. There weren't any large grocery stores nearby, and they had the most business of the smaller stores. Hattie regretted that she lived so far from the store that she couldn't shop there, and seldom went there; she had to conserve gasoline.

When Susan saw her, she said, "I'm sorry Hattie, but Francis isn't here. He found out about a store north of here that's goin' out a business, an' they're sellin' stuff cheap. He won't be back till later, but Richard can watch the store an' I'll go over with you to see the house." Richard was the butcher and he often worked behind the cash register if Francis and Susan weren't there.

Hattie was disappointed. She'd planned to ask Francis for some money to buy food for Friday's breakfast and lunch, and even though she liked Susan, she didn't feel comfortable asking her for money—even for a loan. And she had counted on Francis having supper with her. She felt worried about going hungry for a moment, but saw the little yellow house and forgot about food.

As they walked down the dirt road near the house, a medium-sized, short-haired, white dog with brown spots ran out to greet them, followed by three little white puppies with brown spots. "Aah! Look at them little puppies," Hattie cooed, squatting down to pet them.

"The owner's trying to git rid of 'em," Susan told her. "She already gave four away. You can have one if you want it."

Hattie had never thought of having a dog. Horace didn't want anything around that required food or care. "I might like to have a dog," she said. "It'd keep me comp'ny. It wouldn' complain 'bout ever'thang like ole Horace does, an' it'd prob'ly be a better companion."

Susan laughed. She was surprised Hattie would say that. She knew they didn't have a good relationship, but Francis said Hattie never said a bad word about him.

"If you think you want one, pick it out," Susan said. "I'll tell Miz Hanover so she won't give it to anybody else."

Hattie picked up the smallest one and checked to see if it was a female. "I want this one," she announced. "I like her. She's got a spot right over her left eye, an' she's kindly runty."

The puppy had two more spots, both on her back. She licked Hattie's hand, wagged her little tail, and looked up at Hattie. All remaining doubt about having the puppy disappeared as her heart filled with love. She thought, "She needs a frien' jus' like I do. Some people'd thank she's ugly with a spot on her face like that. Bless her lil heart."

Susan was surprised that Hattie chose the runt. She would've chosen the biggest one. "I'll tell Miz Hanover," she said.

Hattie put the puppy down reluctantly, and they went to the house.

The front yard had a nice lawn, except around the edges. "That's fine," Hattie thought. "I can put my crape myrtles along the driveway an' plant the other kinda flow'rs I wont."

"It has a nice porch," Susan commented. "It's the whole width of the house, an' plenty wide for your swing. Francis said you'd wont the swing out here."

"He thought about that?" Hattie asked, surprised. "I wuz gon' ask 'im ta move it fer me."

"Your brother knows you purty well, Hattie. He sure knows how much you love that swing."

When Susan unlocked the door, Hattie asked, "Do ya need ta lock the doors? We ain't even got keys ta our doors."

"No," Susan answered. "It's jus' that when there's nobody livin' here, it's better to lock it. I'd think, though, that you'd wont to keep it locked at night since you'll be alone." Susan was thinking mostly of Horace.

"That's a good idear," Hattie agreed, thinking of strangers, "although I'm alone part of the time now." She immediately regretted saying that.

"You are?" Susan asked. "Where's Horace at?"

"Well, sometimes he goes down to his brother Darrell's in Mulberry an' stays fer a couple a days." Hattie was grateful that Susan didn't ask any more questions.

The little yellow house was even nicer than Hattie had dreamed it would be. As she'd expected, it was in good shape and just as cute inside as it was outside.

The front door opened into the living room, which was painted a pale yellow. And there were pale yellow curtains with small dark yellow flowers hanging over the two windows. The wood floor was the golden and brown hard Southern pine.

"Oh, this is a nice bright room, an' I love the floor," Hattie said. "My brown furniture will go good in here."

From there they went to the kitchen. "The kitchen's small," Susan said, "but it's got ever'thing you need."

"It's bigger 'an the one we got now," Hattie responded.

The walls were painted the same pale yellow, and the floor was covered with a light brown linoleum, similar to the one in her house, but in good shape. The window over the sink, partially covered by a short frilly white curtain, looked out into the back yard. There were pine cabinets along one wall, top and bottom, with counter space. The white electric stove caught Hattie's eye, and she walked over and ran her hand over the surface. "Oh goodie! An electric stove."

The refrigerator was newer than the one she had. The door was open just a little. "Let me turn that on," Susan said. "You'll need it soon." She filled the two metal ice trays with water and put them in the freezer.

"Oh my," Hattie said, "I cain't wait. It looks jus' beautiful!"

Susan smiled. "I thought you'd be pleased."

By a corner window, also partially covered by a frilly white curtain, was a table and four chairs. A vase of pink roses sat on the table, and their perfume filled the air. "Ain't that Mama's table an' chairs?" Hattie asked.

"Yep," Susan said. "Francis thought you'd be surprised to see them here. They've been sitting in the garage at our house, so when you said you'd come here, Francis cleaned 'em an' brought 'em over."

"Oh my," Hattie said, with tears in her eyes. "I don't deserve all this. Did he bring the flow'rs, too?"

"I brought the flowers," Susan said as she put her hand on Hattie's shoulder. "Francis an' I wont you to be happy, Hattie, an' you deserve to be happy. God knows you've had some hard times."

"Thank you so much," Hattie said. "Ever'thang is plumb perfect. Thank you fer ever'thang!"

"You're welcome, Hattie." Susan looked at her watch. "Let me show you the bedroom. I hafta git back to the store."

The white bedroom, which also had a pine floor, was larger than the one she had. The two outside walls each had one curtain-less window. "A closet with a door," Hattie said as she opened it. "That's great. Lots a space, too." She wondered why that seemed important since she had so few clothes. "Well, I'll git more now," she thought. Now that Horace won't be wastin' our money. Or, *my* money."

"Sorry there aren't any curtains in here, but I didn't have any for this room," Susan said.

"That's okay," Hattie replied. "I wadn' expectin' any at all. I think I might git me some Venetian blinds." She looked around the room. "What's this other door?"

"Open it an' see," Susan said, smiling.

"Why, it's a bathroom! It's got a door from my bedroom, an' another door ta the livin' room. An' look at that bathtub." It was just a plain white clawfoot bathtub, but something Hattie had only had for the brief time she and Horace had lived in the apartment, and it looked beautiful to her. The bathroom walls were painted light green, and it had the same light brown linoleum on the floor that the kitchen had. There was a small window above the toilet, which also had no curtains.

"You can lock the bedroom door if you have company an' wont to," Susan explained.

"Oh, this is so nice," Hattie said, overwhelmed.

Susan walked into the living room. "I'm glad you like it, Hattie. Francis wonts to put a shower in, but he didn't git around to it yet. As you know, he's real busy."

"Oh my! I'll jus' be happy ta have a bathroom an' a bathtub!"

"I have to go to the store now, but I'll be back in a little while," Susan told her. "Why don't you look at the back yard?"

Hattie went out on the back porch, which was small, but large enough for her needs. As she looked at the back yard, she thought, "Well, this will take some work." She felt excited and looked forward to fixing it up the way she wanted. "There's lots a weeds out here, but that's better'n grass. They'll be easier ta take up." She went out into the yard and into the weeds, some of which were almost waist high, pulling a few at the edge of the steps.

She walked around looking at everything. "There's a orange tree on the left side a the house—I thought there was. An' there's plenty a room fer the chicken pen an' a little garden in the back." In her mind, she saw where the chicken pen would be in the left corner and where her vegetable garden would be in the right corner. "There's plenty of space fer both," she thought. "Not much room fer a dog out here with all that, but I'll prob'ly keep her in the house most a the time, an' she can be on the porch. An' there's a clothesline on the other side a the house." Behind the clothesline was a wooden fence, which shielded the yard from the store and the little parking area beside it. "A clothesline already here!" she thought, and her chest swelled with happiness. "Oh, this is so nice. So much better 'an where I live now."

"An' I'm gon' have a dog," she said. "Wonder what I'll name her. One thang I know fer shore—it ain't gon' be 'Spot.' I'll hafta thank about it. Imagine me with a puppy. Oh my." She felt lightheaded. "If I git any happier, I'll jus' bust."

She was still in the backyard when Susan returned. "Don't git lost out there, Hattie," she called. "Those weeds are tall."

"Well, they'll be easier ta take up than grass would. 'Sides, I hope Francis'll move the chicken pen over here fer me. It would be nice in that corner on the left side," she said, pointing. "If I git some hens, I won't hafta take up the weeds in there; they'll prob'ly eat most a 'em."

"I know a woman who wonts to git rid of some chickens," Susan said. "Her husband died an' he was the one who took care of 'em. I think she's got a half dozen."

"Does she have a rooster?" Hattie asked.

"Yep. We hear him crowin' in the mornin's," Susan said, smiling. "I won't miss him."

"That'd be perfect. Absolutely perfect."

"Why, Hattie! You're happy as a lark. I've never seen you like this," Susan said as Hattie entered the kitchen. "You look a lot younger when you're happy. Your purty blue eyes are jus' shinin'. I wish Francis could see you now."

Hattie knew her happiness was showing. "I am mighty happy," she replied. She realized she couldn't stop smiling. "I shoulda done this years ago," she thought.

"You reckon you can settle down enough to eat somethin'?" Susan asked, laughing. "I jus' brought over some baloney an' some bread that I opened yesterday. I'm sorry, it's not much of a supper."

She took a few slices of bologna, the bread, a knife, and a small jar of mayonnaise from a bag and put it on the table. Then she took a small bag of potato chips, two Coca-Colas, and a bottle opener out of the bag.

"This looks good to me," Hattie said. "I wadn' expectin' ta eat. Oh, you brought some tall Cokes!" Hattie bought the regular size when she bought one because they were only a nickel. The tall Cokes were seven cents, and were a treat for her.

"You'd never guess how good it looks ta me," she thought. "I'd be happy jus' ta have a Co-Cola. And she brought potato chips!" Hattie didn't often buy potato chips. They were a luxury, as were Coca-Colas.

Susan handed Hattie the knife and mayonnaise so she could make herself a sandwich. "Use two slices," she said when Hattie only put one piece of bologna on her sandwich.

"Will there be enough fer *you?*" Hattie asked.

"There are four slices, but I'm not gonna eat now, anyway. I'll eat with Francis when he gits home," Susan explained. "I'll just have a Co-Cola with you, and maybe a couple of potato chips."

Hattie added another slice. "Thank you fer this," she said.

"It's nothin'." Susan raised her Coke. "Here's to you, Hattie. May you be happy in your new life."

Hattie took her Coke and clinked Susan's. "You an' Francis are makin' it possible fer me ta have a new life. Ya don't know how much it means ta me. I don't rightly know how I'm gon' be able to thank you."

"No need to," Susan said. "You're makin' us happy, too. Francis has been worried about you for years. He's so relieved that you're comin' here to live an' work."

After a few minutes, Susan said, "I'd better git back to the store. It's closing time an' Richard will be expectin' me to help take in the stuff that's outside. You just take your time here. I know Francis is keepin' Saturday evenin' open to help you move, so don't worry about that."

"That's good," Hattie said. "I'm countin' on 'im."

"You can put that mayonnaise an' baloney in the refrigerator an' you'll have it when you come here Saturday." She handed Hattie the house key. "Lock up when you leave," she said, walking out with her unfinished Coke.

Hattie stopped eating for a moment and just held the key in her hand. "I think I'm gon' bust!" she thought. Her heart was beating fast and she felt warm all over. She couldn't remember ever feeling so happy.

When she finally finished eating, she counted the pieces of bread and bologna. There were nine slices of bread and two slices of bologna. "I can take this fer my lunch tomorrah," she thought. "An' I'm gon' take the mayonnaise, too. I'll need it fer my san'wich, an' I'll try puttin' some on my grits in the mornin'. Maybe that'll taste good." She put the bread, bologna, and mayonnaise in the bag Susan had left on the table. She and Susan had finished the potato chips.

"I'm glad she left this sack here," Hattie thought. "I can use it fer part a my packin'."

"Oh Lord," she said. "I forgot ta ask fer some boxes. I better git over there 'fore they close the store."

She walked out with her unfinished Coke in her hand. As she neared the store, she could see Susan through the front glass, so not wanting Susan to know she was taking the food home with her, she took time to put the bag and the Coke in her car.

Susan gave her four boxes, although Hattie said three would be plenty. "I could prob'ly use a couple a sacks, too, if ya got any extras," Hattie said.

Susan reached under the counter and handed her four paper bags. "You can bring back what you don't need," she said, knowing that Hattie would object to taking that many.

Hattie looked around the store and thought about how nice it would be to work there. She felt relaxed and comfortable in the store. "An' I might git ta be friends with my cousin Sophie ag'in," she thought. "Course, I ain't even seen her in ages, an' she's prob'ly a lot diff'runt now. Francis said her an' J. B. an' their daughter Carla go fishin' wi' that nigger shoeshine boy that shines shoes by their garage. An' they cook the fish in the woods an' eat out there, an' that shoeshine boy eats right there with 'em. Francis said sometimes just Carla an' J. B. go with 'im, an' Carla sits in the middle a the boat wi' them on the ends. I shore wouldn' like that—her bein' that close to that nigger—but I guess Sophie don't care." It didn't make any difference to Hattie that the shoeshine "boy" was sixty-two years old an' had known Carla since she was four.

After Hattie thanked Susan again for showing her the house and for the food, reminded her to tell the lady she wanted the puppy, and thanked her again, she finally left.

♥ ♥ ♥

As she drove home with the Coke bottle balanced between her legs, occasionally taking a sip, she thought about Horace and was filled with dread that he might be there. She didn't think he would be since he knew they didn't have any food, but she was afraid, anyway. When she got home and saw that the house was dark, she breathed a huge sigh of relief. She turned off the engine, and just sat there listening to a whippoorwill and watching the lightning bugs.

"Whippoor-will, whippoor-will, whippoor-will."

"Me an' Francis used ta catch lighning bugs an' put 'em in a jar," she remembered. "When we had a few, we'd watch 'em for a while, then turn 'em loose."

After a few minutes, she went into the dark house with her bag of food and her Coke. She left the empty bags and boxes in the trunk.

When she turned on the light in the kitchen, she saw two empty Coke bottles, a salted peanuts bag, and two Baby Ruth wrappers on the table, and three roaches scurrying away. Again, she picked up the wrappers and smelled the peanuts and chocolate before she threw them away. "At least, I'm not hungry," she said, "or this would be torture. That's what Horace wants it to be an' thanks it is. I got my own Co-Cola. Ha, ha, Horace."

She rinsed the empty bottles and put them under the sink. "Aha," she said. "Now I got five bottles. I can turn 'em in tomorrah mornin' fer ten cents an' buy me sumpin ta eat."

She put the bread in the cabinet, and the mayonnaise and bologna in the refrigerator, feeling certain that Horace wouldn't be back until after she got paid. She finished her Coke, rinsed the bottle and put it under the sink. "Ha, ha," she said. "Mine wuz a tall Coke. Yores was only a small Coke."

Hattie went on the porch and got the clothes she'd washed the night before and the slop jar. "I guess he prob'ly dumped out my drawers ag'in," she thought as she went into the bedroom. He had. She put the slop jar and her pocketbook under the bed.

It took her a few minutes to pick everything up and put it back neatly in the drawers. "You prob'ly thank yo're gittin' me down, don't ya, Horace? Well, Mister, I jus' got two more days ta deal wi' yore nonsense an' then I'll be shed a ya. You ain't gittin' me down. If you can dump it out, I can pick it up." Hattie laughed. "Dumpin' out my stuff is prob'ly the most exercise you had in months, you lazy ole thang."

As Hattie put the drawers away, she was thinking about packing those things. But she decided she'd rather have Horace dump things out than do something more destructive, which he might if the drawers were empty. "Better ta jus' leave it here, an' pick it up after the ole buzzard gits his kicks outta throwin' it all on the floor a'gin," she said. "I only got two more days. Jus' two more days a this crazy mess."

She set up the ironing board and ironed the dress she had washed. When she finished, she exclaimed, "Well, if that don't beat all! It's jus' gon' git wrinkled ag'in when I pack it. Thank, Hattie! You ain't got no time ta waste." She hung up the dress, and made a mental note to take her iron and ironing board with her.

As she yawned, she thought about going to bed, but realized that she was hungry. "I can have some bread an' mayonnaise," she thought. She really liked bread and mayonnaise. So she went in the kitchen and fixed two pieces, happily putting a little more mayonnaise than usual. Then she fixed a little water and syrup, and sat down at the table to eat.

Every now and then, she heard a car pass on the hard road, just two houses away. Once she heard one slow down, and fear gripped her heart. "Could that be somebody bringin' Horace home?" she wondered. But the car didn't stop.

She finished eating the bread, and rinsed the knife and left it to drain. And she drank the rest of the water and syrup. Then, she went on the back porch and brushed her teeth.

She didn't expect Horace to show up, but she figured if he did, she would just deal with it then. As she wound her alarm clock, she smiled as she thought, "My new house has really good locks. I wish there wuz good locks on *these* doors. Ole Mr. Horace'd git locked out! Huh!" But she knew that if she locked him out, he'd make such a ruckus, he'd probably wake up everybody within a mile.

When Hattie went to bed, she was thinking about the little yellow house. She was so happy, it seemed to her that her body might float right off the bed. She was excited about the way the house looked—neat and beautiful—and she could just move right in and not even have to clean. And she was full of ideas for the yard. She didn't even think about Horace.

After she finally started settling down a little, she thought about the puppy and got excited all over again. She tried to think of a name, but nothing came that she thought suited the little dog, or was nice enough for her. It was a long time before Hattie went to sleep and dreamed she went for a walk, and saw a man kicking a puppy. Hattie thought his clothes looked familiar, but she couldn't see his face. She quickly snatched the puppy up, backed away, looked into the face of the man, and froze. She knew she'd recognize those hazel eyes anywhere.

Friday

When Hattie woke up Friday morning, it was six o'clock. She heard the blue jay's song and figured that woke her. She thought about the bologna sandwich she'd had the night before, and then she thought about the picnic with Horace. "That wuz the first time I ever had baloney," she thought. "It woulda been a real nice picnic if it didn' end up the way it did. An' I ain't gon' thank 'bout that now."

Her mind drifted, though, to the early years of the marriage. The first three years had been fairly good. Horace was still working as a mechanic, and Hattie was a homemaker. She loved cooking for him. Right after they married, he began putting on weight from her fried chicken, biscuits, peach cobbler, and all the other things she made. She liked being at home, taking care of the house, and cooking.

When Horace lost his job, Hattie worked for a while as a waitress at the Reececliff Family Diner. But as soon as he got another job, he insisted that she quit. She knew he was jealous of her waiting on men who flirted with her, and she didn't blame him; she knew she'd be jealous if there were women flirting with him at work.

They both wanted children, but after a while, they were beginning to think that Hattie couldn't get pregnant. Her doctor said he couldn't find anything wrong with her, and they kept hoping. It never occurred to either of them, nor apparently to the doctor, that the problem might be with Horace.

They were married four years when she finally got pregnant. She remembered the day she went to the doctor and how she had held her breath until he confirmed the pregnancy.

Horace said he was too nervous to go with her, so he stayed home and waited for the results. They lived in an apartment then, and when Hattie arrived home, he was waiting outside. As soon as the car stopped, he ran to her window. "Well?"

"I'm pergnant," she said. "I'm really pergnant."

Both of them were thrilled. Horace talked constantly about his son and how he'd teach him about cars. "He don't hafta be a mechanic, but he won't ever hafta go ta one, 'cause he'll know how ta fix his own car."

"What if it's a girl?" Hattie would ask, but he'd just give her a look.

She'd laugh at him, but she was excited, too. She didn't care whether they had a boy or a girl; however, at ten weeks, she miscarried.

They were both heartbroken, but they reacted in different ways. Hattie blamed herself and Horace; she saw it as a punishment from God for what happened at the picnic. But Horace just blamed her. He thought she had something wrong with her when she didn't get pregnant, and that she'd done something wrong when she miscarried. He was convinced it was her fault. That was the beginning of his drinking regularly.

For a few years, they kept hoping she'd get pregnant again, but she didn't, and they became more and more unhappy. Until the miscarriage, they had been doing all right financially and had even started saving a little money, hoping to buy a house. However, Horace got fired because of the drinking, and all of the money soon disappeared.

After the happy period passed, Hattie had resigned herself to the marriage and remained basically satisfied for a few years. She was used to her father's way of being, and even though she hadn't wanted to marry a man like him, she got one that was much more like him than she'd imagined. Because of her father, she had low expectations, and after a while, Horace met them all, except hitting her. And Hattie assumed he'd do that if he got mad enough; he'd shoved her two times. After his drinking became a problem, he seemed angry all the time.

During World War II, when he lost another job, he tried to join the Navy but was rejected because he was flat-footed. She was sorry he didn't get accepted because she figured it would limit his drinking, and she thought he might even quit.

On the other hand, she was glad Francis didn't have to be in the war. He was supporting their mother in Georgia, and his wife and two small children. After their grandmother died, their mother remained there, but she only lived another six years before succumbing to a heart attack.

Hattie was jolted back to the present with the ringing of the alarm clock. "Oh good Lord. Now I don't have no extry time this mornin'," she said. "How come I wuz thankin' 'bout all that ole stuff, anyhow? Now I won't have time ta cash in the bottles before work."

She got up, took off her gown and panties, took the slop jar from under the bed, and peed. Then she put on clean panties, her brassiere, stockings and garters, slip, and Friday dress. As she put on her old sandals, she thought, "I musta dreamt 'bout that ole stuff."

"Jus' today an' tomorrah," she said as she made the bed. "Today an' tomorrah—jus' two more days."

She went in the kitchen and washed her hands. "I ain't gone hungry at all, an' I almos' made it ta Saturd'y. A course, Anna did gimme some a her san'wich, an' the Wuthertons gimme two eggs an' a cucumber, an' Susan gimme bread an' baloney an' mayonnaise. I wuz lucky."

After she put water on the stove for the grits and her water and syrup, she went into the bedroom and got the syrup from under her dress in the closet. "If I hadn' a hid it, it'd prob'ly be gone," she thought. She took her pocketbook from under the bed, took it to the kitchen, and took the grits out. "Plenty fer today an' tomorrah, an' I'm gon' have some left. I don't thank I'm gon' be eatin' 'em fer a while, though. I'd like ta have some rice or potatoes, fer a change." She put the bag back in her pocketbook.

While the grits were cooking, she went to the sink, took the washcloth from the nail, and washed her face. She unbuttoned the top of her dress and wiped under each arm. Then she stirred the grits. "Today's Friday," she thought. "I washed downstairs on Wednesday; time ta wash ag'in." When she finished, she washed the washcloth and hung it back on the nail. She stirred the grits again. Then she took the Mum deodorant from the top of the refrigerator and put some under each arm. And she washed her dirty panties, and hung them on the porch.

When Hattie put the cane syrup in the hot water, the smell wafted up to her and she realized she was hungry. She counted the pieces of bread. "I got seven slices, so I can have one now," she said. She slathered some mayonnaise on the bread, and browned it the way she would have with butter.

She put some mayonnaise in her grits and tasted them. "They taste a little better," she thought. Then she remembered the bologna. "I can eat half a one piece now, an' still have enough fer a san'wich an' a half." Her spirits lifted some as she breathed in the aroma from the bologna. It did make the grits taste better.

"That was a purty good breakfast," Hattie thought as she washed, dried, and put away the dishes. She made her lunch, wrapped it in waxed paper, and put it in her pocketbook.

As she put some cold water and syrup in her thermos, she wondered, "What will I do with this little jar of mayonnaise? It needs ta be kept cold, but I don't wont Horace ta see it. I'll hafta thank a sumpin."

Hattie had gone to the bedroom to hide the bread with the syrup on the closet floor and get the slop jar, when she remembered the ice in the refrigerator. "I can put that little jar in a big jar an' put ice in it. I'll wrap it in sumpin an' put it in that ole bucket under the porch. It's cool under there." She took a gallon jar, put ice and the little jar in it, wrapped it in a piece of old sheet she'd saved when the sheet got torn too badly to repair anymore, and put it in the bucket that sat under the porch. "It's hot today," she thought, "but it'll be in the shade, an' it'll stay cool with that ice." She pushed the bucket a little further under the porch so that the sheet could not be seen. Then she took the slop jar to the outhouse to empty it. A squirrel sitting on the fence scampered up a tree as she got near.

"This must be the last house in Lakeland that don't have no bathroom," she thought. "If Horace woulda asked Mr. Wilkins ta put one in, I thank he woulda. After all, he has ta know he shoulda done it, but Horace wouldn' say nothin' to 'im."

She heard the blue jay's shrill call as she walked back to the house. It was sitting on the roof. "That mus' be where he was at when he woke me up," she thought. "No wonder he sounded so loud."

"Hello up there," she crooned. His call came again as though it were an answer. She smiled as she rinsed the pot and set it on the doorstep.

Back in the house, she put on her good sandals. "I really oughta git some white shoe polish from the store ta put on these shoes," she thought. "They're lookin' bad."

On her way out, she grabbed the five Coke bottles. "I don't have time ta stop nowhere now, but I'll take 'em to the grocery store later."

As she drove, Hattie was thinking about how different things would've been if Horace didn't spend so much money on alcohol. "I don't know how much Francis is gon' charge me fer rent, or how much he's gon' pay me, but he'll prob'ly give me more bent cans an' ole fruit an' veg'tables 'cause I'll be livin' right there. I know I'll have more money, whatever he pays me, 'cause Horace won't be spendin' any of it, an' I won't hafta buy groceries fer him. I can buy some new shoes, new dresses, a washing machine, a fan, an' maybe a television set. What do ya thank, ole car? Ole Hattie with a bathroom an' a television set."

"Jus' today an' tomorrah fer you an' me, ole car," she said as she waited at a red light. "You been a good ole car an' I'm gon' miss ya. Maybe I'll even be able to save enough ta buy me a used car some day, one all my own. Ya know, Horace knows how to spot a good used car, but I shore ain't askin' him. I'll ask Francis."

The light turned green and Hattie shifted into first gear. "Oh, look at that beautiful crape myrtle in that yard. It's all white," she said. "So, ole car, I jus' got two more days ta work in the dime store. Then I'm gon' work fer my brother an' live in his little yeller house, which ain't really that little; it's bigger 'an where we live at now. It's real nice. Sorry I cain't take you wi' me, but you hafta stay wi' ole Horace. Least he likes *you*, ole car." She patted the steering wheel. "Lord knows when I'll have a car, but I won't need one ta git to work. An' when I do git one, it'll be mine. Jus' mine!"

♥ ♥ ♥

Mr. Simmons was at Carolyn's counter when Hattie entered the store. "I don't know how come I didn' notice before how much time he spends 'roun' Carolyn's counter. I'm glad I won't hafta see that no more after tomorrah," she thought. "I don't know what's goin' on, but I bet she told 'im I'm leavin' Horace."

Hattie cleaned and fixed her counter and went to get a drink of water. As she passed Carolyn's counter, she heard Mr. Simmons say something about a quarter. "Oh Lord," Hattie thought, "he musta gon' over the receipts an' found out I wuz a quarter short ag'in. Or maybe Carolyn told 'im she thought I wonted ta borry some money from her, but I never said a quarter."

Back at her counter, she noticed the rhinestone heart with the silver chain again. "I got a good mind ta buy that fer myse'f. It's so purty. Maybe I will after I git paid."

The morning was busy. Hattie liked it that way because the time flew by. When Mr. Simmons went to her counter, she had no idea that it was almost noon.

"You got a telephone call, Hattie," he said in a harsh voice.

"I do?" she asked.

"It's your brother. You know how much I don't like this."

As they started to his office, she was looking at the pencil behind his ear. "Well, Mr. Simmons," she said, "I been here fer almost eight years, an' this is the first time I ever got a telephone call, 'cept fer when my mama died, an' Francis callin' the other day ta tell me he couldn't come ta see me. An' I'll grant ya one thang: if Francis is callin' me, it's important."

"What's also important, Hattie," Mr. Simmons said sarcastically, "is that you were short a quarter in your receipts yesterday. An' that makes the second time this week."

"Well, I tol' you I found a quarter on the floor an' I turned it in to you," Hattie responded. "Did you forgit that?"

"No, I certainly didn't. I know what you *told* me."

Hattie realized that she didn't even care if Mr. Simmons didn't believe her. "Let 'im thank what he wonts to," she thought. "I couldn' care less what he thanks about me. He don't like me, nohow, an' I ain't gon' be here after tomorrah."

She could smell the old smoke before she entered the office. She took a deep breath, knowing it would be worse in there. She was tempted to go behind the desk and sit down in his chair, but she did what was expected and stood beside the desk.

"Hello, Francis," she said.

"Hey, gal." His serious tone scared Hattie. She wondered if something had happened that would change all of her plans. "Did he decide he don't want me ta work in his store, or live in his house? Oh my Lord!"

"Listen, Hattie. I took some stuff over to the house this mornin', an' when I went to put it in the refrigerator, I noticed it was empty. Susan tol' me she lef' some bread an' baloney an' mayonnaise with you last night so you'd have somethin' when you got there tomorrah night. So what happened to that stuff? Did ya take it home wi' you?"

"Yeah, I did," she replied sheepishly. She sighed in relief that he hadn't changed his mind.

"Why, Hattie? You got plenty a food, don't ya?"

"I got a little."

"A little? I jus' took a box of stuff over there Sunday. An' I saw some stuff there. I know I had some cans a tuna fish an' sardines in that box, an' some fruit an' vegetables. If what I took was all you had, there still oughta be some left." He paused. "What's goin' on, Hattie? If I went over to yore house right now, what would I find? An' tell me the truth."

"Well, it's kindly . . . it's kindly hard ta say right now," she said hesitantly, glancing at Mr. Simmons. Francis' questions made her nervous. "I don't wonta tell 'im Horace tuk all the food," she thought.

"Is Mr. Simmons in the office?"

"Yeah."

"Let me talk to 'im," Francis said in his no-nonsense tone.

"He wonts ta talk ta you, Mr. Simmons," she said, and handed the phone to him.

Mr. Simmons looked surprised. Since his right side was closer to Hattie, he took the telephone receiver in his right hand and jerked it to his right ear. Hattie watched as the receiver hit the pencil, which went flying behind him. "Finally!" she thought, and put her hand over her mouth, trying to conceal her laughter.

She looked around the office to see if any smoke was visible. She didn't see any and assumed the smell was just from stale smoke.

His "Hello" had a question in it. Hattie watched him closely as her brother talked. He said, "Yessir" a couple of times, then handed the receiver to her and walked out of the room.

"What 'id you say ta him?" Hattie asked.

"I asked 'im to leave the office for a couple of minutes so my sister an' I could talk in private. So talk, Hattie."

Hattie couldn't think of any excuse, so she just blurted it out: "Horace tuk the food. He got mad at me, an' he's been gon' since Tuesday. I guess he either sold it or tuk it ta Darrell's."

"That son-of-a-bitch! I oughta skin his hide!"

"That's why I didn' tell ya before, Francis. Promise me ya won't do nothin'. You know I'm leavin' 'im! Jus' don't do nothin'." She glanced at the office door to see if there was any sign of Mr. Simmons.

Francis could tell by Hattie's tone that she was scared and that calmed him down a little. "All right, Hattie. Calm down," he said patiently. "You're right. I won't do nothin' to the jerk, but he's a sorry piece a trash."

"I jus' don't wont you ta git in no trouble," Hattie said. "I couldn' stand it if you got in trouble 'cause a me."

"All right, all right. I won't do nothin'," he assured her. "But tell me 'bout the food. How you been eatin'?"

"Well, he left the syrup an' some grits an' some crackers . . . oh! an' a jar with a little mayonnaise, an' some salt, an' a egg." Hattie wasn't about to tell him the whole truth. "An' I borryed two eggs from the Wuthertons. Oh, an' they gave me a cucumber, but I didn' tell them he tuk my food. An' I got some oranges from the Wuthertons' tree in the back that they don't use."

"Dried up oranges," Francis thought. He had to wait until the lump in his throat went away before he could say anything.

"Francis? Are you there?" Hattie asked.

"Yeah," he said softly. "You shoulda called me, Hattie."

"I knew you'd be mad."

"I said I wouldn' do anything an' I won't, but, jus' so you know, I'd like ta kill 'im!"

"I git paid today," Hattie said. "An' Francis, I ain't gon' hungry. A few years ago, I did go hungry fer a while, but not now."

"Good Lord, Hattie! I cain't imagine what all you've gone through with that man. An' I cain't imagine why you've stayed with 'im all this time—twenty years, fer Christ sake!"

Hattie winced when he said, "Christ." She didn't like to hear it used as a swearword. "It ain't all been bad," she replied. "Me an' Horace had some good times in the beginnin'. If I hadn' a had that miscarriage, I thank thangs woulda been all right."

Mr. Simmons entered the office.

"Oh, I'm almost done, Mr. Simmons."

"Well, I should hope so. You know, I *will* deduct this time from your pay," he said.

"Francis, wuz there anythang else? Mr. Simmons is back."

"Well," he said, and paused. "This is what I'm gonna do, Hattie. Horace knows you git paid today. Does he know you're leavin' 'im?"

"No, he don't."

"Well, I'm guessin' he'll be home tonight lookin' fer money. I'm gonna talk ta Mr. Simmons an' tell him to only give you two dollars today. That'll be plenty to buy you food till tomorrah. He can give you a check for the rest tomorrah, an' I'll be at yore house when you git home tomorrah. That way, you won't hafta worry about Horace gittin' any a yore money."

"All right," Hattie said, looking at Mr. Simmons who was motioning for her to get off the phone.

"You take that baloney to work?" Francis asked.

"Yeah. Francis, I got ta go."

"That ole goat's botherin' you, huh? All right, I reckon we got things worked out. I'll see you tomorrah. Let me talk to him now."

She was about to hand the receiver to Mr. Simmons, when she heard Francis say something.

"Hattie, are you afraid Horace'll do anything to ya when he finds out you ain't got no money an' you're leavin' 'im?"

"No," Hattie said, "I'll be all right." But she *was* concerned.

"Tell 'im I said if he touches a hair on yore head, I'm comin' for 'im. Will ya tell 'im that?"

"Yeah. If I need to, I will. Bye now," she said, and handed the receiver to Mr. Simmons.

Hattie only heard a little of their conversation, but she stopped in the hall for a moment when she heard Mr. Simmons say "quarter."

"That ole buzzard's tellin' 'im 'bout the quarter," she thought. "How come he thanks he needs ta tell him that?"

Carolyn looked at Hattie funny when she walked past her counter, but neither of them said anything. Hattie did not intend to say anything else to Carolyn about her business, and regretted telling her that she was leaving Horace. "Stuck-up ole thang," she thought. "Thanks she's better 'n ever'body else 'roun' here, 'cept maybe Mr. Simmons. She seems to like him a whole lot all of a sudden."

♥　♥　♥

Hattie was glad it was time for her lunch break. She went to the park alone, no one joined her, and Mr. Simmons didn't go, so she had her lunch in peace. After she ate, she walked around the statue and the fountain. "I shoulda did this more," she thought as she stood in the shade and watched the water falling from the tiers. "This is so purty and peaceful." Then she went to smell the red roses. After a few moments, she mumbled, "All right, I can go back ta work now."

A lot of people were in the store that afternoon and she was busy constantly with customers until three o'clock. Then she went to the "White" water fountain and to the bathroom. She took a couple of minutes to think about what Francis had said to her. "If he comes home tonight," she thought, "I will tell 'im what Francis said."

When she left the bathroom, she heard loud voices and went quickly down the stairs. She saw a man at Carolyn's counter, talking to her, and even though his back was to her, she knew immediately that it was Horace. "Oh my Lord!" she thought. "What in tarnation?" Her heart was in her throat and she felt a rush of adrenaline.

She approached them just in time to hear Carolyn say, "An' she's leavin' you tomorrah."

"Carolyn Peabody!" Hattie said angrily, glaring at her, "You got a big, fat mouth."

Horace turned around to face her.

"What are you doin' here, Horace?" she demanded.

"Well, what day is today, Hattie?" Carolyn asked sarcastically. "Don't you know he come after yore money?"

"You shut yore mouth, an' stay outta this, Carolyn," Hattie shrieked. "This ain't none a yore business, nohow."

Hattie looked around to see who might be looking at them. Everybody was. When her eyes met Anna's, Hattie flushed. She could tell that she was concerned.

"Come over here, Horace," Hattie said. She went behind her counter. "An' no more yellin'. Mr. Simmons is already mad at me." Her knees felt weak, and she knew her hands were shaking. She leaned against the counter.

Mr. Simmons must have heard the yelling because he suddenly appeared. He stopped at Carolyn's counter and talked to her for a moment. Hattie noticed that the pencil was back.

"What's she sayin' 'bout you leavin'?" Horace asked.

"What do you expect after the way you been treatin' me?" Hattie was talking in a low, stern voice. "I ain't livin' like that no more, Horace. You stole the food—left me wi' no money, no food, an' no gas, fer Christ sake." She remembered Francis' voice saying "Christ," and was immediately sorry she said it. She realized she was extremely upset.

"What 'id you do fer food?" he asked, with a smirk.

Hattie looked at him with eyes full of hatred. He didn't dare say anything else, and his smirk vanished. He tried a different tack: "I find out yo're leavin' me from that bitch, Carolyn?" He glanced at her.

"You ain't been home since Tuesday, Horace. An' I had ta try ta borry a quarter from her ta buy gas. If you recall, you used all the gas goin' ta Darrell's! An' she said she weren't loanin' me no more money as long as I wuz wi' you, an' that's how come I tol' her."

"When you plan on leavin'?"

"I'm leavin' tomorrah, Horace."

"Well, I guess Mr. Francis is smack dab in the middle a this."

"He didn' have nothin' ta do with it," Hattie said angrily, but quietly. "But you did. You had a lot ta do with it, Horace." She felt tears in her eyes and knew they were angry tears. "You tuk my food! You knew I didn't have a penny to my name an' you tuk my food, an' poured the grits all over the floor." With one rough swipe with the back of her hand, she wiped the tears away. "An' you dumped out all my stuff. Twice!"

Horace watched her dumbfounded. He'd never seen her so angry.

She continued, "I know you don't care 'bout me, Horace—prob'ly never have—but nobody oughta be treated like that. Nobody!"

Mr. Simmons walked over to her counter.

"What is that smell?" Horace asked, sniffing the stale-smoke odor around Mr. Simmons, and knowing exactly what it was. Hattie felt the blood rush to her face. She figured Mr. Simmons would feel insulted and she'd pay a price for that, but he ignored the question, if he'd even heard it.

"Listen, Horace," he said. "You can't come in here an' talk to my employees like that, yellin' an' carryin' on. I could hear you from my office.

Now, you git outta here, an' if I ever see you in this store ag'in, I'll call the police."

"I wadn' the only one yellin'," Horace said. "An' I didn' start it either; that ole bitch did."

Hattie's mouth flew open as she gasped. She thought Mr. Simmons was going to hit Horace, and she wouldn't have cared if he had. His face turned red and he looked like he was about to explode.

"I guess he really likes Carolyn," she thought, somewhat amused in spite of the tense situation.

He threw his hands up, hitting the pencil behind his ear, which went flying. It hit the floor, bounced, and rolled over to Carolyn's counter. "That's the second time today," Hattie thought, repressing a smile. "He looks kindly lopsided without his pencil."

"Don't you git smart wi' me, or you'll regret it, Mister," Mr. Simmons said angrily. "I don't allow people talkin' like that in my store. Such language! Hattie, y'all take this outside, and when you're done, come see me. I meant what I said, Horace. You're lucky I don't call the police right now with you talkin' like that."

As they were leaving, Hattie saw Carolyn leave her counter and pick up the pencil. She smiled inwardly, but her face showed her embarrassment.

When they got outside, Horace started laughing. They walked across to the park and sat down on the bench under the oak tree. "He must be sweet on that woman," Horace said. "I thought he wuz gon' explode."

"Me, too," Hattie said. "He even knocked that pencil from behine his ear," she said, and started laughing, in spite of her effort not to.

When they stopped laughing, they sat silently for a minute. Then Hattie asked, "What happened ta us, Horace?"

"You really leavin'?" he asked.

"I ain't got no choice," she answered with sadness in her voice. "I done my best, Horace." She noticed that his eyes were moist.

"What am I gon' do, Hattie?" he asked.

Hattie hadn't counted on this. She expected him to be furious; she hadn't expected him to care.

"Would you git a job an' stop drinkin' if I stayed?" she asked softly. She immediately thought, but didn't say, "Good Lord! What am I sayin'? There ain't no way I'm stayin' with him! I'm leavin' tomorrah!"

He turned away from her and sat silently for a moment. Then he asked, "Are you sayin' this is my fault? You ain't takin' no blame, even though you ain't ever bore me no babies? Nary a one!"

That was like a knife in Hattie's heart, and her blue eyes filled with tears. "I couldn' he'p that, Horace. I ain't God. Don't you thank I wonted babies? I woulda had a whole slew a 'em if I coulda."

Hattie thought, "How could I even thank fer one second 'bout stayin' wi' him any longer? I mus' be outta my head. If I went back ta him, I'd send *myse'f* ta Chattahoochee!"

She stood up. "This ain't gittin' us nowhere, Horace, an' I got ta git back ta work."

"You thank you can jus' walk out after all these years?" he asked in a threatening tone. "Twenty years, Hattie!" His hazel eyes looked darker with his anger.

That was more like what Hattie had expected, and suddenly, she felt afraid. "You need ta know sumpin, Horace. I tol' Francis you tuk my food, an' he said ta tell you sumpin, an' you better listen 'cause I know he means it. He said ta tell you if you touch me, he's comin' after you."

"Well, that jus' scares me half to death," he said, smirking. "I'm shakin' in my boots."

"He means it, Horace," she said.

"So, you gon' go live wi' Francis'?" he asked sarcastically.

"No, I ain't. Francis has got a wife an' children."

"Well, where you goin'?"

"Horace, that ain't none a yore concern now. But let me tell you sumpin: I know it's been twenty years—twenty *long* years—an' the truth is, I never shoulda married you, but since I did, I shoulda lef' long ago. Years ago! Fer a long time now, you treated me like dirt, an' I let you. What 'id I ever do ta you to deserve that?" She paused.

Horace sat stunned, his eyes wide, staring at her.

"By tomorrah night, I'll be gone, an' outta yore life. I'm startin' over, Horace, an' that's what you oughta do. An' right now, I'm goin' back ta work." She turned and started to walk away.

"Hey, sugar," he called. "Gimme some money."

Hattie stopped and her back stiffened. He hadn't called her that in years, and she felt insulted to the depth of her being that he'd call her that now. She thought, "He thanks he can sweet talk me after all he done!"

She whirled around and sneared, her voice shaking, "Carolyn wuz right, wadn' she?" She took a deep breath. "You ain't got one bit a pride. Anyhow, you mus' be crazy, Horace. You steal all my food, an' then thank I'm gon' give you money. Well, you got another thank comin'! I wouldn' give you one red cent, Mister! I ain't crazy, but if I was, I couldn' give you none, 'cause I ain't gittin' paid till tomorrah." She didn't dare tell him that Francis was behind that, nor that she was getting two dollars. "An' I figgered out you stole lots a food, an' my hen, too, you ole buzzard."

He just stared at her, dumbfounded, his mouth hanging open.

"I'm startin' over, Horace. You need ta start over, too. Git you a job."

She turned and left, not stopping even when she heard him say, "Hattie, wait," although it hurt her heart. After she entered the store, she looked to see if he was still there. When she saw him sitting on the bench, now bent forward with his head in his hands, she shook her head. "I don't know how come I feel sorry fer 'im," she thought. "I guess it's the twenty years; that's a long time ta live wi' somebody. An', I guess I prob'ly still love 'im a little, although I know that's crazy. Jus' plain crazy."

Hattie went back to her counter. "Oh, my head hurts," she thought, "an' I ain't got no more aspirin." She needed a minute before she went to see Mr. Simmons. "No tellin' what he's gon' say. Maybe he'll fire me. I thank he's mad enough. At least, that'd save me havin' ta quit."

Carolyn saw her and said, "Hey, Hattie, Mr. Simmons said for you to go to his office."

"What a busy body!" Hattie thought, and she didn't even look at her as she said between clenched teeth, "I heard 'im, Carolyn. I'll go in a minute, not that it's any a yore business."

Carolyn could tell from her tone that she was angry, and she didn't say anything else. But when Hattie walked past her counter, she asked, "What happened? Are you leavin' 'im?"

Hattie looked straight ahead, as though she hadn't heard anything. "Of all the nerve!" she thought. "She cain't he'p her sorry se'f."

She dreaded going into that smelly office almost as much as she dreaded facing Mr. Simmons. He was sitting at his desk. His face wasn't red anymore and he'd replaced the pencil, but he still looked angry.

He got right to the point. "What's goin' on, Hattie? You're makin' calls an' gittin' calls, an' Horace is in here makin' a scene an' cussin'. I'm not at all happy with what's been goin' on with you this week. Your receipts have been short twenty-five cents two times. That's very suspicious, Hattie, very suspicious. I'm afraid I have no choice but to fire you."

"All right," she said. "I wuz plannin' ta quit tomorrah, anyhow."

"You were plannin' to quit tomorrah an' you weren't goin' to give me two-weeks notice?"

"I didn' say that," Hattie said. She thought, "That ain't a lie. I didn' say I would or I wouldn', or nothin' else."

"Well, you know I need two-weeks notice when you quit," he said.

"Mr. Simmons, you jus' fired me," Hattie said, amazed that he was still talking about two-weeks notice. "I'm goin' now." "My goodness," she thought. "I never thought about two weeks notice."

"No, I wont you to work tomorrow," he said. "I can't hire anybody on this short notice. I got some people waitin' that I can call tomorrow."

"How come you cain't call 'em today?"

"You just come in tomorrow, Hattie."

She started to leave. "So, I'm fired, but you wont me ta work tomorrah?"

"That's right. What's goin' on with you, anyway? You're quittin' your job, an' you're leavin' your husband?"

She turned around to face him. "I didn' tell you that, Mr. Simmons. How do you know I'm leavin' my husband?"

"Well, that don't matter," he said sheepishly. "I just know."

Hattie looked him straight in the eye and just shook her head.

"Oh, Hattie, here's the two dollars your brother said to give you," he said, handing her the bills.

She took the money and went to the bathroom. No one was in there, and she stood for a little while just staring at the mirror. "Well, it's over, Hattie," she said, "with Horace an' Mr. Simmons. Tomorrah's gon' be my leavin'-an'-startin'-over day." She smiled at her reflection.

When she passed Carolyn's counter, Carolyn didn't say anything, but Hattie knew she was dying to ask what happened. "Mr. Simmons'll tell her soon enough," Hattie thought.

After a while, Anna went to see Hattie. "Are you all right?" she asked.

"Yeah, I am. Thanks," Hattie said, nodding her head. "Thangs didn' turn out the way I planned. I hadn' even tol' Horace I wuz leavin' 'cause he ain't been home since Tuesday, an' Carolyn blurted it out, even though I asked 'er not ta tell anybody. An' she tol' Mr. Simmons. An' he jus' fired me, which don't matter since I wuz gon' quit tomorrah, anyhow."

"Is today your last day, then?" Anna asked.

"No," Hattie smiled. "After he fired me, he said he wonted me ta work tomorrah. So I will. I can use the money."

"Well, Hattie," Anna said softly, "I'm sorry you're leaving, but at least, after tomorrow you won't have to worry about any of that anymore."

"That's right." Hattie said. A big smile spread across her face as she suddenly felt the euphoria of her coming freedom.

♥ ♥ ♥

ON THE WAY HOME, HATTIE STOPPED AT PUBLIX Super Market. She knew, with the deposit for the bottles, she'd have $2.10. "I got three slices a bread left, so I don't need no bread." She bought the smallest chicken she could find, which she figured she could have for supper, and then breakfast and lunch on Saturday. It was $.70. She bought a dozen eggs for $.24, mostly to pay back the Wuthertons, and a handful of string beans for $.15. Hattie added the cost up as she went. She got a can of coffee for $.39 and a can of evaporated milk for $.14, so she'd have it when she got to her new place. She decided to try coffee without sugar for a few days. She picked up a tube of toothpaste. "I'll leave that ole tube; it's almost empty an' Horace can have it. That's $.28. All right, that makes $1.90."

She still had grits for supper and breakfast. She wished she could buy butter, but she knew she could make some chicken gravy after she fried the chicken. "Anyhow," she thought. "'If wishes were horses, all beggars would ride,' as Mama used to say." She bought a five-cent bag of salted peanuts and a small Coke. Her bill was $2.00. "Ten cents left," Hattie thought. "I can buy a cup a coffee tomorrah at the store." When the clerk handed Hattie the dime for the five bottles, and her green stamps, she started thinking about what she might get with them. "Maybe I can save enough stamps ta git a fan, an' then I won't hafta buy one," she thought.

Lake Mirror was her next stop. She opened the Coke with an opener Horace kept in the glove compartment, and took it and the salted peanuts, and sat on a bench in the shade of a palm tree. She poured the salted peanuts into the bottle of Coke and drank the fizz before it could spill over. Nearby, a teenage boy sat on the grass strumming a guitar. She thought it sounded vaguely like "Love Me Tender."

Hattie watched the ducks and geese in the lake. "It's awf'ly peaceful here," she thought, "even though I hear the cars drivin' past. I shoulda done stuff like this more often, but I always rushed home ta make supper fer Horace. I wuz always thankin' 'bout him, but he never thought about me."

She looked over and through the concrete slats of the low wall surrounding the lake, searching for the pair of white swans, which had arrived in February. A Lakeland woman, living in England, was upset that all the local swans had been killed by dogs or alligators, and she requested that Queen Elizabeth donate a pair of the royal swans on the Thames to Lakeland. The city paid $300 for capture and shipping charges, inoculated them for disease, and provided food and safe habitat for them. Hattie hadn't seen them, and as she looked, she remembered that they were in Lake Morton. "I'll go there sometime, maybe on the bus," she thought.

Several sparrows lit in front of her looking for food. She watched them as she drank her Coke and munched on the peanuts. Sitting in the peaceful place, her mind got still. The boy with the guitar left, and for a while, the only sounds she heard were the chirping of the sparrows, and the steady, hypnotic drone of passing cars. She watched some anhingas light near the edge of the lake and start swimming and diving; one lit on the wall and spread its wings to sun itself, its black feathers shining in the sunlight. The sparrows gave up on her and started looking for food on the cement walkway that circled the lake, but when a man walked too close to them, they flew to another area. Occasionally, people walked past and she could hear snatches of their conversations.

After a while, no one passed. Hattie was alone. "I'm feelin' plum peaceful," she thought, and she realized her headache was gone. "Don't know when I felt like this." After she finished her Coke and peanuts, she sat watching the lake, the anhingas, some ducks that swam over from the other side, and the sparrows, which had returned and were a little further away from her. She could hear their soft chirping. The only other time Hattie had that kind of peace was when she was in the yard with her flowers.

♥　♥　♥

"I DON'T RIGHTLY KNOW HOW LONG I SAT THERE," she thought as she drove home, surprised to see how low the sun was in the sky. "It's almost sunset."

When she pulled into her driveway, the Wuthertons were walking past her house and she remembered the hibiscus cuttings and the eggs. She called to them, "Hey there. I got yore eggs," and took two out of the carton. "Thank you so much," she said, handing them to Mrs. Wutherton. "I really 'preciated 'em."

"Oh, Hattie, you didn' hafta do this," Mrs. Wutherton said. "You gave us eggs lots of times when you had chickens."

"Well, you gave me lots a scraps fer my chickens," Hattie replied. "By the way," she announced, "I'm gon' have chickens ag'in."

"You are?" Mr. Wutherton asked. "I b'lieve yore brother took down yore chicken pen this afternoon. When we got up from a nap, I saw 'im puttin' it in his truck an' yore swing was in there, too."

"He did?" Hattie asked, turning to look at the empty place on her front porch. "I didn' know he wuz gon' do that today."

The Wuthertons just looked at her. "Where you plan to put chickens?" he asked.

"Oh," Hattie said. "The truth is, I'm leavin' Horace an' I'm movin' to a house Francis owns, an' I'm gon' work in his store. I woulda tol' y'all before, but Horace didn' even know I wuz leavin' till today. It didn' seem right ta tell other people 'fore I tol' him."

Mrs. Wutherton handed the eggs to her husband. "Hold these while I give Hattie a hug," she said.

She hugged Hattie hard. "I'm so happy for you, Hattie. We've been so worried about you; I'm so glad you're leavin' him."

Mr. Wutherton added, "We'll miss you, but I think you're doin' the right thing." He handed the eggs back to his wife.

"So do I," Mrs. Wutherton agreed. "You know I just hated it when Horace killed your chickens. I knew how much you loved those hens. An' you know, Hattie," she added in a quiet voice, "we didn' say anything to you, but yesterday an' Wednesday, we saw Horace go into the house with a blond woman while you were at work."

"Goodness gracious! Well, I cain't b'lieve that!" Hattie said, her eyes filling with tears. "That rascal! I put up with a lot a stuff from Horace, but I wouldn' a put up with that, an' he knows it. The ole buzzard!"

"I'm so sorry, Hattie," Mrs. Wutherton said. "The only reason we didn' tell you is because we knew it would just hurt you. An' to tell the truth, we knew you already had plenty to worry about."

"Well, I'm glad you tol' me now," Hattie said. "If I ever thank I made a mistake leavin' 'im, I'll jus' thank a this an' know I didn'.'"

"I'm so sorry, Hattie," Mrs. Wutherton said again.

"It's all right," Hattie replied. "I shoulda left 'im long ago, but I b'lieve people oughta stay together if they can, an' not git a divorce."

"That's what we think, too," Mr. Wutherton said. "An' nobody can say you didn' try, Hattie."

"That's shorely the truth!" Hattie exclaimed. "I did do my best." She nodded her head. "Well, I need ta git yore cuttin's from my white hibiscus. Can I use yore knife, Mr. Wutherton?"

He reached in his pocket and pulled out his knife. He opened it and handed it to Hattie as they walked to the hibiscus bushes. Hattie cut five limbs and gave them to Mrs. Wutherton. "Will that be enough?" she asked.

"That's plenty," Mrs. Wutherton replied. "I figured I'd plant three, so that gives me two extra, if I need 'em."

"Well, I got ta git my groceries in. Miz Wutherton, do ya wont some more zinnias?"

"Oh, thank you, Hattie, but the ones you gave me are still purty."

"Well, they'll be here if ya wont ta git some more. I know Horace ain't gon' take care a 'em, so pick 'em any time you wont some. An' y'all come by ta see me sometime. You know where my brother's store is. I'll be workin' there, an' livin' in that little yeller house behine the store. But don't tell Horace," she added.

"Oh, don't worry 'bout that," Mrs. Wutherton said. "We wouldn' give him the time a day."

As Hattie walked back to her car, she heard Mr. Wutherton say, "I'm so glad she's leavin' that bum."

Hattie thought, "There were lots a times I wouldn' a wonted nobody callin' him a bum. But him with another woman in my house, an' ever'thang else he done! He is a bum, a worthless bum! I'm so glad she tol' me that 'cause I won't ever doubt that I did the right thang leavin' 'im. He takes all the food an' leaves me ta go hungry, an' brings another woman in my house, an' him an' her got Co-Colas an' candy, an' they leave the bottles an' wrappers on the table fer me ta see an' ta take care of. An' that wuz *her* cigarette! An' she sat in my chair. *My* chair! She must be a witch, herse'f. An' then he acts like he don't wont me ta leave 'im? I hope I never lay eyes on him ag'in, ever!"

Hattie took the groceries into the kitchen. "Well, at least he wadn' here today," she said. "I guess he jus' went back ta Darrell's, or ta that witch's house. If she's even got a house."

She went back outside and took the bucket with the mayonnaise from under the porch. She took the big jar out of the bucket and took the mayonnaise out of the jar. Then she took the jar around front, and poured the water from the melted ice on the smallest one of the crape myrtle plants. "I cain't wait ta see y'all's buds open up," she said. "I shore hope they're gon' be white. I'm gon' git Francis ta move y'all fer me ta my new house. Y'all'll be happy there. We all will. Oh, I cain't wait ta git over there, and have y'all there."

Hattie noticed that the heat of the day was gone and the air was pleasant. "I love this time a day, this time a year," she said, straightening up and breathing deeply. She went over to the zinnias. "I'm gon' miss y'all, but you'll be okay."

A pair of mourning doves flew over her head and lit in the field across the road. After a little while, she heard their mournful call. She always felt melancholy when she heard mourning doves, so she went to the back porch, got the mayonnaise and the slop jar, and took them into the house. "Anyhow," she thought, "I need ta make my supper." She put the mayonnaise in the refrigerator and the slop jar under the bed.

Hattie went in the living room to turn on the radio. "Oh, I see Francis wuz in here, too," she said. The picture of her parents and the lamp, as well as the table they sat on, were gone. "Thank you, Francis. It's nice ta thank that's already in my livin' room. The couch an' chair go tomorrah." Francis had put the radio on the floor. She changed from the country station, when she heard Kitty Wells singing some mournful song about love gone wrong, to a rock and roll station. Elvis Presley's "Heartbreak Hotel" had just come on. Hattie started to sing along, but she stopped.

"That's a sad ole song, but there ain't gon' be no Heartbreak Hotel fer me. It's gon' be Hattie's Hallelujah Hotel!"

As she cut up the chicken, she said, "I never used chicken ta flavor beans before, but I'm gon' do it tonight. I ain't got no salt pork or ham, an' it oughta be good." She lit a burner, put some water and salt in a pot and set it on the stove. When the water boiled, she added the neck and the back, which she'd cut into two pieces. She turned the burner down and let the chicken simmer for a while.

"I oughta check the bedroom ta make sure Horace wadn' here," she thought. As she looked around the room, she said, "Thank God. Nothin' ta pick up tonight." She took off her sandals and hose, and went back to the kitchen barefoot.

"Ummm, that chicken smells good cookin'," she said. She broke the stems off the green beans, snapped and rinsed them, and put them in the pot. When Elvis' "Blue Suede Shoes" came on, Hattie started moving her feet and hips to the music.

The can of lard did not have much left in it, so she scraped all of it into the frying pan. She salted the chicken and dumped the little bit of flour Horace had left into a shallow aluminum pan. Then, she floured the chicken, and put it, piece by piece, in the hot grease. "I have jus' enough flour left ta make a little gravy," she thought as she put some grits on to cook. The smell of the frying chicken made her mouth water, and when she turned it, it was the brown color she wanted.

After she took the chicken out of the frying pan, she took a few spoonfuls of lard out of the pan and put it back in the can so she'd have some to fry her egg and warm some chicken for breakfast. Then she sprinkled some flour in the hot grease to make gravy, and when it was brown, she added some water. She stirred it rapidly and added a sprinkle of salt and black pepper. Then she fixed her water and syrup, and everything was ready.

Hattie sat down to eat feeling very grateful for the food. She decided it was important for her to say grace. "Dear Lord, I thank you fer this wonderful food. I'm real grateful. I know I ain't always thanked you an' I'm sorry. An' I'm gon' try ta thank you from now on. An' thank you fer Francis an' the little yeller house an' my new job. An' please take care a Horace. Amen."

"Well, I got a whole chicken fer myse'f," Hattie said. "An' it's delicious, even if I did cook it." Her mother had taught her not to brag on her own cooking. "The only thang missin' is some good ole buttermilk biscuits an' butter, but I can have a piece a light bread. Oh, an' some ice tea—that'd be good. I bet Horace ain't got a meal this good. A course, if he's at Darrell's, he's prob'ly too drunk ta care 'bout eatin'." Enjoying the gizzard, liver, and heart, she realized that when Horace was there, he always ate them."

When she finished eating, she cleaned up the kitchen. As she'd been doing, she dried the dishes and put them away. Then, she took her toothbrush and toothpaste from the cup on top of the refrigerator, put some toothpaste on the toothbrush, put some water in a glass, went on the back porch, and brushed her teeth. She left the light on, and after she put the toothbrush away, she went to the car and got the boxes and bags she needed for packing.

"It's time ta pack," she said. "Horace knows I'm leavin' now, so he prob'ly won't do nothin'. Anyhow, I don't thank he wonts ta pick a fight wi' Francis, in spite a his big talk. Francis is eight years younger 'an him, an' he works hard, so I know he's a lot stronger. Horace used ta be strong when he was a mechanic, but he don't do nothin' ta keep hisse'f strong no more."

She went to the bedroom. When she looked at the bed, she imagined Horace there with another woman. She was surprised to find that she really did not care much. "I guess I'm through wi' him," she thought. "I don't care what he does if it don't involve me. I wonder if she likes him pawin' her. That there woman shore ain't got good sense, nohow!"

As she turned away from the bed, she thought of the jar of zinnias that she'd had on the table. "He musta give them flow'rs ta that woman," she thought. "Now that, I care about. I don't care what he does wi' her, but he ain't got no right givin' her my flow'rs. An' right off my kitchen table! He wouldn' even lift a finger ta he'p me plant 'em, an' he give 'em ta her like some kinda big shot, I bet."

She packed everything that was in her drawers in one of the cardboard boxes. As she emptied the drawers, she thought, "I bet that woman wuz in here wi' Horace when he wuz emptyin' out my stuff. She prob'ly saw my personal thangs. She may even a been emptyin' stuff, herse'f. Now that makes me mad — her seein' my thangs, an' maybe dumpin' 'em on the floor." Hattie took one of Horace's undershirts from his drawer and ripped the front of it. Then she folded it neatly and put it back in the drawer. "Stupid ole bastard," she said, and she didn't feel the least bit guilty.

She grabbed his dirty clothes from the clothes hamper and threw them on the closet floor. "My goodness," she said, "if Francis had a come here yestiddy an' seen my stuff all over the floor an' them Coke bottles, no tellin' what he woulda done. Lord, am I glad he didn' come!"

She folded her sweater and all her dresses, except Saturday's, and put them in the hamper. She put her housedress on top, and decided to just carry her winter coat. It would take too much room folded up.

Hattie saw the electric heater in the closet. It was their only source of heat in the winter. "I'm takin' that fer shore," she thought. "I bought it with my hard-earned money." She put it next to the clothes hamper.

"Well, I'll leave out my ole sandals ta wear while we're movin' stuff, an' these dungarees an' pink shirt," she said. "I don't wont them ole blue curtains, so they can stay here. I'm takin' my crocheted bedspread, but that'll wait till tomorrah. I'll leave them sheets on the bed; the bed's made up, but that woman musta been on it. I shore don't want 'em if she wuz. Lord knows if they'll ever git washed ag'in. Oh," she remembered, "my other set a sheets is on the closet shelf. An' the towels." She put the sheets in a bag and put the four towels and four washcloths on top of them. "Well, that's it fer the bedroom," she said.

She went into the kitchen. "I shoulda got some newspaper ta pack the dishes with," she thought. "Good gracious! How could I forgit that? Well, it ain't like I'm movin' ta Georgia. It's jus' the other side a town. It ain't that far an' Francis'll drive careful. I know what! I can use the towels an' dishrags fer packin' the dishes. An' the sheets, if I need 'em. They all hafta be packed, anyhow. Might as well use 'em." She packed most of the dishes before she quit to go to bed. "It wuz a rough day an' I'm tired," she thought, changing into her nightgown.

As she wound the alarm clock, she remembered Horace's eyes and angry tone, and she felt afraid again. She closed the wooden doors even though it was warm in the house. She pushed the little latch over on each one, doubting that the locks would hold if someone jiggled the knobs, so she propped a kitchen chair under each of the doorknobs. "He might git in," Hattie thought, "but I'd shore hear 'im, so I could be up an' not lyin' in bed. My last night here, an' I'm goin' ta bed scared ha'f ta death!"

Hattie turned her pillow over just in case the woman's head had been on it. She lay on top of the sheets, but didn't feel comfortable and she didn't sleep well. Lying in bed, she kept thinking of Horace giving another woman her flowers and his being there in *her* bed with her. "I guess I do care," she thought. It wasn't that he was with another woman that bothered her; it was simply the betrayal. It was also the utter lack of concern for her welfare, while he was obviously being charming to the other woman. He hadn't been charming with Hattie for years.

She wondered what kind of woman would be attracted to him now; what did he have that would attract anyone, and if he had something so great, why didn't he let her see it? As she thought about it, she felt nauseous and nervous, and she could feel her hands trembling..

"The very nerve a him," she moaned. "I work an' give him money, cook, clean, an' wash his filthy clothes. An', I cut the grass! An' he comes in here with another woman? An' ta top it all off, he gives her my flow'rs. Flow'rs that he never lifted a finger ta he'p me fix a place fer. He better not come in this house tonight, 'cause, jus' like Francis, I'd like ta kill 'im! An' I bet anythang he give her my food, too. I shoulda listened ta Mama. She tol' me when I wuz sixteen not ta let a boy kiss me till we wuz engaged. I thought that wuz stupid, an' I let 'im kiss me. I wanted 'im to, but I shouldn' a let 'im! The ole bastard . . . son of a bitch!" Her hands were busily twisting the sheet. "I know I said it, an' I don't care."

The phrase, "Girls havta be careful," popped into her mind, and she remembered a story her grandmother told her: "My mama's cousin wuz with child, an' the father wouldn' marry her. Her daddy wuz plannin' a shotgun weddin', but the boy run off, so she had a bastard child. That pore ole soul wuz eighty years old when she died, an' people were talkin' 'bout that at her funeral. Girls havta be extry careful, honey."

Hattie took a deep breath and sighed. "Thank about happy thangs now, Hattie! You need some peace. I need a angel ta brang me some peace." And as she began to relax, she suddenly sat up and laughed. "That's what I'm gon' name my little puppy. Angel. I'm tradin' Horace fer a little angel an' some peace. An' I'm gittin' a real good deal. Angel. Oh! I like that name."

After she finally went to sleep, she woke up a couple of times, thinking she heard a car in the driveway. She was too tired and too scared to get up and look, so she just lay there and listened, her body still and stiff, all of her senses alert, until she was sure that Horace wasn't trying to get into the house. Each time, she calmed herself by saying, "This is the last night. Tomorrah I'll be free. I'll be free."

Saturday

Hᴀᴛᴛɪᴇ ᴡᴏᴋᴇ ᴜᴘ ᴀɴ ʜᴏᴜʀ ʙᴇꜰᴏʀᴇ sʜᴇ ʜᴀᴅ ᴛᴏ ɢᴇᴛ ᴜᴘ. Although she was tired, she was too excited to go back to sleep. "This is the last day a my ole life," she thought. "I better git up an' finish packin'. I jus' got the kitchen stuff lef' ta do."

She stood up, stretched, and yawned. "Boy! I didn' sleep much at all last night. I wuz too nervous. It's no wonder I'm so tired."

When she took the slop jar from under the bed and peed in it, she thought, "I thank I'll take this ole thang wi' me fer a keepsake a life wi' Horace. It purty much sums up the last few years." She laughed. "Maybe I'll plant a flower in it, an' make it smell sweet."

Since she'd already packed her housedress, Hattie decided to just leave her gown on, and she went to the kitchen barefoot. She moved the chair from the door and put it back by the table. "I hafta remember to move that other chair, too," she thought. "I don't wont Francis or Horace ta know I wuz scared."

She packed the rest of her dishes, and took out the pots and pans, but decided to have her breakfast before packing them since she needed some for cooking. She took the chicken and an egg from the refrigerator and went into the bedroom to get her pocketbook with the grits.

"Well, at least I ain't got much food ta pack. I'll eat all a that chicken. There is that little jar a mayonnaise, the eggs, an' that coffee an' can a milk I bought. An', a course, the grits in my pocketbook safe." She smiled. "Ain't this a ridiculous way ta live! Well, it don't matter, nohow; today's the last day, an' at least today, I got plenty a food. Thank God fer that."

She lit two burners, put water and salt in a pot for the grits, and put a spoonful of the used lard in the frying pan. It was a small chicken and she had eaten the drumsticks, short thighs, and giblets for supper, and used the neck and back in the beans. She'd also eaten the meat off the back with her supper; she liked the dark meat on the lower back. The two wings and the breast were left. "Well I'm gon' have one piece a breast an' the wings fer breakfast, an' the other piece a breast fer work." She cut the smaller piece of breast in half and put the two pieces in the hot grease to warm. The water was boiling and she poured some grits in it and turned the burner down. After she stirred them, she went to the sink to wash up.

She got the washcloth from the nail and washed her face. She rinsed it and wiped under each arm. Then she put the cloth in the sink, turned the chicken, and stirred the grits. "When I have my bathtub tonight, I'll jus' take a bath, an' I won't hafta do this ever' mornin'. Hallelujah!" She rinsed the cloth and hung it back on the nail. "I hafta remember ta pack it," she said. She put on her deodorant and washed her hands.

She took the chicken out of the pan, turned the burner down, stirred the grits, and broke the egg in the pan. She went quickly to the bedroom and got the syrup from the closet. She salted the egg and turned it. Then she put some syrup in a glass and filled it with water, put that in her thermos, and made a second glass. "I don't need no hot water," she thought. "It got purty warm in here last night with the doors closed." She looked at the syrup bottle. "There ain't much a this syrup left," Hattie thought. "I wouldn' even care if Horace got that." She put the bottle under the sink.

Hattie said grace before her breakfast. "I remembered," she said. "I hafta remember ta say a blessin' from now on." She ate her breakfast, feeling very grateful for the food. Then she washed and dried the breakfast dishes. She packed them and the rest of the pots and pans and the silverware. "Well, that's purty much it, I thank," she said. "Time ta git ready fer work."

After she got dressed, she took the slop jar to the outhouse. The yard looked strange without the chicken pen. Hattie heard the blue jay and looked for it, automatically, where the chicken fence had been. She finally saw it sitting in a long-needle pine tree in the neighboring field.

As she left the outhouse, she thought about the two oranges that she hadn't eaten. "I wonder if I can git one a 'em." She waded through the weeds and looked for the big yellow and black spider. It was there in almost the same place. She went past it and noticed that one of the oranges was above a low limb that she could easily stand on. "I'm gon' git that an' leave it on the table fer Horace ta see. A course, he prob'ly won't even remember the picnic, but I don't care."

She went back to the house with the orange and the slop jar, looking around as she walked. "Sumpin seems diff'runt," she thought, her mind uneasy. "It mus' jus' be 'cause the chicken pen's gone." She rinsed the slop jar and set it on the step to drain. "Fer the last time," she said.

In the kitchen, she noticed the chair was still missing. "I hafta move that chair from the front door after I git my chicken." She took the paper bag from her pocketbook and used the waxed paper in it to wrap the piece of chicken breast, and she put it and the two slices of light bread in the paper bag and put it in her pocketbook. And so Horace wouldn't see them, she put the chicken bones in a bag and put the bag in her pocketbook, and she put it and her thermos on the table. "The chair," she remembered.

She went into the living room, moved the chair, and opened the door to peek out at her beautiful zinnias. "Oh my Lord!" she screeched when she saw them. Her whole body began to shake. She shoved the screen door open and ran out on the porch. "Oh my Lord! Oh my Lord! What in tarnation?" she cried as she flew down the steps and into the yard. "What in the worl' happened?" The row of zinnias was broken and crushed and lying all over the ground. As Hattie frantically inspected them, she saw the tracks. "Oh my Lord! They been run over," she moaned, her hands over her heart. "Somebody run over my zinnias."

Hattie's first thought was that somebody had an accident. Then she noticed her crape myrtles. They'd also been run over and were broken and crushed. She knew that was suspicious. Standing over the crape myrtles, she finally noticed that the car was gone. "Oh my Lord!" she cried, "Horace done it. That ole buzzard done it! Oh my Lord!" She could tell that the car had been over the crape myrtles three times. "He done it on purpose. He had ta back up, go forward, an' back up ag'in. An' he done the same thang with my zinnias," she said, looking at the ground there. "That's how come I heard a car durin' the night," she thought as she remembered waking up.

Hattie picked up one of the crape myrtle blooms, still closed, but she forced it open enough to see white. She sank down onto the ground, crying. She'd forgotten about work and everything else. "Now I know why sumpin looked diff'runt earlier," she thought. "The car was gone."

After a little while, the Wuthertons, who were just beginning their morning walk, saw the devastation. Hattie was still sitting on the ground crying. Mrs. Wutherton said softly, "Oh, Hattie." Hattie looked up and Mrs. Wutherton knelt down and put her arms around her. Hattie didn't want to cry with the Wuthertons there, but she couldn't help it.

"Oh my goodness! I'm so sorry," Mrs. Wutherton said.

"He done it on purpose," Hattie sobbed. "On purpose."

After Hattie cried for a little while, Mr. Wutherton said, "Hattie, I think we can save one of these crape myrtles." She looked up. "Most of the limbs are broke off, but the trunk's still okay. I think it'll come back. An' there's plenty a limbs here. You said they were jus' little twigs when you got 'em, so you can start 'em over ag'in."

Hattie's spirits lifted a little. "Yes, sir, I can," she said through her tears. "I'm startin' over, so I can start my flow'rs over, too."

She looked at the hibiscus by the porch. "Thank God he didn' hurt the hibiscus. I wont ta git some clippin's from them, too."

"Are you goin' to work today?" Mrs. Wutherton asked.

"Oh my Lord! I forgot all about work. Can I use yore telephone ta call Francis ta see if he can gimme a ride?"

"Oh, don't be silly, Hattie," Mr. Wutherton said. "You can use our telephone to call 'im if ya need to, but I'll take you to work."

Hattie needed to hear her brother's voice. "I would like ta call 'im," she said, and they walked next door in silence.

"Y'all been so kind ta me," she said softly as they entered the house. "I don't know how to repay ya."

"Jus' knowin' you're goin' to be workin' with yore brother an' livin' in his house is all we care about. We're so happy 'bout that," Mrs. Wutherton said.

Hattie sat down on a chair near the phone. She felt like she'd just heard about the death of a relative. Her knees felt weak and she was still on the verge of tears.

"Let me git you a cup of coffee," Mrs. Wutherton said. "I think there's still some in the pot. I b'lieve you take cream an' sugar, don't you, Hattie?"

"Yes, ma'am," Hattie said, grateful for the older woman's concern.

Hattie picked up the phone and hung it up. "Someone's on the line."

"Was it a woman?" Mr. Wutherton asked.

"Yes, sir," Hattie replied.

Mr. Wutherton picked up the phone. "Excuse me, Miz Melton. We need to make an important call. Could you hang up an' give us a few minutes, please?"

After a moment, he said, "Thank you," and handed the phone to Hattie. "I shore wish that woman wadn' on our party line. Ever' time I wanna use the phone, she's talkin' to somebody."

Fortunately, Francis was at the store. As soon as Hattie heard his voice, she started crying. Mr. Wutherton was still standing near her and she handed the receiver to him. He told Francis what had happened.

Hattie could hear Francis say, "Damn! I cain't say I'm surprised. I knew he'd be mad as a wet settin' hen when he found out she was leavin'. Damn it all! I'd like ta talk to 'er if she can talk now."

Mrs. Wutherton gave Hattie the coffee and she took a sip. She looked at Mr. Wutherton who said, "I'm givin' the phone back to her."

Francis asked, "Have you packed yore stuff yet?"

"Yeah, I'm all packed," she said.

"This is what I wont you to do. Ask them to he'p you move ever'thing you packed over to their house. Don't worry 'bout the furniture, but take ever'thing else you wont over there. Maybe you can put it on their front porch."

"I cain't ask that," Hattie said, glancing at the Wuthertons.

"Well, let me talk ta Mr. Wutherton ag'in. An' Hattie, I'll pick you up after work. We won't be goin' back to yore house, so be sure to git ever'thing you wont outta there."

Mr. Wutherton nodded his head as he listened to Francis. "Yes, sir, I'll be here," he said. "I'll be more than glad to."

Hattie drank the coffee and wondered what Francis was saying.

"Of course we'll help her."

When he hung up the telephone, Mr. Wutherton said, "Okay, Hattie. The wife an' I are gonna help you bring yore stuff over here."

"Oh no," Hattie declared. "That's too much trouble for y'all."

"No, it's not," Mr. Wutherton insisted. "That's exactly what we're goin' to do. When you finish yore coffee, we'll git started. You don't want yore stuff left in the house. What if Horace came home an' saw ever'thing? That man's awf'ly mad, an' there ain't no tellin' what he might do."

It only took two trips for the three of them to take all of Hattie's belongings. She got her crocheted bedspread, her coat and the other clothes she hadn't packed, and she decided to take the oilcloth off the table. "That red, yeller, an' white will look nice in the kitchen with them yeller walls," she thought. And she took the little bit of food she had left.

Mrs. Wutherton said she had room in her refrigerator for a few things, but Hattie only had the eggs and mayonnaise. She grabbed her washboard and her washtub from the back porch, and he got her lawn mower.

The Wuthertons didn't say a word, but they noticed how little food she had to move. Hattie didn't see the look they shared, nor the tears in Mrs. Wutherton's eyes.

Mrs. Wutherton suggested that Hattie use their bathroom to wash her tear-stained face. Then Mr. Wutherton took her to work. On the way, he told Hattie that Francis was coming and he was going to help him load her furniture. "He wonts to know if there's anything else besides the couch an' chair in the livin' room, an' the bed an' dresser in the bedroom."

"I don't wont that bed," Hattie said. "Not after what Horace done. The couch opens up an' I'll sleep on that till I can buy me a bed. I do wont that chair that's in the bedroom, though, and the dresser. I forgot to take out Horace's stuff; he's got stuff in two drawers on the left side. You know, Mr. Wutherton, Horace dumped my stuff all over the floor twice this week, so jus' dump his on the floor." Hattie was surprised at herself for telling him that, but she was so angry at Horace for ruining her plants that she didn't care anymore. However, she didn't tell him about Horace taking the food or dumping the grits on the floor—she felt ashamed that she'd married someone who'd stoop that low.

"I'll do it, gladly," he said. "An' please tell me if there's anything else you wont me to dump."

Hattie laughed, in spite of herself. "There's not," she said, and added, "This may sound funny, but I wont the slop jar that's on the back step, an' I forgot ta take it to yore house. I'm gon' put a plant in it."

He laughed. "I guess you'll have a bathroom at yore new house."

"Yes, sir," Hattie replied. "A real nice one. I wont y'all ta come over an' see me. When I git a telephone, I'll call an' y'all can come over fer dinner some Sunday, an' see my new place."

"That would be nice, Hattie," Mr. Wutherton said. "But you don't hafta go to all that trouble."

"I wont ta fix dinner for y'all some Sunday," Hattie responded. "I'd like ta do that."

"It's a deal, Hattie," he said as he pulled up in front of the store.

Hattie was over an hour late, and the store was open. "Mr. Simmons is gon' yell at me," she said to Mr. Wutherton.

"Well, you'll soon be away from the men who yell at you," he said, and smiled at her.

"Yes, sir, I will," Hattie replied, returning his smile. "Thank you an' Miz Wutherton for all yore help. I shore do 'preciate it."

♥ ♥ ♥

WHEN MR. WUTHERTON ARRIVED HOME, he saw his wife in Hattie's yard. She was trying to see how much she could salvage of the broken plants.

"Pore Hattie," she said, looking around the yard. "This jus' broke her heart. It was a mean, mean thing to do."

"It shore was," he agreed. "Plain cruel. He knew how much she loved those plants, an' that's why he did it."

Mrs. Wutherton looked at the pathetic remainder of Hattie's treasured bushes. "I know the main thing she wonted was the crape myrtles. We can take up one of these bushes an' it'll be okay, but the other two are done for. However, there are plenty of good limbs. An', you know what, I bet if we put these limbs in some water, the flowers will open up in a few days. That way, at least Hattie'll be able to enjoy 'em for a little while."

"I'll go git yore clippers an' a bucket with some water in it for ya," Mr. Wutherton said, turning to go back to their house.

While she waited for her husband to return, she picked up some of the zinnias that were still attached to their stems. "We can make Hattie a nice bouquet," she thought.

Mr. Wutherton returned with the clippers, a shovel, and Hattie's slop jar with water in it. "Hattie said she wonted this, so we might as well use it for the flowers."

Mrs. Wutherton laughed. "Are you serious?"

"Why not?" he asked. "She was gonna take it, so it might as well serve a purpose."

She shook her head. "Well, the flowers won't care what kind of container they're in."

She had collected all of the zinnias that she could save, and she clipped their stems so they were the right length for a nice bouquet while Mr. Wutherton dug up the salvageable crape mrytle. "I'll put these zinnias in a quart jar," she said. "I've got one that has a little chip out of the top an' I cain't use it for cannin' anymore, nohow."

She cut four crape myrtle limbs that looked sturdy and put them in the slop jar. "These oughta root, but I've got four of 'em, just in case." She cut off the other blooms and added them. When she was finished, the pot was full, and she nodded her head in approval. "That was a good idea," she said. "That white pot with the red rim makes 'em look nice even now. When they open, they'll look real purty."

The two of them were about to go back to their house when Francis arrived. He backed his truck into the driveway and got out. He stood for a minute just looking at the yard. Then he went over and shook hands with the Wuthertons, and greeted them as though they were at a funeral. Shaking his head, he said, "This is hard to believe, even for Horace."

Mr. Wutherton nodded, "It shore is. We knew Horace was unpredictable, but he really surprised us this time."

"Hattie was so upset," Mrs. Wutherton said. "When we came, she was jus' sittin' on the ground cryin'."

Francis turned to face the row of zinnias to hide the tears in his eyes. After a moment, he wiped his eyes and said, "I cain't tell you what I'd like ta do to 'im, but I hafta swallow it. I'd prob'ly jus' git myse'f in trouble."

"I know how you feel," Mr. Wutherton said.

Francis added, "But I'll tell you one thang. If he's got any sense, he'll steer clear a me fer a long time."

"I expect he knows that," Mr. Wutheron said, and laughed softly.

"How do you like the bouquet of crape myrtles?" Mrs. Wutherton asked. "She was jus' tellin' us the other day that she was anxious to see what color the blooms would be, an' she hoped they'd be white. An' they are."

"That's great," Francis said, smiling as he noticed the slop jar.

"Hattie wonted the pot, so I figured we might as well use it," Mr. Wutherton offered.

"Good idear," Francis agreed, nodding his head. "Do you have the lid?"

"It's at our house with her things."

"Are you sure you can he'p wi' that furniture?" Francis asked the older man. "No bad back or anything?"

"My back's fine, an' I'd like to help," Mr. Wutherton assured him.

"Well, I got a lot to do today, so I'm ready to git started."

Mrs. Wutherton went home to get the jar for the zinnias. She returned shortly with the jar, which had water in it, a pencil, and some newspaper.

Francis and Mr. Wutherton went in the house, and Mr. Wutherton told Francis what Hattie said about dumping out Horace's stuff.

"I can take care of that," Francis said, an' he threw stuff all over the bedroom, making sure that some stuff went under the bed, some on the bed, and some on the window sills, but most of it went on the floor.

Mr. Wutherton laughed. "I b'lieve you're even madder than I am."

"I hope you're not as mad as me," Francis replied. "It ain't good for yore blood pressure."

They quickly loaded Hattie's dresser and the chair from the bedroom on the truck. "I'll get the living room couch and chair, an' anything else that's left, in the next trip," Francis said. "I'll drive the truck over to yore house now so we can git some of the stuff she's got packed."

"Francis," Mrs. Wutherton called. "Hattie said she wonted some cuttin's from her hibiscus bushes, so I'm gittin' some for 'er. I'm labelin' them so she'll know what color they are. Also, I put some crape myrtle limbs, which she can use for cuttin's, in the pot with the blooms."

"Thank you, ma'am. I know she'll 'preciate that," Francis said. "You can put 'em in the truck on the floorboard when you're done."

Mrs. Wutherton labeled the newspaper that she wrapped the clippings in, and stuck in at least one limb with a flower, and one with a flower coming, from each plant. She knew the flowers would only last for a day, but it would help Hattie identify the colors.

After they put most of Hattie's packed stuff in the truck, Mrs. Wutherton brought out the bag from the refrigerator. "This must be all the food she had," she said softly, with a question in her eyes.

Francis felt his body stiffen as he took the bag. "Yes, ma'am. I jus' found out yesterday that Horace took almost all the food on Tuesday, an' he's been gone since then. I'd jus' brought her a box a stuff on Sunday. She said she made out all right, but I wanted to kill the son of a bitch." He put his hand on Mrs. Wutherton's arm. "Excuse me, ma'am. I cain't kill 'im, so I hafta cuss some."

"I understand, Francis," she replied, with tears in her eyes. "That makes me so mad I cain't hardly stand it, myself."

Mr. Wutherton's face was the picture of anger. "Pore Hattie. I wish we'd knew it. I cain't b'lieve even Horace would pull a stunt like that. That's jus' low-down mean! An' sorry!" He paused for a moment. "I started to call you Tuesday mornin', Francis. Sumpin happened between 'em an' Horace was *out in his underwear* yellin' an' chasin' after Hattie while she was drivin' off. I wuz scared he'd catch her."

Francis just shook his head. "Lord, I'm glad she's gittin' outta that mess! An' I'm glad you didn' call me; I prob'ly woulda ended up in the pokey. I knew they had problems, but this is jus' ridiculous now." He turned to leave. "I gotta git goin'. Thank you both for helpin' me with Hattie's things, an' for all y'all've done for her."

"Well, I'll go help you unload all this stuff," Mr. Wutherton said.

"Oh no," Francis said, holding up his hand. "I can git my butcher away from the store long enough to he'p wi' this. You've done enough. I 'preciate it, an' all you've done."

"We were glad to do it, an' woulda done a lot more if we knew how bad things were," Mr. Wutherton said. "Francis, you comin' right back to git the rest of the stuff?"

"Yes, sir," Francis replied.

"Well then, I'm goin' with ya'," he said, and Mrs. Wutherton handed him the jar of zinnias.

On the way to the house, he told Francis that they'd seen Horace go in the house with a blond woman twice that week, and that his wife had told Hattie.

After Francis got over his outrage, he said, "There must be some hard-up women 'round here. Who in the world would choose to be wi' that bum? It ain't fer money, that's fer shore! And it ain't fer looks."

Mr. Wutherton said, "I had the same thought. It ain't fer looks, or personality, either. Of course, the woman he was with was a cheap-lookin' floozy. She had on a dress that left nothin' to the imagination. The wife said it looked sprayed on."

They took the boxes and bags in first. Francis peeked in the ones that were closed to see whether they belonged in the bedroom or kitchen. He put the ones with clothes in them in the closet so the room would still look neat. The ones for the kitchen got stacked neatly next to the wall. After they put the dresser in the bedroom, he moved the vase of roses from the kitchen table to the dresser and put the jar of zinnias on the kitchen table.

Mr. Wutherton could not stop expressing how much he liked the house. "Hattie's gonna be so happy here. It's such a nice little house."

"She likes it," Francis said.

Mr. Wutherton looked in the back yard. "You already put up the chicken pen!" he exclaimed. "I woulda he'ped you take it down if I knew you were there. The wife an' I were takin' a nap an' we didn' see you till you were puttin' it on the truck. An' by the time I got my shoes on, you were gone. Boy! Hattie's gonna be surprised."

"I didn' really have the time, but I put it up yesterday. I wuz determined it'd be here when she comes. By the time she sees it, there'll be chickens in there."

"You already got chickens for her?"

"One of our neighbors died recently, an' his wife don't wont to bother with the chickens. There's a rooster an' half a dozen hens, an' frankly, I'll be glad not to hear that ole rooster crowin' on Sunday mornin'."

Mr. Wutherton laughed, "Killin' two birds with one stone, huh?"

Francis smiled, "That's the idea."

Mr. Wutherton looked at the kitchen ceiling. "Francis, I don't b'lieve I ever saw a kitchen with a ceilin' fan."

"I've got one in my house an' my wife loves it. Says it makes cookin' bearable in the summer heat. Hattie's gonna be surprised to see that, too. An' the ones in the livin' room an' bedroom. I just had 'em put in yesterday."

"My goodness! She was already braggin' to us 'bout how nice the house was. Those fans are like frostin' on the cake."

"Well, I wuz plannin' to have it done, an' when I called the electrician, he said he had a couple a hours yesterday afternoon, so he came over, an' we got it done. I thought it would be a nice surprise fer 'er. An' I tell ya, after the mornin' she had, I'm really glad I did it."

"She's gonna be thrilled," Mr. Wutherton said. "I'd like to have the name of yore electrician. Maybe I'll have some put in our house."

"They make a world a difference. Put one in the bedroom."

"I think I will."

"I guess in a few years, everybody'll have air conditionin' in their houses, but I don't think you even need it with ceilin' fans. I *am* plannin' to put it in the store purty soon, though," Francis said. "It'll he'p keep the produce longer, an' my employees'll prob'ly be happier."

Francis put the jar with the hibiscus cuttings on the kitchen counter for Hattie to deal with. He set the slop jar full of crape myrtles next to the wall in the living room, near the doorway to the kitchen. As he did that, Mr. Wutherton put the chair in the bedroom, and they were ready to go back for the rest of her things.

They had the living room chair and couch on the truck by the time Mrs. Wutherton went over and announced that she'd prepared some food for them. Francis thanked her and said he'd join them after he took a last look around the house. He looked in the bedroom closet and saw Horace's dirty clothes on the floor, and a couple of shirts and pants hanging up; he looked on the back porch and saw the clothesline, but decided to leave it there, knowing there was a nice one in Hattie's new yard; he looked in the refrigerator, the kitchen cabinets, and the metal cabinet. He noticed the orange on the table, picked it up, smelled it, and put it back. He wondered why Hattie had put it there, but it seemed clear to him that she intended to leave it; he knew it was half dry.

When he saw the syrup bottle under the sink with about an inch of syrup in it, he took it. "I don't care if she did mean to leave that, I ain't leavin' it, nohow. Not fer him." He took the washcloth from the nail and put it and the syrup in the truck.

He took a piece of paper and a pencil from the glove compartment and went back into the house. He sat down at the table, stared at the orange for a minute, and then wrote a note to Horace. He signed it, Francis Bridges, and put his telephone number after his name.

> Horace,
>   You've been lucky to have Hattie for a wife for almost 20 years!! She was NOT lucky!! You know you've been a lousy husband, AND a sorry excuse for a man!!!

Forget Hattie and forget about the past. She's moving on and that's what you need to do. Don't even TRY to contact her. If you need to talk to her FOR ANY REASON, call ME.

Horace, I'm not messing around here. You've done enough damage. If you even try to contact Hattie, I'll be talking to the police about what you did last night, and some other things!! You know what I mean. Remember, I'm a man of my word.

♥ ♥ ♥

Mr. Simmons was standing behind her counter, wearing his pencil and waiting on a customer when Hattie entered the store. "Now my counter's gon' smell," Hattie thought.

When the customer left, he turned to Hattie and said, "You're late, Hattie!"

"I know that, Mr. Simmons. I'm sorry, but I had an emergency at my house. It couldn' be he'ped."

"What kind of emergency would make you an hour late?"

"Mr. Simmons, if I stand here talkin' ta you, I'll be even later gittin' my counter set up. It was an emergency."

"Well, you know you're not gittin' paid for that time. In fact, I don't believe you should git paid for this whole week."

"Just a minute here," Hattie said. "Yo're tellin' me I ain't gon' git paid fer this whole week. You thank I'm gon' work today when yo're tellin' me I ain't even gon' git paid?"

His face flushed. "I said I don't believe you *should* git paid for the week. You know you've made telephone calls an' got telephone calls, an' now you're an hour late."

"Well, you better decide 'cause I shore ain't about ta work if I ain't gone git paid. An' I thank my brother would find that mighty int'restin'—you not payin' somebody when they already worked. I 'spec' he'd talk ta his lawyer 'bout that."

"I didn' say I wouldn' pay you, Hattie. I jus' don't believe it's right."

"So, am I gittin' paid?"

"Yes, except for the time you were late, an' a half hour for the telephone call yesterday."

"All right then," Hattie said, and she went behind her counter and started rearranging the jewelry. She breathed a sigh of relief when he left. She felt proud of the way she stood up to him, but she was trembling for several minutes afterwards. And she was angry that he was planning to deduct time for the telephone call, but she didn't think there was anything she could do about it.

Saturday was their busiest day and Hattie had customers pretty steadily, so she didn't have much time to think about the morning. And Carolyn stayed busy, so she didn't bother Hattie.

When it was time for lunch, Hattie saw Anna leave the store. "She must be goin' to the park," she thought. "I'm gon' buy two doughnuts wi' that dime I have an' Anna an' me'll have doughnuts after we eat our dinner." She bought the doughnuts at the lunch counter and went to the park, but she didn't see Anna. "Well, I'll give her the doughnut later," she thought. "She musta had sumpin ta do."

She sat under her favorite oak tree, looking at the Confederate soldier statue. "I'll miss seein' that ole statue an' the beautiful fountain. A course, I can always come ta the park when I come ta town, if I wont to. I might even be able ta come eat wi' Anna sometime if I take a day off."

She'd finished eating her chicken, and was watching a squirrel and listening to birds chirping nearby, when Anna joined her. Anna was carrying a bag, which she put on the ground beside the bench.

Hattie smiled. "I looked fer you."

"I had to run an errand," Anna said, looking at the breastbone on Hattie's bag. "Looks like you had chicken today."

"It wuz left over from my supper last night," Hattie said. "Wont ta pull the pulley bone?" They both made wishes and Hattie got the longer piece.

"Well, Hattie, I guess you'll git your wish."

"I thank I already did," Hattie said, smiling. "Oh Anna, I bought some doughnuts fer us to have fer dessert."

Anna could tell by her voice that she thought she'd done something very special. "Oh, thank you, Hattie. That's so nice of you," she said.

"It ain't much."

"Well, I'm looking forward to having a doughnut. It'll be a nice treat."

Anna thought about how a small gesture can have a big effect on people—both the giver and the receiver, and how sometimes something one thinks is a big thing doesn't mean anything to others. Hattie was giving her a gift that cost a nickel, but clearly, it was worth much more to Hattie, and Anna knew that, so it was worth more to her. She was reminded of something her mother told her.

When she was fifteen, Anna gave her grandmother a doily she'd crocheted for her. When her grandmother barely looked at it, Anna's feelings were hurt and her mother noticed. She told her later, "Anna, honey, the *value* of your gift is not determined by the way someone receives it. You gave that gift from your heart, an' that makes it extra special."

Anna knew that Hattie was giving from her heart. She thought maybe she should say more to assure her that she appreciated the gift. "I'm so glad you got the doughnuts for us to share, Hattie. That was very thoughtful."

Hattie smiled self-consciously. "I wonted to give you sumpin since I'm leavin'."

"Well, thank you, Hattie. I appreciate it."

They sat quietly for a moment watching a squirrel across the park jump up on a bench and then onto a tree.

"Isn't that fountain lovely," Anna said.

"It shore is. I walked 'round it yesterday. An' I smelled the roses. They really smell good. All these years, I shoulda done that more often. I'm gon' miss seein' the park."

"I'm sorry you're leavin', Hattie," Anna said softly.

"Well, it's a good thang fer me. I'm leavin' Horace an' goin' ta work fer Francis. I'm startin' over ag'in, kindly."

"I'm happy for you, but I'll miss you."

"I'll miss you, too, Anna," Hattie said sincerely. "Maybe I can come eat wi' you sometime, an' maybe you can come see me. If you give me yore telephone number, I'll call ya after I git settled."

"That would be nice," Anna responded, and she took some paper and a fountain pen from her pocketbook and wrote her number down for Hattie.

Hattie realized that, after eight years of working in the dime store, Anna was the only person who worked there that she actually would miss, and Anna had only been there a year. Even though she was half Hattie's age, she was very mature. Hattie had liked her as soon as she started there, and Anna had made Hattie's last year more enjoyable.

♥ ♥ ♥

THE AFTERNOON WAS BUSY ALSO, with things finally slowing down around four o'clock. When Hattie finished waiting on an elderly white woman, she noticed a young Negro man standing back from her counter. "That's that boy that wuz here the other day," she thought nervously. "He looked at the necklaces." She could tell he was about to go to the counter, but she wanted some water, so she pretended she hadn't seen him, and just left. "I'm hot an' thirsty," she thought. "He'll hafta wait, or maybe he'll go away."

As she drank the cool water, she wondered how many times she'd gotten a drink from that fountain. She noticed the one beside it under the "Colored" sign looked dirty. Whoever was supposed to clean it obviously hadn't. When it was Hattie's turn to clean the fountains, she always cleaned both of them—the white one first, and then, the colored. "Well, I ain't cleanin' it," she thought. "I'm done wi' that. 'Sides, if they're thirsty, they'll drink. The water ain't dirty." Still, it bothered her a little.

She looked at her counter, and no one was there. "I guess that nigger boy left. He prob'ly ain't got no money, nohow."

Walking up the stairs to the bathroom, she thought, "What a day. Horace run over my flow'rs an' Mr. Simmons threatened ta not pay me fer the whole week. Good thing I thought about mentionin' Francis, or he might notta. This is one a my wors' days an' one a my bes' days."

When she went back downstairs, Hattie saw the young Negro man standing near the side of the store. He was looking at a little white girl who was drinking from the "Colored" fountain. "Good gracious! That little girl's drinkin' outta that dirty, colored fountain," she thought. She went over to her and said softly, "Honey, this is the colored fountain."

The little girl looked at her and then at the sign. "Oh," she whispered, clearly embarrassed. "I'm sorry."

"That's all right," Hattie said. "Jus' be careful." She looked at the Negro man to see if he was watching, but he was looking at something else. After she returned to her counter, she saw him drinking from the fountain.

She looked around the store for the little white girl and saw her standing at the toy counter. Hattie could tell her dress was homemade. When she walked away from the toys, she was walking funny, and Hattie noticed that one of her sandal straps was broken. "Oh Lord," she thought, "don't that brang back memories. Seemed like I wuz always needin' a new pair a shoes when I was little. Course, I didn' have sandals back then, but sumpin on my shoes would break or a heel would come off, an' I never got a new pair till they didn' fit anymore or sumpin was bad wrong with 'em. Sometimes I had ta wear the broke one fer days 'fore I got new ones. An' thangs ain't been much better since I got grown. If a strap woulda broke this week, I'd a had ta wear these broke, or else wear them ole shabby, ever'day ones, an' them are almost broke."

When she thought of that, her next thoughts were of the morning and the destruction of her flowers. "I don't know how Horace could do that to my pore flow'rs. He mus' really hate me, or else he jus' really wonted ta hurt me." She could feel her heart pounding and the tears welling up in her eyes. "Thank a sumpin else, Hattie," she silently commanded herself. As she wiped her eyes, the little girl approached her counter and stood quietly, just looking around.

Hattie didn't say anything until she calmed down a little. "That's that little girl who was in here the other day lookin' at the rings," she thought. "I didn't recognize her at first. Her an' her mama were talkin' to Anna, an' Anna said they useta be her neighbors."

"Oh Lord, that nigger boy's comin' over here, too," she thought as she saw him walking toward her counter. Her heart started racing. She watched him walk around the counter and stop a few feet behind the little girl. "At least he's good lookin'," Hattie thought. She took a deep breath.

"Can I he'p ya with sumpin, honey?" she asked, as she walked slowly over to the girl.

"I wanna buy that ruby ring, please," she said softly, pointing at the rings.

"Okay," Hattie said, but she thought, "I wonder how she could have money ta buy a ring, when she don't even have decent shoes or a nice dress. I 'member the other day she had on a ole faded dress." She put the rings on the counter.

"I wont that one," the girl said, pointing to a ring. "The ruby one."

"Try it on," Hattie said, handing her the ring.

The little girl slipped it on her finger. "It fits," she said, smiling. "I'll take it." She put a quarter, a nickel, and five pennies on the counter.

"Of course, it fits—it's adjustable," Hattie thought. She noticed how the little girl's eyes lit up when she put the ring on. "She must've had her money all ready. This means a lot ta her."

"It's adjustable," Hattie said, and looked at the change on the counter. "You owe another penny. It's thirty-six cents."

"Did you say 'thirty-six'?" the girl asked, her eyes wide.

"Yes, honey," Hattie replied. "It's thirty-six cents. You need another penny."

"You tol' me thirty-five cents the other day."

"Well, there's a penny tax," Hattie explained. "She oughta know that," she thought.

"Oh," the girl said softly.

Hattie noticed that her eyes weren't sparkling anymore.

"I only got thirty-five cents," the girl said with a plea in her voice. And she just stood there looking at Hattie. Hattie glanced at the Negro man, who was also looking at her. He lowered his eyes.

"I'm sorry," Hattie said in an unconvincing tone. She could see sweat on the little girl's forehead.

"He prob'ly thanks I oughta give her a penny," Hattie thought. "Who does he thank he is? That ain't part a my job." She looked at the blue shirt he was wearing. "Well, that's another really nice shirt, but he's got some spots on this one. He musta got that on there when he drank from that dirty fountain—I don't care if it was dirty. That's a purty blue shirt; Francis would look great in it."

She looked at the girl who was still looking at her, and thought, "She wonts me ta give 'er a penny, an' if I had one, I would. Land sake! I been needin' a quarter all week, an' now she's needin' a penny—just a penny—an' I ain't got one red cent ta give her. But it ain't my job ta give out pennies, nohow. I got my own troubles."

Hattie glanced around the store to see if anyone was looking at them. No one was, but when she saw Anna, she thought, "Oh my goodness! I hope she don't tell Anna 'bout this. Anna wouldn' understand how come I didn' give 'er a penny."

When she looked at the little girl again, she was just standing there looking at her. Hattie thought she saw tears in her eyes. "Good Lord! I cain't stand here in front of that nigger boy an' tell 'er I ain't got a penny. Why don't she jus' go away?"

After a moment, Hattie heard a man's voice say, "Ah got a penny."

She looked at the Negro man who was holding out his hand with a penny in it. "Well, if that don't beat all!" she thought. "I guess he'll thank he's better 'an me now."

The girl turned and looked up at him. "Oh, thank you," she said, clearly relieved. When he stepped forward and placed the penny on the counter, Hattie noticed the girl's face was glowing with gratitude.

"You welcome, Miss," he said as he stepped back, smiling.

Hattie swallowed, relieved that the crisis was over. "Ya wanna wear it?" she asked.

"Yes, ma'am," the girl said, the light back in her eyes, as she slipped it on her finger. She looked at the Negro man and smiled.

Hattie rang up the sale as the girl left. She saw her talking to Anna, and showing her the ring. Anna didn't look at Hattie, so she figured the girl must not have said anything about the penny. "She was prob'ly too embarrassed to mention it," she thought. Anna gave her what looked to Hattie like a nickel, and she heard the girl say, "Thank you, Anna."

"You're welcome, Lora Lee," Anna said.

"That's right," Hattie thought. "Anna said her name was Lora Lee." She watched her buy a bag of popcorn and start to skip out of the store. Then the sandal with the broken strap came off and she had to stop and put it back on. "Pore little thang," Hattie thought. When she saw her looking around to see if anyone saw her, Hattie quickly looked at the Negro man who was looking at her, and she realized he'd moved closer to the counter. She was just about to wait on him when a white woman walked up to the part of the counter with the clocks, and Hattie immediately went to wait on her. The woman hadn't looked at anything, and she had no idea what she wanted, but Hattie didn't care.

She took some satisfaction from the fact that it took a while for the woman to make up her mind. Normally, she would've been a little annoyed, but knowing that the Negro man was waiting gave her a lot of patience with the white woman. "He may have embarrassed me," she thought, "but I can make him wait."

When the customer finally left, Carolyn went to Hattie's counter. "I don't know if I'll see you after work, so I jus' wonted to say goodbye," she said. "I hope you'll be happy."

Hattie noticed her tone did not wish her happiness. Hattie just looked at her for a moment. "I will be," she said matter-of-factly, and turned her back, and went to wait on the Negro man.

"Did ya wanna see sumpin?" she asked.

"Yes, ma'am," he said, looking at the counter. "I'd like ta see dem necklaces, please."

Hattie took the display case out and placed it on the counter. "I'd like da heart wit' di'mon's, please," he said softly, glancing at Hattie.

"Oh no! That boy's gon' buy that beautiful necklace I wont," she thought, her brow wrinkling. "I shoulda tuk it out a the case an' put it aside. I'd have the money ta buy it when I git paid."

"Dere sumpin wrong, ma'am?" he asked.

Hattie realized her face must have shown her disappointment. "Oh no," she responded, and swallowed.

"He prob'ly thanks they're real di'mon's," she thought. And she asked, "You know they ain't real di'mon's, don't ya?"

"Yes'm," he said.

As she took the necklace from the display case and put the case away, Hattie thought, "I prob'ly shouldn' spend that much a my money, nohow."

"Is it fer yore wife?" she asked.

"It fuh my girlfrien'," he answered. "Ah ain't got married."

"Is it her birthday?"

"No, ma'am. It jes' a present."

"It's a nice present. When ya git married, keep givin' her nice thangs," Hattie said, surprising herself.

"Yes, ma'am, Ah sho will," he responded.

After he left, Hattie thought, "He wuz nice ta give that little gal a penny. An' he shore bought his girlfriend a nice necklace, an' he said it wuz fer no reason. How could a Nigra thank about thangs like that? I bet Horace never spent that much money on me. He never bought me nothin' 'cept at Christmas, an' he ain't done that fer years. Lord knows that boy's prob'ly gon' be a better man than Horace is. I guess I shoulda been nicer ta 'im. After all, God's the one that made 'im a Nigra. I'm shore glad he didn' make me one—I got enough troubles as it is."

She was pleased when other customers came to her counter. "I don't need ta thank about that stuff," she thought. "I already know Horace weren't a good husband. I don't need no more evidence a that."

♥   ♥   ♥

JUST BEFORE CLOSING TIME, HATTIE LOOKED UP from her cash register to see Francis standing there. He greeted her with a big smile.

"Hey, gal. You ready to go to yore new place?" he asked.

"Well, you're a sight fer sore eyes," she said. "I just have a few more minutes an' then I can go an' we can git ever'thang moved."

Francis laughed, and Hattie saw a twinkle in his eyes. "Yore furniture's already in yore livin' room, an' yore swing's hangin' on yore porch."

"Really? What about all my boxes an' stuff?"

"It's all there. I tol' you this mornin' to git ever'thing together that you wonted, that we wadn' goin' back there."

"I don't even remember that," Hattie confessed. "I guess I wuz too upset."

"Don't matter," Francis said. "I got a couple a surprises for you."

"Oh, please tell me. This has been a awful day an' I could use some surprises," Hattie pleaded.

"Who you think you're talkin' to, gal?" Francis asked, with a twinkle in his eyes. "You'll hafta wait till you git there."

"All right, but are they good? I need sumpin real good after today."

"Of course, they're good! Who do you think planned 'em? An' what kinda surprise would it be if it wadn' good?"

"All right," Hattie grinned. "Time will tell."

"So, did somethin' happen at work that made yore day worse?"

"Well, Mr. Simmons threatened ta not pay me fer the week. An', by the way, he still ain't paid me."

"I'll jus' go git yore pay," Francis said, and he didn't wait for a response.

"Well, be careful," Hattie called as he left. "He's got a pencil!"

Carolyn looked at her crossly and Hattie laughed. "She oughta be ashamed a herse'f," she thought, "fer carryin' on with a married man."

Hattie had a customer while Francis was gone, but she was still able to worry about what was happening with him. When he returned a few minutes later, no one was at the counter. He handed her the check.

"Mr. Simmons is awf'ly considerate, an' he didn' even touch his pencil," he said, smiling. "He decided he didn' need to deduct any time, 'cause you've been such a good employee for eight years."

"You mean he didn' deduct anythang?" Hattie asked.

"Jus' the two dollars he gave you yesterday, an' you'll get yore full pay next week. He saw how wrong he'd been, thinkin' that he should charge you for the time you spent on the phone call, an' for this mornin'. He happened to remember that you often came in early."

"He remembered that, huh? Francis, yo're amazin'!" Hattie was shaking her head and smiling.

"Boy! His office stinks!" he said.

"I know. Smells jus' like him."

They laughed.

"You know," he said, "I won't need you in the store till Monday week."

"But Francis," Hattie pleaded, "I thought I wuz startin' on Monday."

"No, ma'am," he declared. "You're havin' a week to unpack an' git ya place fixed up, an' jus' relax."

"You mean like a vacation?" she asked. "I ain't never had a vacation. But I don't need a whole week to unpack an' fix up the house; I can do that in one day."

"Well, you've got plants ta plant an' dresses ta buy, ya know," he reminded her. "An', don't worry 'bout payin' rent for the next month. If you weren't movin' in, the house would be empty."

"Oh, thank you, Francis. That means I can buy a bed, git my hair cut, an' buy some new shoes an' a new dress or two."

Francis smiled. "Or three or four. Ya know, you could use some new dresses, gal."

"I shore could!" she agreed. An' the bus goes right by yore place, so I don't even need a car."

"Seems ta me like you're gonna be lookin' like a new woman purty soon."

"I already feel like a new woman," she said. She was smiling while she got her cash ready for Mr. Simmons. As she put in the quarter she owed, she thought, "Okay, that's it. Now I don't owe nobody nothin'."

When Mr. Simmons went to her counter for her cash and receipts, he said, "Well, Hattie, we'll miss you. I hope ever'thing goes well for you."

Hattie thought, "You thank I don't know yo're sayin' that 'cause my brother's standin' here?" She looked him straight in the eye and said, "I'll miss you, too, Mr. Simmons," but she added in her mind, "An' I'll be happy missin' you an' that blamed ole pencil, an' yore ole stinkin' se'f."

He was just about to turn around when Hattie said sweetly, "Oh, by the way, Mr. Simmons, please tell yore wife I'm leavin', an' give 'er my regards."

She watched as his face turned red. "Sure," he muttered, and went and closed the doors, hung the closed sign, and went back upstairs.

"Well," Francis said, "I think you touched a sore spot."

Hattie laughed. "I'll tell you about it later." She looked at Carolyn, who Mr. Simmons hadn't even looked at as he passed by. She was glaring at Hattie, who smiled, thinking, "There's a little comeuppance fer ya, Miss too-big-fer-yore-britches flirt."

On her way out, Carolyn went over and told her goodbye again. Hattie wondered why, and then she watched as Carolyn turned to face Francis and started talking just to him. "Why! she's flirtin'," she thought. "Don't she know he's married?" She was amused watching her try to impress him.

Several of the other employees said goodbye to her, as well. Anna was last. She handed Hattie a neatly wrapped box with a matching ribbon. "It's for your new place," she said.

"Oh, Anna," Hattie said. "You didn' hafta git me a present."

"I know," Anna said. "That's what made it so much fun. I did it only because I wonted to. Open it, Hattie."

"I hate ta mess it up, it looks so beautiful," Hattie said, with tears in her eyes. "This is the most beautiful present I ever got." The wrapping paper was full of flowers, including some zinnias.

Hattie removed the ribbon, and carefully removed each piece of Scotch tape. Anna watched her, savoring the moment; she knew that Hattie would save the ribbon and paper, and she was happy that she had spent the time to wrap the present nicely. She'd brought the paper and ribbon to work with her and wrapped the present after she bought it on her lunch break.

When Hattie finally opened the box, she exclaimed, "Why, it's a vase! Francis, look at this beautiful vase! It's jus' perfect, Anna. I don't have no vases fer my flow'rs; I always use a ole jar." It was a lovely clear-glass vase, adorned with intricate etchings of flowers.

Anna was surprised when Hattie burst into tears. She looked at Francis. "She had a rough day," he said. "Horace ran over her flowers."

Hattie walked to the other side of her counter to get a handkerchief out of her pocketbook. Francis leaned close to Anna and said softly, "Her neighbor rescued some of the flowers, an' they're sittin' in her house now. She'll be surprised when she gits there."

"That's great," Anna said. "Did he run over her white crape myrtles?"

"Yep, but we managed to save one of 'em an' there's a lot of clippin's," Francis replied. He paused for a moment and looked at her curiously. "How did you know they were white?"

Anna smiled. "My mother has some, too."

"I see," Francis said, smiling. "Do you mind if I tell Hattie? She always wondered where they came from."

"You can tell her. I wore a little piece of one to work once an' Hattie went on an' on about how much she jus' loved white crape myrtles. When I told Mama, she rooted three cuttings for her. Hattie wasn't home when I dropped them off at her house. I was planning to tell her, but she was so excited an' curious about who had left them, it seemed more fun for her not to know."

After she blew her nose, Hattie went back to where they were. "Anna," she said, but she started crying again.

Francis smiled. "What she means to say, Anna, is that you chose the perfect present for her, an' she thanks you a lot."

Hattie nodded her head, and the three of them laughed.

Anna gave her a big hug and said, "I'm so happy for you, Hattie. Be sure you remember to call me. An' if you lose my number, you know where to find me."

Hattie finally managed to say, "I will. An' you know where ta find me. I shore hope you'll stop by the store sometime, Anna. An' thank you a lot fer ever'thang."

As Francis and Hattie were leaving the store, Hattie said, "Ain't that the most beautiful vase you ever saw?"

"I b'lieve it is," he replied. "An' I cain't think of nobody who deserves it more, or would appreciate it more."

Hattie smiled. "I shore do 'preciate it."

As soon as Francis opened the door, Hattie saw Horace across the street, leaning against the back of her favorite bench. He stood with his arm around a woman that Hattie immediately classified as a "bleached-blond floozy," and both of them were looking at her. She had a moment of embarrassment when she realized that Carolyn and Anna would have seen them, too. "I won't forget this," she thought. She glanced to the right and saw the little white girl sitting on a bench a little further down, just looking around. Hattie's thoughts went to her, "Wonder where her mama and daddy are. Lora Lee, that's her name." Then she looked back at Horace and the woman with him.

"Uh, wait," Francis said, taking her arm.

"I see 'em," she said. "It don't matter one bit ta me."

Horace had a silly grin on his face and the woman looked half amused and half frightened.

"The nerve a him!" Francis said. "I'd like ta knock that stupid grin right off his face."

"Jus' look at 'em, Francis," Hattie said softly. "She looks like a cheap floozy, an' don't they look pathetic! Both a 'em." She stared for a moment. "I guess he thanks I'll be upset seein' my replacement, but he's got another thank comin'. It jus' makes me wonder: if that's the kinda woman he wonts, how come he was ever wi' me?" She paused, and then said in a voice loaded with revulsion, "I'm actually glad they're here 'cause if I ever start ta feel lonesome an' thank I made a mistake, this is one more thang fer me ta remember."

They all stood there for another moment, just looking at each other, and Horace's smile faded. The woman moved to stand right beside him, her shoulder touching his, her amused look gone. Suddenly, she just looked scared.

"Ya know what, Francis," Hattie said with a lilt in her voice, and a smile on her face. She looked into eyes filled with apprehension. "I'm ready ta go ta my new house."

Francis took a deep breath. And his mood shifted as he started thinking about her full refrigerator, the pot of crape myrtle blooms, the ceiling fans, and the chicken pen's new residents.

Hattie turned around for a long, last look at the store, and her counter. She sighed. Then she walked out with her shoulders back and her head held high, and closed the door behind her.

CPSIA information can be obtained
at www.ICGtesting.com
Printed in the USA
FFOW03n1823071015
17526FF